Welcome to
FERAL

LITTLE TOWN. BIG SCARES!

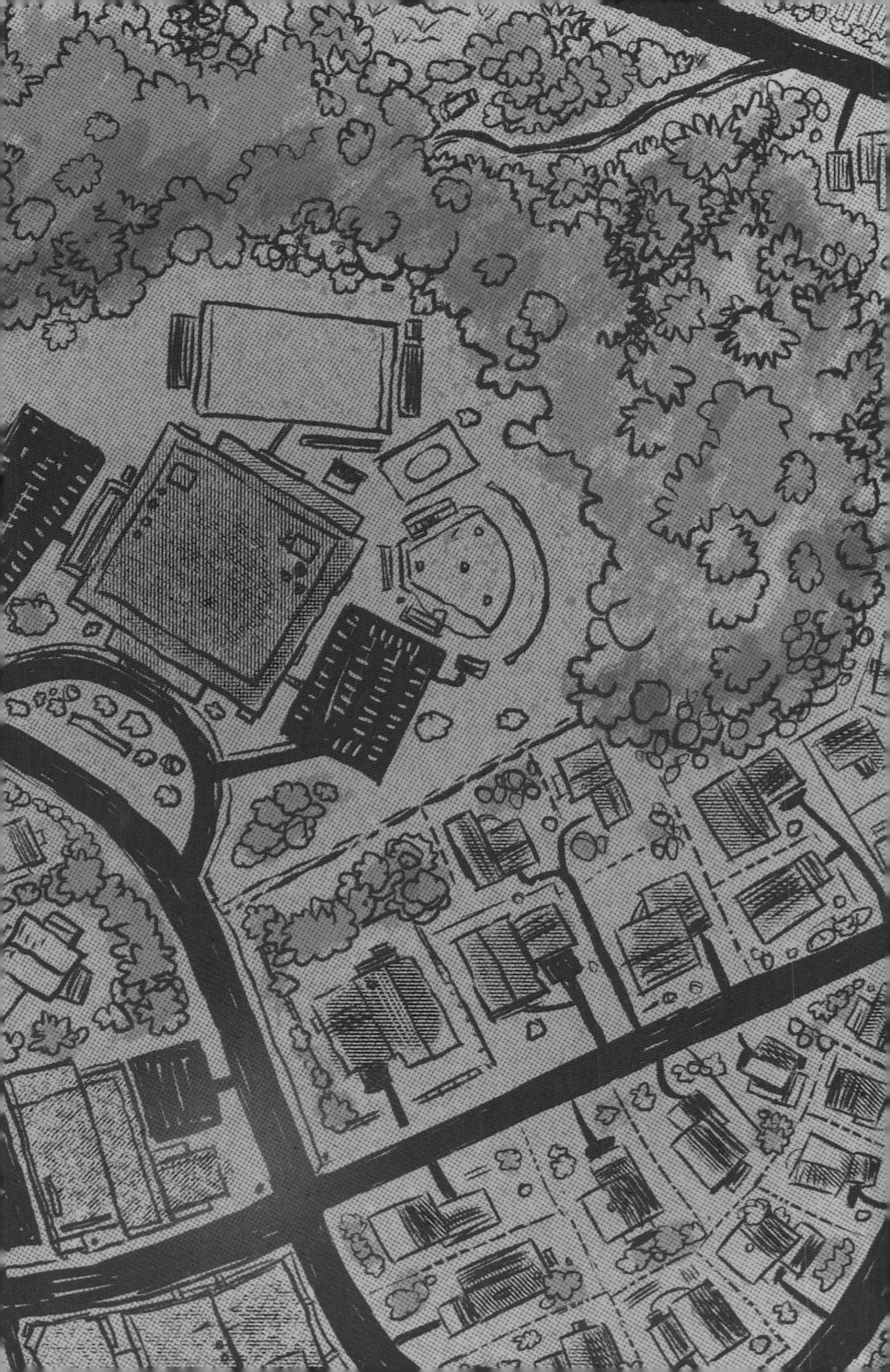

Welcome to FERAL

LITTLE TOWN. BIG SCARES!

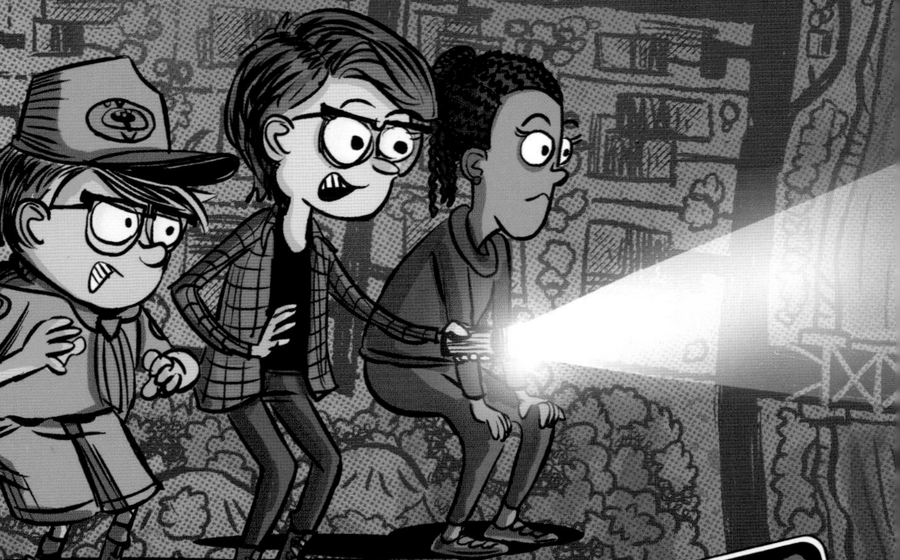

FRIGHTS FROM FERAL

MARK FEARING

HOLIDAY HOUSE NEW YORK

Dedicated to everyone in Otisville, and every small town where people enjoy a good scary story.

Thanks to Lily Fearing for her color work on this book.

HOLIDAY HOUSE is registered in the U.S. Patent and Trademark Office.

Printed and bound in July 2022 at Toppan Leefung, DongGuan, China.

The artwork was created with pencil and finished with digital ink and paint.

www.holidayhouse.com

First Edition

10 9 8 7 6 5 4 3 2 1

Library of Congress Cataloging-in-Publication Data

Names: Fearing, Mark, author, illustrator.

Title: Welcome to Feral : little town, big scares! / Mark Fearing.

Description: First edition. | New York : Holiday House, 2022. | Series:
    Frights from Feral ; 1 | Audience: Ages 8–12. | Summary: "In five spooky
    stories, an intrepid young resident invites readers to look a little
    closer at this scenic rural town's secrets, mysteries, and unexplained
    disappearances"— Provided by publisher.

Identifiers: LCCN 2021062895 | ISBN 9780823448654 (hardcover)

Subjects: CYAC: Graphic novels. | Horror stories. | LCGFT: Horror fiction.
    | Graphic novels.

Classification: LCC PZ7.7.F42 We 2022 | DDC 741.5/973—dc23/eng/20220311

LC record available at https://lccn.loc.gov/2021062895

ISBN: 978-0-8234-4865-4 (hardcover)

ISBN: 978-0-8234-5490-7 (paperback)

CONTENTS

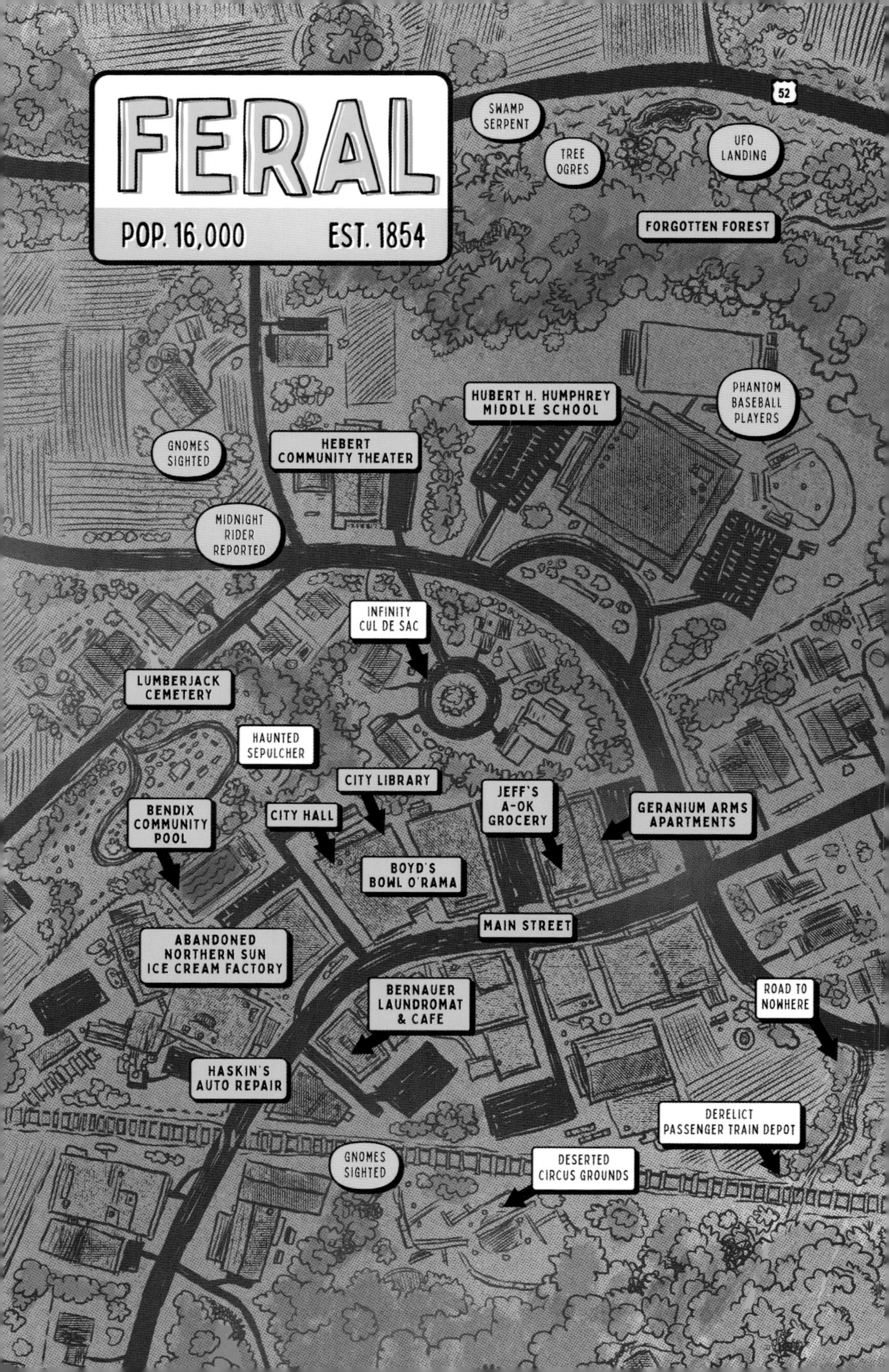
FERAL
POP. 16,000
EST. 1854
52
SWAMP SERPENT
TREE OGRES
UFO LANDING
FORGOTTEN FOREST
HUBERT H. HUMPHREY MIDDLE SCHOOL
PHANTOM BASEBALL PLAYERS
GNOMES SIGHTED
HEBERT COMMUNITY THEATER
MIDNIGHT RIDER REPORTED
INFINITY CUL DE SAC
LUMBERJACK CEMETERY
HAUNTED SEPULCHER
CITY LIBRARY
BENDIX COMMUNITY POOL
CITY HALL
JEFF'S A-OK GROCERY
GERANIUM ARMS APARTMENTS
BOYD'S BOWL O'RAMA
MAIN STREET
ABANDONED NORTHERN SUN ICE CREAM FACTORY
BERNAUER LAUNDROMAT & CAFE
ROAD TO NOWHERE
HASKIN'S AUTO REPAIR
DERELICT PASSENGER TRAIN DEPOT
GNOMES SIGHTED
DESERTED CIRCUS GROUNDS

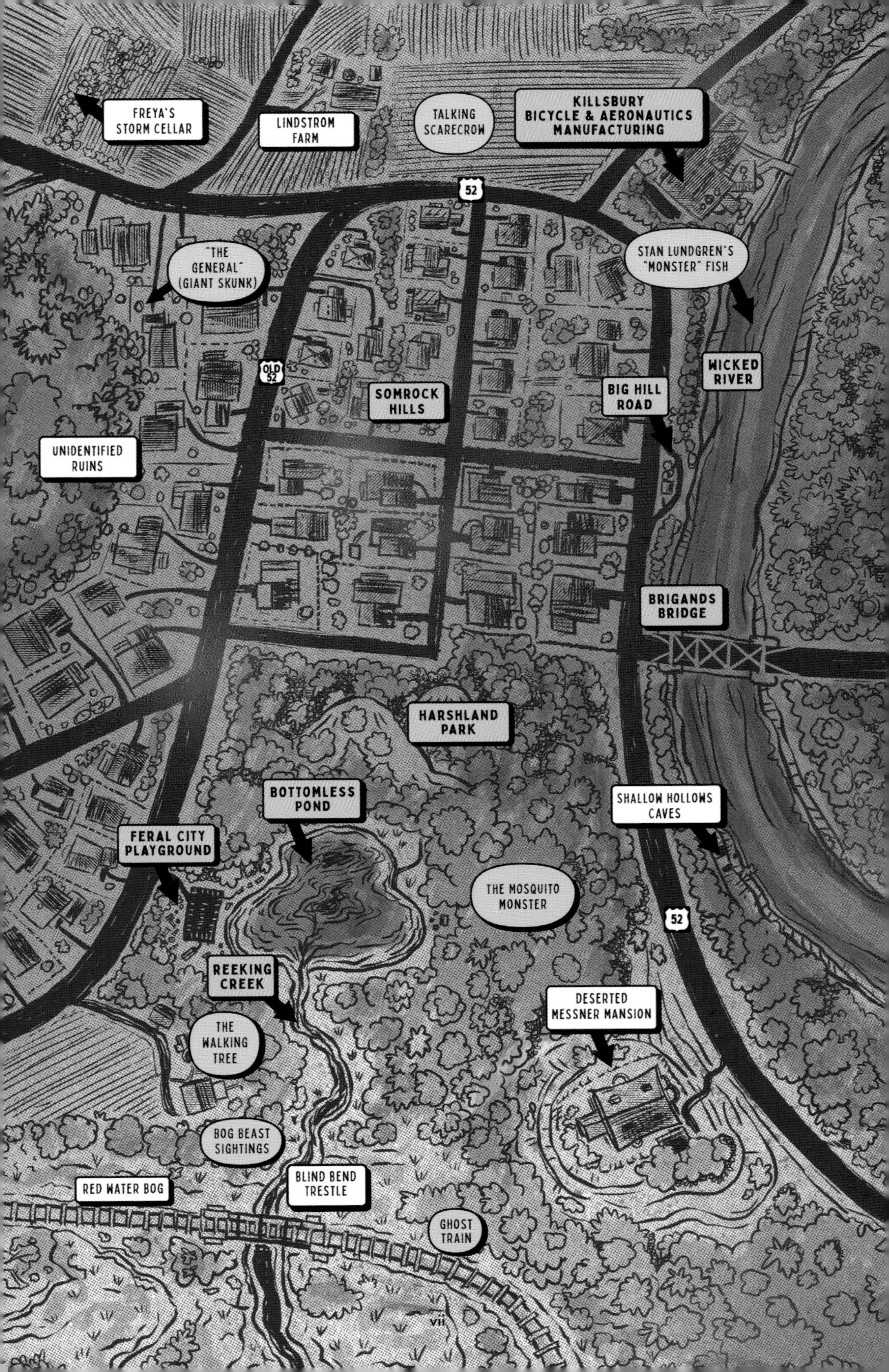

FREYA'S STORM CELLAR
LINDSTROM FARM
TALKING SCARECROW
KILLSBURY BICYCLE & AERONAUTICS MANUFACTURING
52
"THE GENERAL" (GIANT SKUNK)
STAN LUNDGREN'S "MONSTER" FISH
OLD 52
SOMROCK HILLS
BIG HILL ROAD
WICKED RIVER
UNIDENTIFIED RUINS
BRIGANDS BRIDGE
HARSHLAND PARK
BOTTOMLESS POND
SHALLOW HOLLOWS CAVES
FERAL CITY PLAYGROUND
THE MOSQUITO MONSTER
52
REEKING CREEK
DESERTED MESSNER MANSION
THE WALKING TREE
BOG BEAST SIGHTINGS
RED WATER BOG
BLIND BEND TRESTLE
GHOST TRAIN

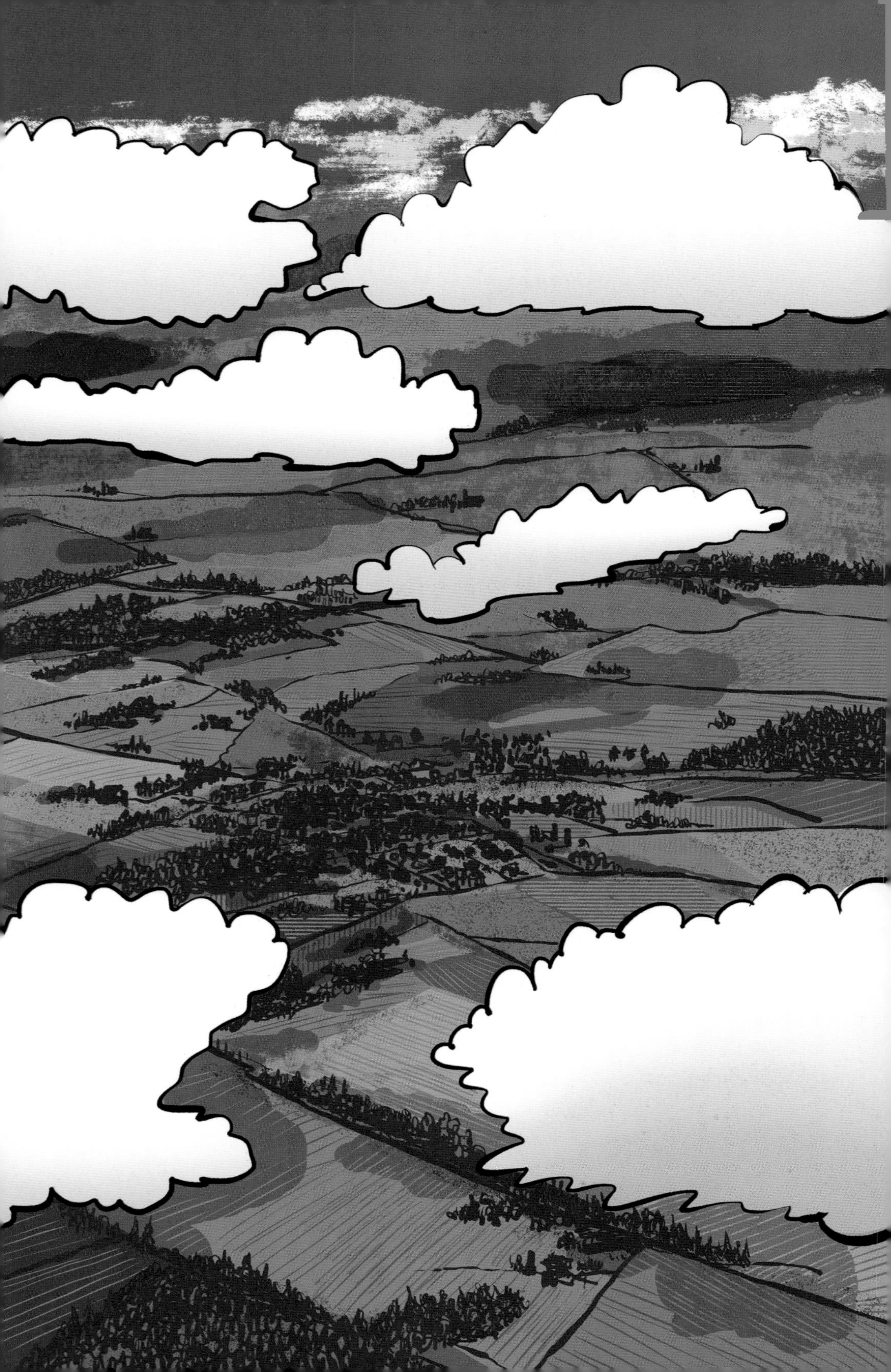

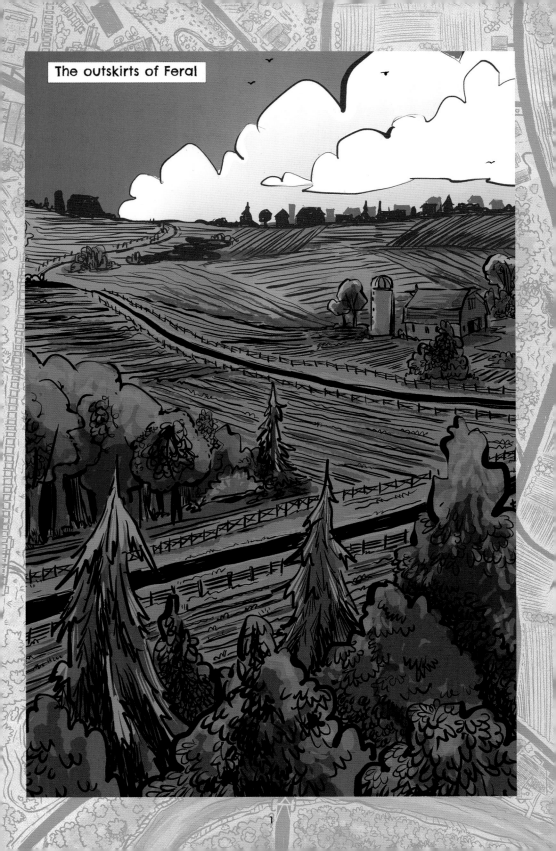

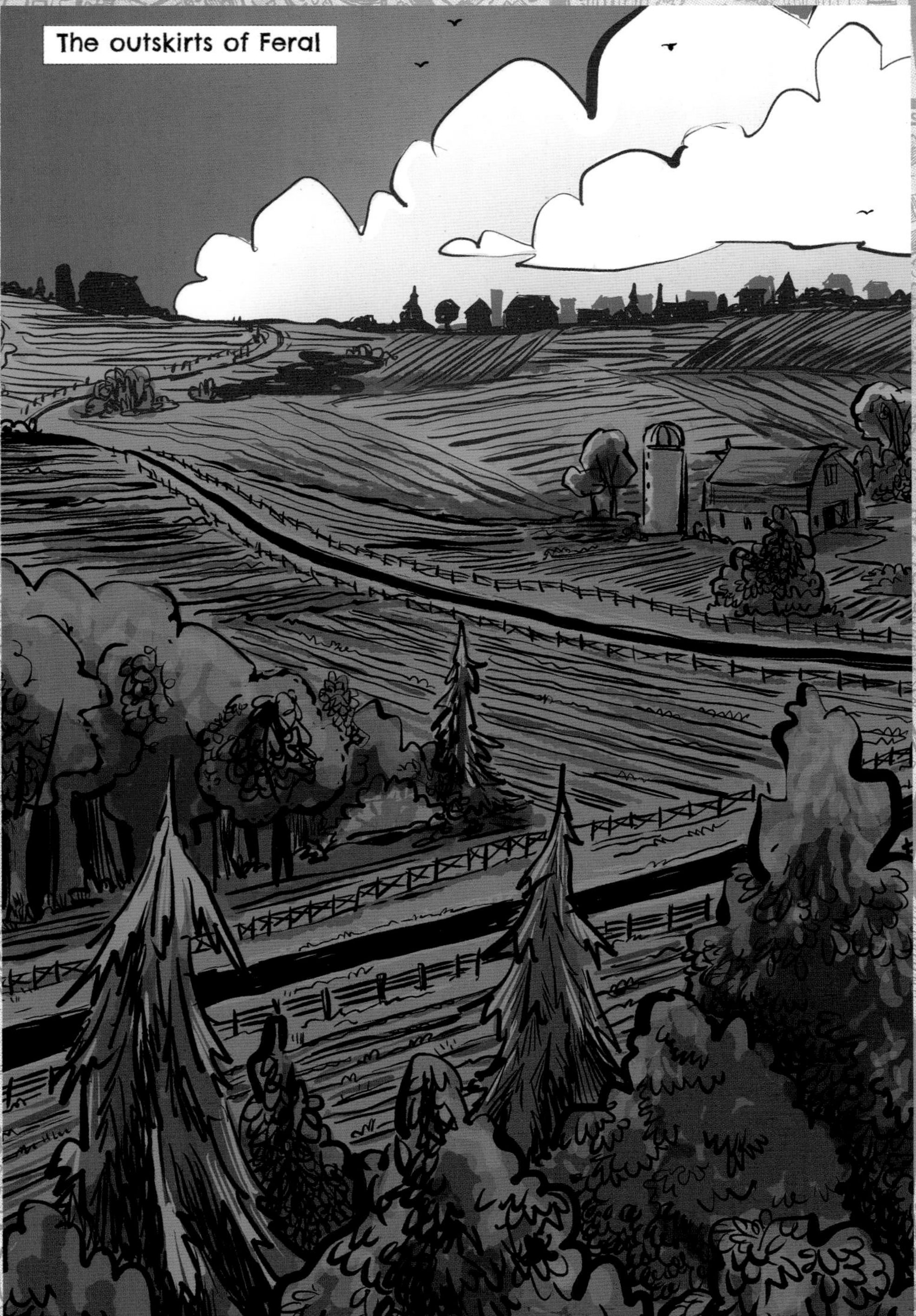
The outskirts of Feral

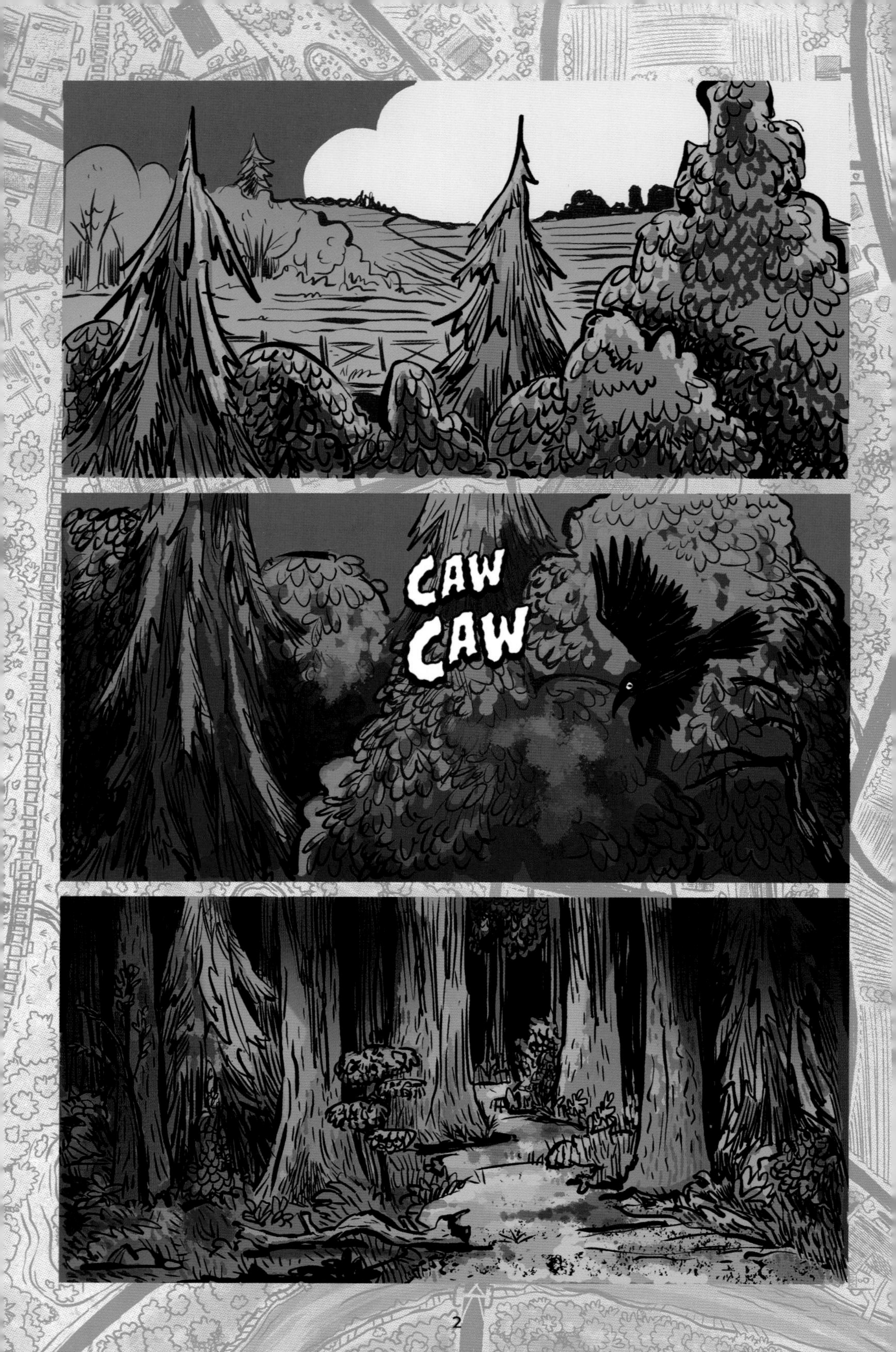
CAW
CAW

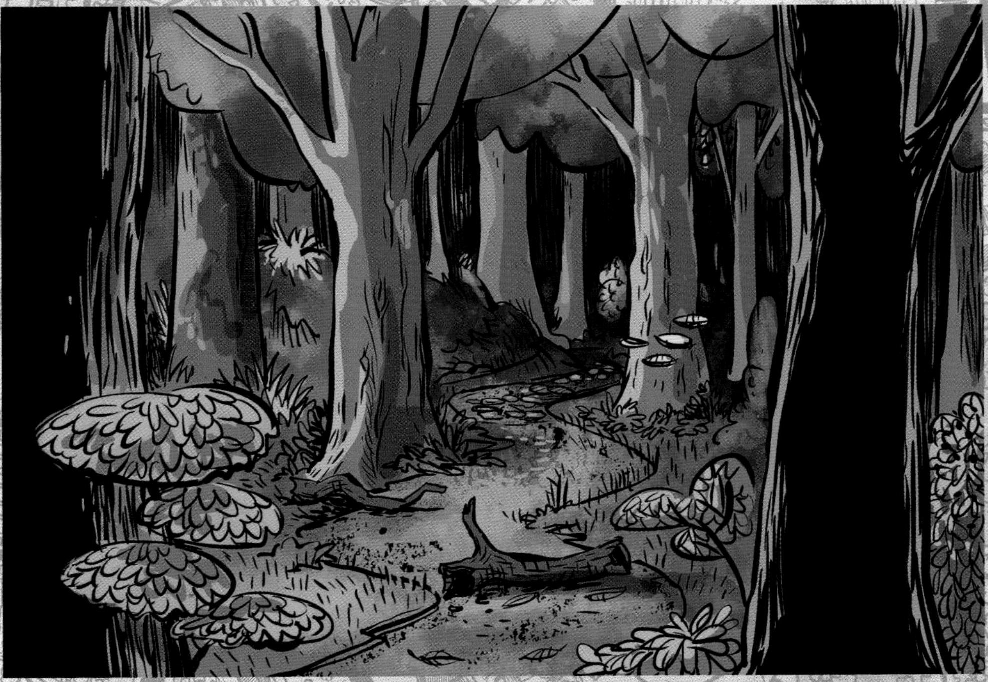

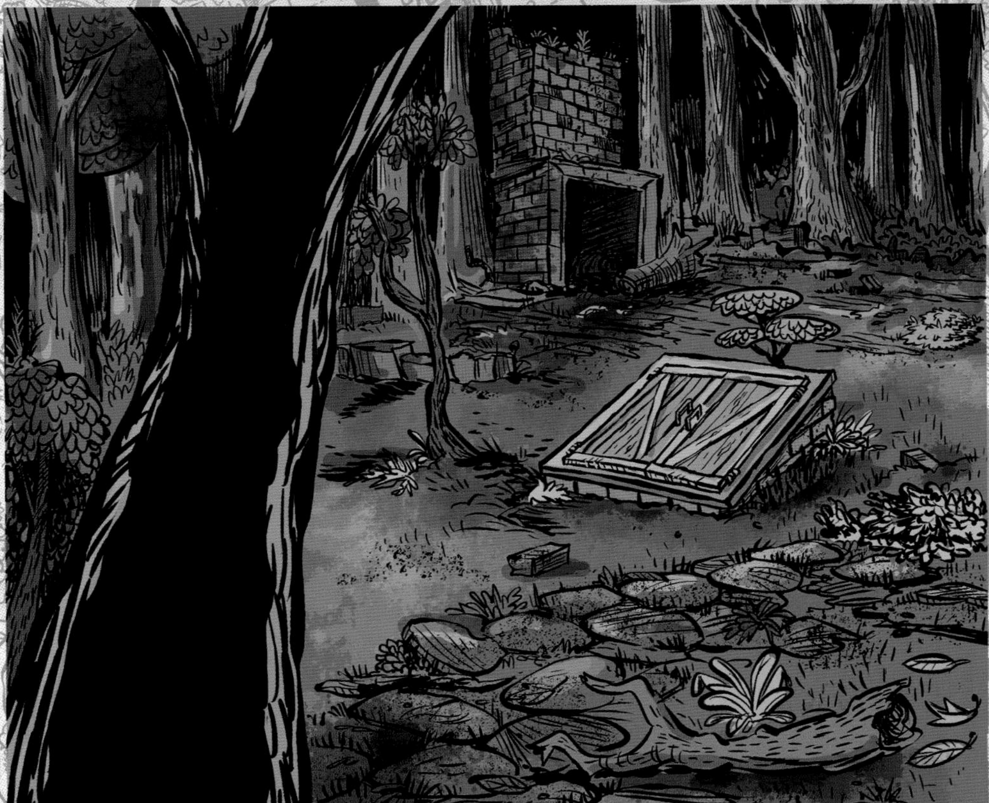

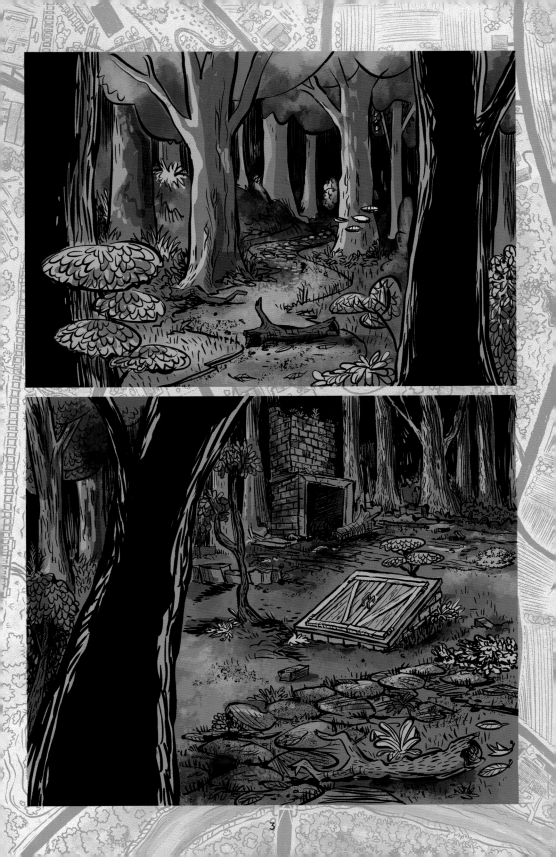

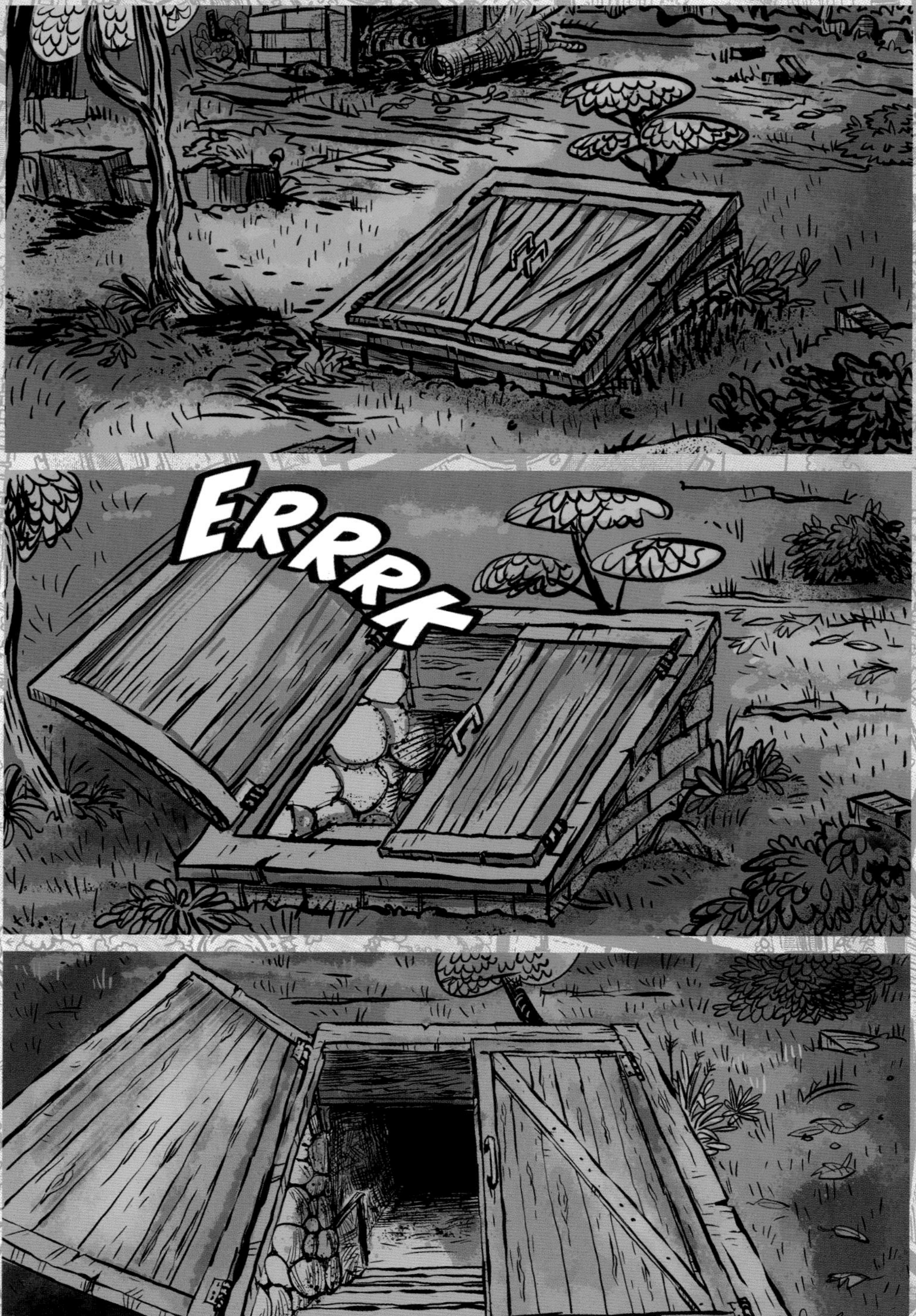
ERRRK

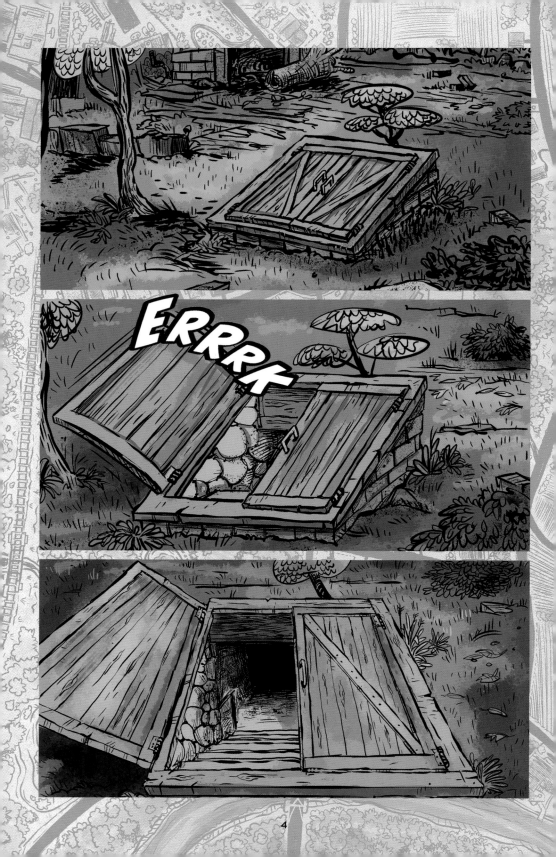

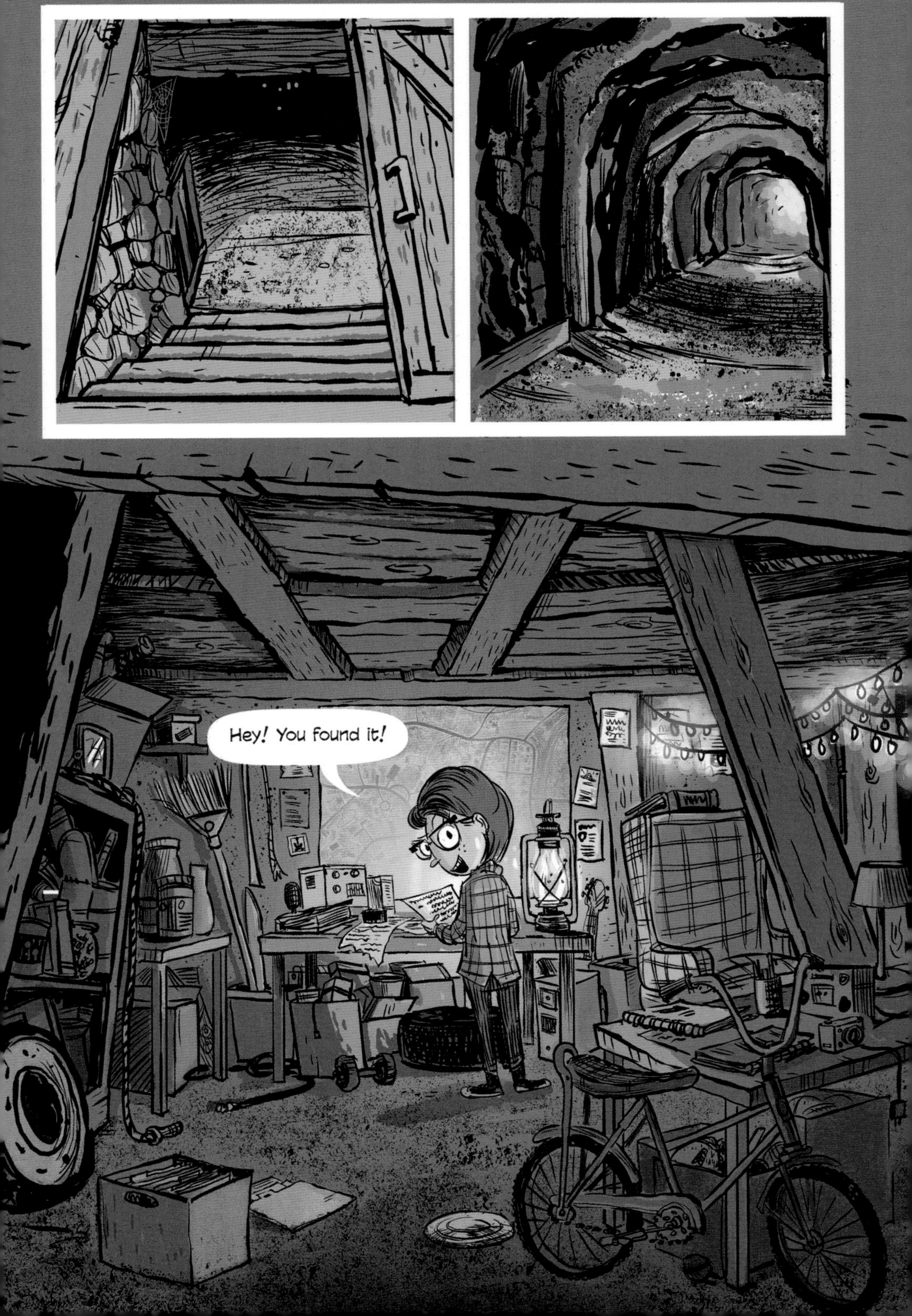
Hey! You found it!

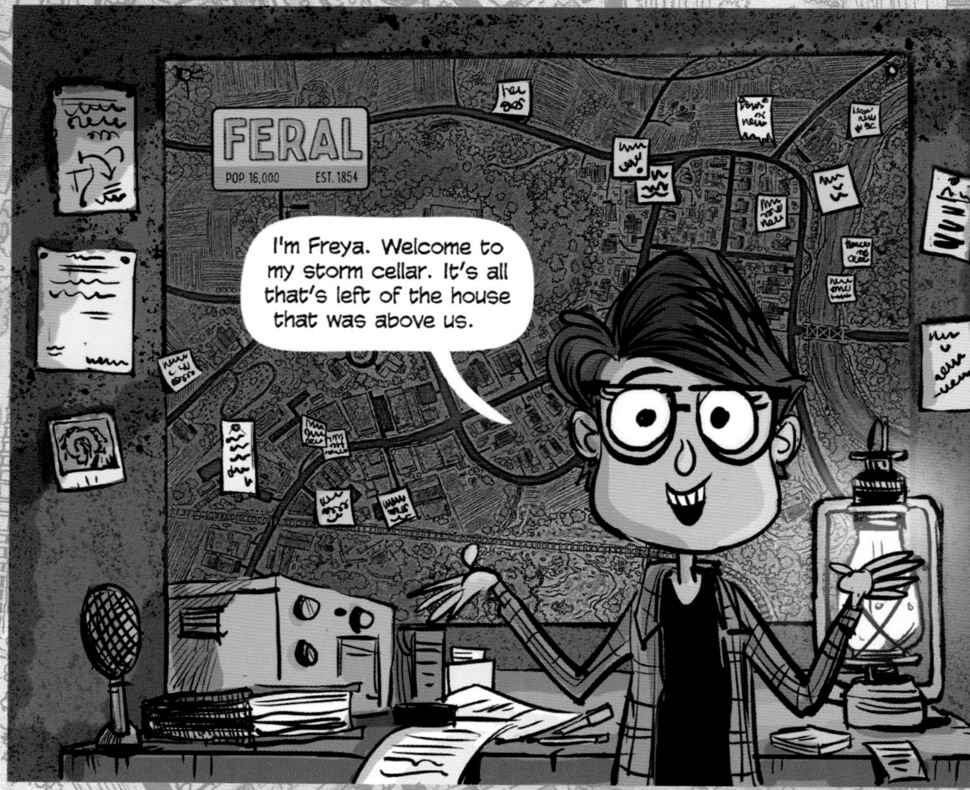
FERAL
POP. 16,000
EST. 1854
I'm Freya. Welcome to my storm cellar. It's all that's left of the house that was above us.

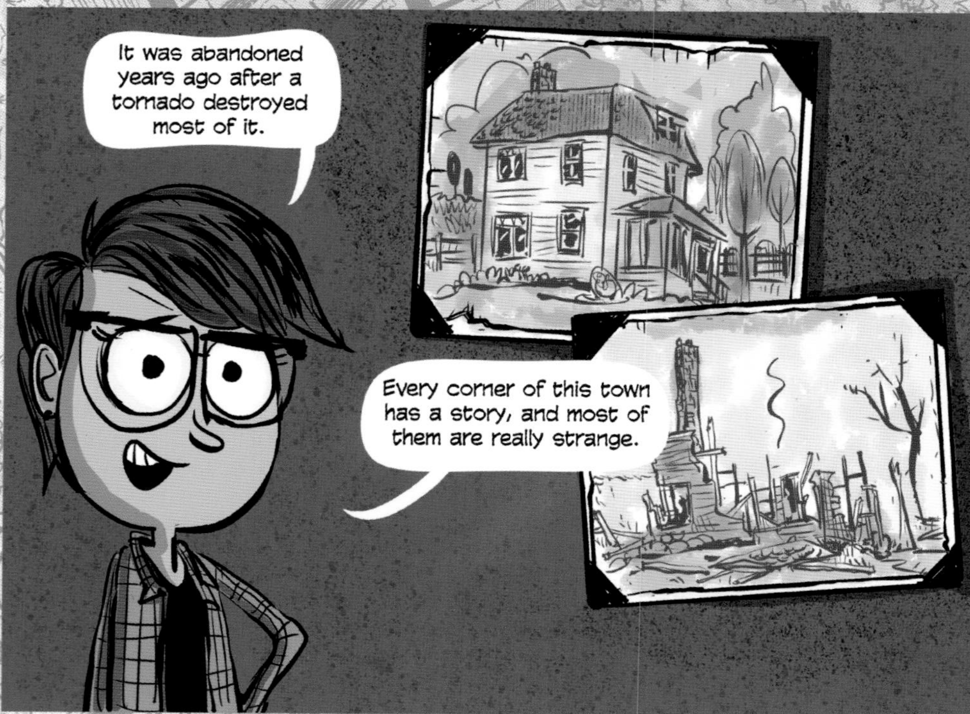
It was abandoned years ago after a tornado destroyed most of it.
Every corner of this town has a story, and most of them are really strange.

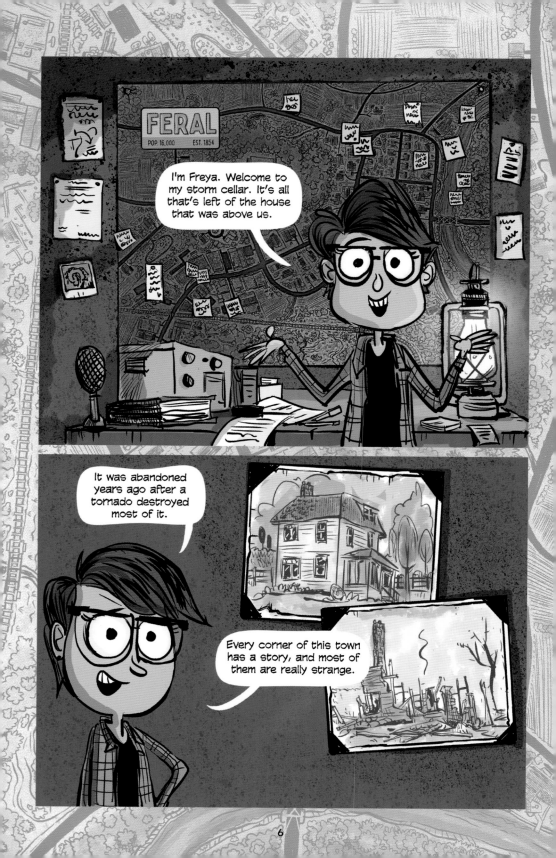

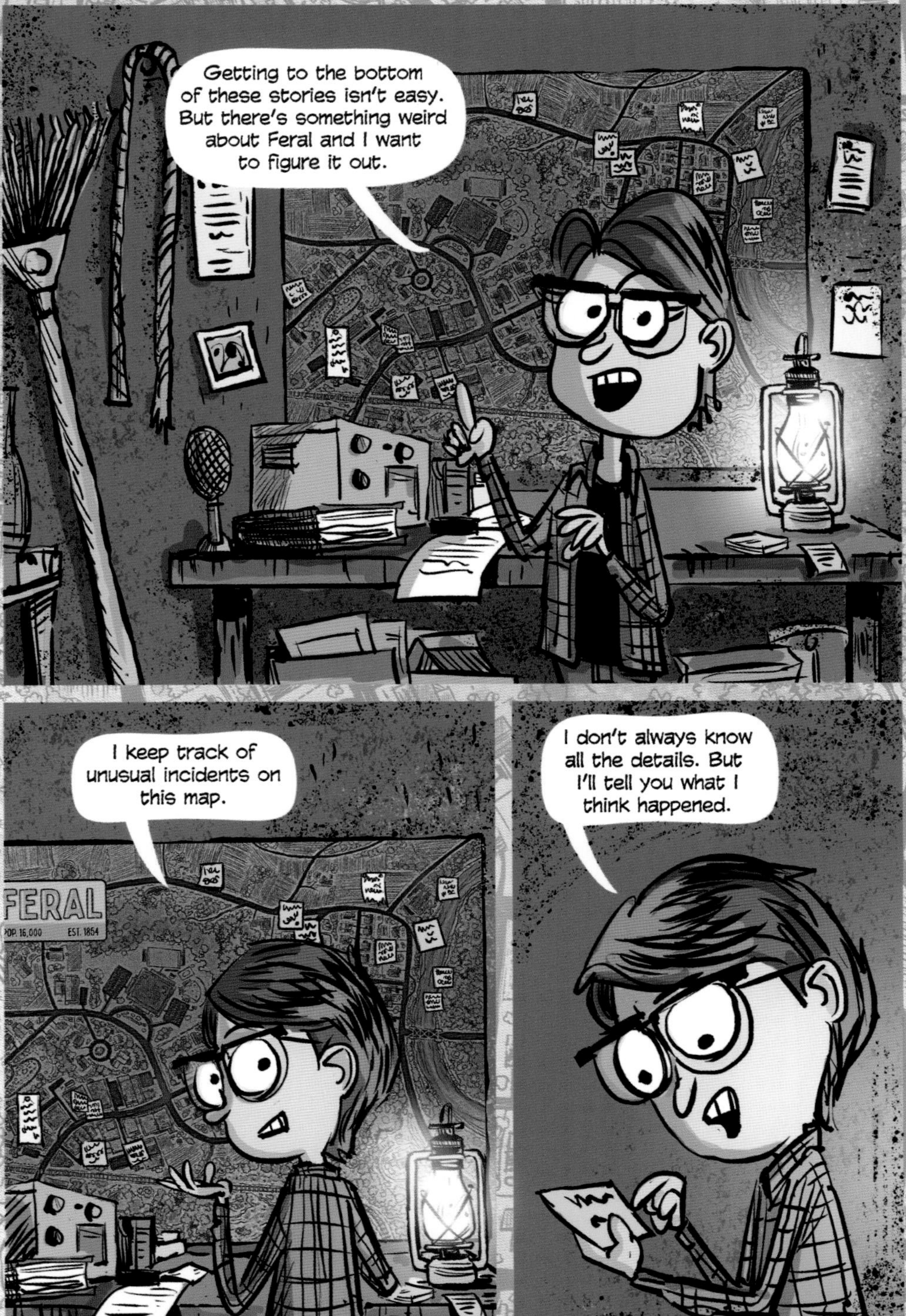
Getting to the bottom of these stories isn't easy. But there's something weird about Feral and I want to figure it out.
I keep track of unusual incidents on this map.
FERAL
POP. 16,000
EST. 1854
I don't always know all the details. But I'll tell you what I think happened.

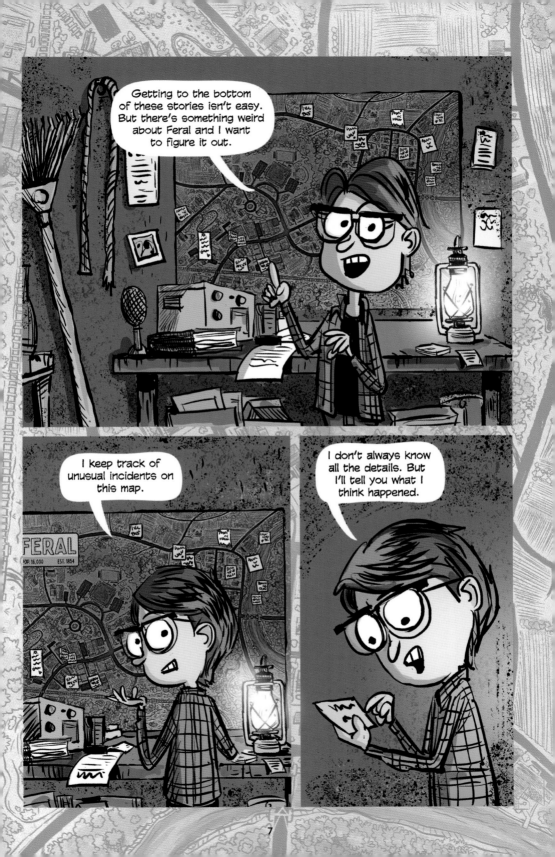

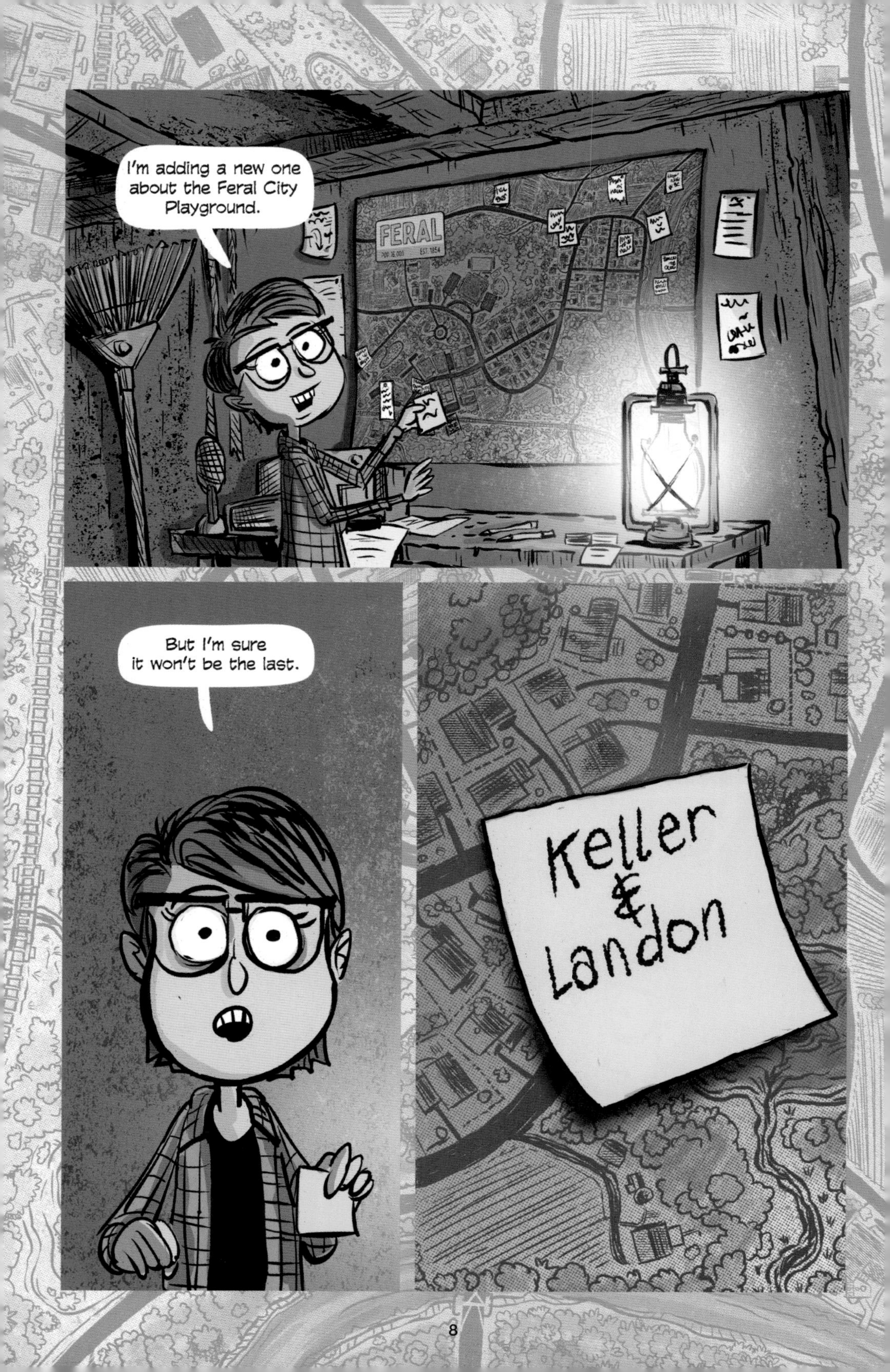

I'm adding a new one about the Feral City Playground.
FERAL
But I'm sure it won't be the last.
Keller
&
Landon

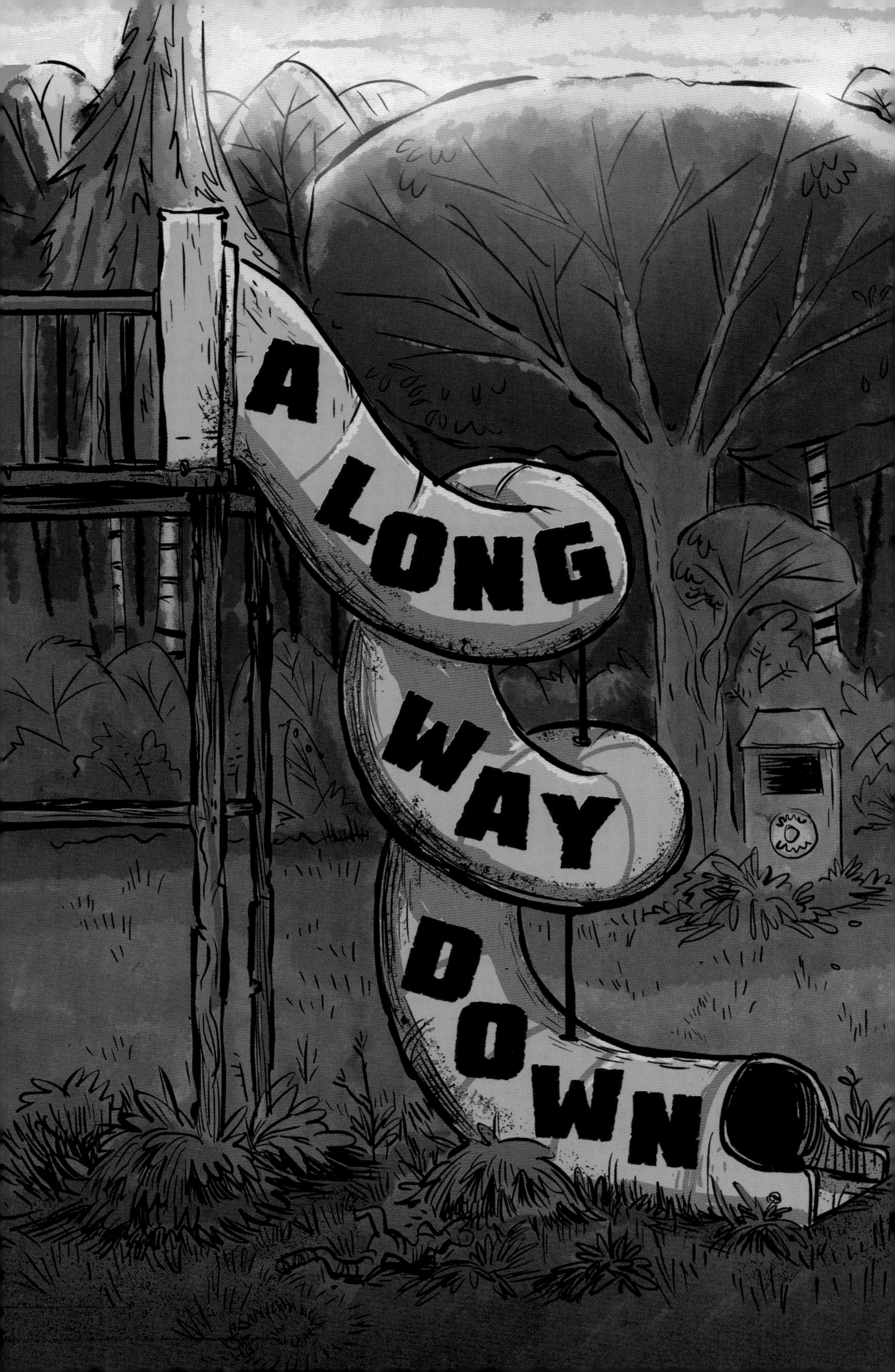
A LONG WAY DOWN

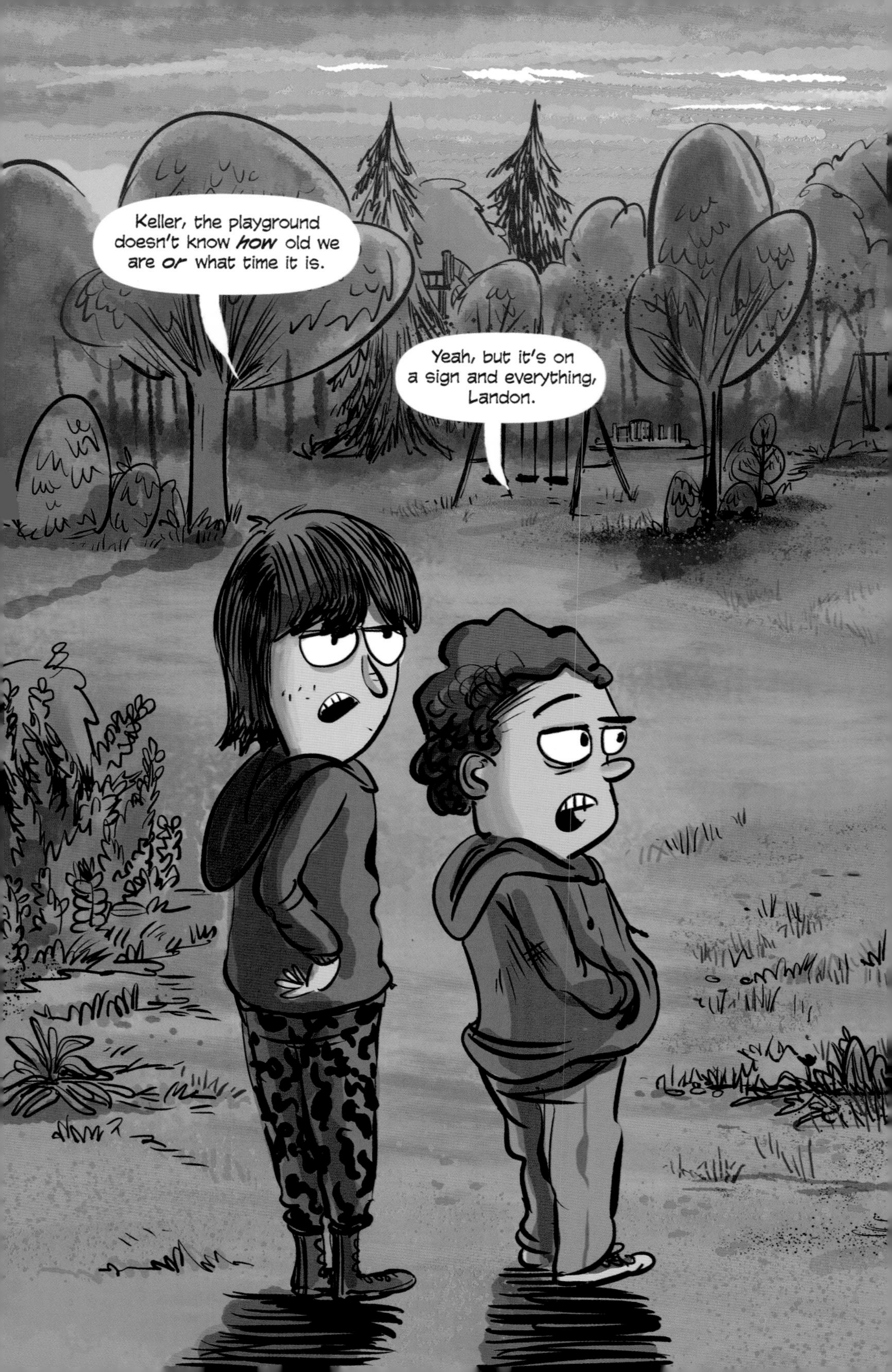
Keller, the playground doesn't know *how* old we are *or* what time it is.
Yeah, but it's on a sign and everything, Landon.

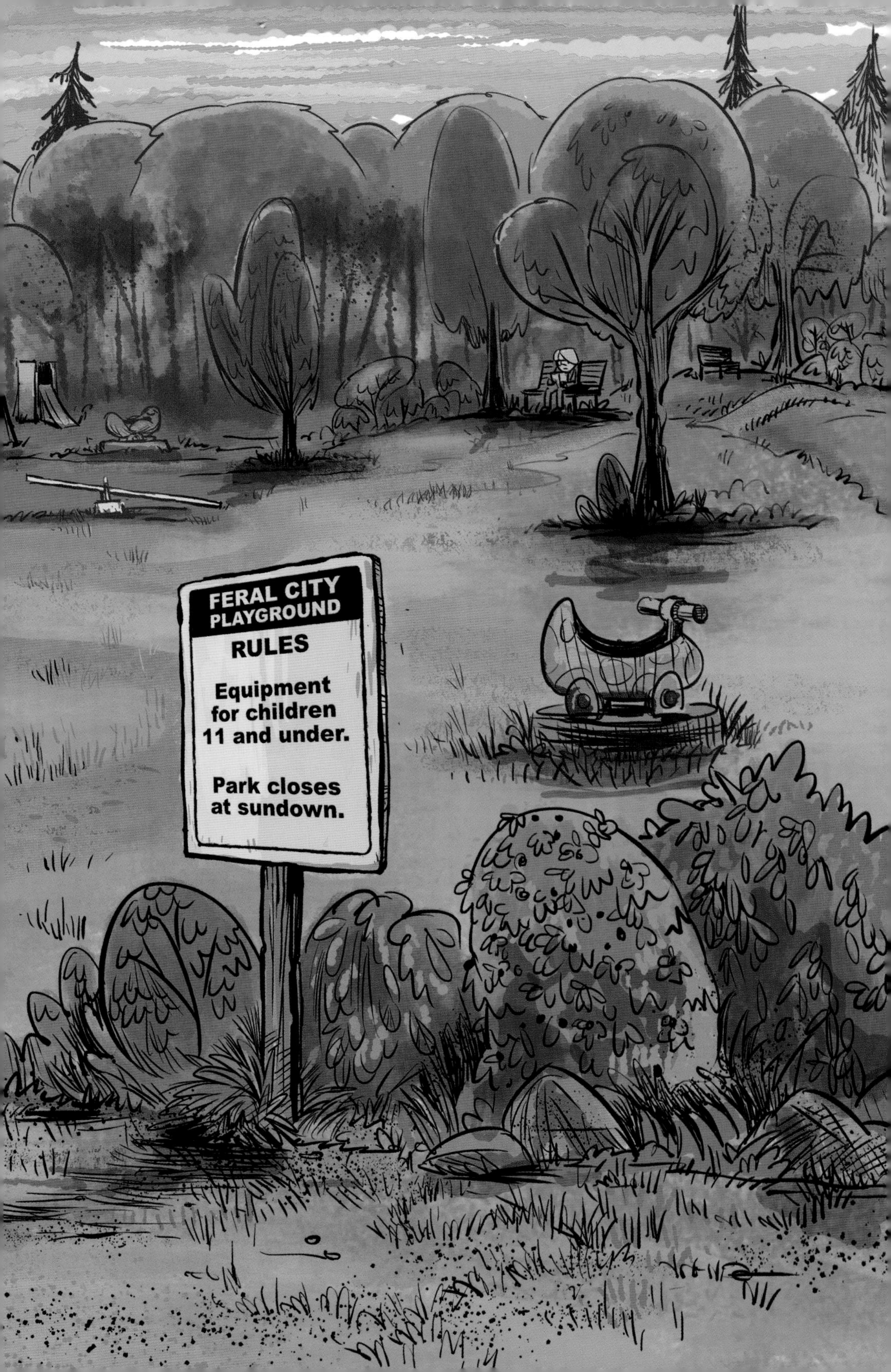
FERAL CITY
PLAYGROUND
RULES
Equipment
for children
11 and under.
Park closes
at sundown.

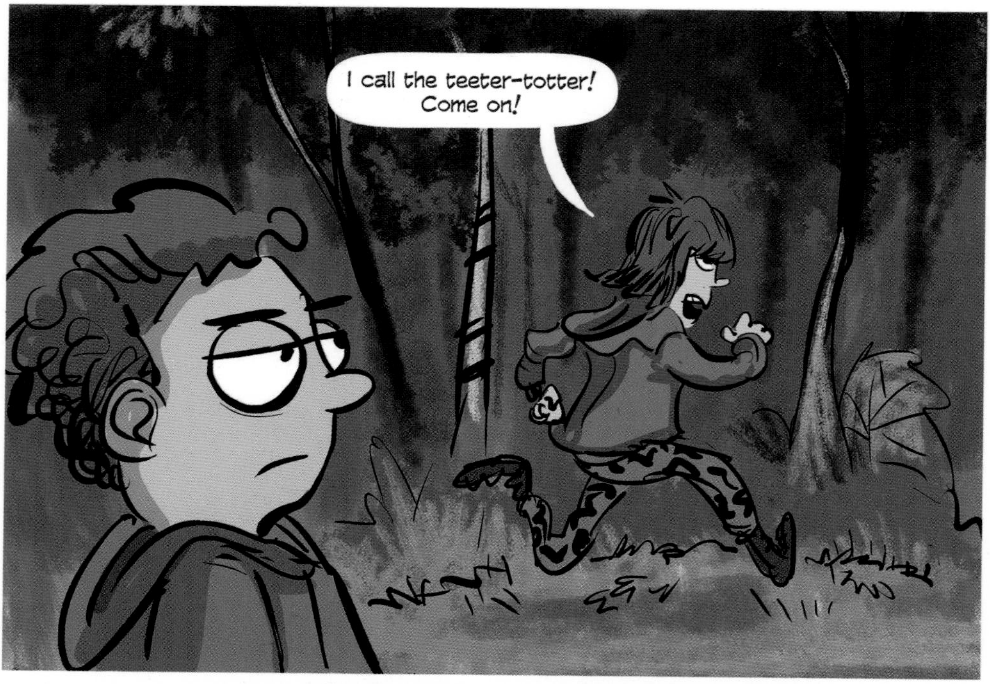
I call the teeter-totter! Come on!

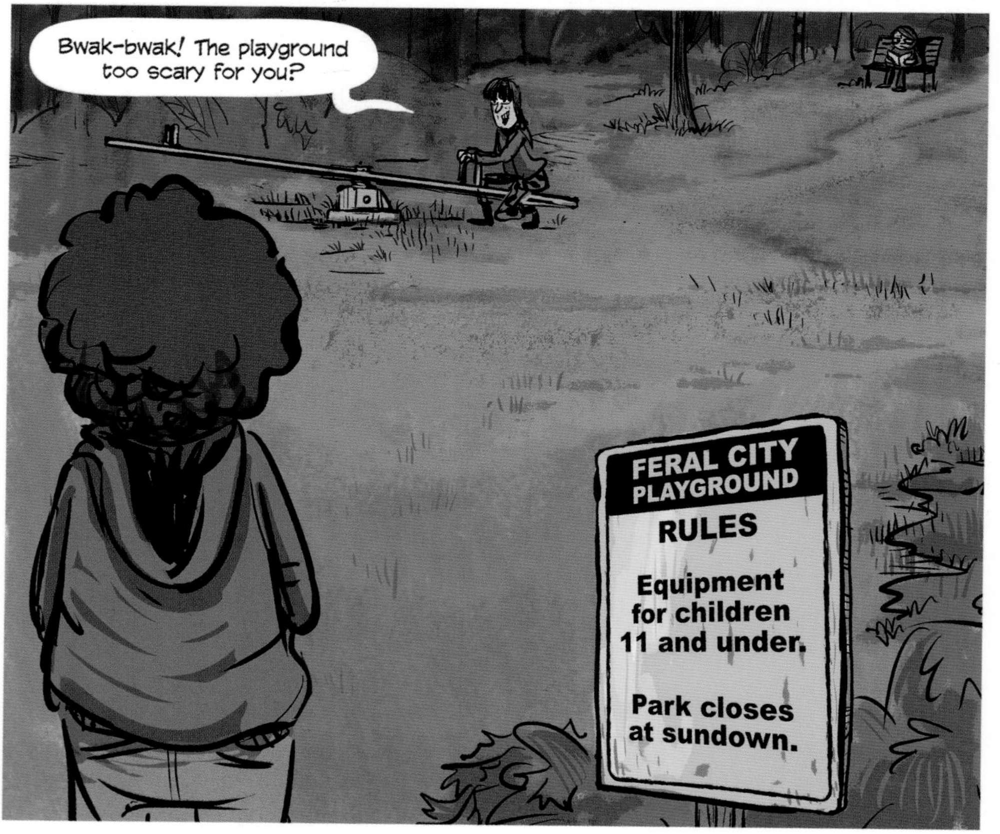
Bwak-bwak! The playground too scary for you?
FERAL CITY PLAYGROUND
RULES
Equipment for children 11 and under.
Park closes at sundown.

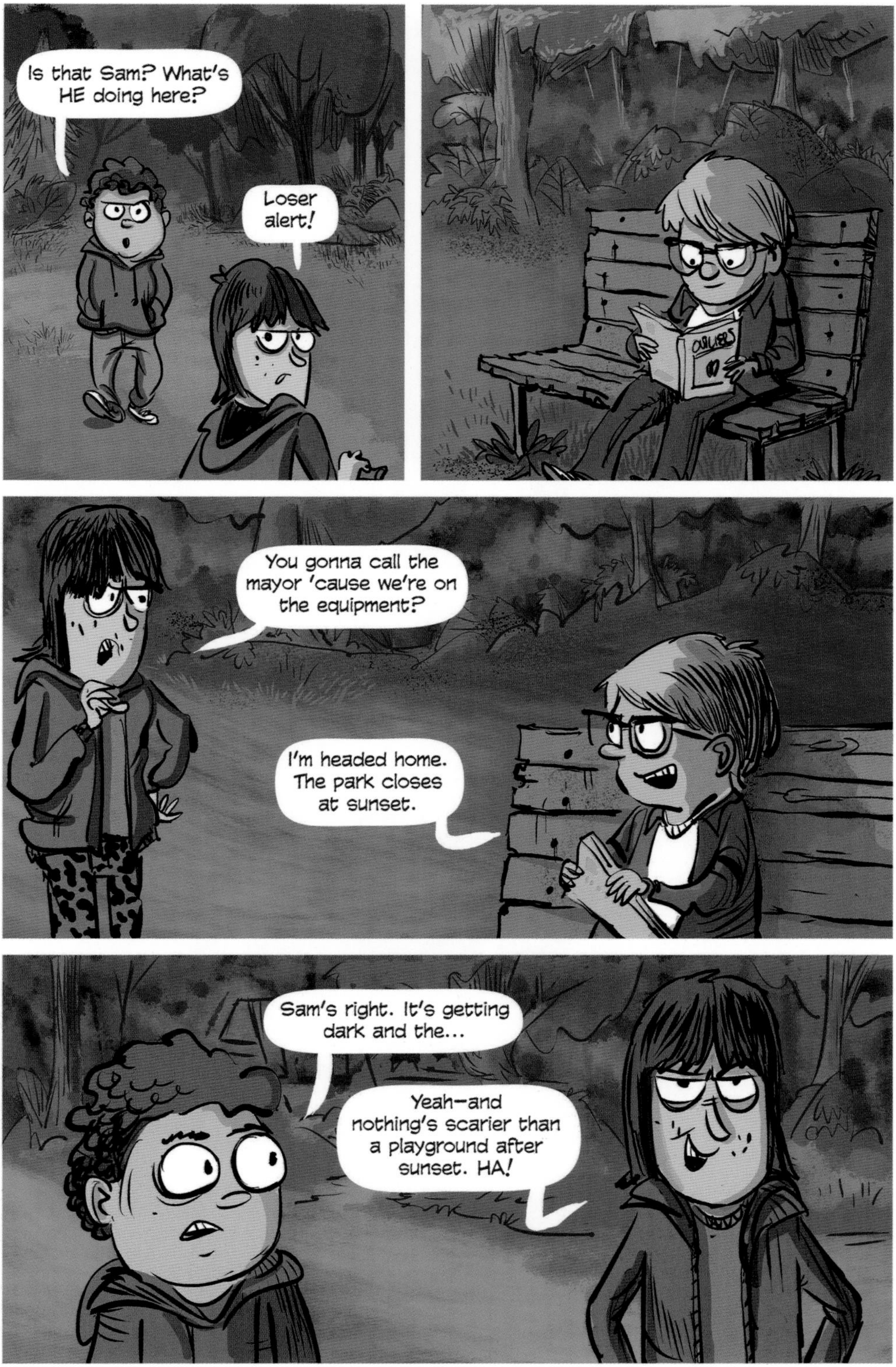
Is that Sam? What's HE doing here?
Loser alert!
You gonna call the mayor 'cause we're on the equipment?
I'm headed home. The park closes at sunset.
Sam's right. It's getting dark and the...
Yeah—and nothing's scarier than a playground after sunset. HA!

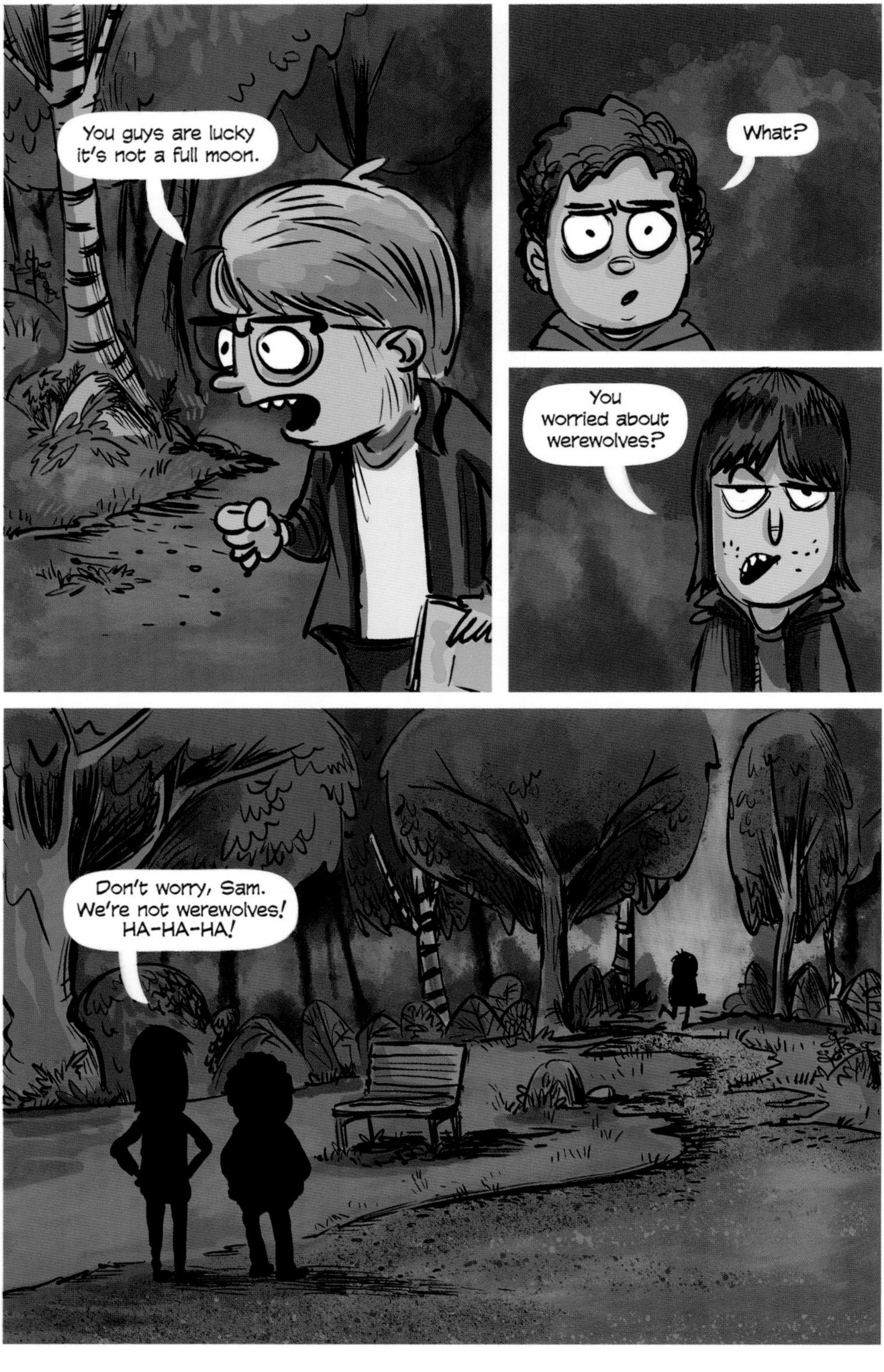
You guys are lucky it's not a full moon.
What?
You worried about werewolves?
Don't worry, Sam. We're not werewolves! HA-HA-HA!

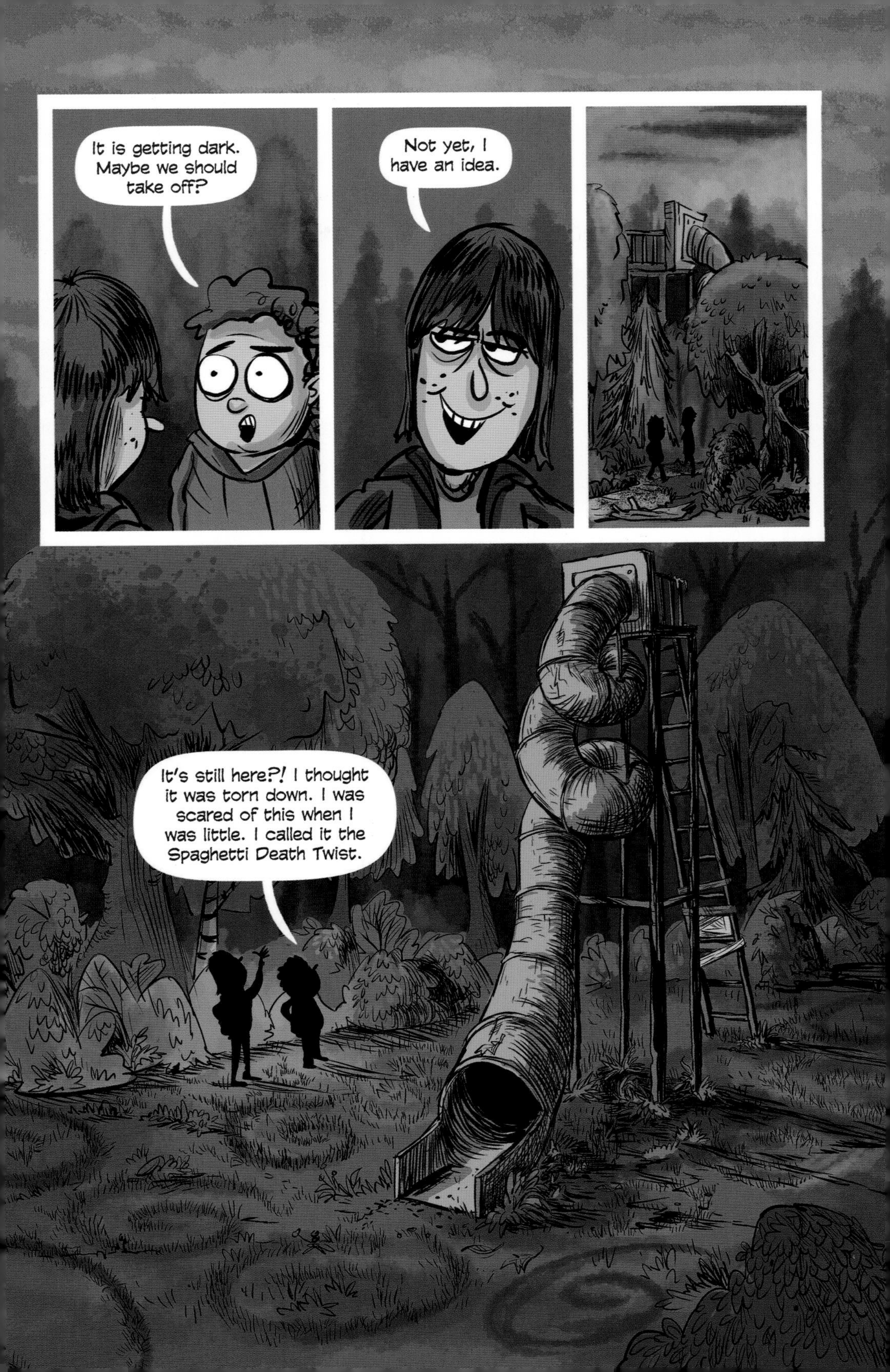
It is getting dark. Maybe we should take off?
Not yet, I have an idea.
It's still here?! I thought it was torn down. I was scared of this when I was little. I called it the Spaghetti Death Twist.

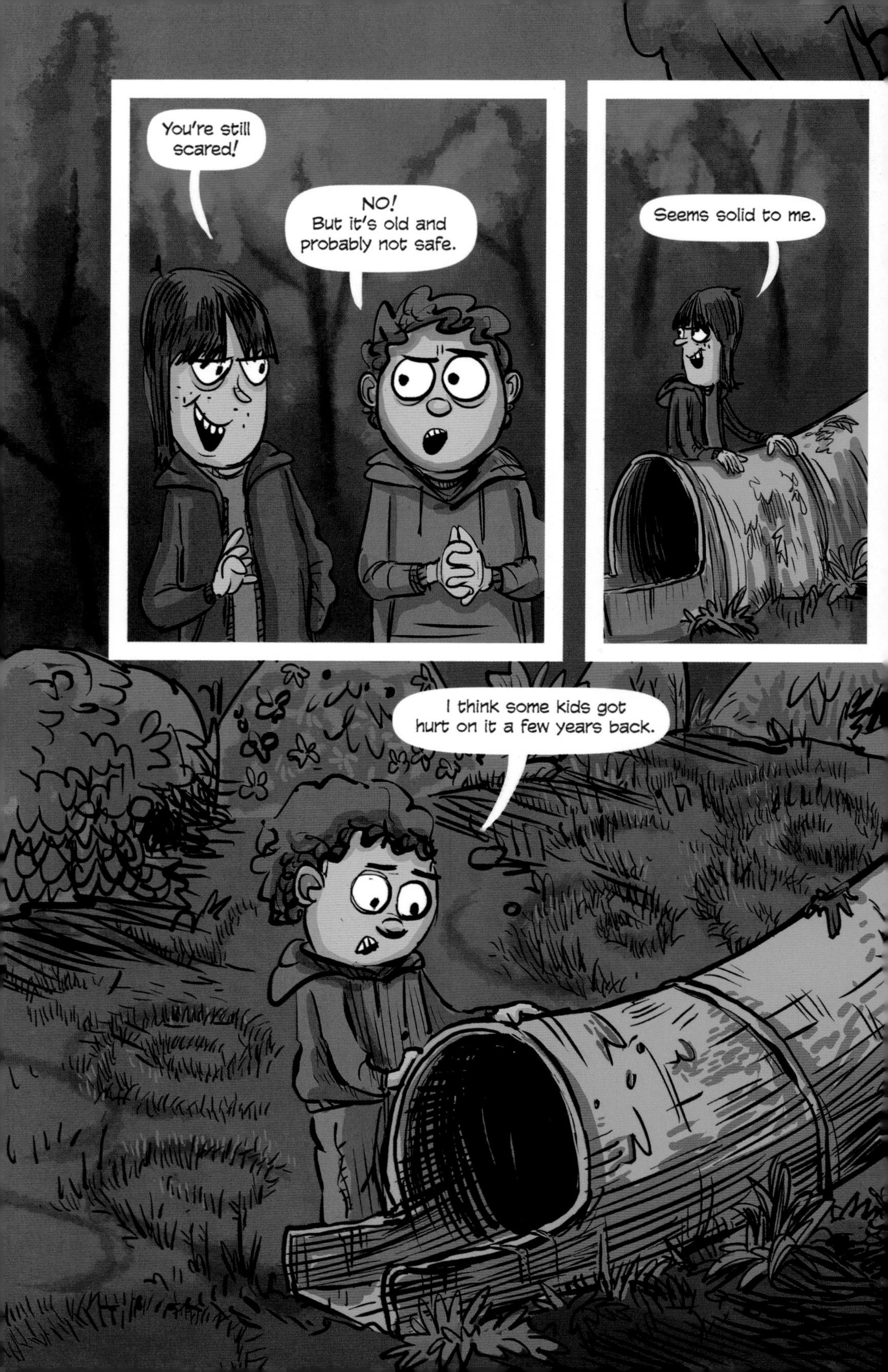

You're still scared!
NO! But it's old and probably not safe.
Seems solid to me.
I think some kids got hurt on it a few years back.

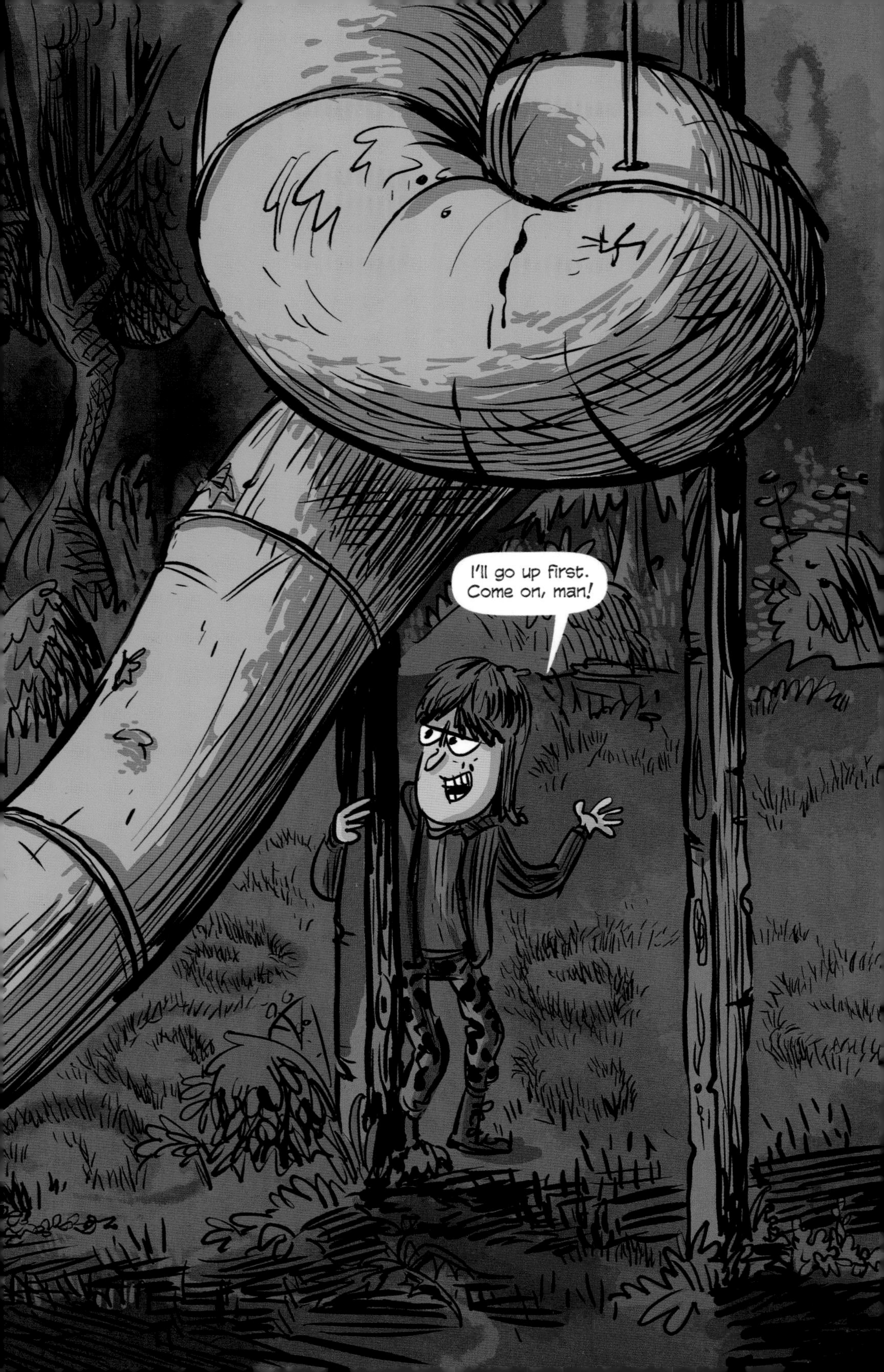
I'll go up first. Come on, man!

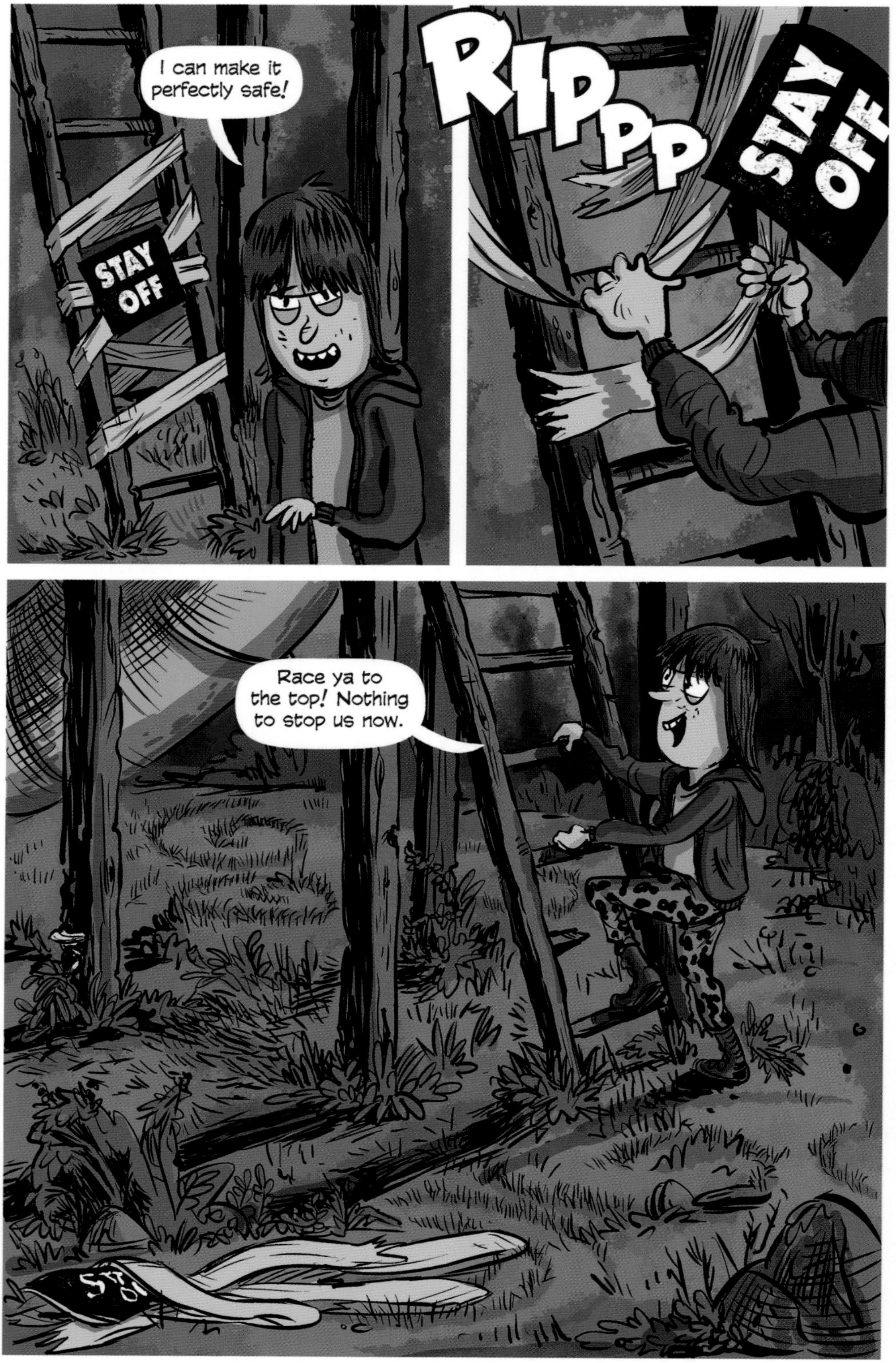
I can make it perfectly safe!
STAY OFF
RIPPP
STAY OFF
Race ya to the top! Nothing to stop us now.

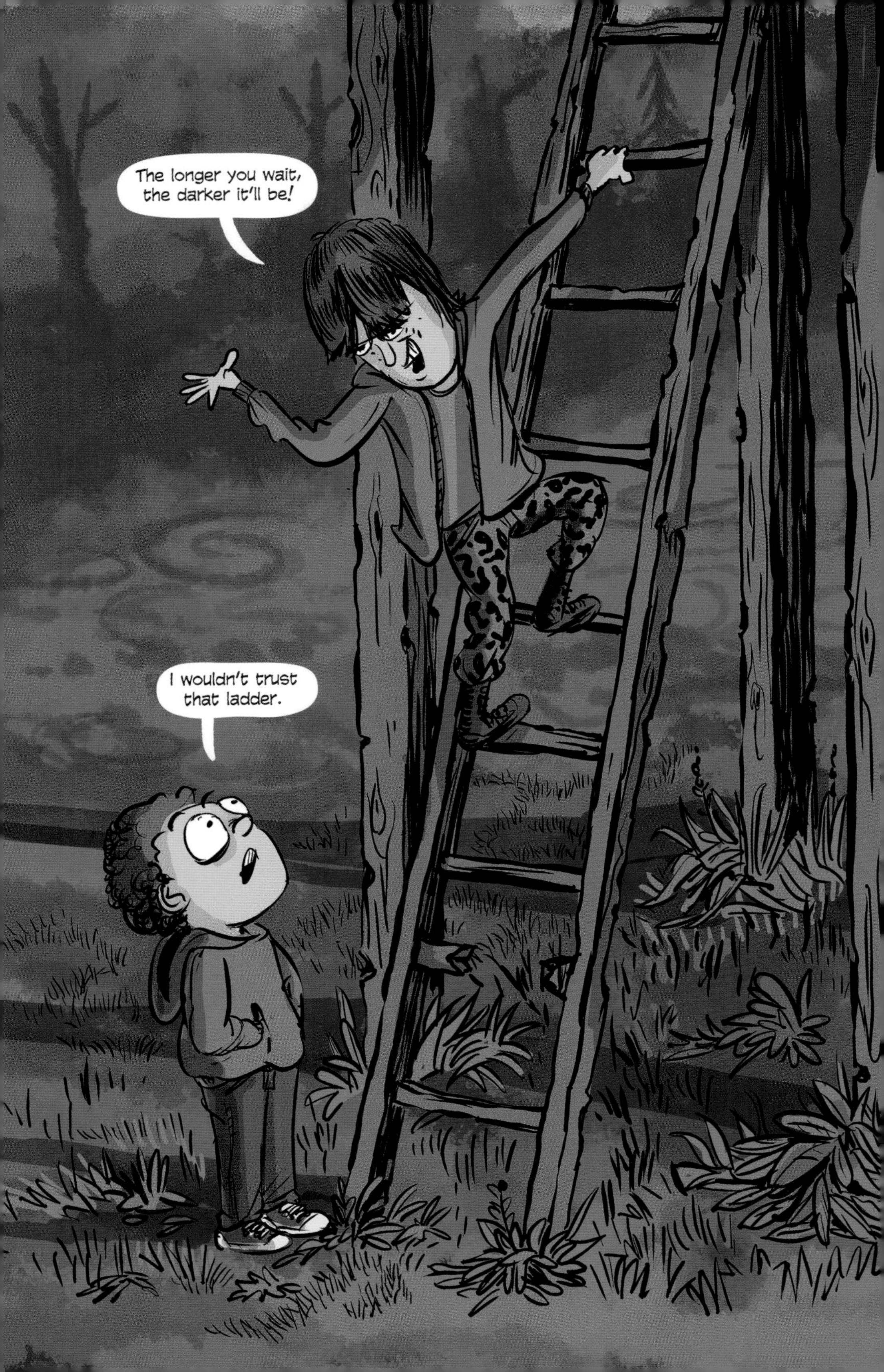
The longer you wait, the darker it'll be!
I wouldn't trust that ladder.

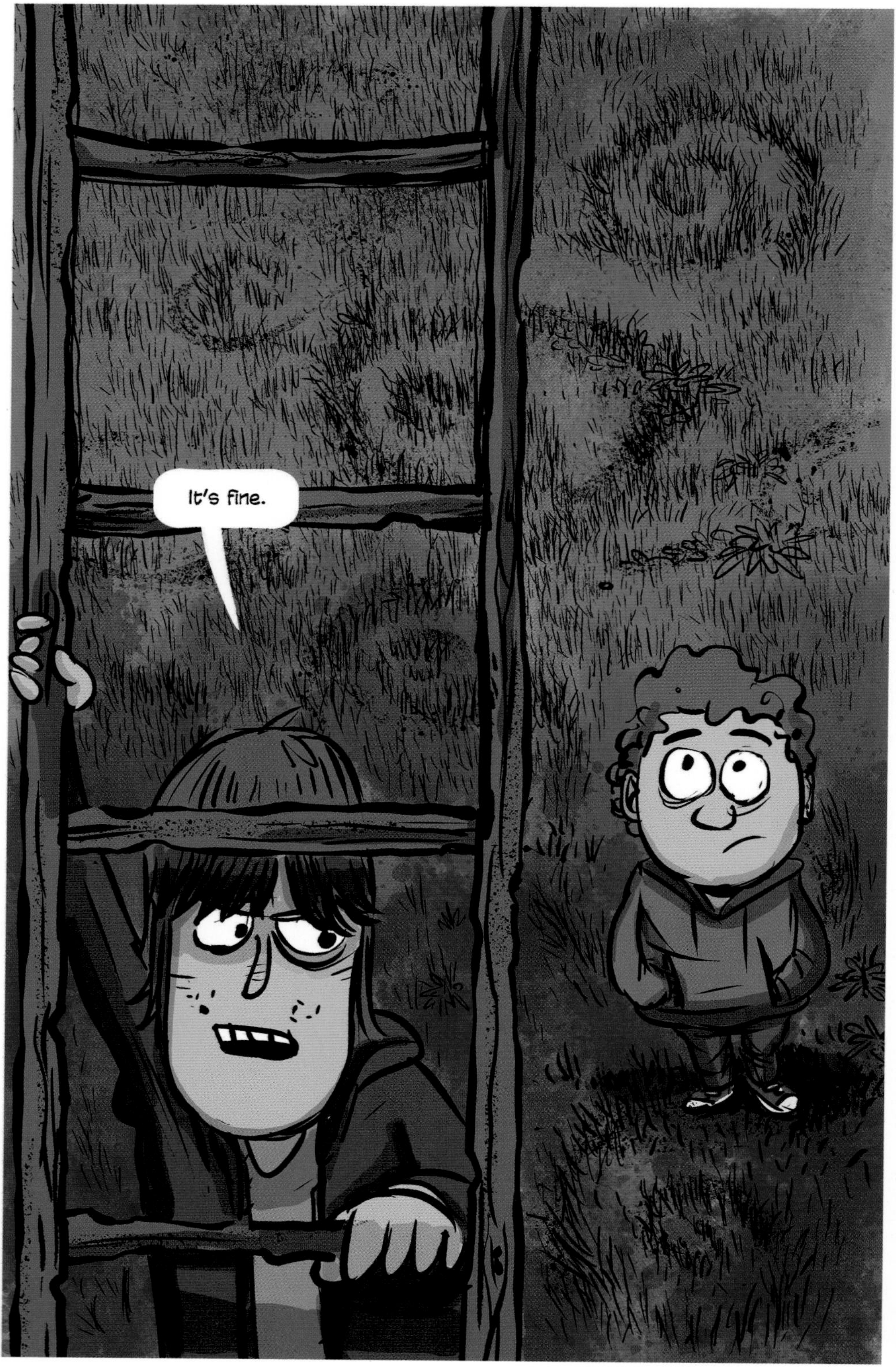
It's fine.

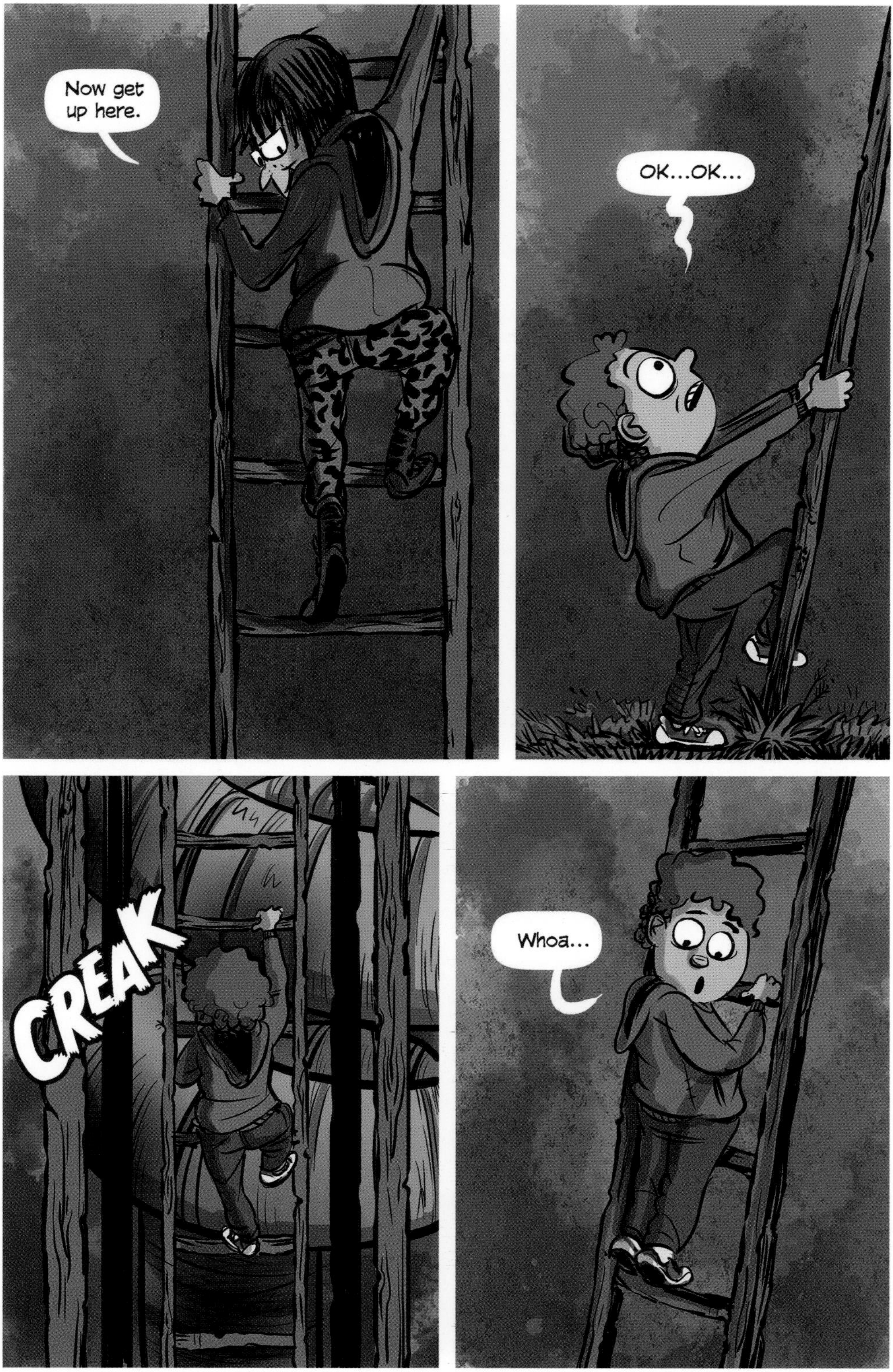
Now get up here.
OK...OK...
CREAK
Whoa...

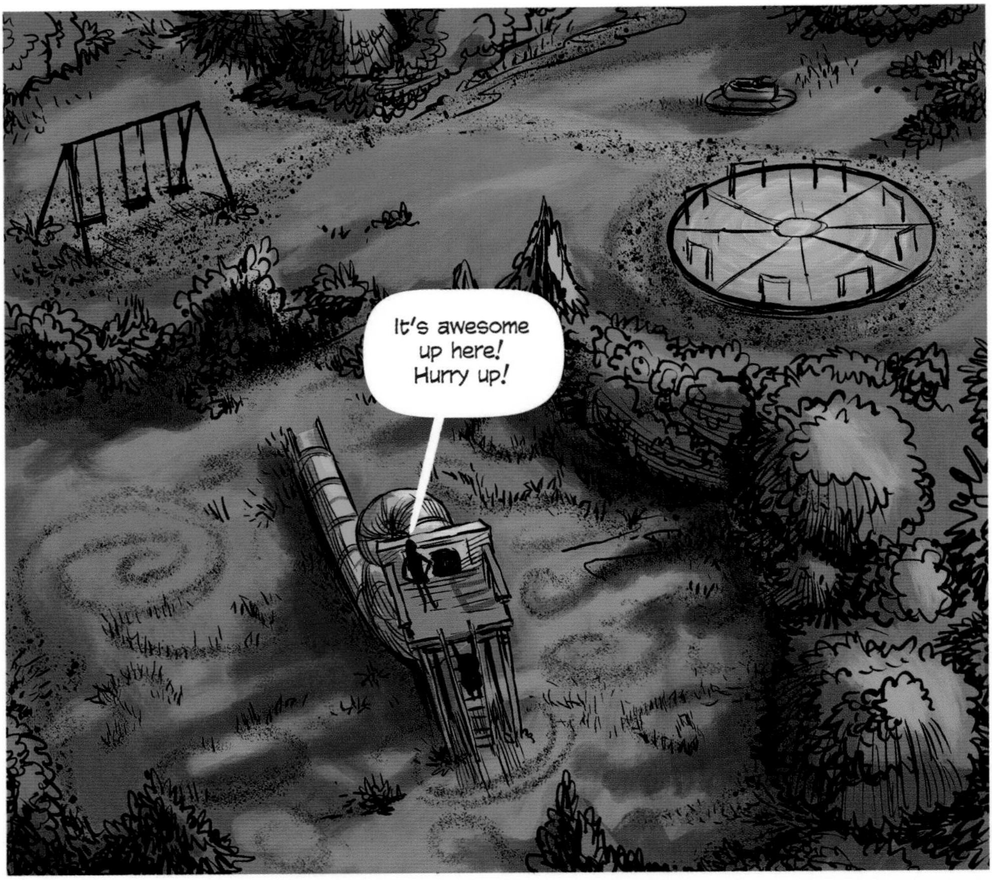
It's awesome up here! Hurry up!

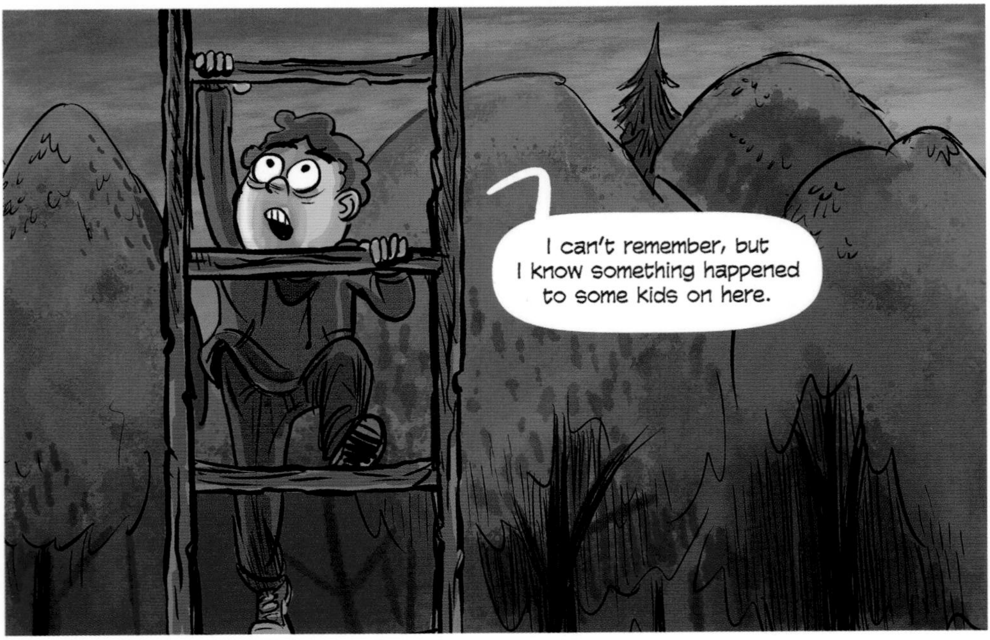
I can't remember, but I know something happened to some kids on here.

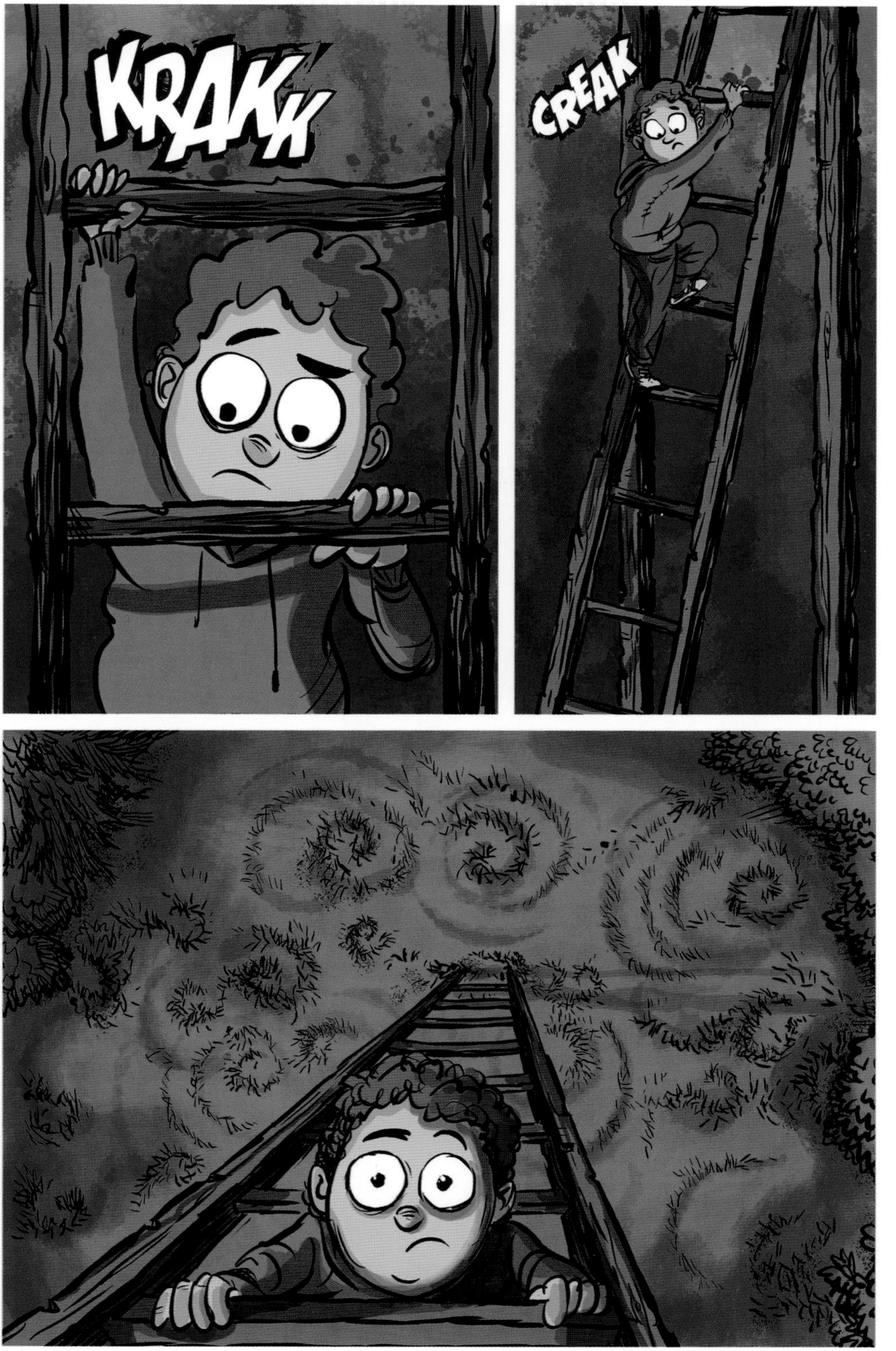
KRAKK
CREAK

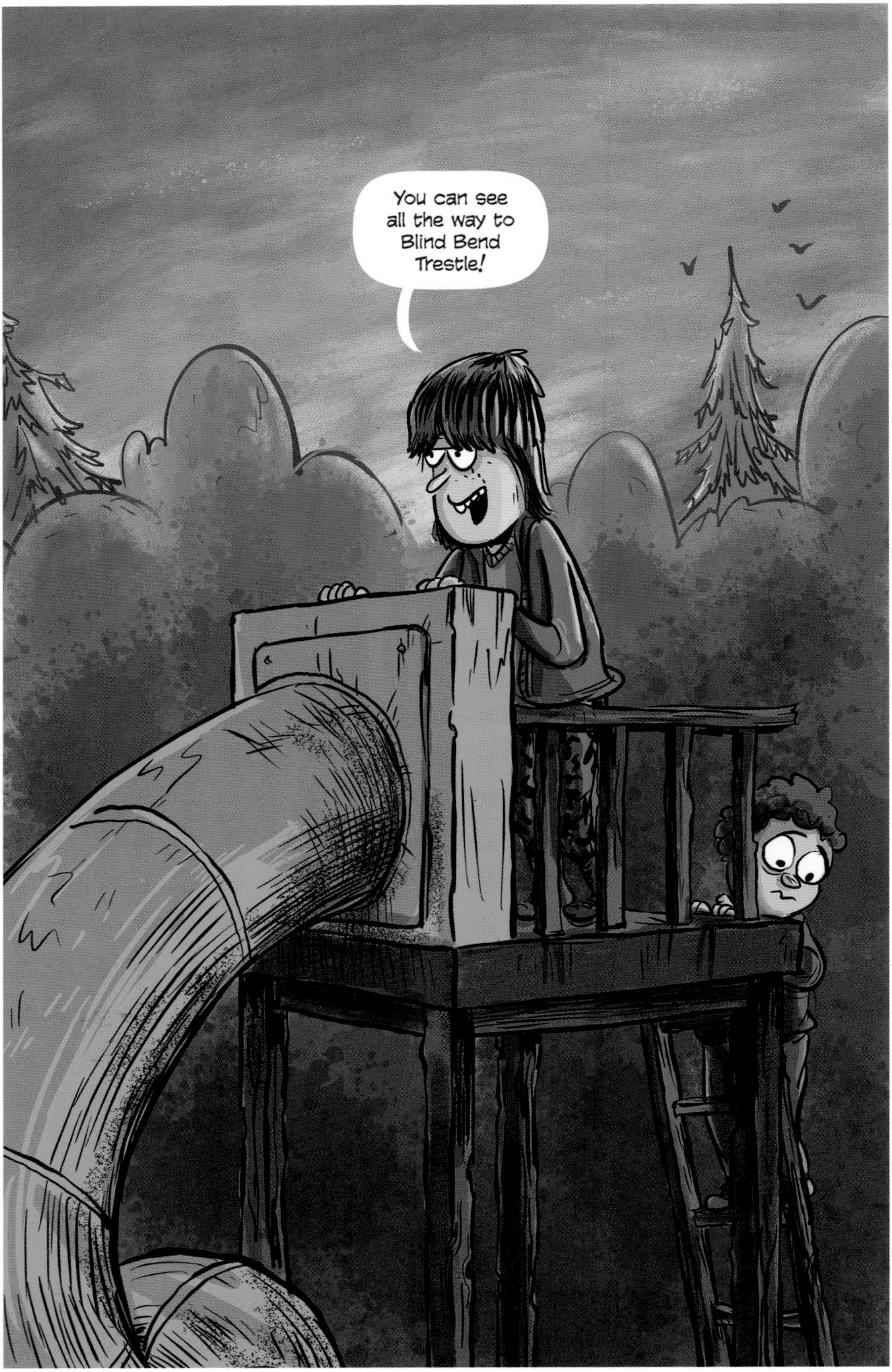
You can see all the way to Blind Bend Trestle!

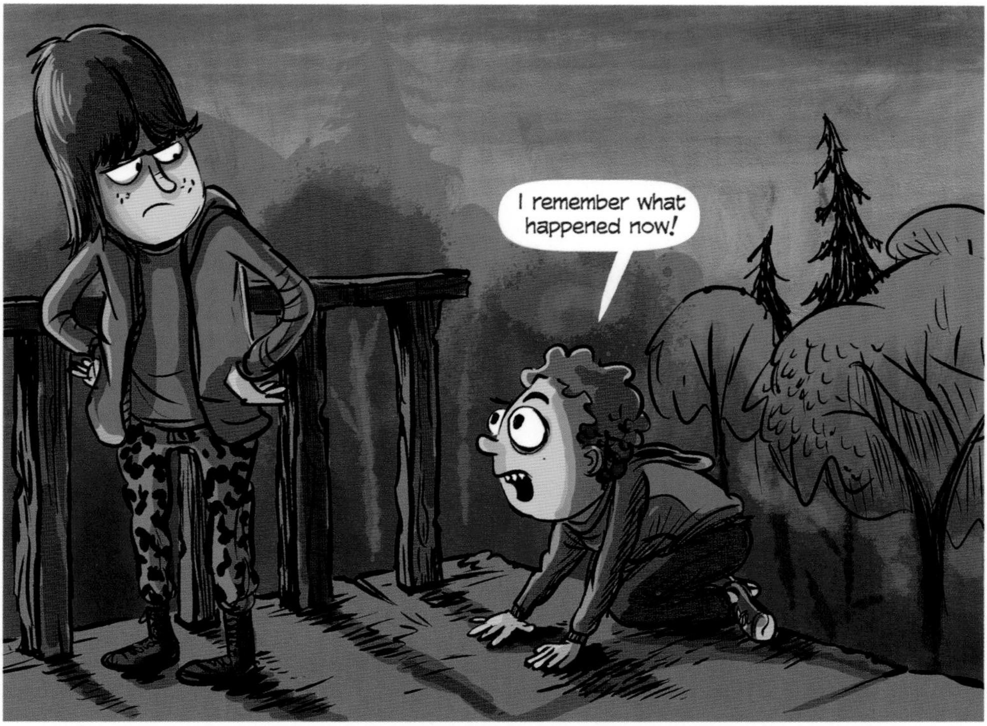
I remember what happened now!

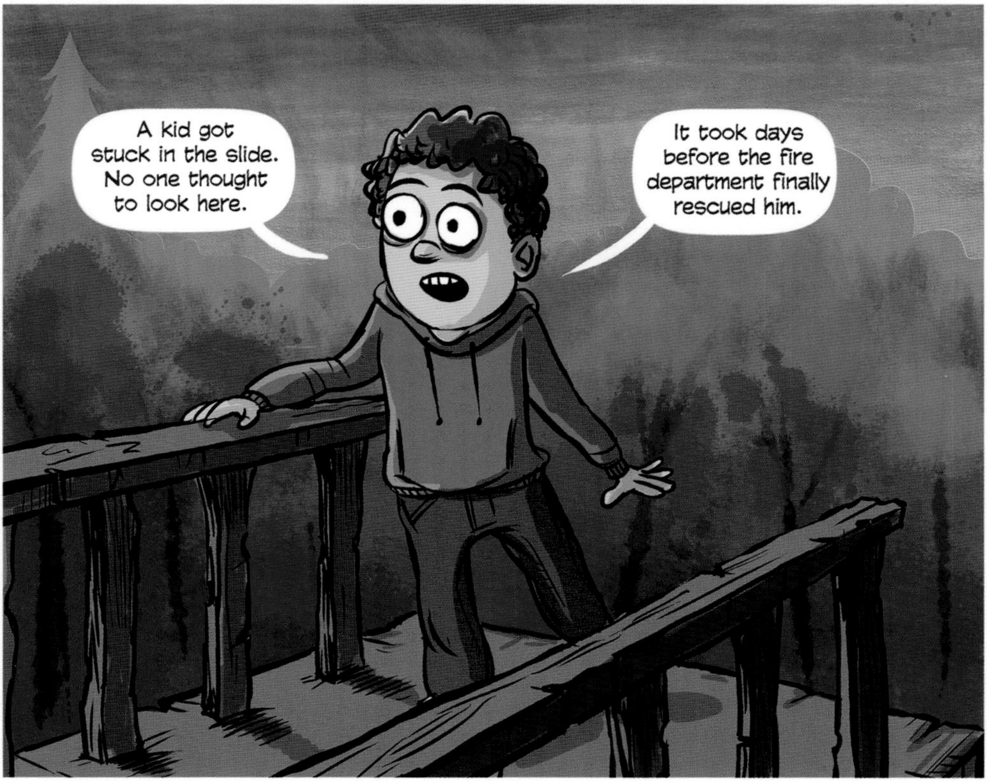
A kid got stuck in the slide. No one thought to look here.
It took days before the fire department finally rescued him.

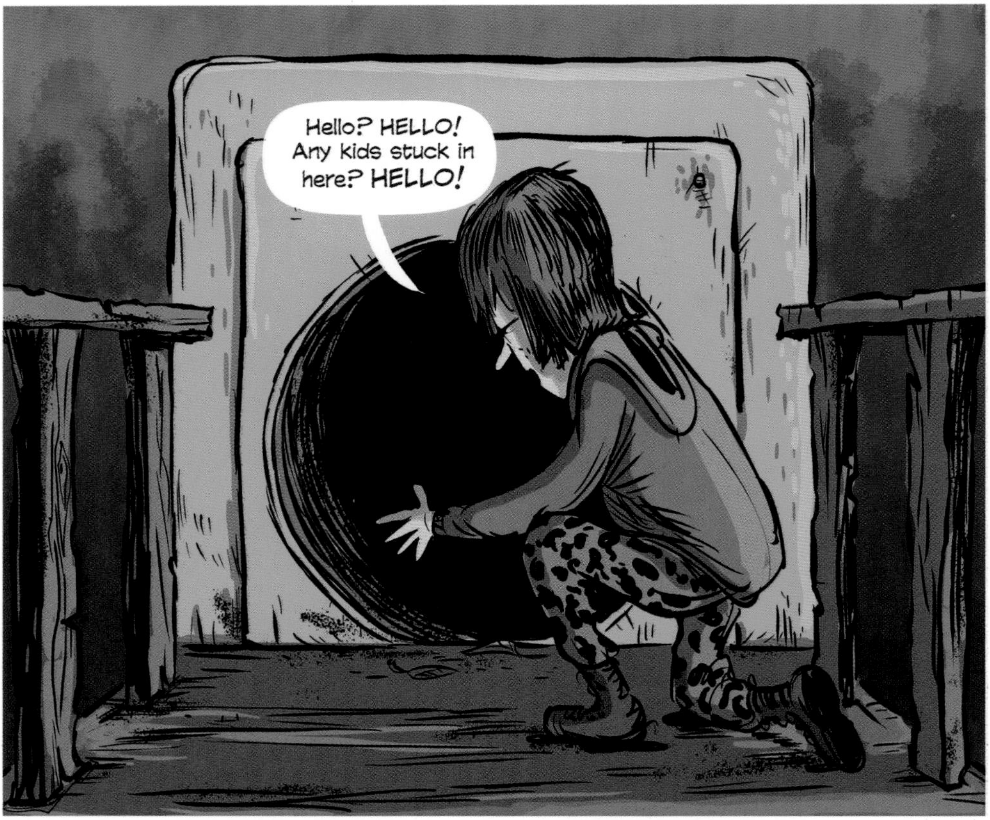
Hello? HELLO! Any kids stuck in here? HELLO!

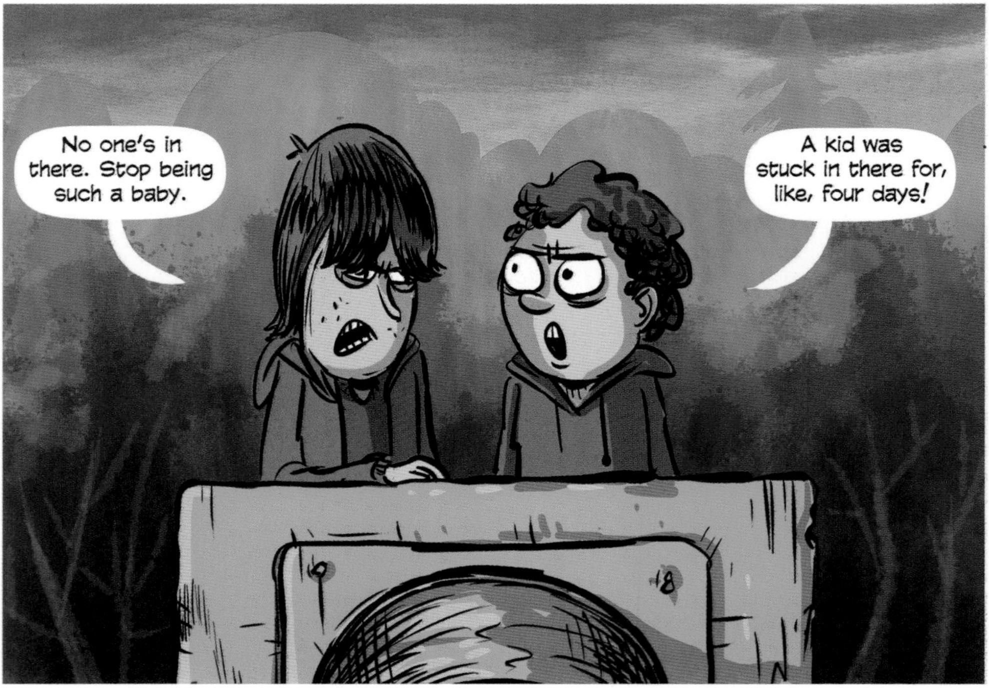
No one's in there. Stop being such a baby.
A kid was stuck in there for, like, four days!

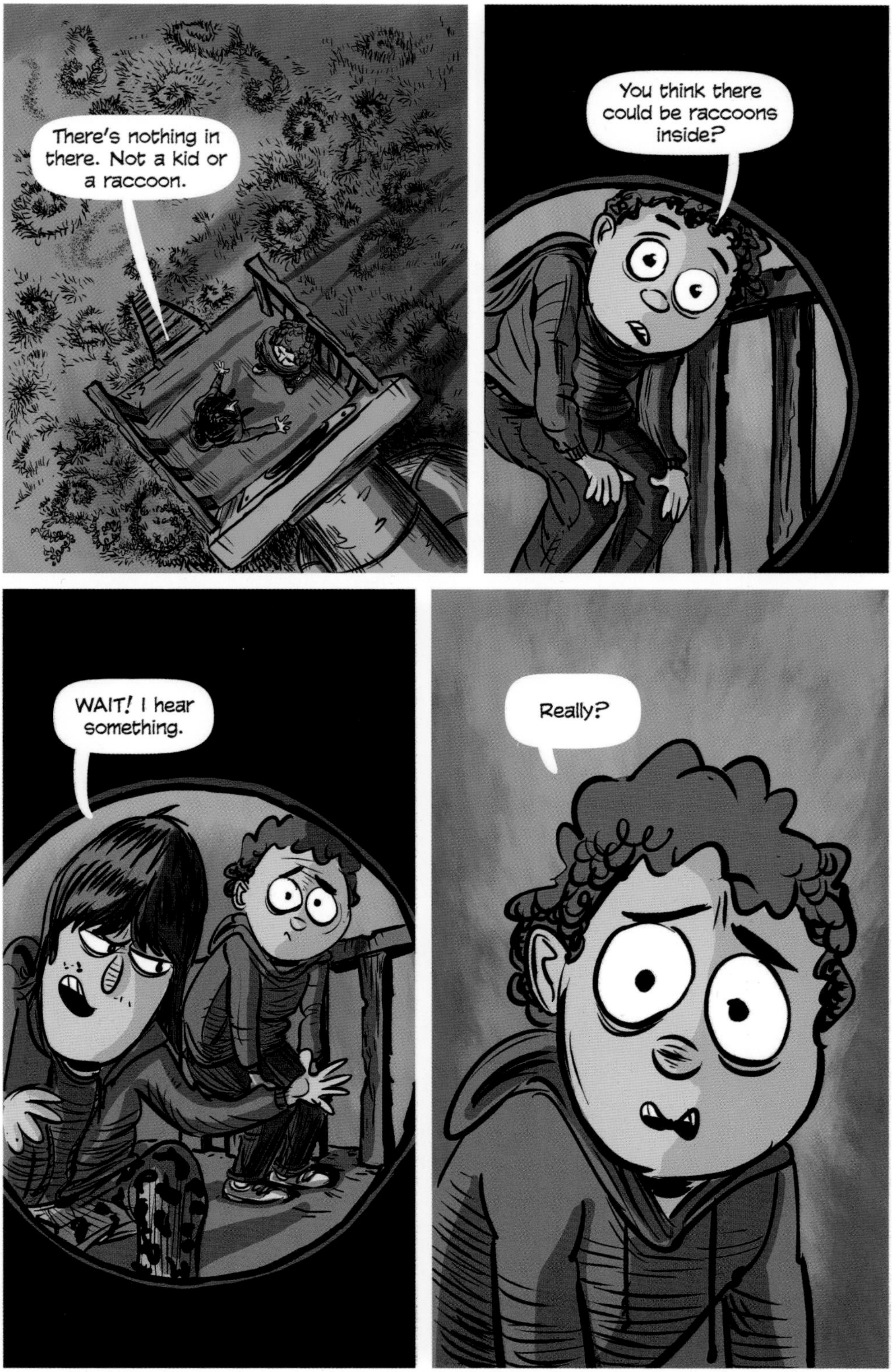
There's nothing in there. Not a kid or a raccoon.
You think there could be raccoons inside?
WAIT! I hear something.
Really?

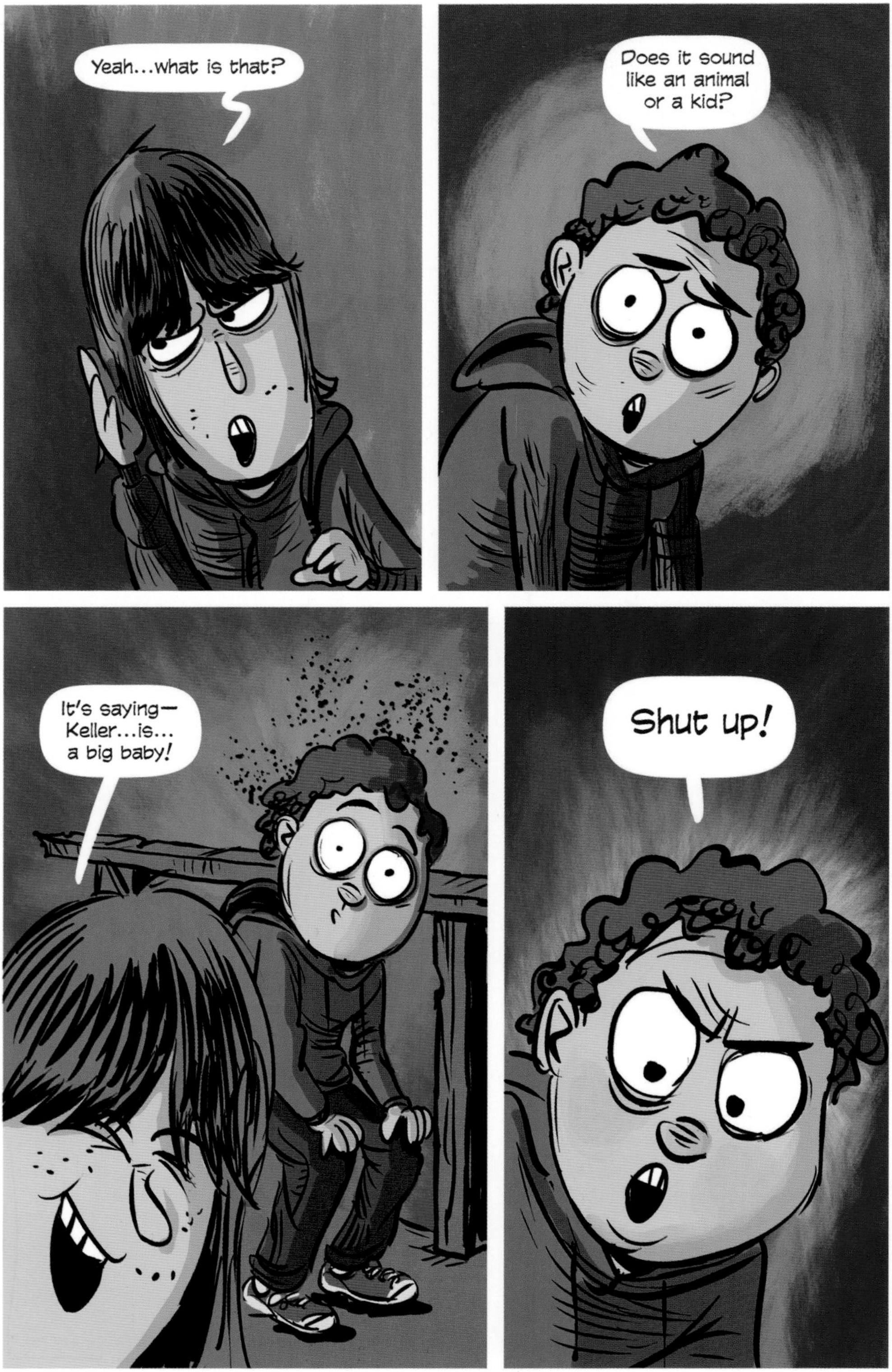
Yeah...what is that?
Does it sound like an animal or a kid?
It's saying—Keller...is... a big baby!
Shut up!

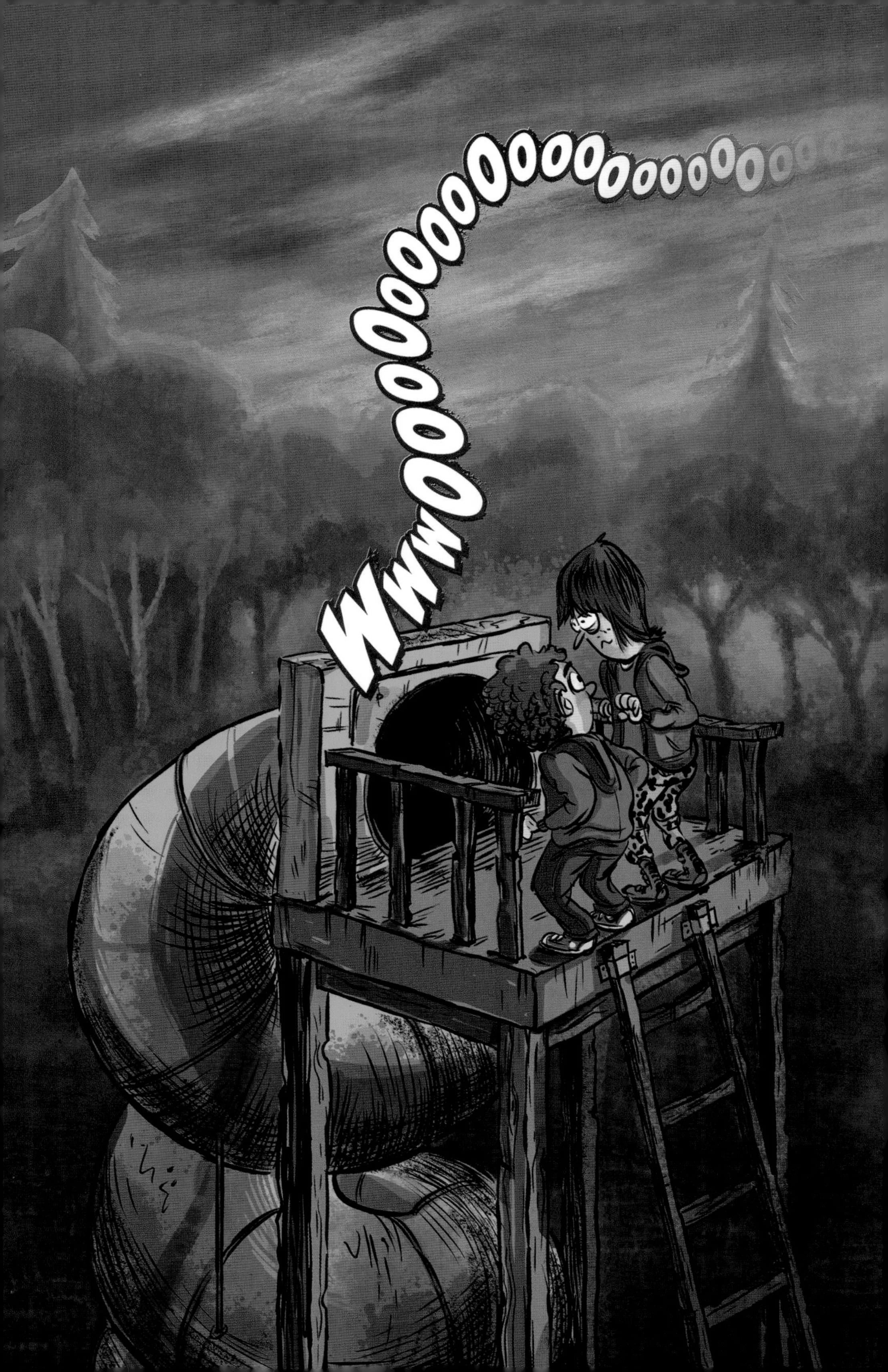
WWWOOOOOOOOOOOOOOOOOOOOOOOOOOO

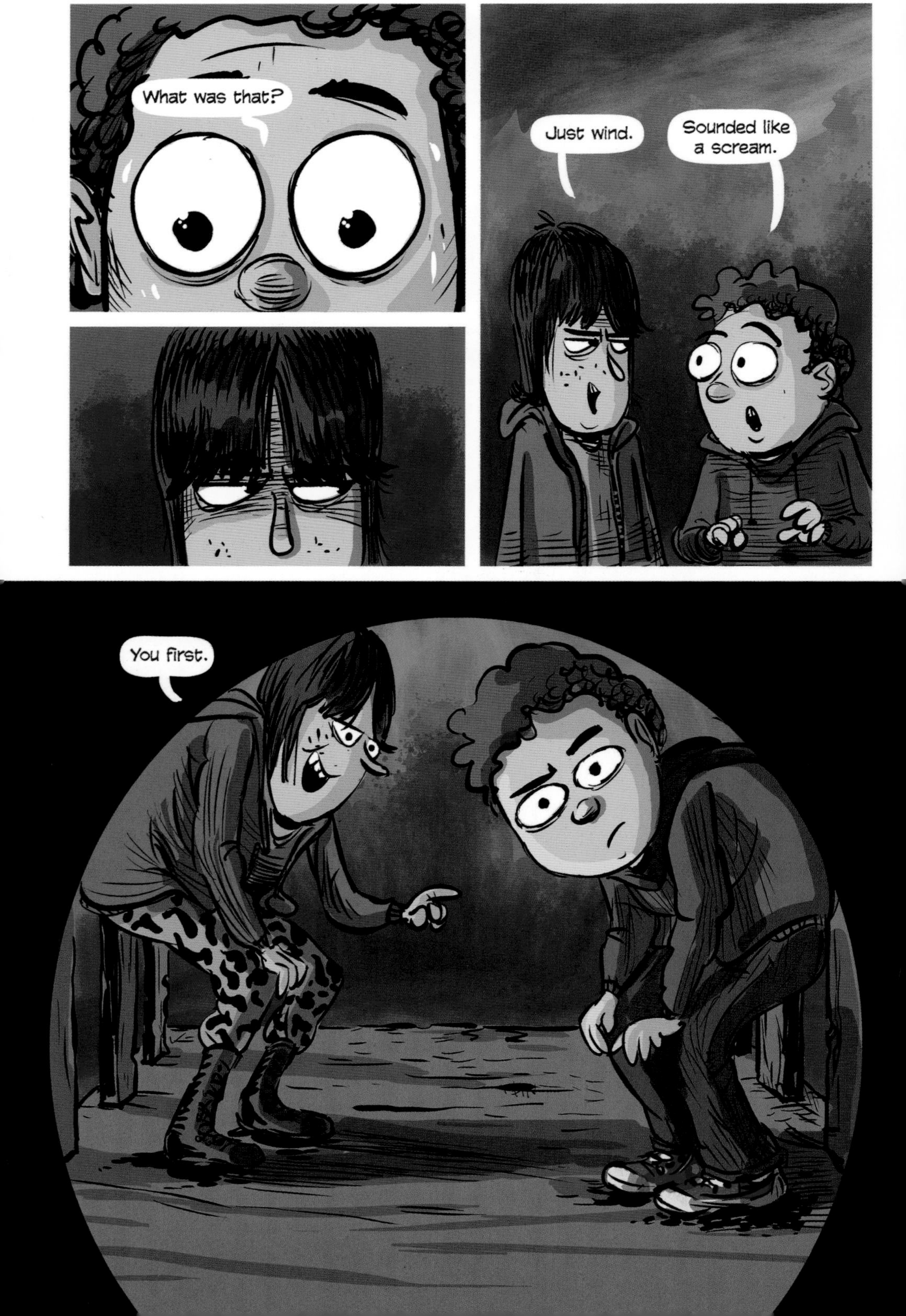
What was that?
Just wind.
Sounded like a scream.
You first.

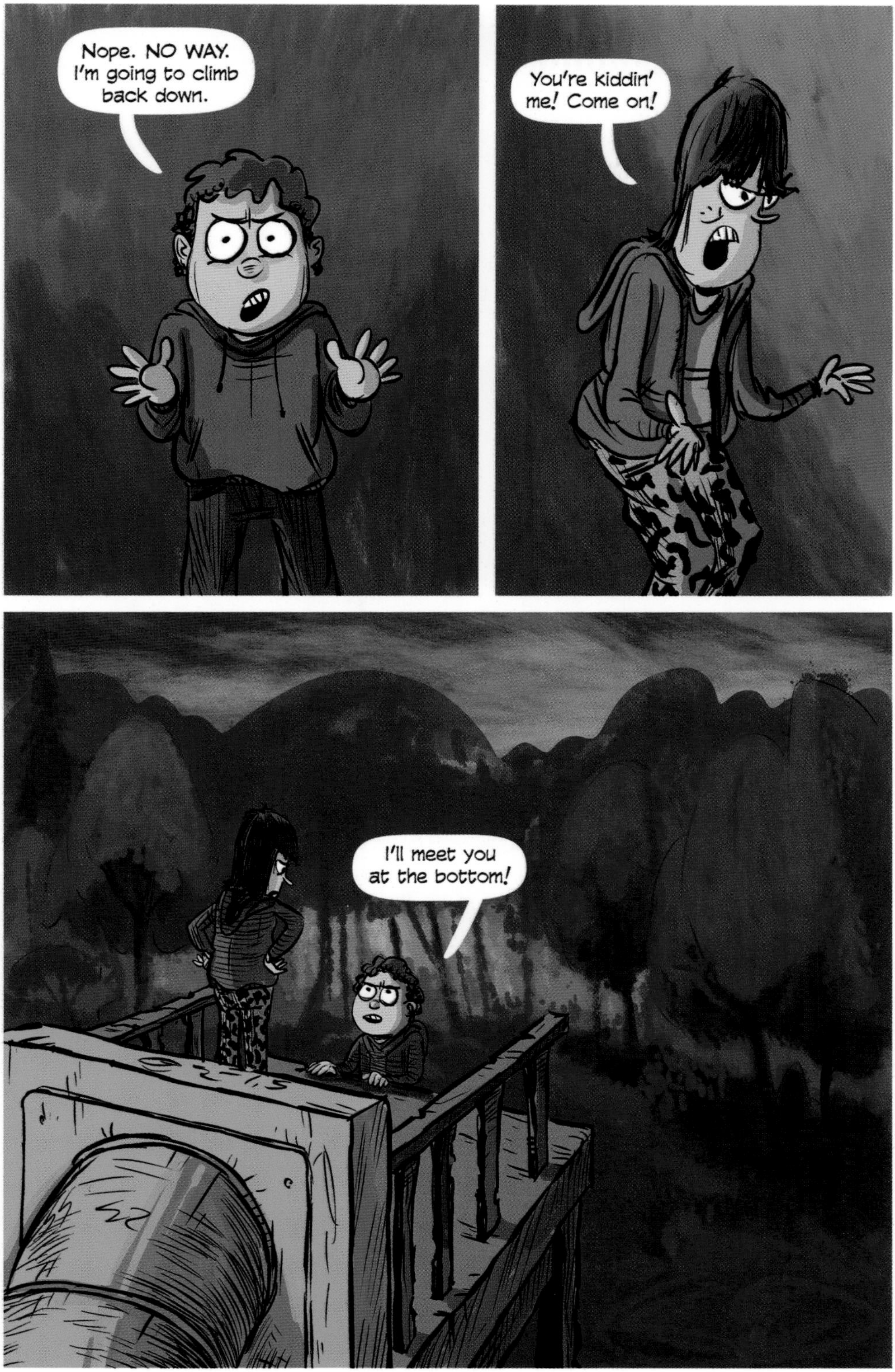
Nope. NO WAY. I'm going to climb back down.
You're kiddin' me! Come on!
I'll meet you at the bottom!

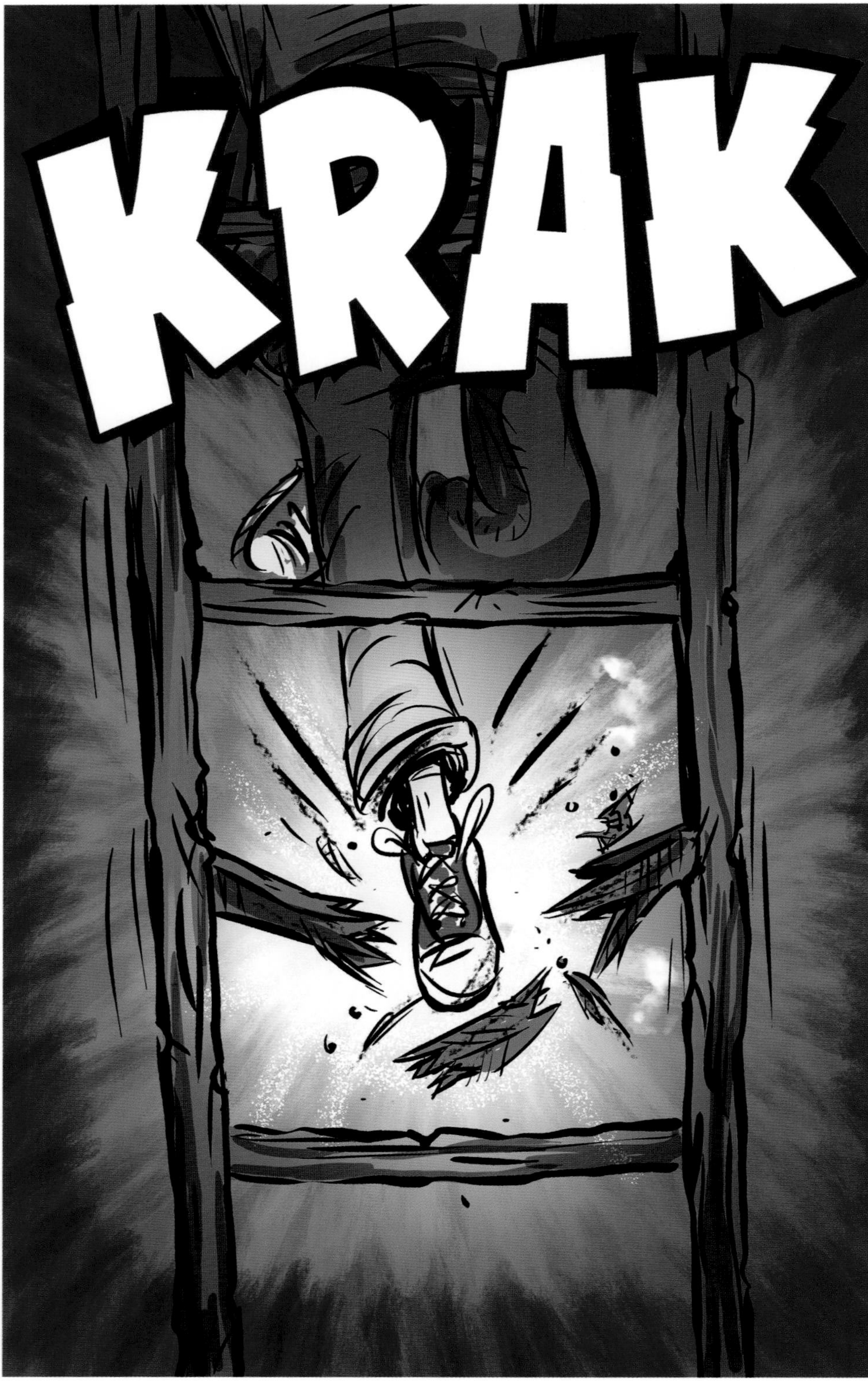
KRAK

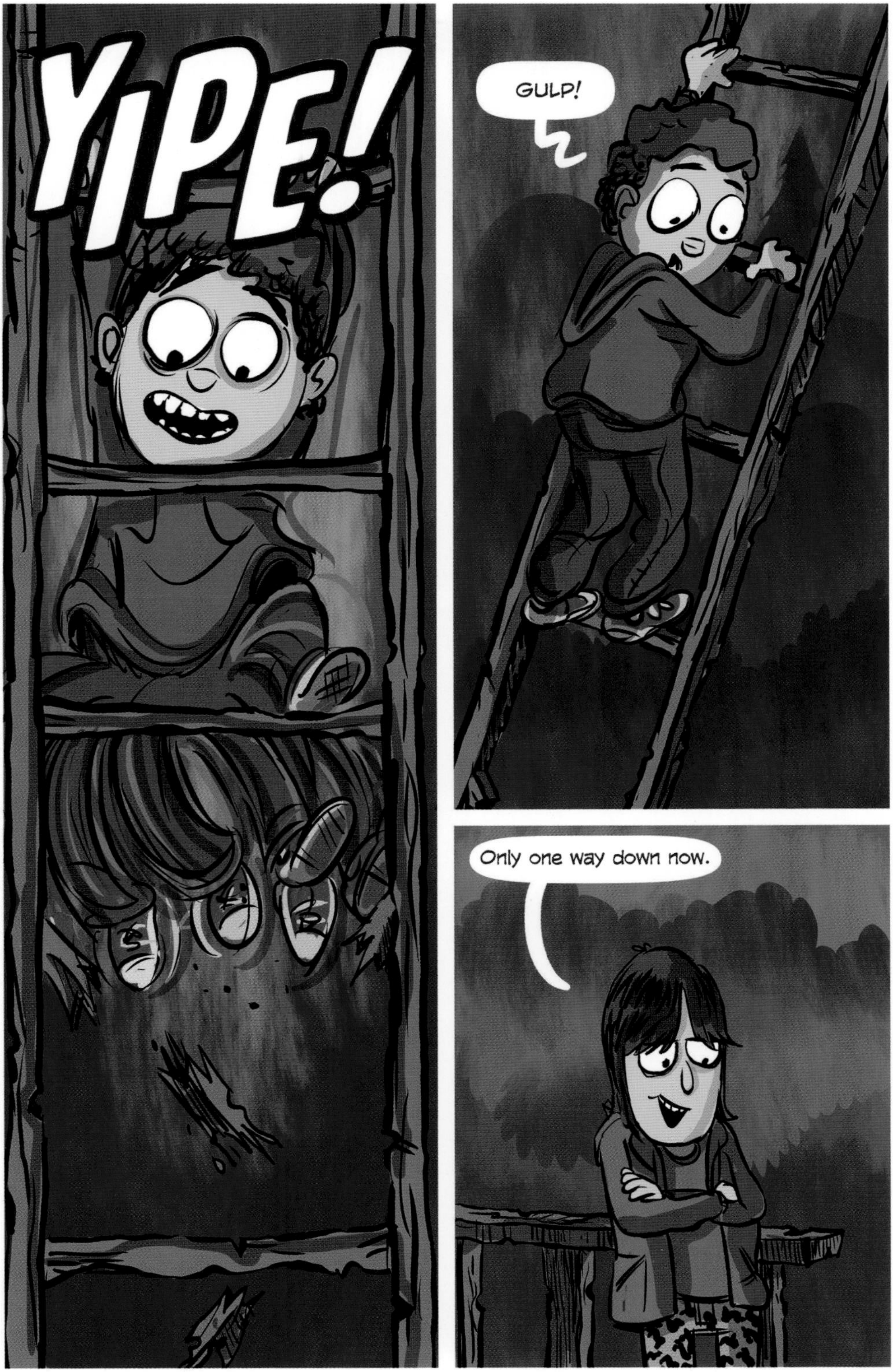
YIPE!
GULP!
Only one way down now.

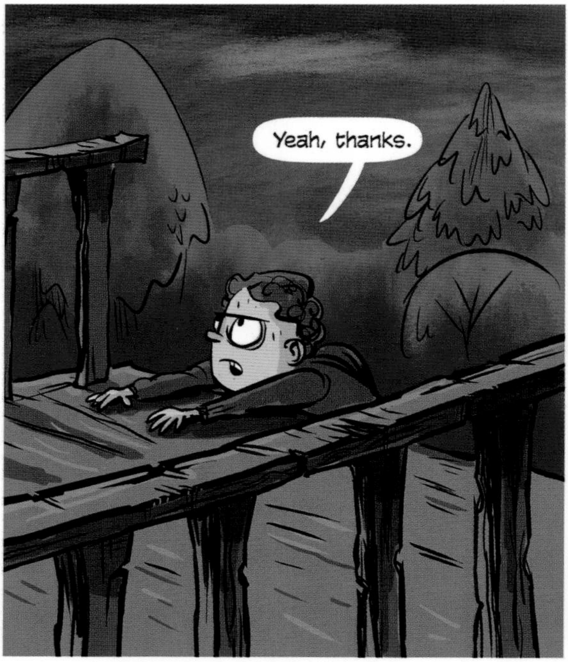
Yeah, thanks.

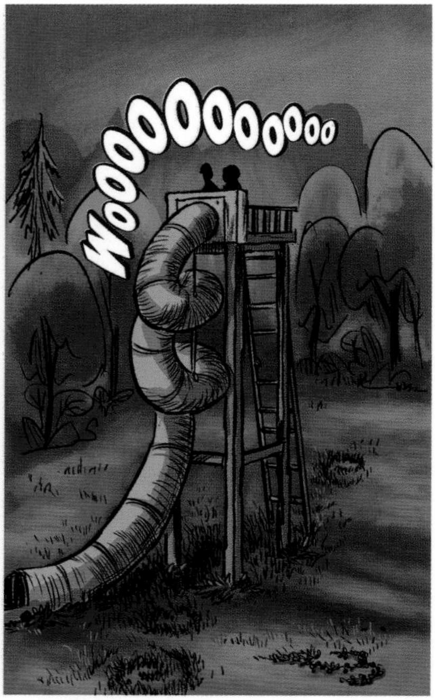
WOOOOOOOOOoo

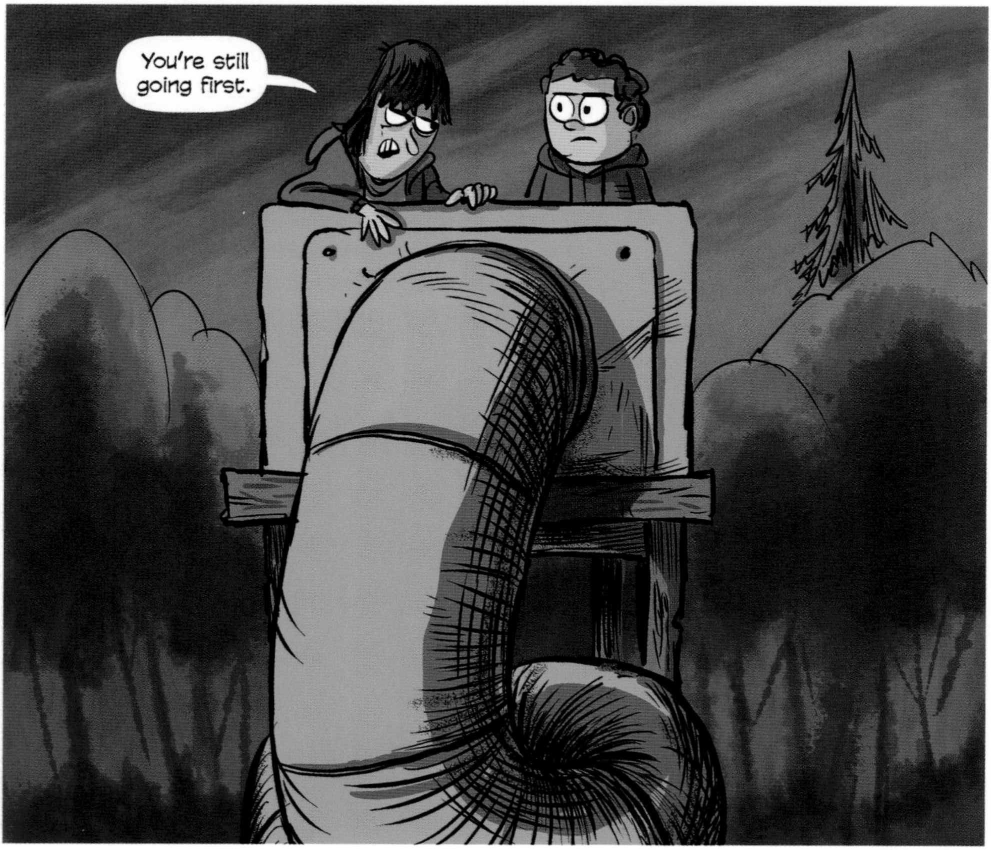
You're still going first.

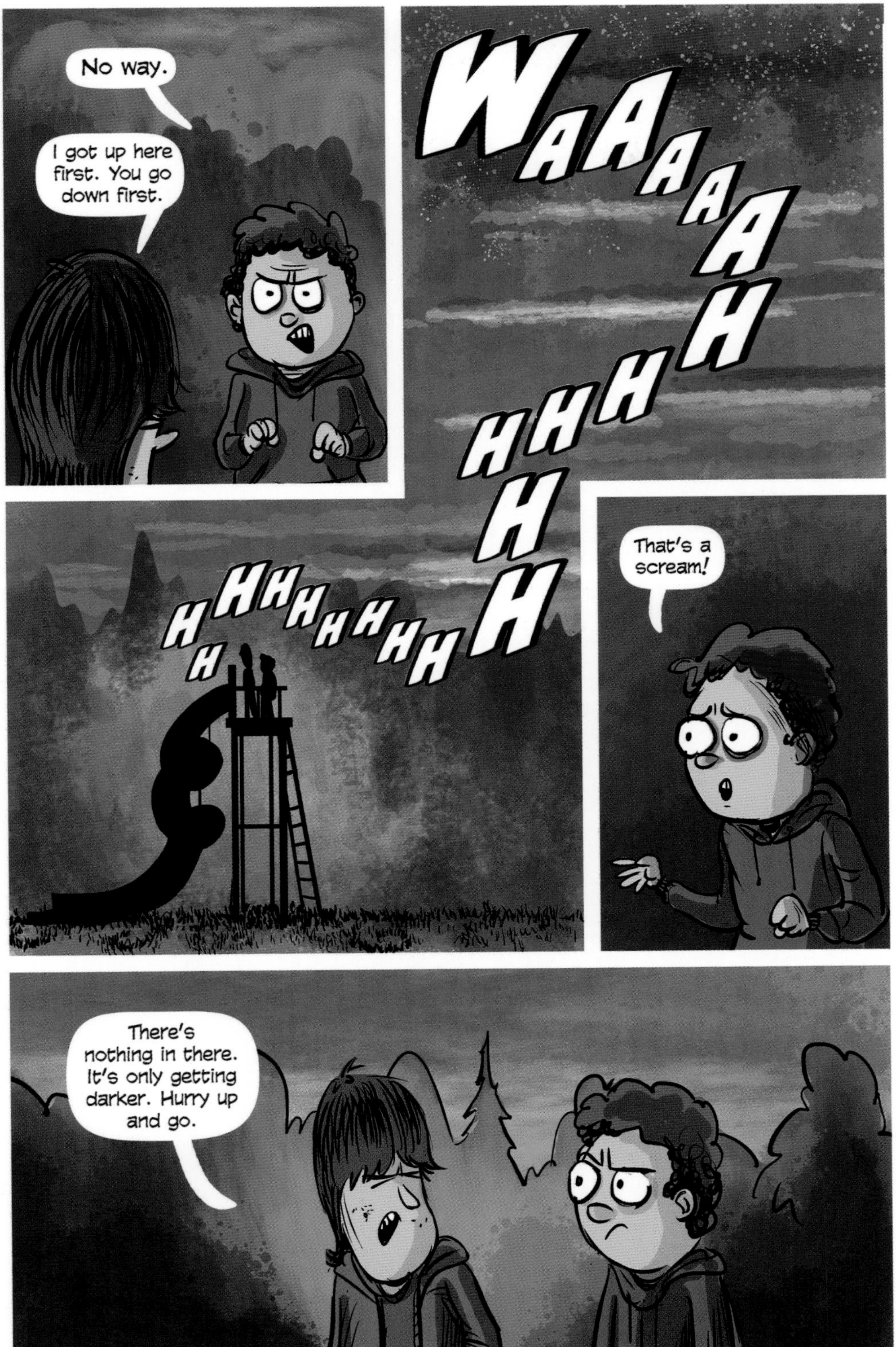
No way.
I got up here first. You go down first.
WAAAAAAHHHHHHHHHHHHHHHHHHH
That's a scream!
There's nothing in there. It's only getting darker. Hurry up and go.

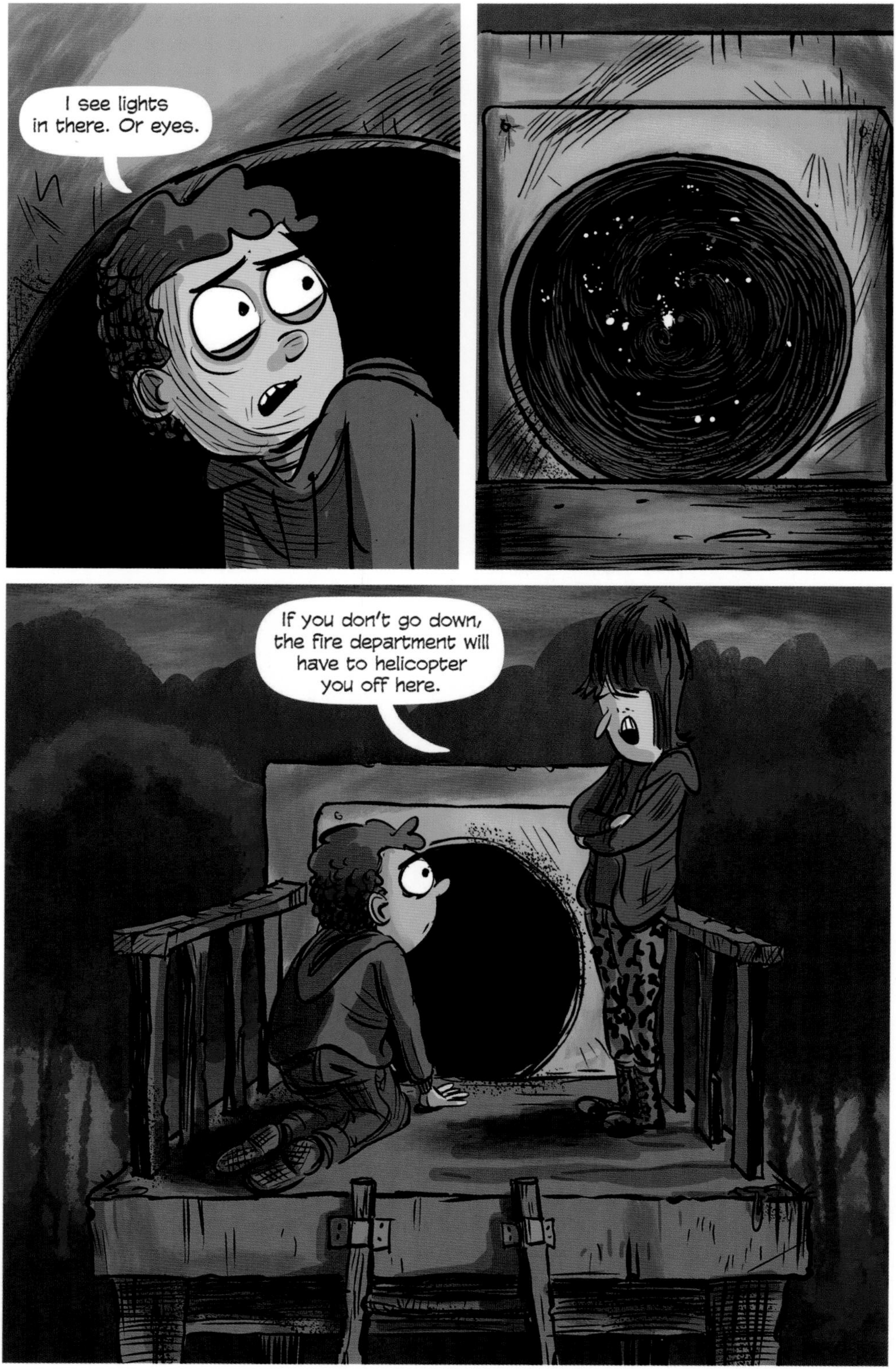
I see lights in there. Or eyes.
If you don't go down, the fire department will have to helicopter you off here.

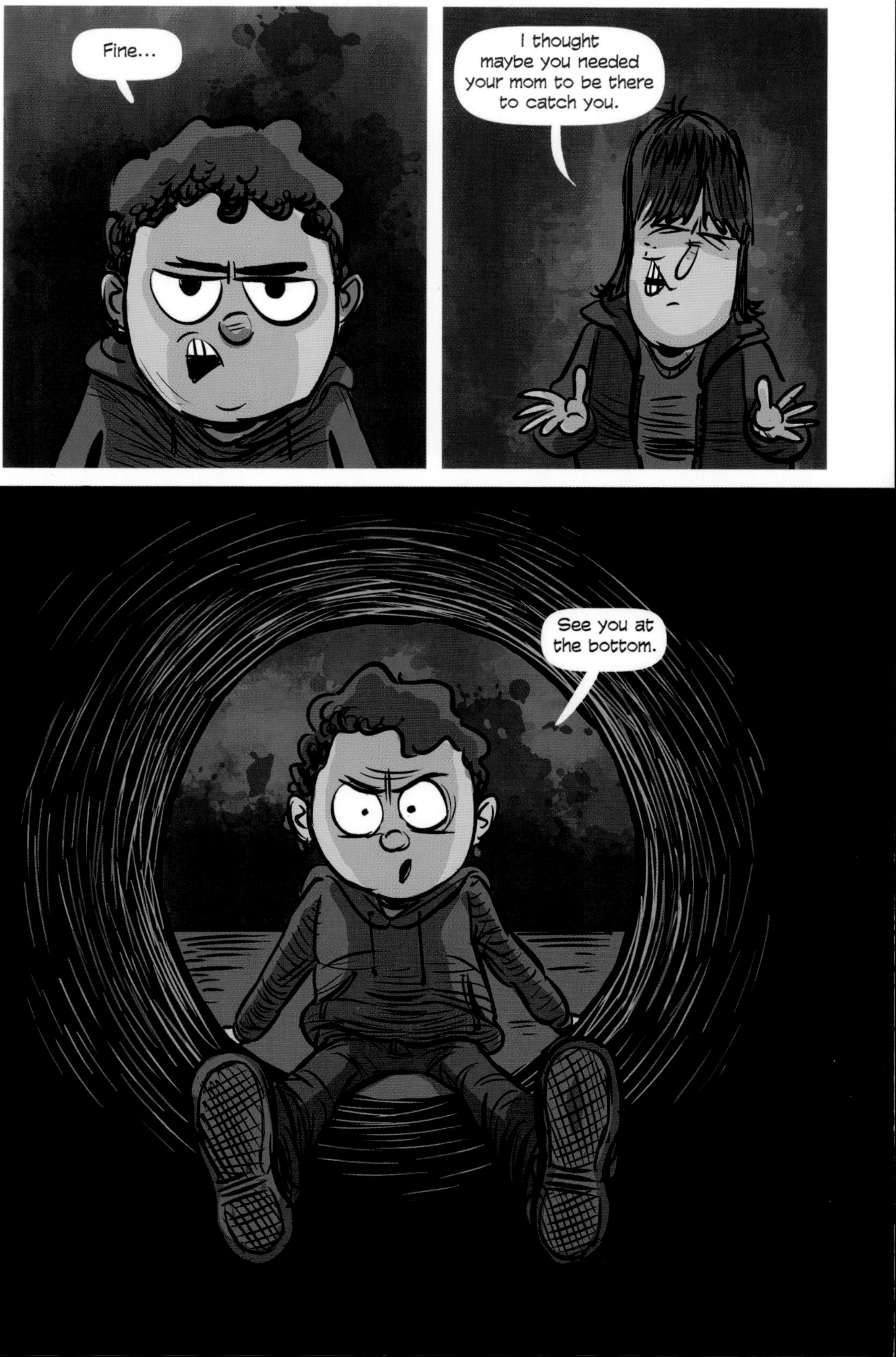
Fine...
I thought maybe you needed your mom to be there to catch you.
See you at the bottom.

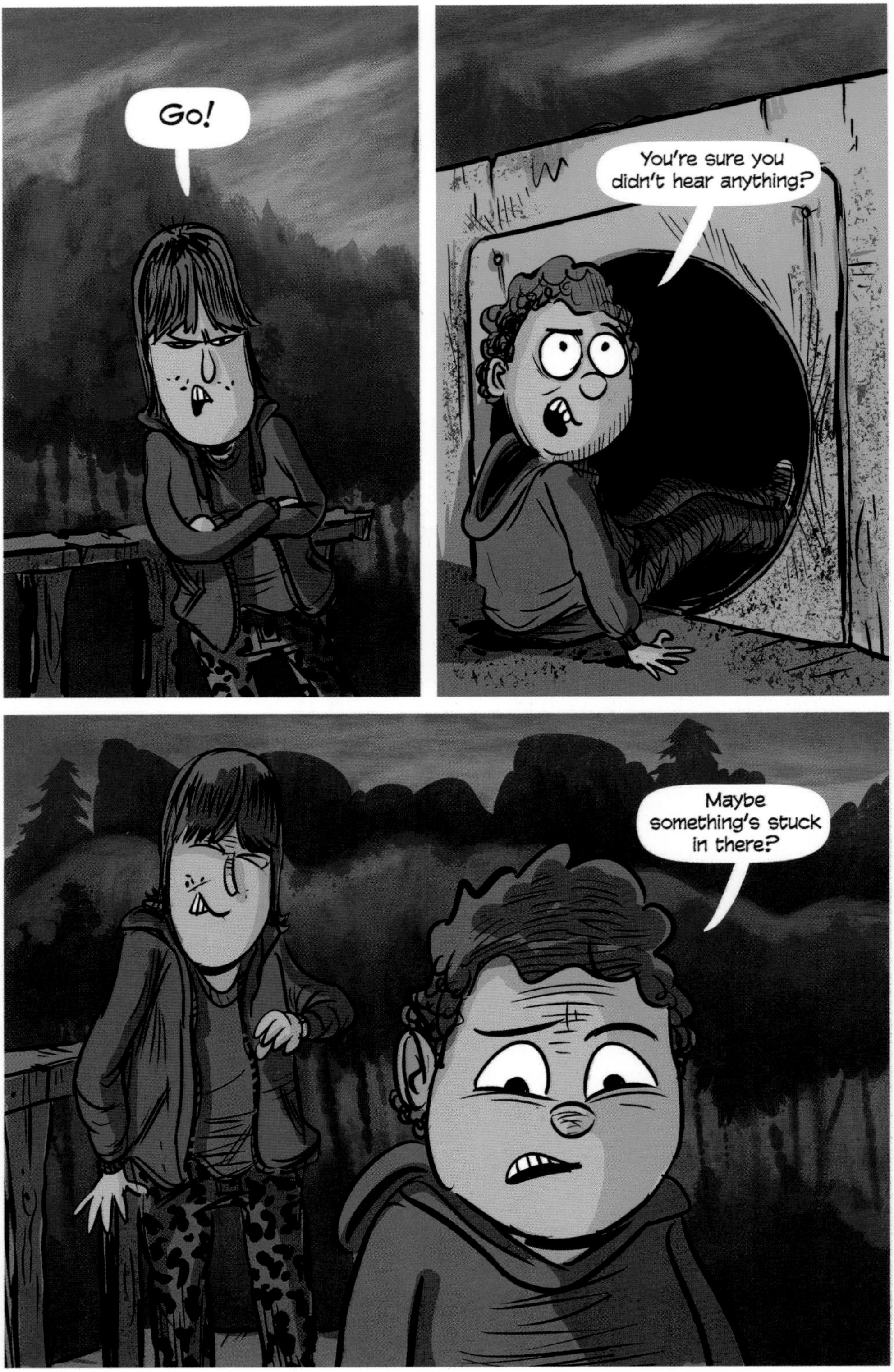
Go!
You're sure you didn't hear anything?
Maybe something's stuck in there?

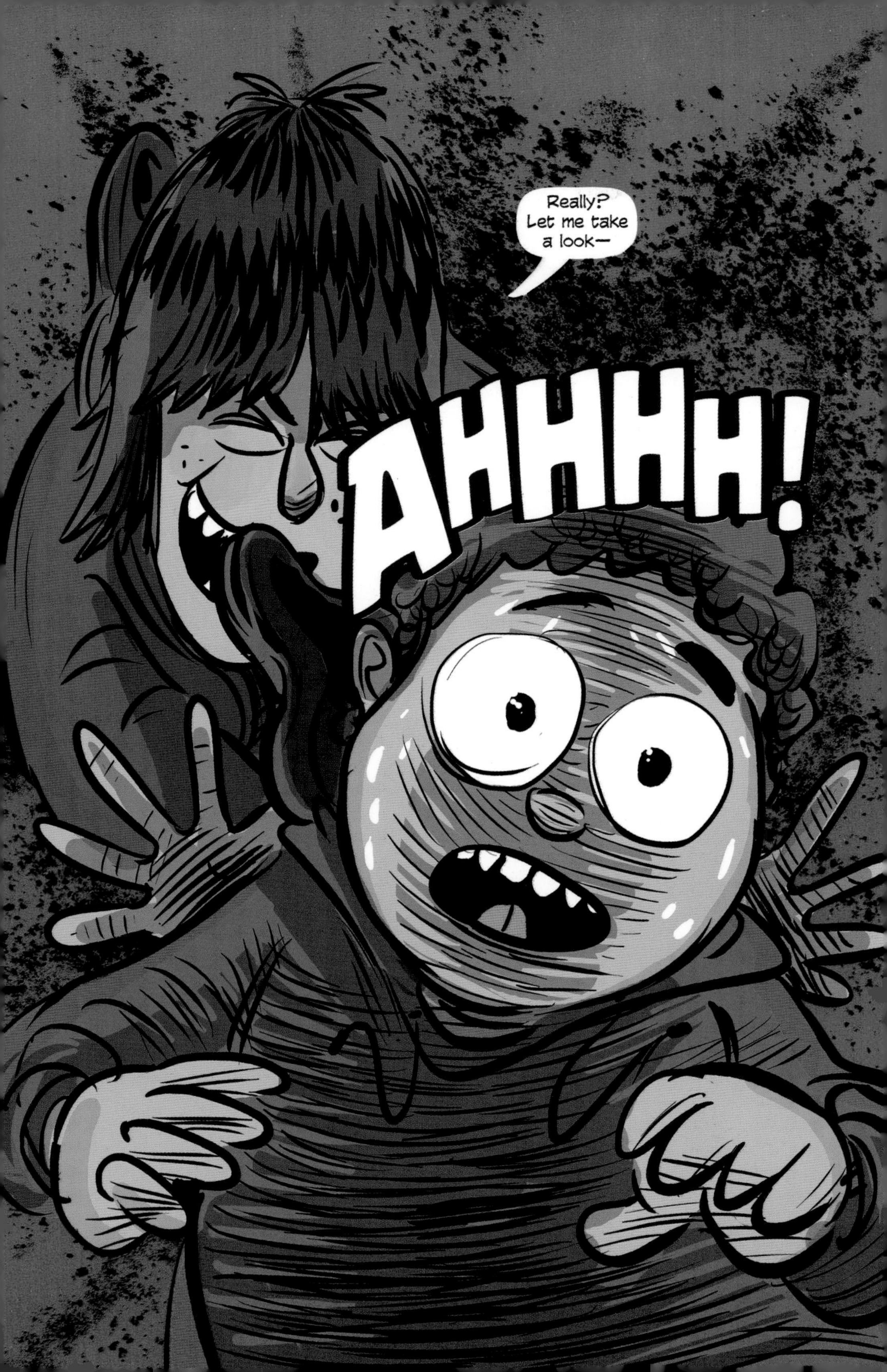
Really? Let me take a look—
AHHHHH!

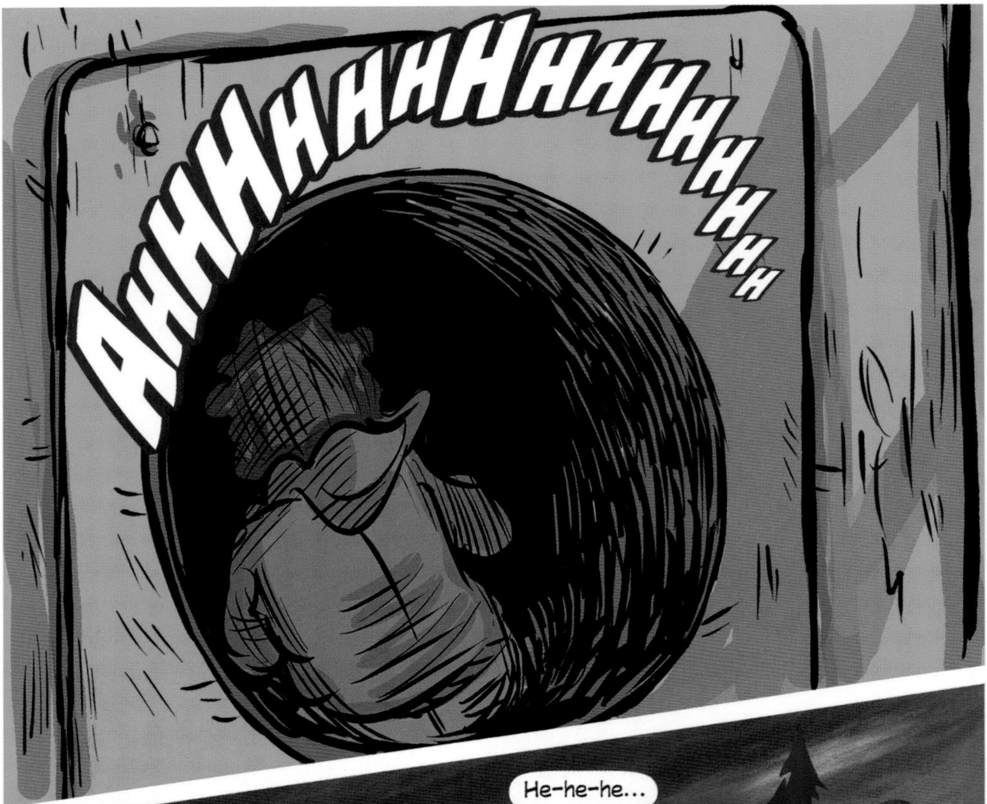
AHHHAAHHHHHHHHHHH

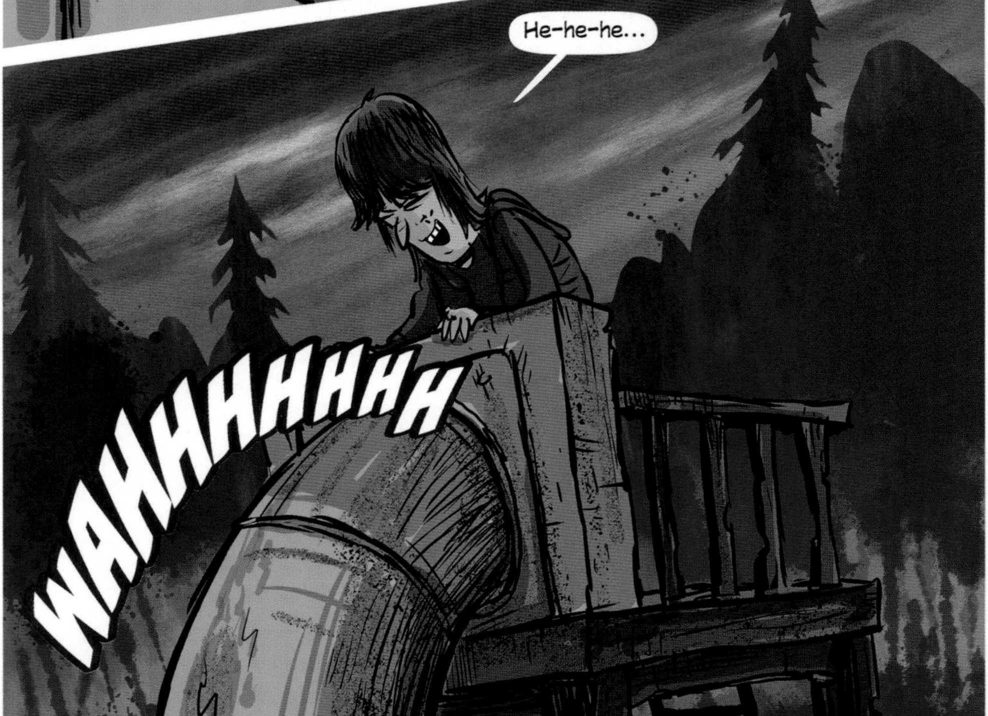
He-he-he...
WAHHHHHHHH

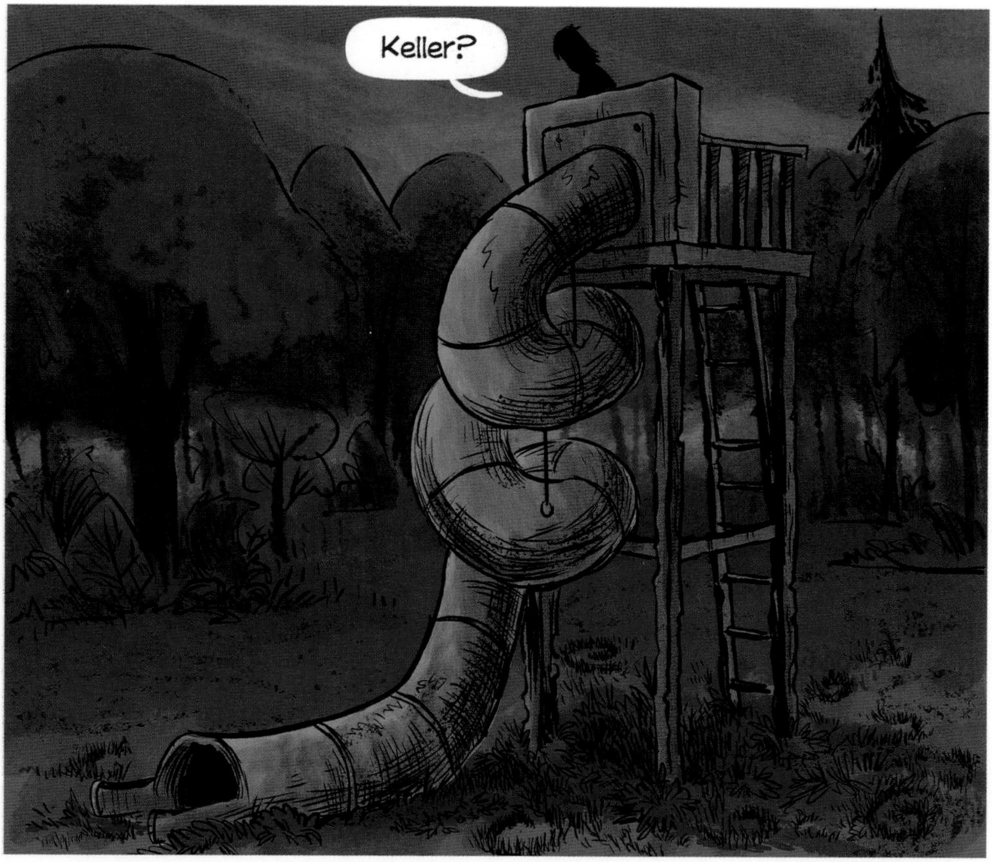
Keller?

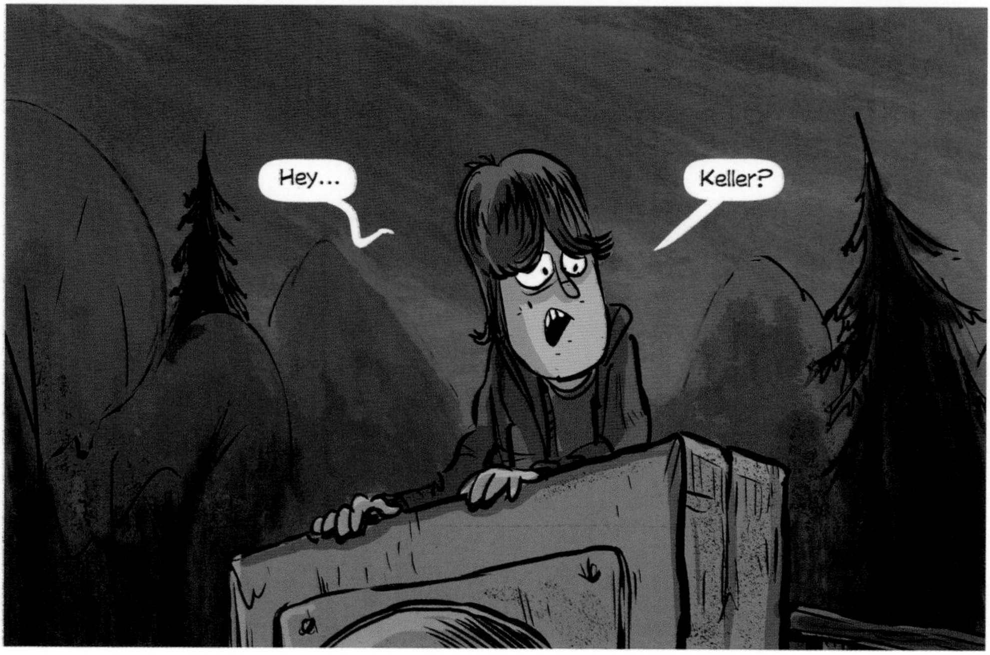
Hey...
Keller?

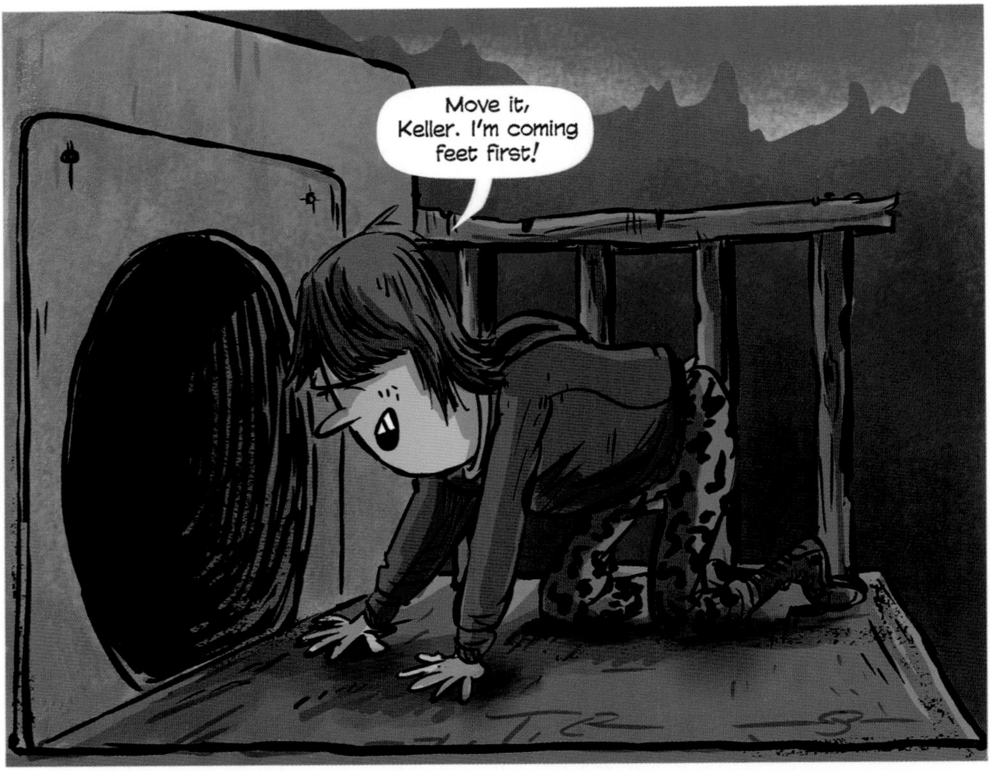
Move it, Keller. I'm coming feet first!

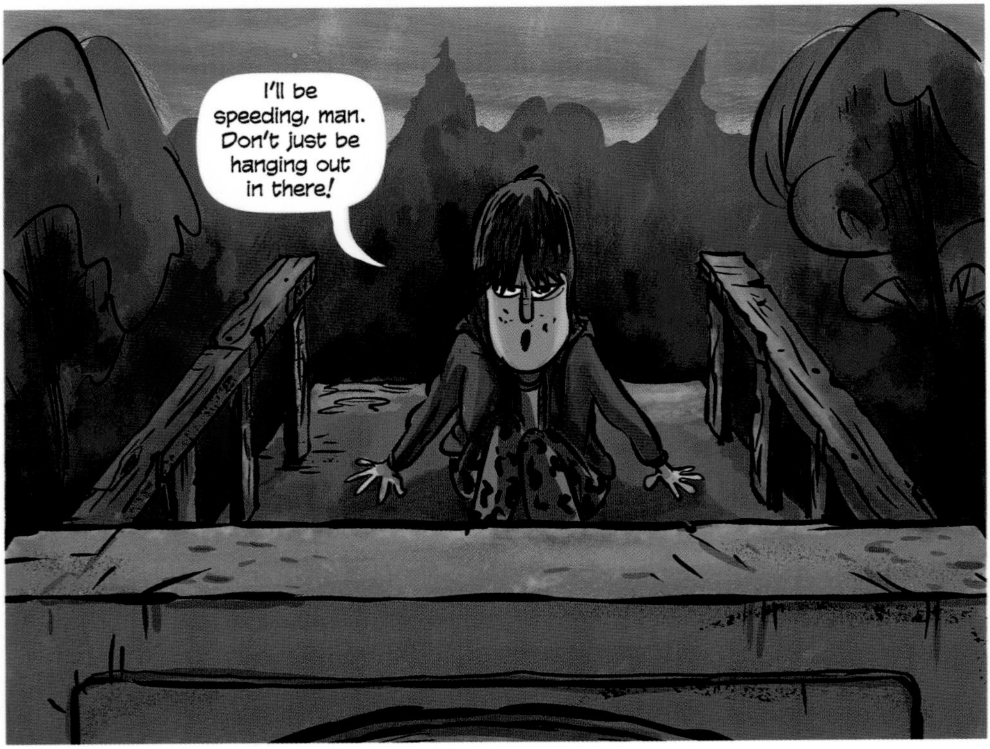
I'll be speeding, man. Don't just be hanging out in there!

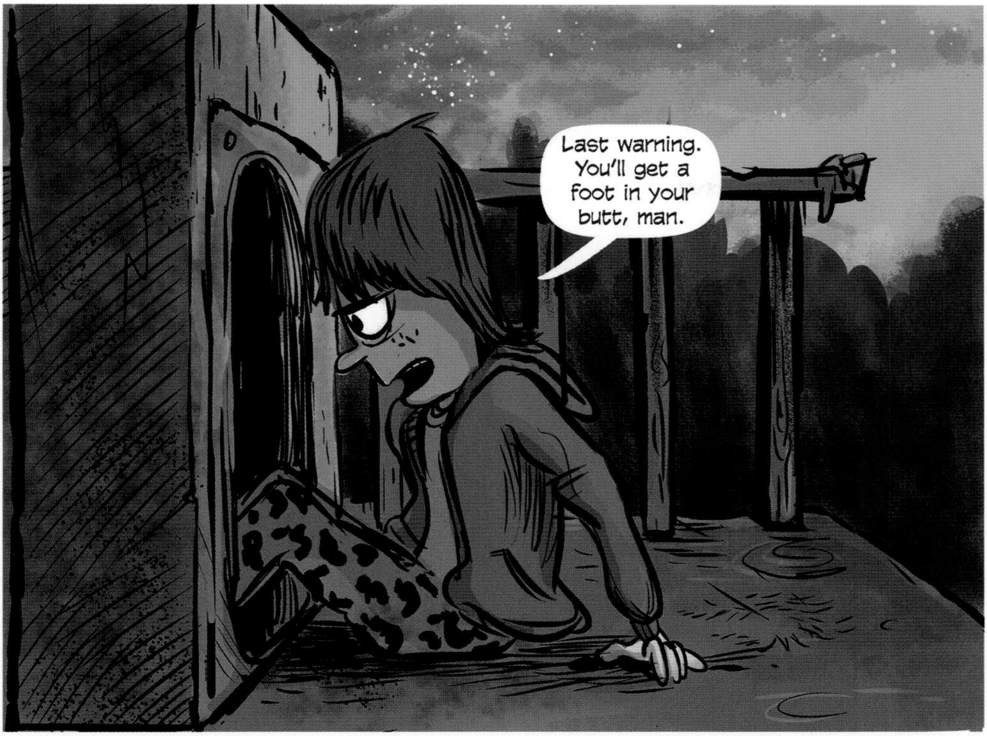
Last warning. You'll get a foot in your butt, man.

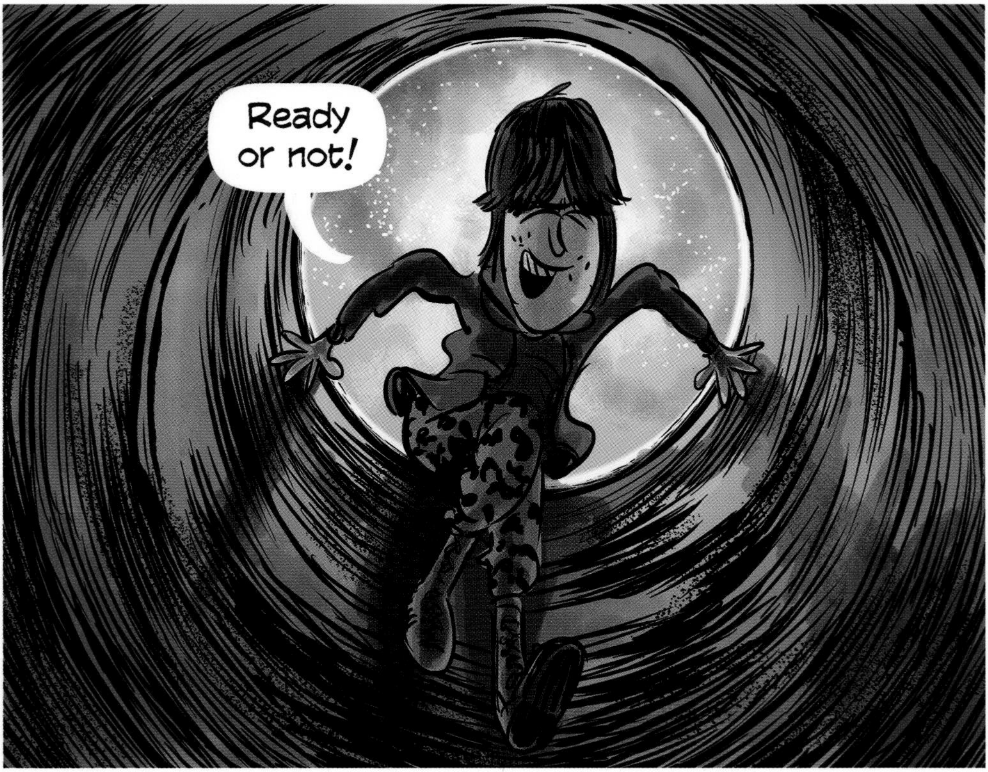
Ready or not!

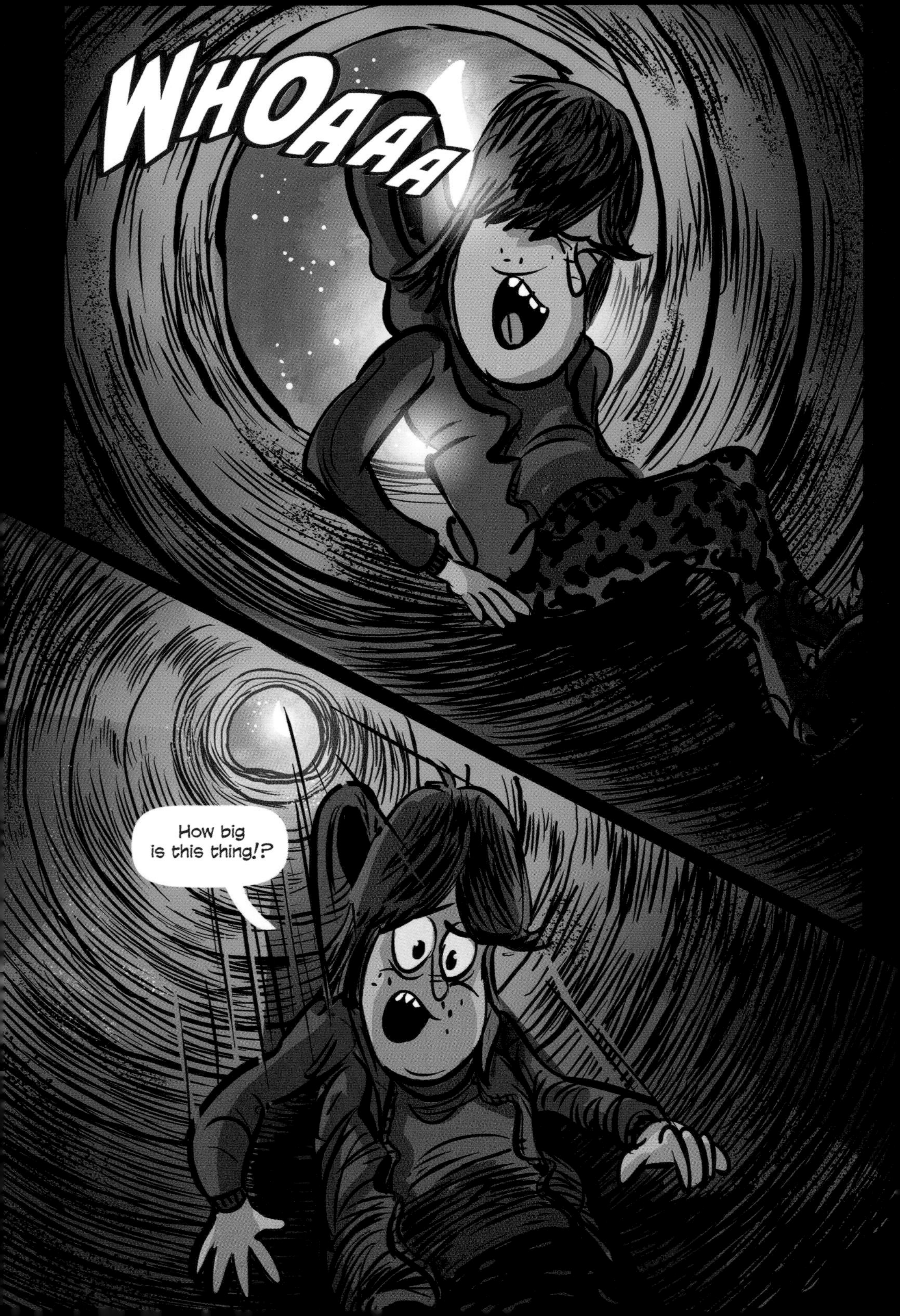
WHOAAAA
How big is this thing!?

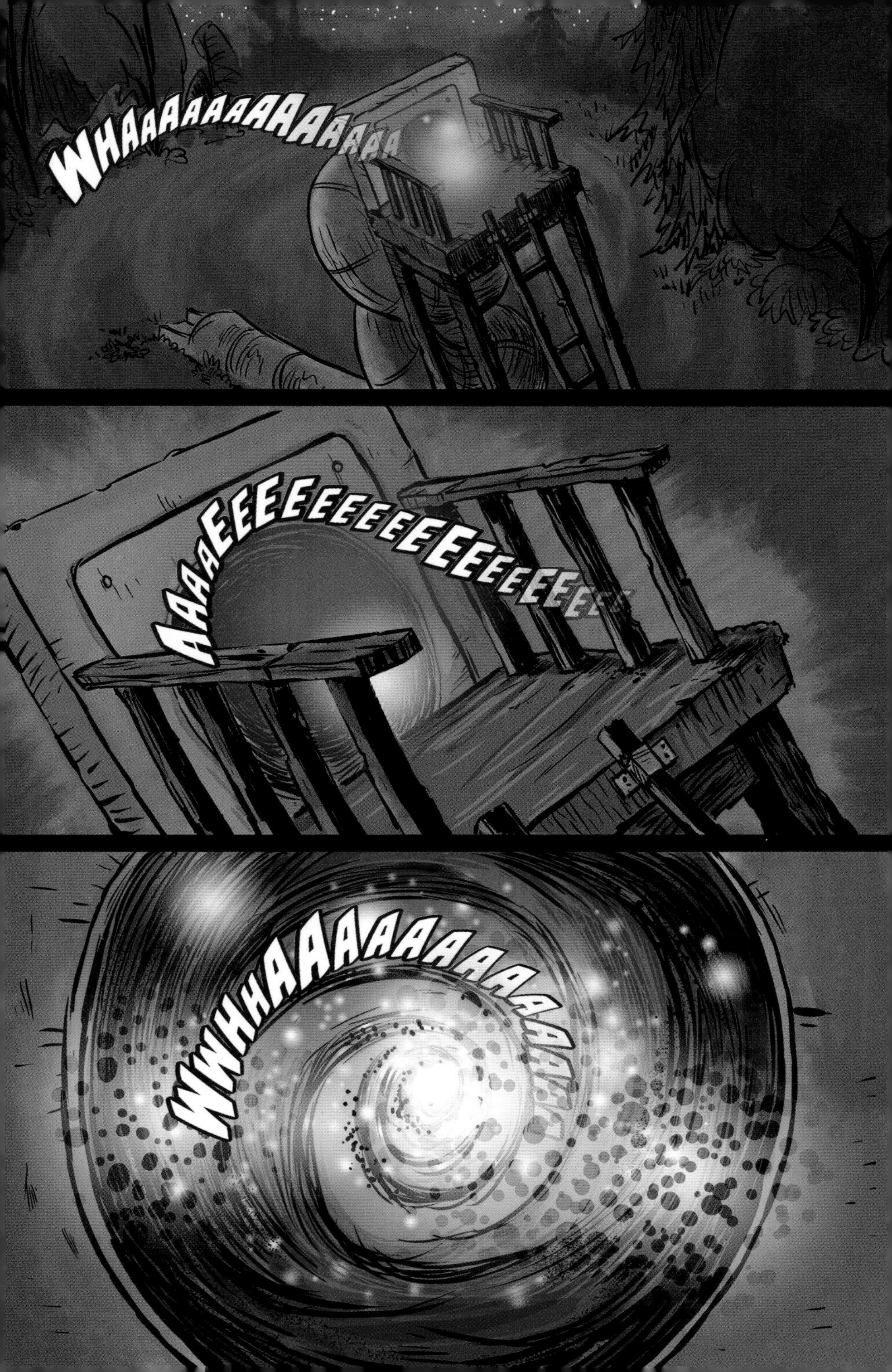
WHAAAAAAAAAAAAA
AAAEEEEEEEEEEEEEEEE
WWHAAAAAAAAAAAAA

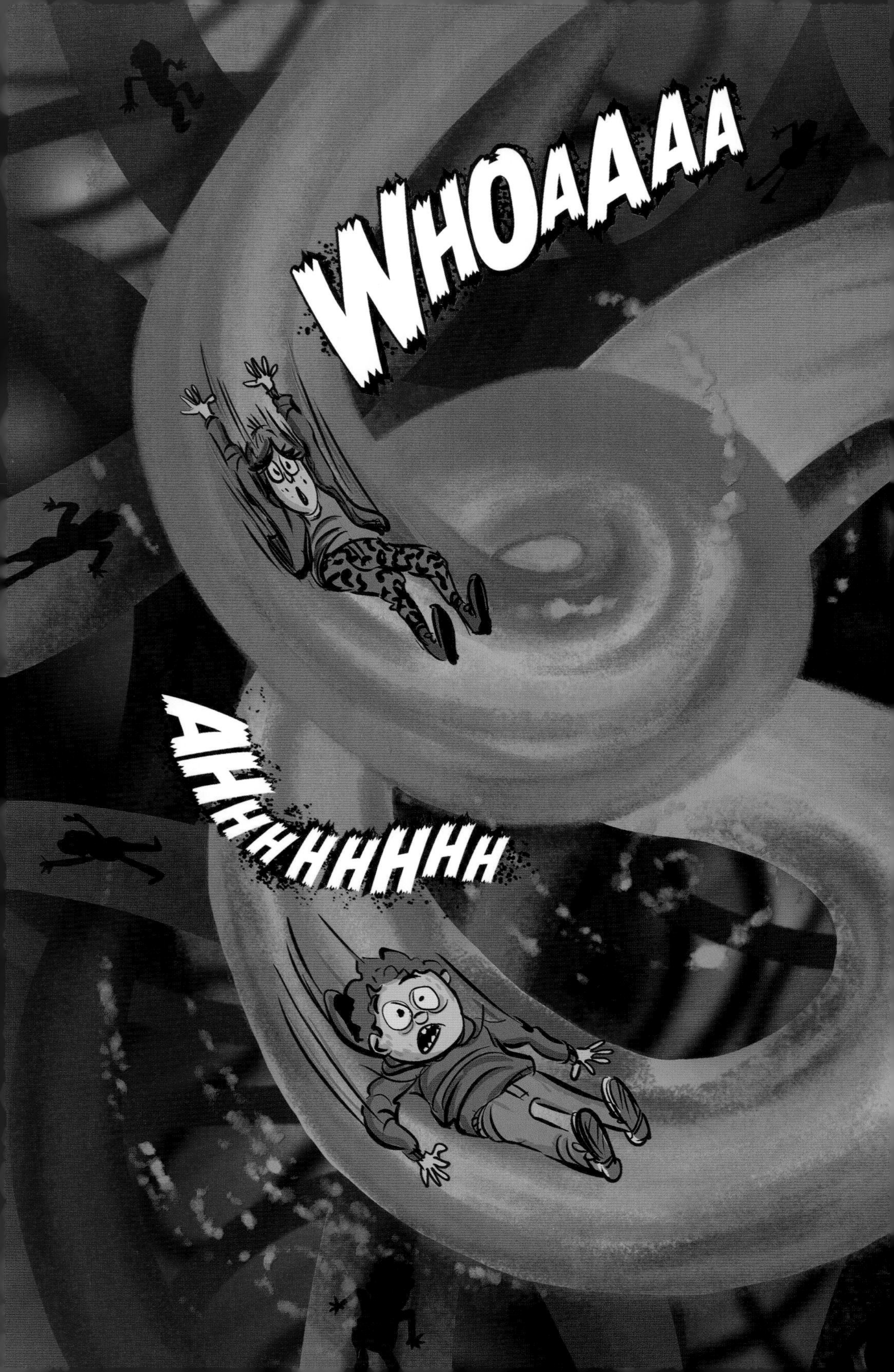
WHOAAAA
AHHHHHHHH

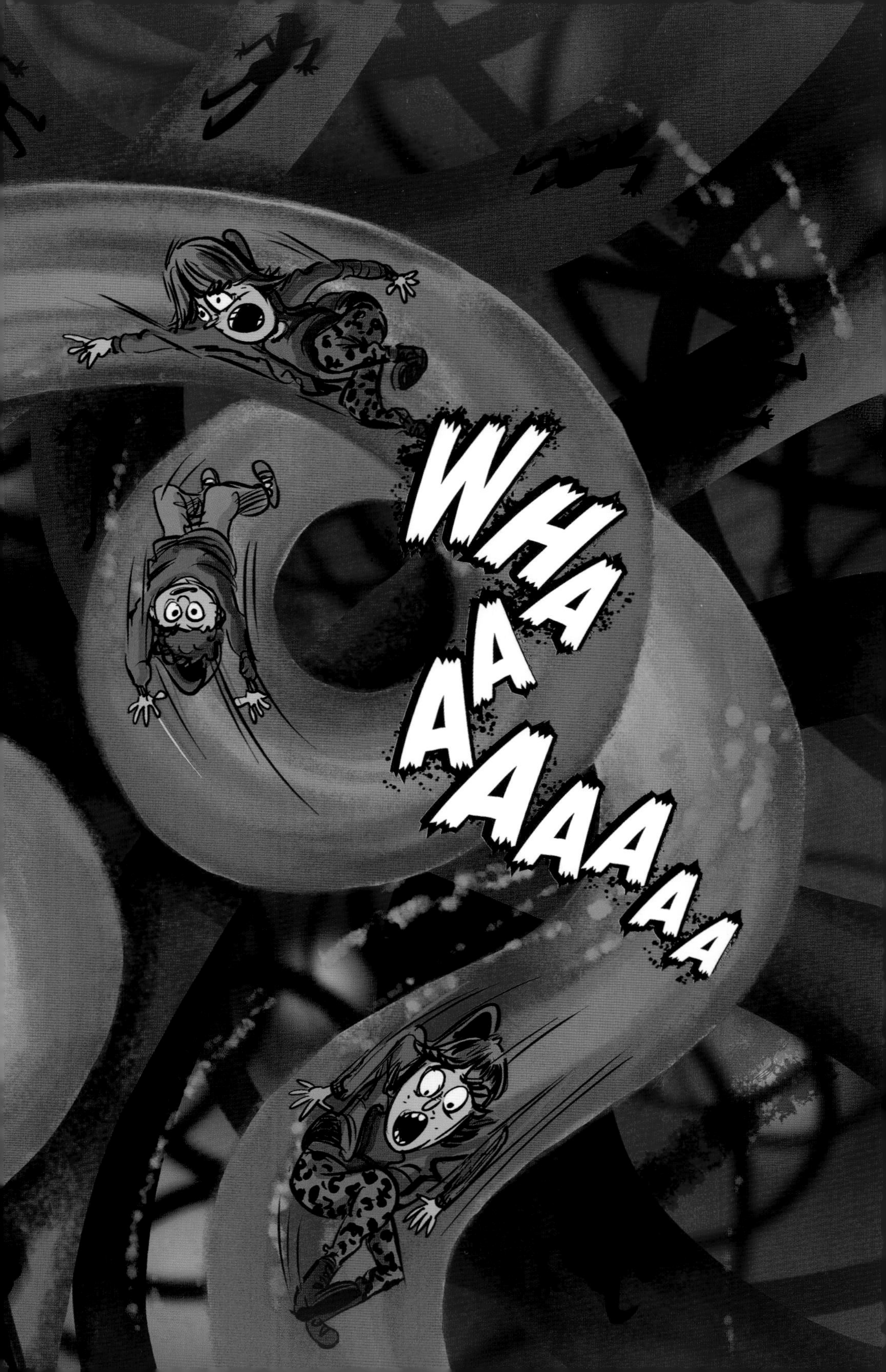
WHAAAAAAAA

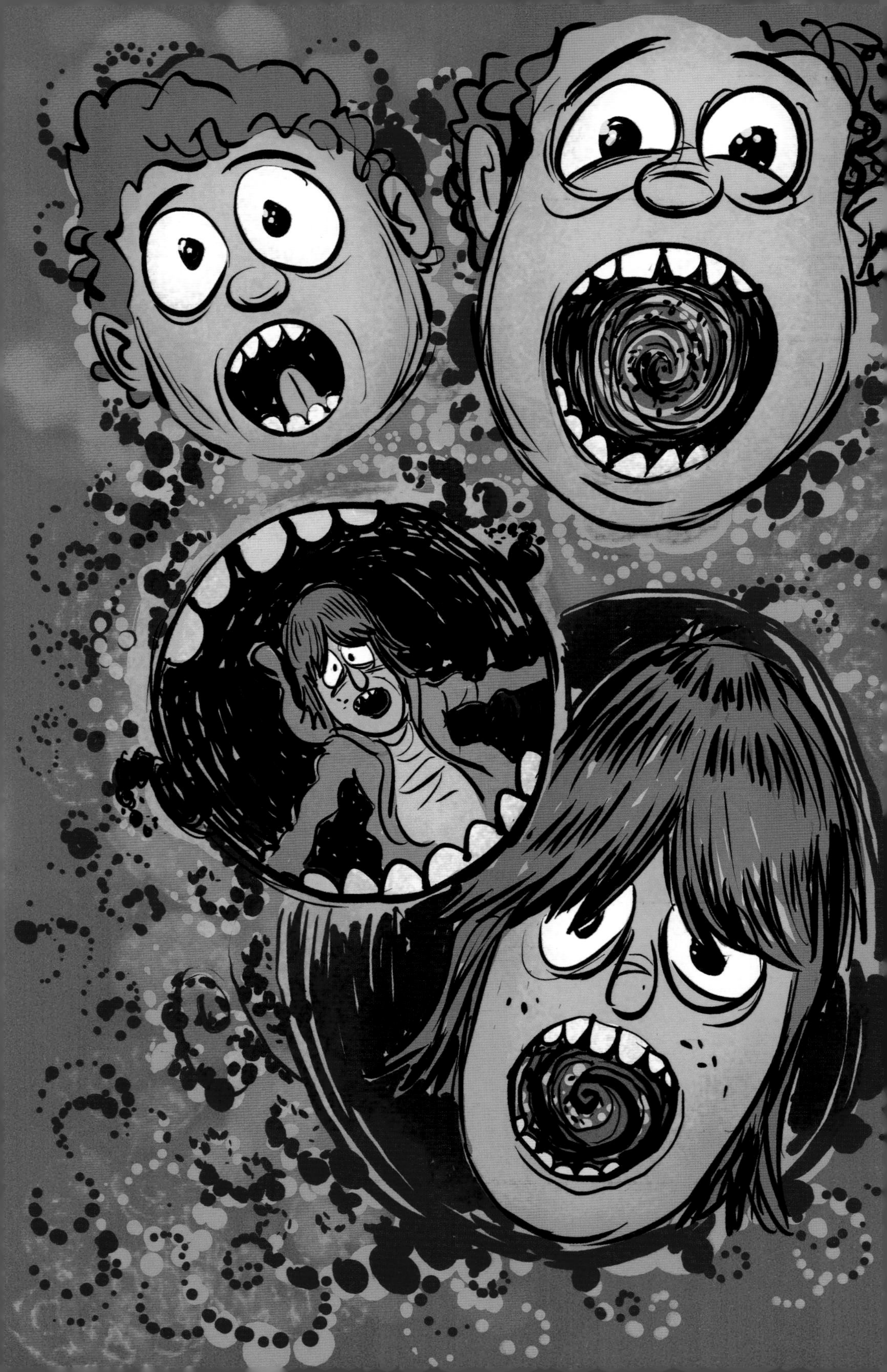

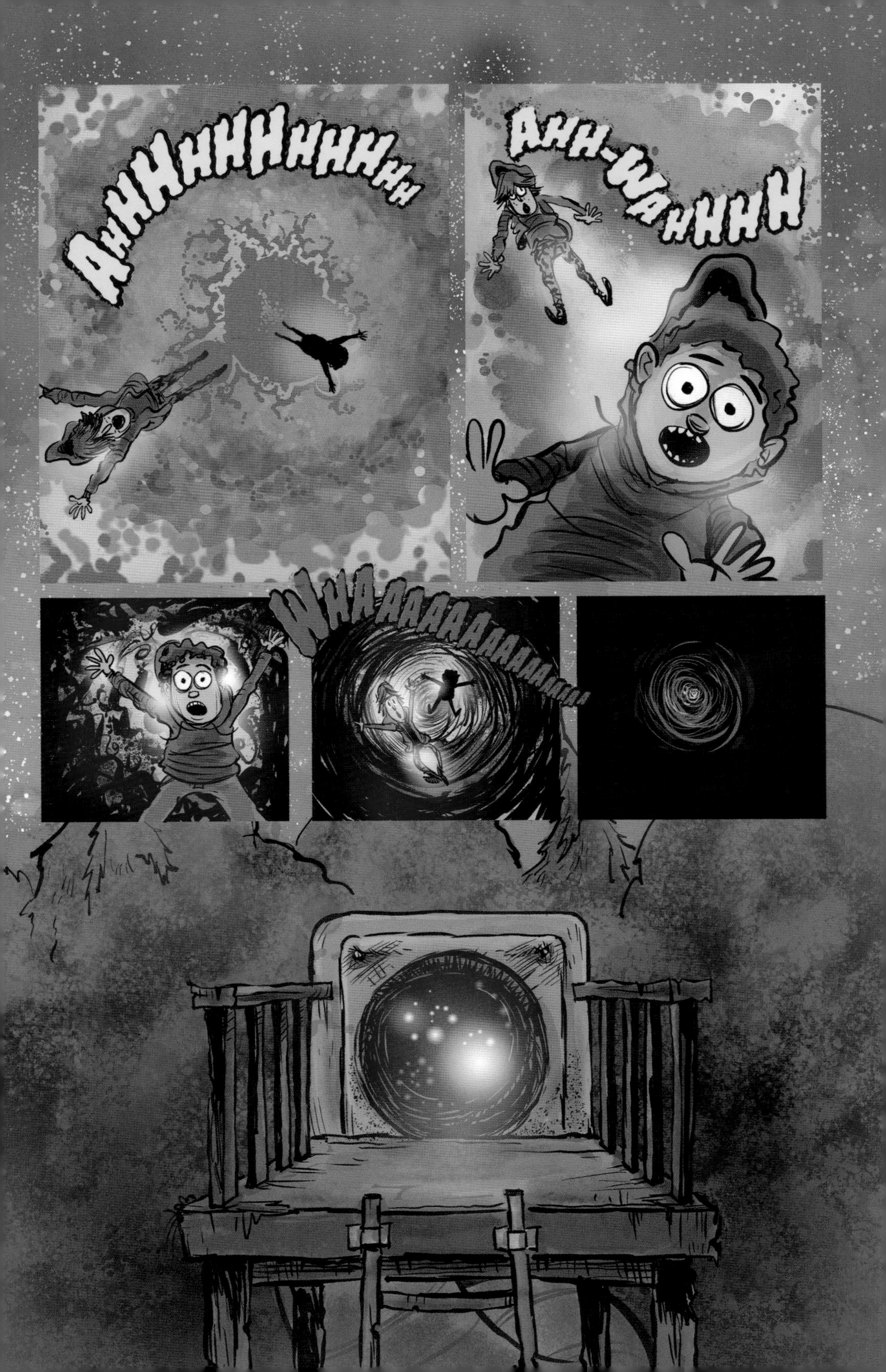
AHHHHHHHHHHH
AHH-WAHHHH
WHAAAAAAAAAAAA

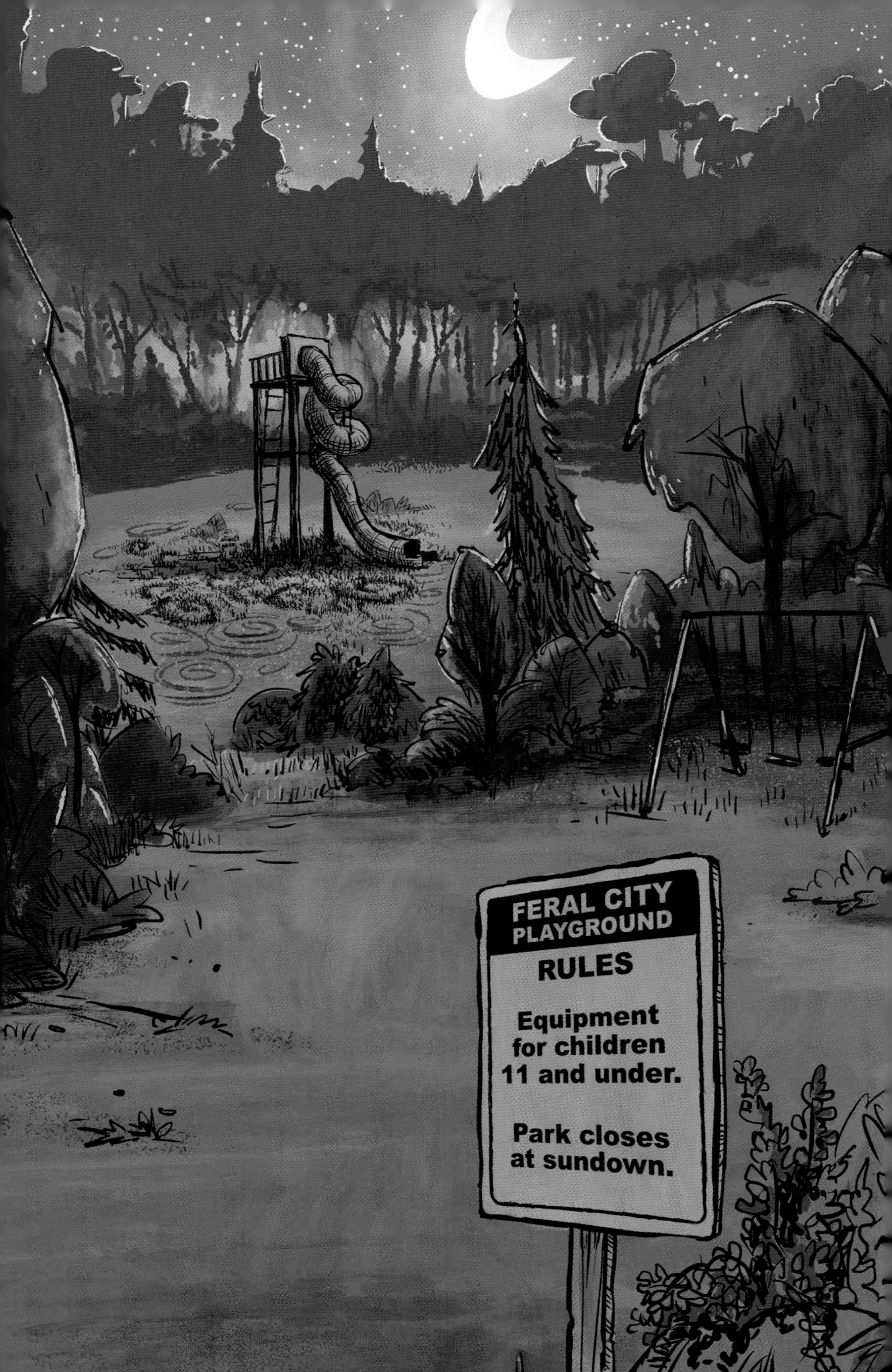
FERAL CITY
PLAYGROUND
RULES
Equipment
for children
11 and under.
Park closes
at sundown.

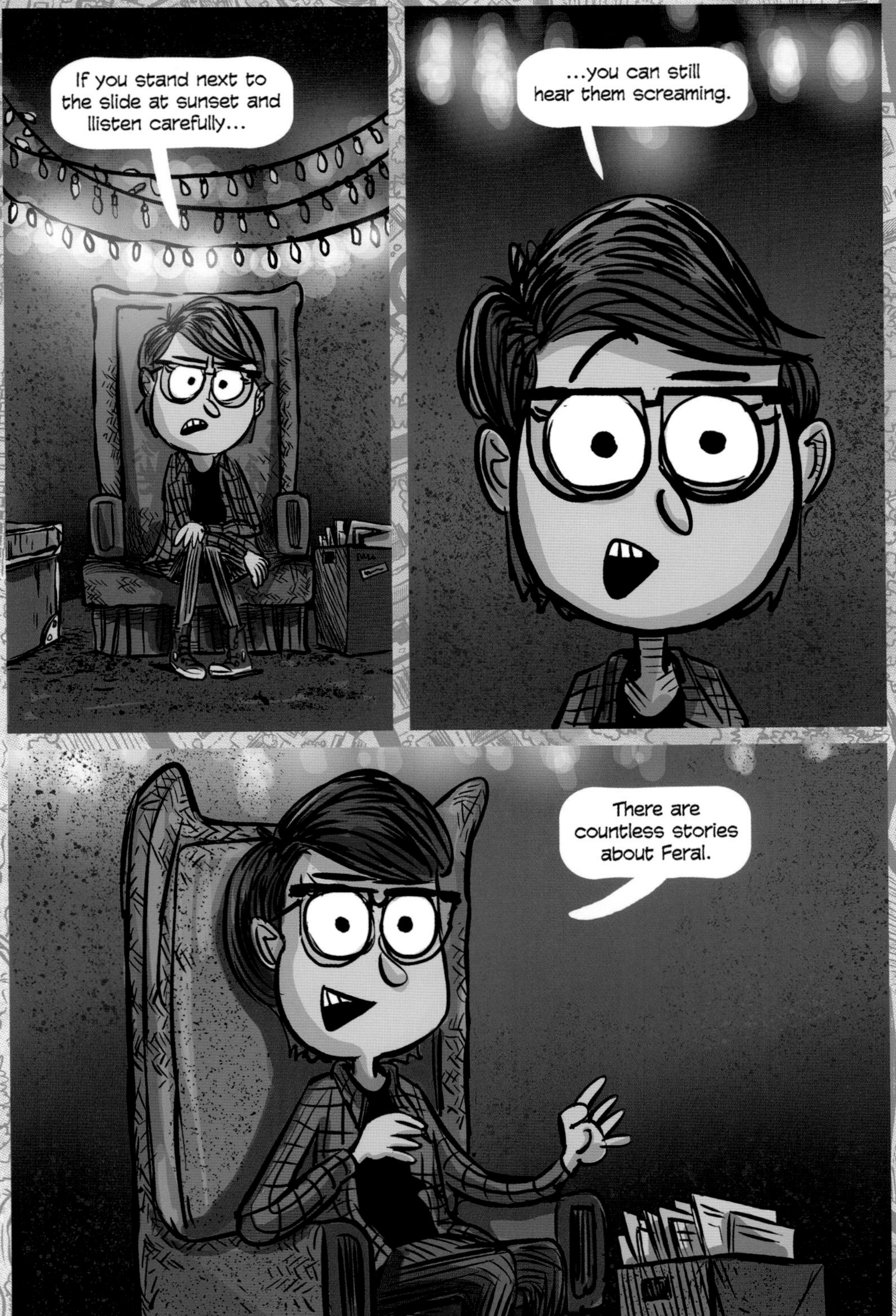
If you stand next to the slide at sunset and llisten carefully...
...you can still hear them screaming.
There are countless stories about Feral.

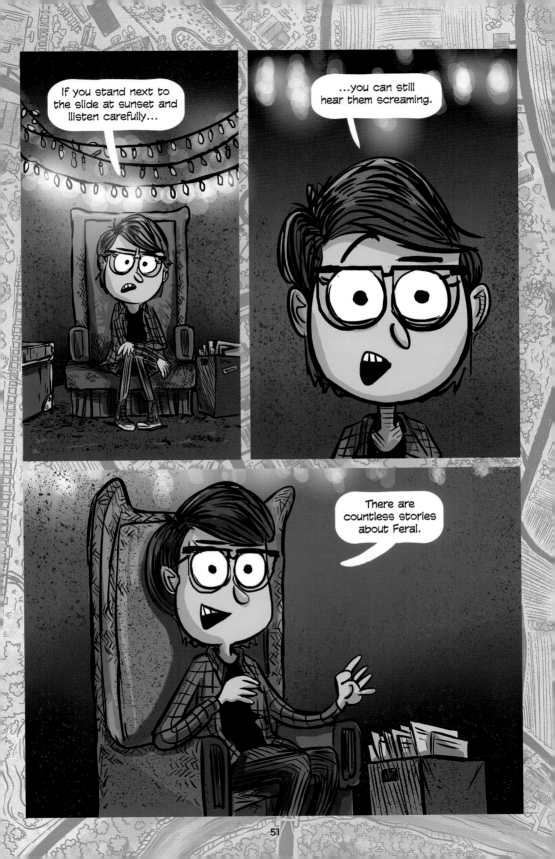

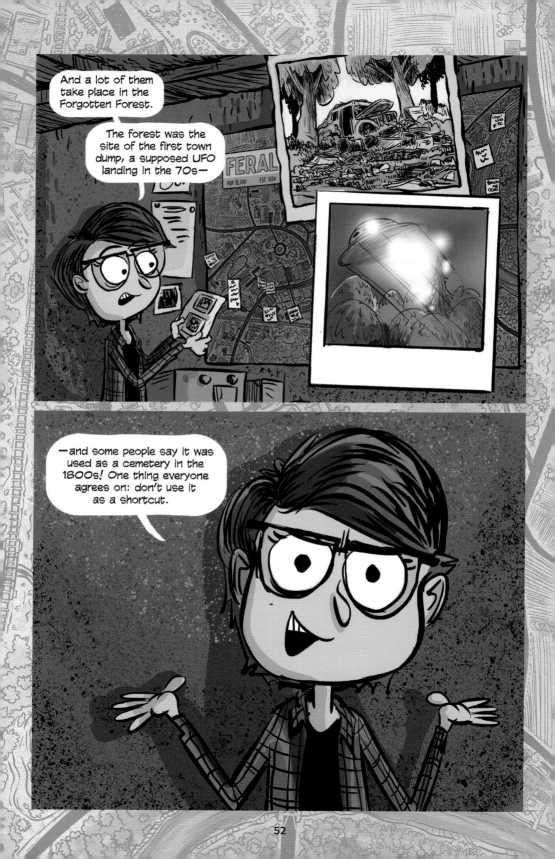

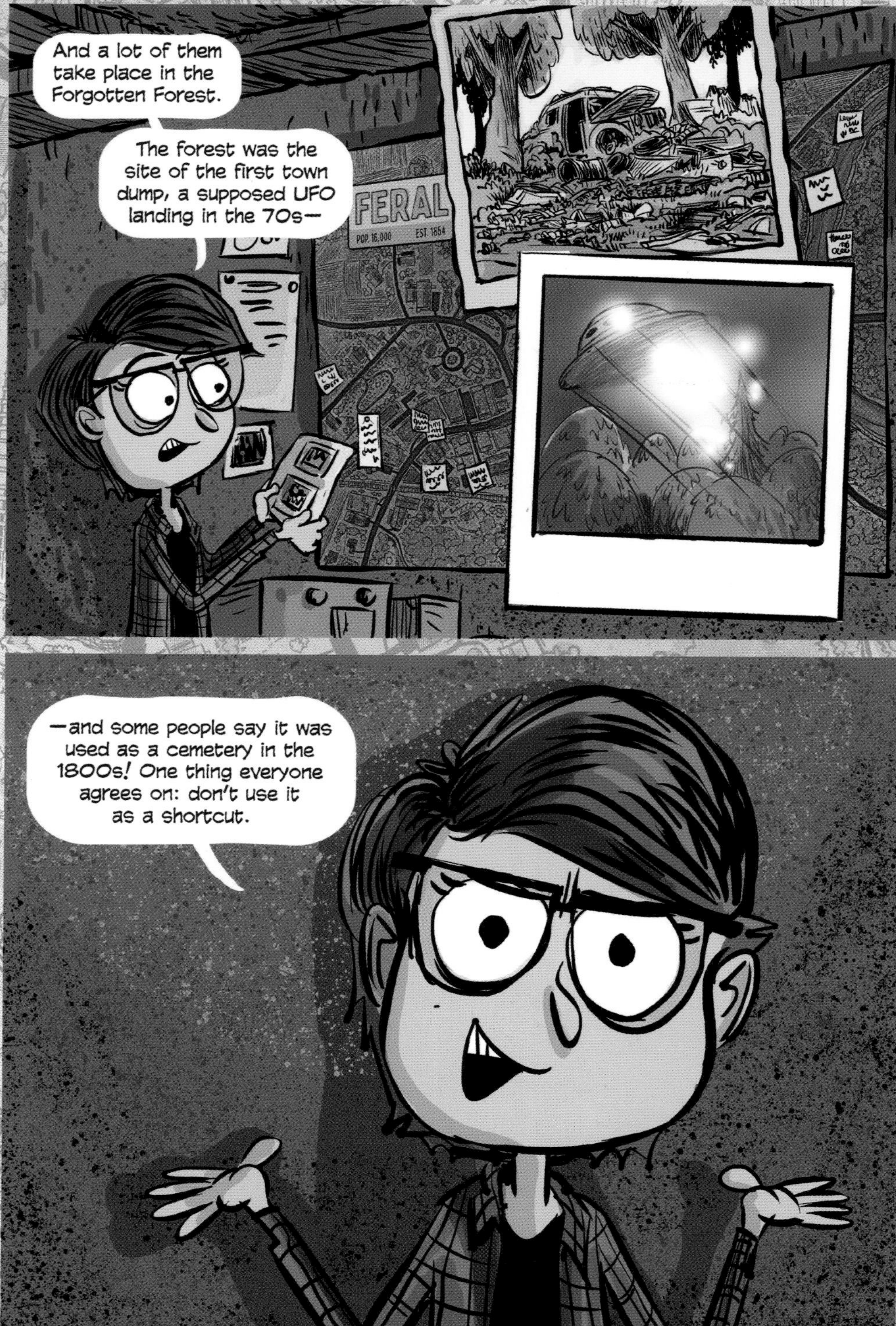
And a lot of them take place in the Forgotten Forest.
The forest was the site of the first town dump, a supposed UFO landing in the 70s—
FERAL
POP. 16,000
EST. 1854
—and some people say it was used as a cemetery in the 1800s! One thing everyone agrees on: don't use it as a shortcut.

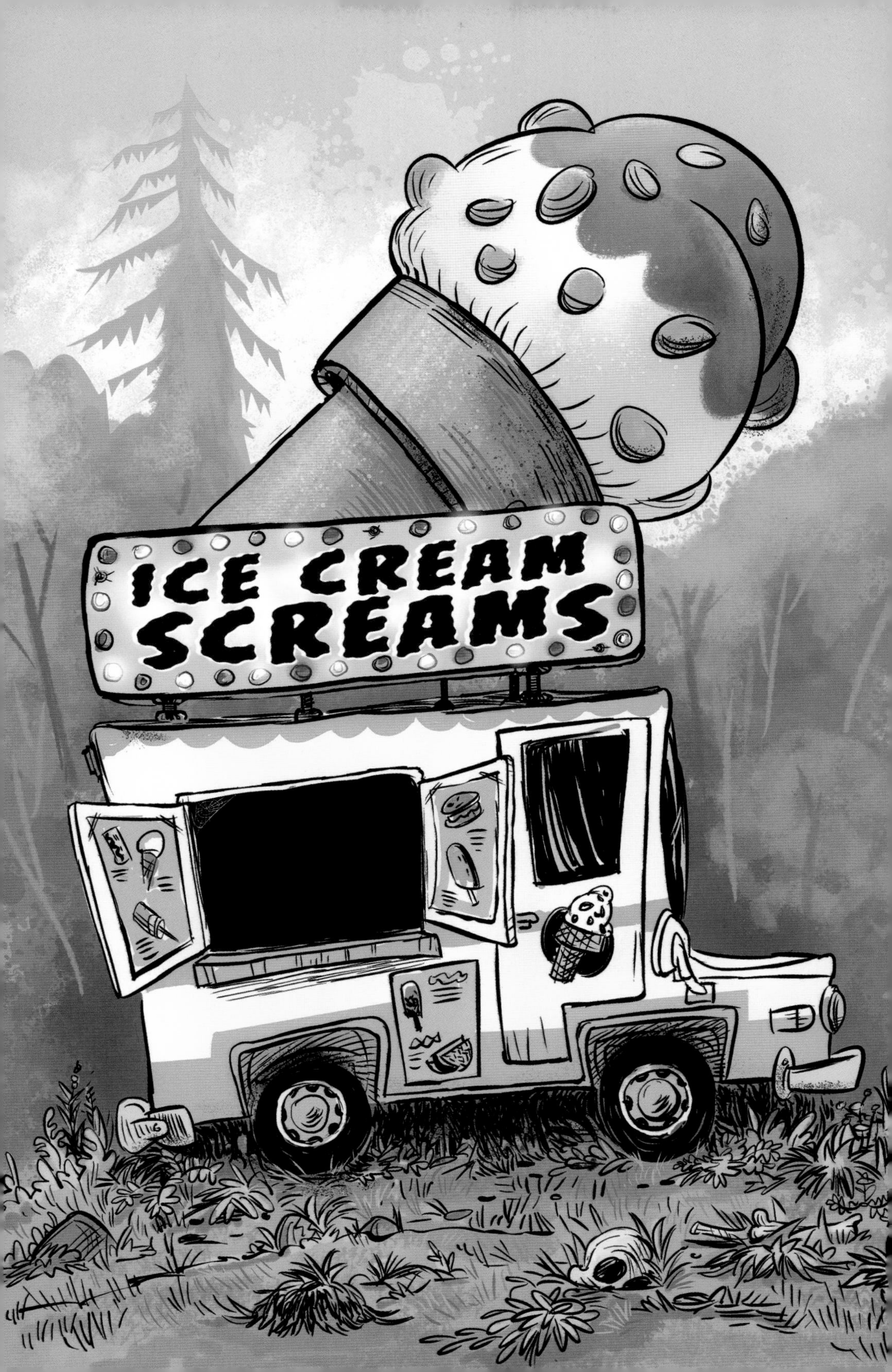
ICE CREAM
SCREAMS

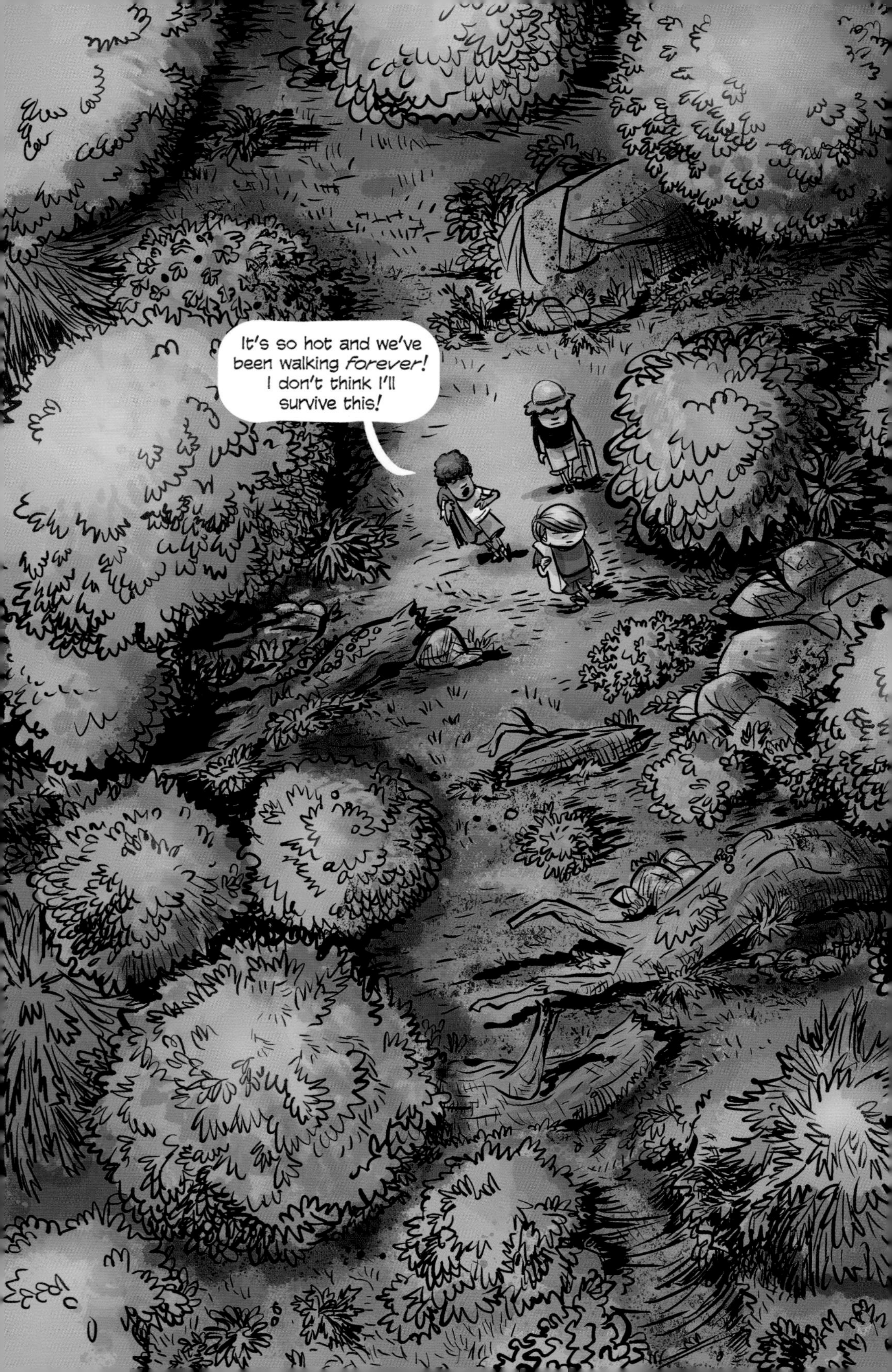
It's so hot and we've been walking *forever*! I don't think I'll survive this!

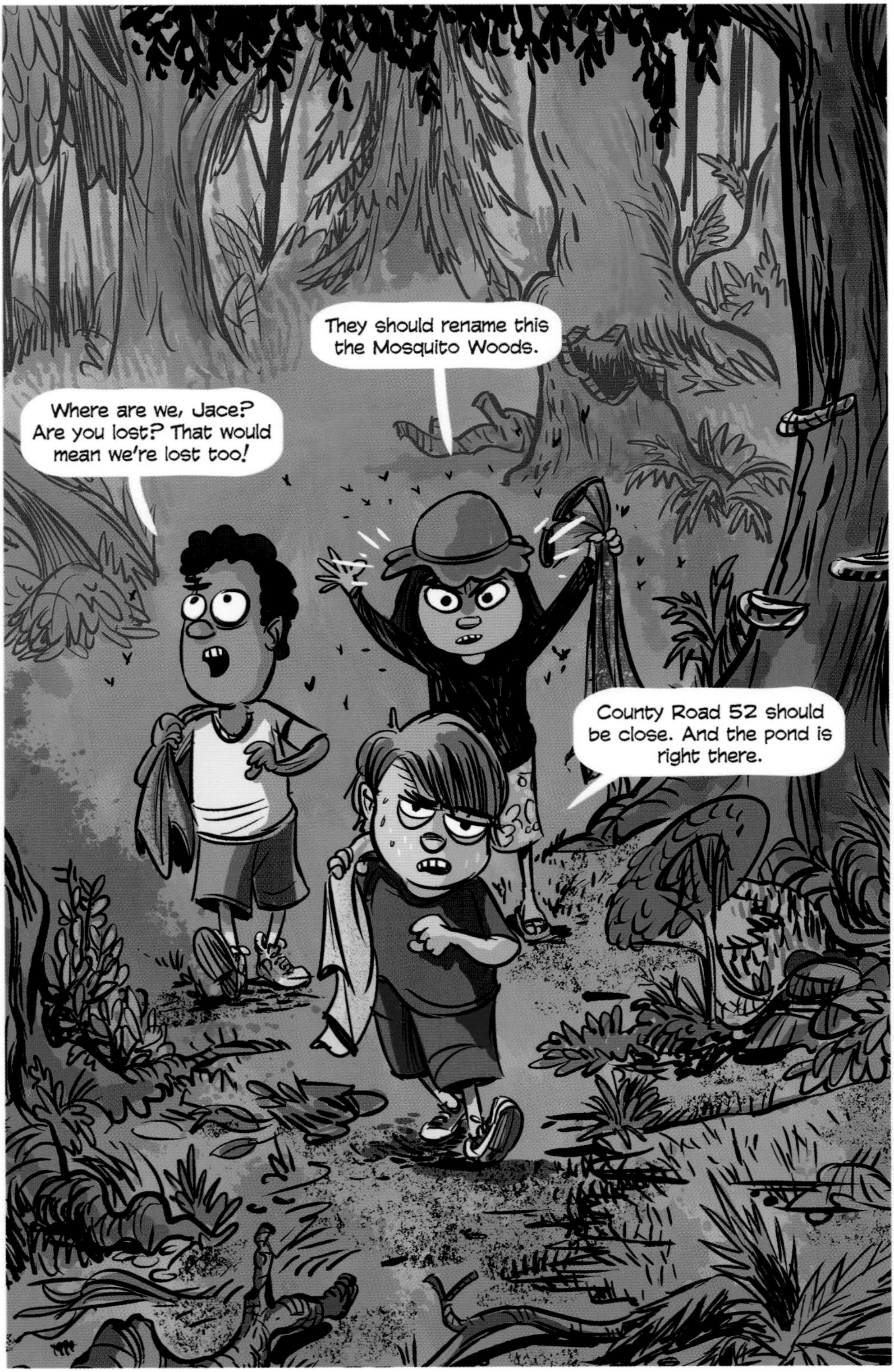
Where are we, Jace? Are you lost? That would mean we're lost too!
They should rename this the Mosquito Woods.
County Road 52 should be close. And the pond is right there.

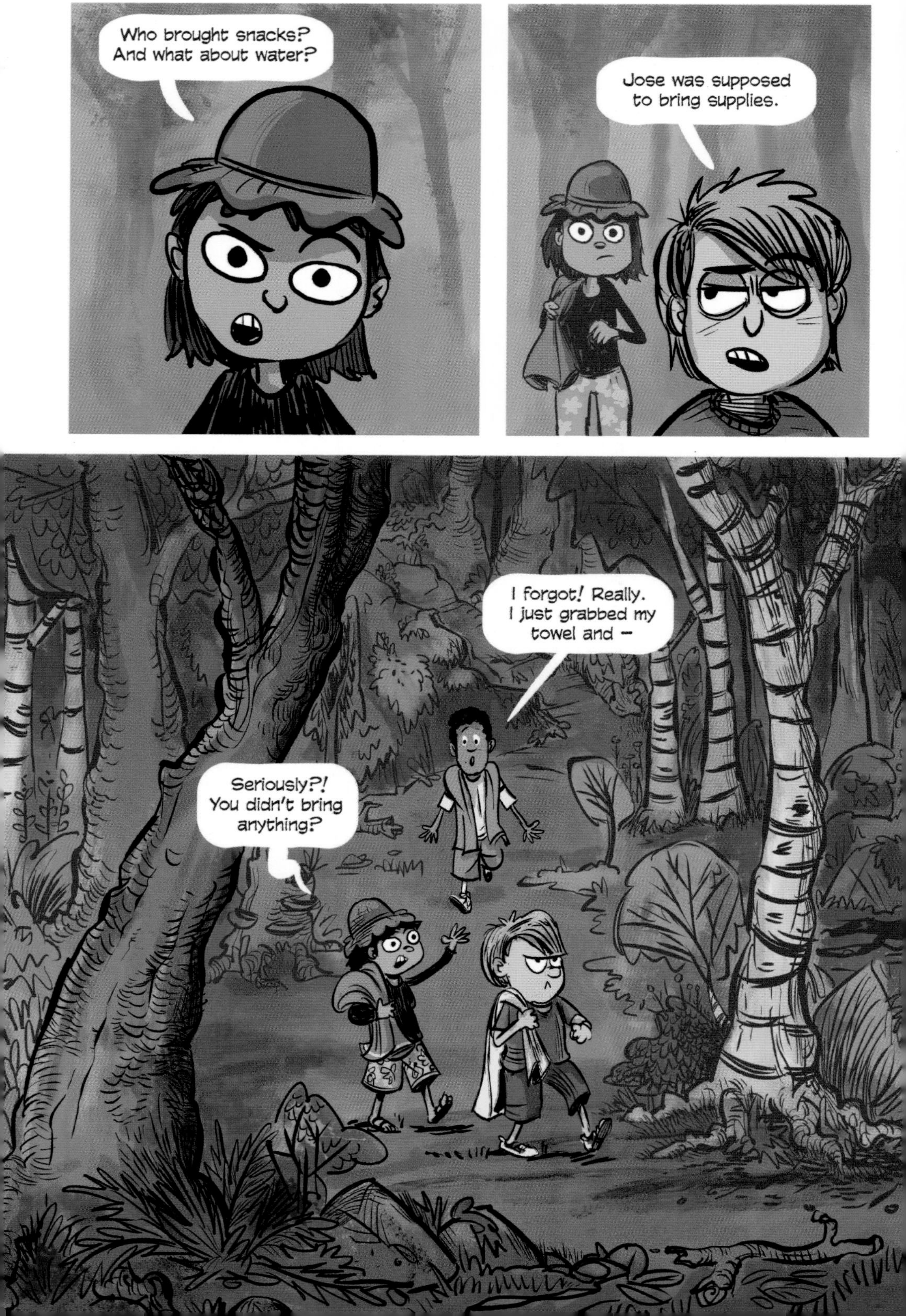

Who brought snacks? And what about water?
Jose was supposed to bring supplies.
I forgot! Really. I just grabbed my towel and –
Seriously?! You didn't bring anything?

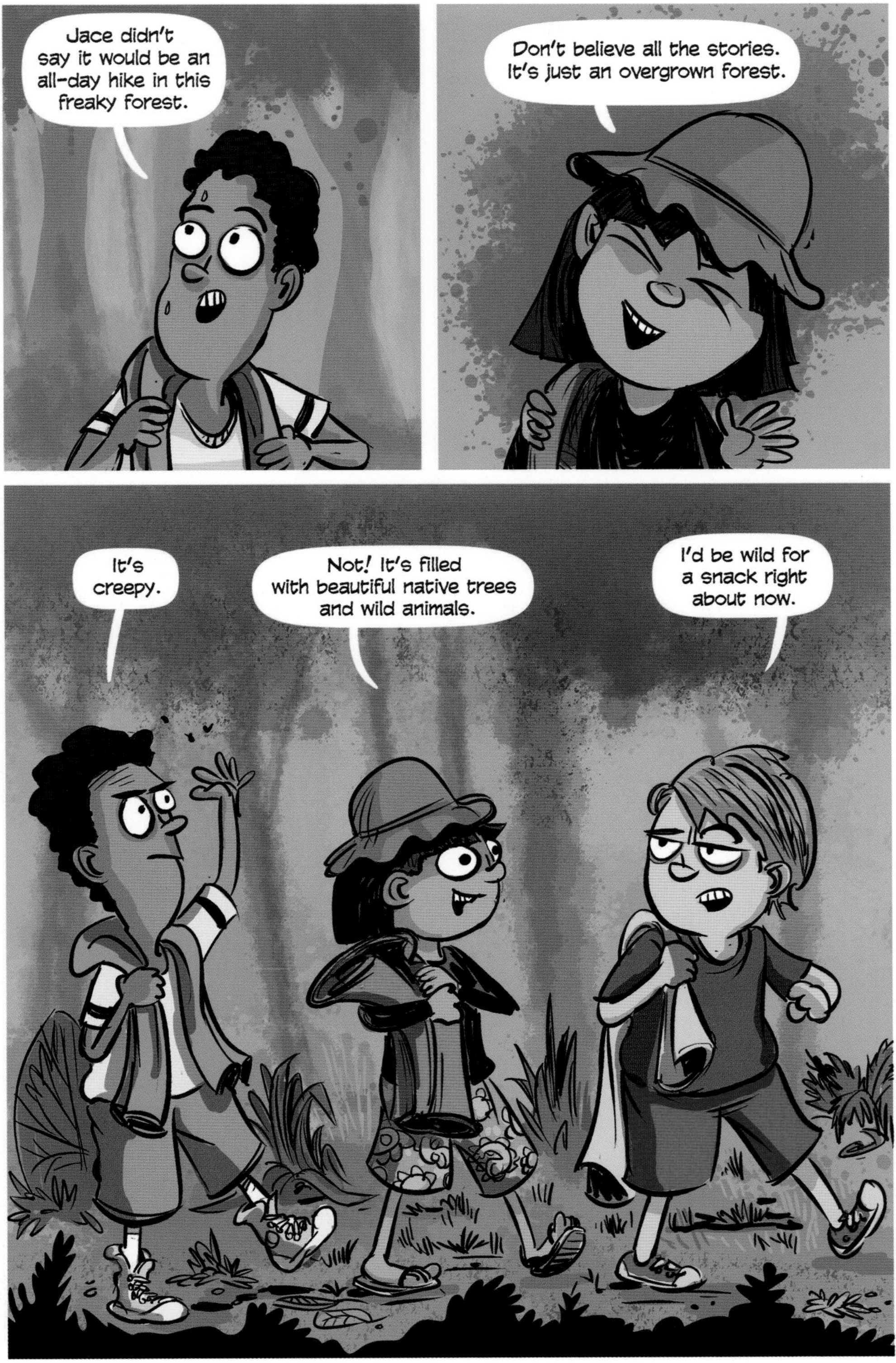
Jace didn't say it would be an all-day hike in this freaky forest.
Don't believe all the stories. It's just an overgrown forest.
It's creepy.
Not! It's filled with beautiful native trees and wild animals.
I'd be wild for a snack right about now.

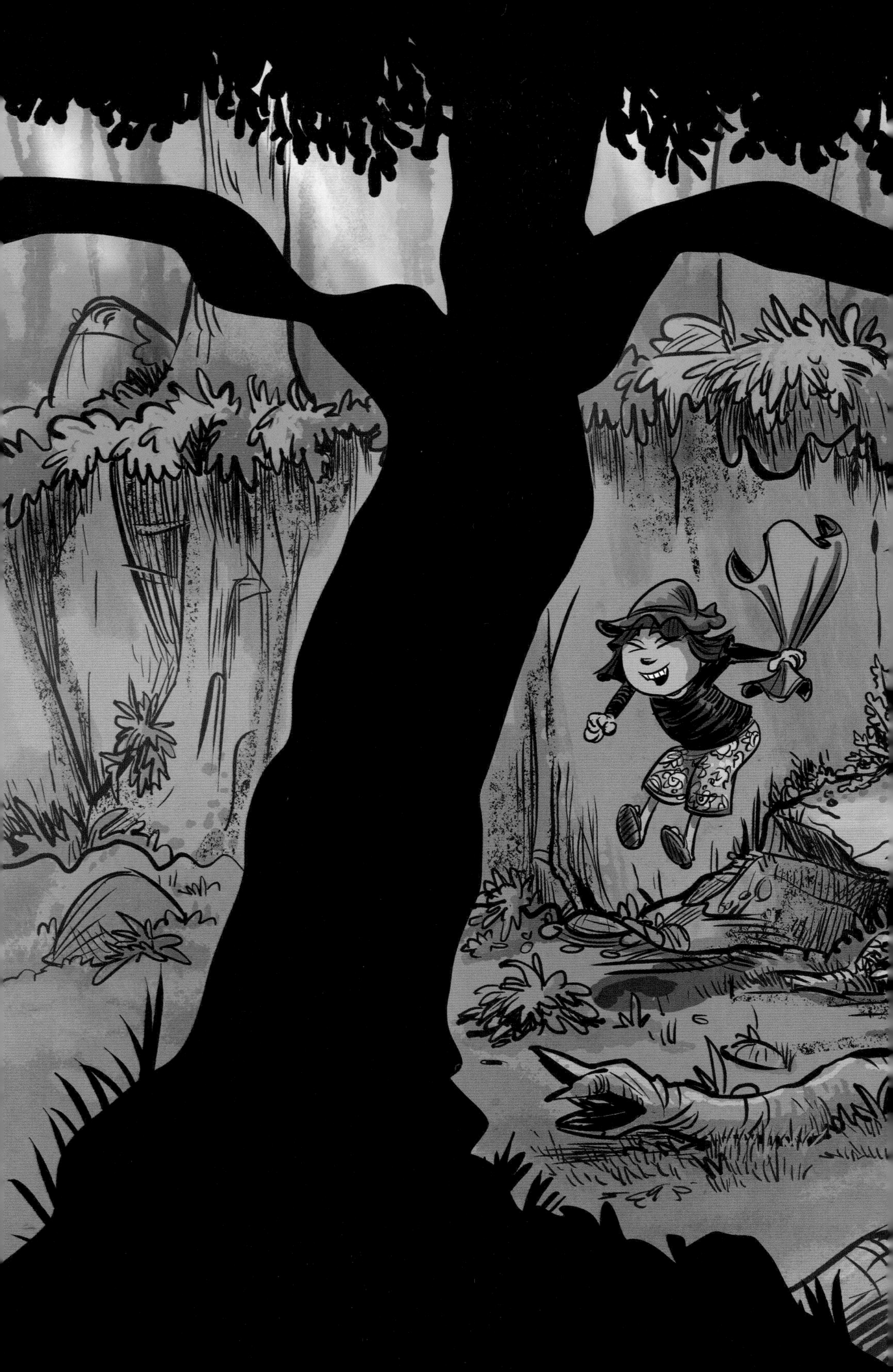

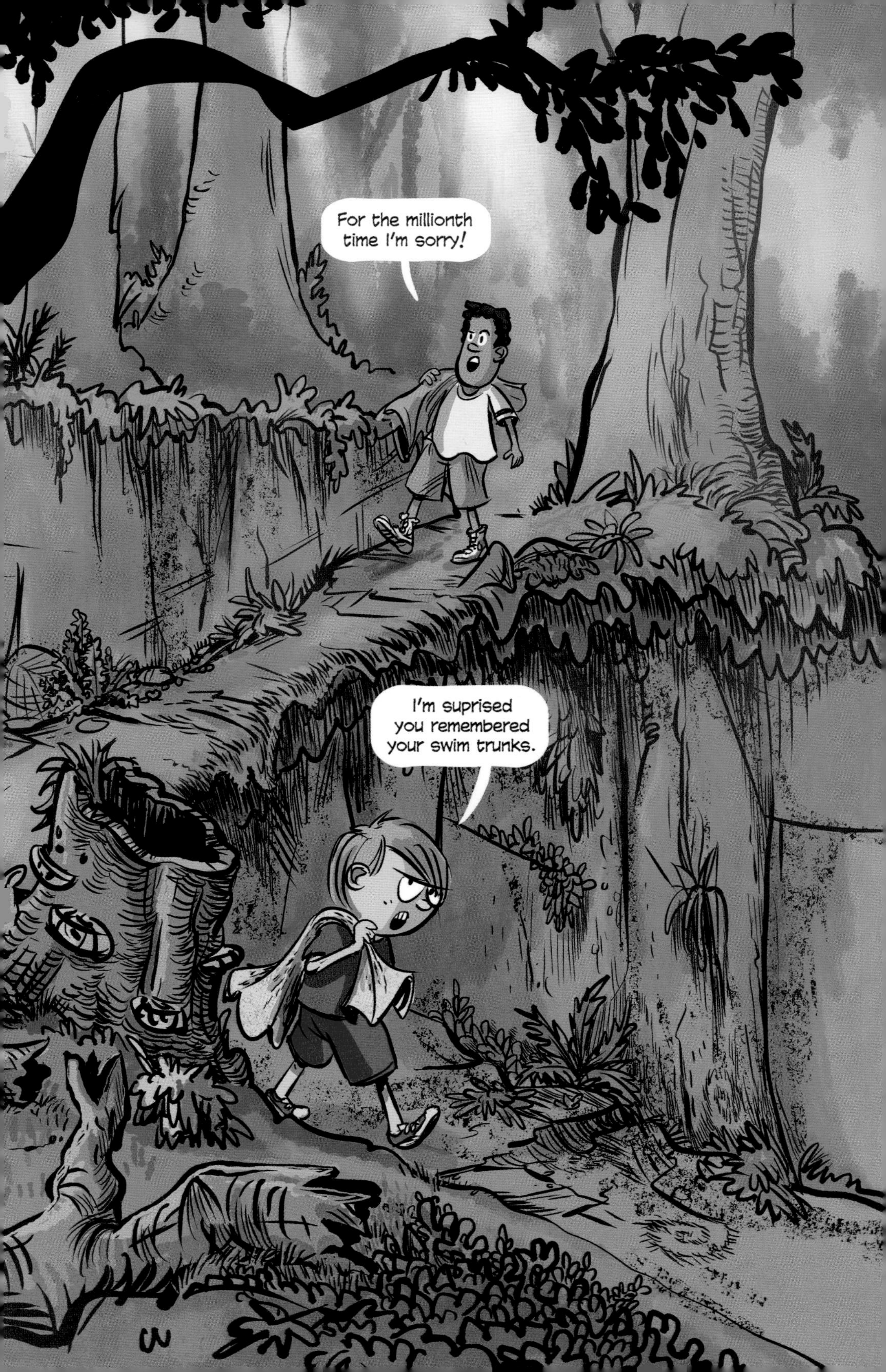
For the millionth time I'm sorry!
I'm suprised you remembered your swim trunks.

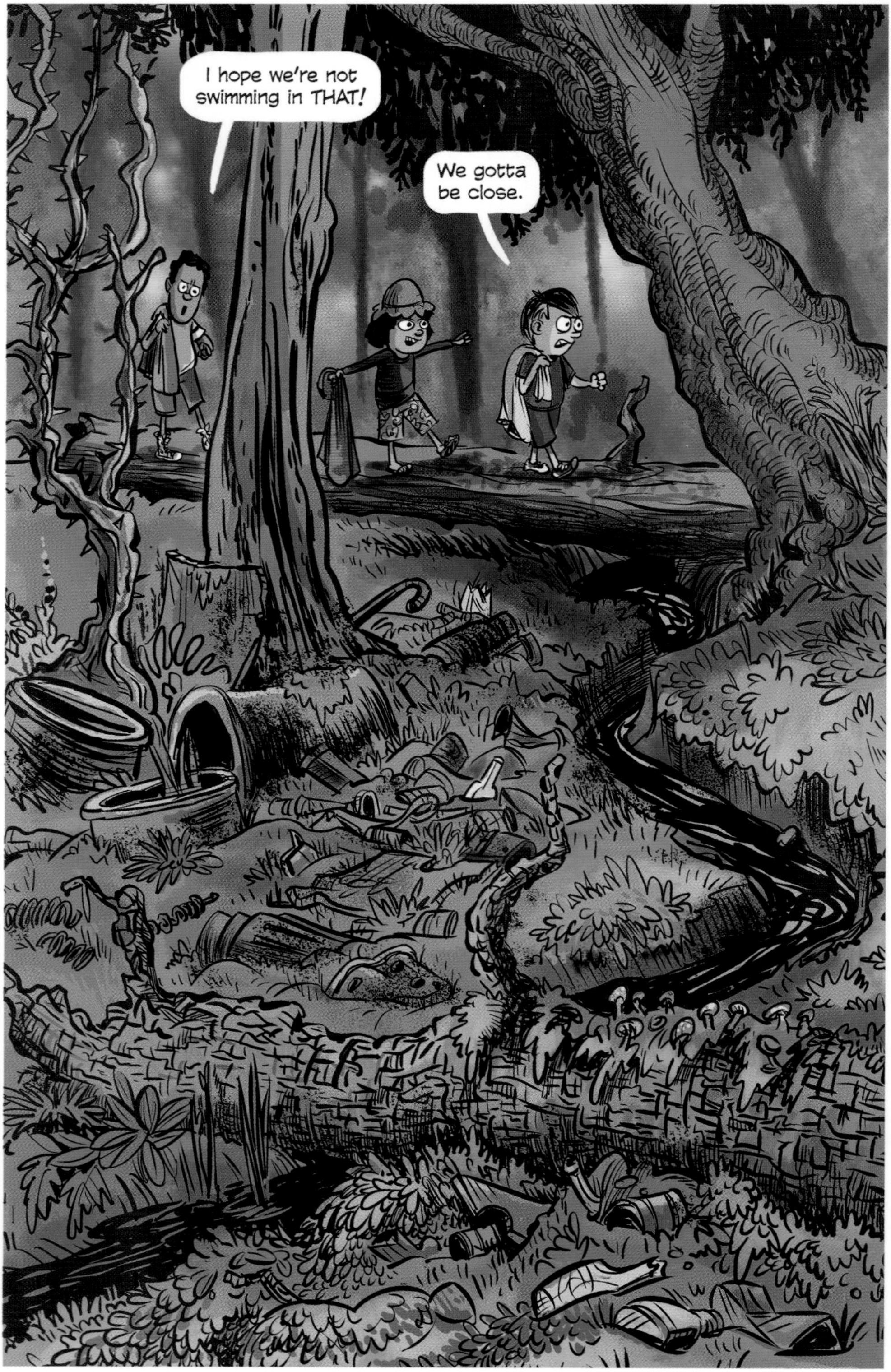
I hope we're not swimming in THAT!
We gotta be close.

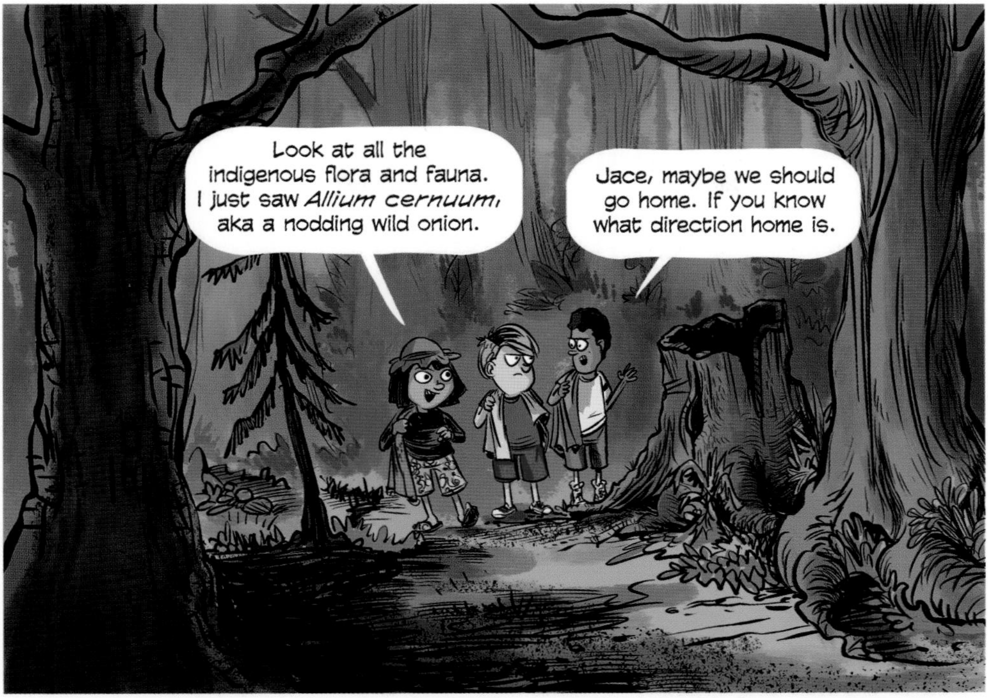
Look at all the indigenous flora and fauna. I just saw *Allium cernuum*, aka a nodding wild onion.
Jace, maybe we should go home. If you know what direction home is.

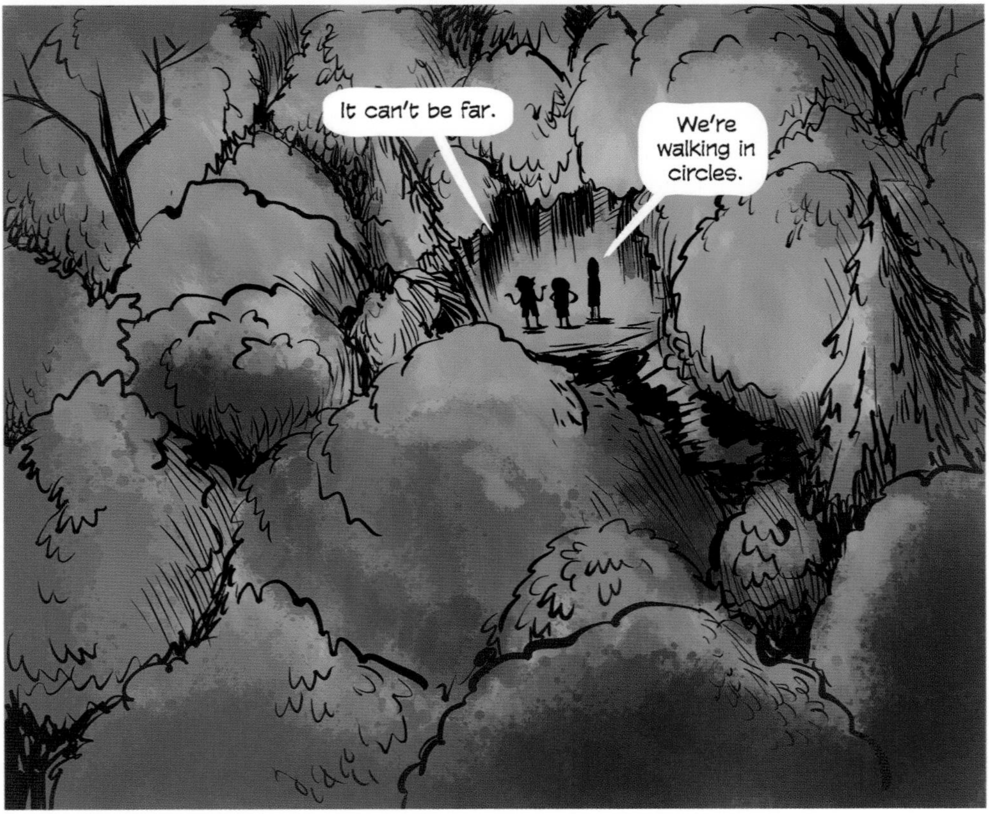
It can't be far.
We're walking in circles.

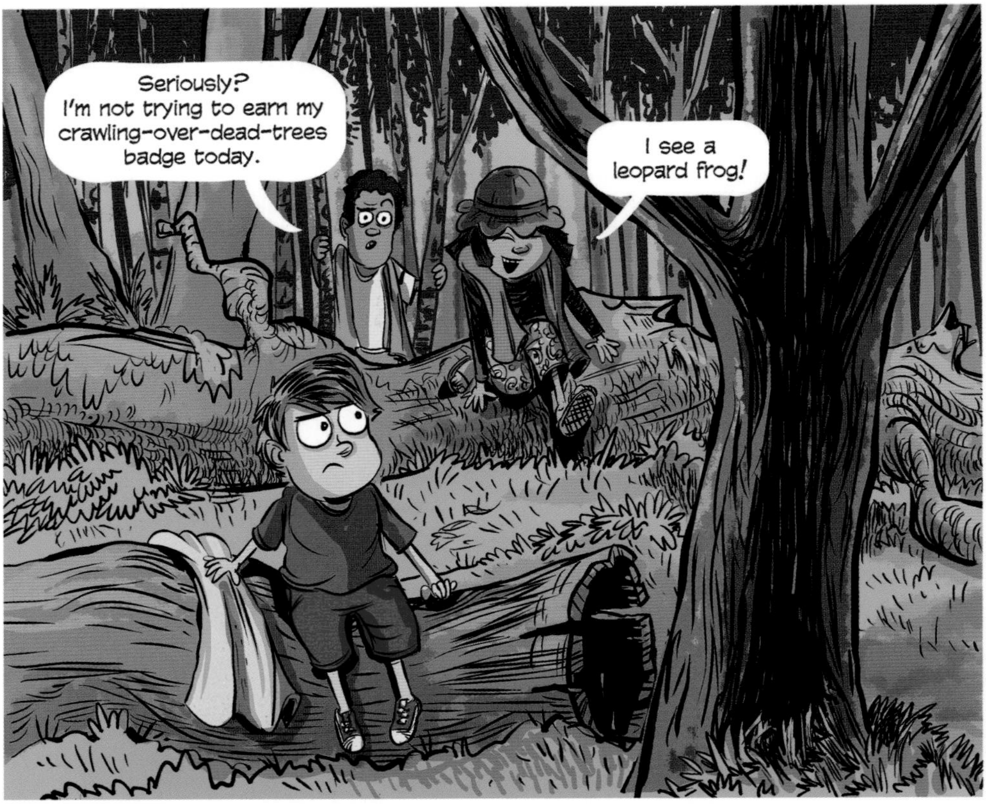
Seriously? I'm not trying to earn my crawling-over-dead-trees badge today.
I see a leopard frog!

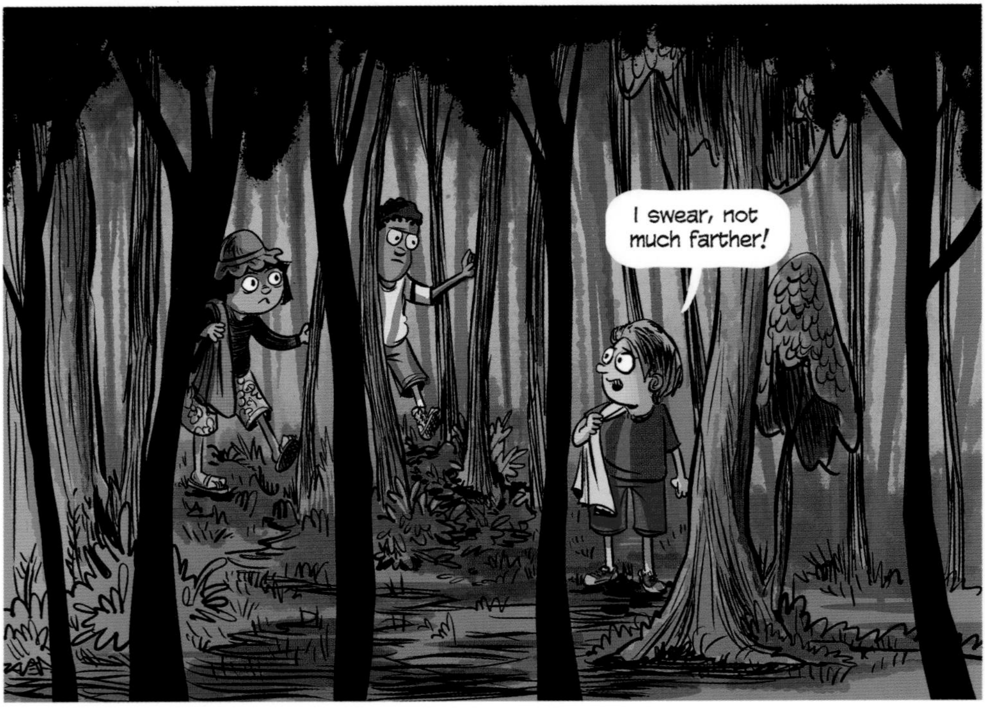
I swear, not much farther!

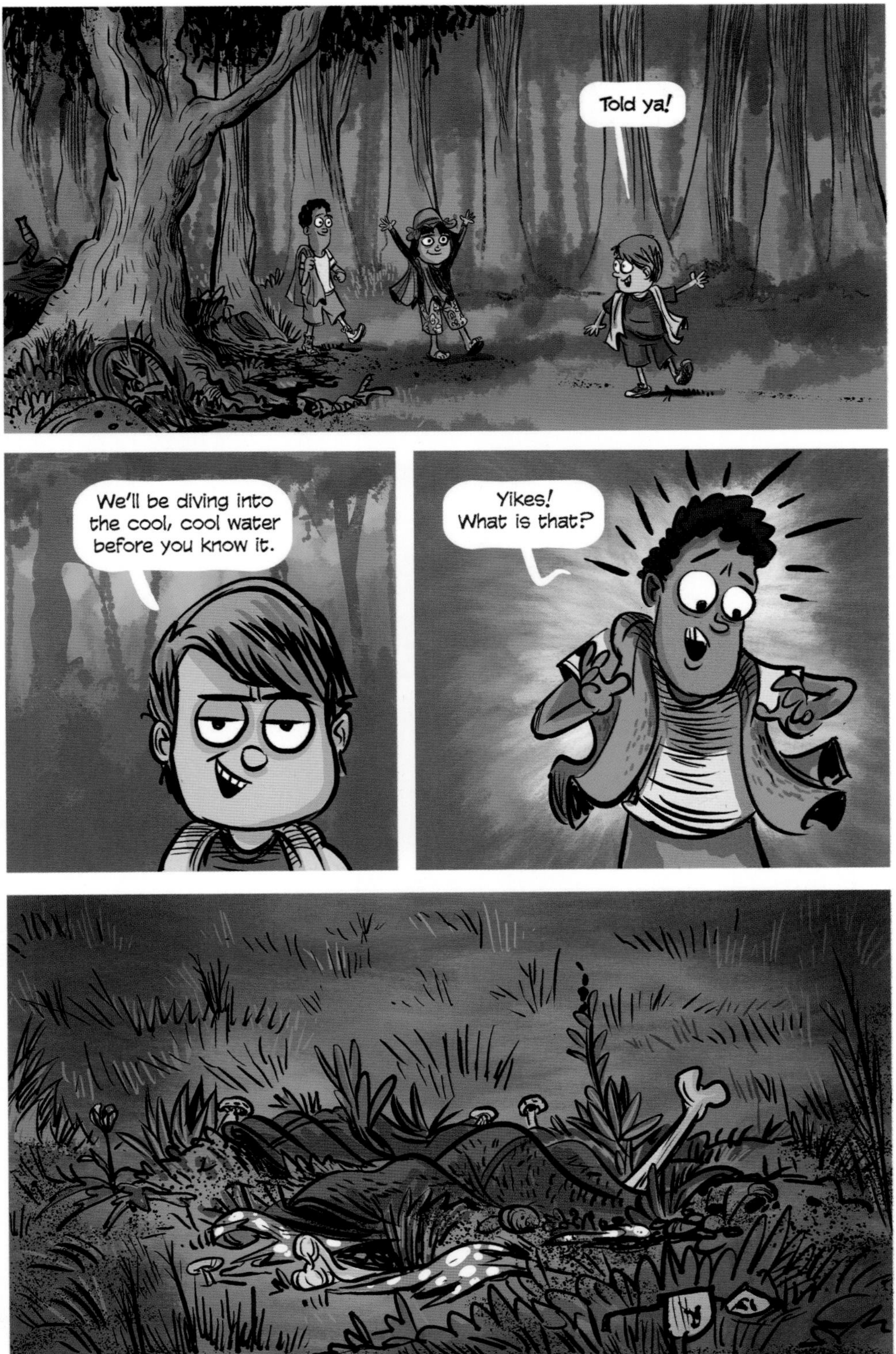
Told ya!
We'll be diving into the cool, cool water before you know it.
Yikes! What is that?

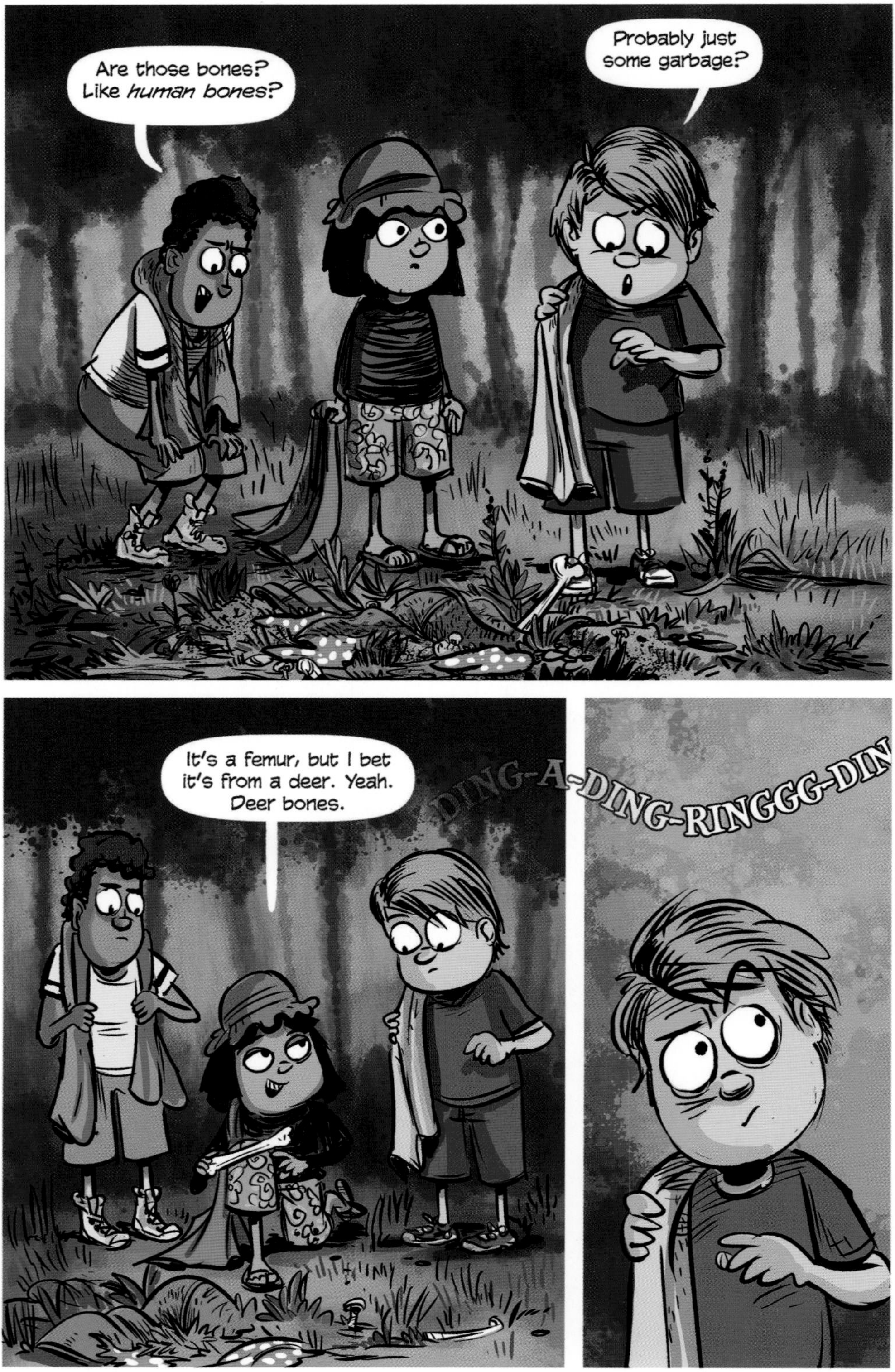
Are those bones? Like *human bones*?
Probably just some garbage?
It's a femur, but I bet it's from a deer. Yeah. Deer bones.
DING-A-DING-RINGGG-DIN

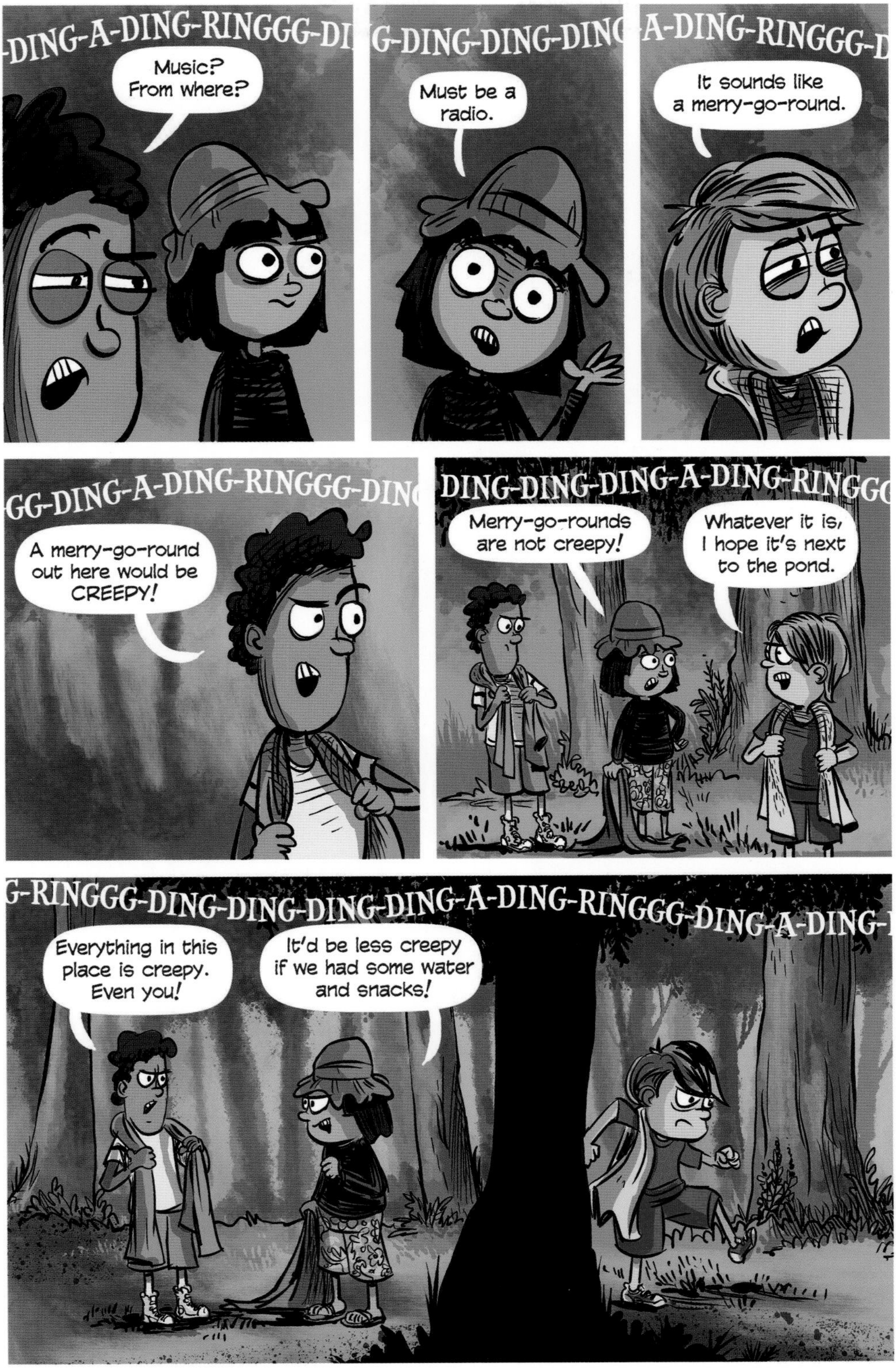
-DING-A-DING-RINGGG-DI
Music? From where?
G-DING-DING-DING
Must be a radio.
A-DING-RINGGG-D
It sounds like a merry-go-round.
GG-DING-A-DING-RINGGG-DIN
A merry-go-round out here would be CREEPY!
DING-DING-DING-A-DING-RINGG
Merry-go-rounds are not creepy!
Whatever it is, I hope it's next to the pond.
G-RINGGG-DING-DING-DING-DING-A-DING-RINGGG-DING-A-DING-
Everything in this place is creepy. Even you!
It'd be less creepy if we had some water and snacks!

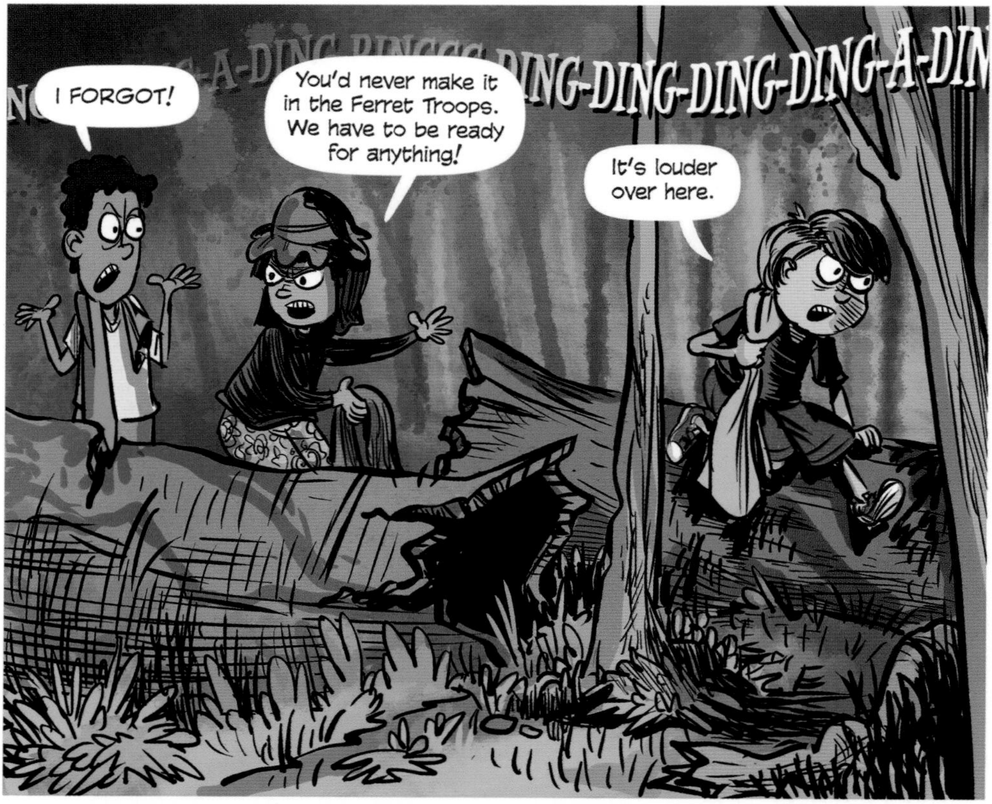

NG-A-DING RINGGG-DING-DING-DING-DING-A-DIN
I FORGOT!
You'd never make it in the Ferret Troops. We have to be ready for anything!
It's louder over here.

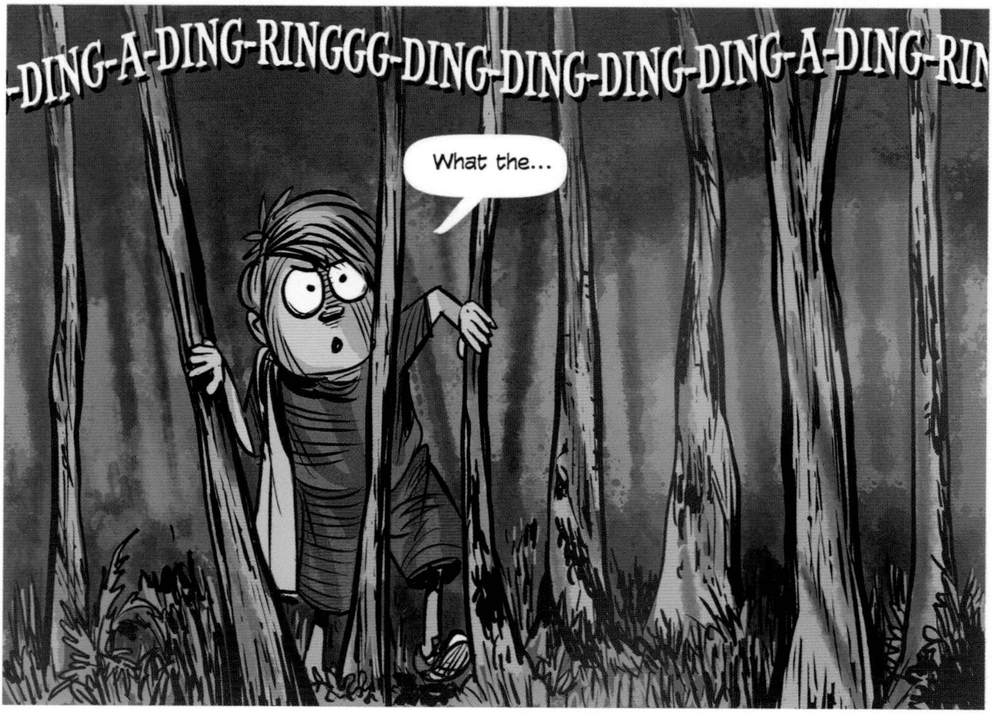

-DING-A-DING-RINGGG-DING-DING-DING-DING-A-DING-RIN
What the...

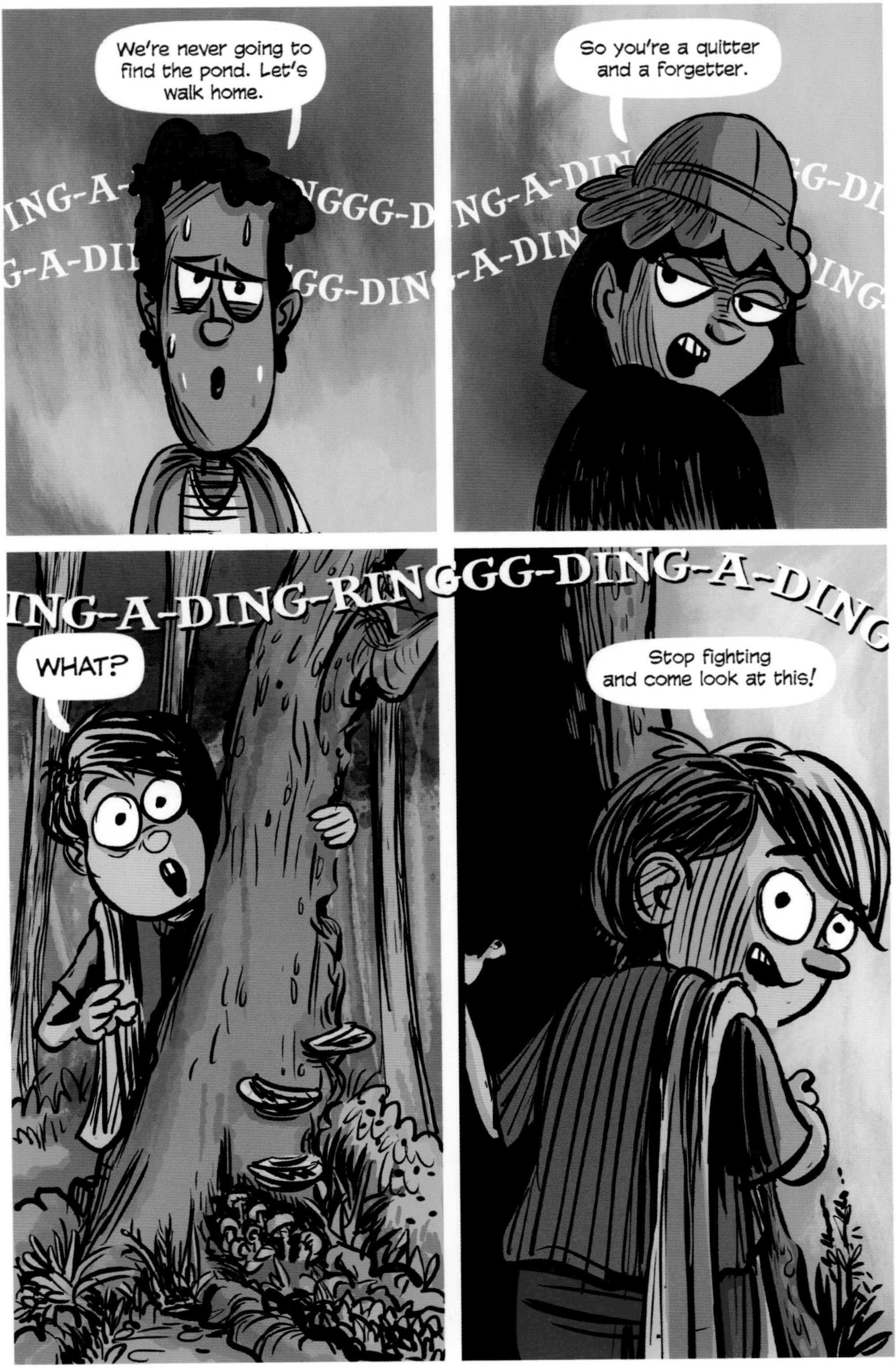
We're never going to find the pond. Let's walk home.
So you're a quitter and a forgetter.
ING-A-DING-RINGGG-DING-A-DING
WHAT?
Stop fighting and come look at this!

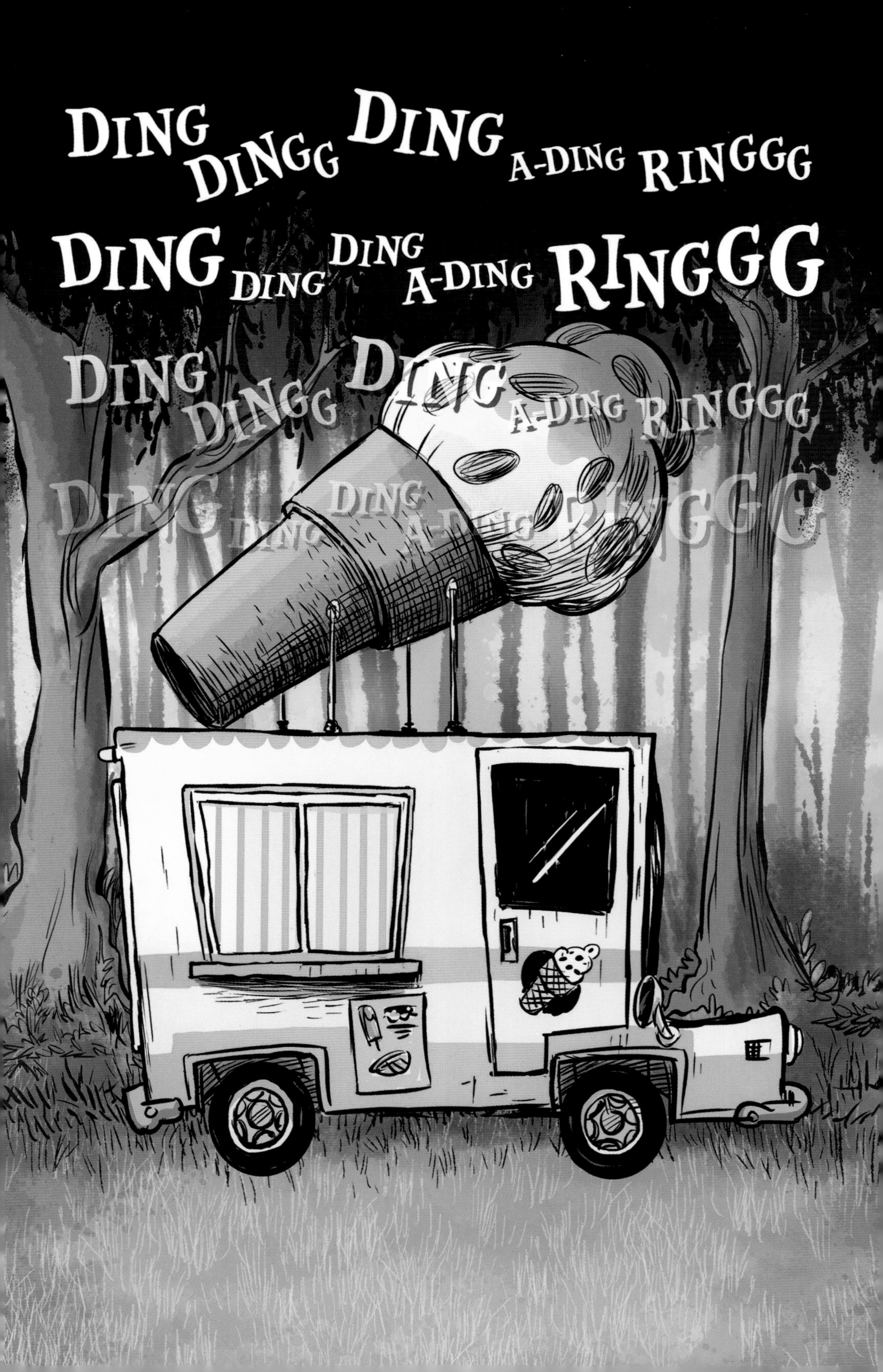
DING DINGG DING A-DING RINGGG
DING DING DING A-DING RINGGG
DING DINGG DING A-DING RINGGG

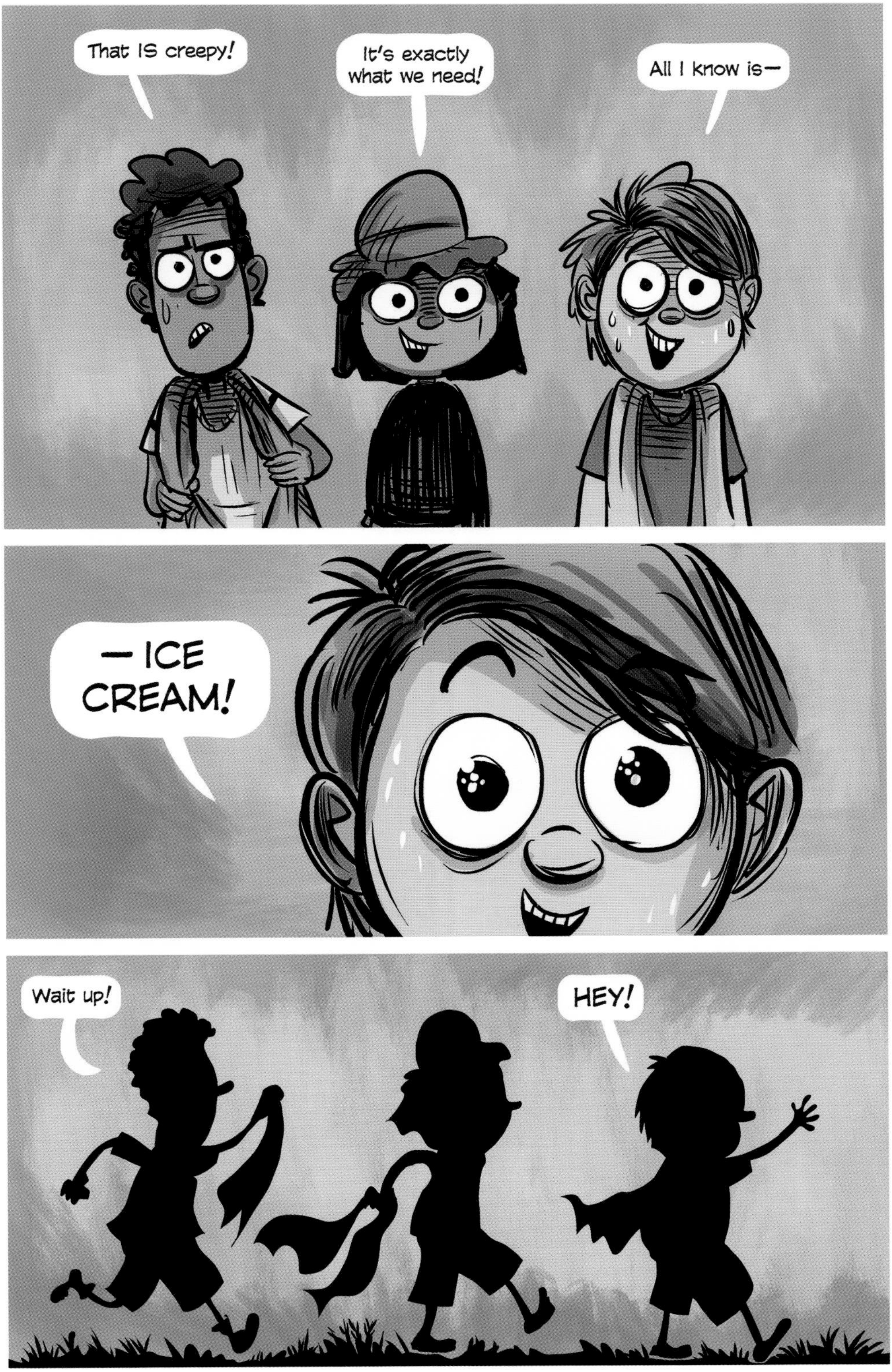
That IS creepy!
It's exactly what we need!
All I know is—
—ICE CREAM!
Wait up!
HEY!

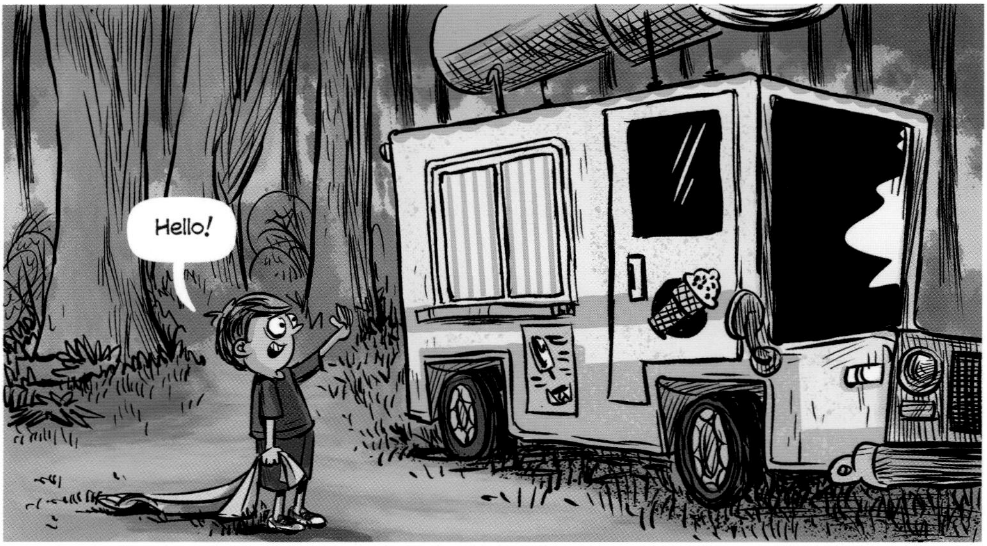
Hello!

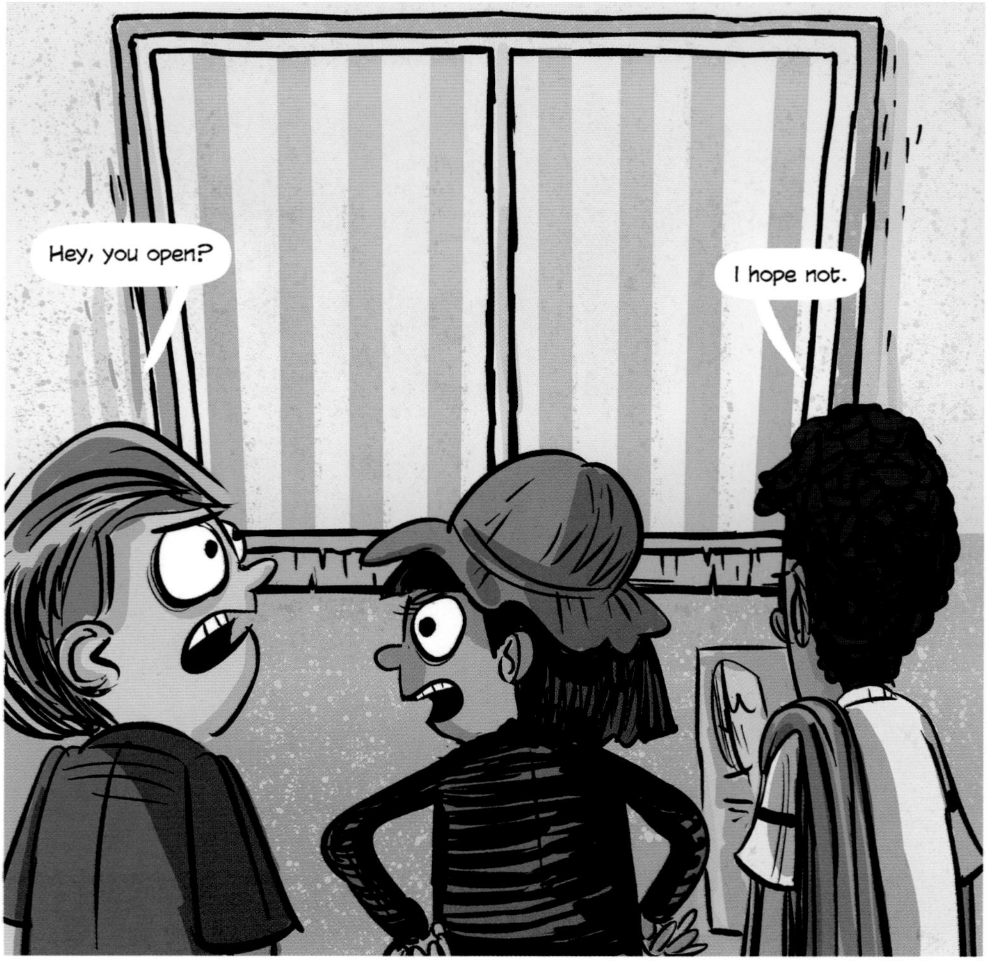
Hey, you open?
I hope not.

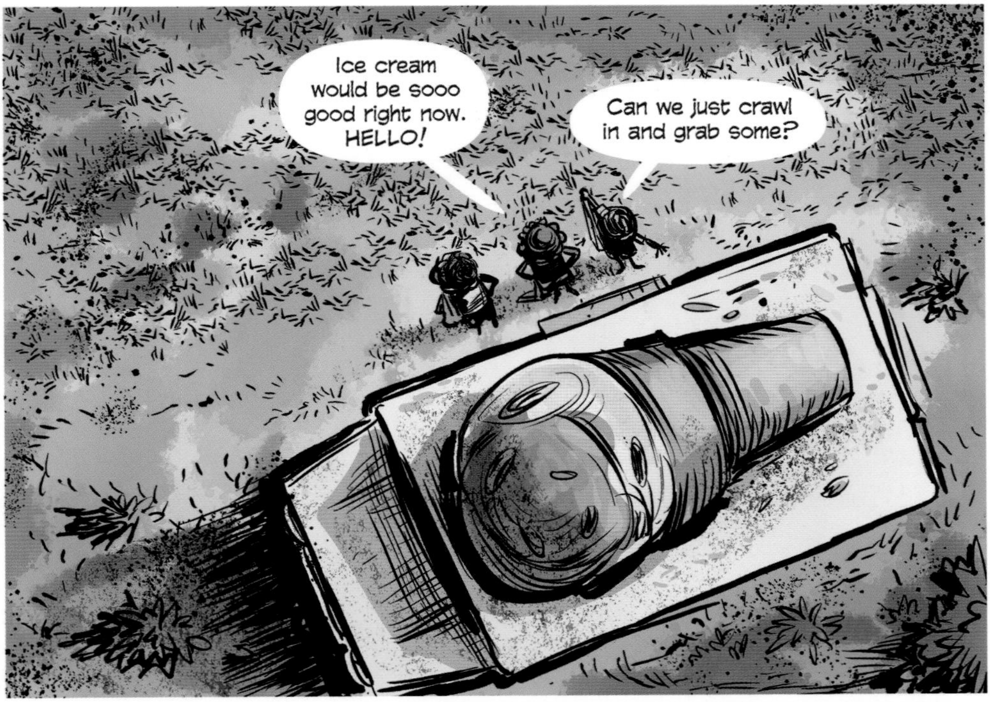
Ice cream would be sooo good right now. HELLO!
Can we just crawl in and grab some?

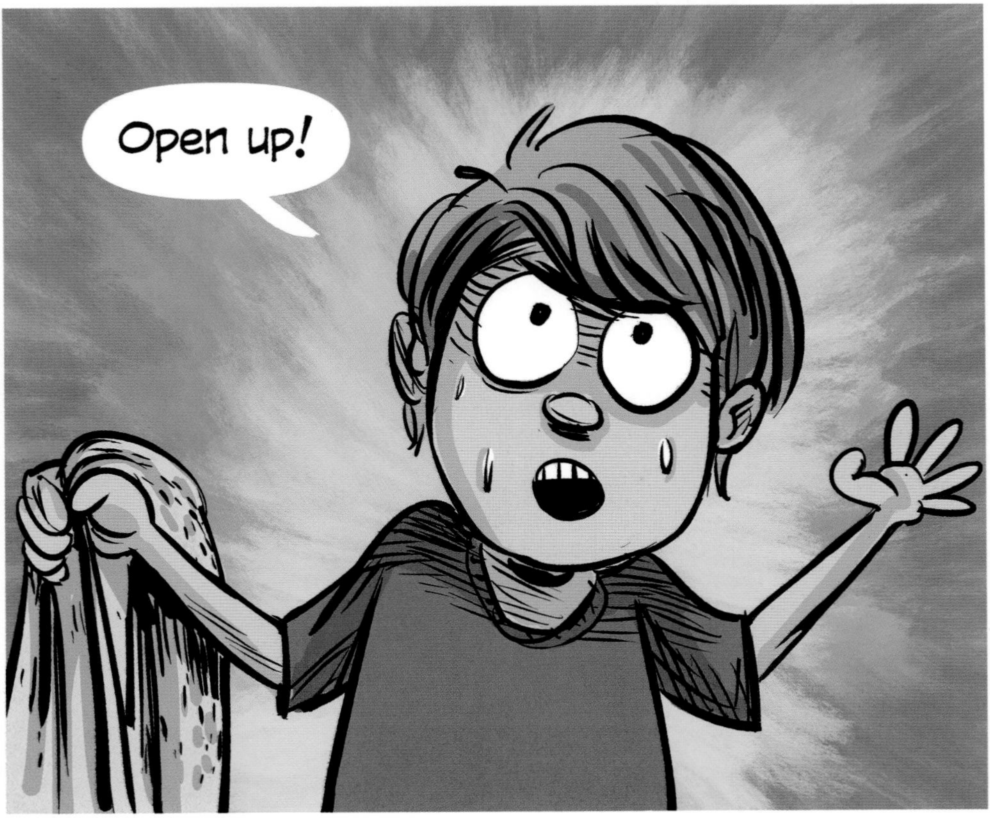
Open up!

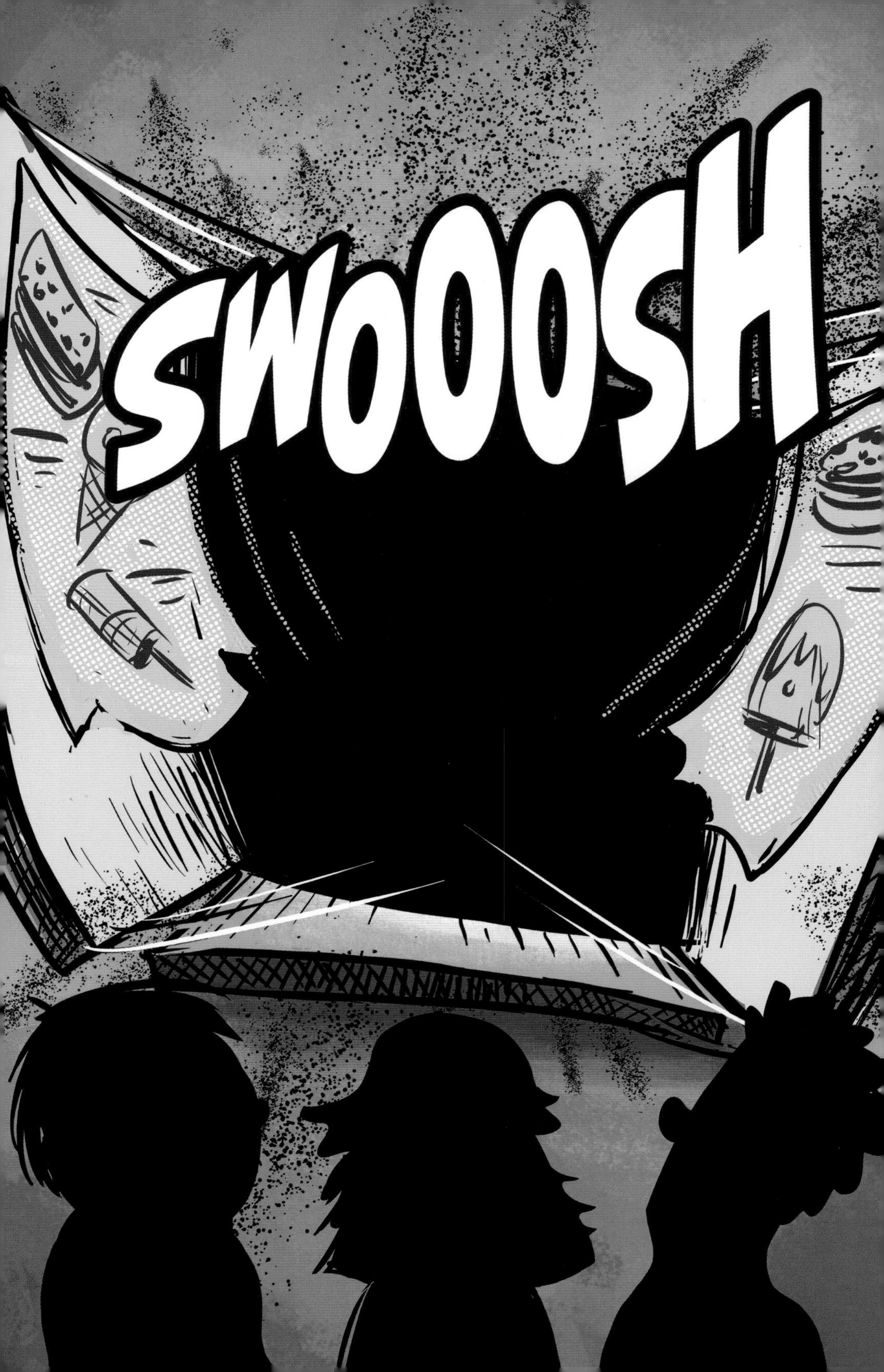
SWOOOSH

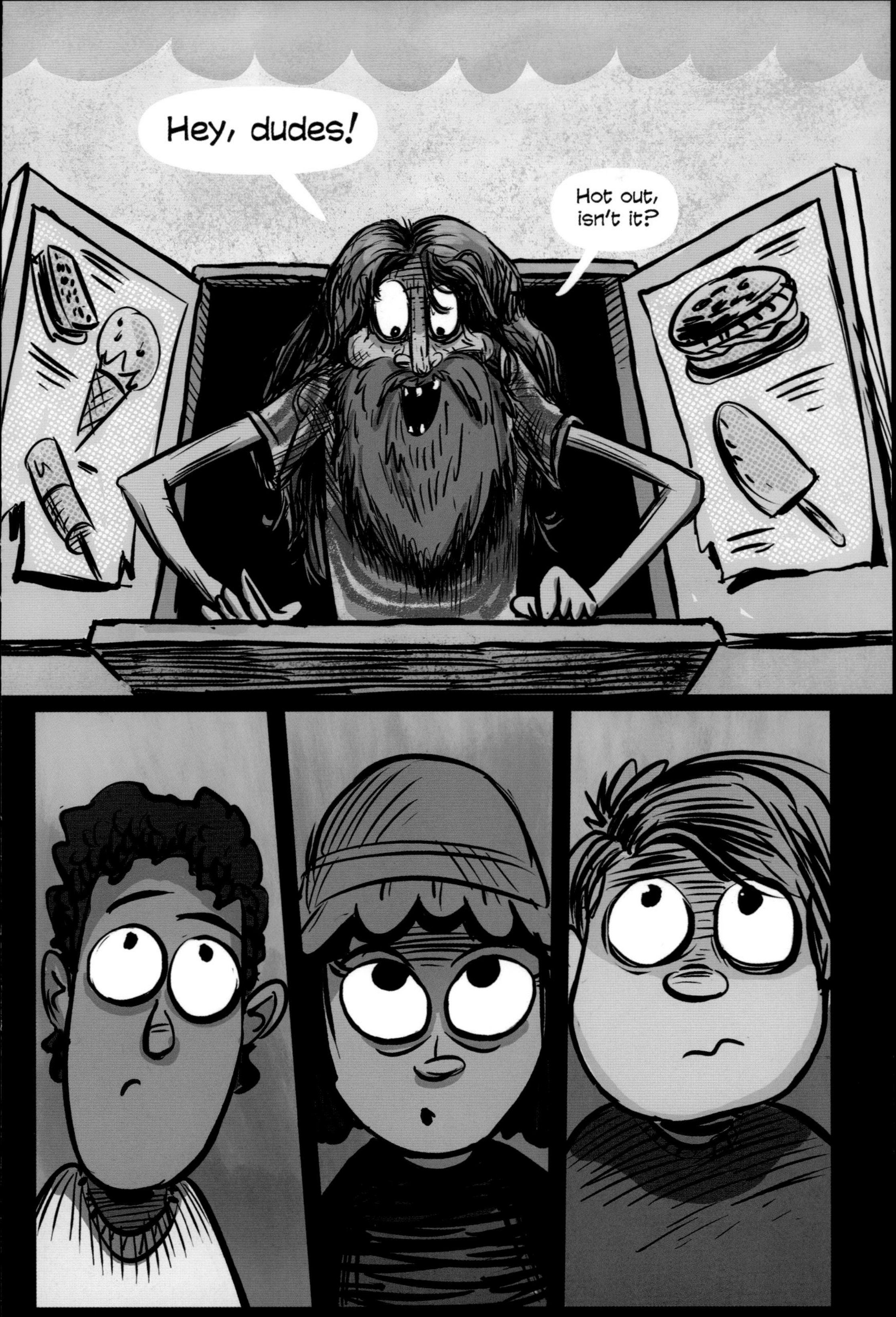
Hey, dudes!
Hot out, isn't it?

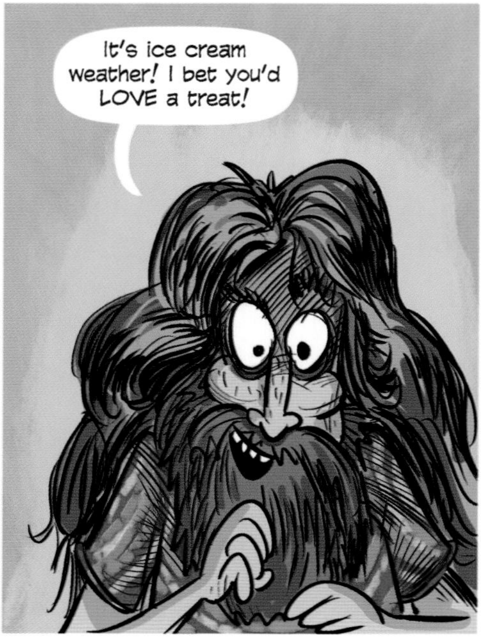
It's ice cream weather! I bet you'd LOVE a treat!

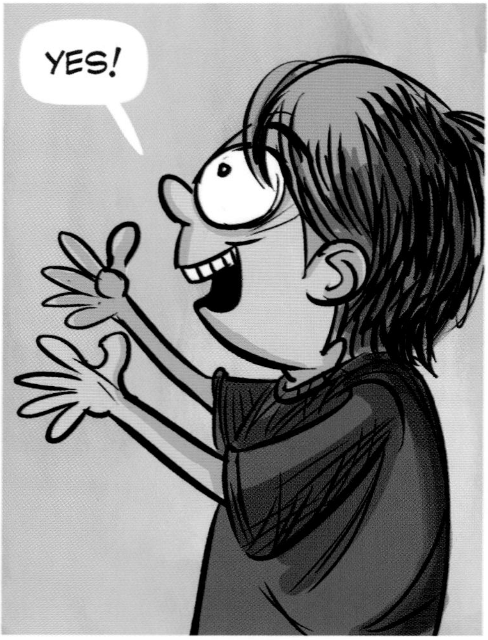
YES!

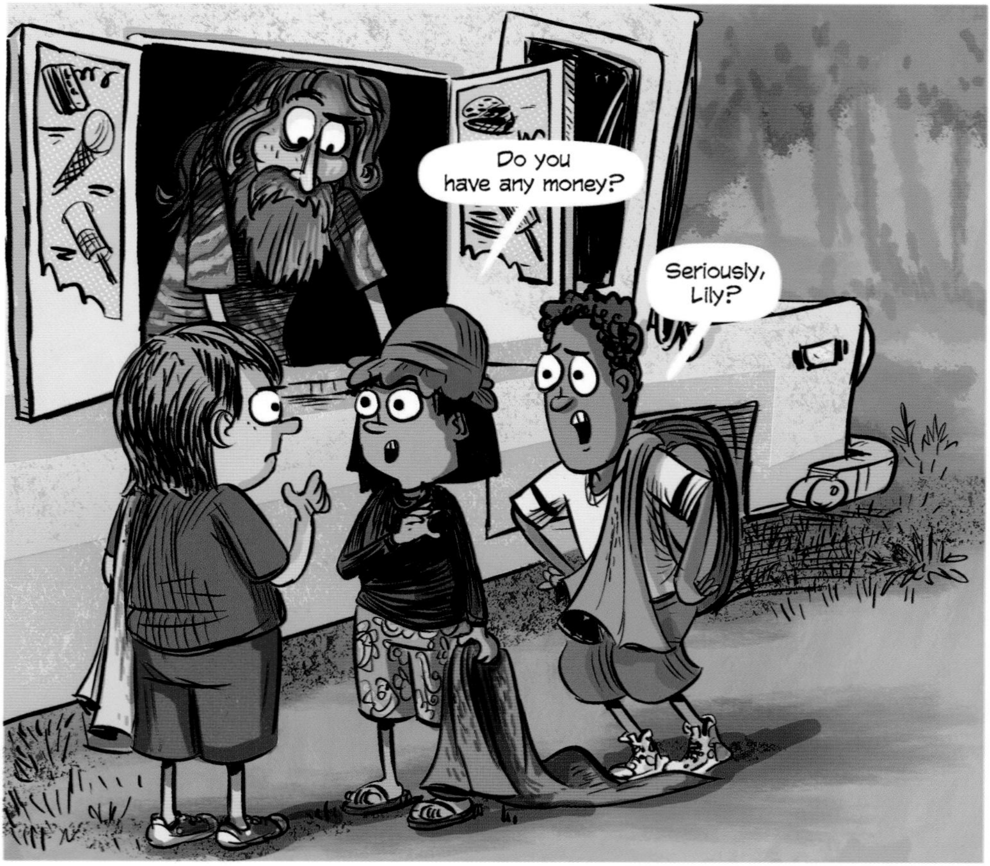
Do you have any money?
Seriously, Lily?

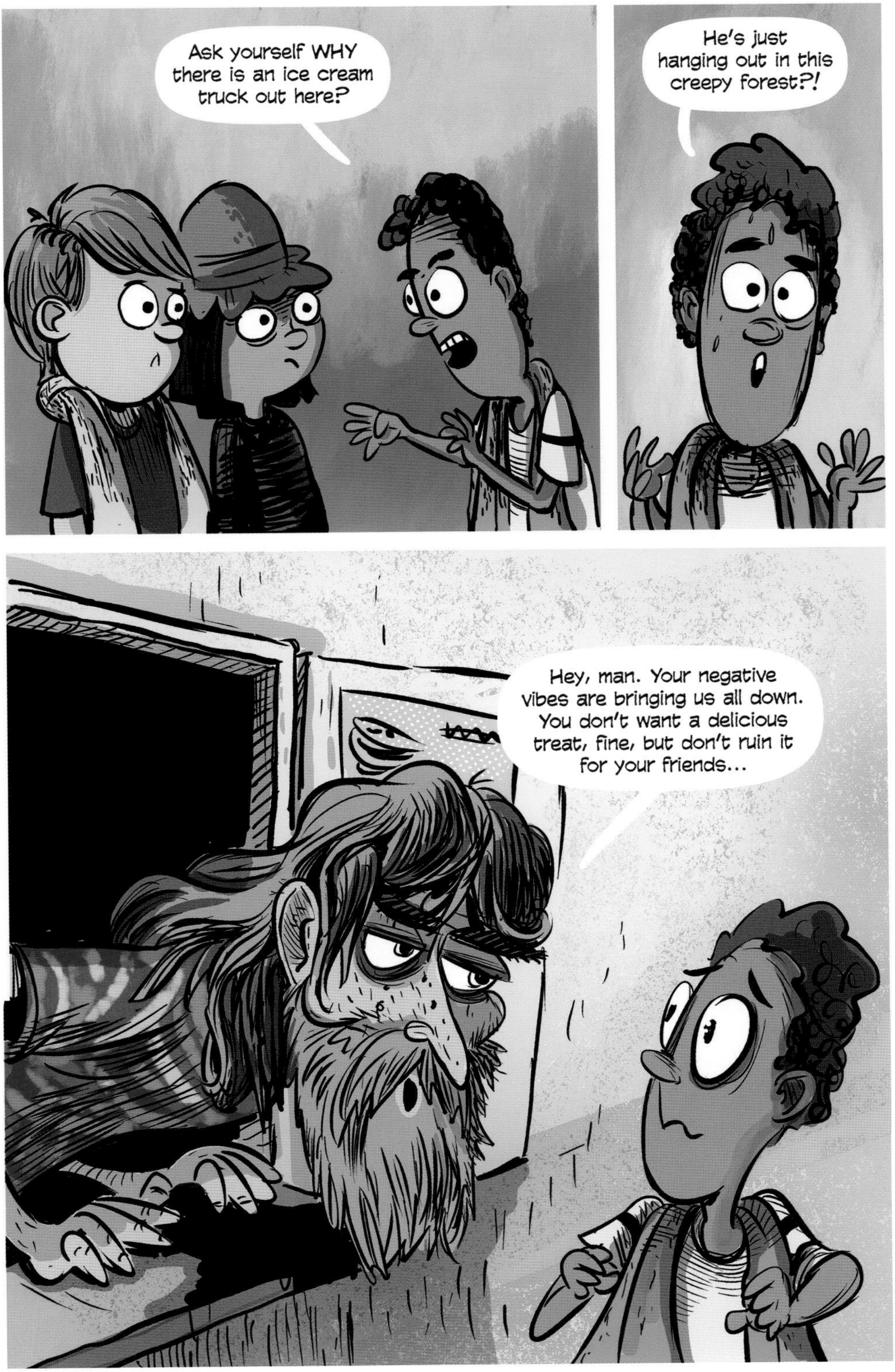
Ask yourself WHY there is an ice cream truck out here?
He's just hanging out in this creepy forest?!
Hey, man. Your negative vibes are bringing us all down. You don't want a delicious treat, fine, but don't ruin it for your friends...

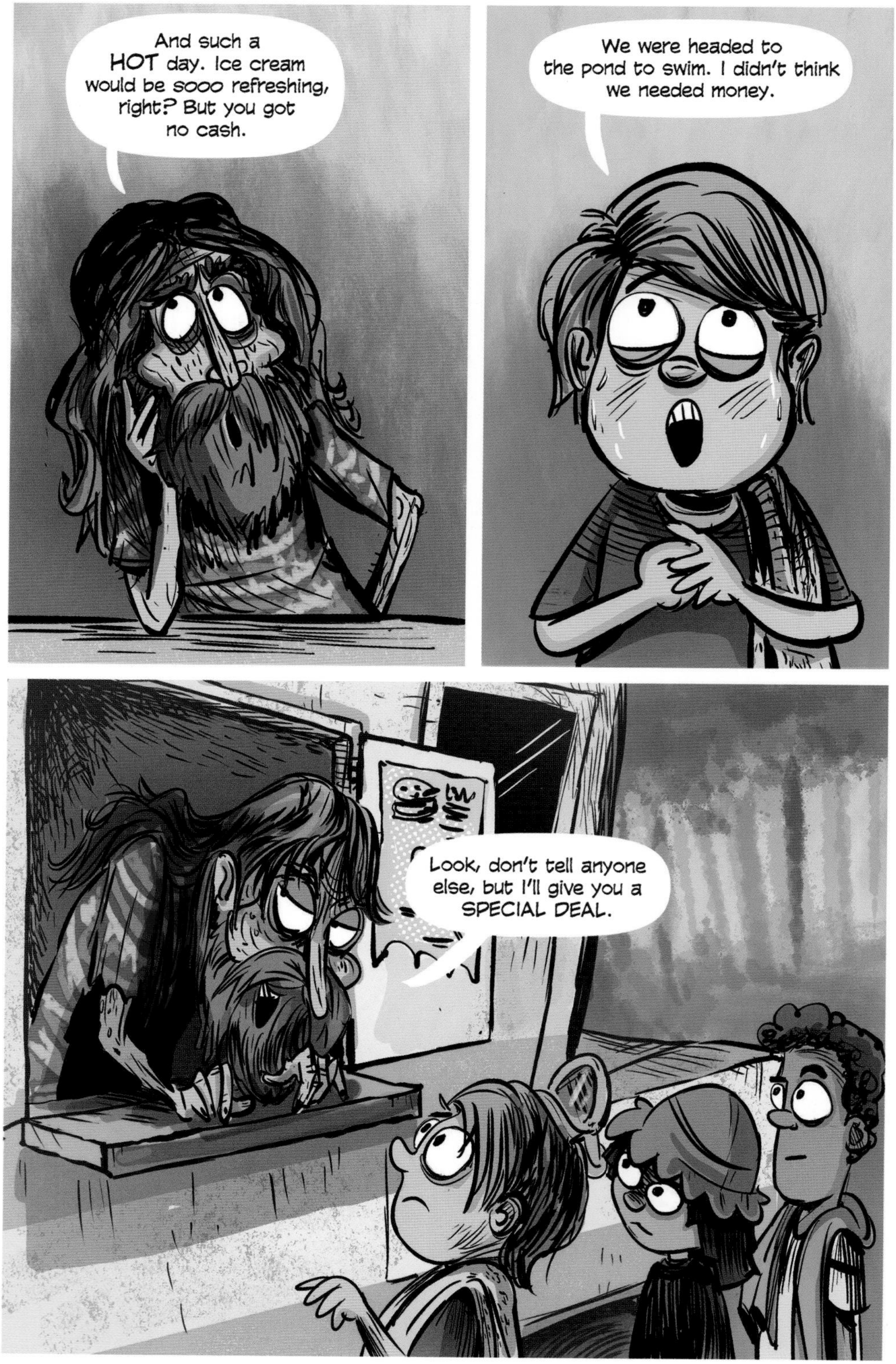
And such a HOT day. Ice cream would be sooo refreshing, right? But you got no cash.
We were headed to the pond to swim. I didn't think we needed money.
Look, don't tell anyone else, but I'll give you a SPECIAL DEAL.

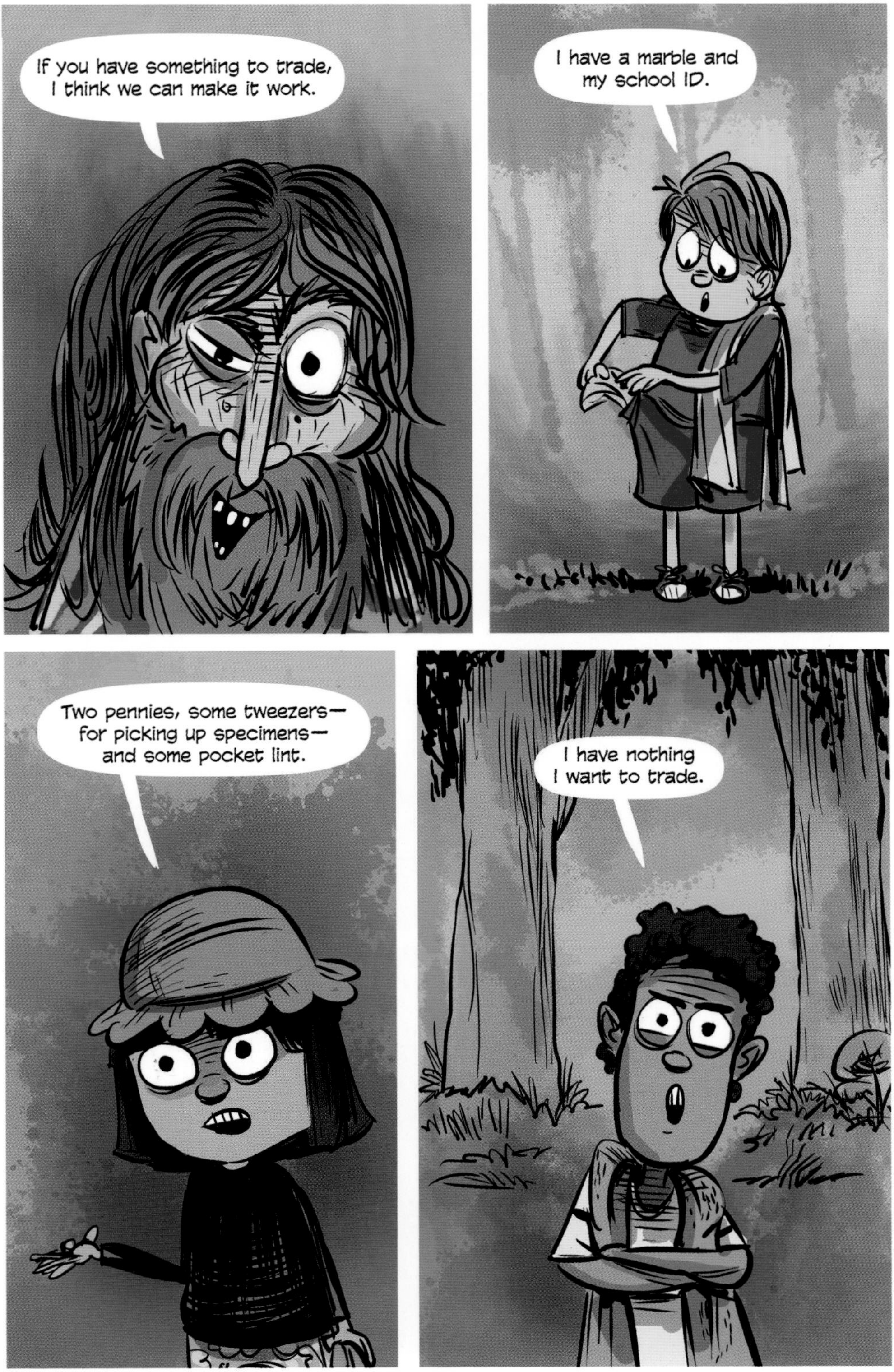
If you have something to trade, I think we can make it work.
I have a marble and my school ID.
Two pennies, some tweezers—for picking up specimens—and some pocket lint.
I have nothing I want to trade.

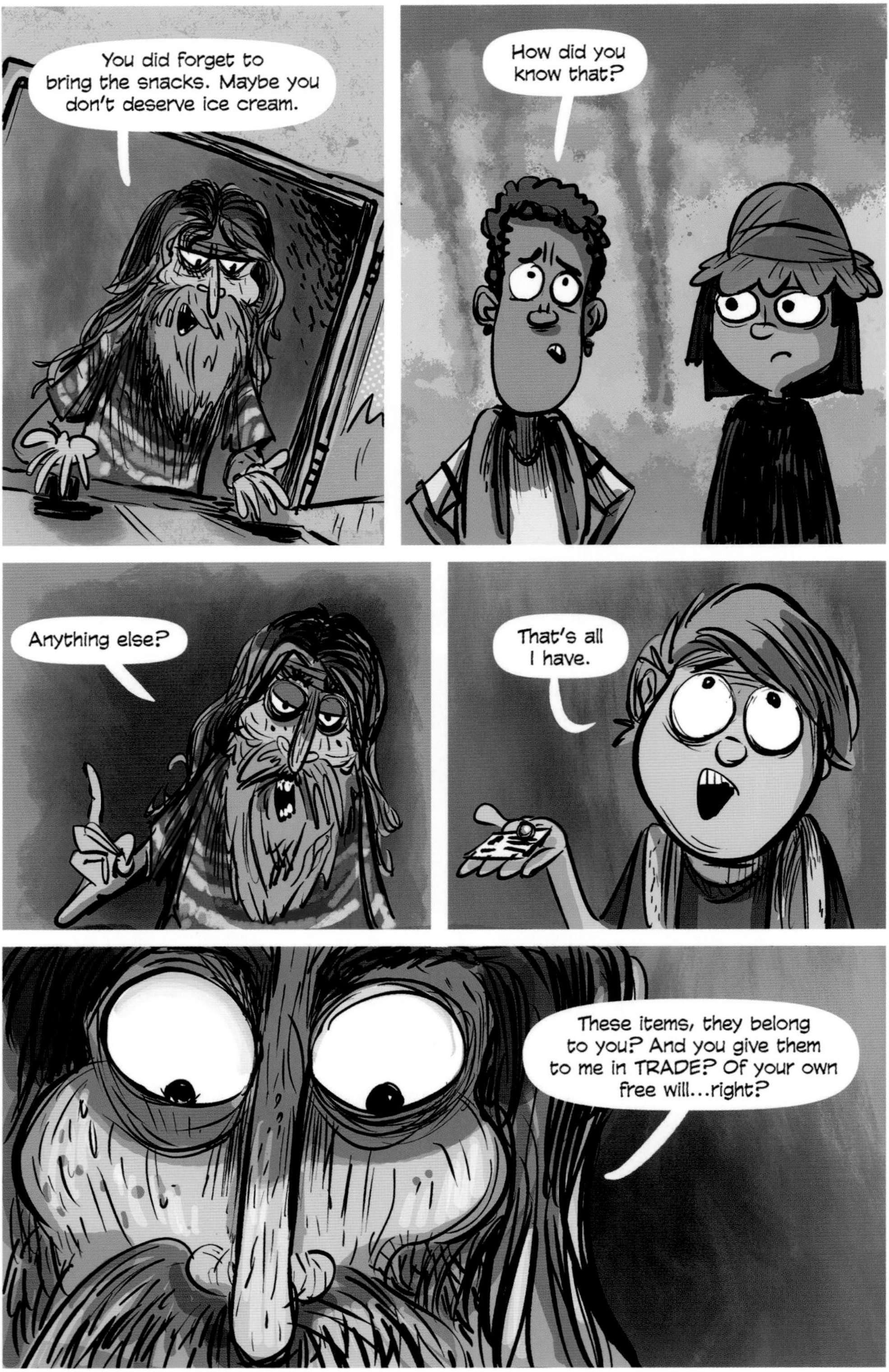
You did forget to bring the snacks. Maybe you don't deserve ice cream.
How did you know that?
Anything else?
That's all I have.
These items, they belong to you? And you give them to me in TRADE? Of your own free will...right?

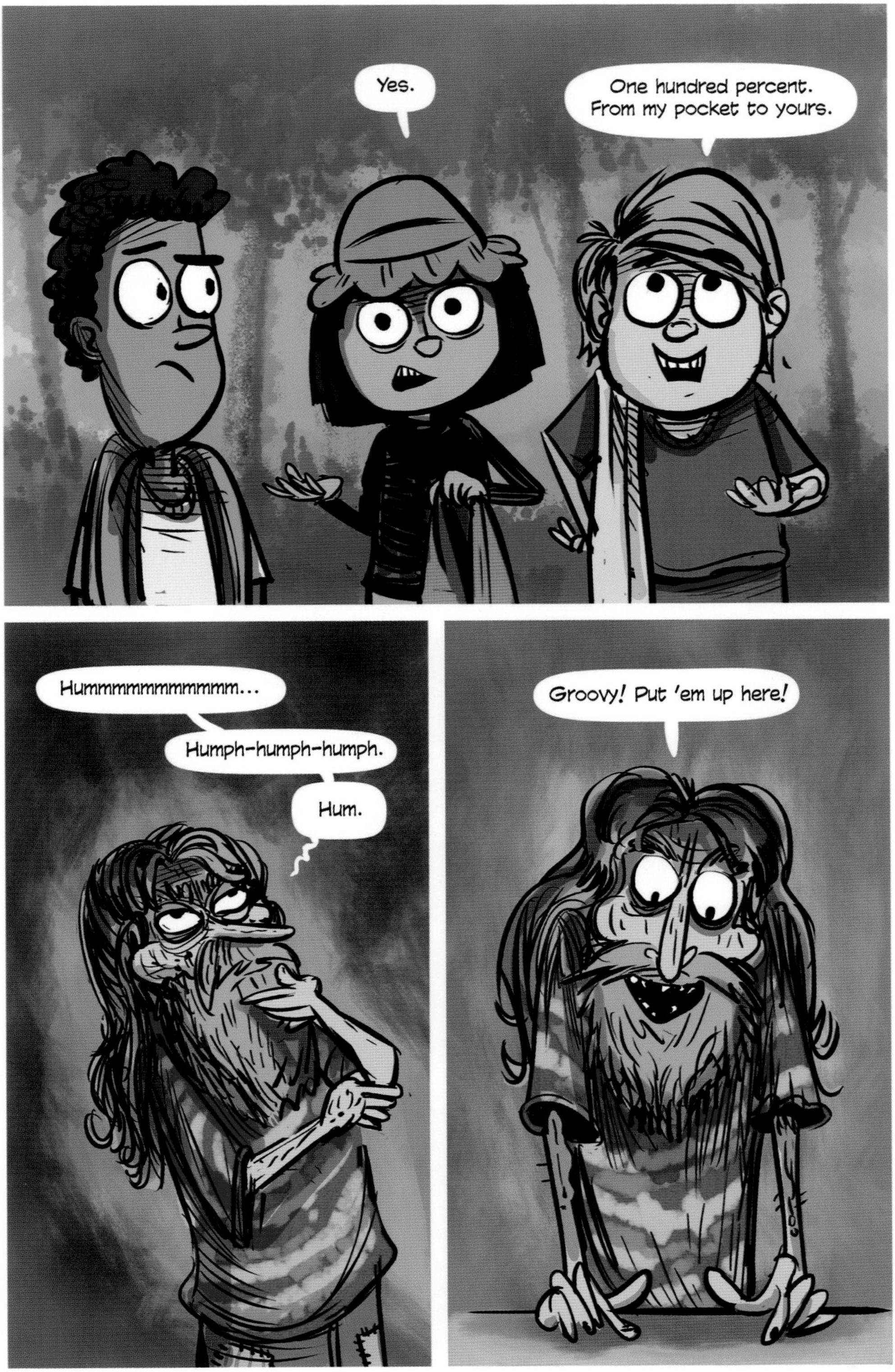
Yes.
One hundred percent. From my pocket to yours.
Hummmmmmmmmmm...
Humph-humph-humph.
Hum.
Groovy! Put 'em up here!

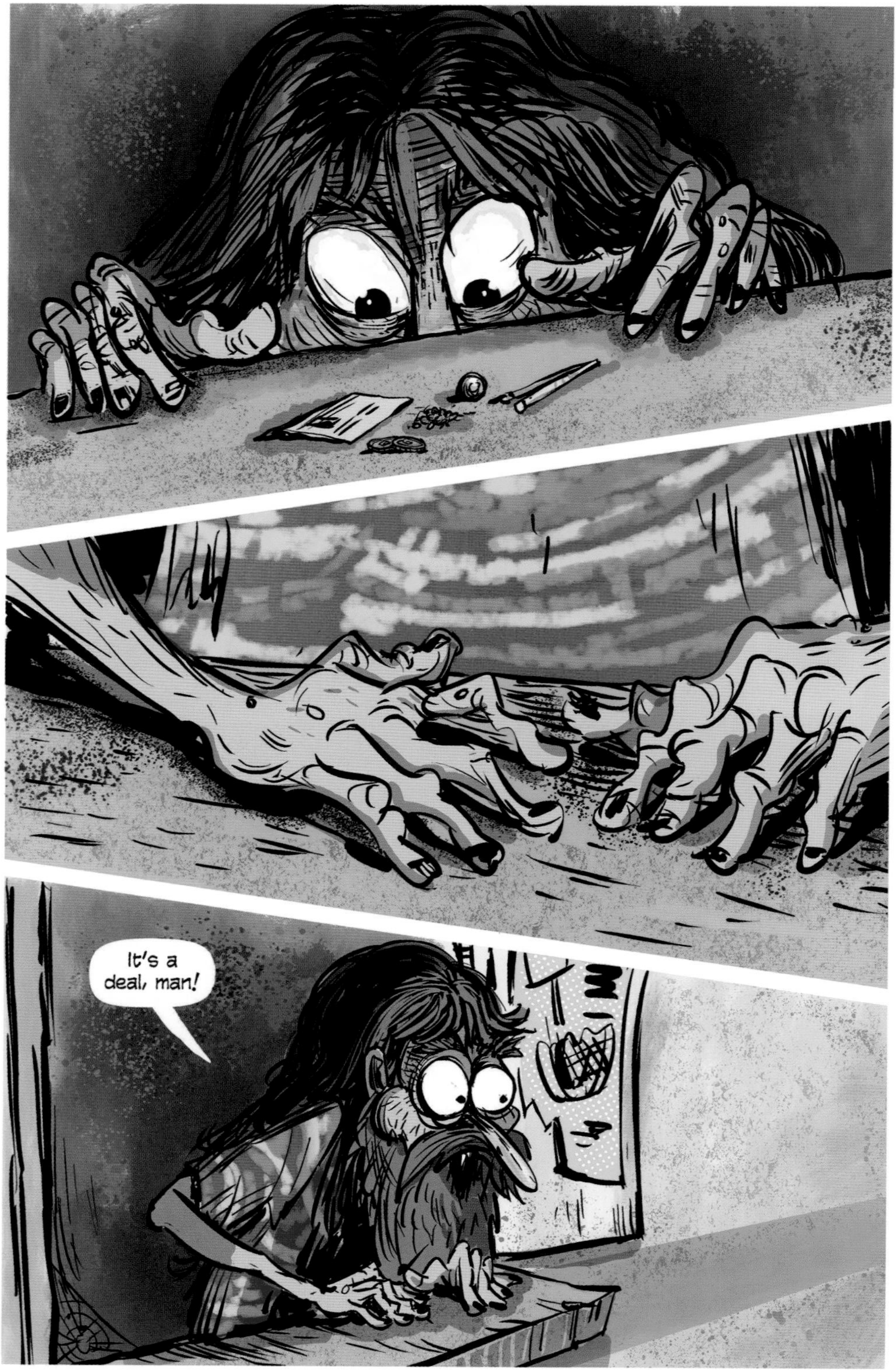
It's a deal, man!

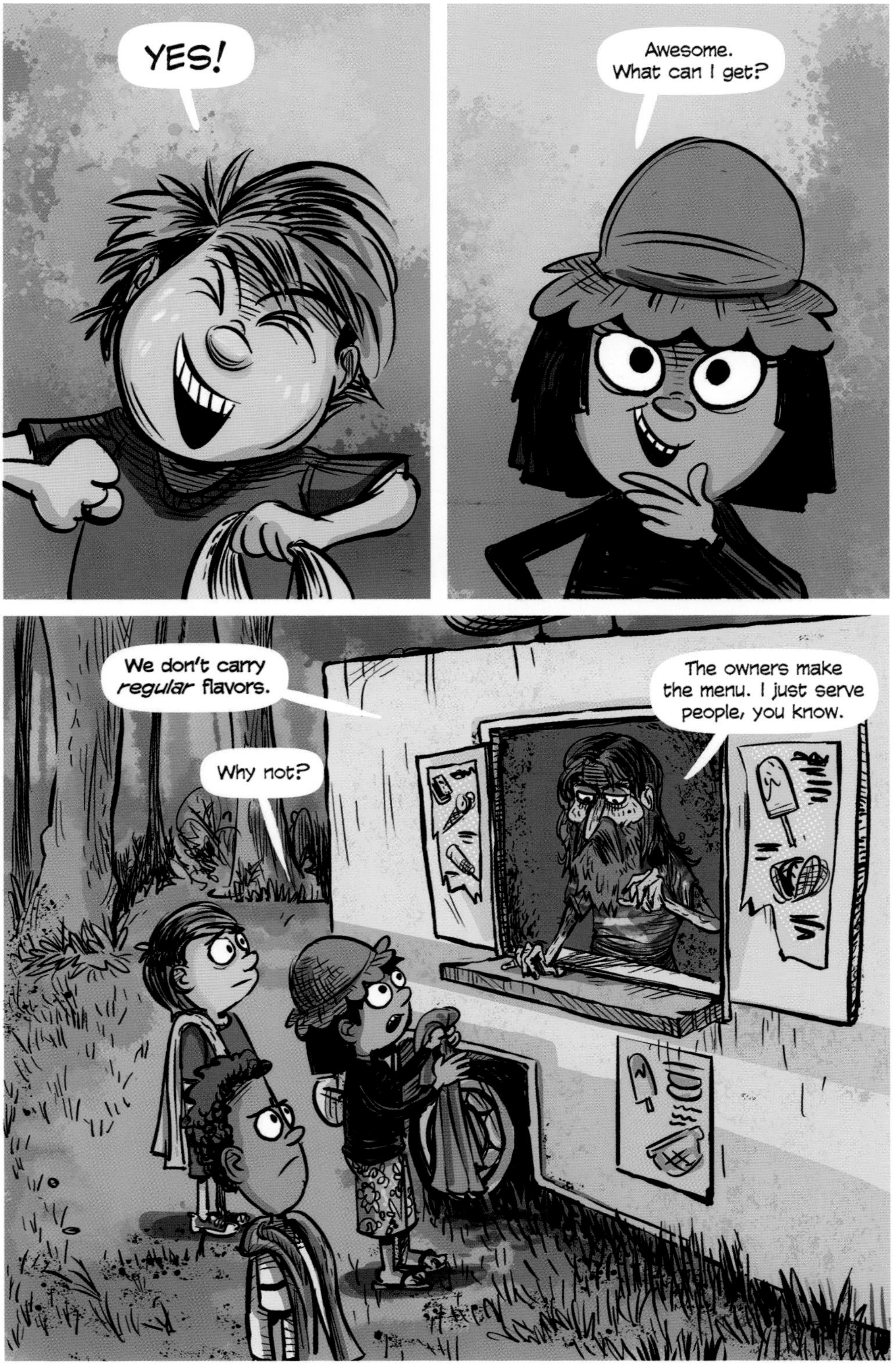
YES!
Awesome. What can I get?
We don't carry *regular* flavors.
Why not?
The owners make the menu. I just serve people, you know.

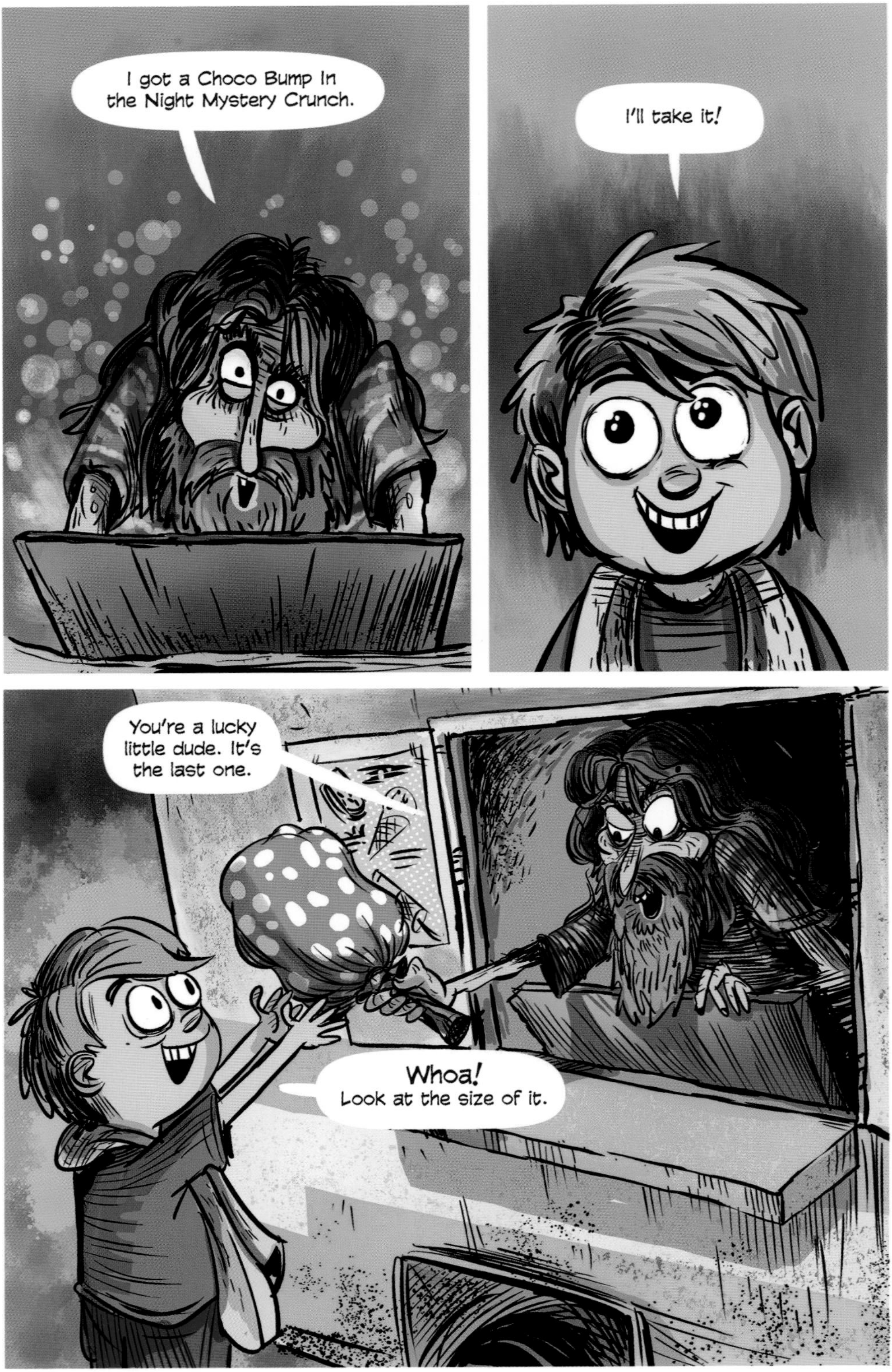
I got a Choco Bump In the Night Mystery Crunch.
I'll take it!
You're a lucky little dude. It's the last one.
Whoa! Look at the size of it.

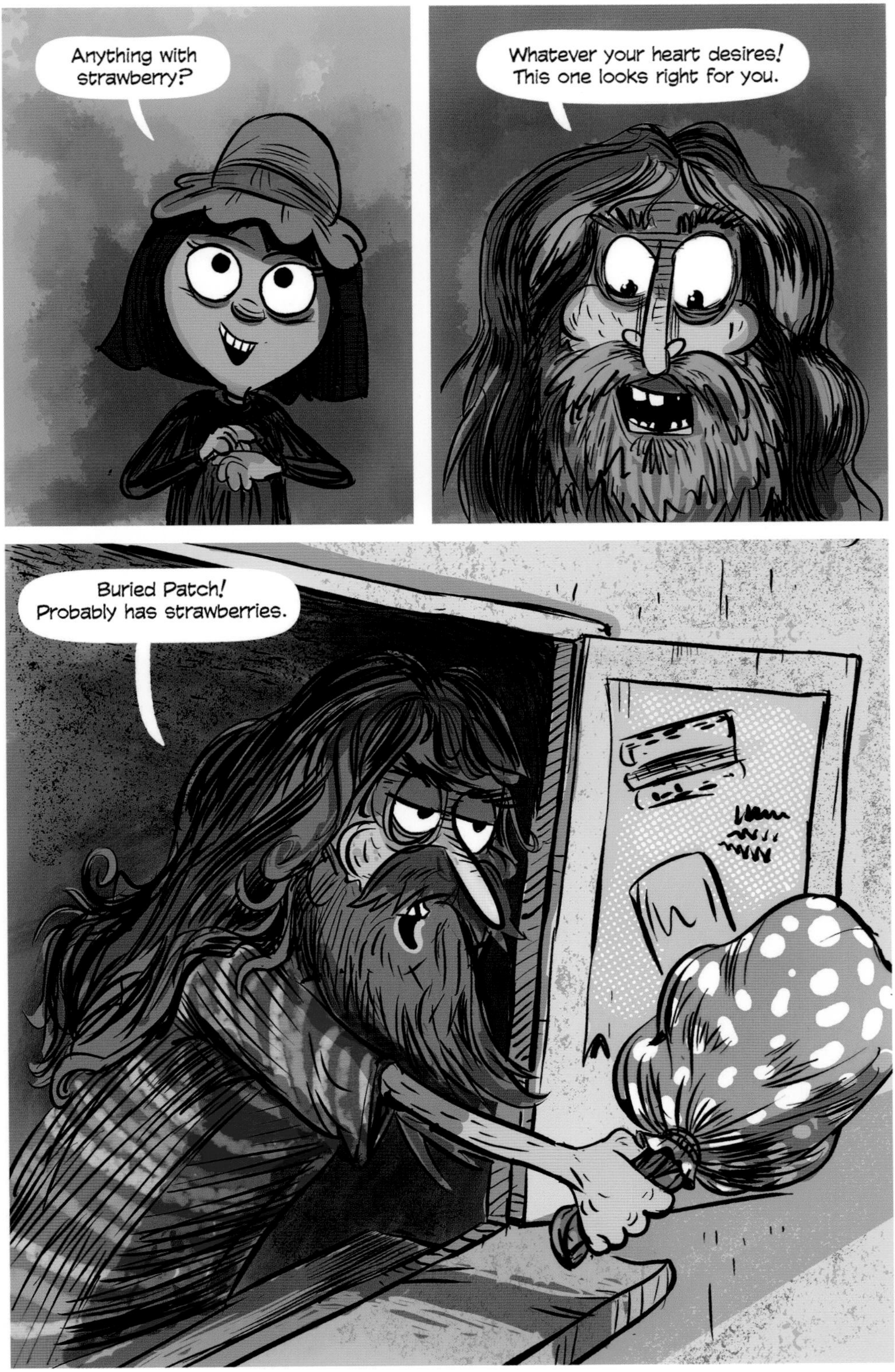
Anything with strawberry?
Whatever your heart desires! This one looks right for you.
Buried Patch! Probably has strawberries.

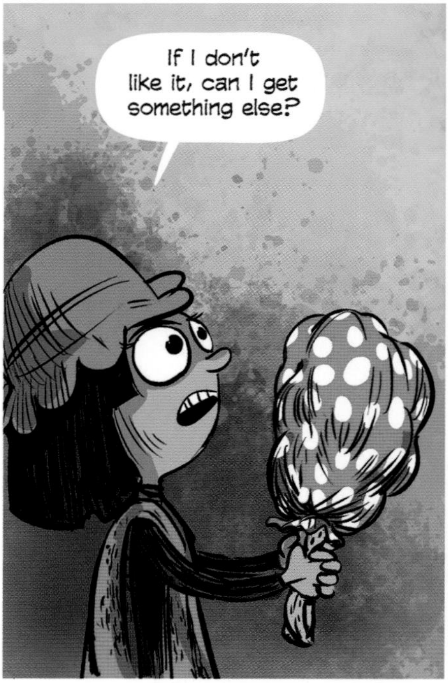
If I don't like it, can I get something else?

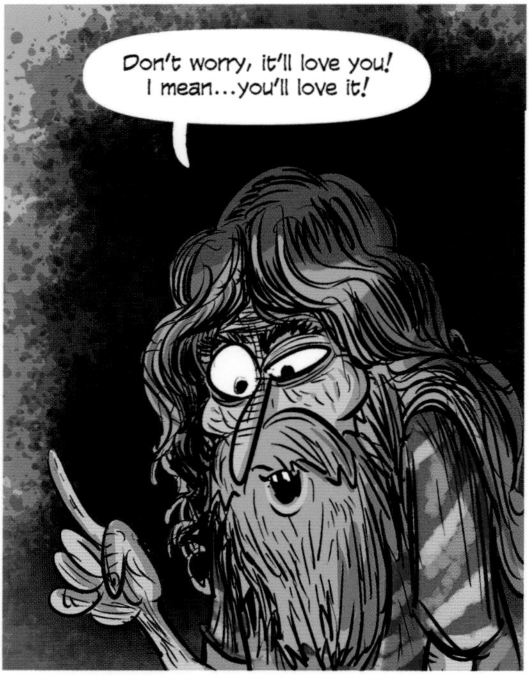
Don't worry, it'll love you!
I mean...you'll love it!

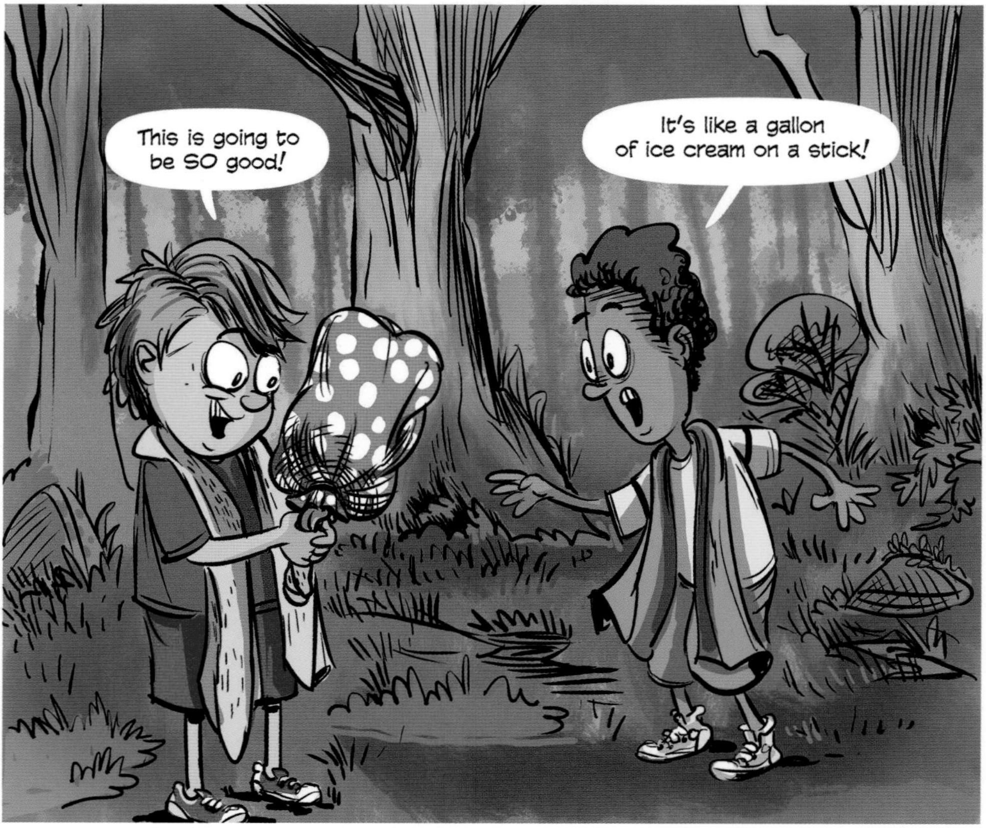
This is going to be SO good!
It's like a gallon of ice cream on a stick!

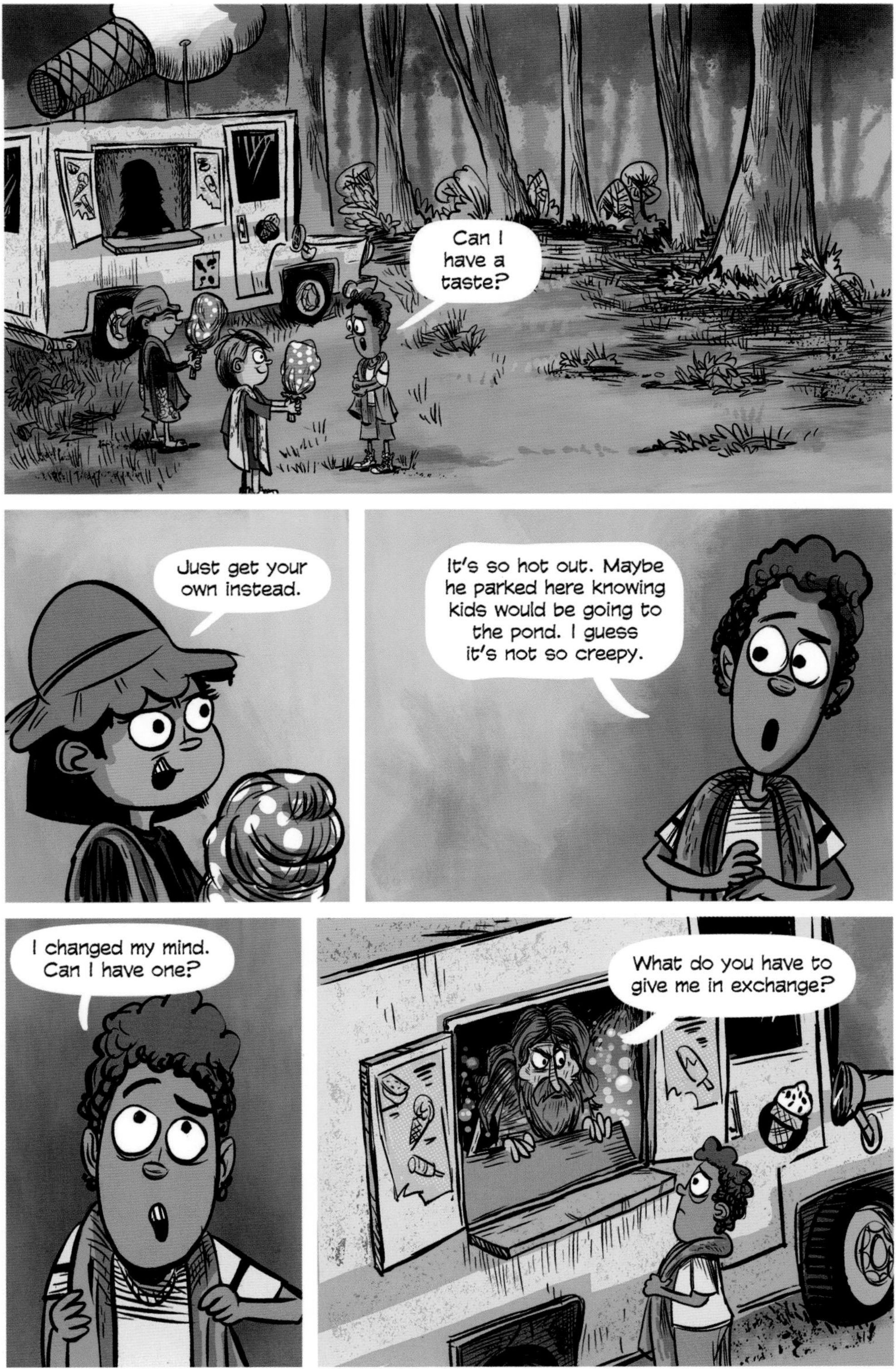
Can I have a taste?
Just get your own instead.
It's so hot out. Maybe he parked here knowing kids would be going to the pond. I guess it's not so creepy.
I changed my mind. Can I have one?
What do you have to give me in exchange?

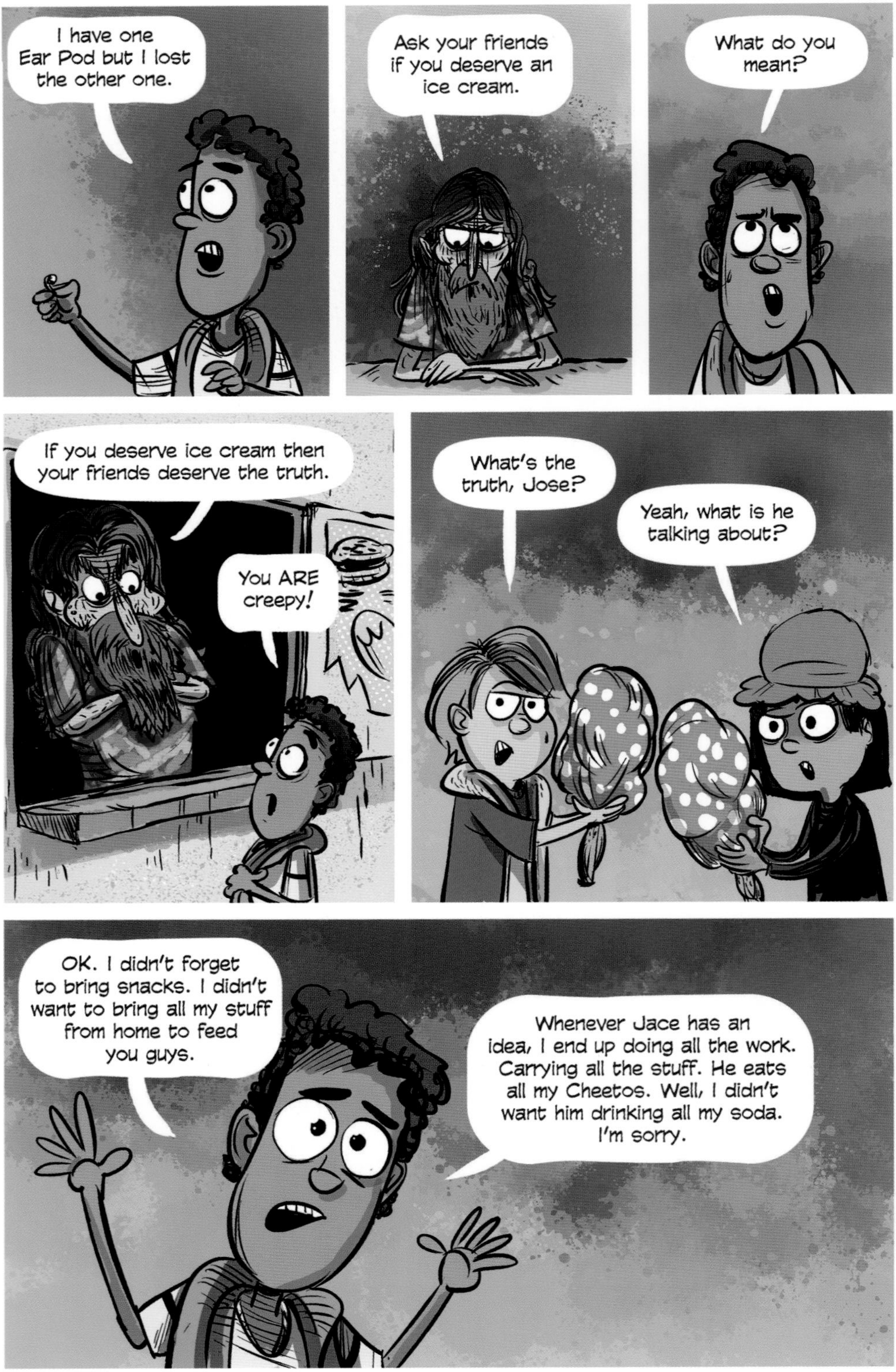
I have one Ear Pod but I lost the other one.
Ask your friends if you deserve an ice cream.
What do you mean?
If you deserve ice cream then your friends deserve the truth.
You ARE creepy!
What's the truth, Jose?
Yeah, what is he talking about?
OK. I didn't forget to bring snacks. I didn't want to bring all my stuff from home to feed you guys.
Whenever Jace has an idea, I end up doing all the work. Carrying all the stuff. He eats all my Cheetos. Well, I didn't want him drinking all my soda. I'm sorry.

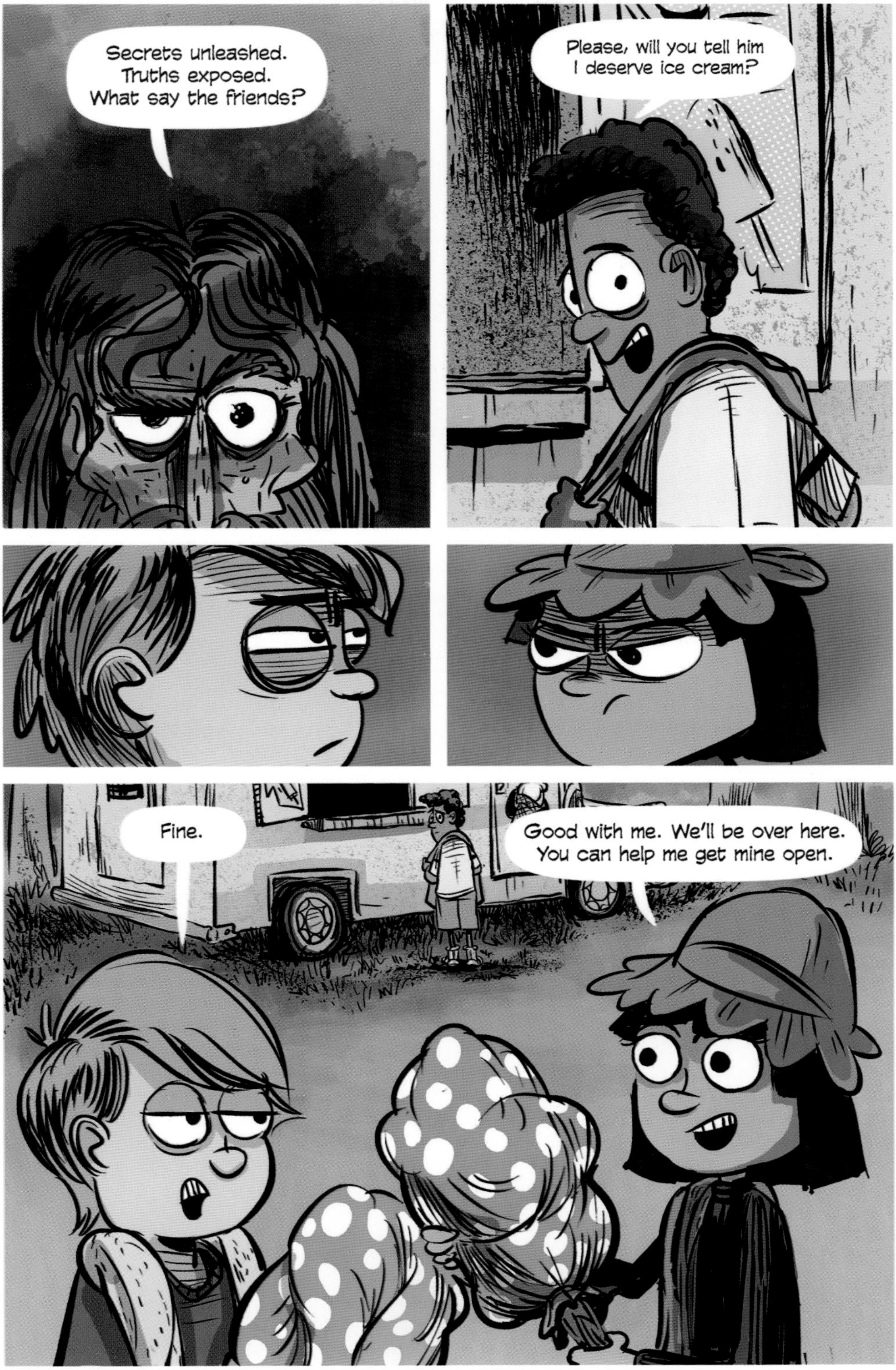
Secrets unleashed. Truths exposed. What say the friends?
Please, will you tell him I deserve ice cream?
Fine.
Good with me. We'll be over here. You can help me get mine open.

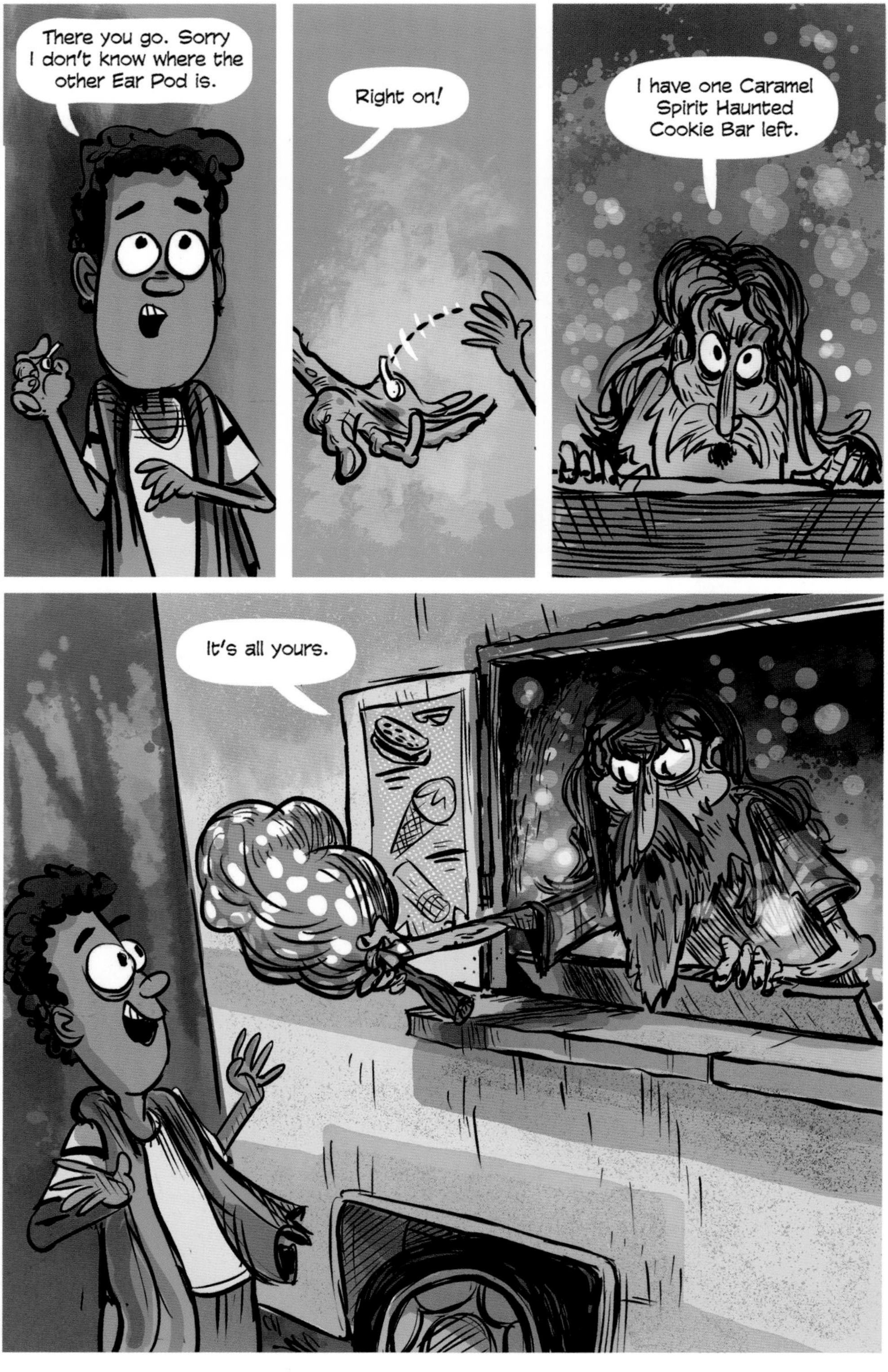
There you go. Sorry I don't know where the other Ear Pod is.
Right on!
I have one Caramel Spirit Haunted Cookie Bar left.
It's all yours.

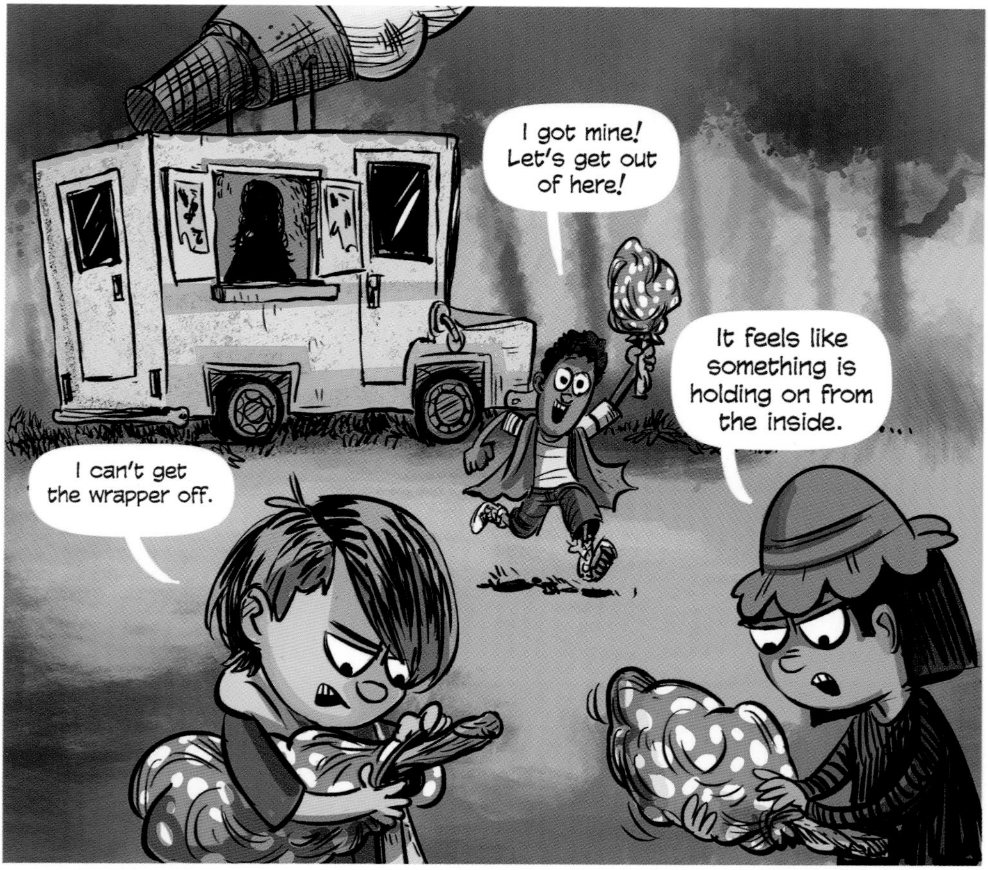
I got mine! Let's get out of here!
It feels like something is holding on from the inside....
I can't get the wrapper off.

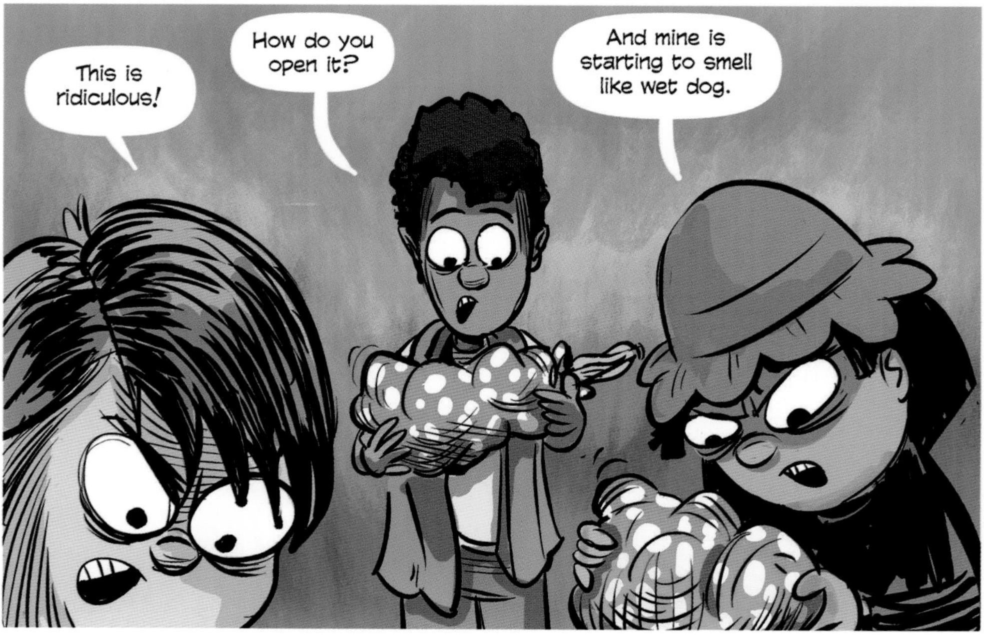
This is ridiculous!
How do you open it?
And mine is starting to smell like wet dog.

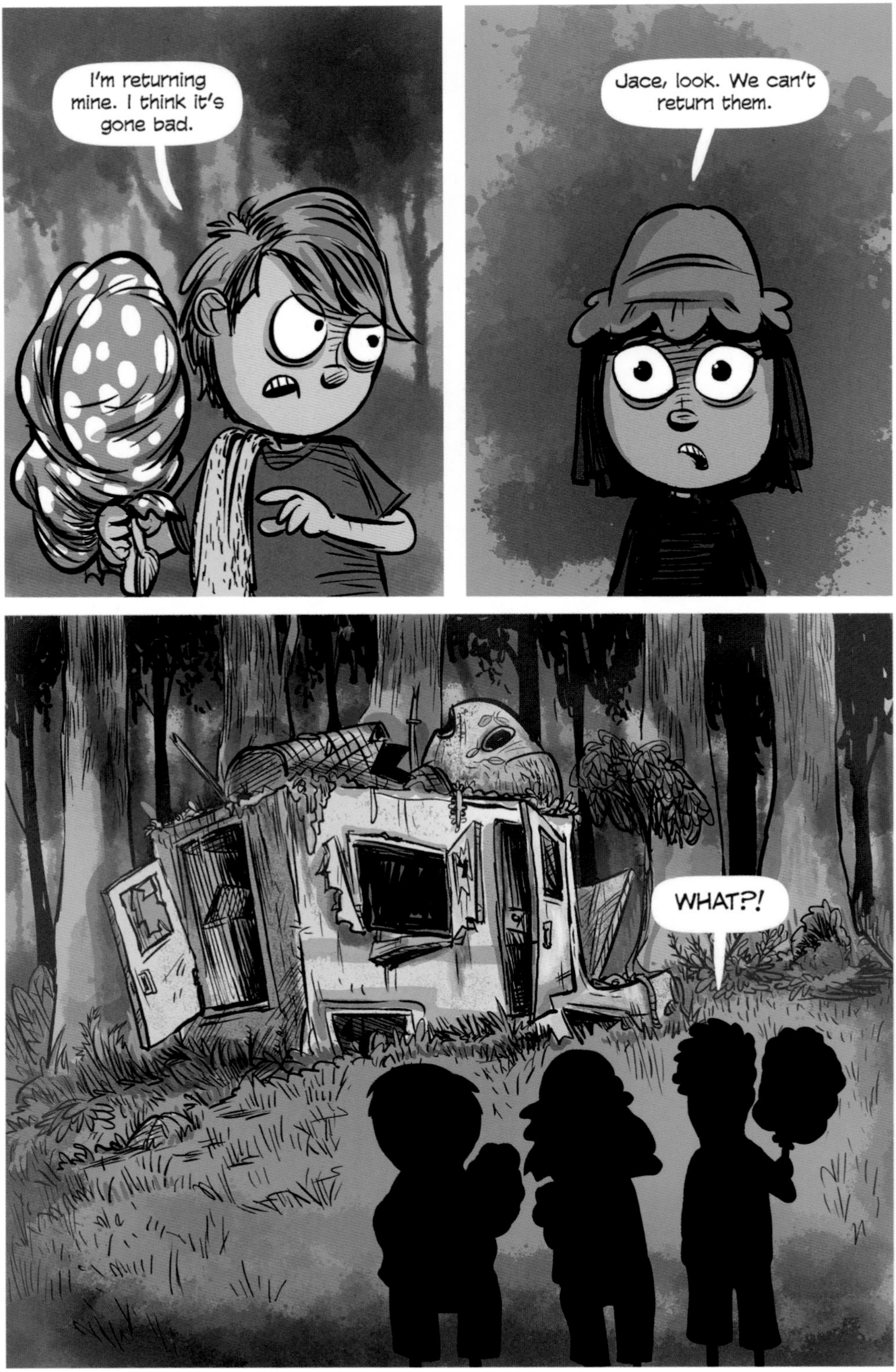
I'm returning mine. I think it's gone bad.
Jace, look. We can't return them.
WHAT?!

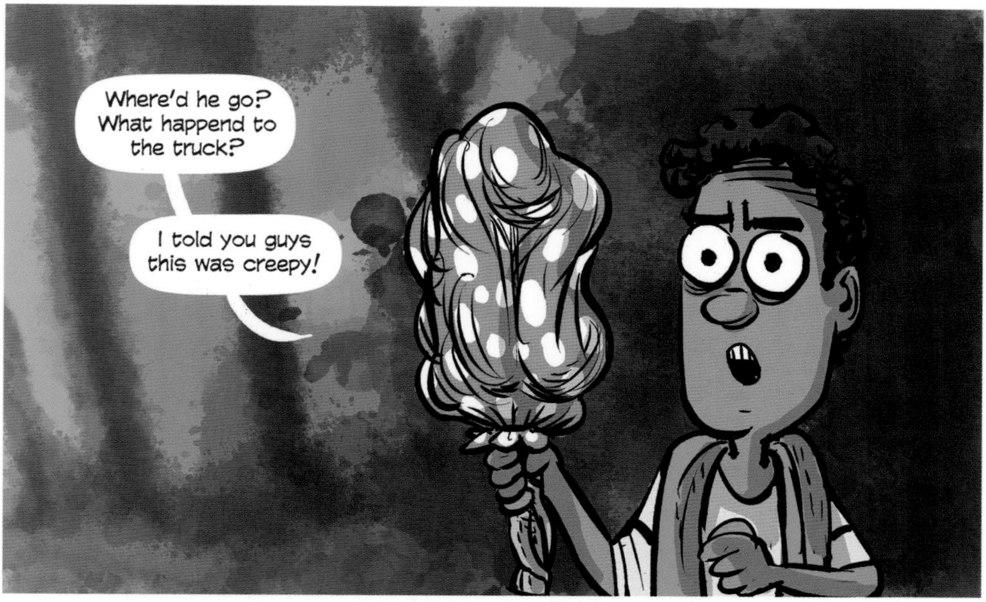
Where'd he go? What happend to the truck?
I told you guys this was creepy!

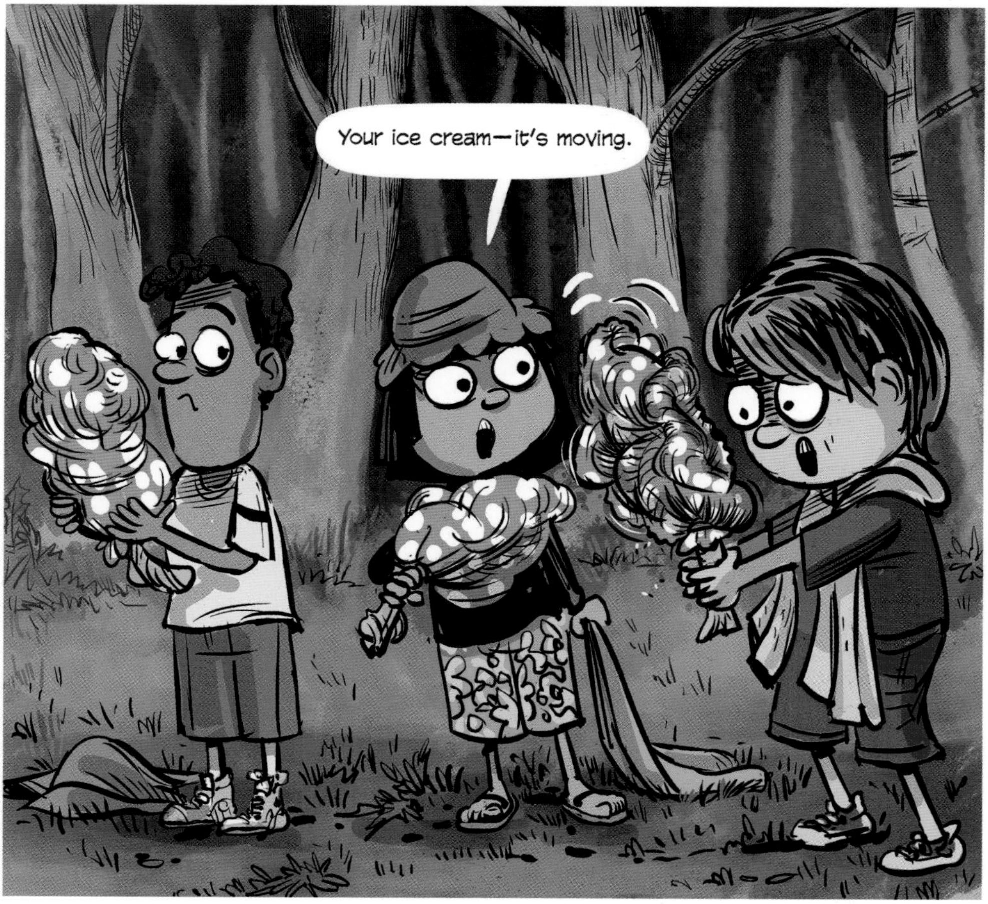
Your ice cream—it's moving.

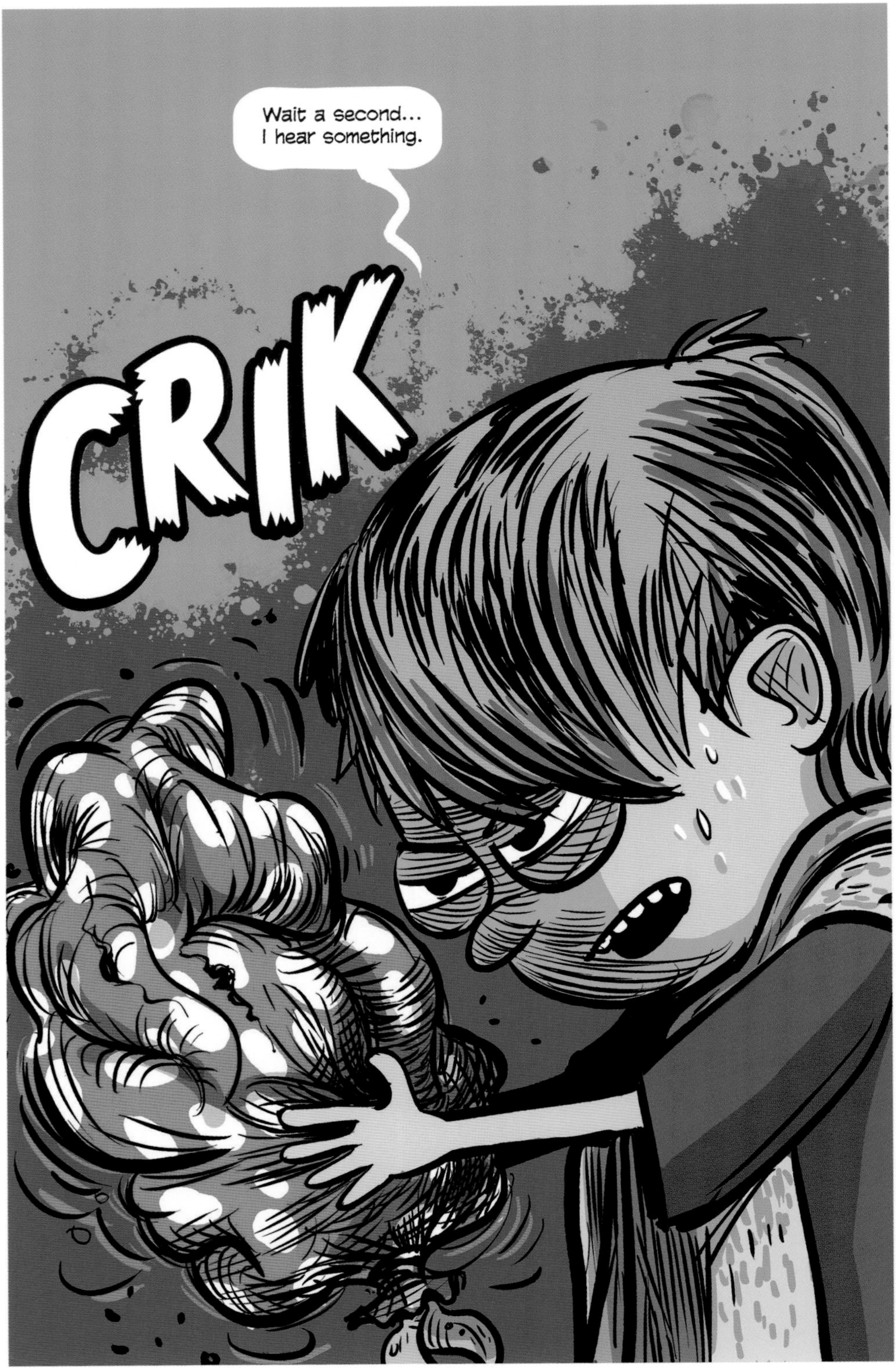
Wait a second...
I hear something.
CRIK

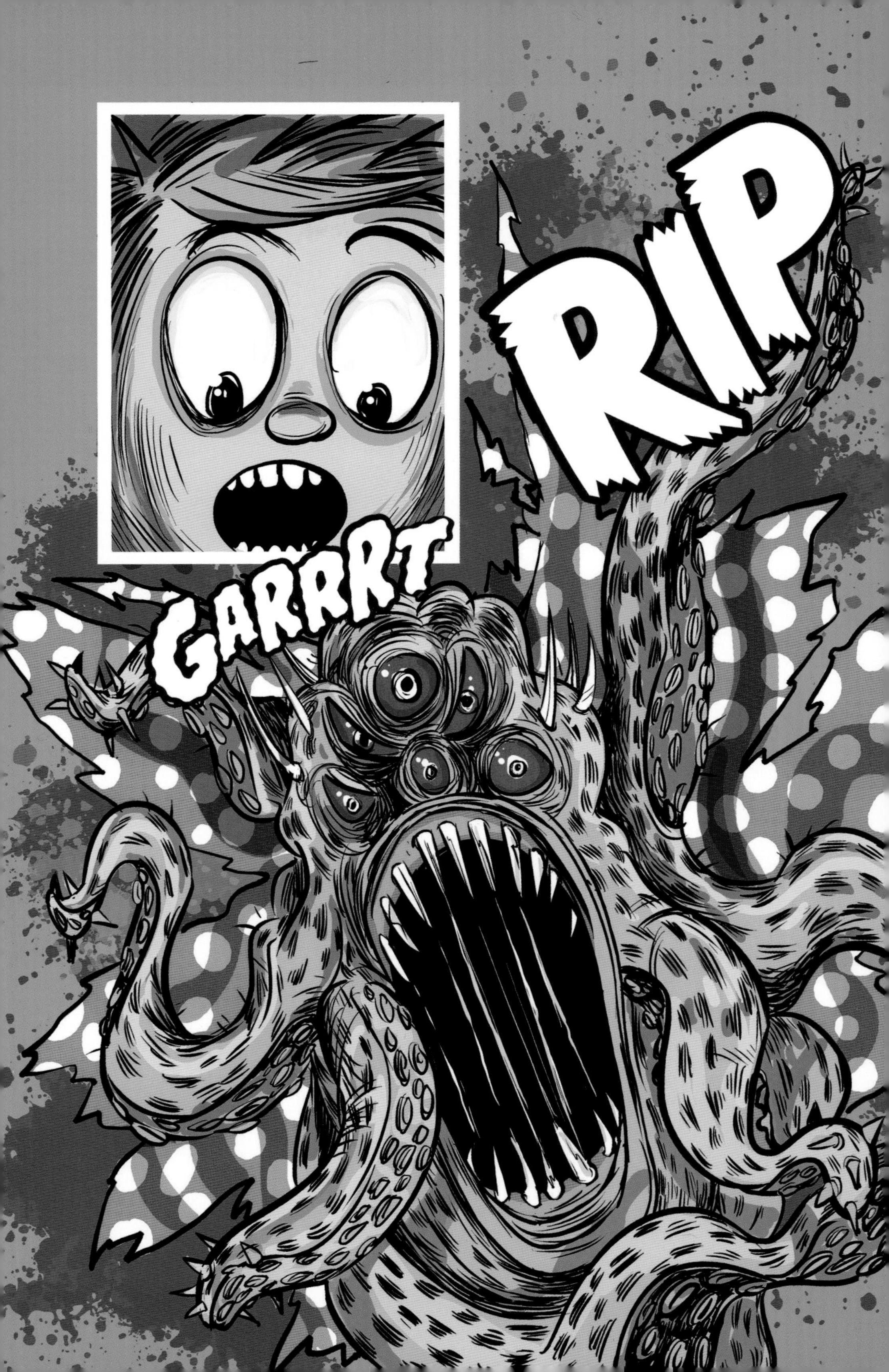
RIP
GARRRRT

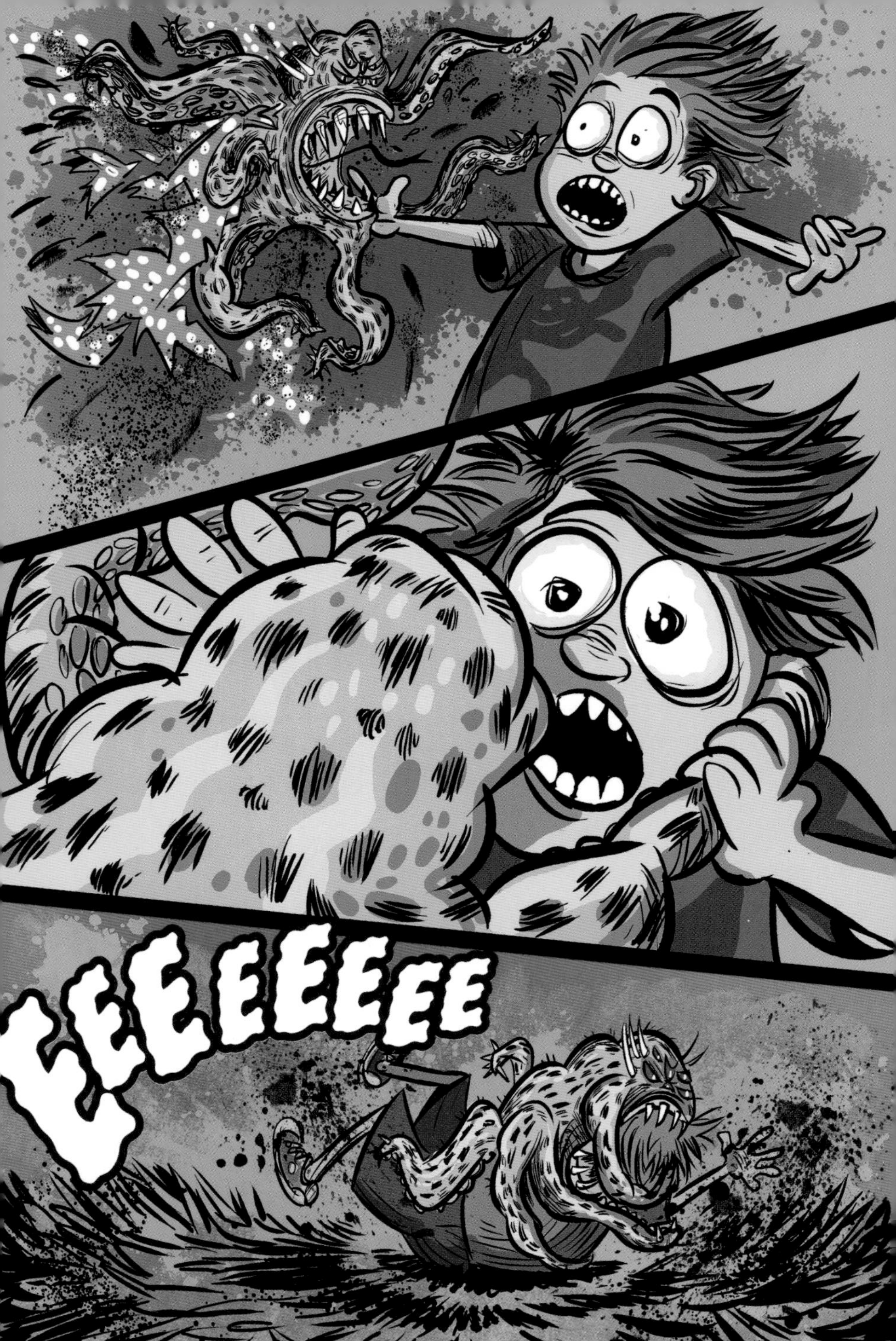
EEEEEEEE

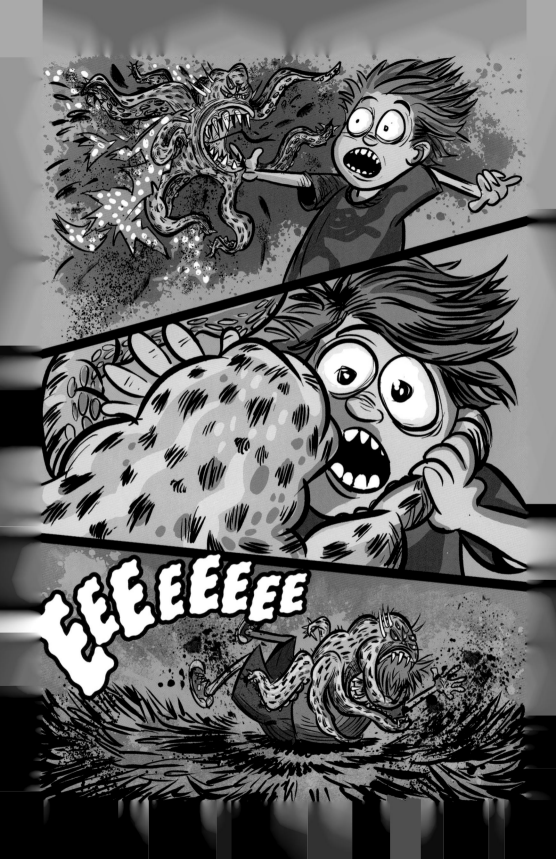

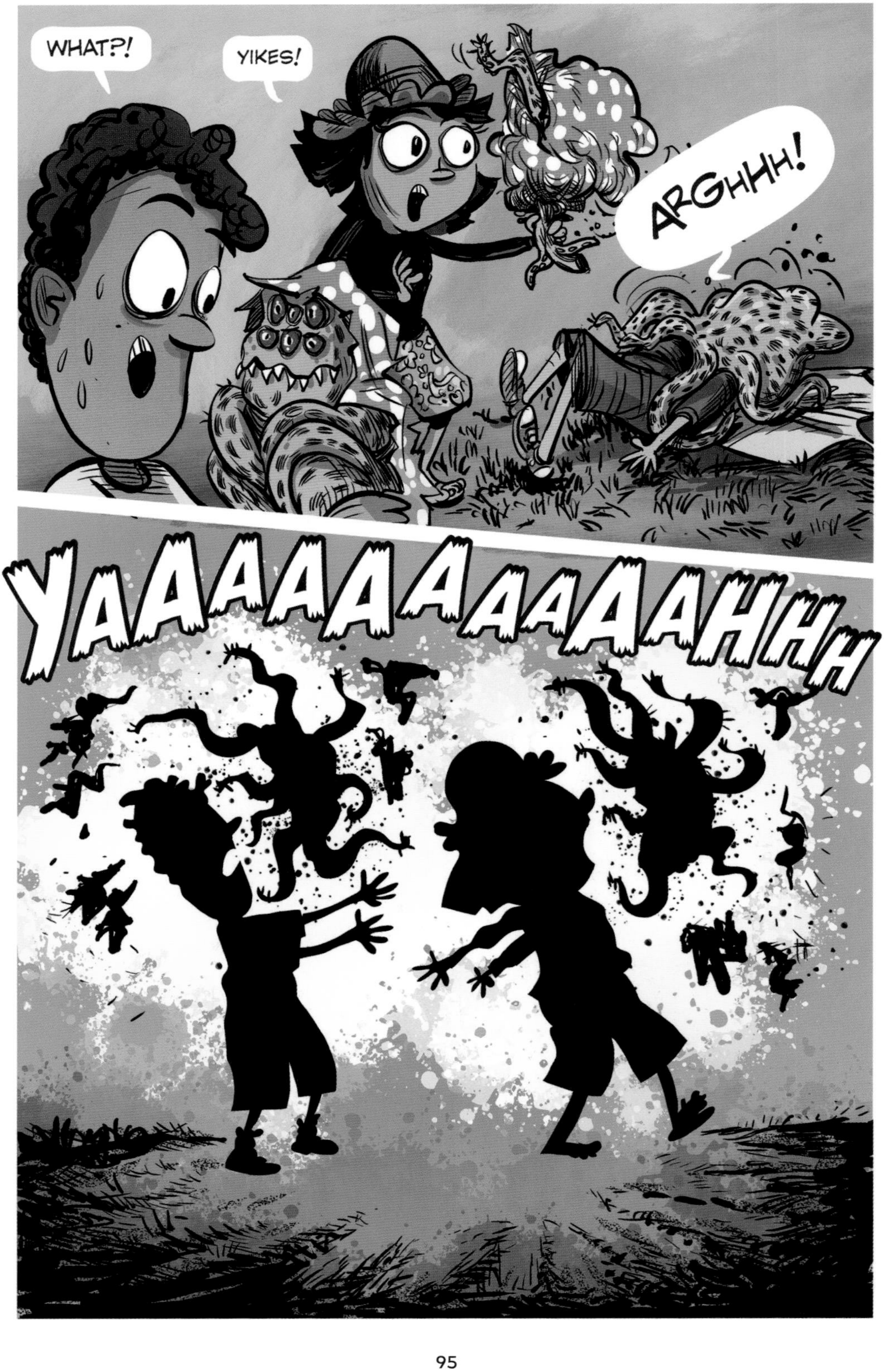
WHAT?!
YIKES!
ARGHHH!
YAAAAAAAAAAAHHH

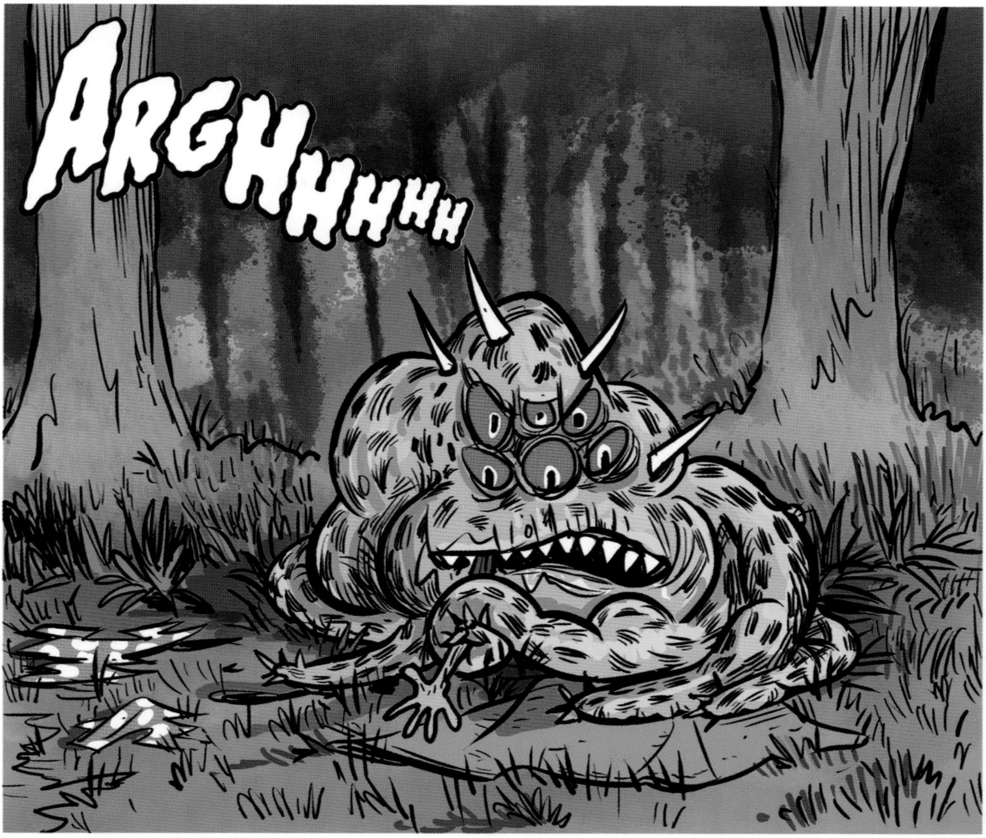
ARGHHHHH

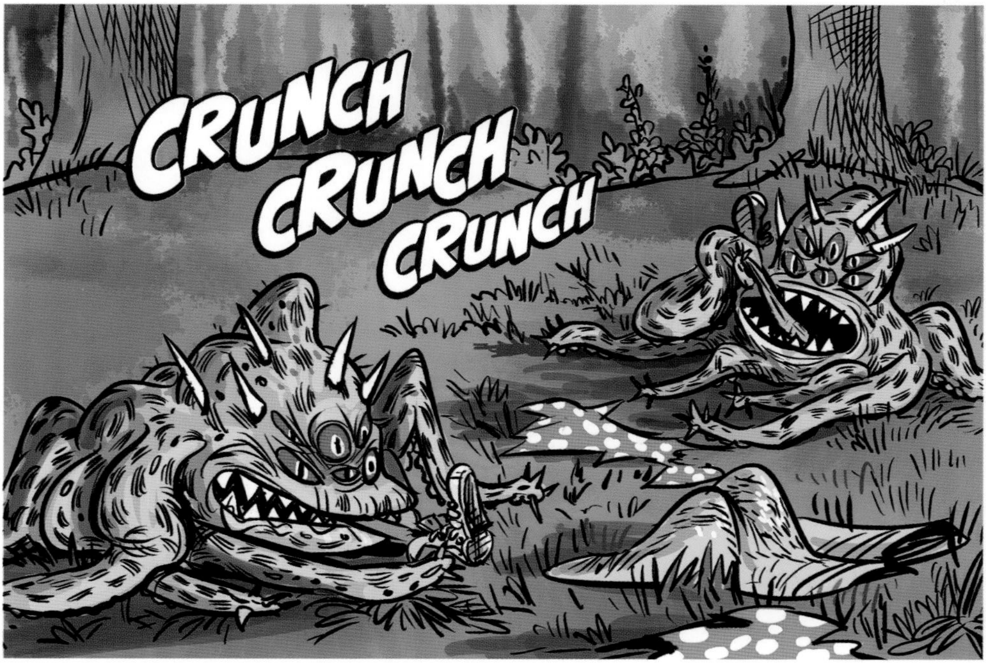
CRUNCH
CRUNCH
CRUNCH

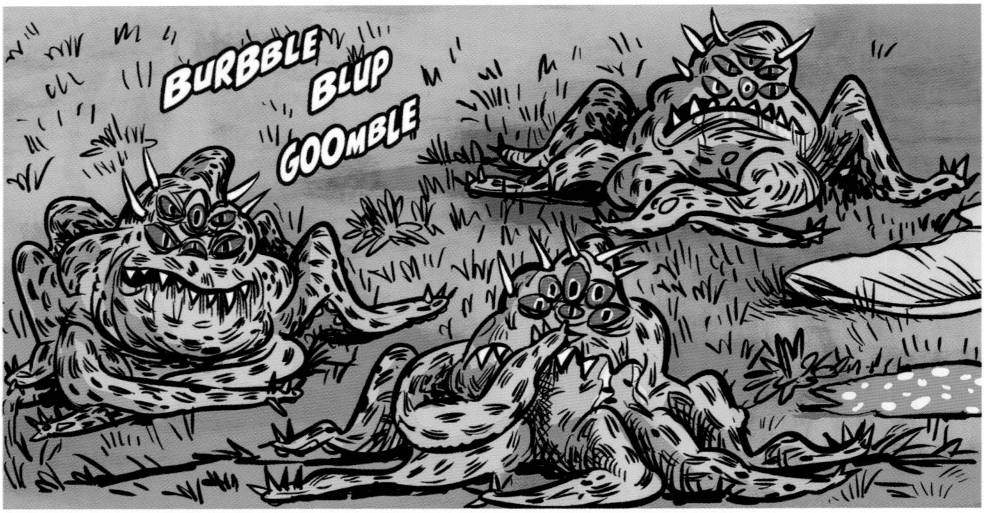
BURBBLE
BLUP
GOOMBLE
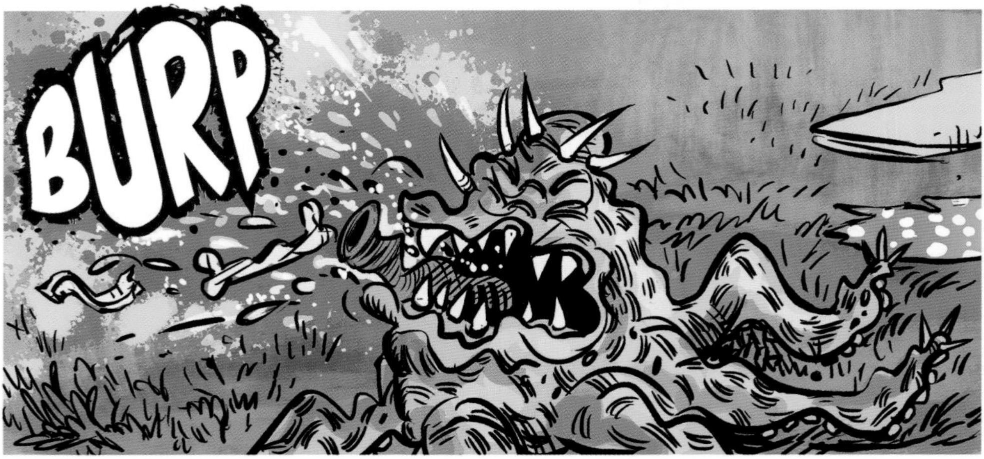
BURP
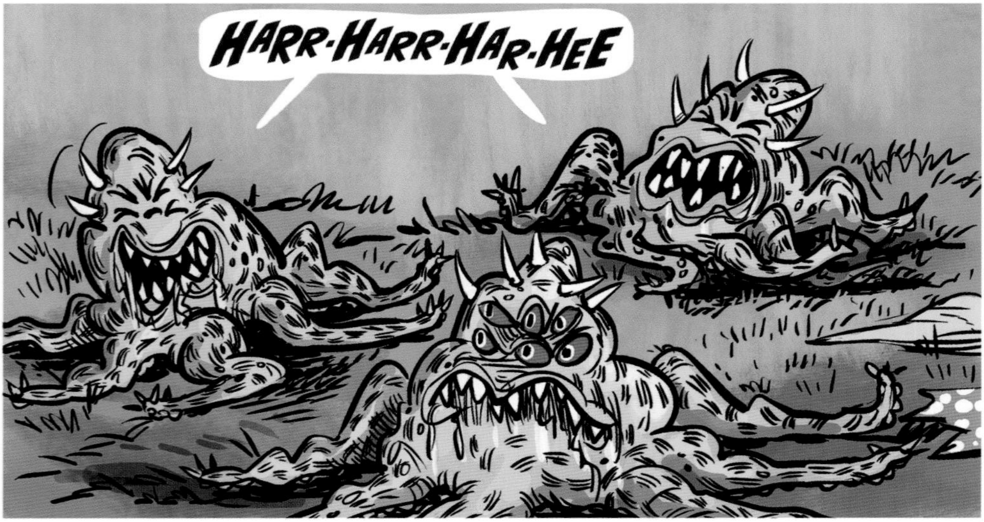
HARR-HARR-HAR-HEE

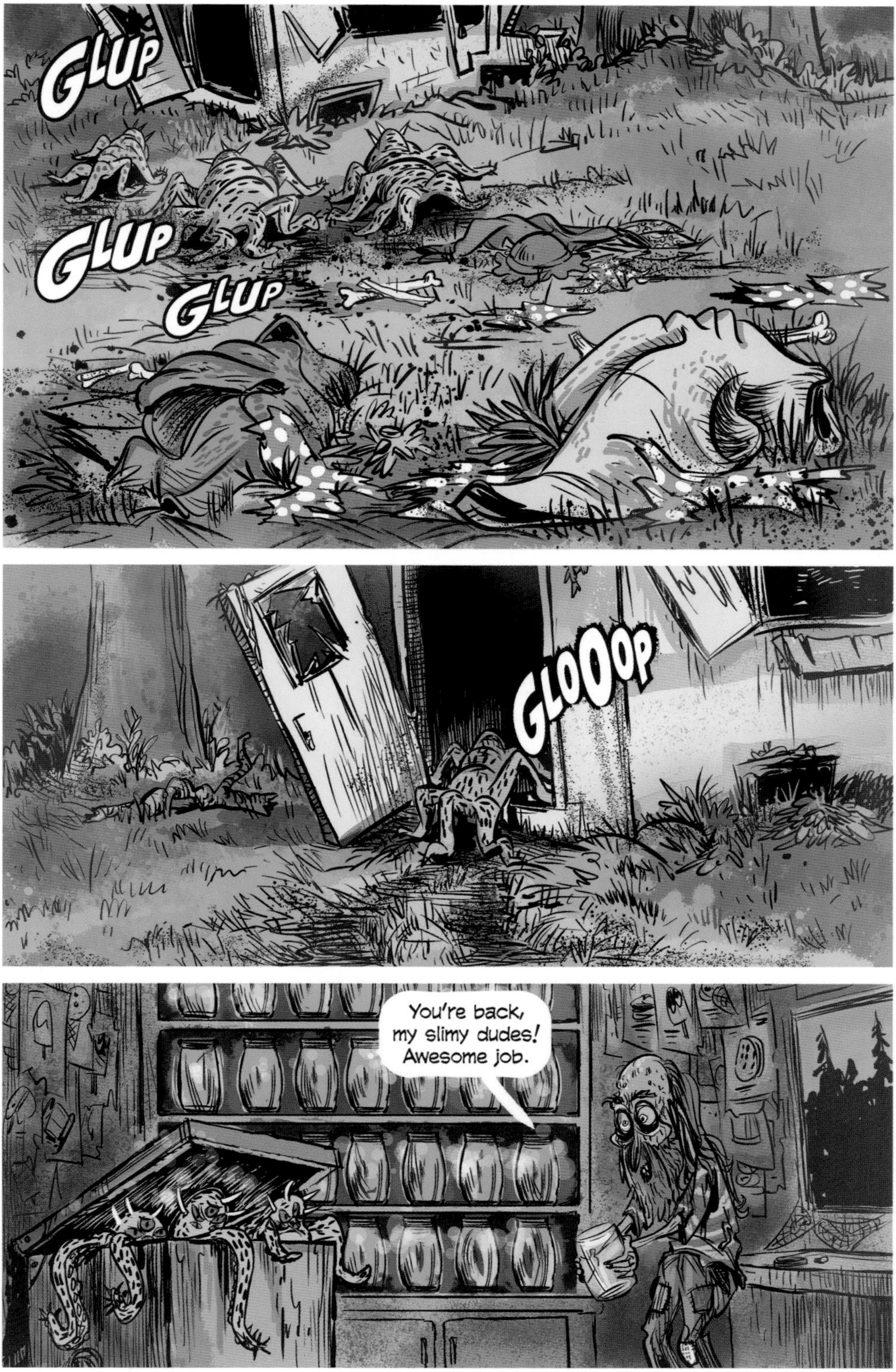
GLUP
GLUP
GLUP
GLOOOP
You're back, my slimy dudes! Awesome job.

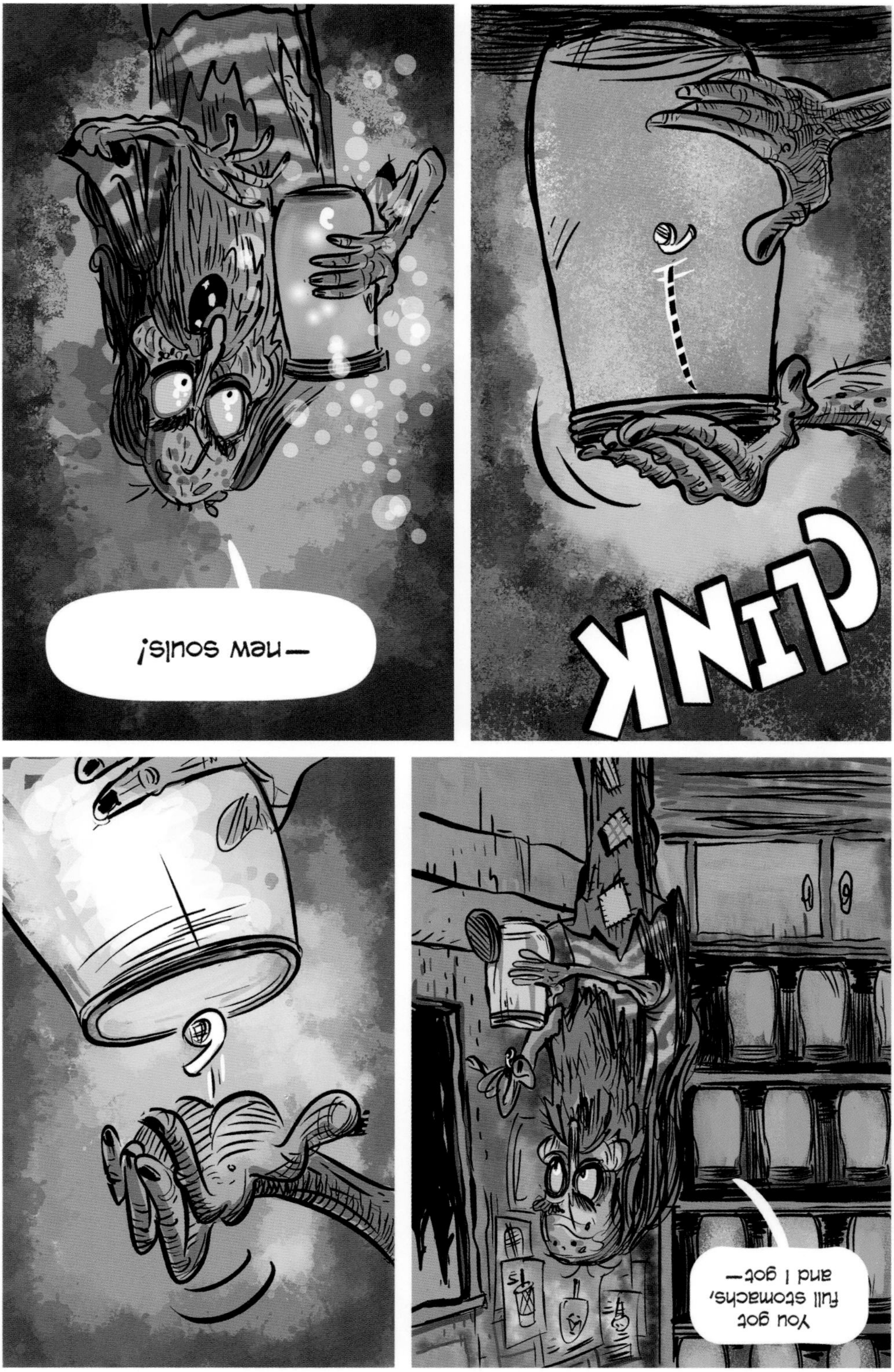
You got
full stomachs,
and I got—
CLINK
—new souls!

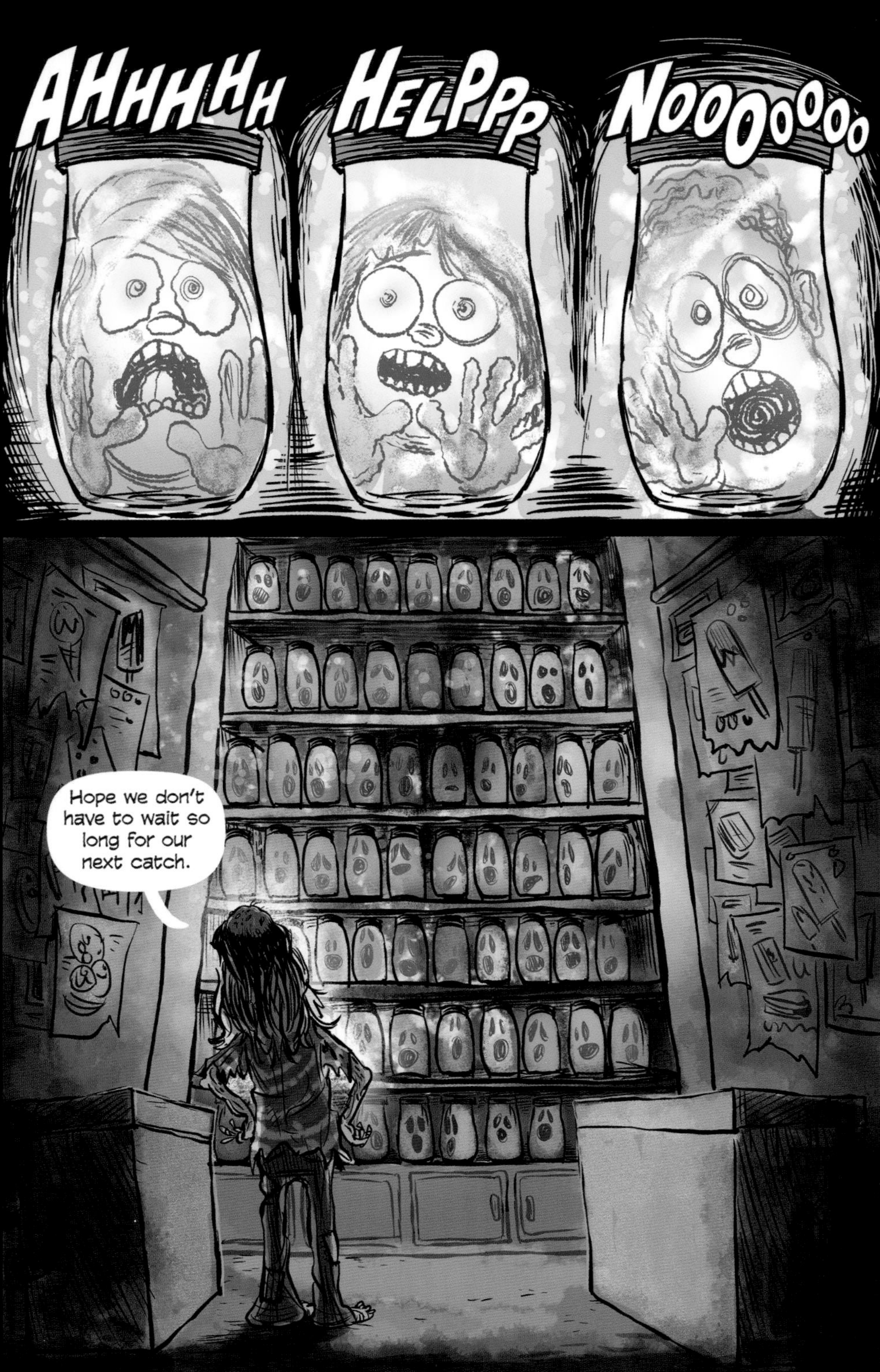
AHHHHHH
HELPPPP
NOOOOOOO
Hope we don't have to wait so long for our next catch.

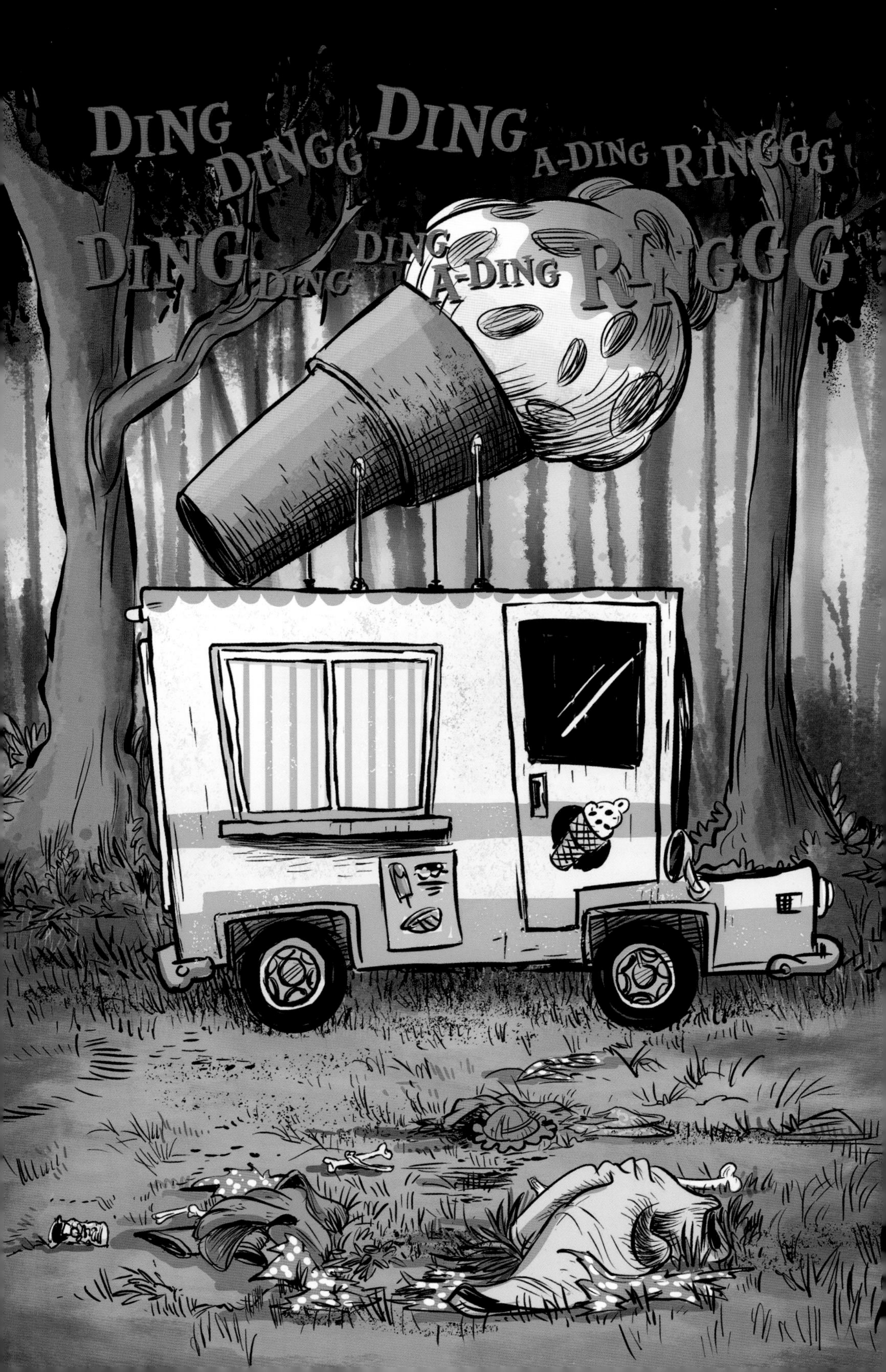
DING DINGG DING A-DING RINGGG
DING DING DING A-DING RINGGG

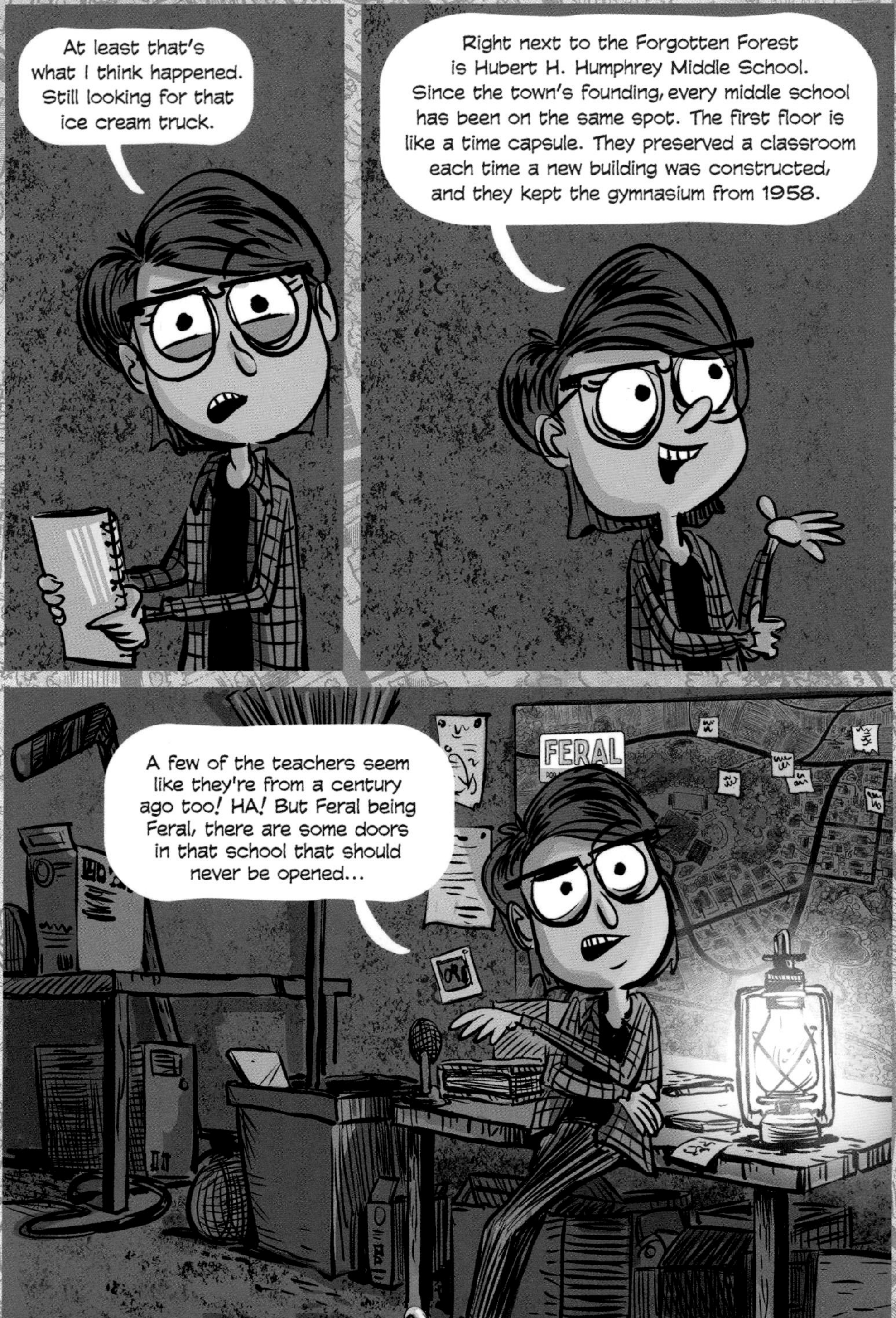
At least that's what I think happened. Still looking for that ice cream truck.
Right next to the Forgotten Forest is Hubert H. Humphrey Middle School. Since the town's founding, every middle school has been on the same spot. The first floor is like a time capsule. They preserved a classroom each time a new building was constructed, and they kept the gymnasium from 1958.
FERAL
A few of the teachers seem like they're from a century ago too! HA! But Feral being Feral, there are some doors in that school that should never be opened...

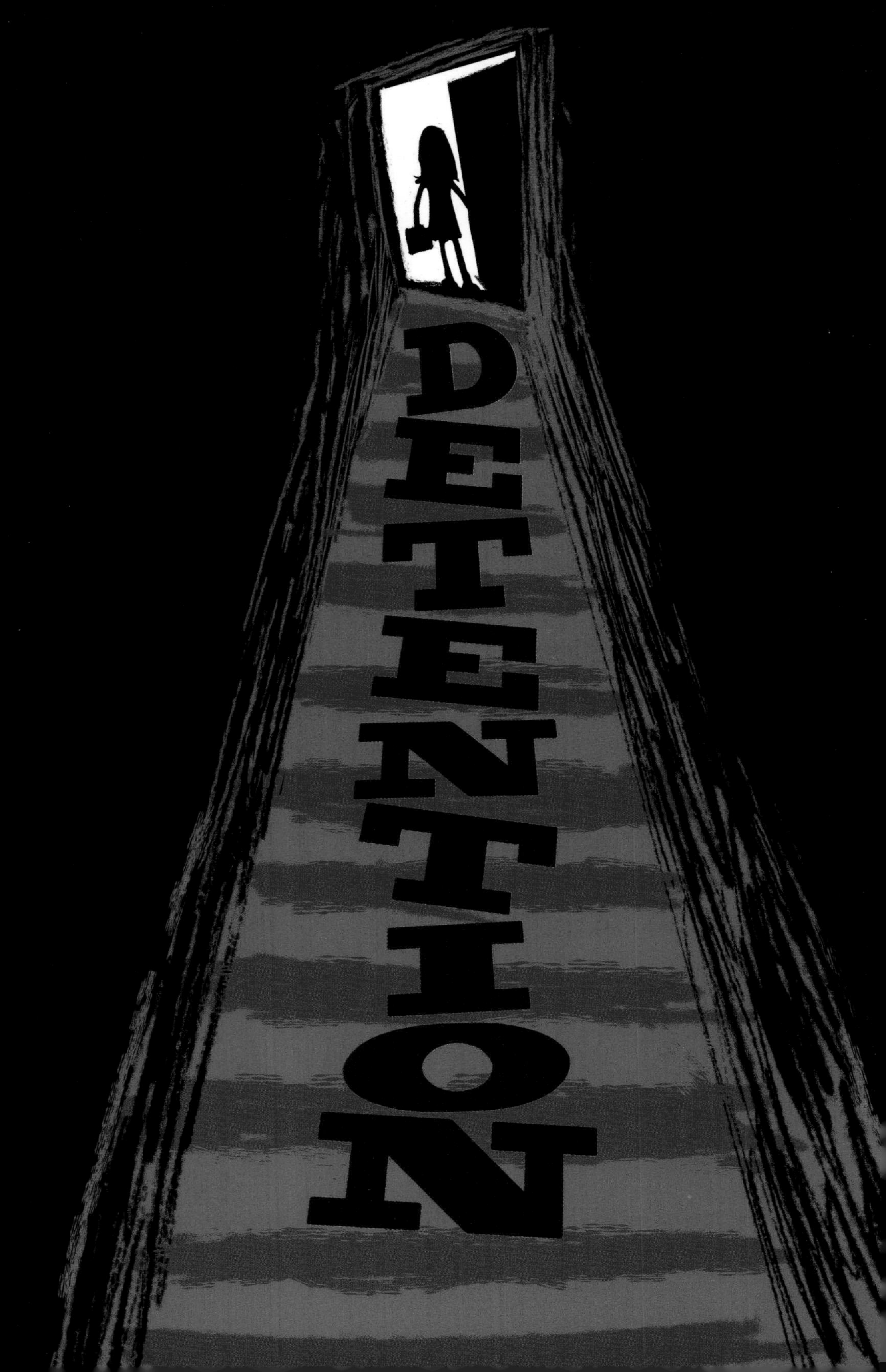
DETENTION

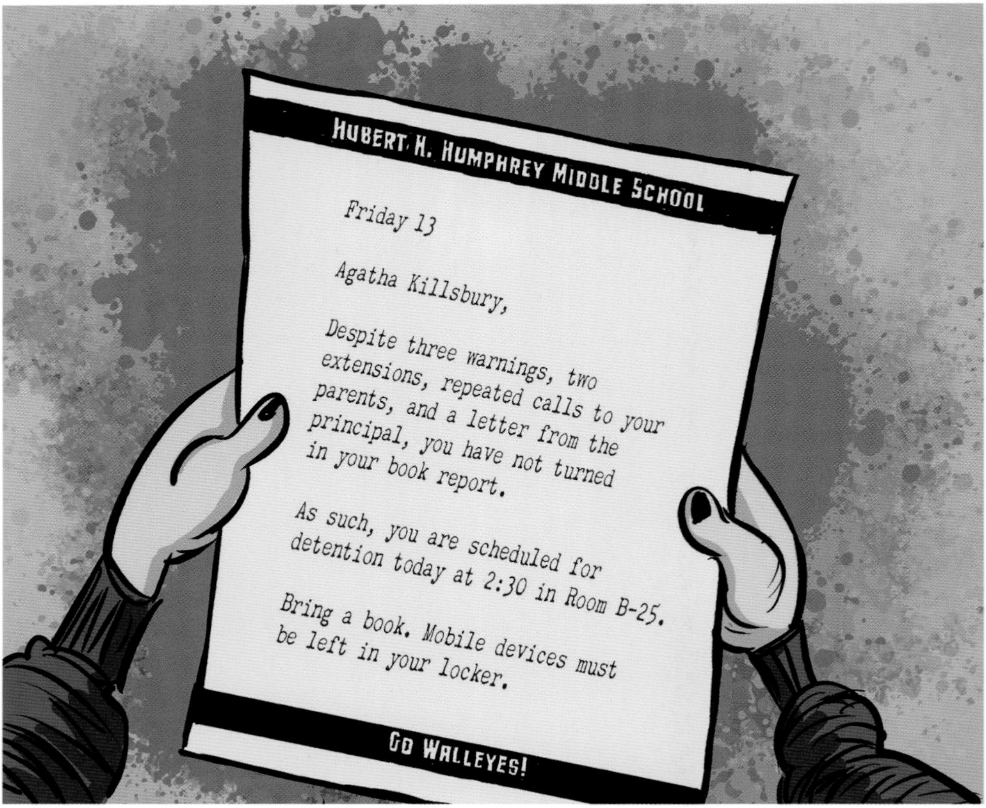
HUBERT H. HUMPHREY MIDDLE SCHOOL
Friday 13
Agatha Killsbury,
Despite three warnings, two extensions, repeated calls to your parents, and a letter from the principal, you have not turned in your book report.
As such, you are scheduled for detention today at 2:30 in Room B-25.
Bring a book. Mobile devices must be left in your locker.
GO WALLEYES!

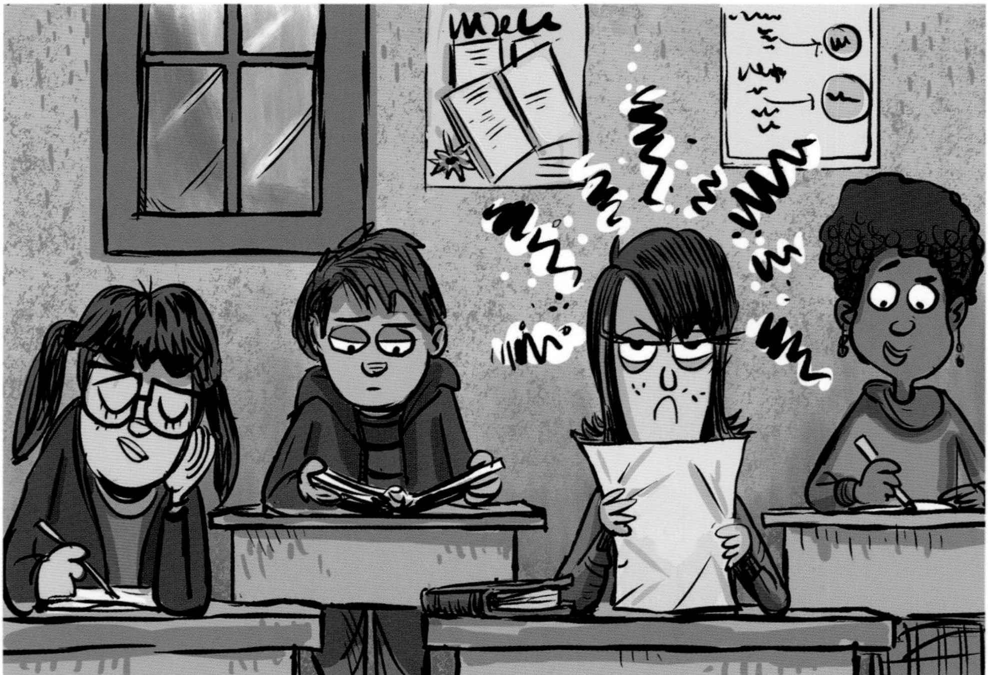

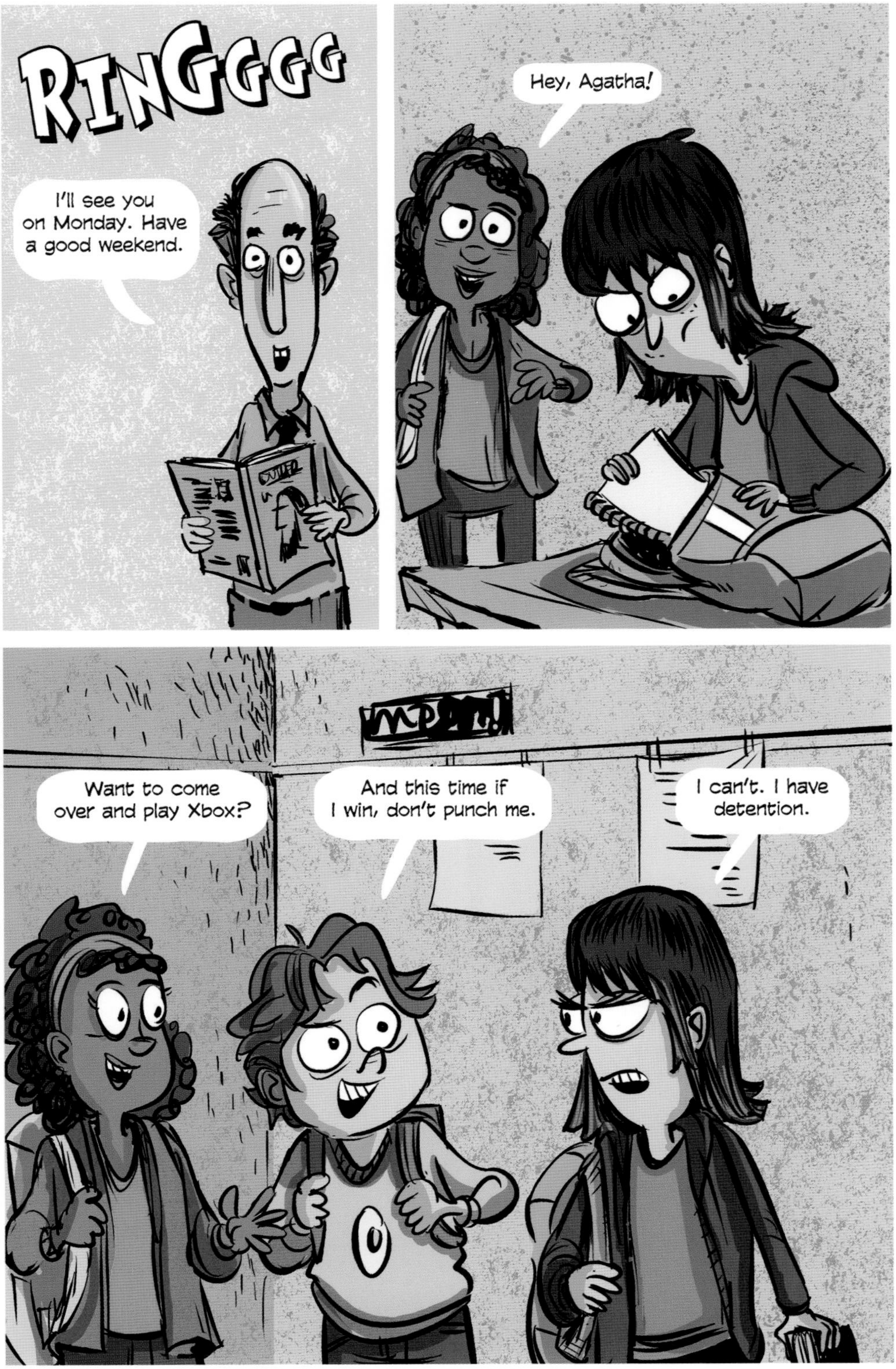
RINGGGG
I'll see you on Monday. Have a good weekend.
Hey, Agatha!
Want to come over and play Xbox?
And this time if I win, don't punch me.
I can't. I have detention.

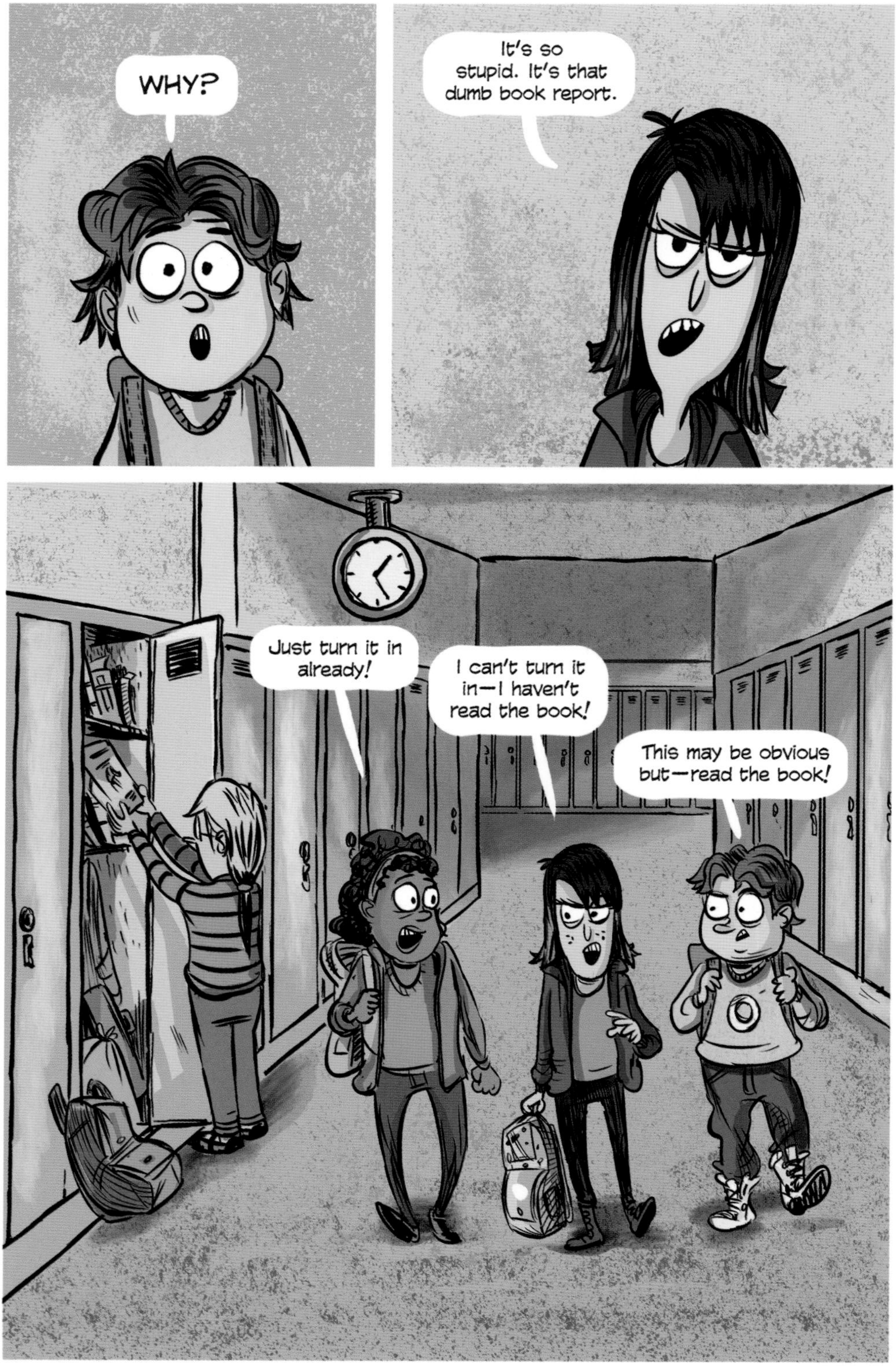
WHY?
It's so stupid. It's that dumb book report.
Just turn it in already!
I can't turn it in—I haven't read the book!
This may be obvious but—read the book!

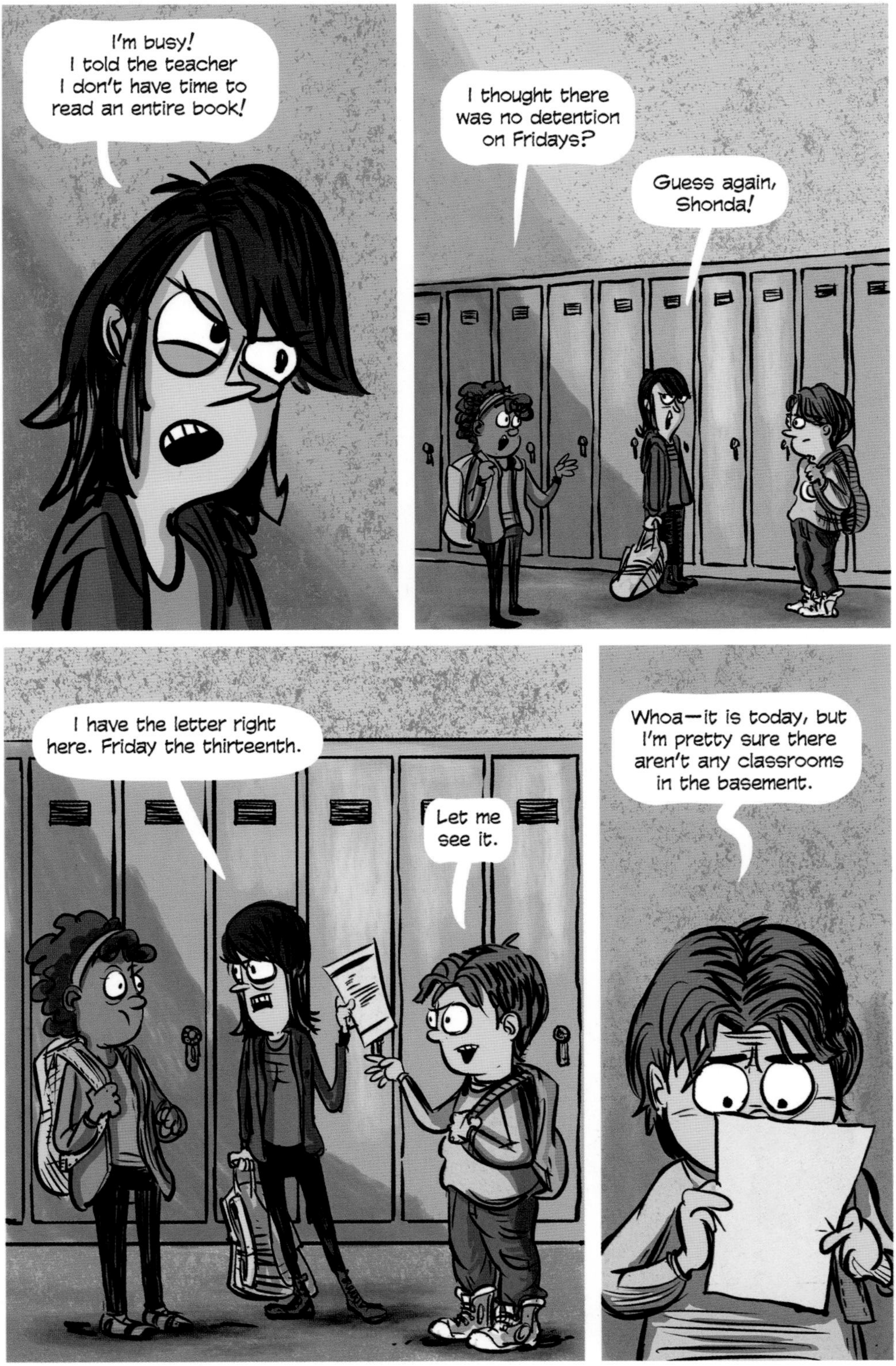
I'm busy! I told the teacher I don't have time to read an entire book!
I thought there was no detention on Fridays?
Guess again, Shonda!
I have the letter right here. Friday the thirteenth.
Let me see it.
Whoa—it is today, but I'm pretty sure there aren't any classrooms in the basement.

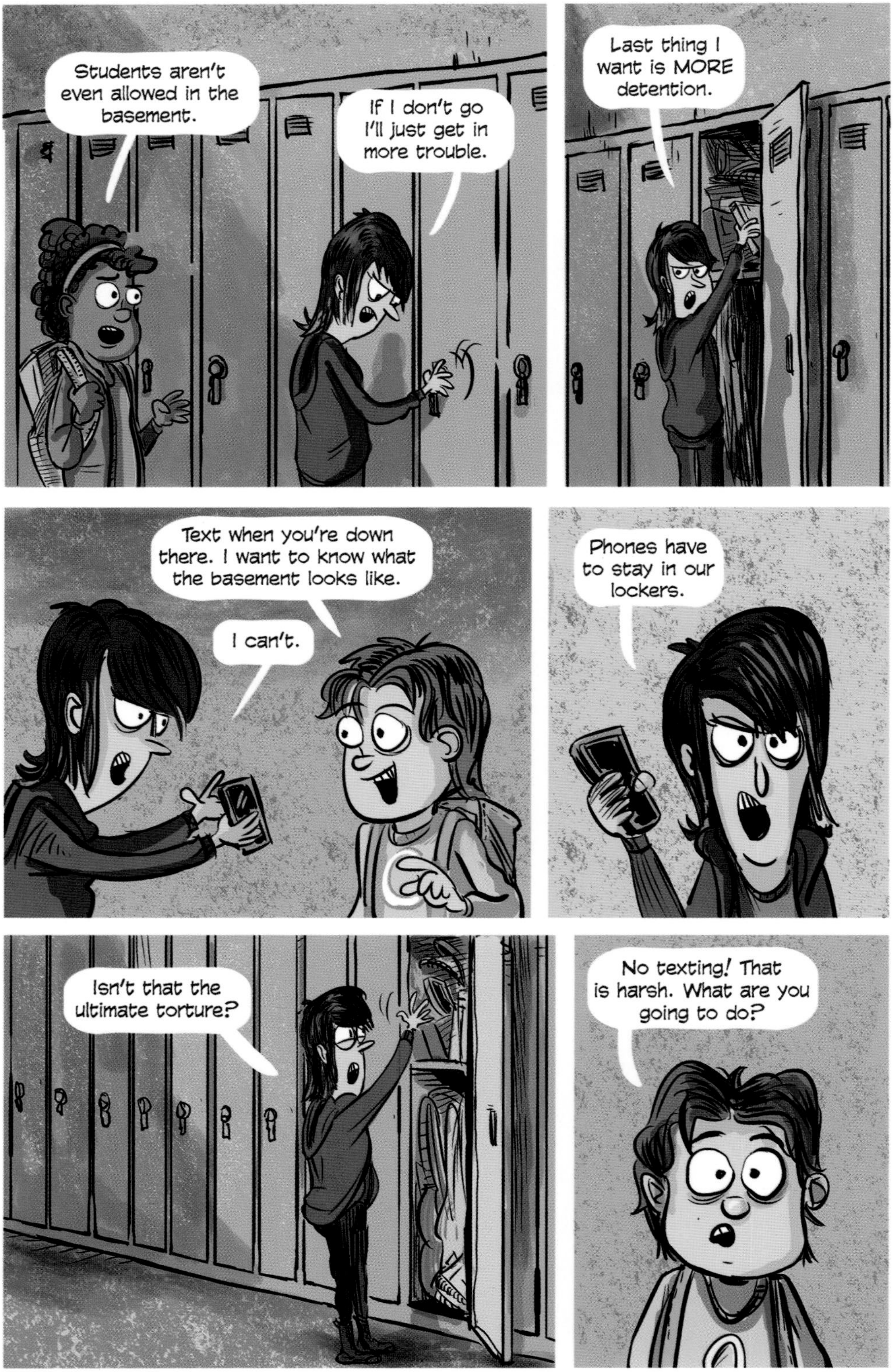
Students aren't even allowed in the basement.
If I don't go I'll just get in more trouble.
Last thing I want is MORE detention.
Text when you're down there. I want to know what the basement looks like.
I can't.
Phones have to stay in our lockers.
Isn't that the ultimate torture?
No texting! That is harsh. What are you going to do?

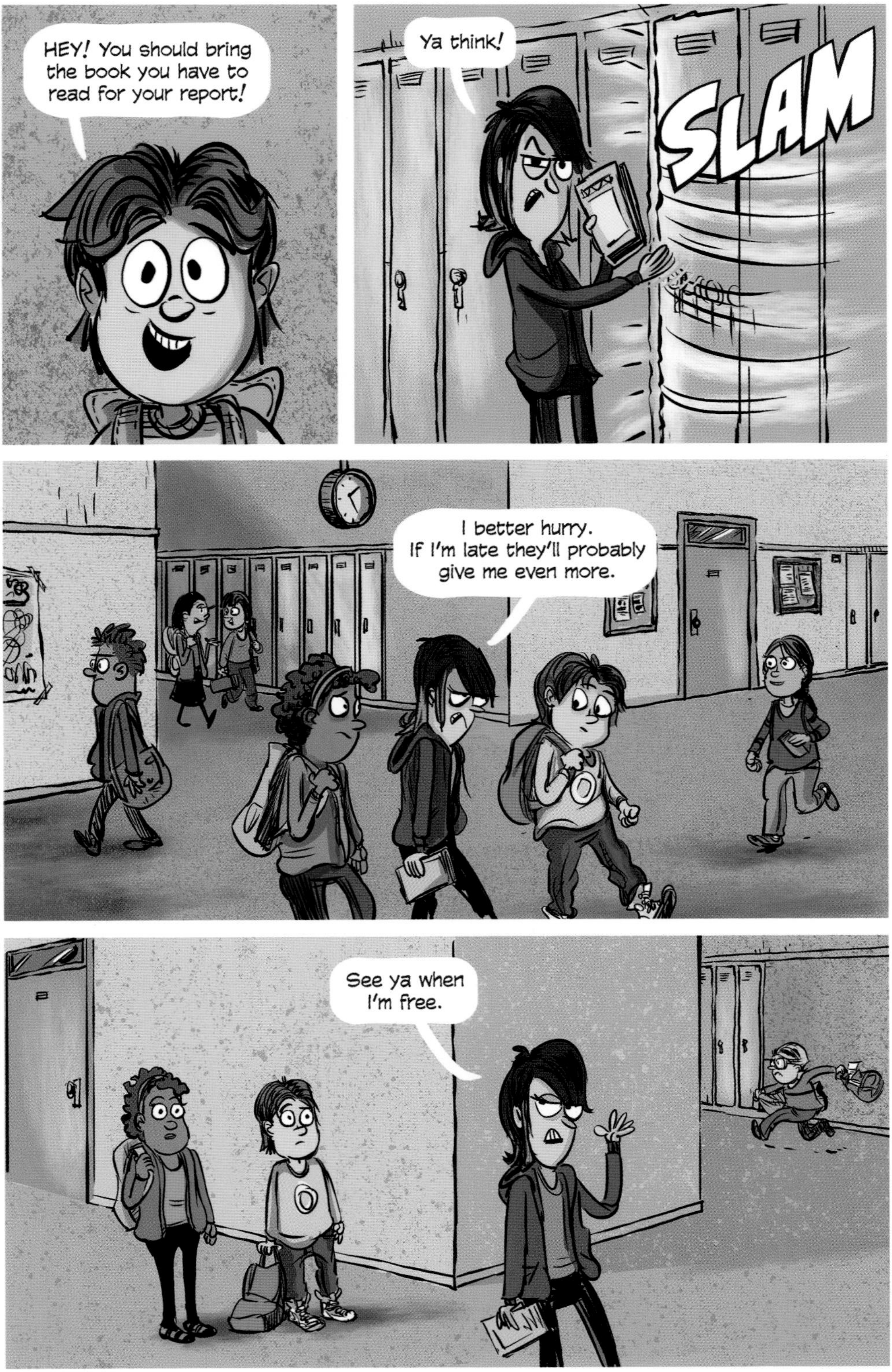
HEY! You should bring the book you have to read for your report!
Ya think!
SLAM
I better hurry. If I'm late they'll probably give me even more.
See ya when I'm free.

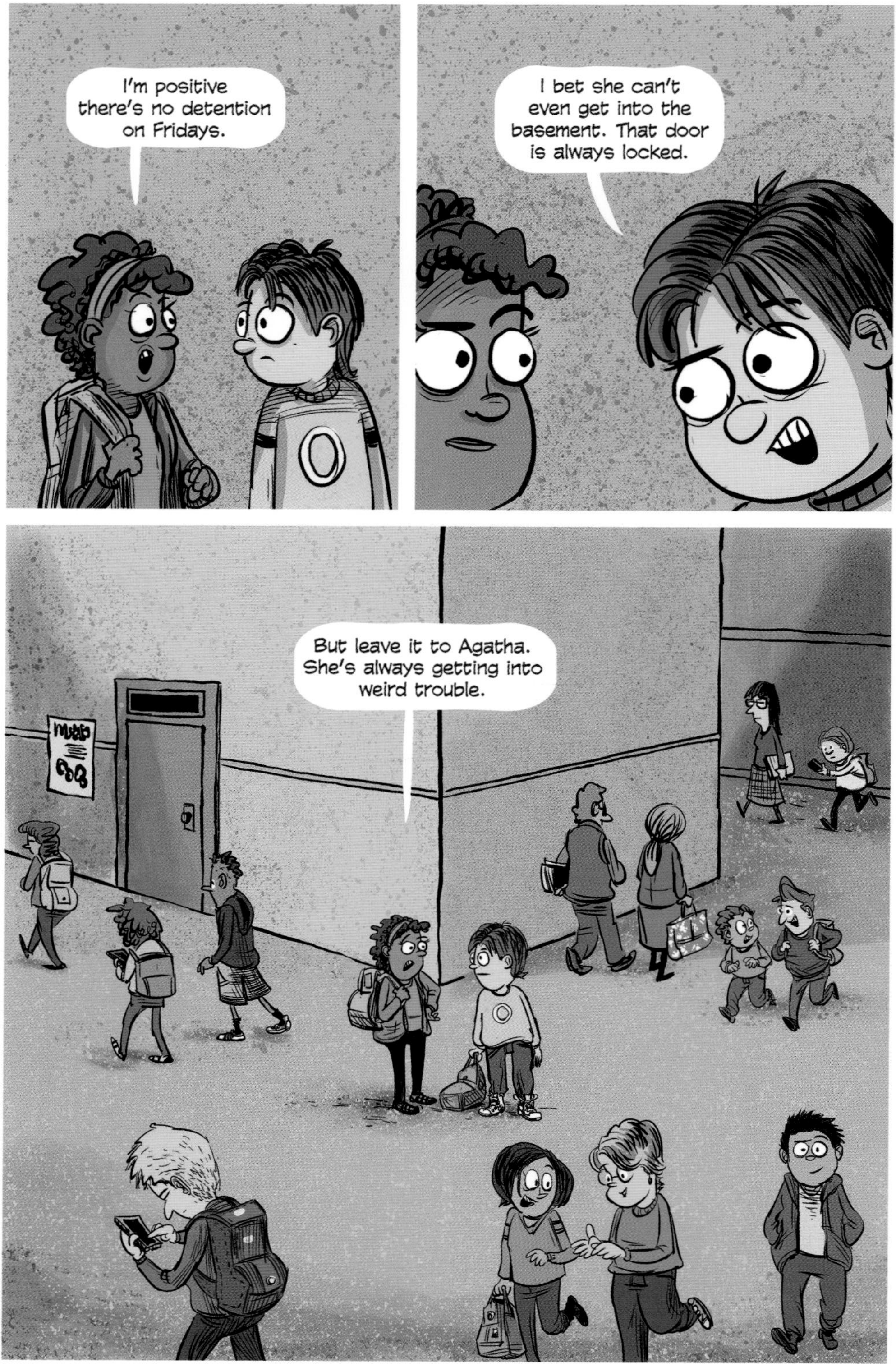
I'm positive there's no detention on Fridays.
I bet she can't even get into the basement. That door is always locked.
But leave it to Agatha. She's always getting into weird trouble.

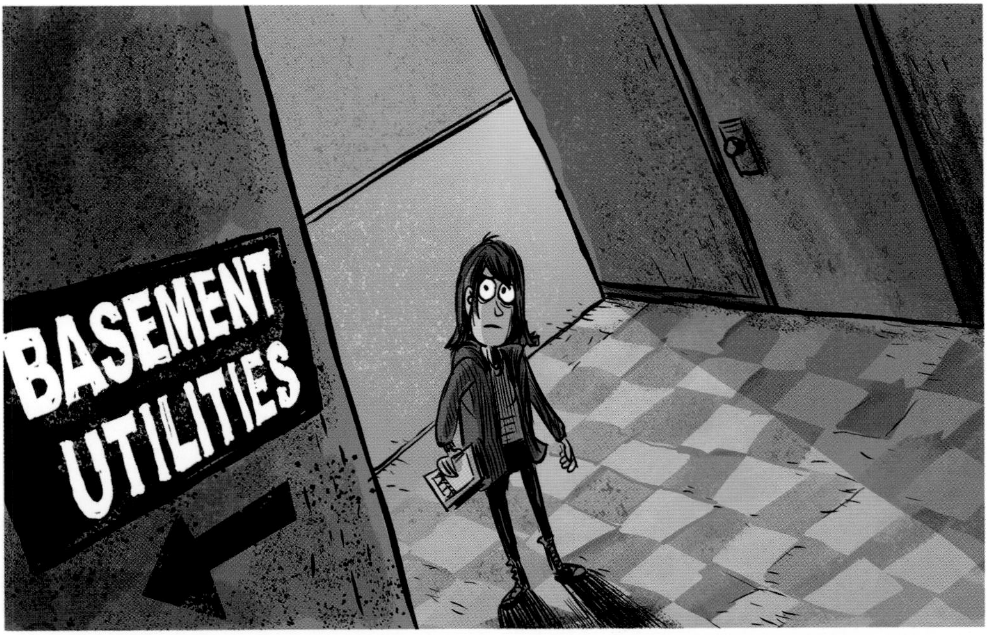
BASEMENT UTILITIES

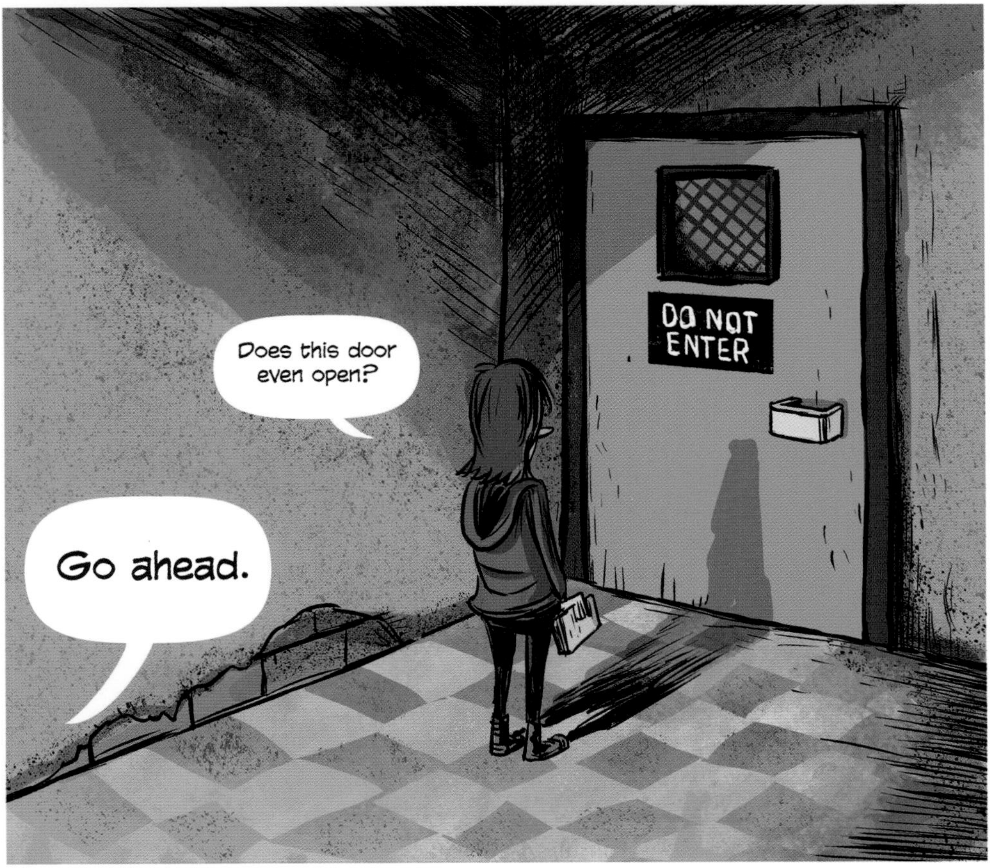
DO NOT ENTER
Does this door even open?
Go ahead.

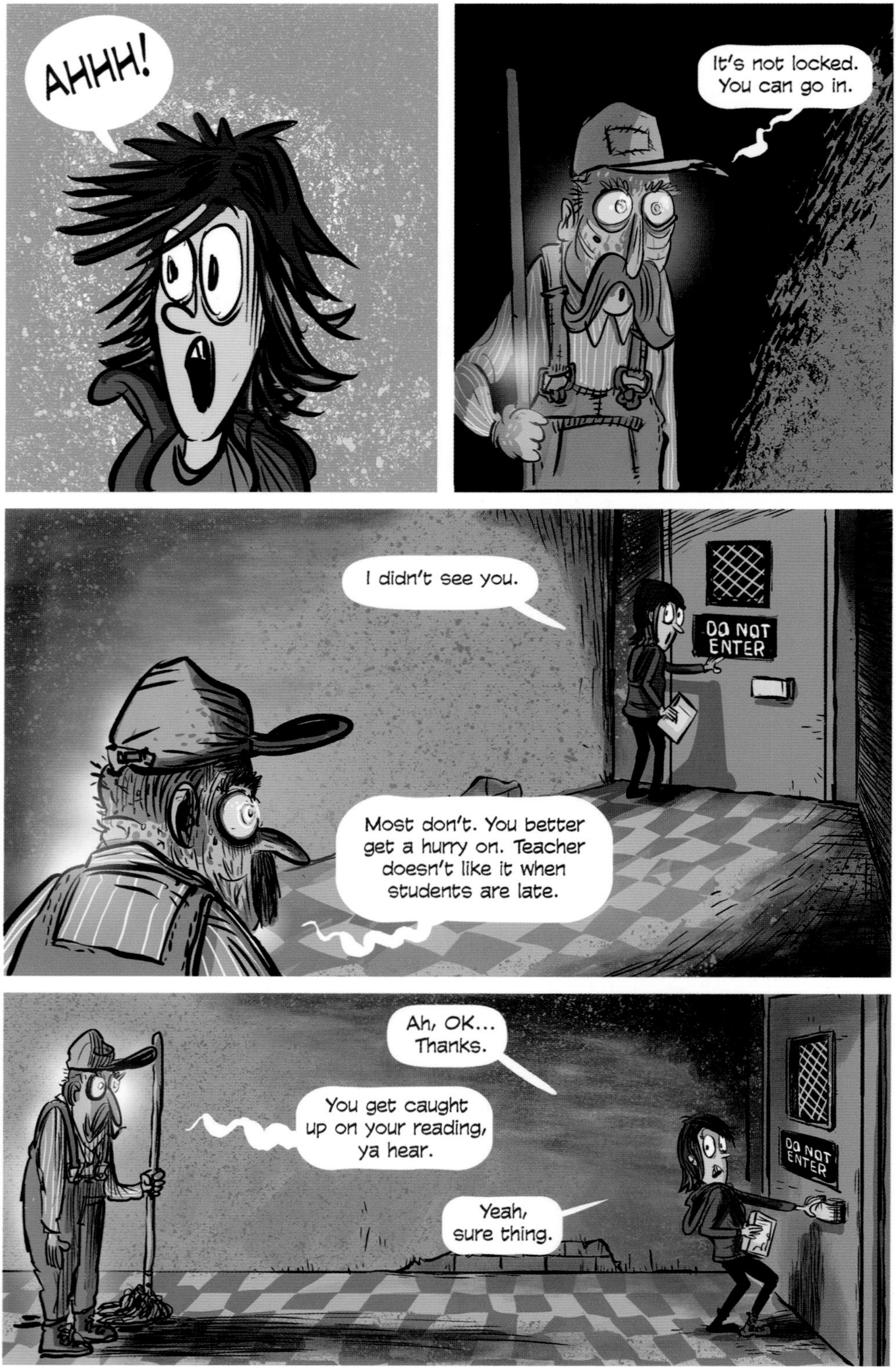
AHHH!
It's not locked. You can go in.
I didn't see you.
DO NOT ENTER
Most don't. You better get a hurry on. Teacher doesn't like it when students are late.
Ah, OK... Thanks.
You get caught up on your reading, ya hear.
DO NOT ENTER
Yeah, sure thing.

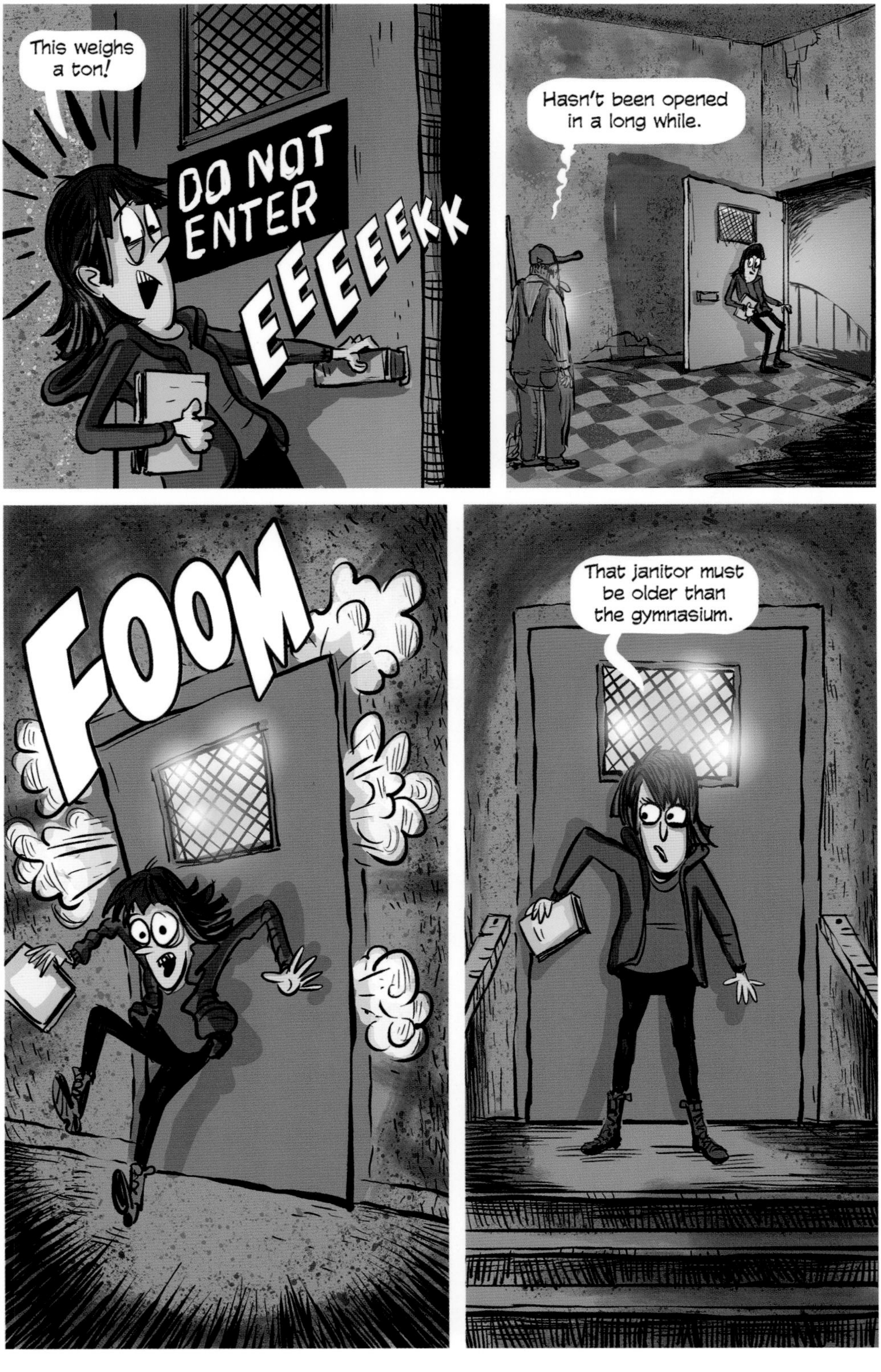
This weighs a ton!
DO NOT ENTER
EEEEEKK
Hasn't been opened in a long while.
FOOM
That janitor must be older than the gymnasium.

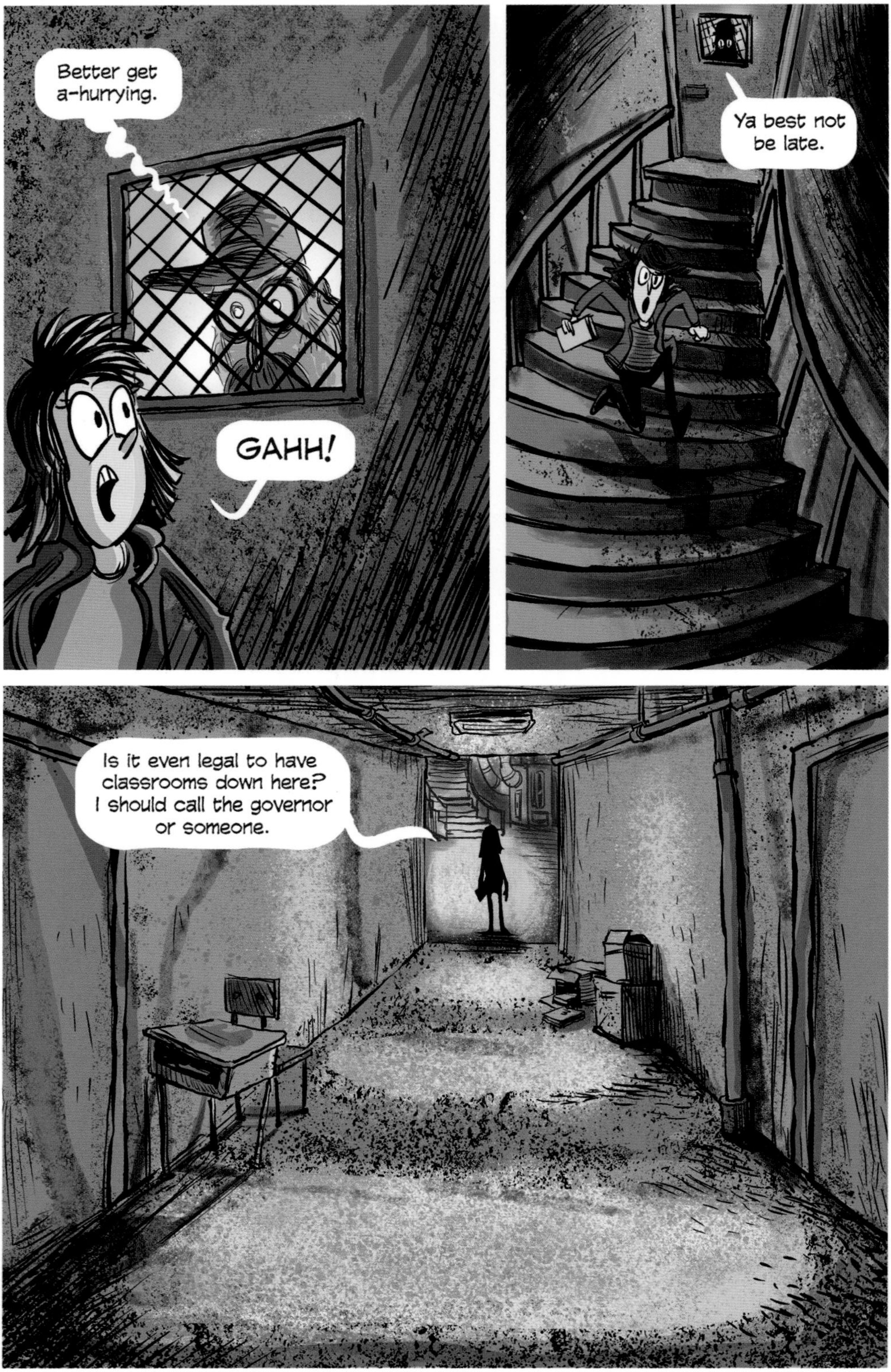
Better get a-hurrying.
GAHH!
Ya best not be late.
Is it even legal to have classrooms down here? I should call the governor or someone.

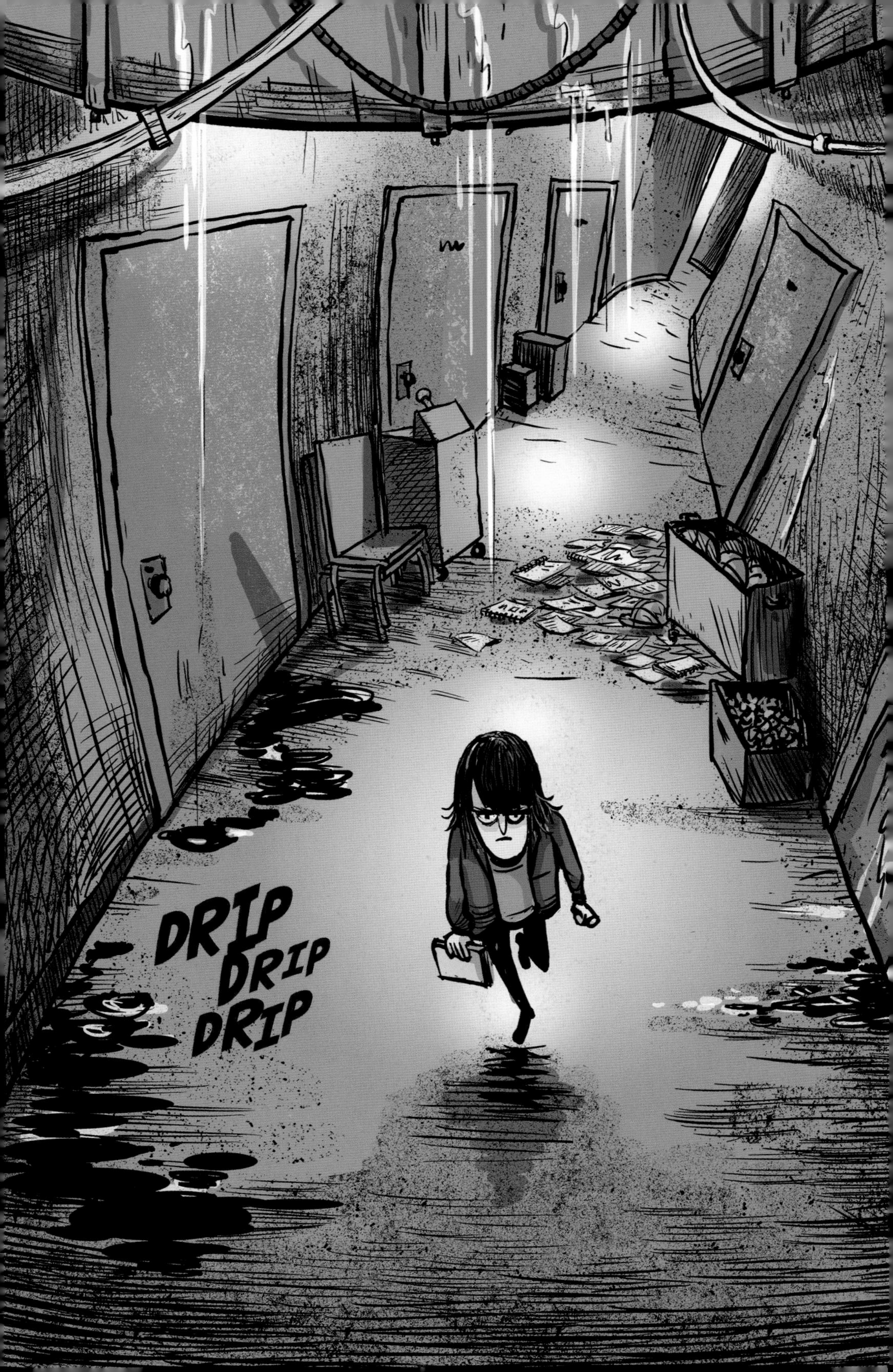
DRIP
DRIP
DRIP

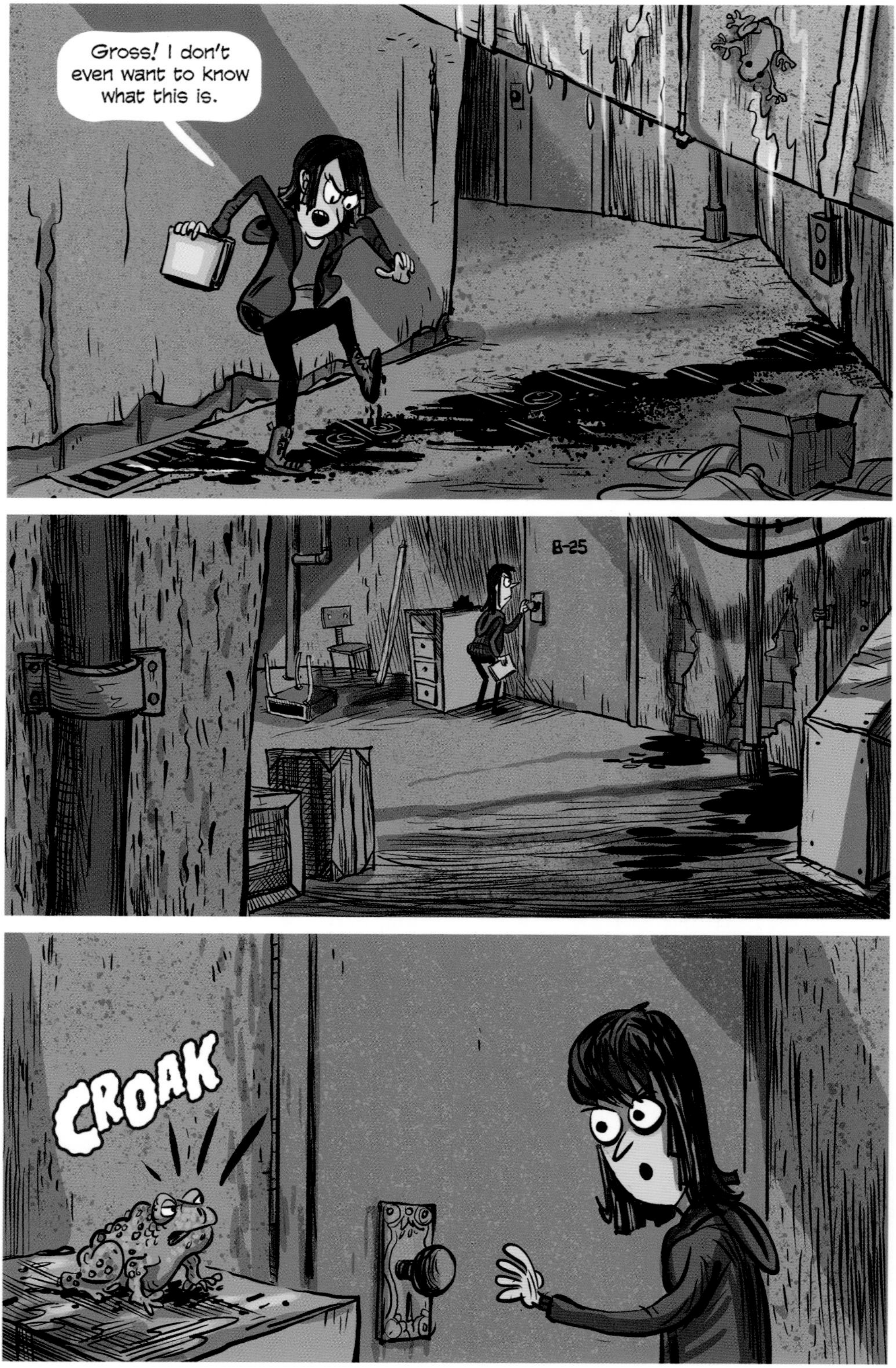
Gross! I don't even want to know what this is.
B-25
CROAK

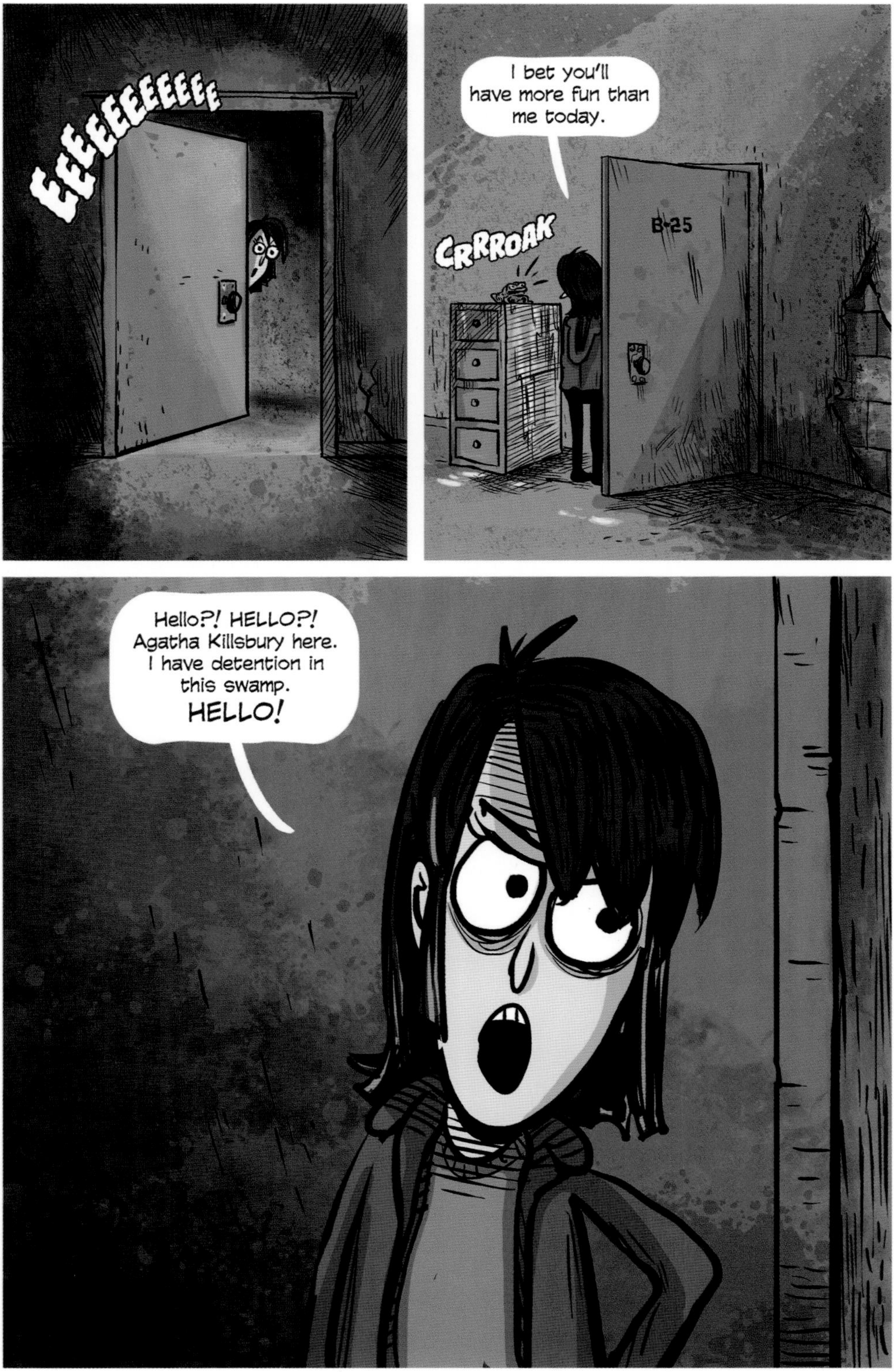
EEEEEEEEEEEE
I bet you'll have more fun than me today.
CRRROAK
B-25
Hello?! HELLO?! Agatha Killsbury here. I have detention in this swamp. HELLO!

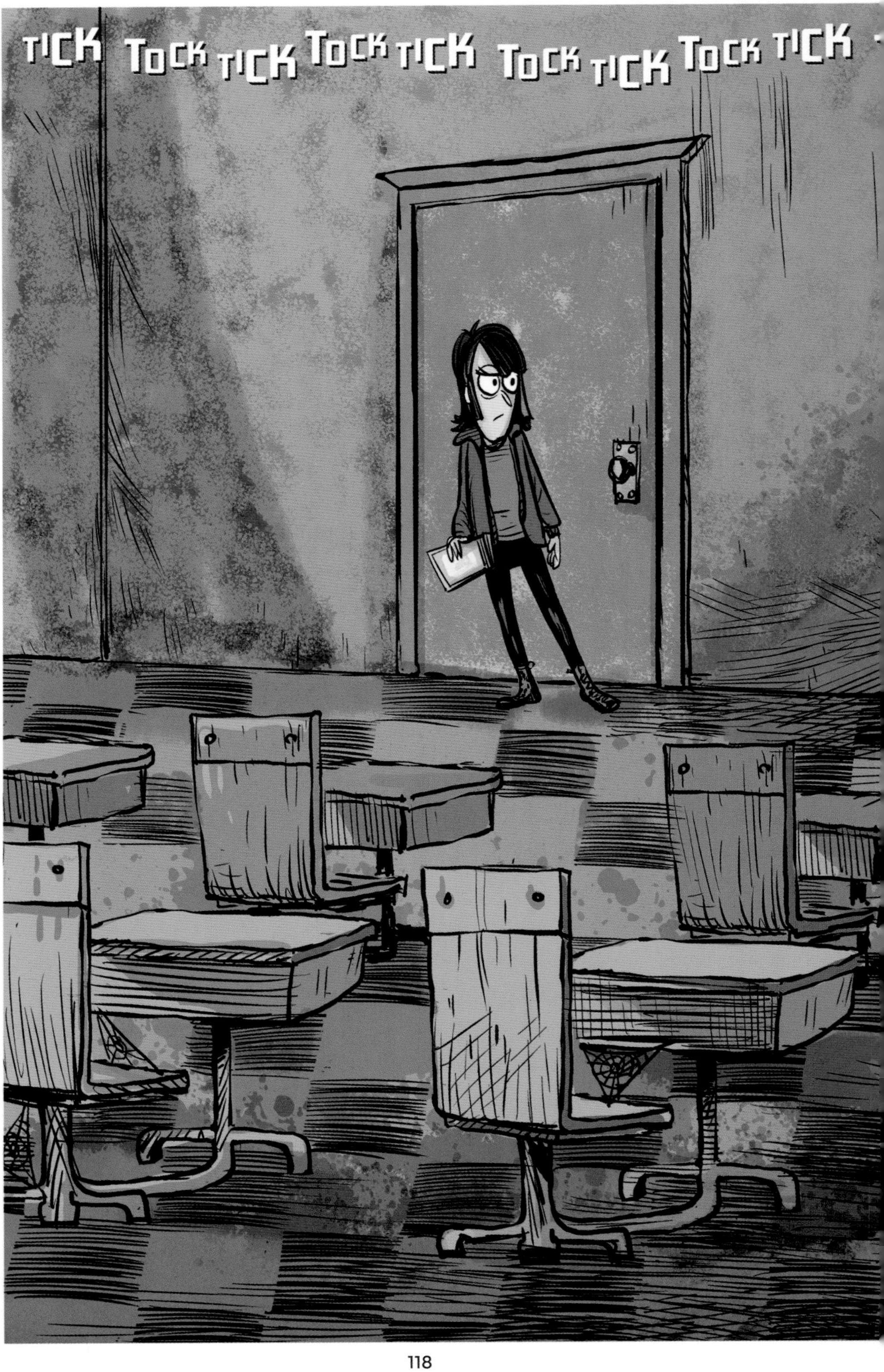
TICK TOCK TICK TOCK TICK TOCK TICK TOCK TICK

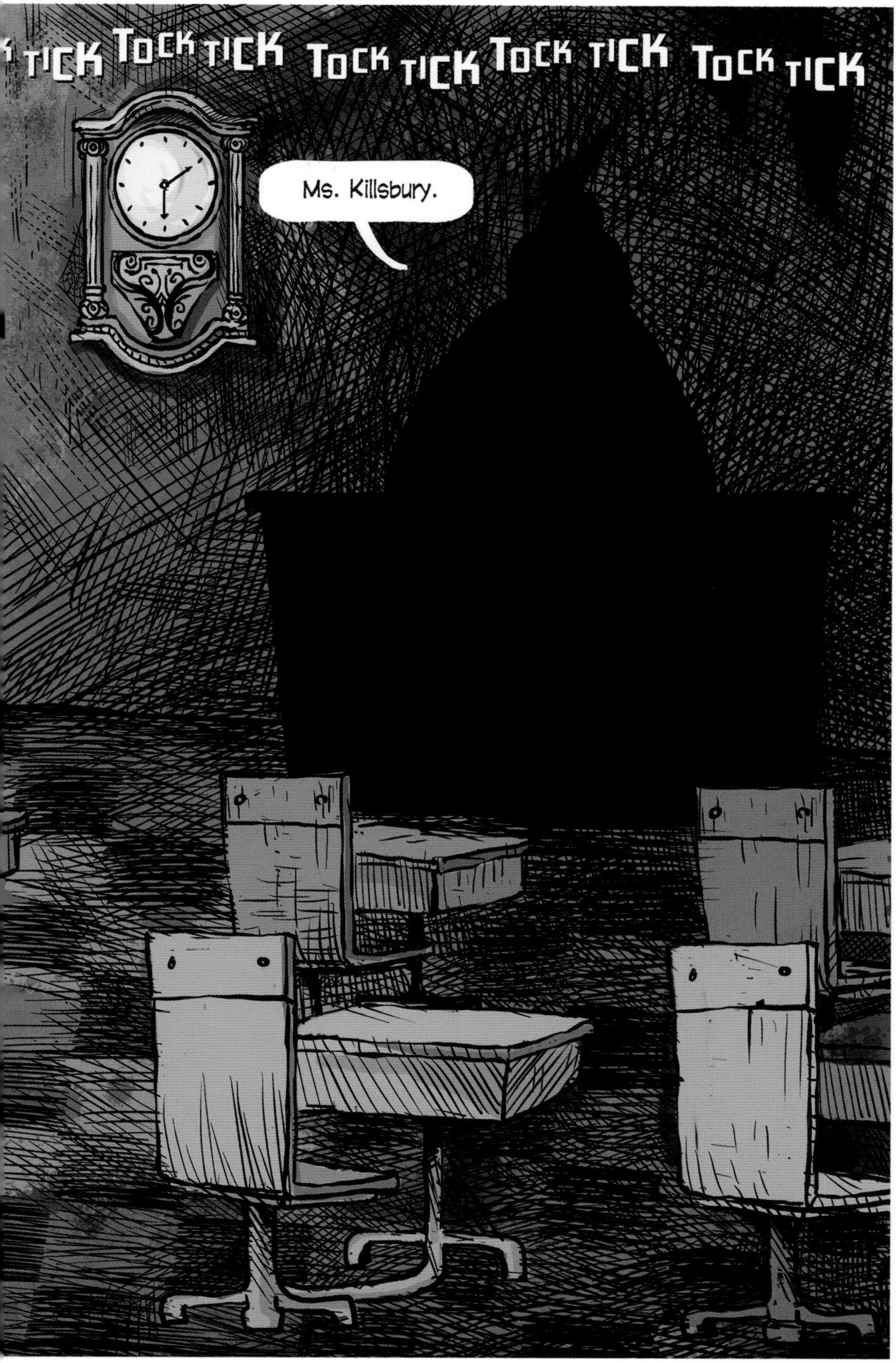
TICK TOCK TICK TOCK TICK TOCK TICK TOCK TICK
Ms. Killsbury.

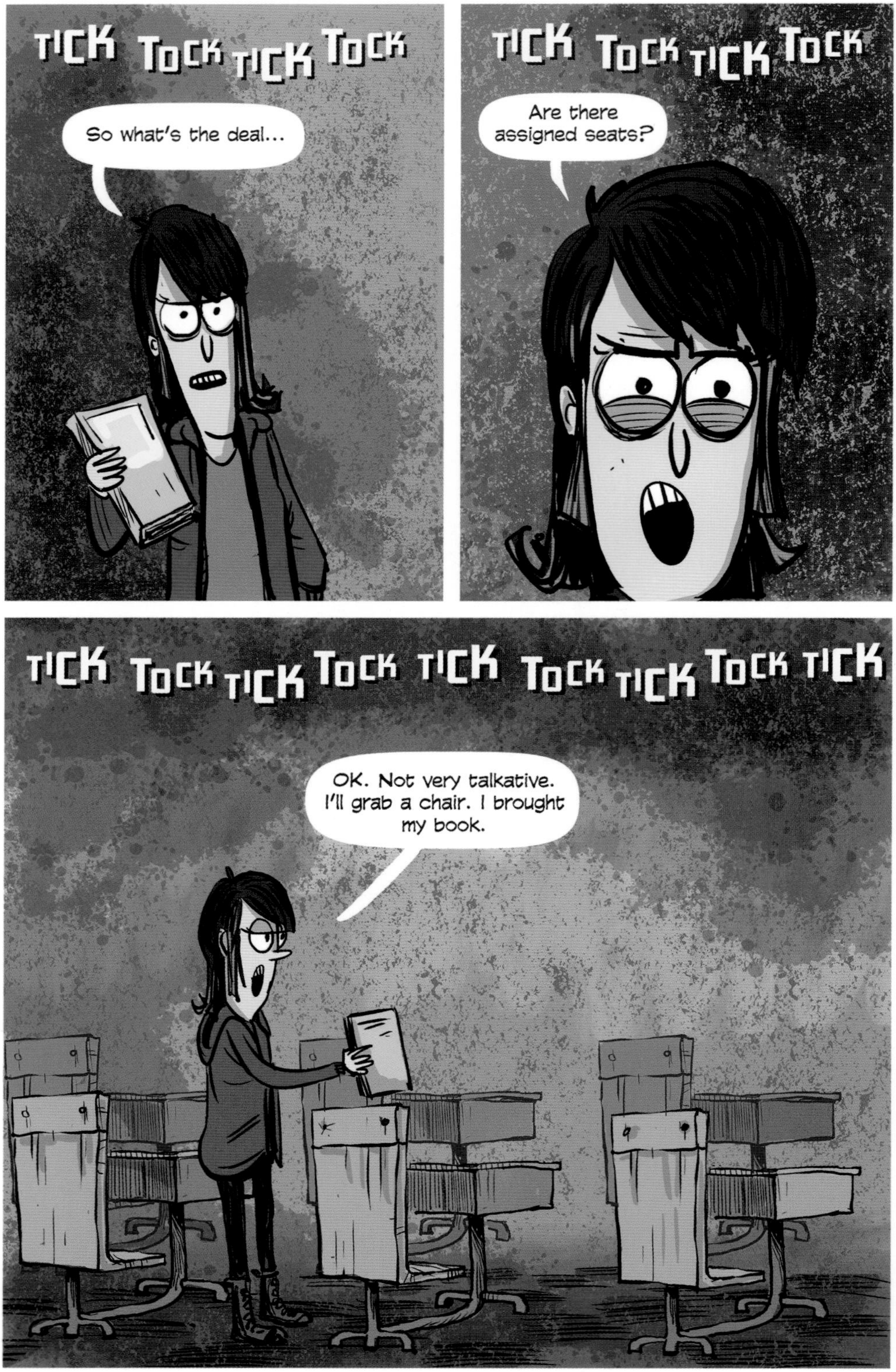
TICK TOCK TICK TOCK
So what's the deal...
TICK TOCK TICK TOCK
Are there assigned seats?
TICK TOCK TICK TOCK TICK TOCK TICK TOCK TICK
OK. Not very talkative. I'll grab a chair. I brought my book.

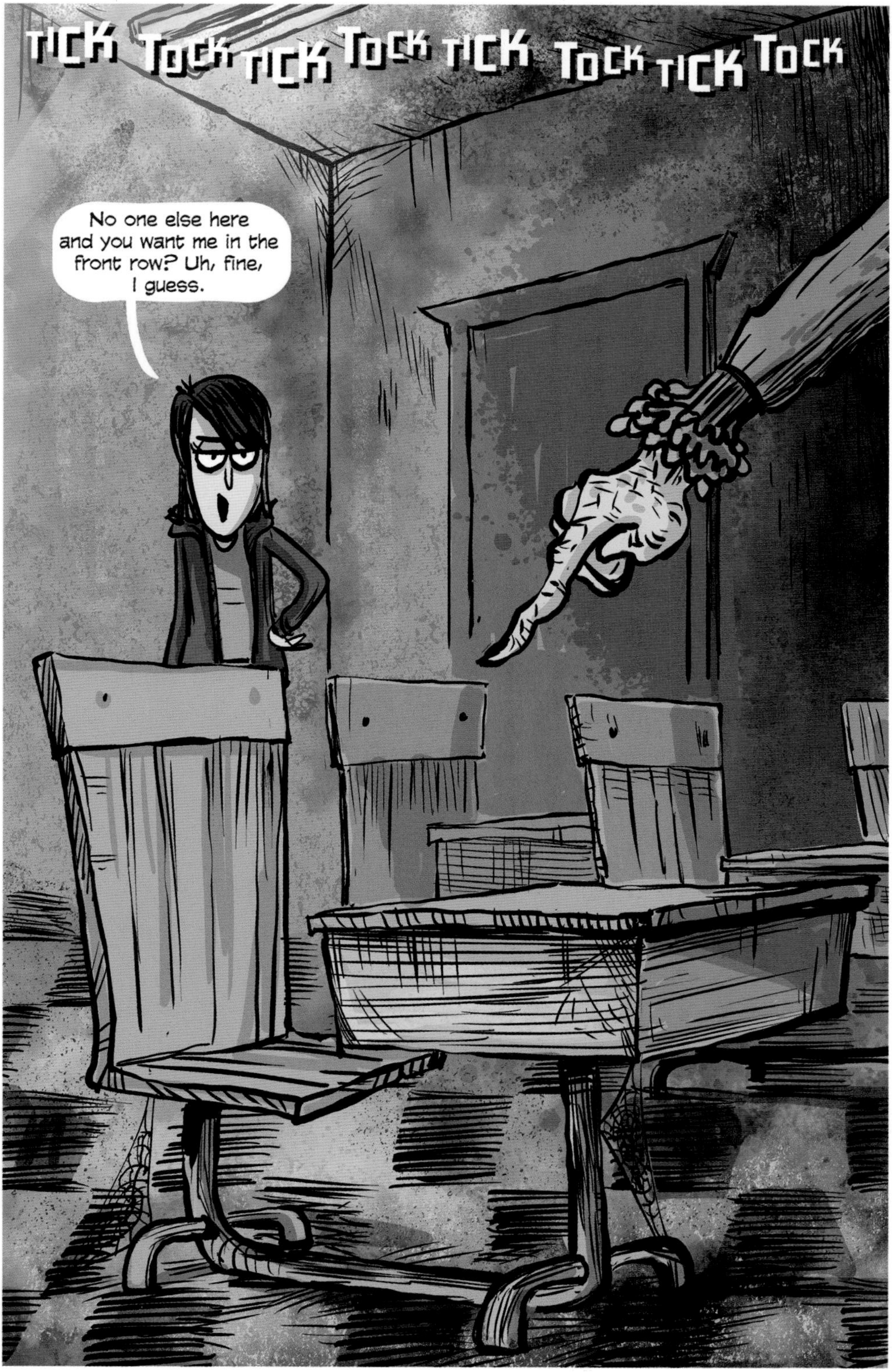
TICK TOCK TICK TOCK TICK TOCK TICK TOCK
No one else here and you want me in the front row? Uh, fine, I guess.

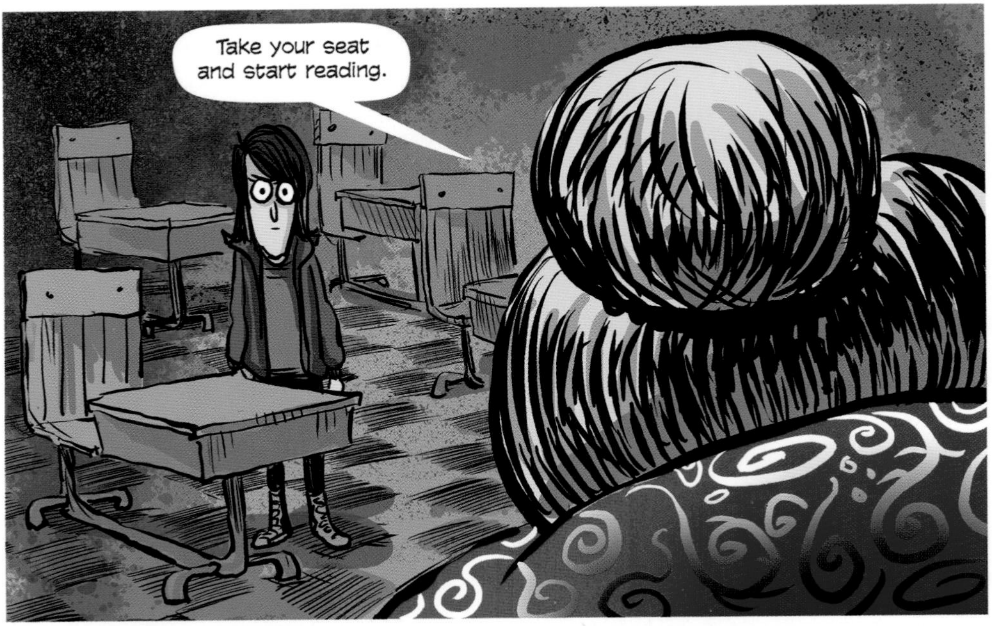
Take your seat and start reading.

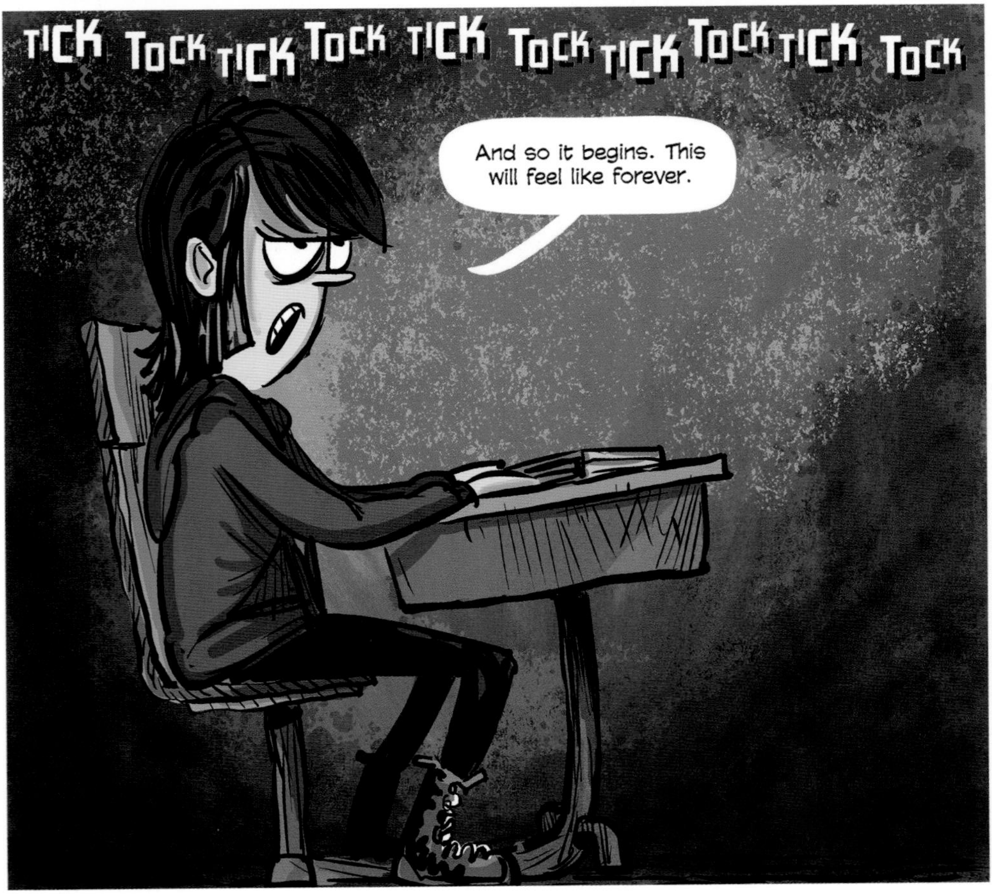
TICK TOCK TICK TOCK TICK TOCK TICK TOCK TICK TOCK
And so it begins. This will feel like forever.

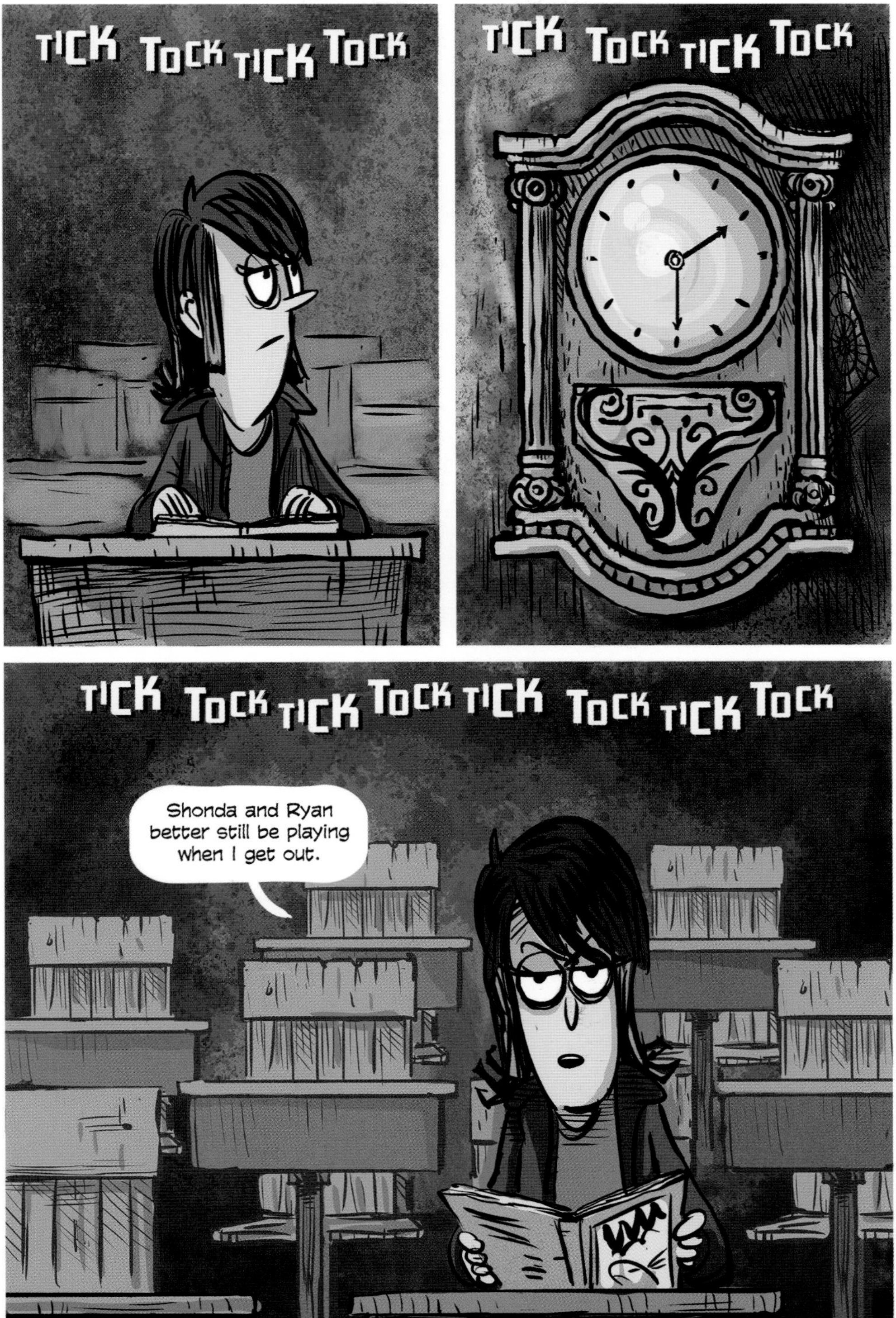
TICK TOCK TICK TOCK
TICK TOCK TICK TOCK
TICK TOCK TICK TOCK TICK TOCK TICK TOCK
Shonda and Ryan better still be playing when I get out.

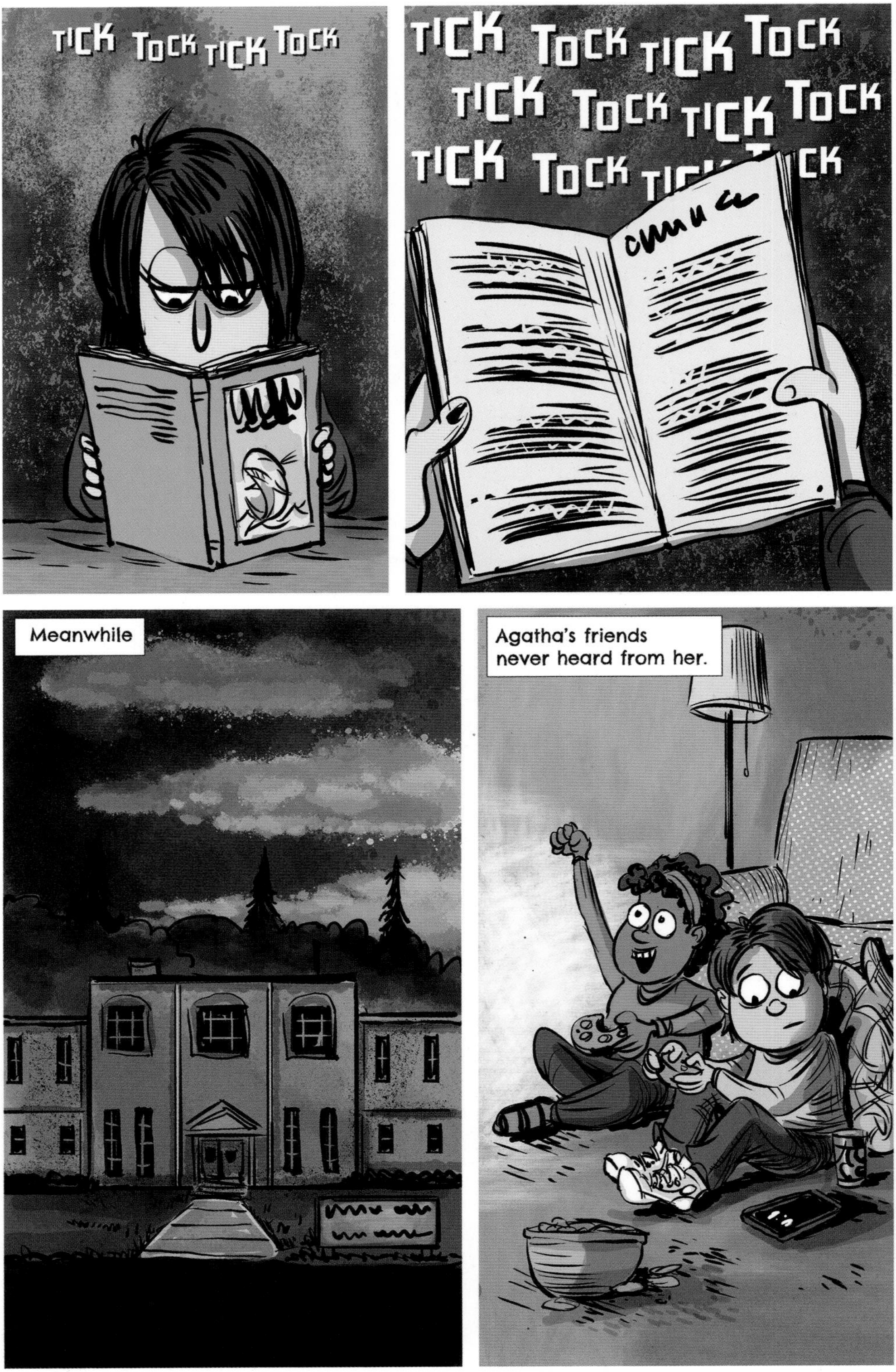
TICK TOCK TICK TOCK
TICK TOCK TICK TOCK
TICK TOCK TICK TOCK
TICK TOCK
Meanwhile
Agatha's friends never heard from her.

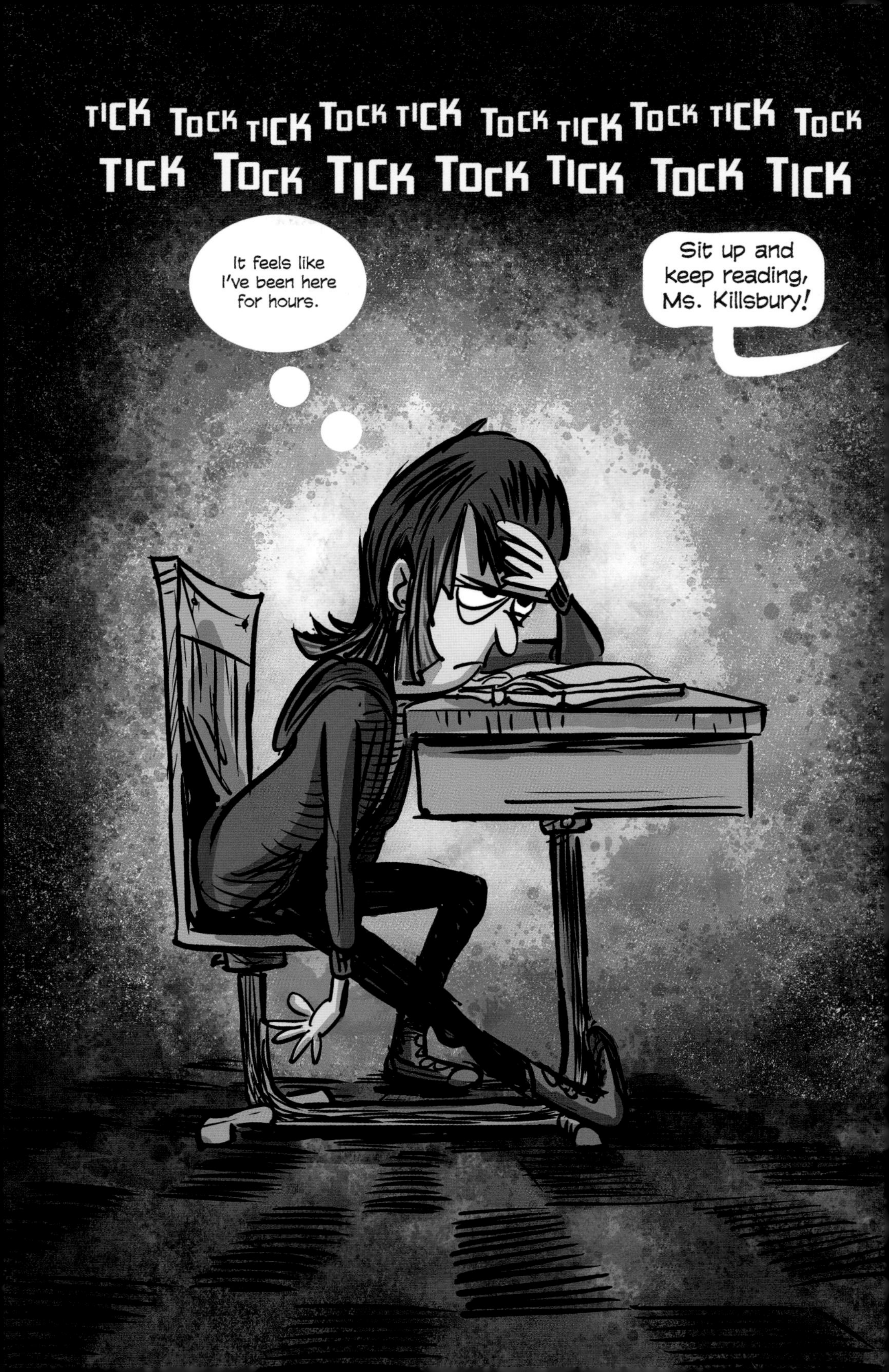
TICK TOCK TICK TOCK TICK TOCK TICK TOCK TICK TOCK
TICK TOCK TICK TOCK TICK TOCK TICK
It feels like I've been here for hours.
Sit up and keep reading, Ms. Killsbury!

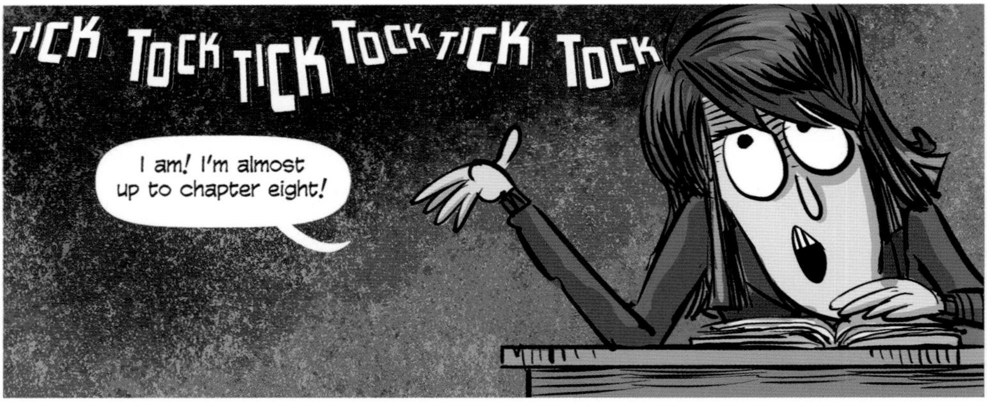
TICK TOCK TICK TOCK TICK TOCK
I am! I'm almost up to chapter eight!

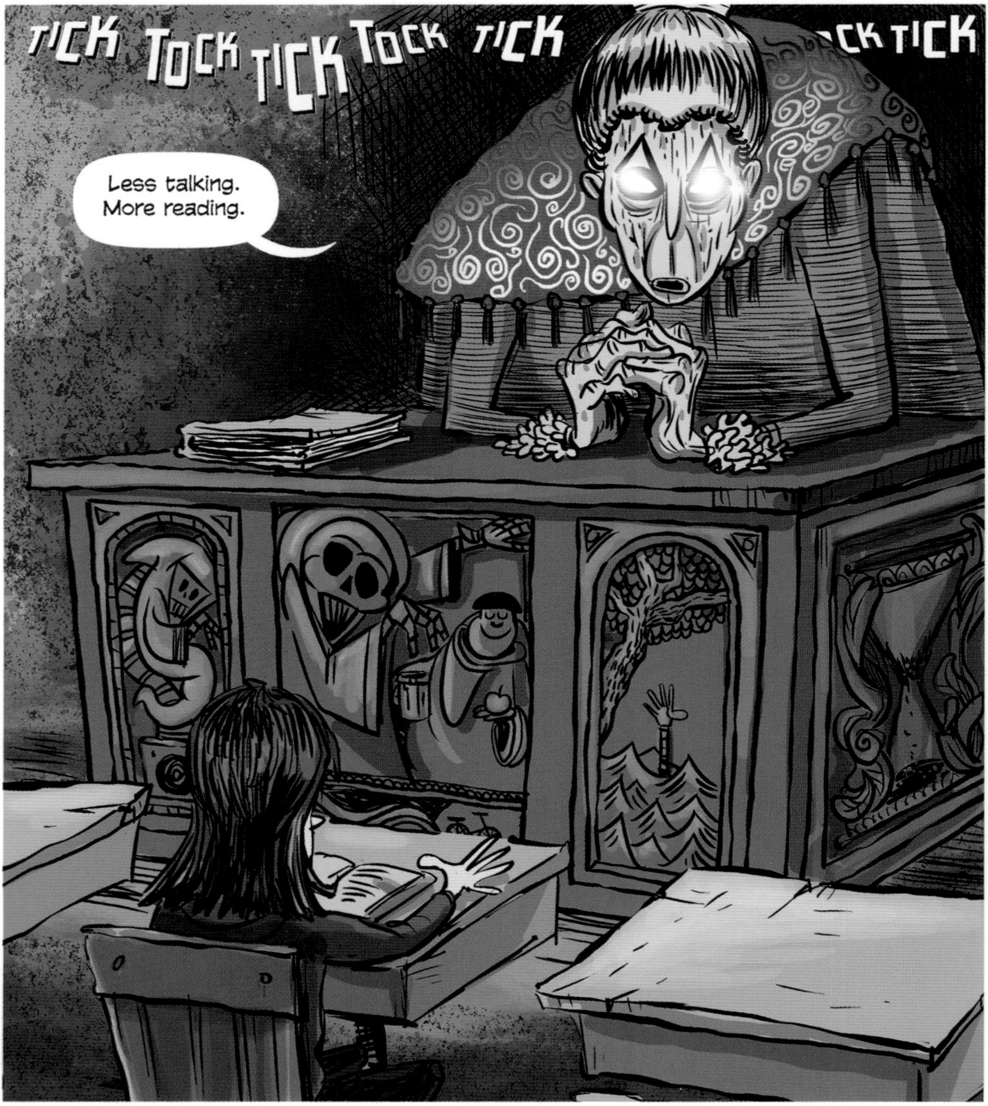
TICK TOCK TICK TOCK TICK
CK TICK
Less talking. More reading.

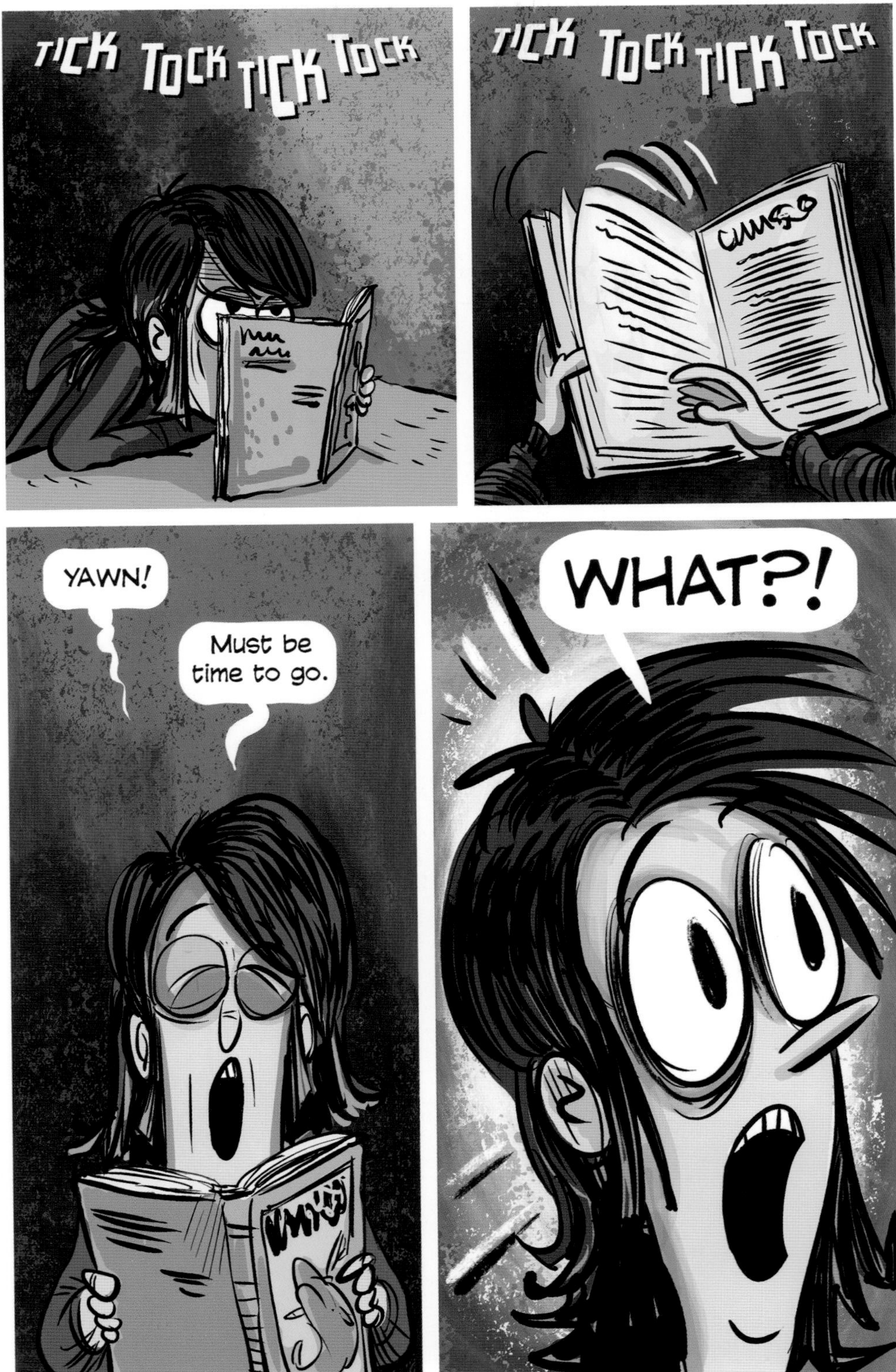
TICK TOCK TICK TOCK
TICK TOCK TICK TOCK
YAWN!
Must be time to go.
WHAT?!

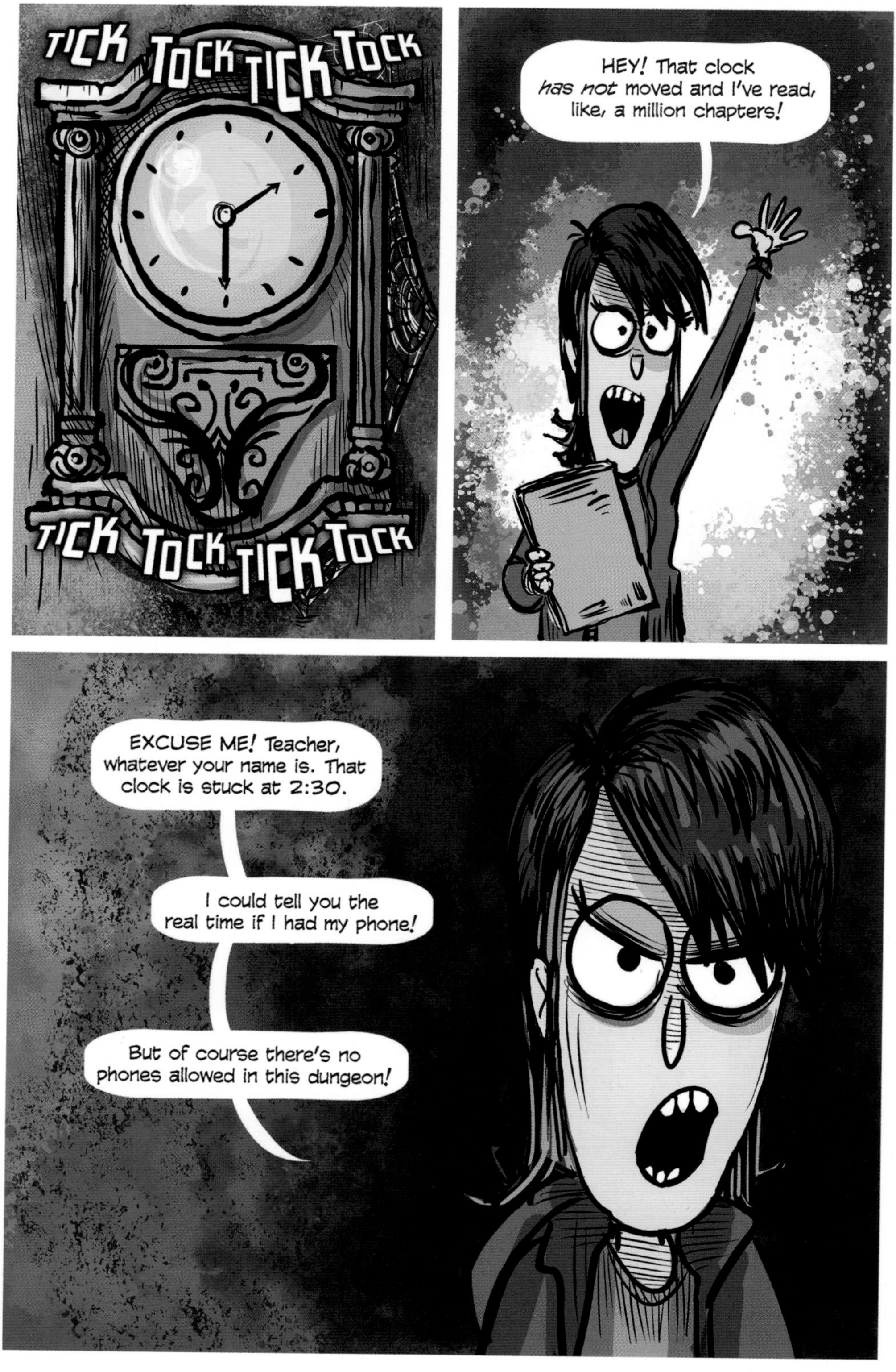
TICK TOCK TICK TOCK
HEY! That clock *has not* moved and I've read, like, a million chapters!
TICK TOCK TICK TOCK
EXCUSE ME! Teacher, whatever your name is. That clock is stuck at 2:30.
I could tell you the real time if I had my phone!
But of course there's no phones allowed in this dungeon!

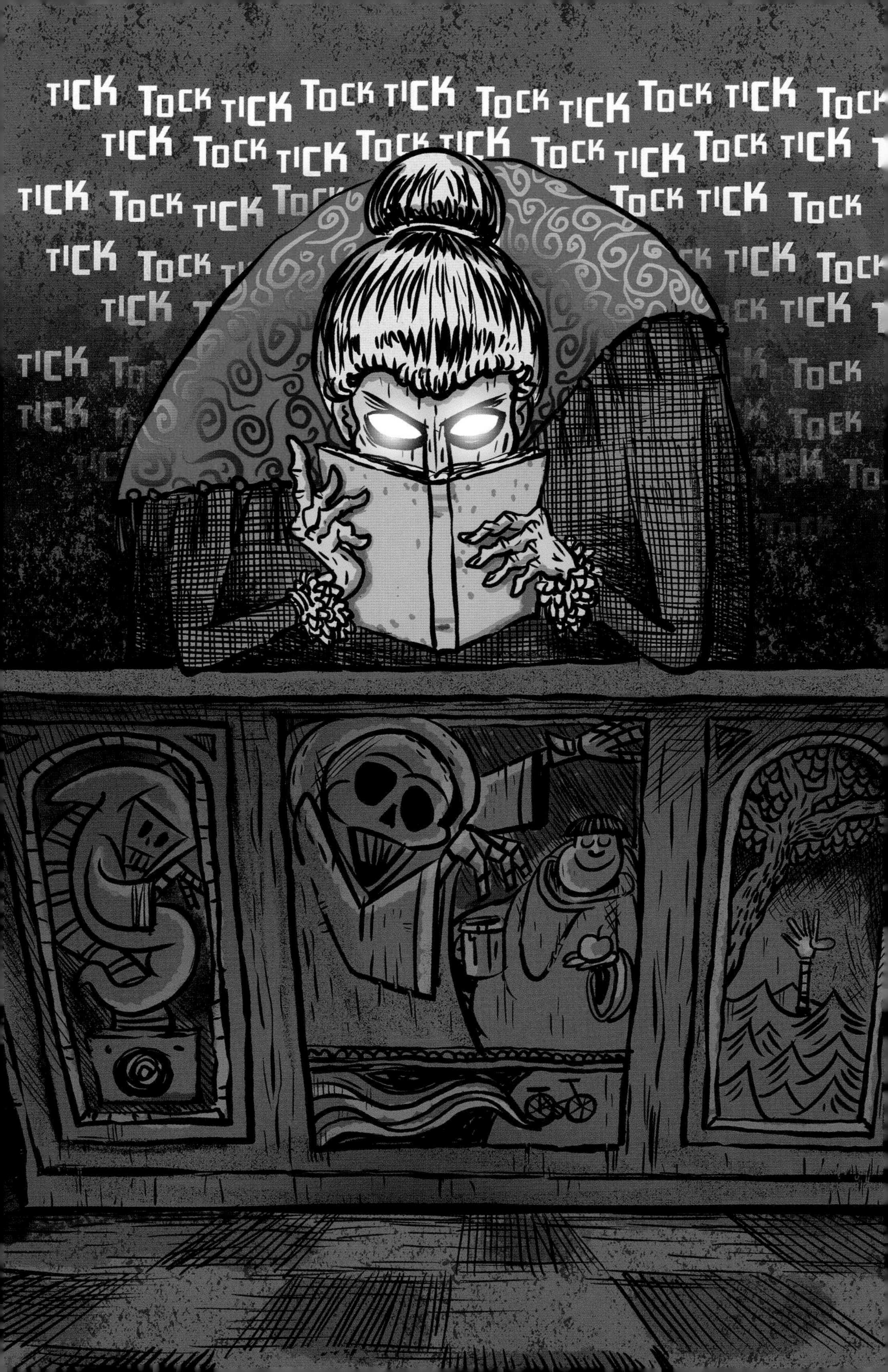
TICK TOCK TICK TOCK TICK TOCK TICK TOCK TICK
TICK TOCK TICK TOCK TICK TOCK TICK TOCK TICK
TICK TOCK TICK TOCK TICK TOCK
TICK TOCK TICK TOCK
TICK TICK
TICK TOCK
TICK TOCK

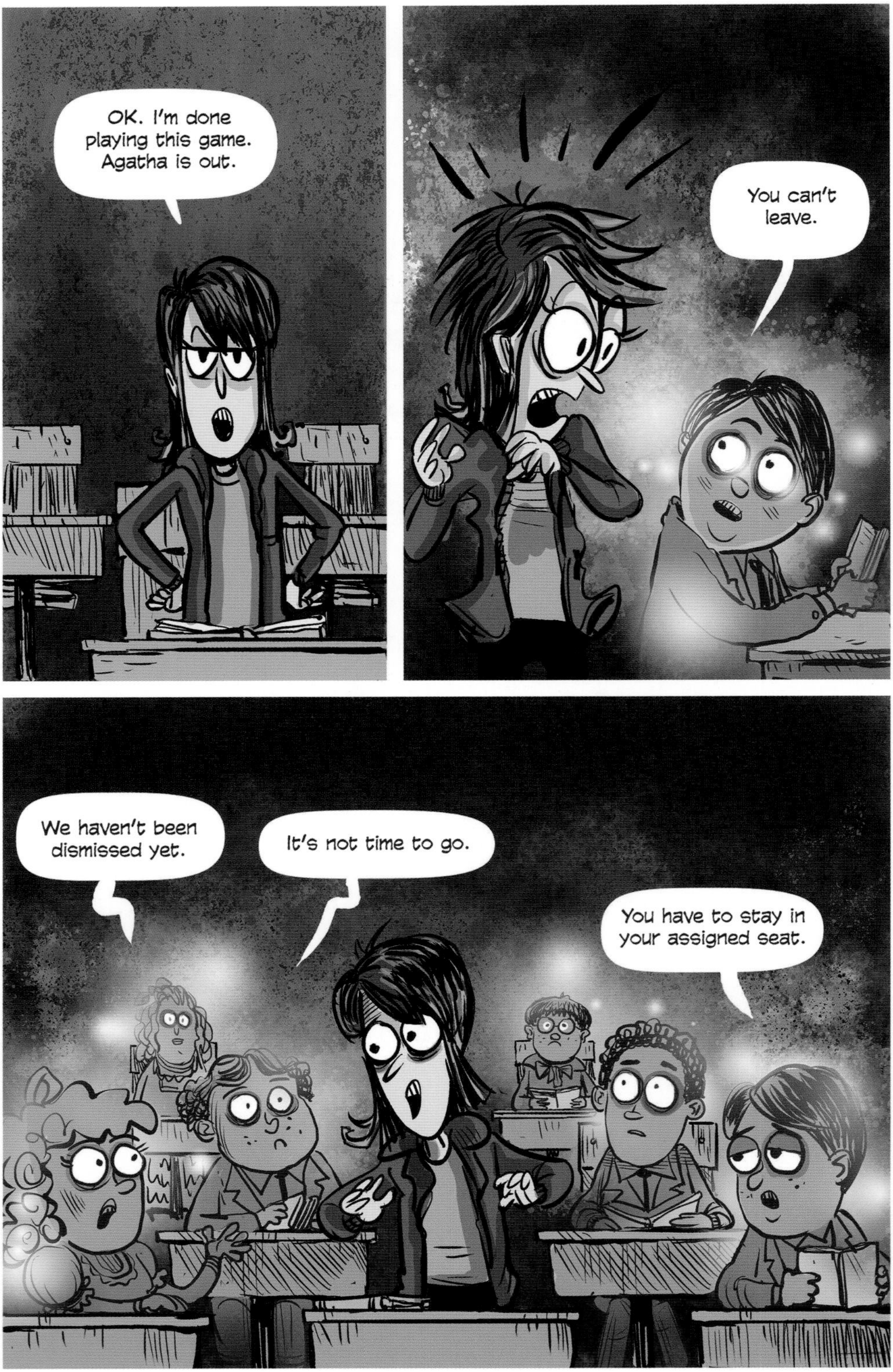
OK. I'm done playing this game. Agatha is out.
You can't leave.
We haven't been dismissed yet.
It's not time to go.
You have to stay in your assigned seat.

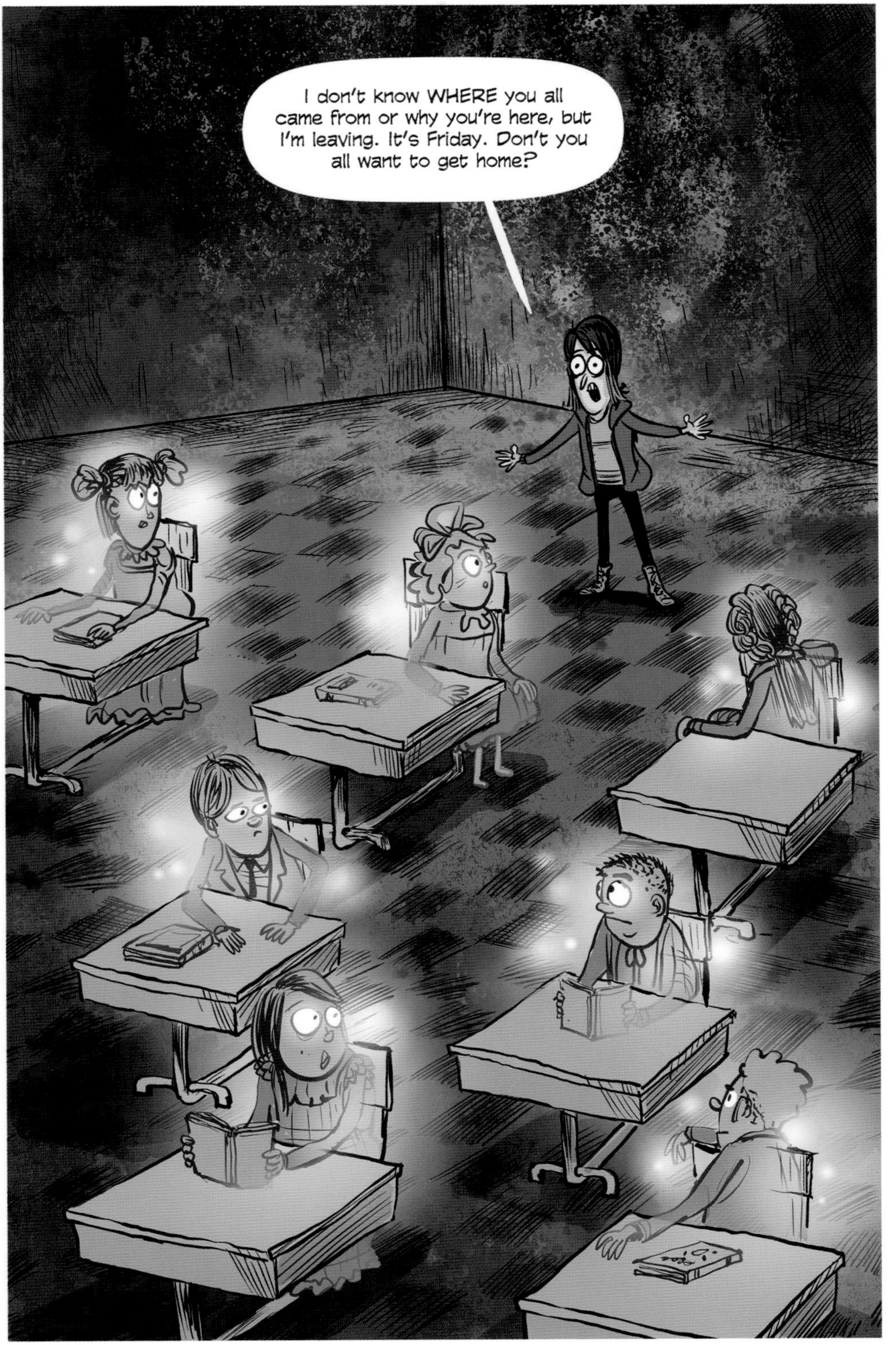
I don't know WHERE you all came from or why you're here, but I'm leaving. It's Friday. Don't you all want to get home?

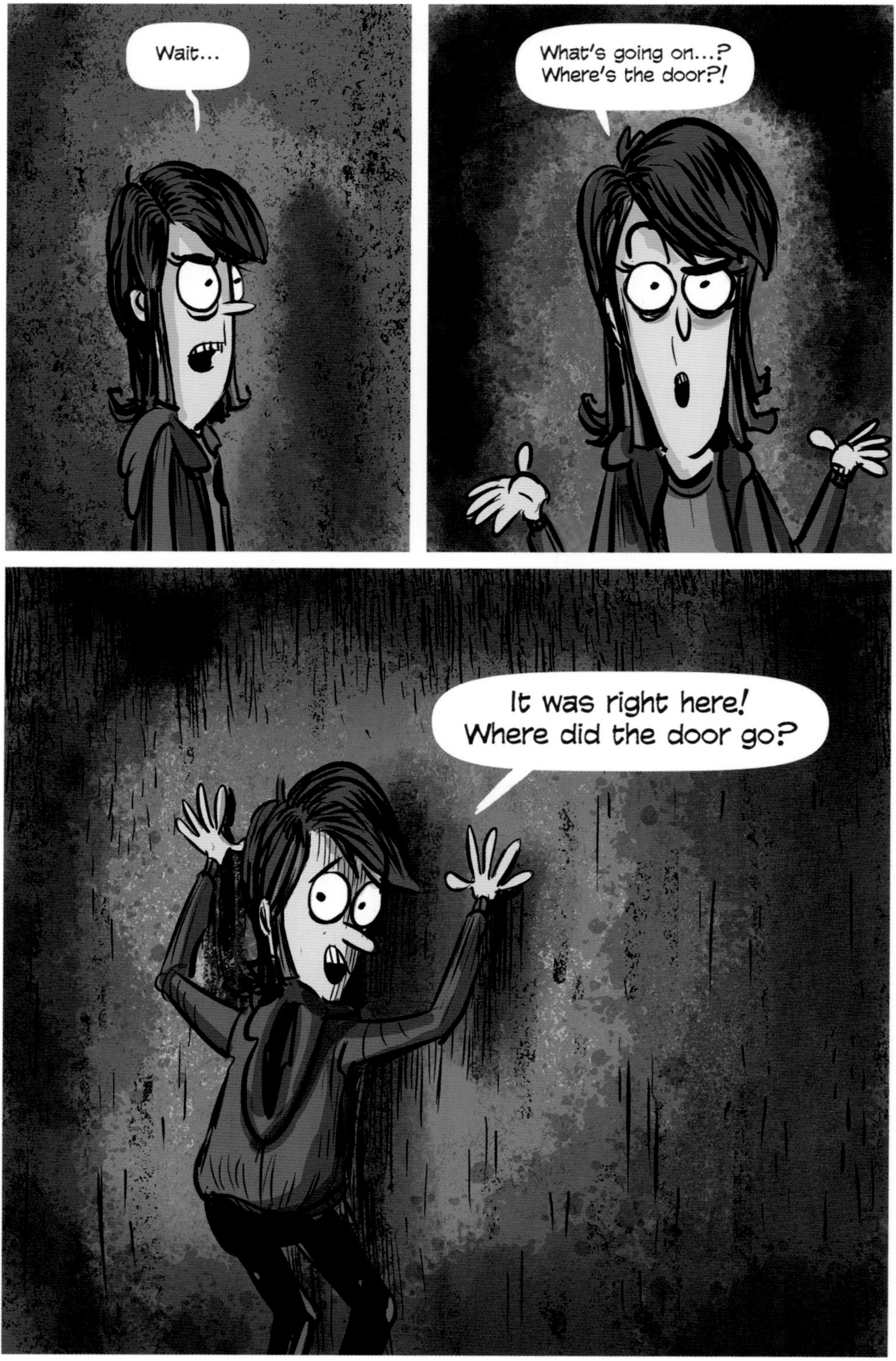
Wait...
What's going on...?
Where's the door?!
It was right here!
Where did the door go?

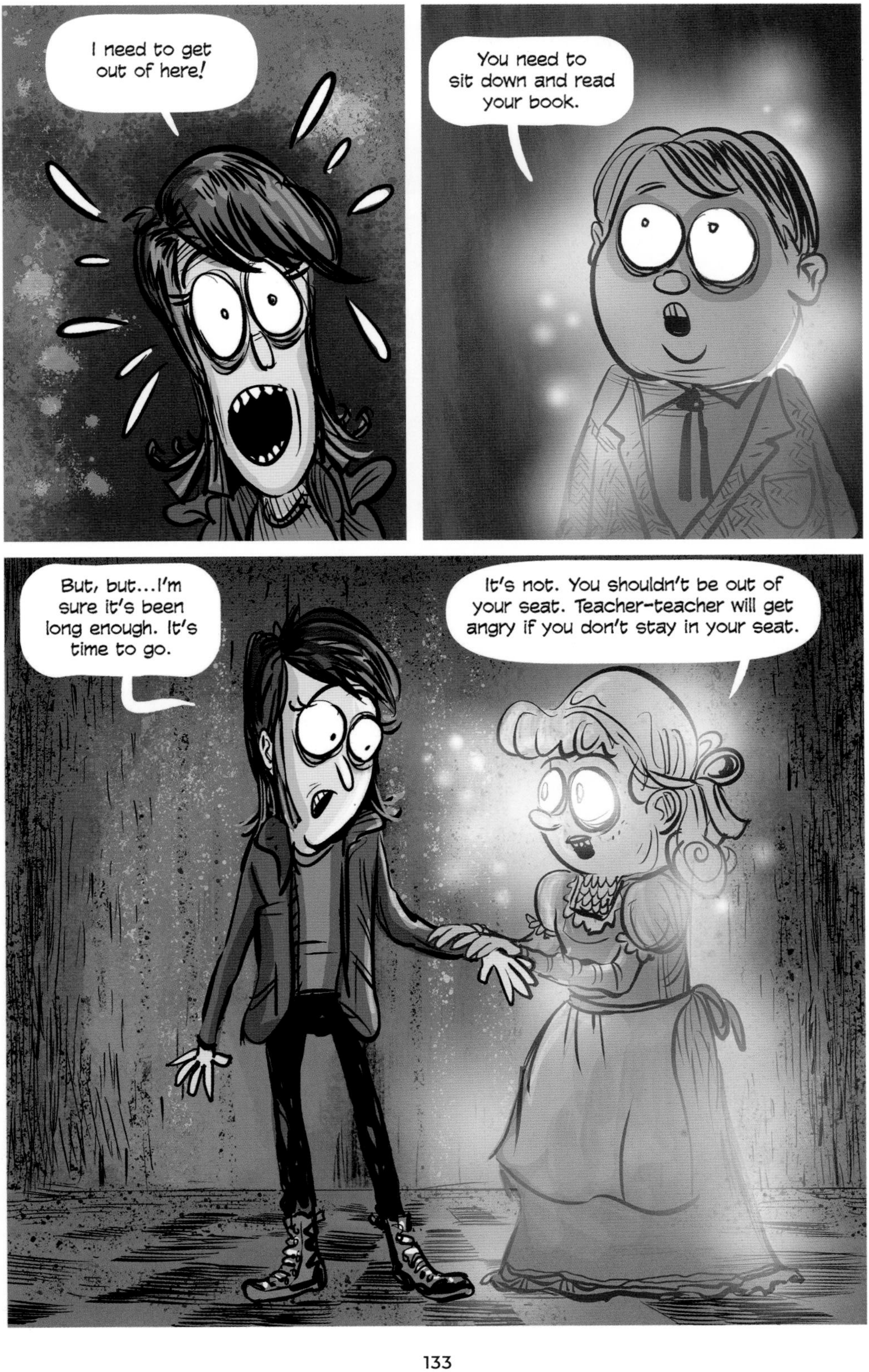
I need to get out of here!
You need to sit down and read your book.
But, but...I'm sure it's been long enough. It's time to go.
It's not. You shouldn't be out of your seat. Teacher-teacher will get angry if you don't stay in your seat.

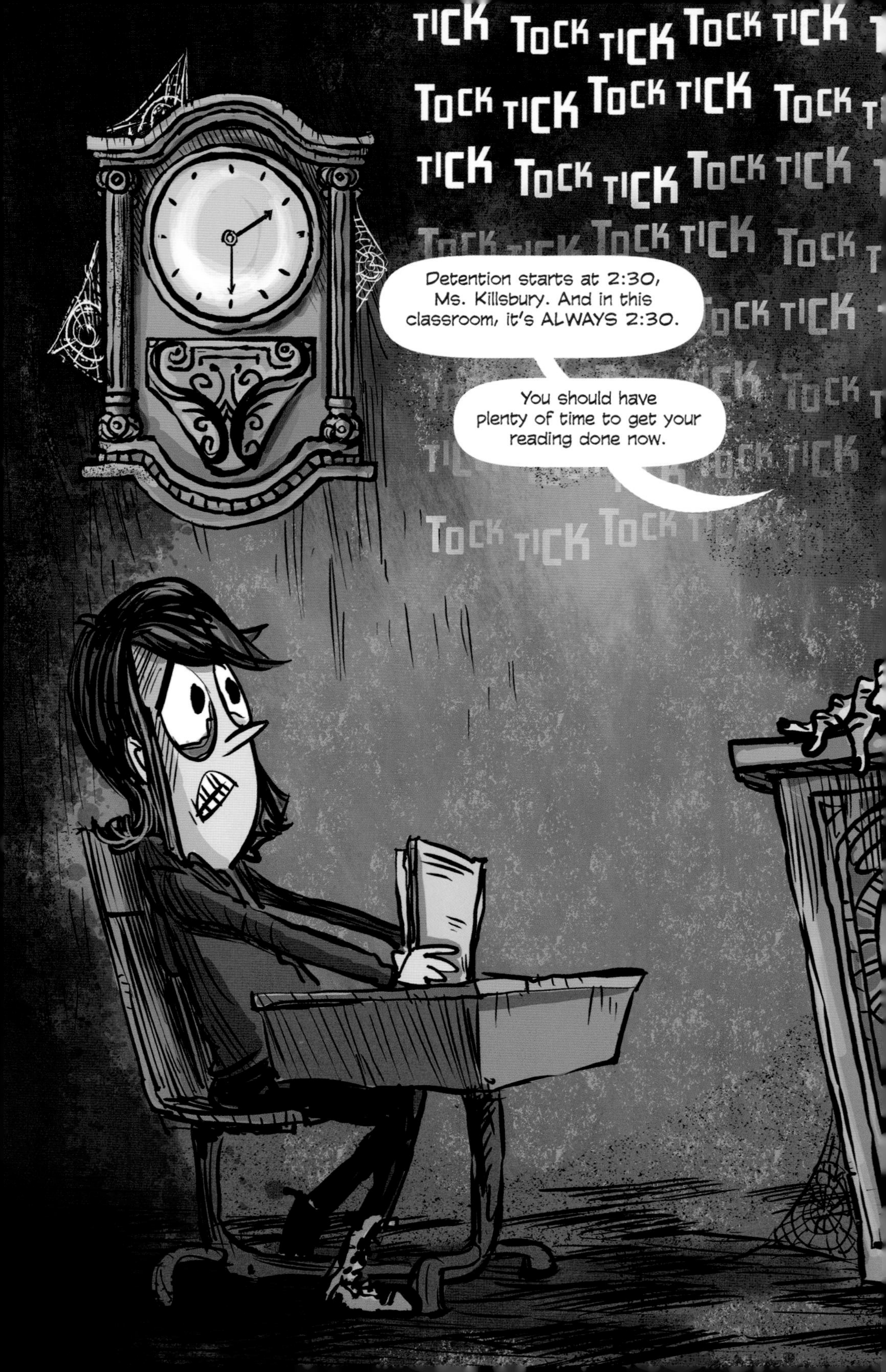
TICK TOCK TICK TOCK TICK
TOCK TICK TOCK TICK TOCK
TICK TOCK TICK TOCK TICK
Detention starts at 2:30, Ms. Killsbury. And in this classroom, it's ALWAYS 2:30.
You should have plenty of time to get your reading done now.

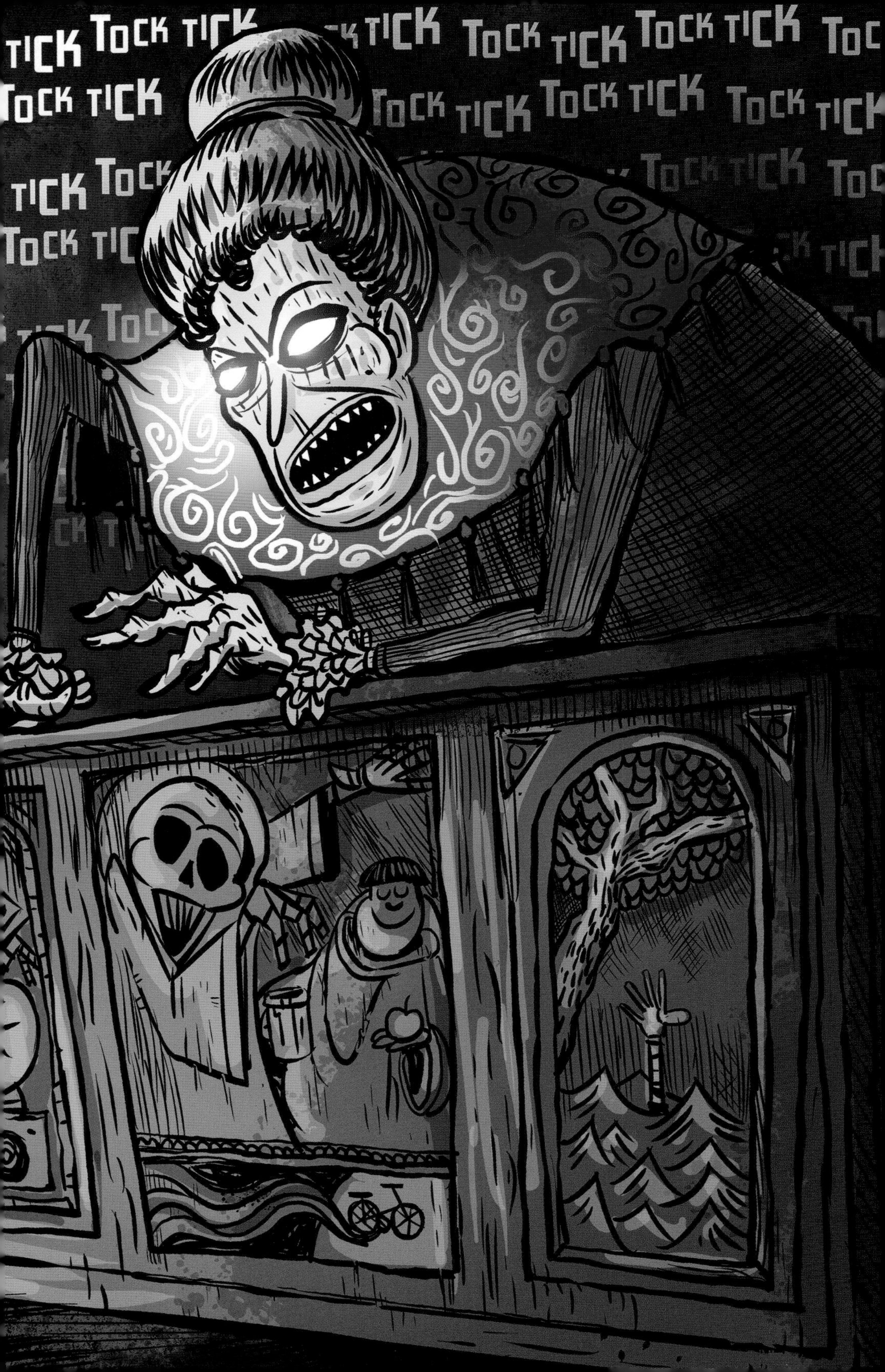
TICK TOCK
TICK
TOCK TICK TOCK TICK TOCK TICK
TOCK TICK
TOCK TICK TOCK TICK TOCK TICK TOCK TICK
TICK TOCK
TOCK TICK
TICK
TOCK TICK
TICK

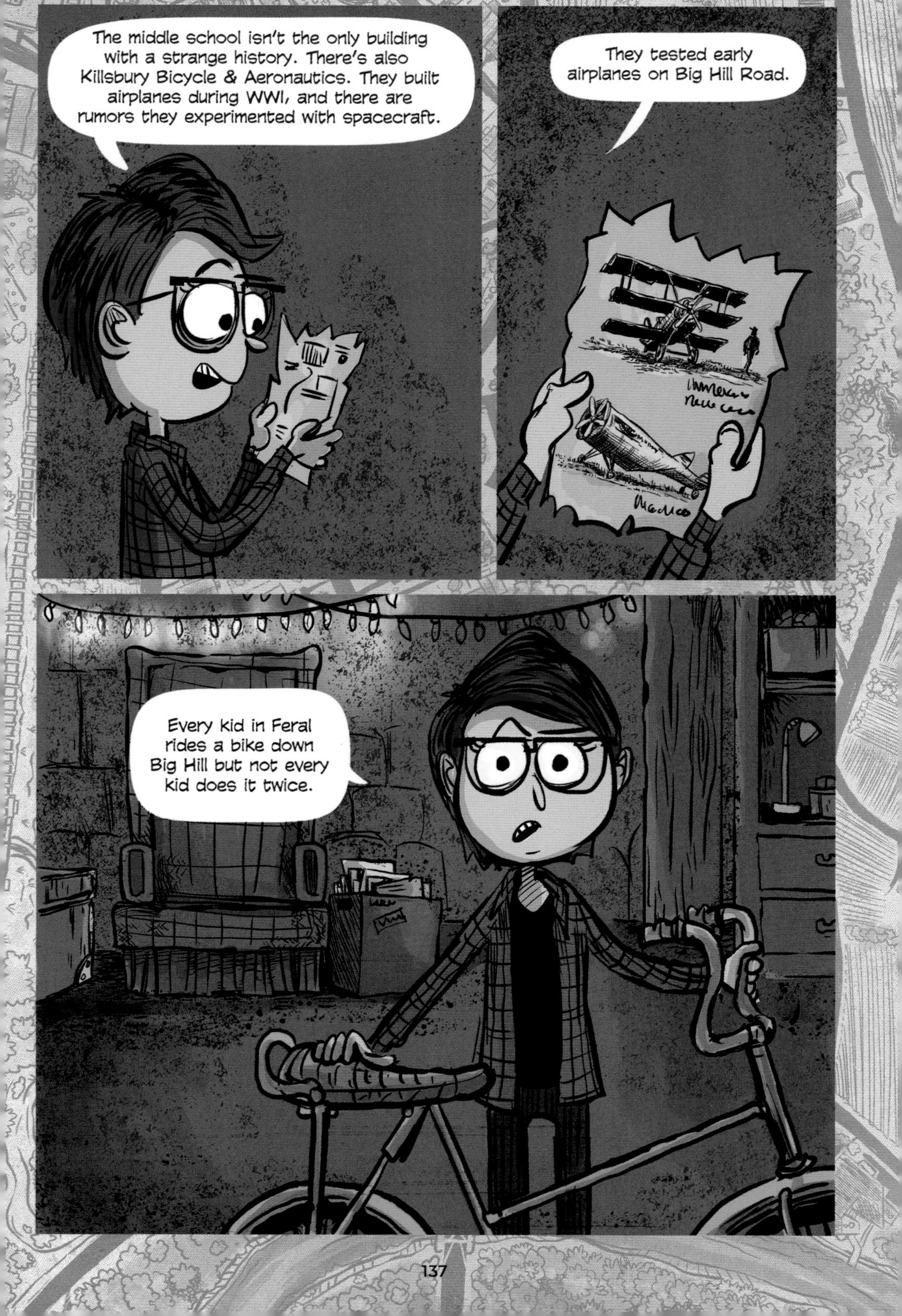
The middle school isn't the only building with a strange history. There's also Killsbury Bicycle & Aeronautics. They built airplanes during WWI, and there are rumors they experimented with spacecraft.
They tested early airplanes on Big Hill Road.
Every kid in Feral rides a bike down Big Hill but not every kid does it twice.

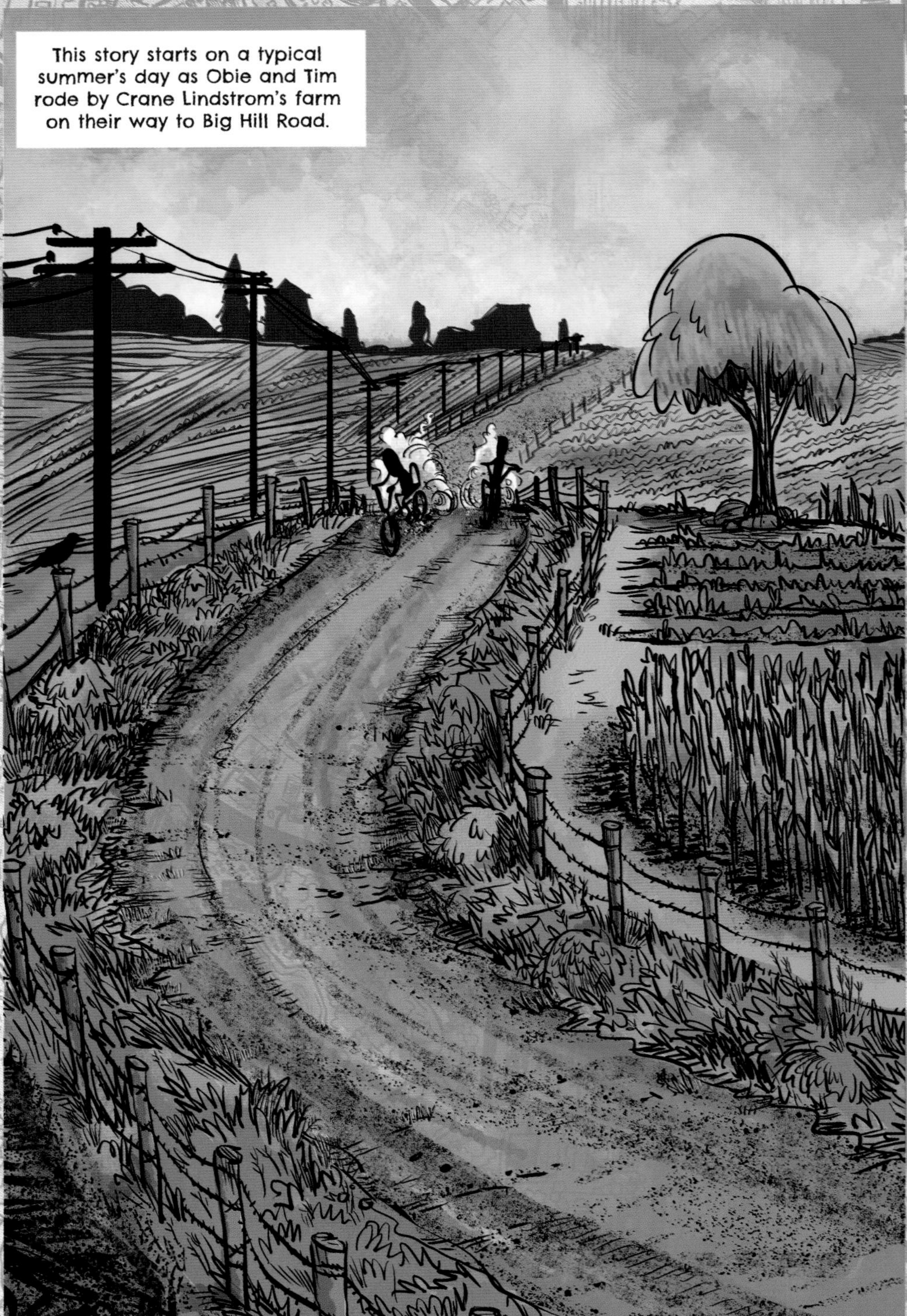
This story starts on a typical summer's day as Obie and Tim rode by Crane Lindstrom's farm on their way to Big Hill Road.

the Old bike

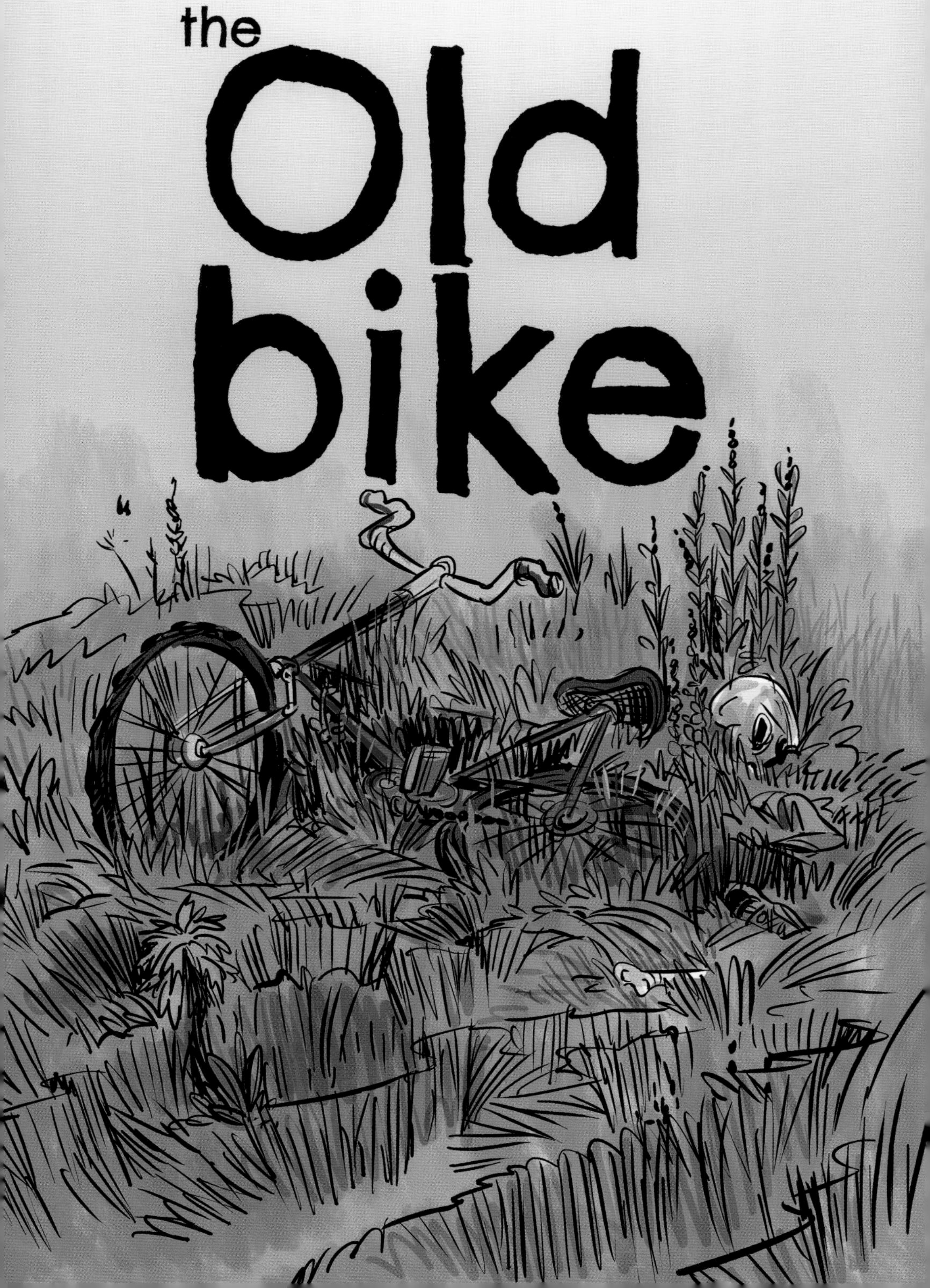

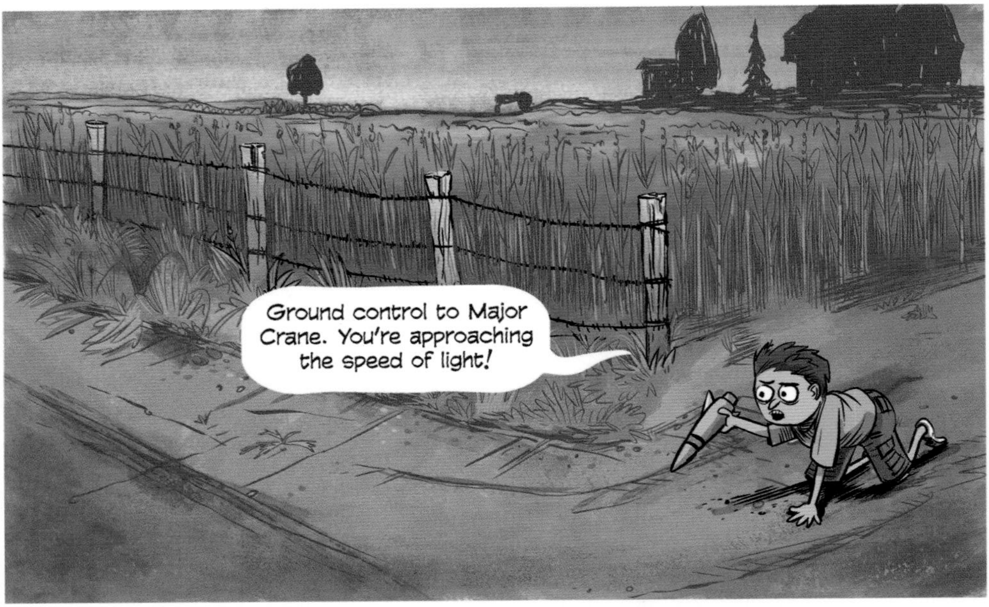
Ground control to Major Crane. You're approaching the speed of light!

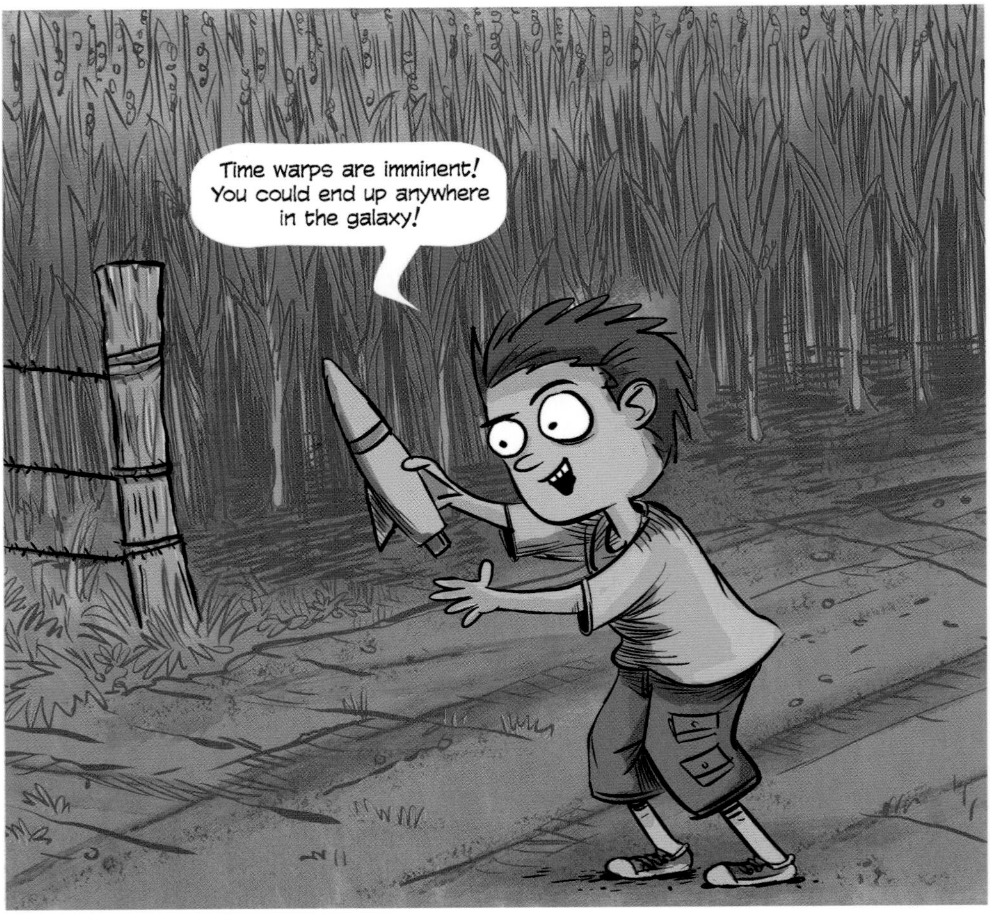
Time warps are imminent! You could end up anywhere in the galaxy!

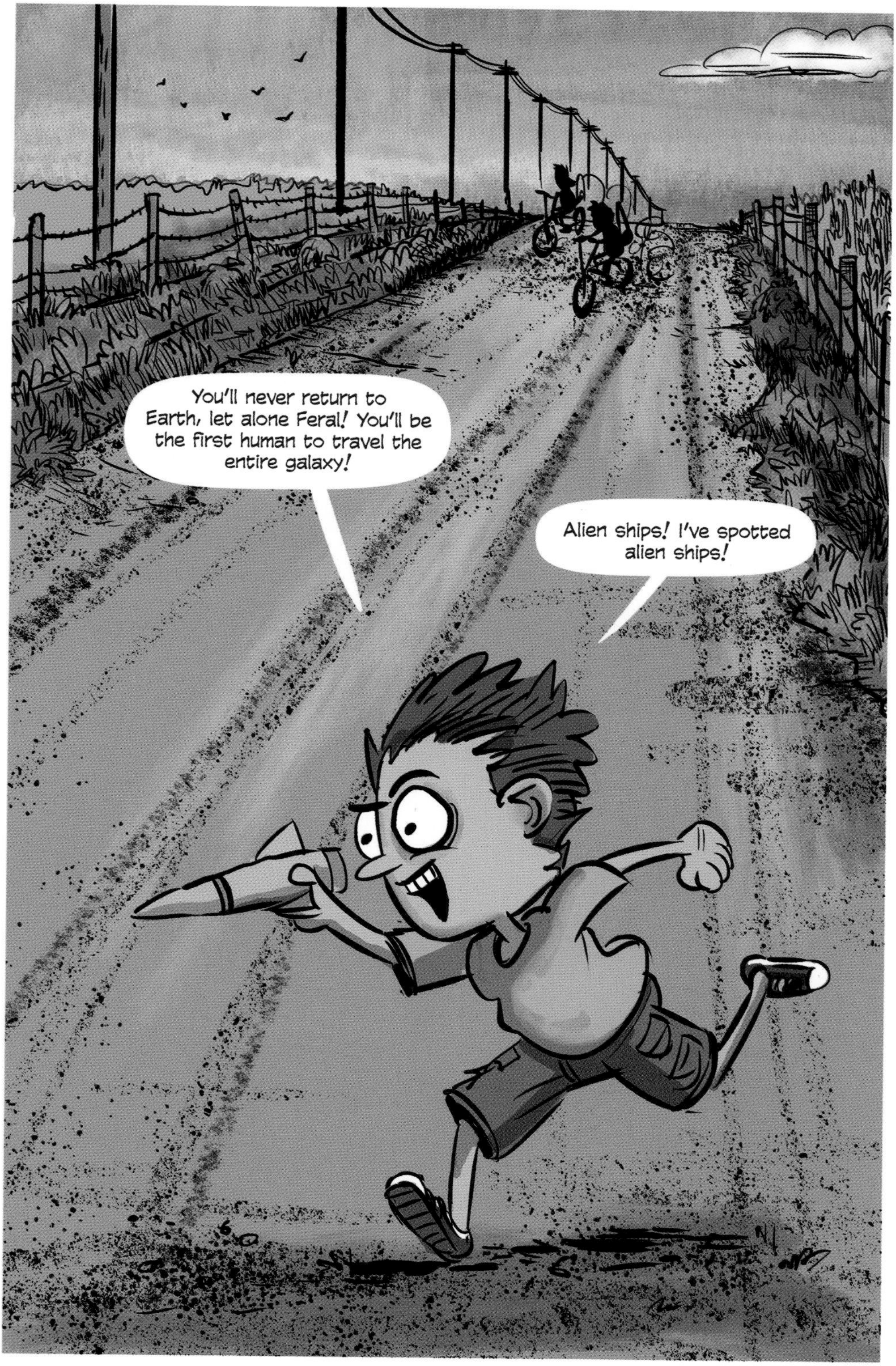
You'll never return to Earth, let alone Feral! You'll be the first human to travel the entire galaxy!
Alien ships! I've spotted alien ships!

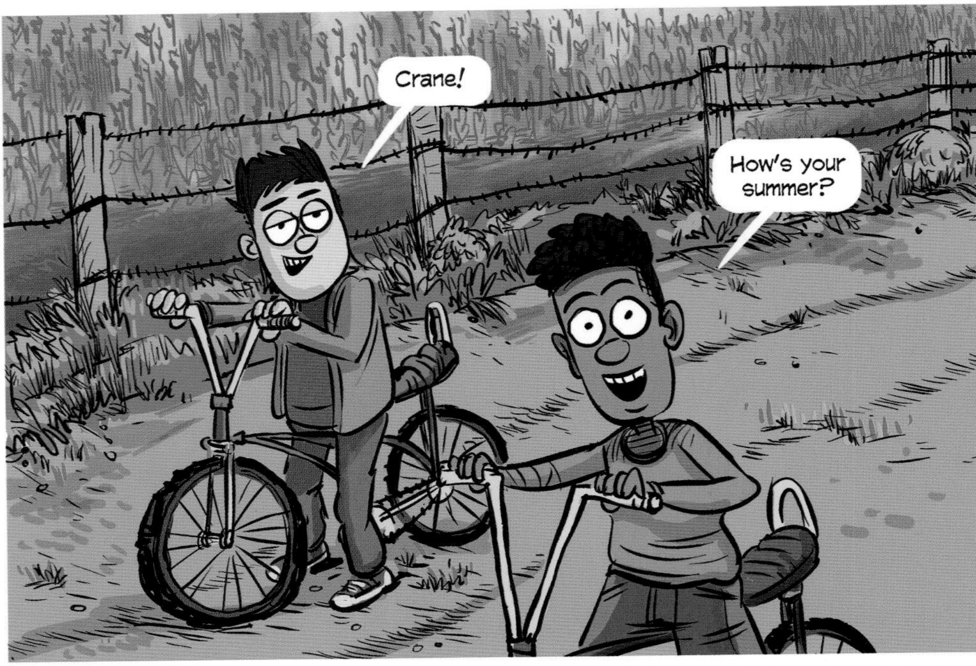
Crane!
How's your summer?

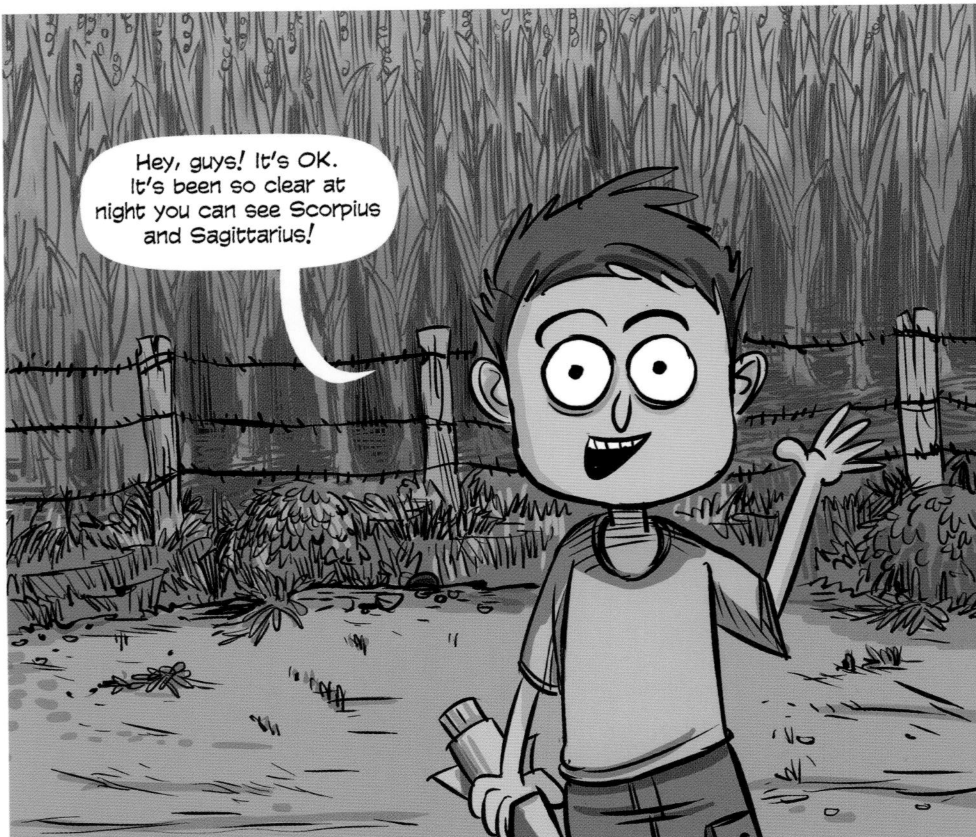
Hey, guys! It's OK. It's been so clear at night you can see Scorpius and Sagittarius!

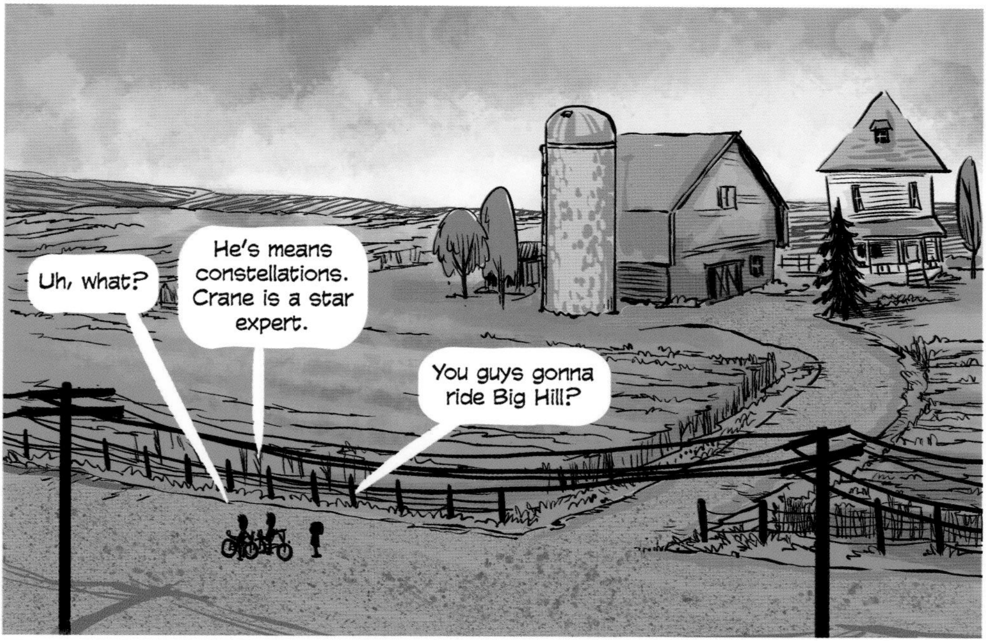
Uh, what?
He's means constellations. Crane is a star expert.
You guys gonna ride Big Hill?
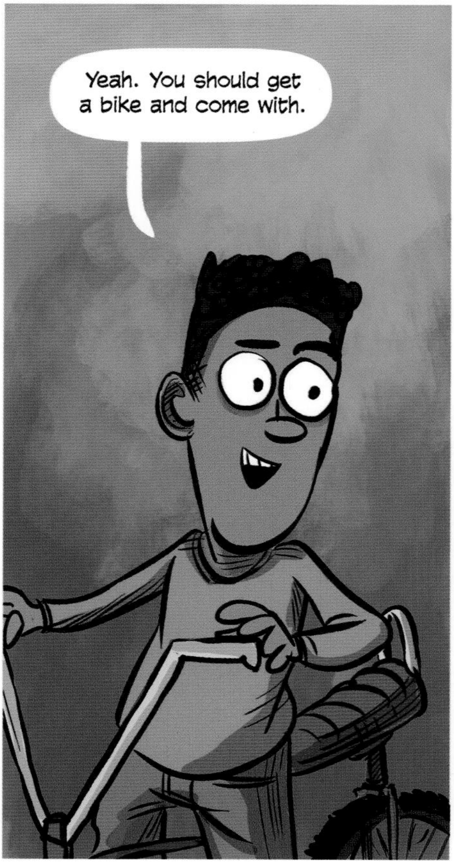
Yeah. You should get a bike and come with.
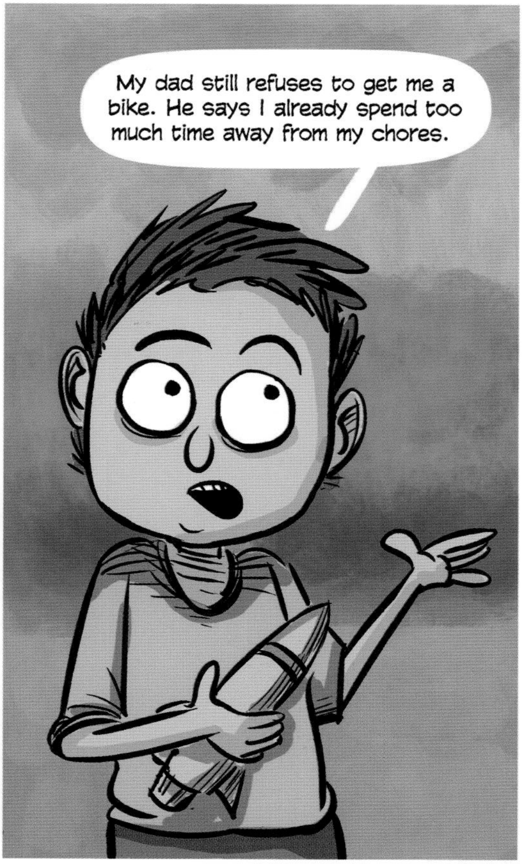
My dad still refuses to get me a bike. He says I already spend too much time away from my chores.

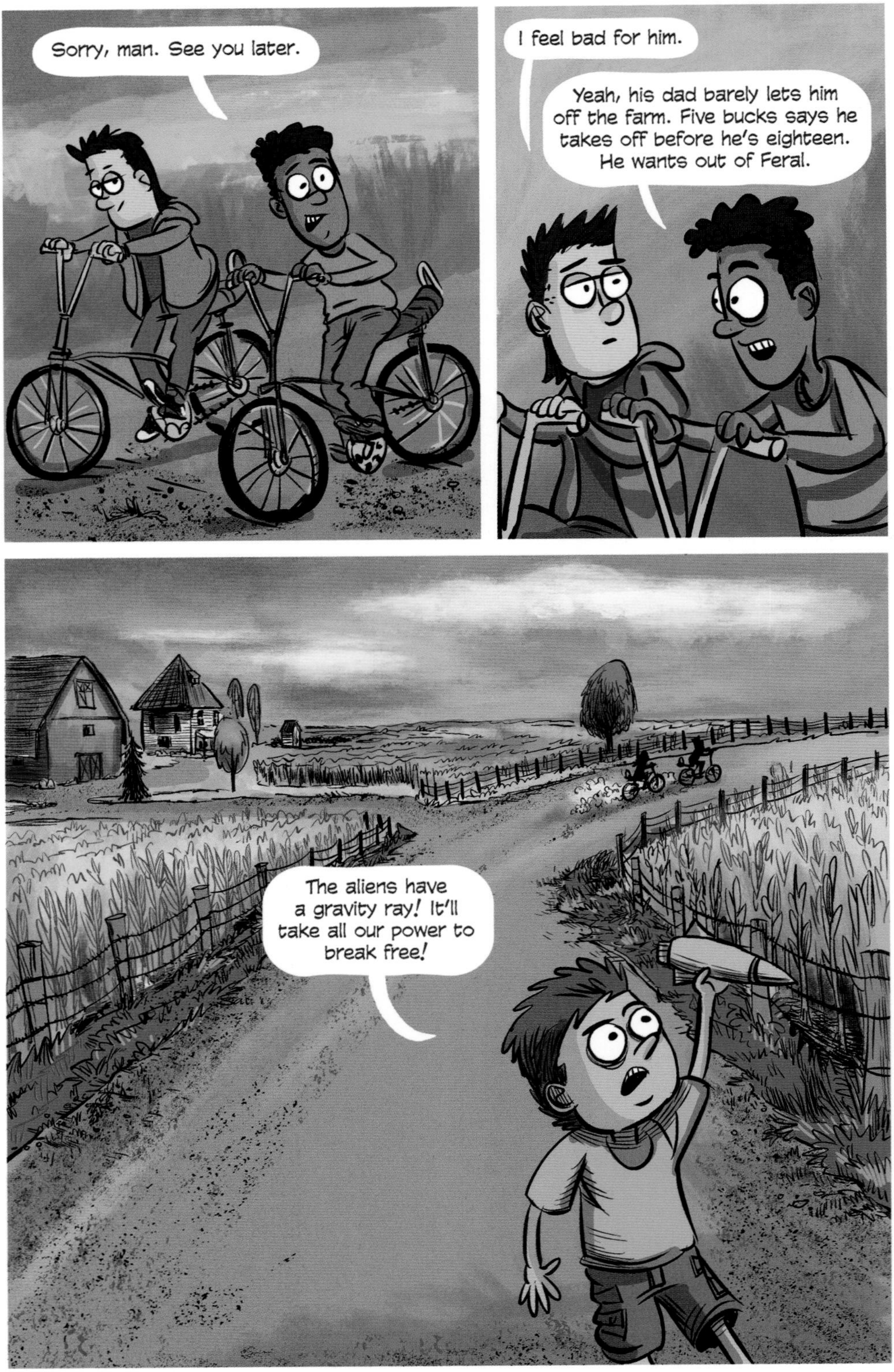
Sorry, man. See you later.
I feel bad for him.
Yeah, his dad barely lets him off the farm. Five bucks says he takes off before he's eighteen. He wants out of Feral.
The aliens have a gravity ray! It'll take all our power to break free!

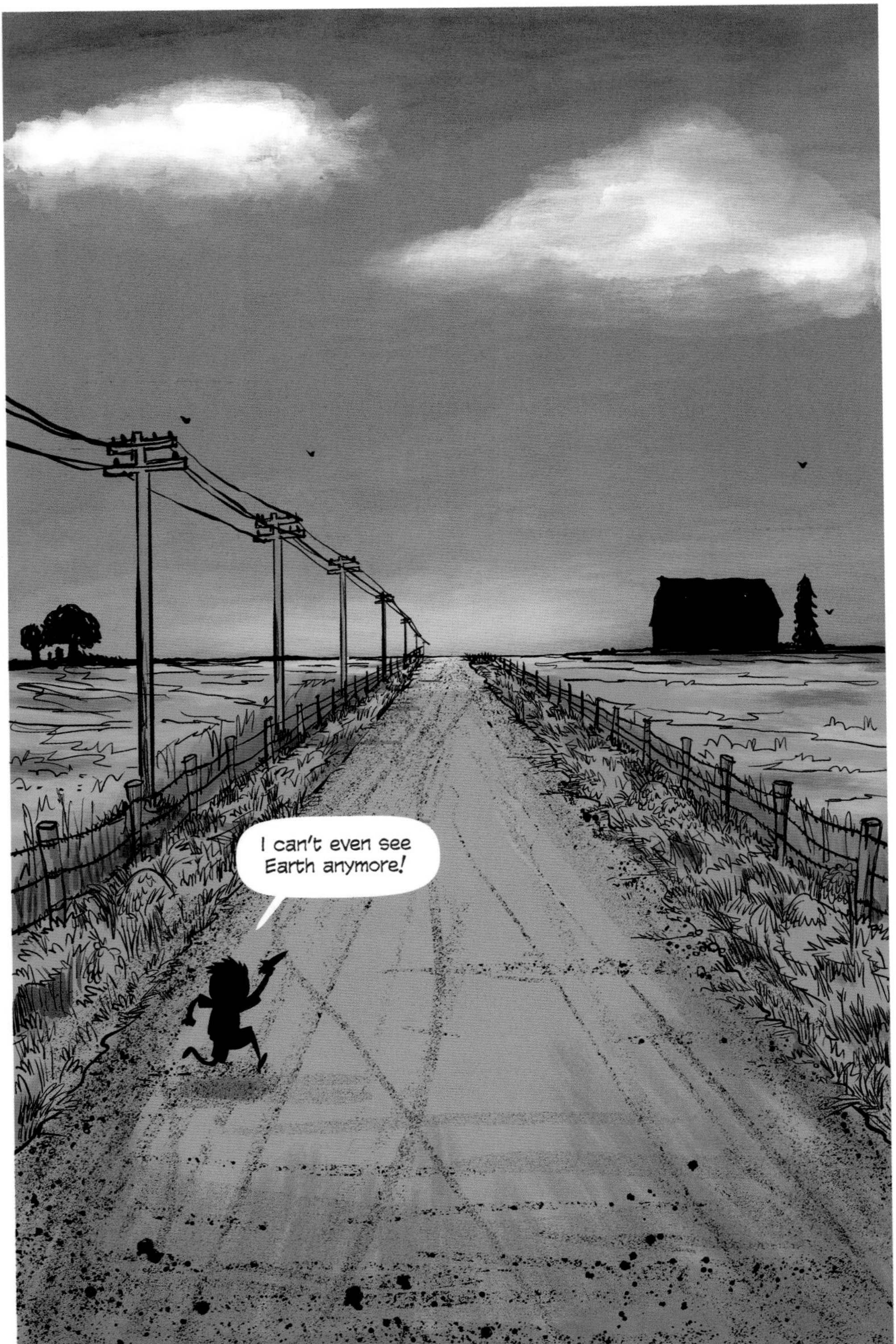
I can't even see Earth anymore!

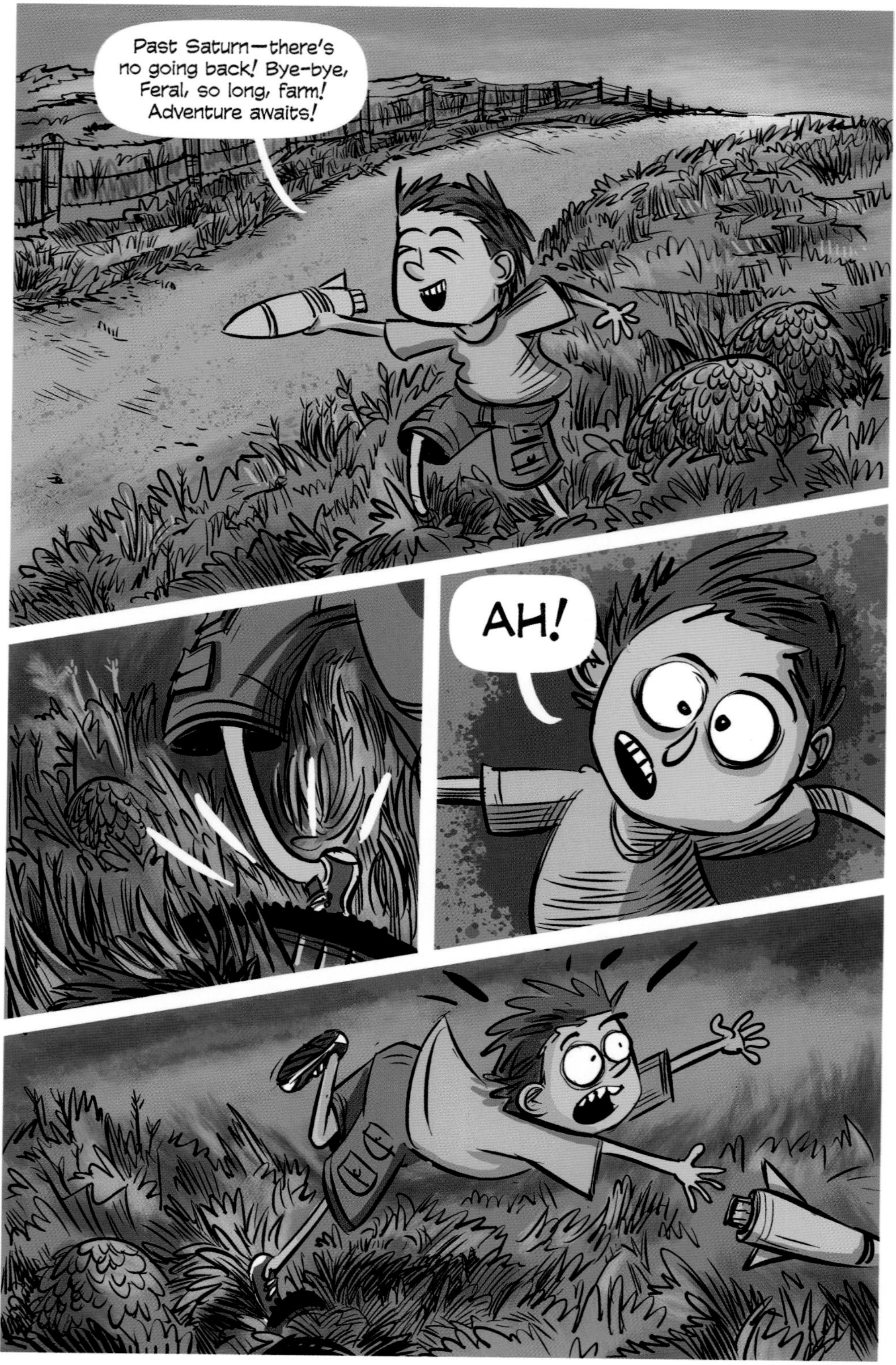
Past Saturn—there's no going back! Bye-bye, Feral, so long, farm! Adventure awaits!
AH!

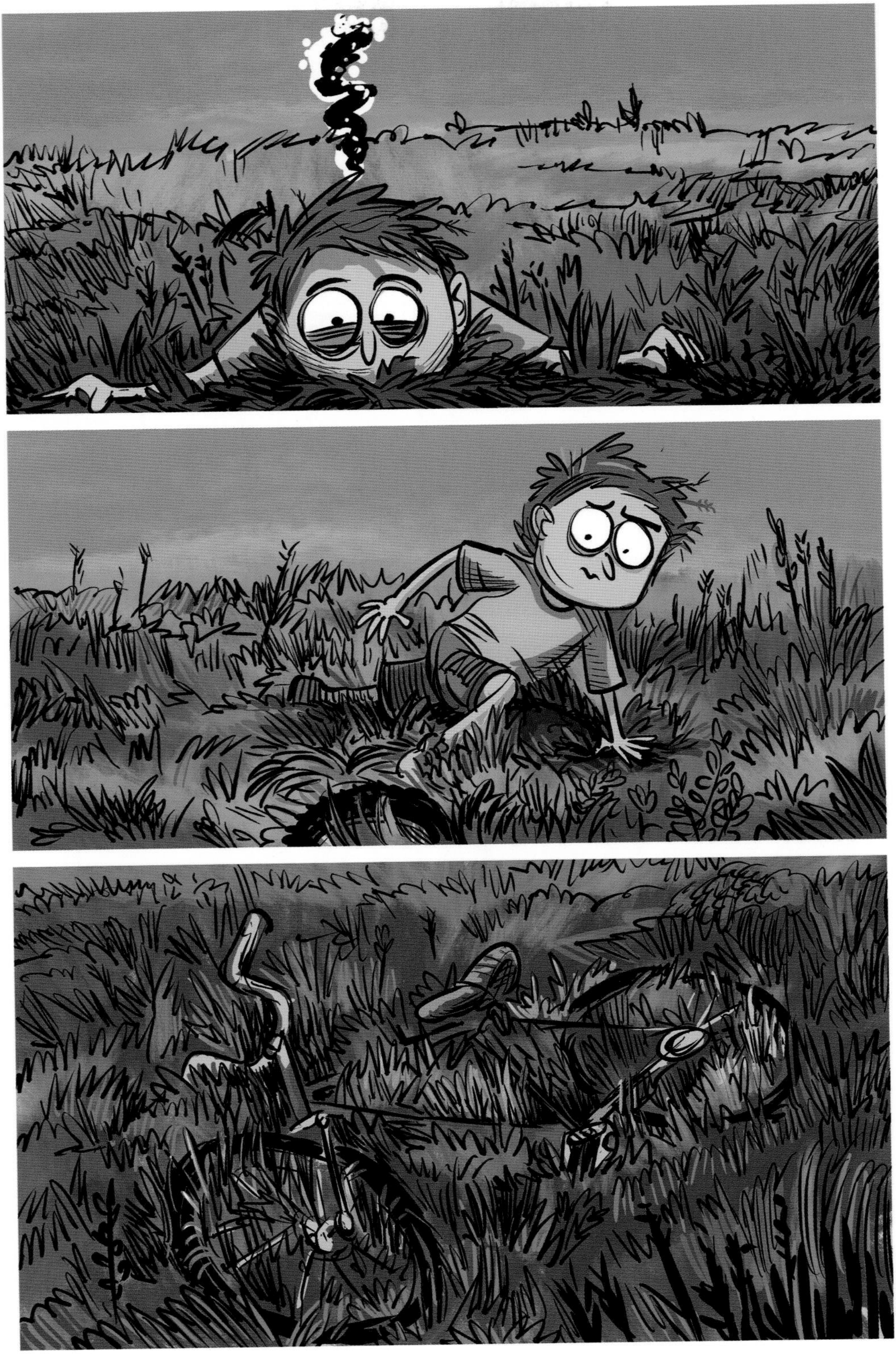

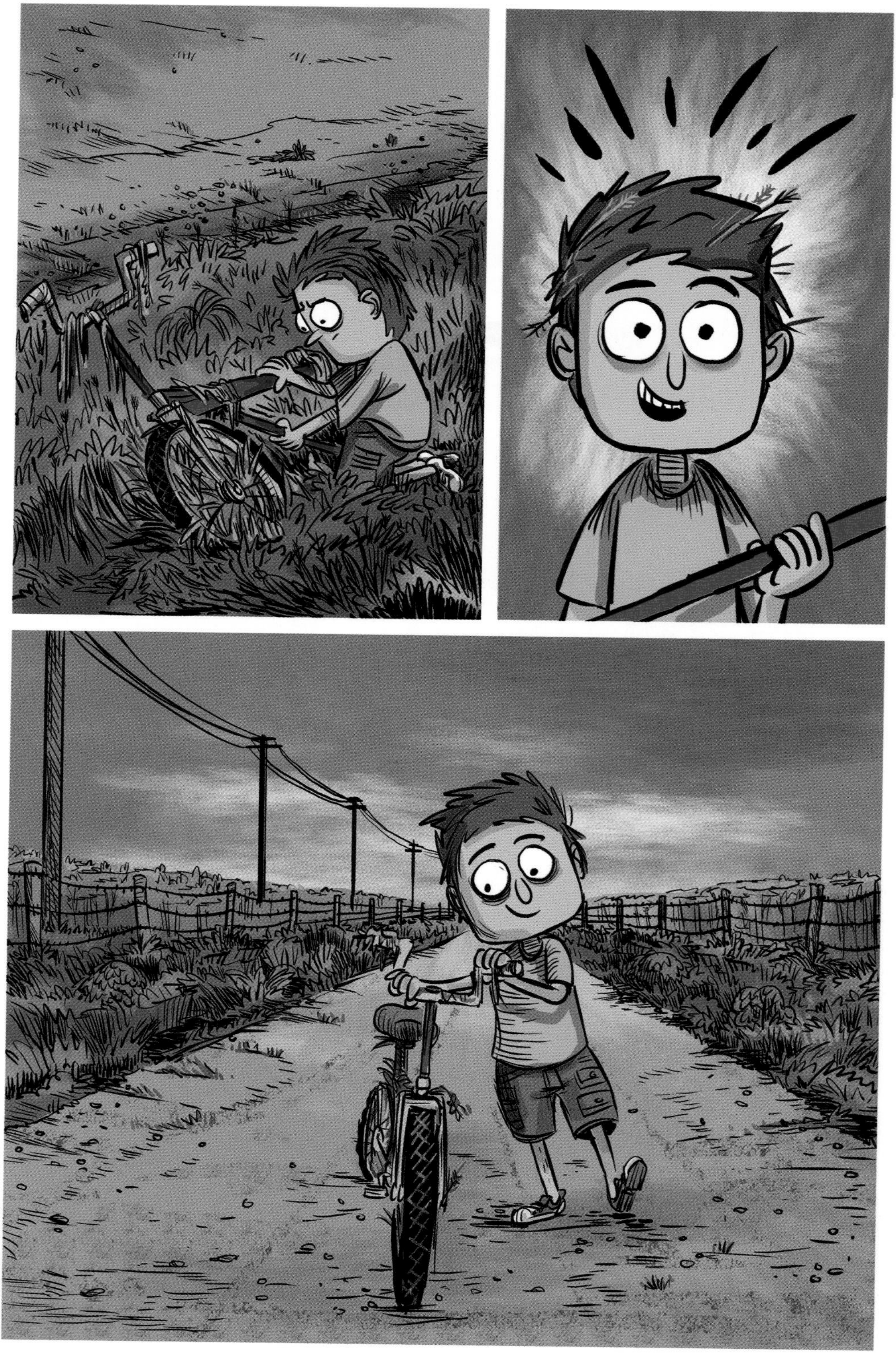

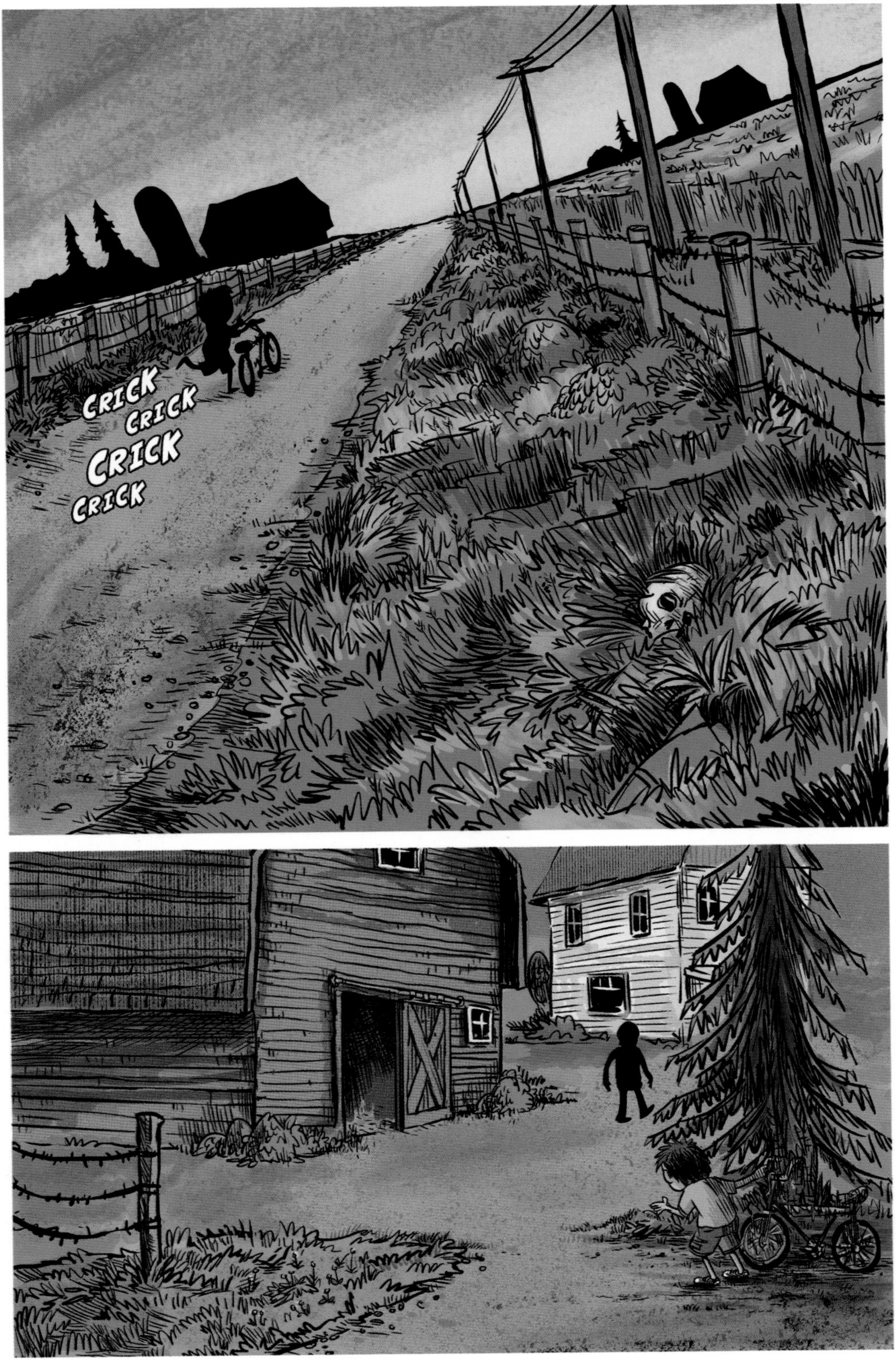
CRICK
CRICK
CRICK
CRICK

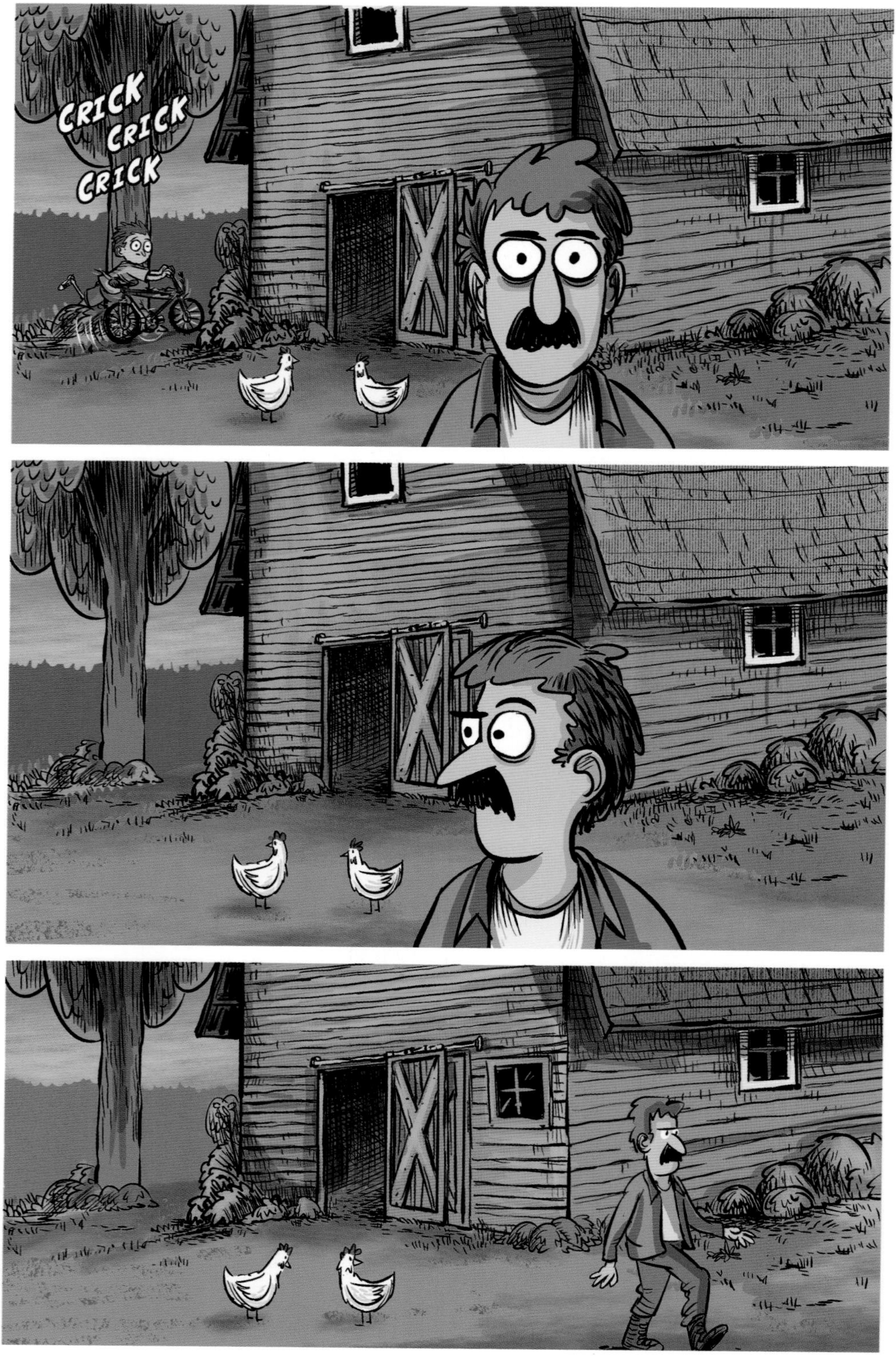
CRICK
CRICK
CRICK

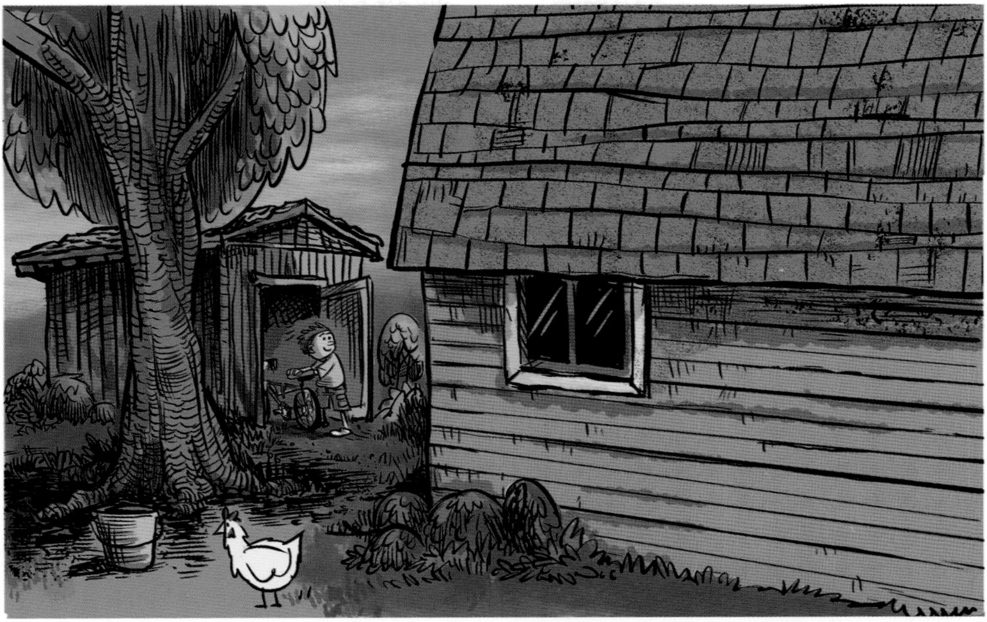

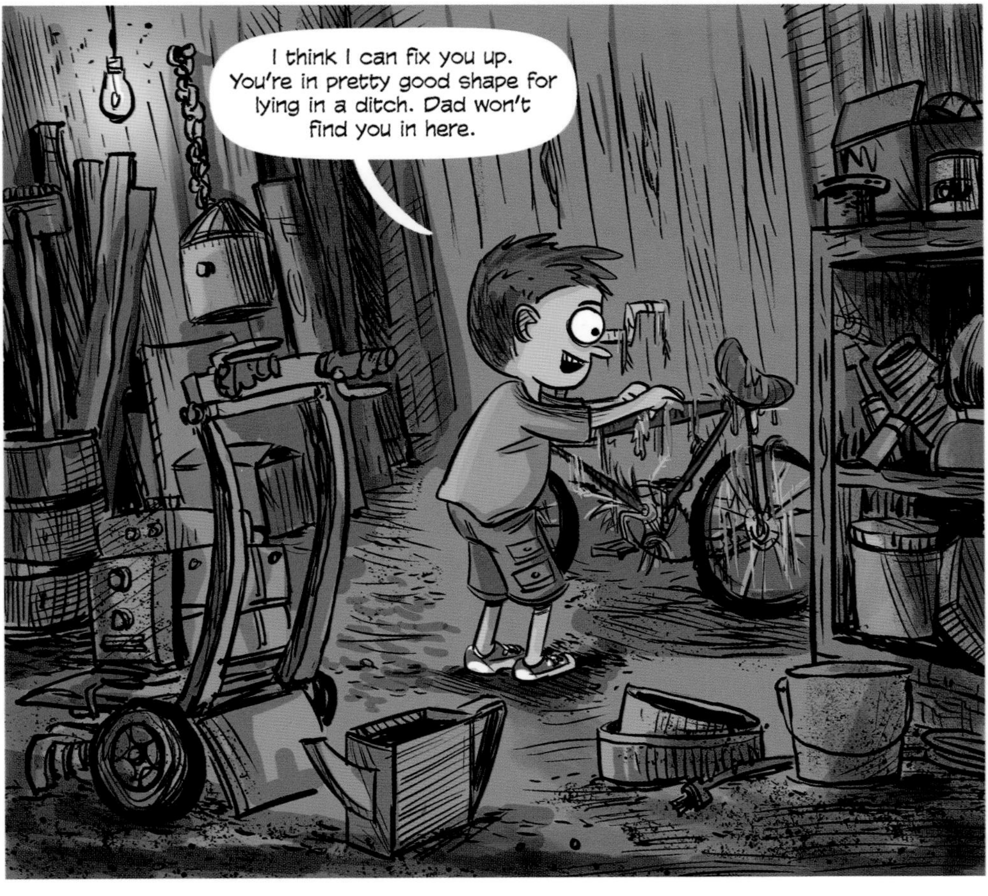
I think I can fix you up. You're in pretty good shape for lying in a ditch. Dad won't find you in here.

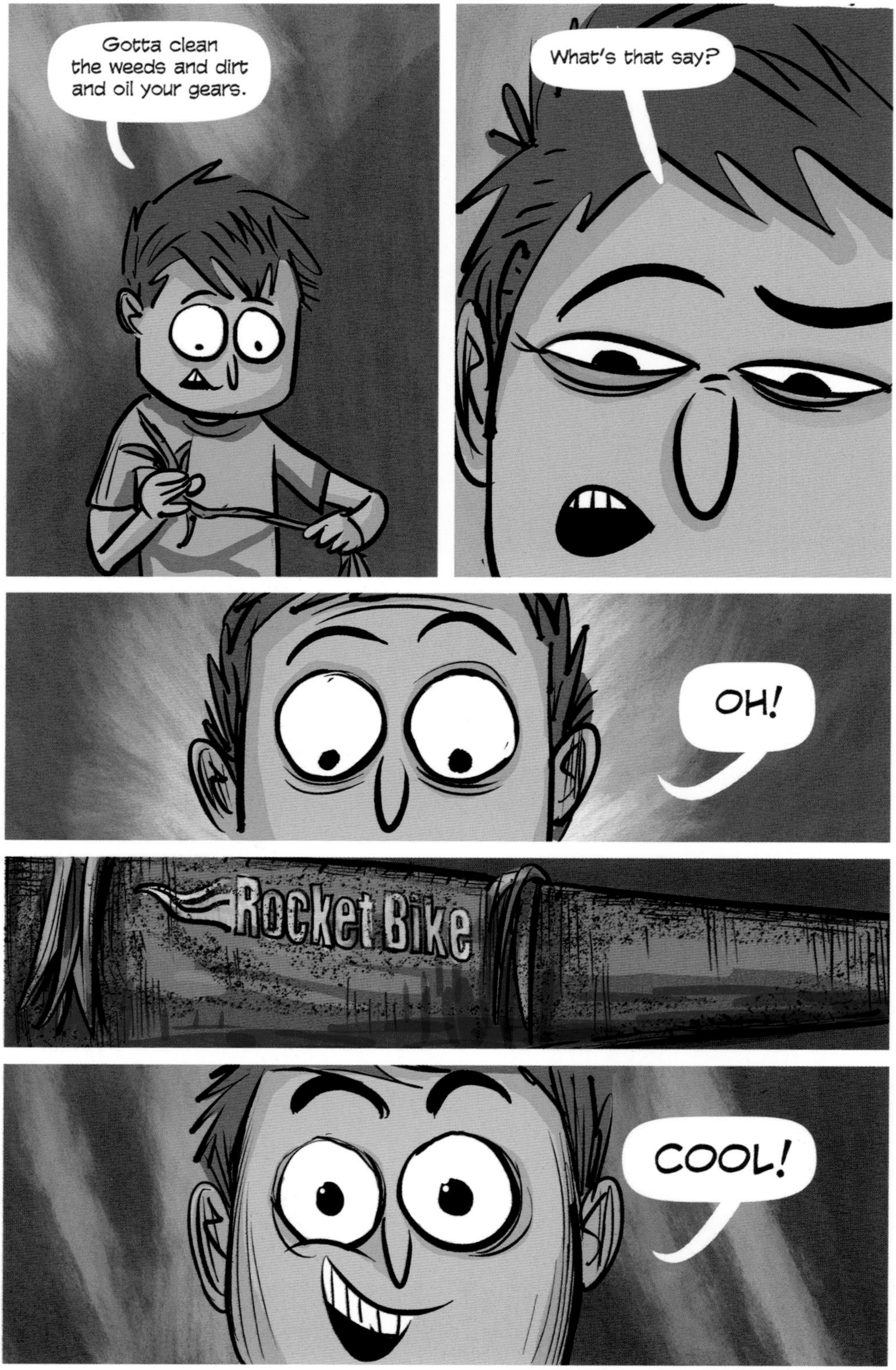
Gotta clean the weeds and dirt and oil your gears.
What's that say?
OH!
Rocket Bike
COOL!

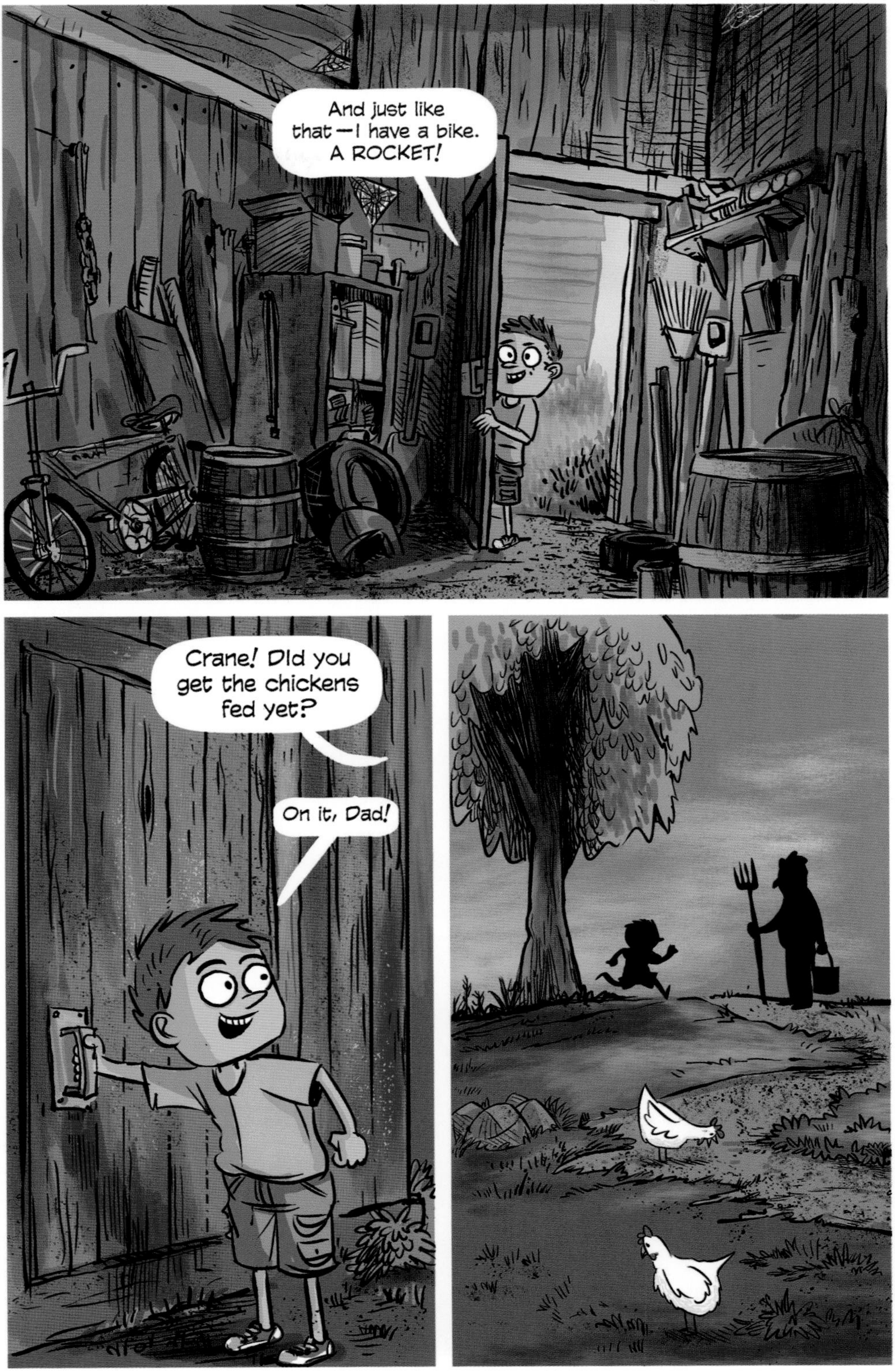
And just like that—I have a bike. A ROCKET!
Crane! Did you get the chickens fed yet?
On it, Dad!

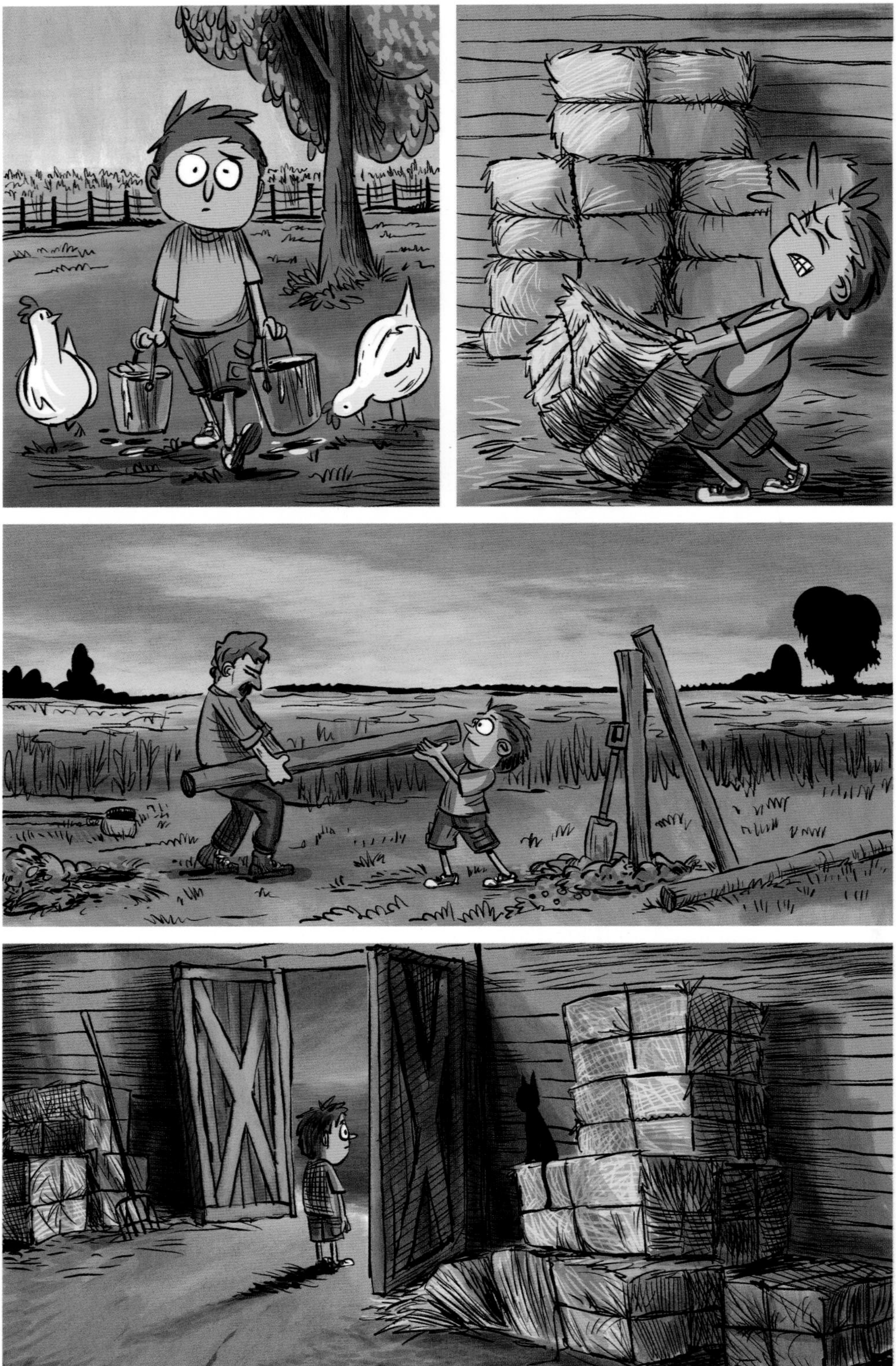

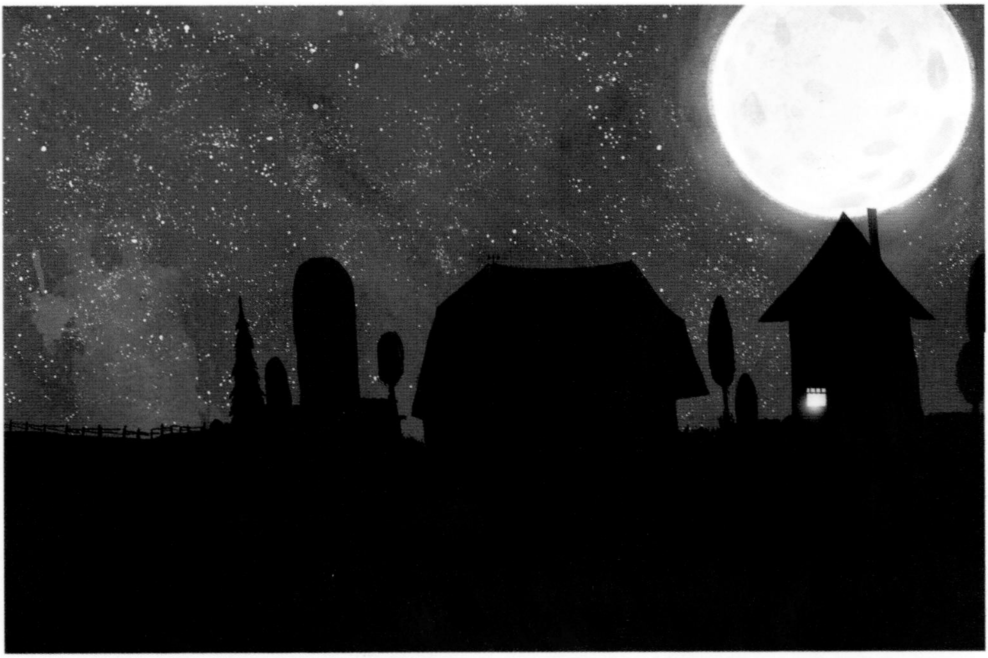

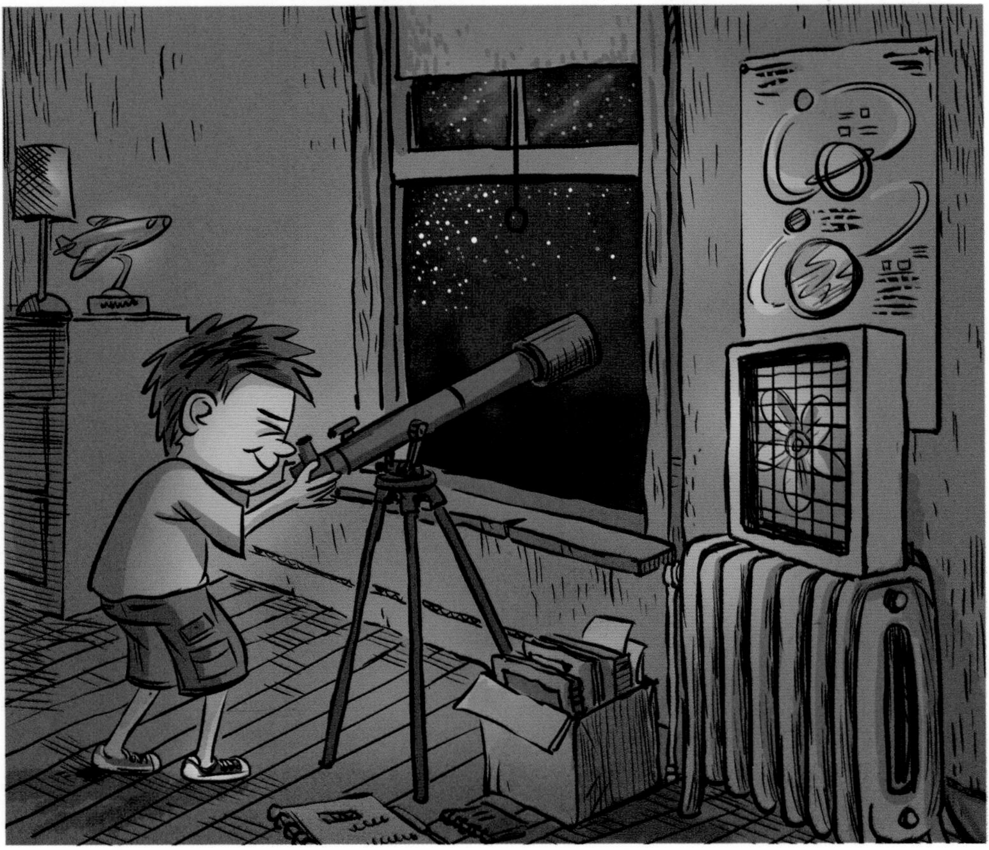

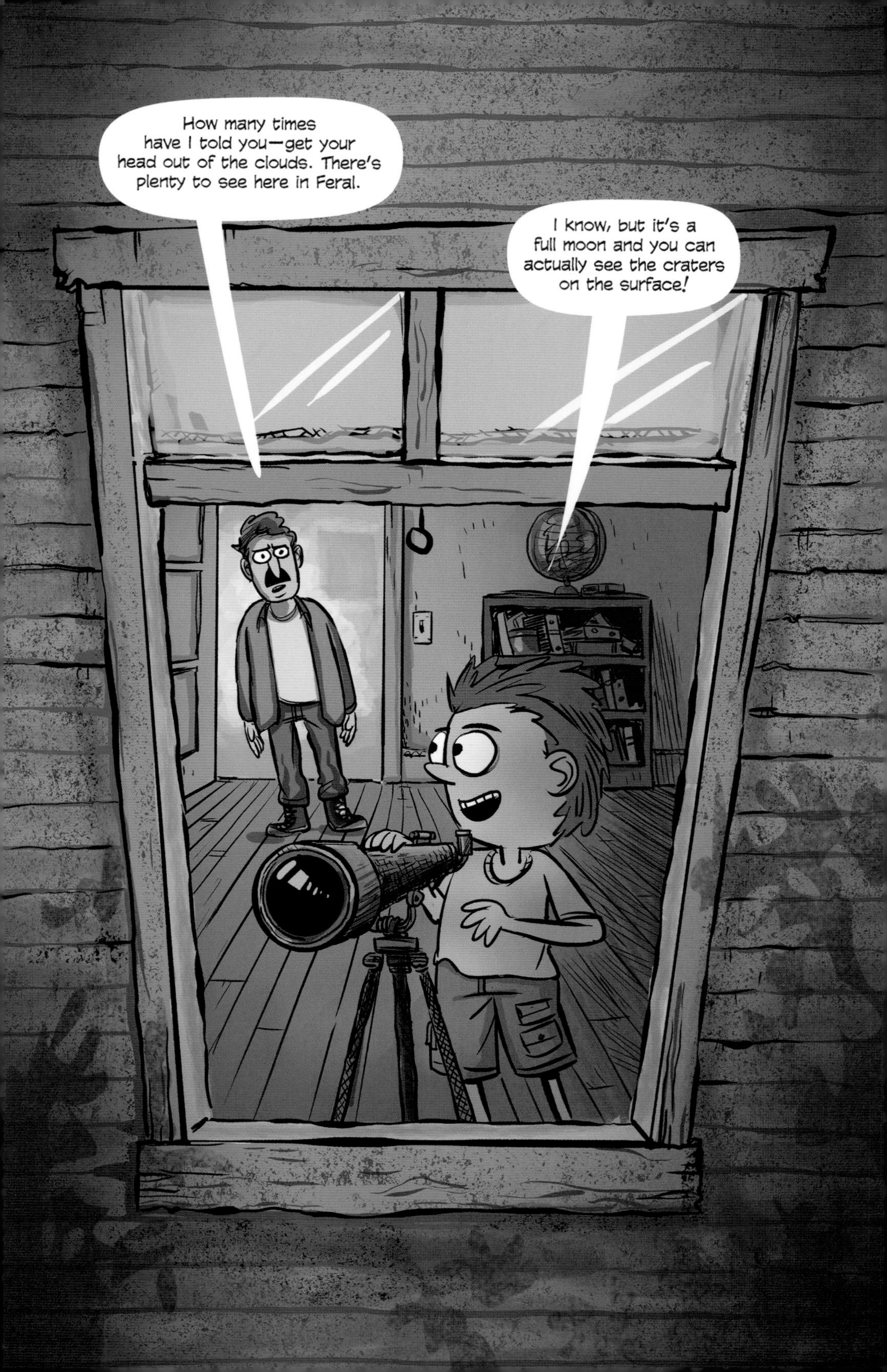
How many times have I told you—get your head out of the clouds. There's plenty to see here in Feral.
I know, but it's a full moon and you can actually see the craters on the surface!

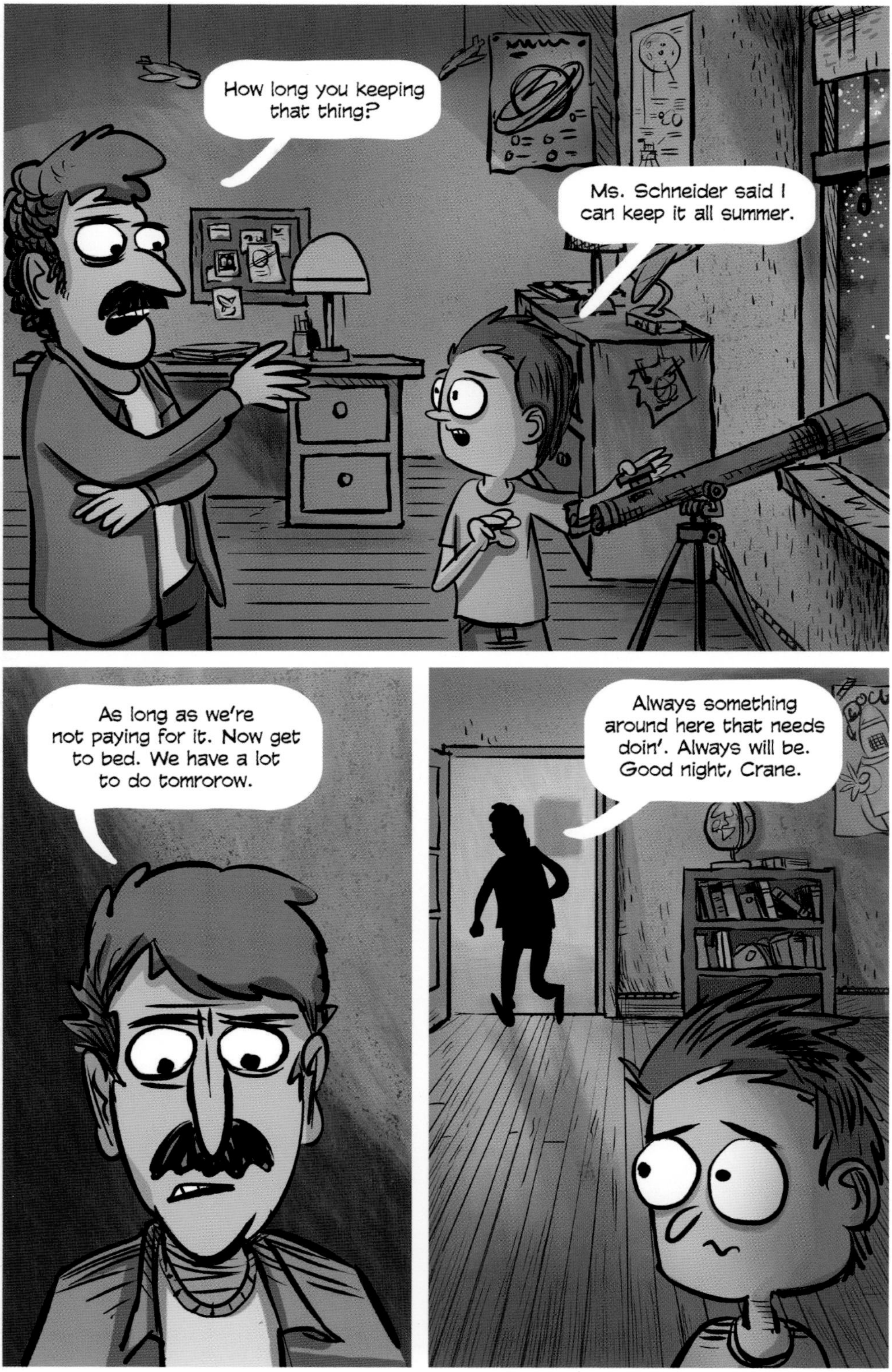
How long you keeping that thing?
Ms. Schneider said I can keep it all summer.
As long as we're not paying for it. Now get to bed. We have a lot to do tomrorow.
Always something around here that needs doin'. Always will be. Good night, Crane.

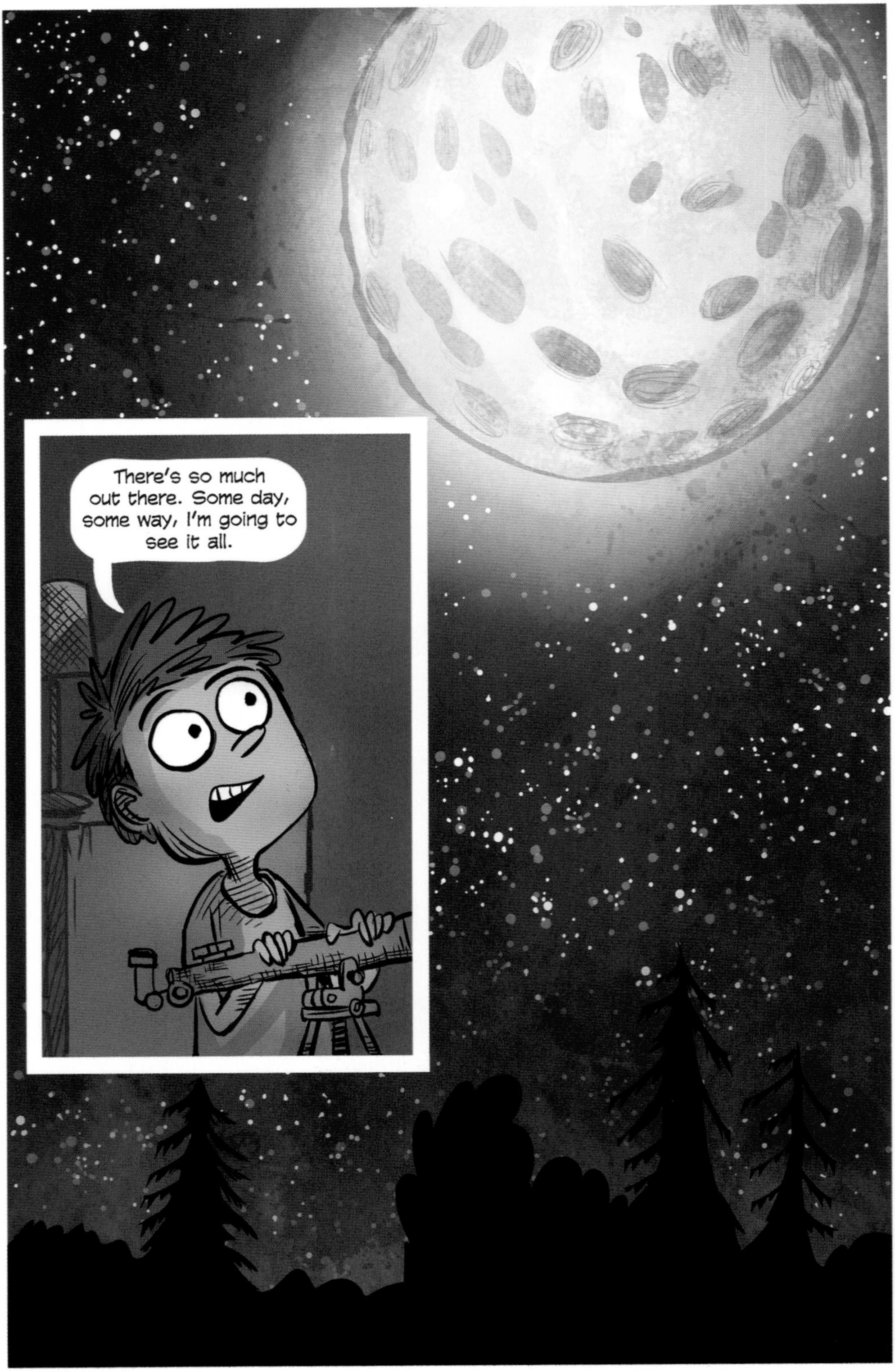
There's so much out there. Some day, some way, I'm going to see it all.

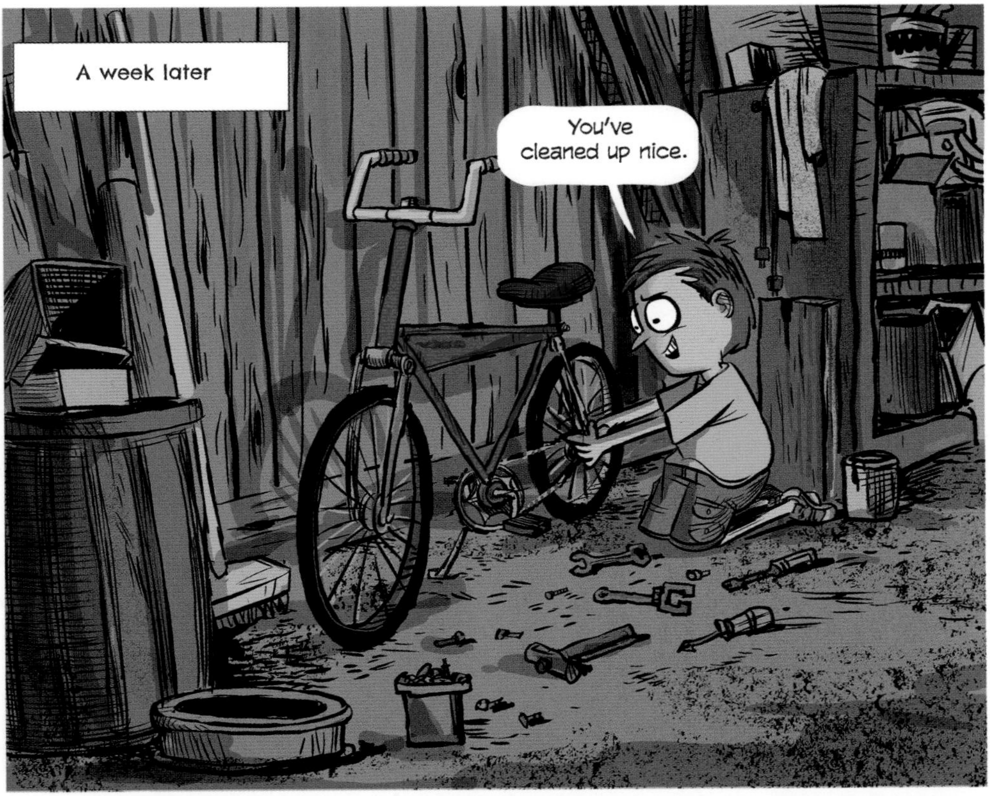
A week later
You've cleaned up nice.

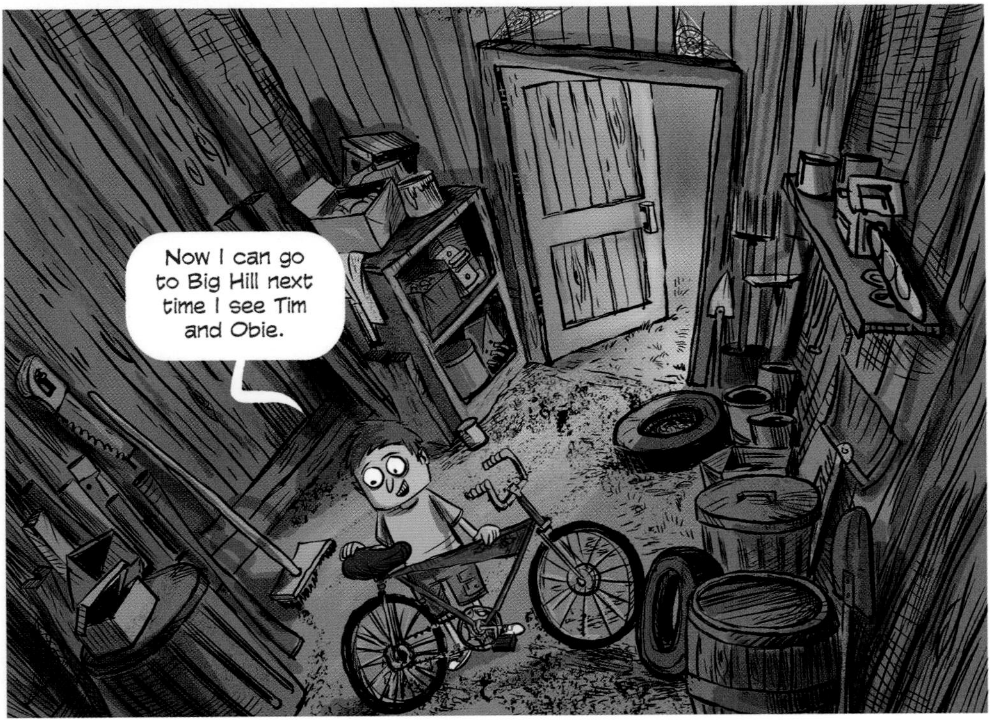
Now I can go to Big Hill next time I see Tim and Obie.

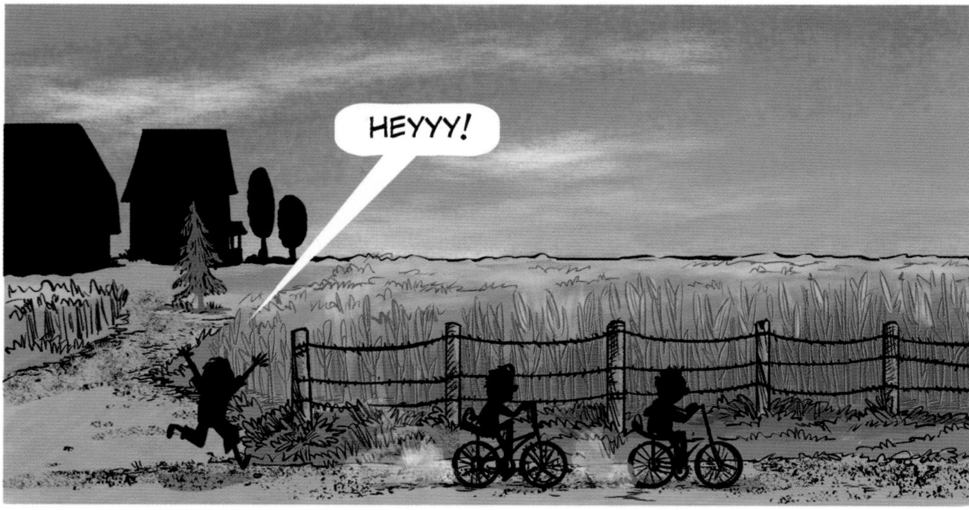
HEYYY!

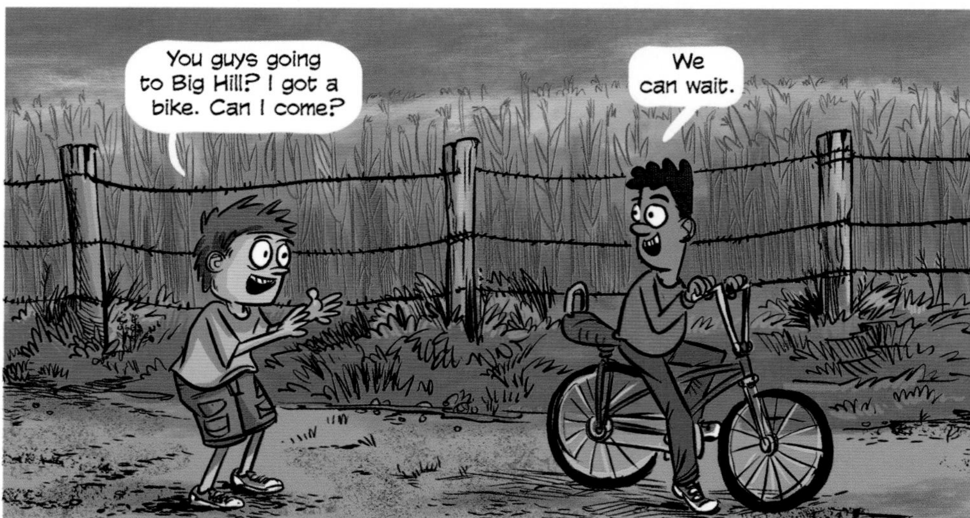
You guys going to Big Hill? I got a bike. Can I come?
We can wait.

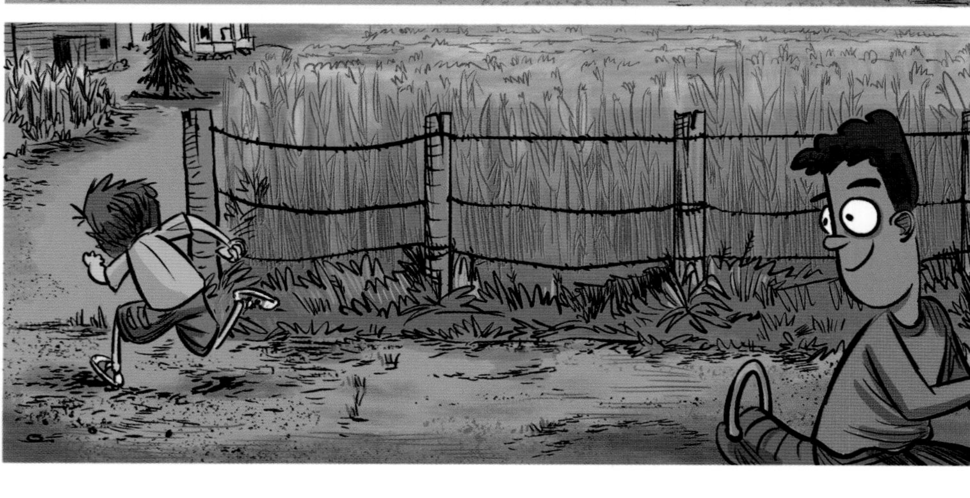

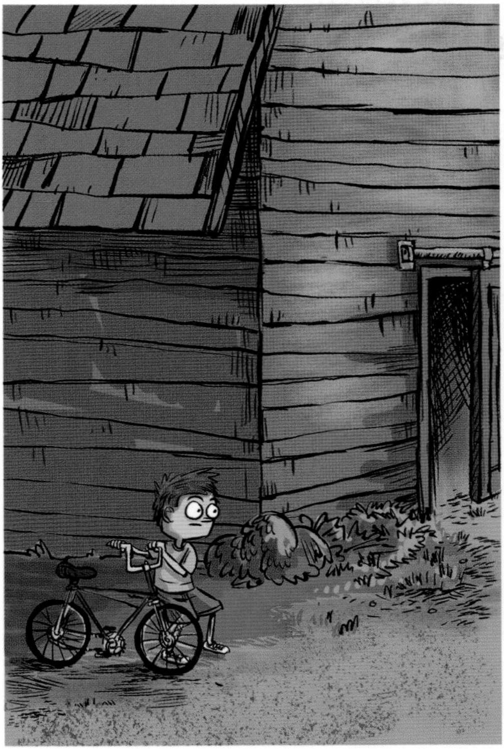

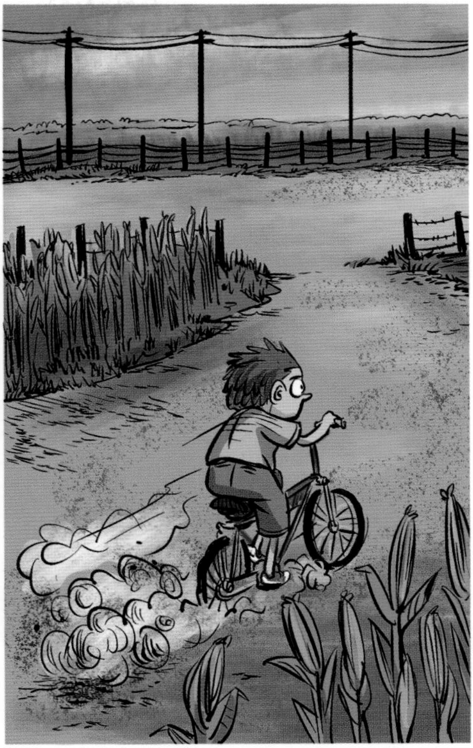

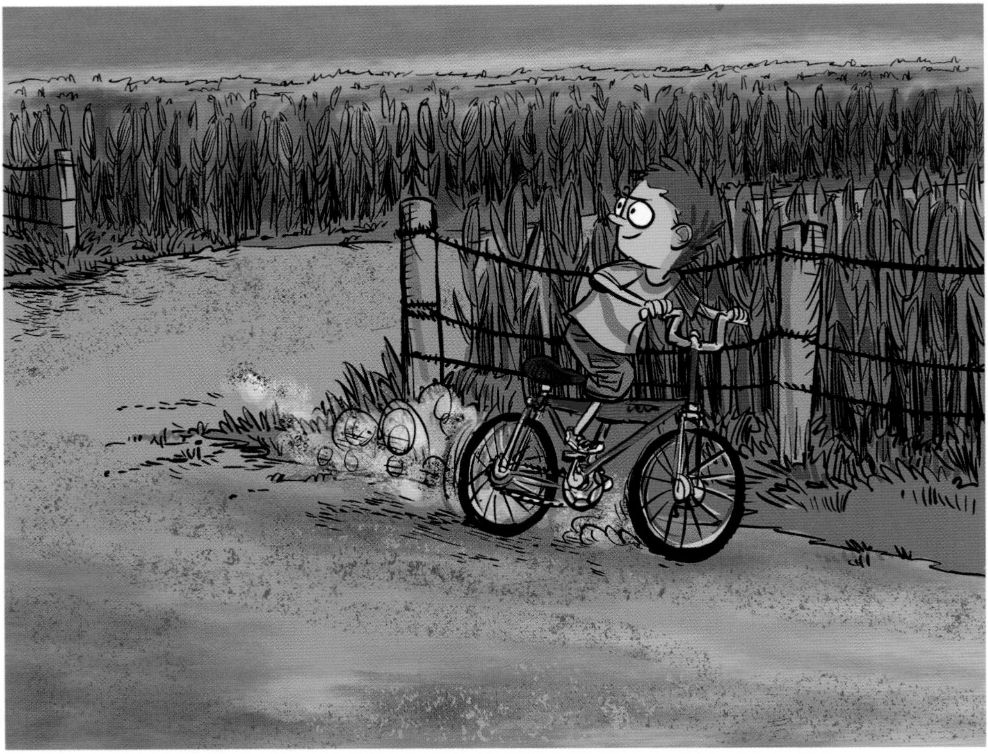

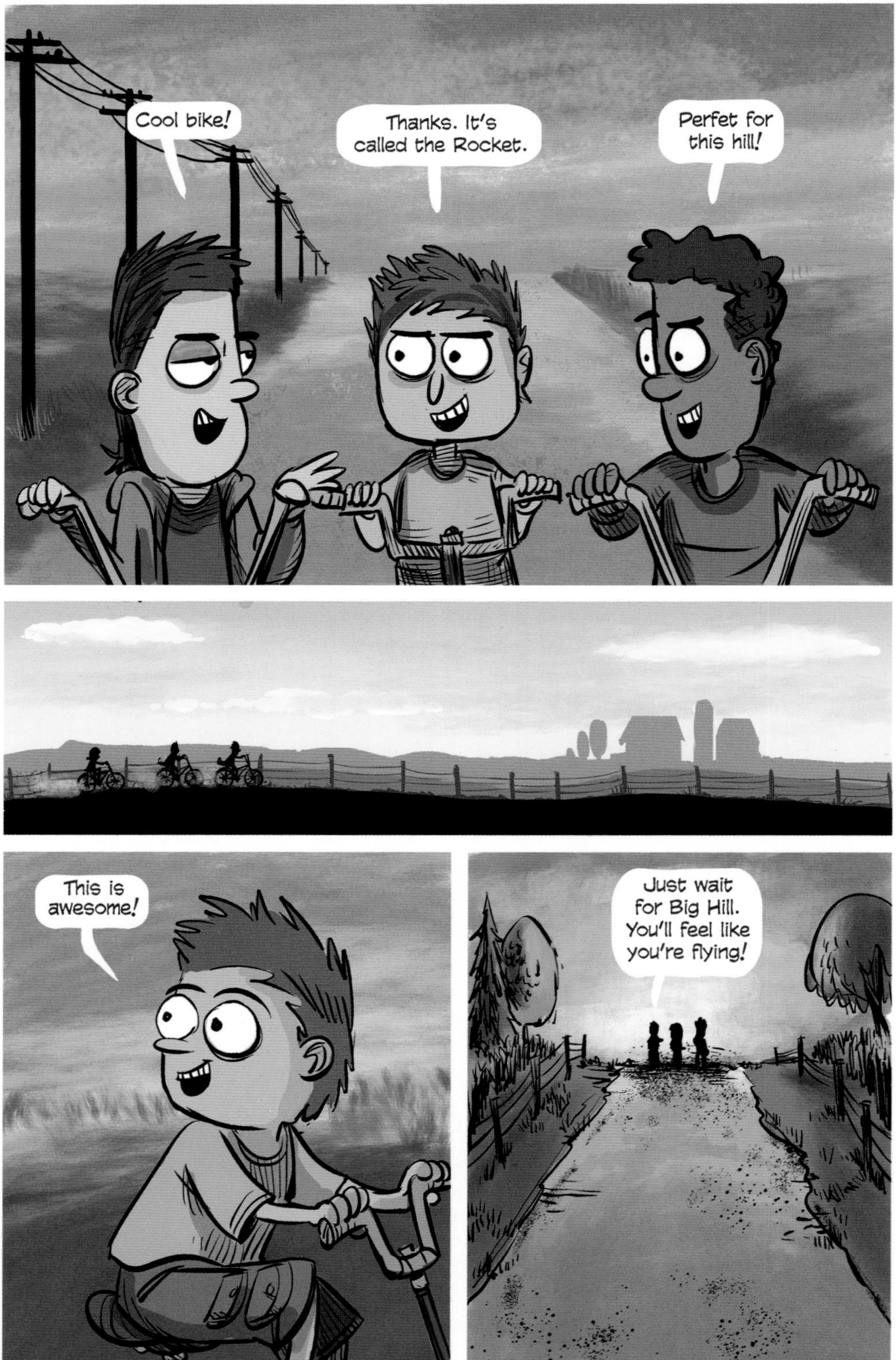
Cool bike!
Thanks. It's called the Rocket.
Perfet for this hill!
This is awesome!
Just wait for Big Hill. You'll feel like you're flying!

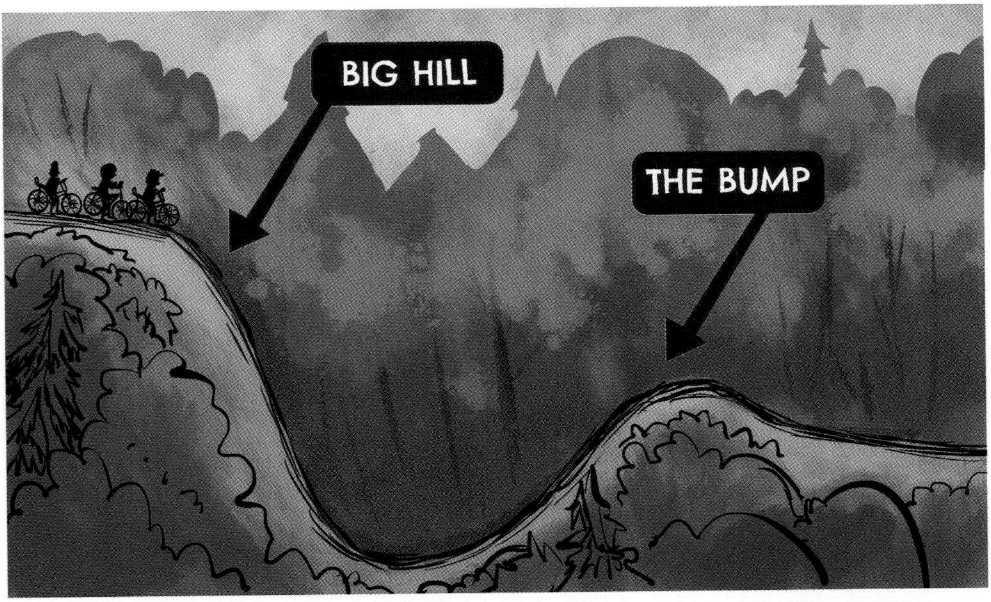
BIG HILL
THE BUMP

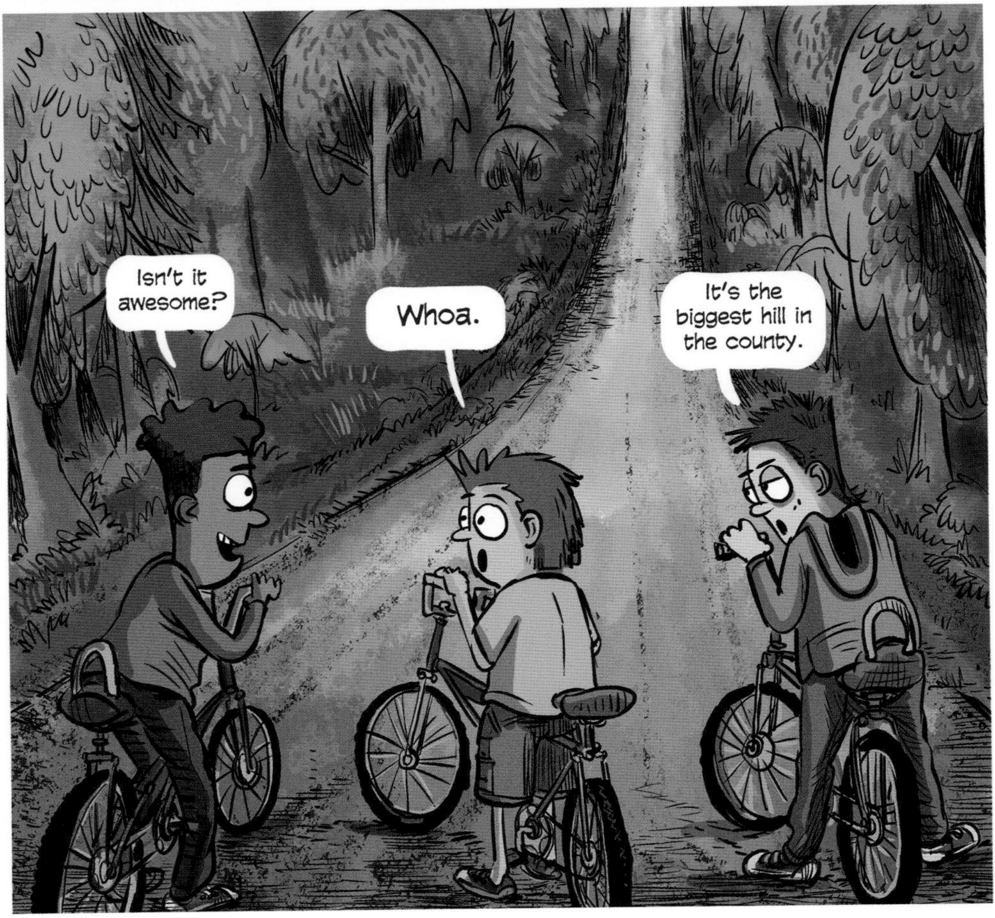
Isn't it awesome?
Whoa.
It's the biggest hill in the county.

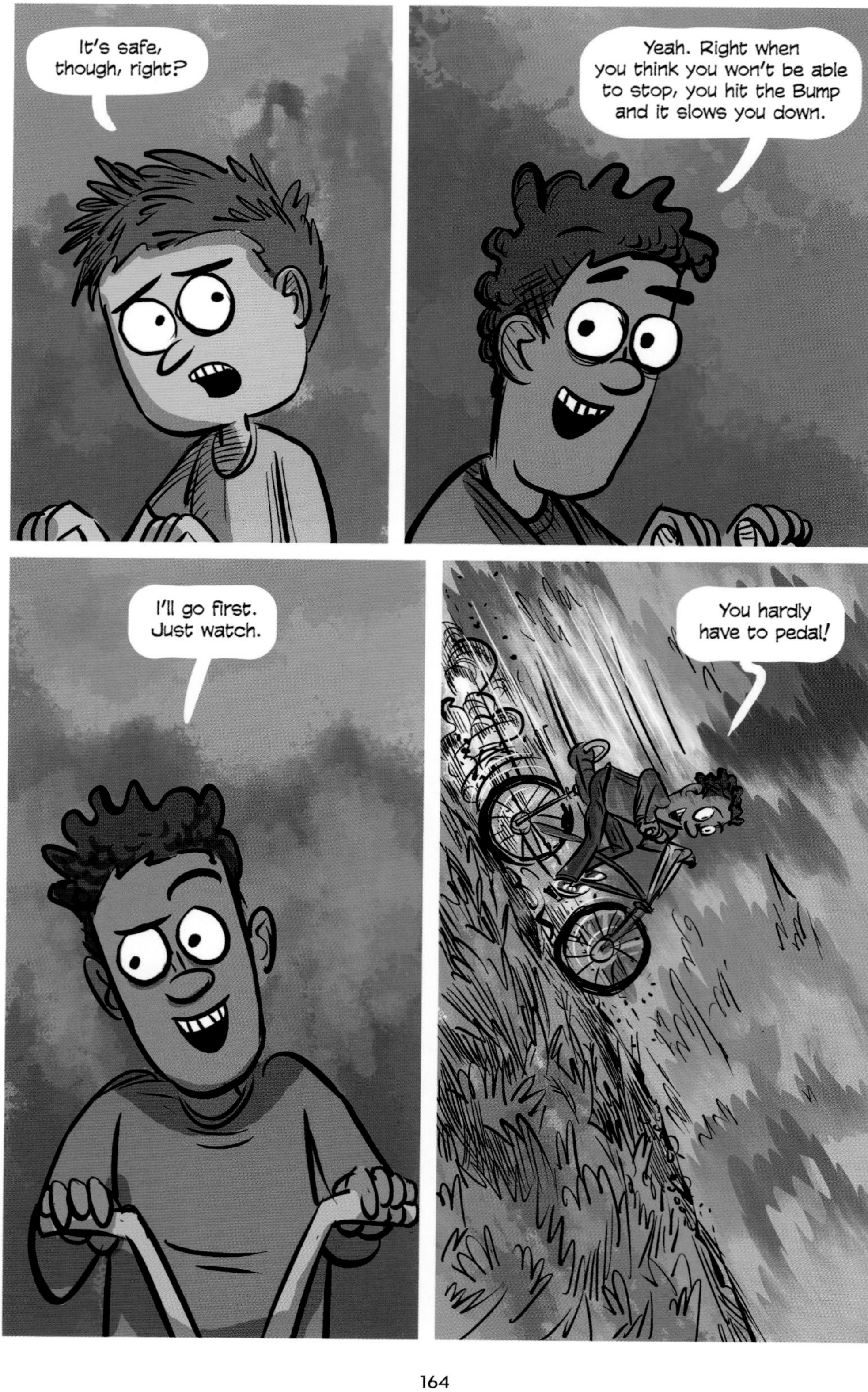
It's safe, though, right?
Yeah. Right when you think you won't be able to stop, you hit the Bump and it slows you down.
I'll go first. Just watch.
You hardly have to pedal!

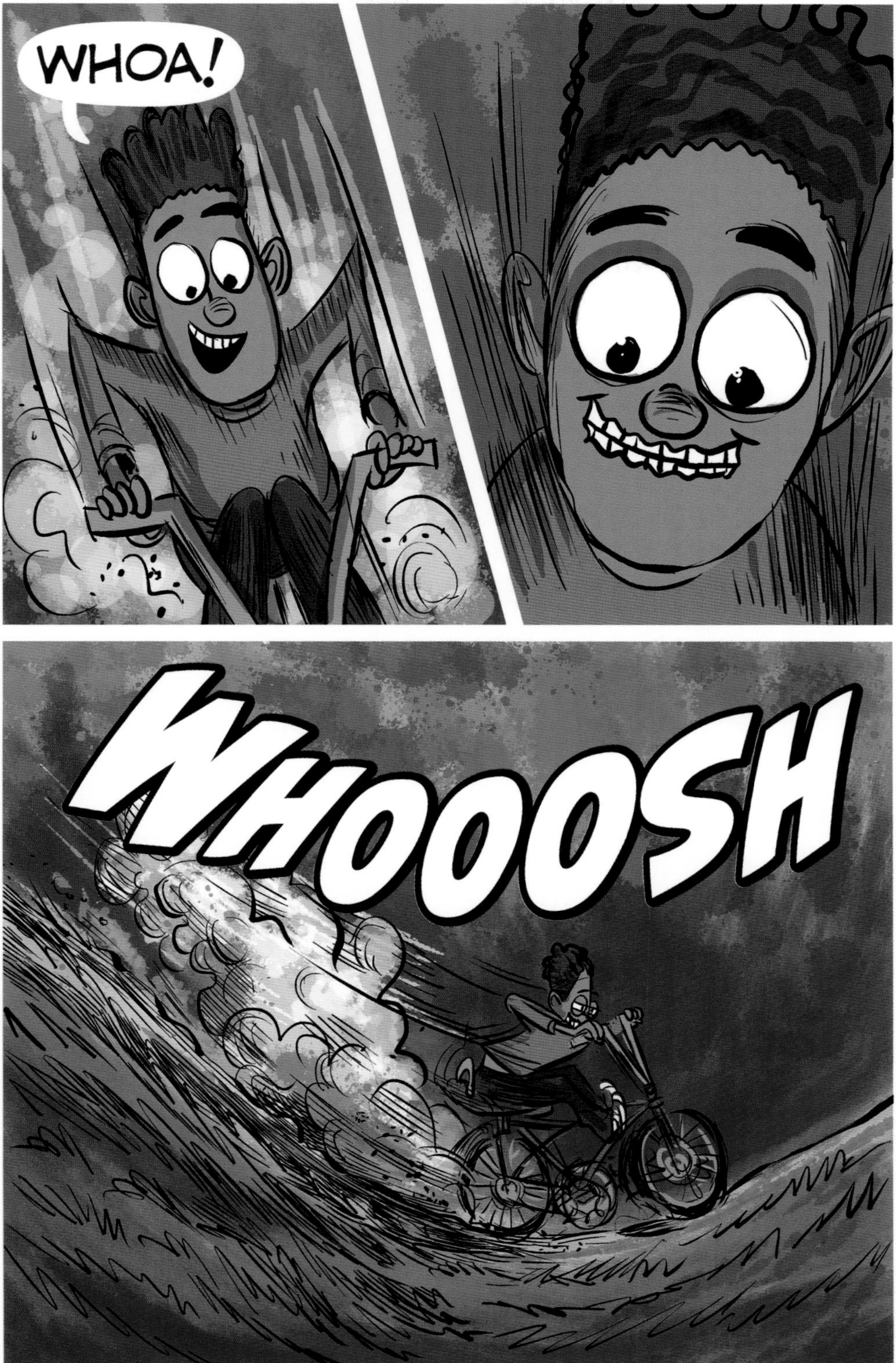
WHOA!
WHOOOSH

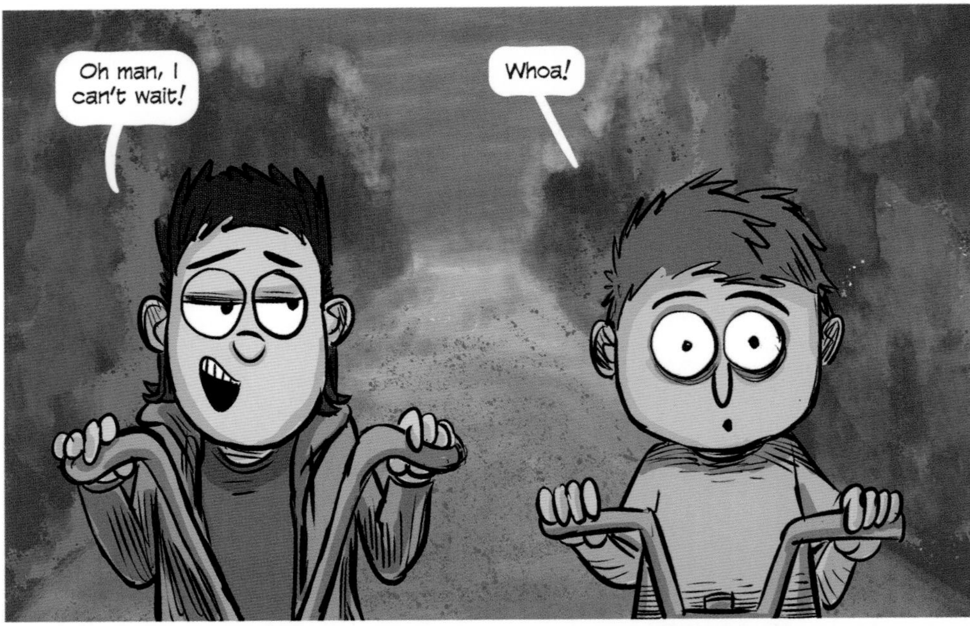
Oh man, I can't wait!
Whoa!

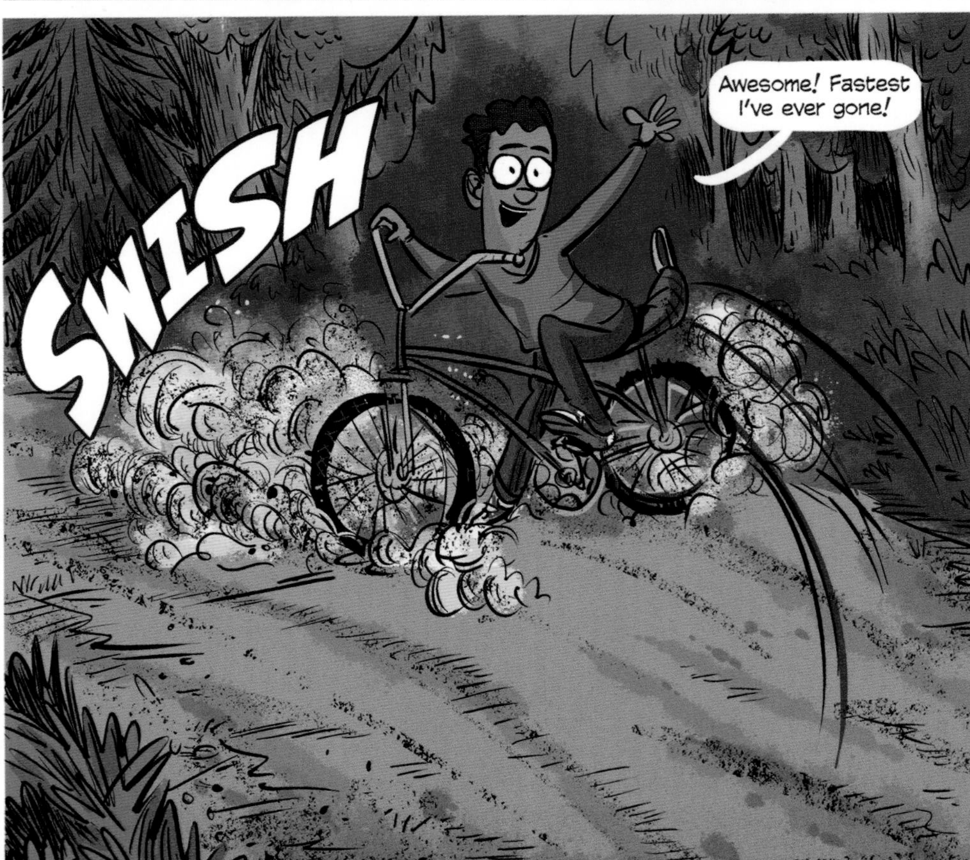
SWISH
Awesome! Fastest I've ever gone!

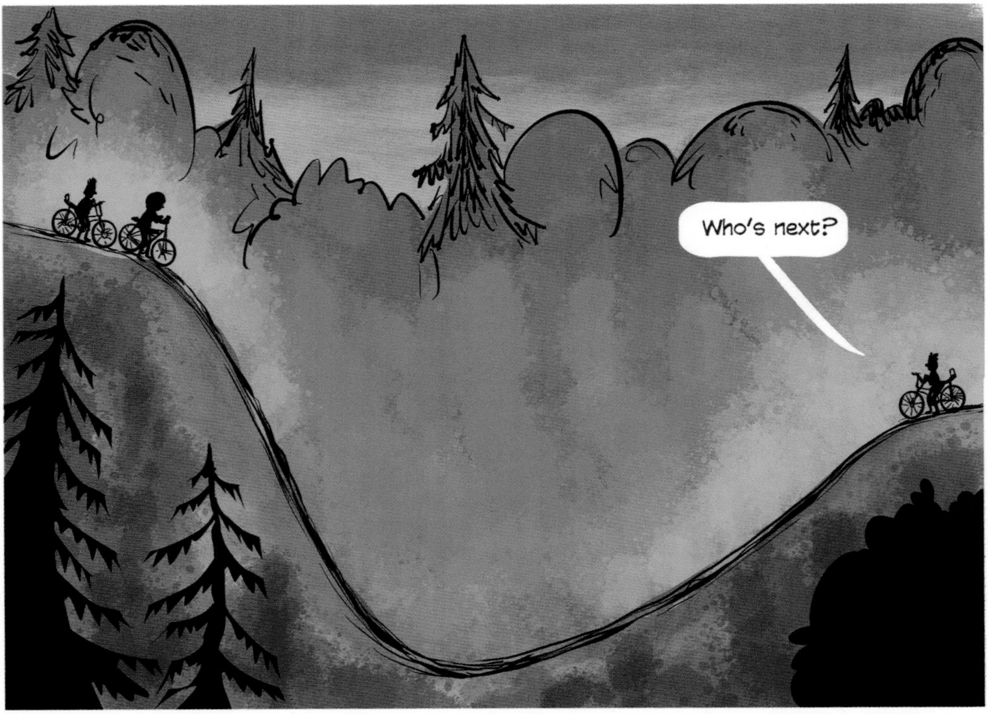
Who's next?

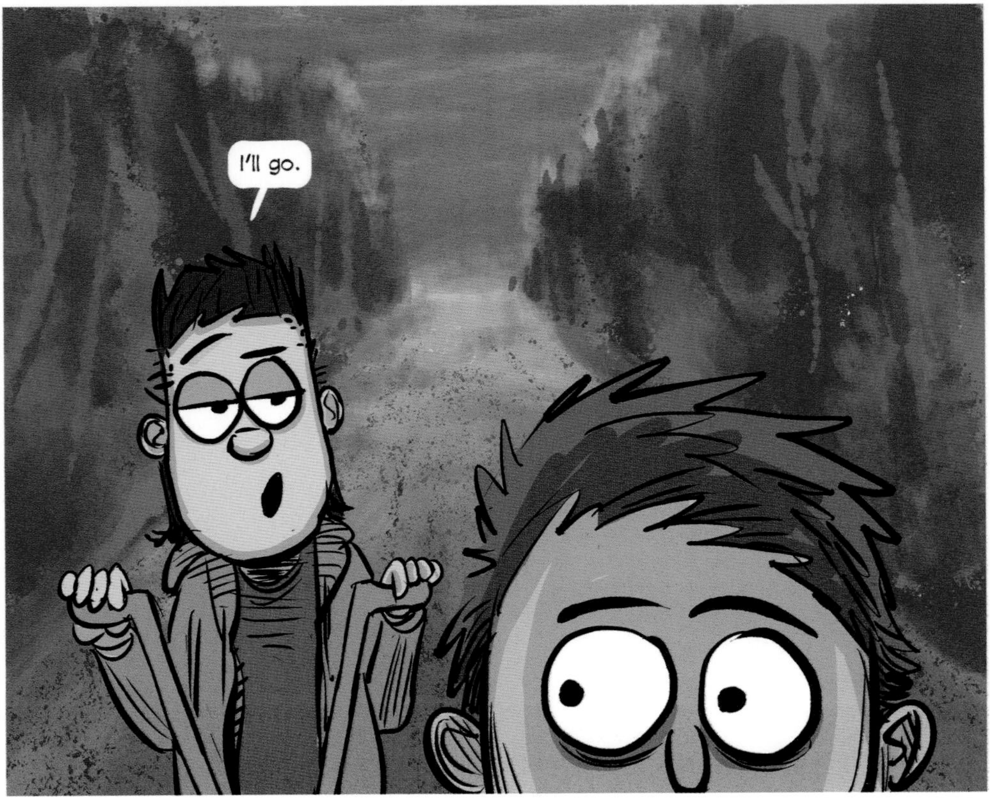
I'll go.

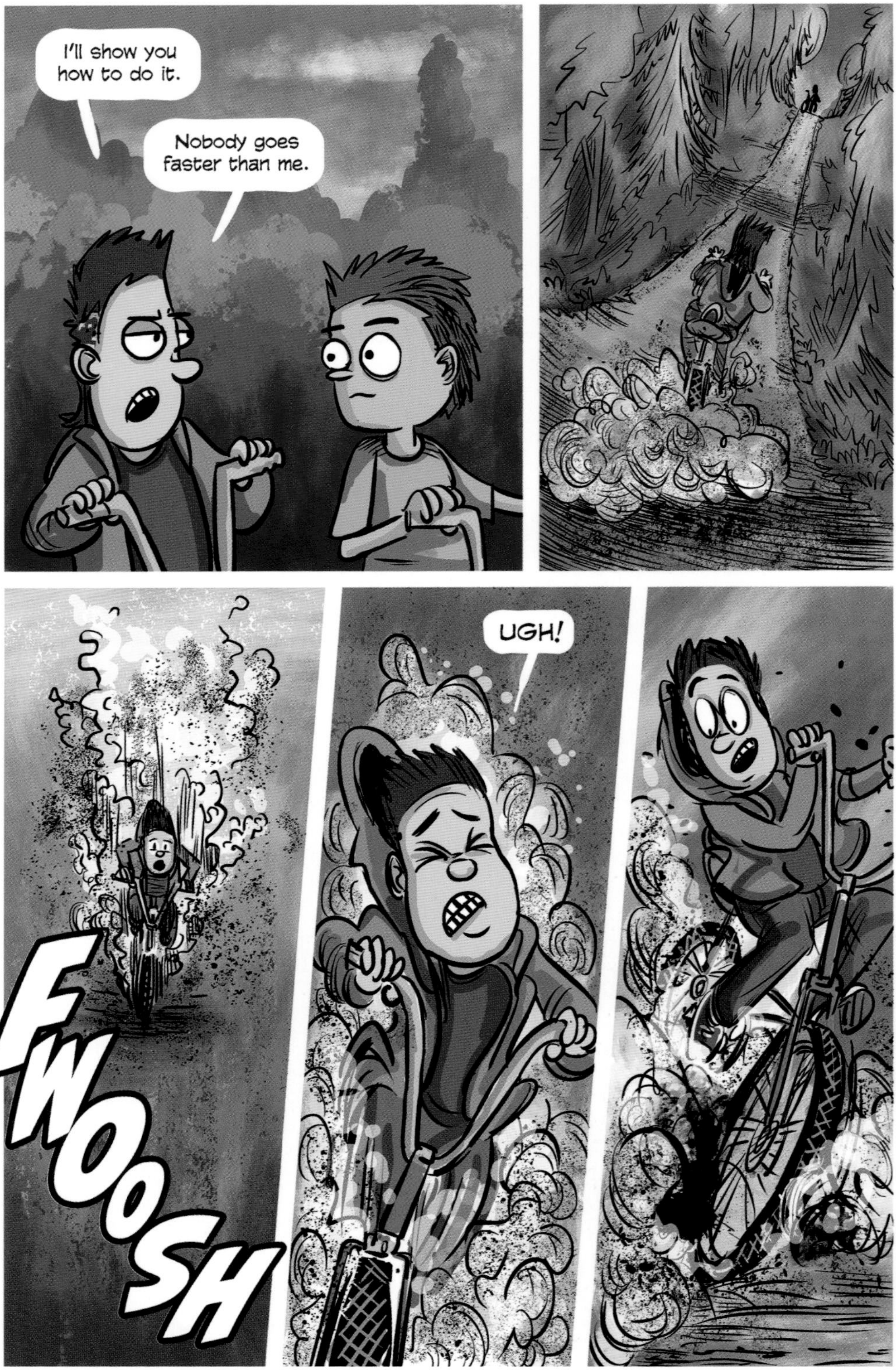
I'll show you how to do it.
Nobody goes faster than me.
FWOOSH
UGH!

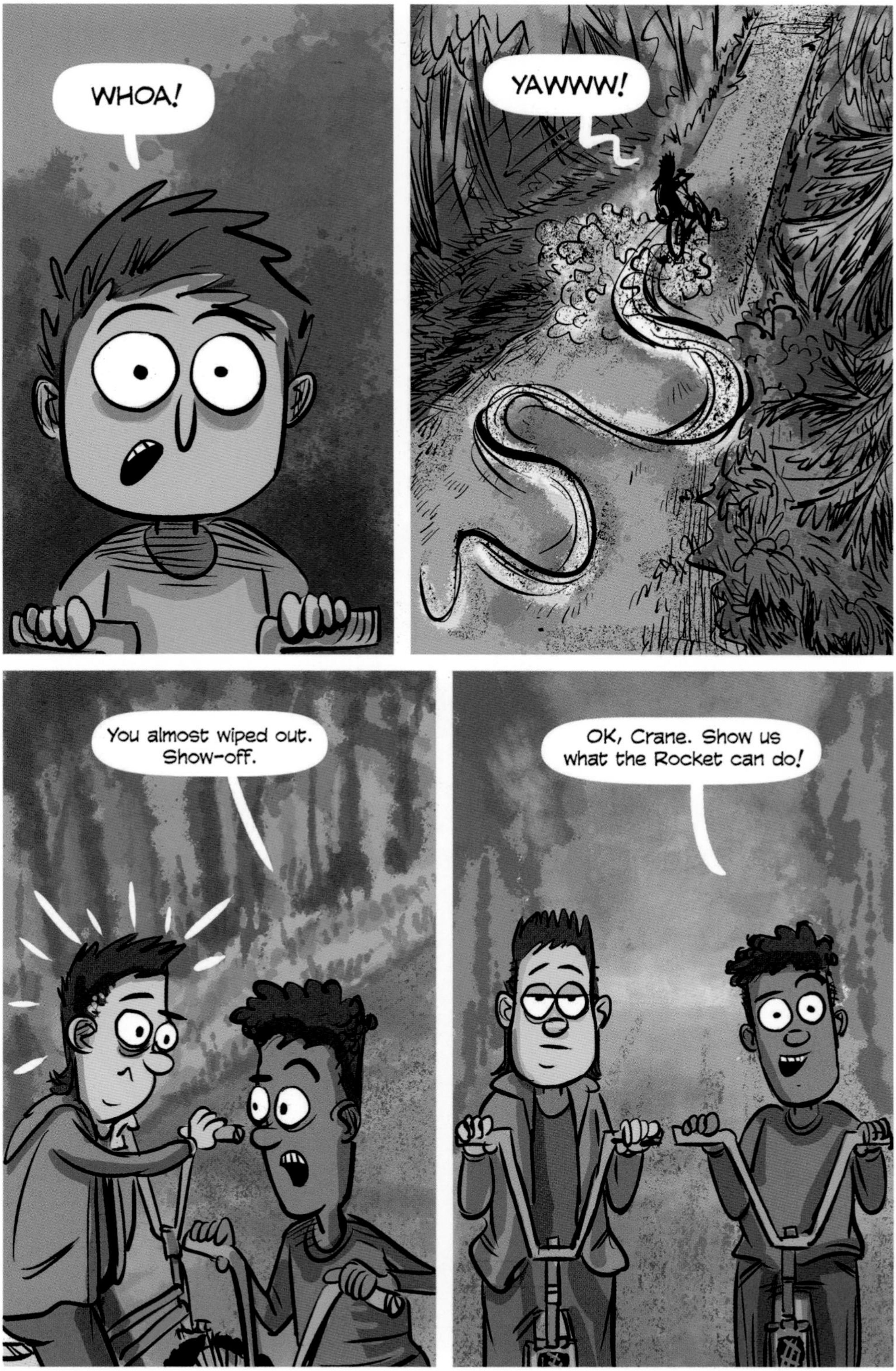
WHOA!
YAWWW!
You almost wiped out. Show-off.
OK, Crane. Show us what the Rocket can do!

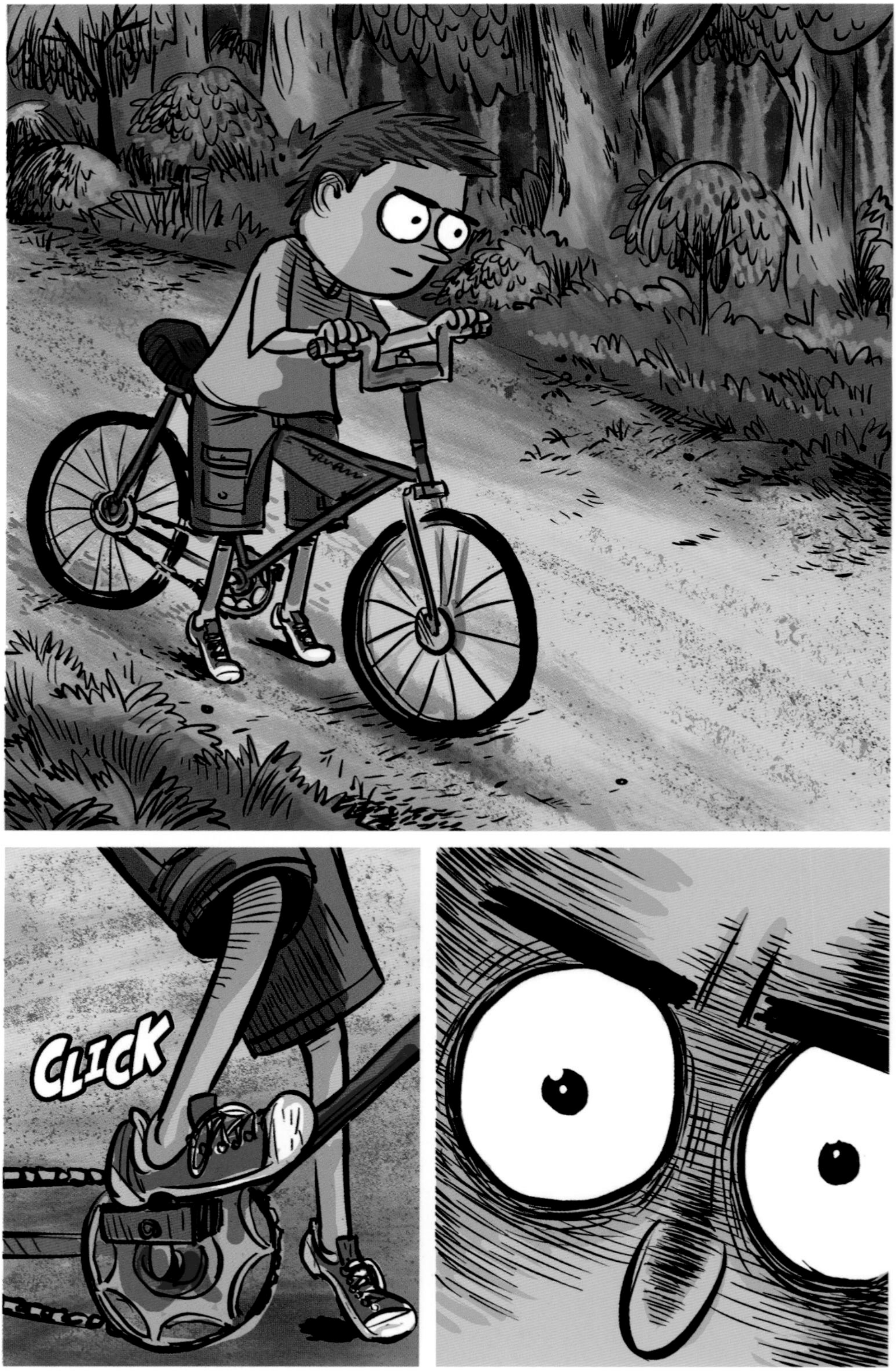
CLICK

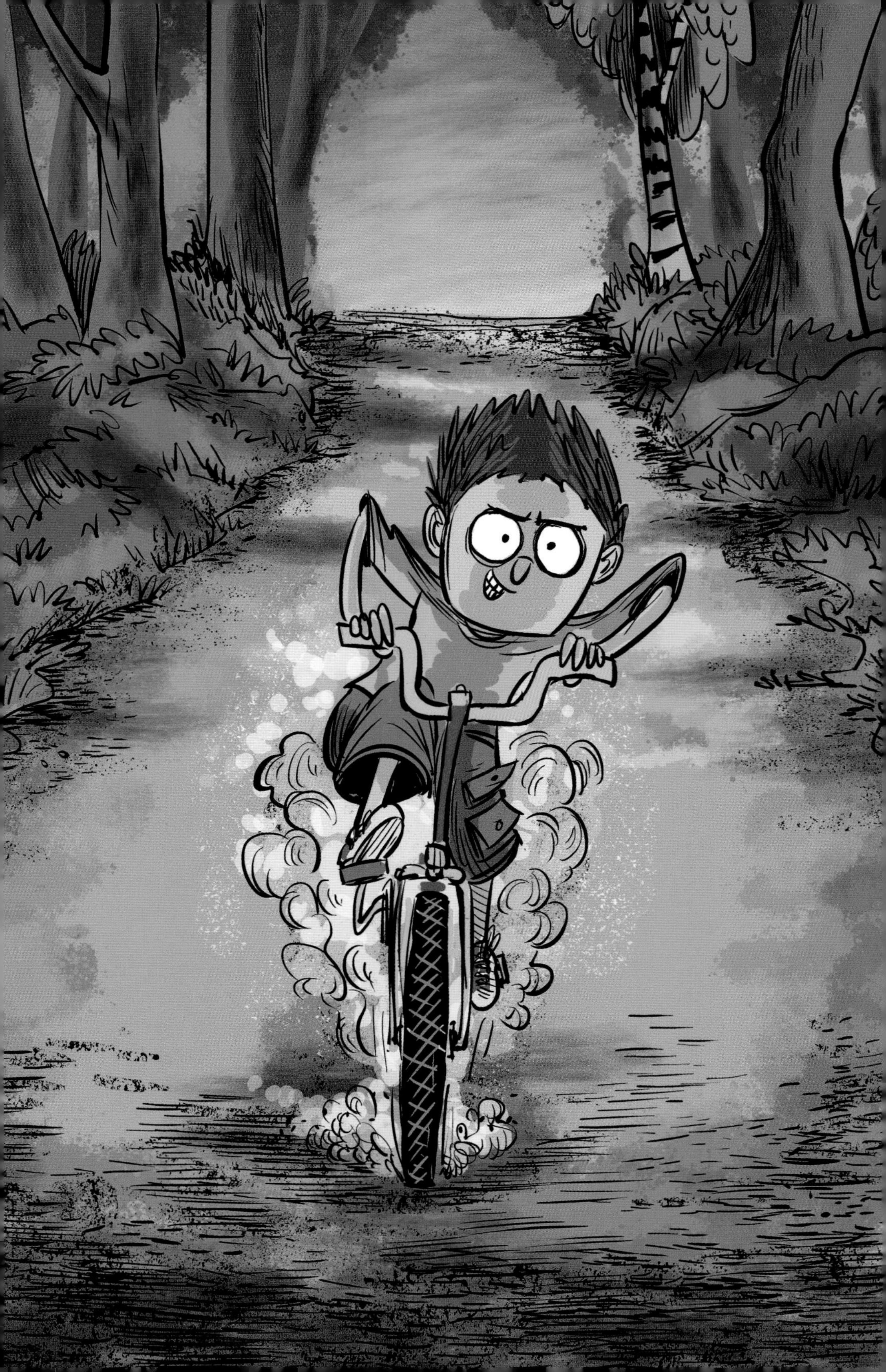

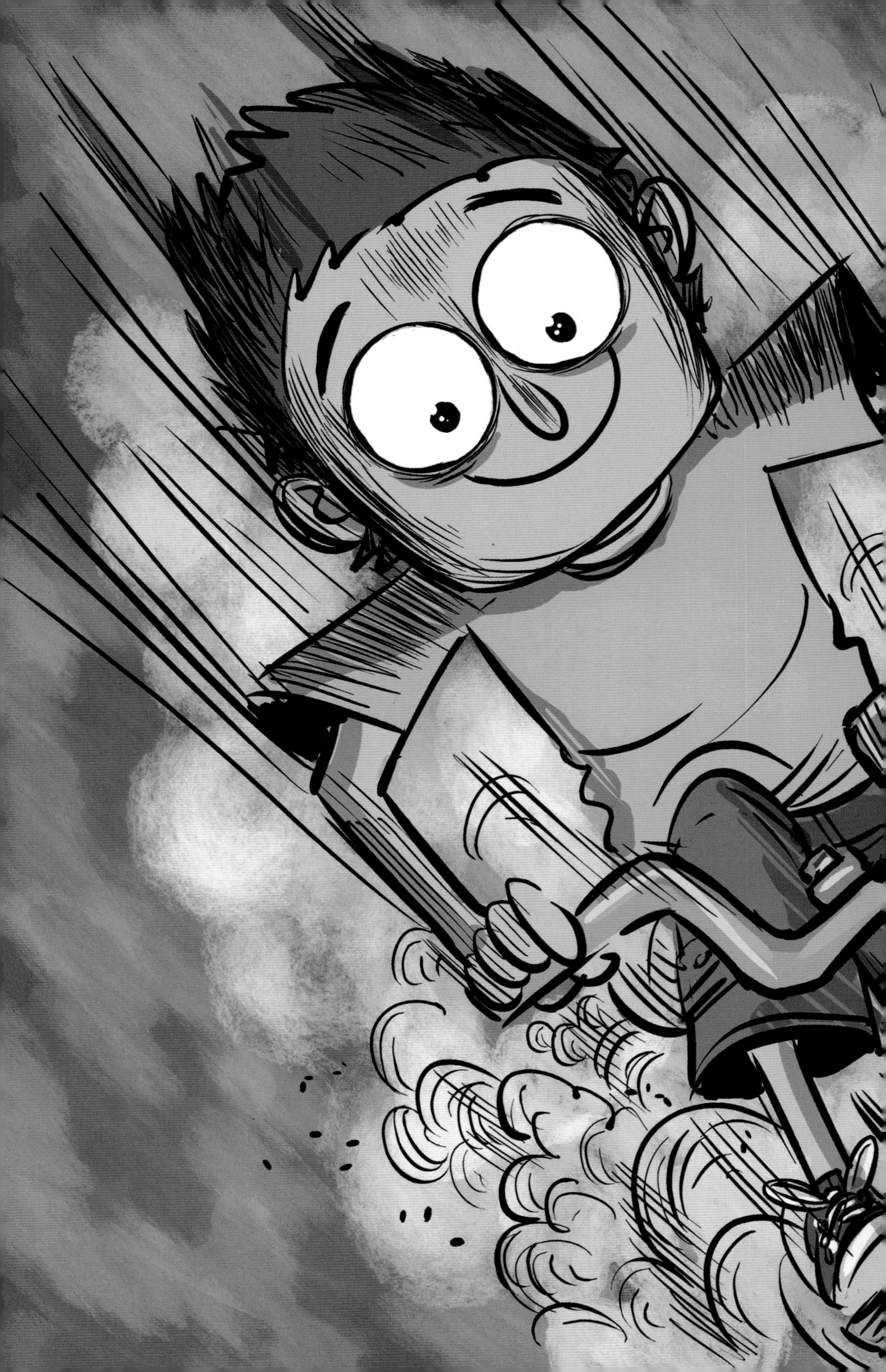

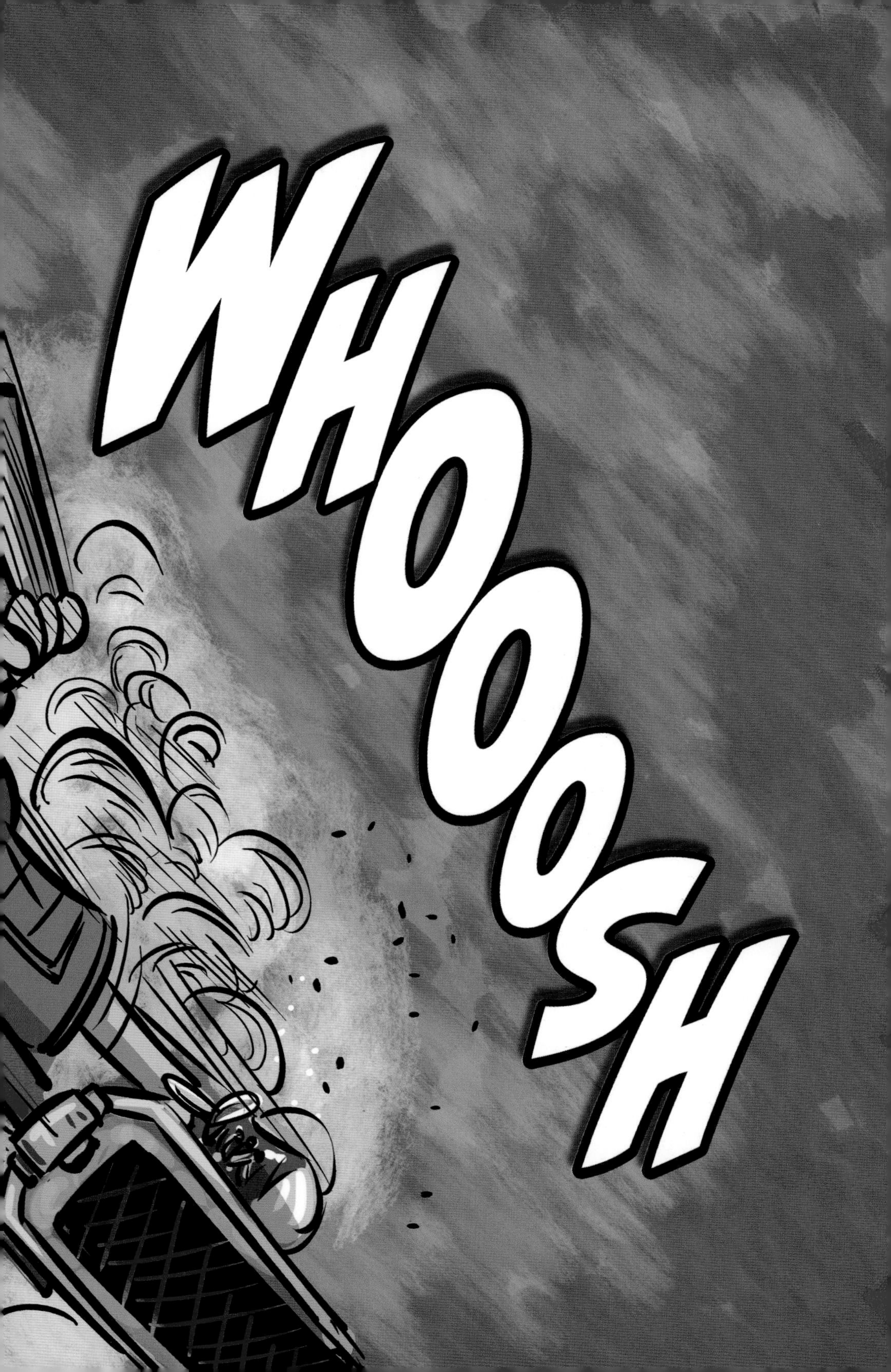
WHOOOOSH

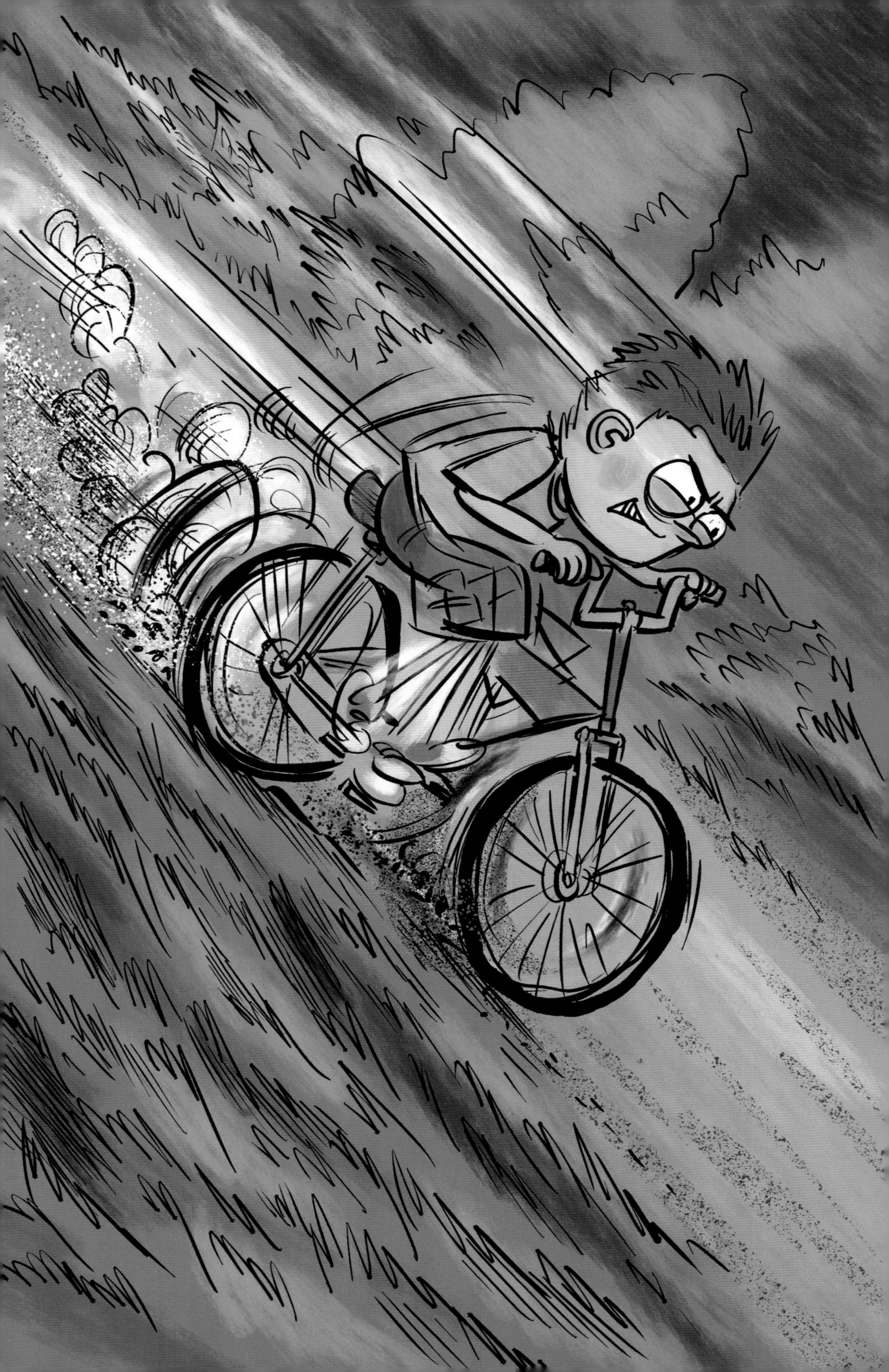

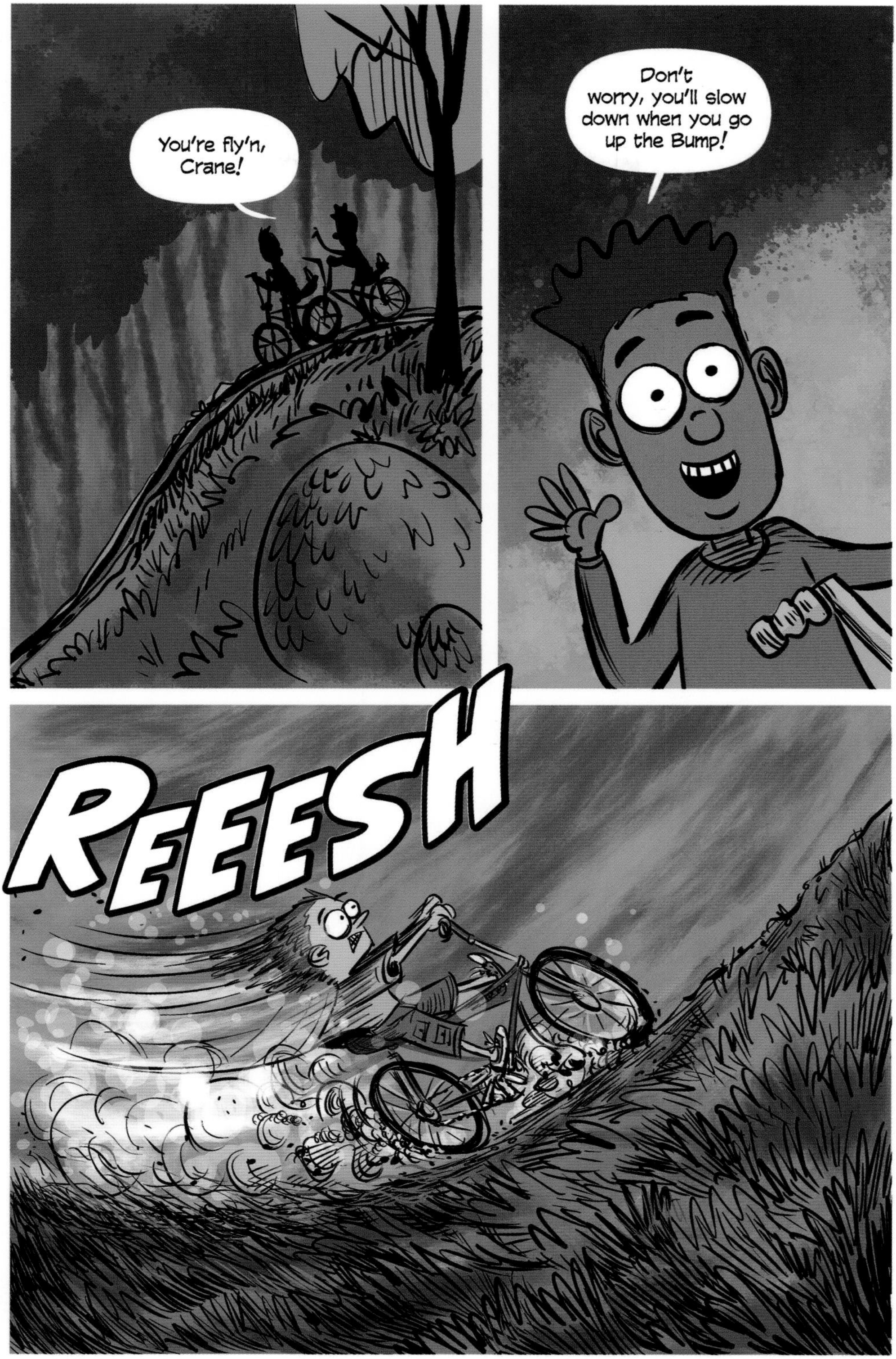
You're fly'n, Crane!
Don't worry, you'll slow down when you go up the Bump!
REEESH

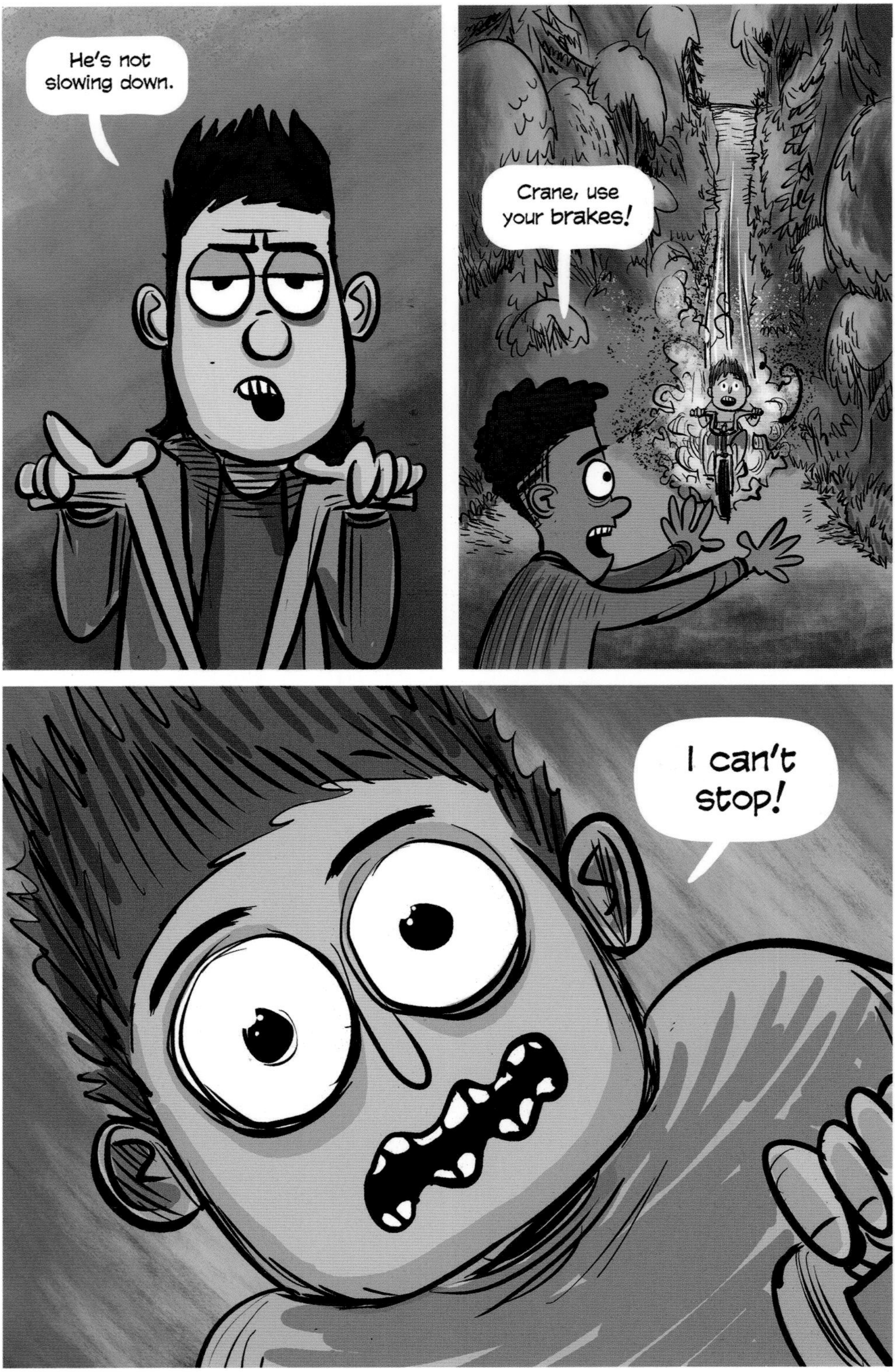
He's not slowing down.
Crane, use your brakes!
I can't stop!

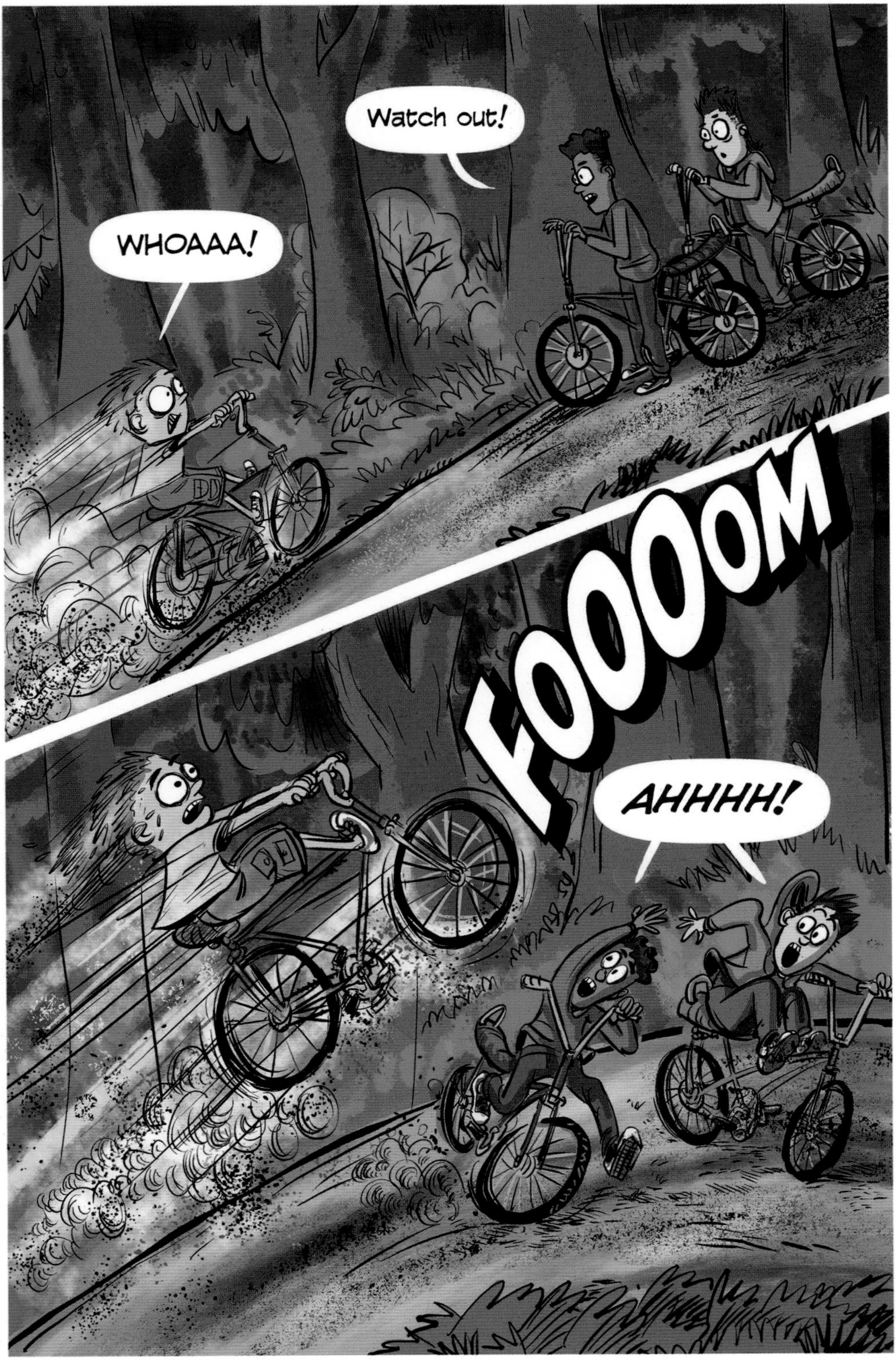
Watch out!
WHOAAA!
FOOOOM
AHHHH!

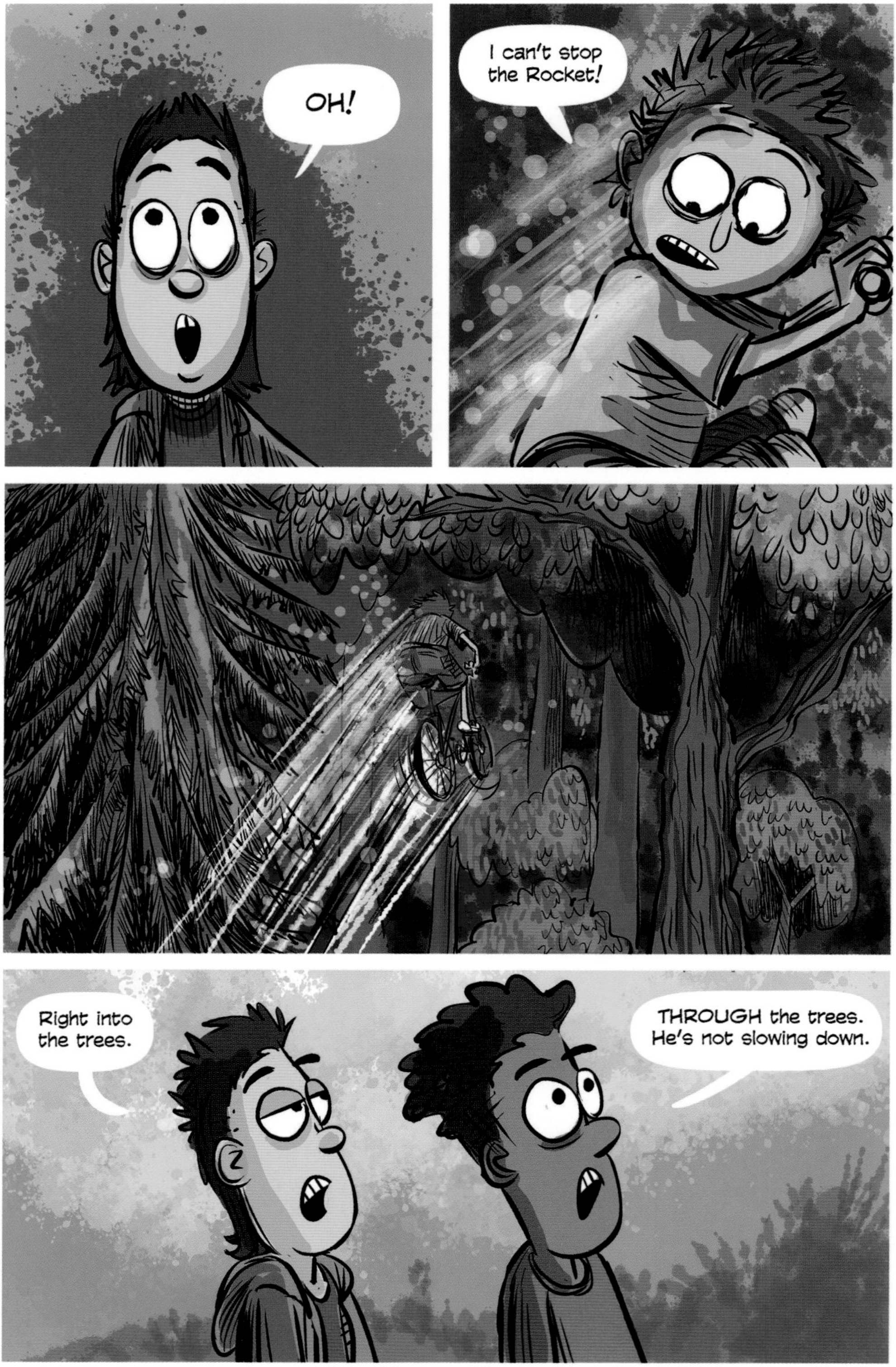
OH!
I can't stop the Rocket!
Right into the trees.
THROUGH the trees. He's not slowing down.

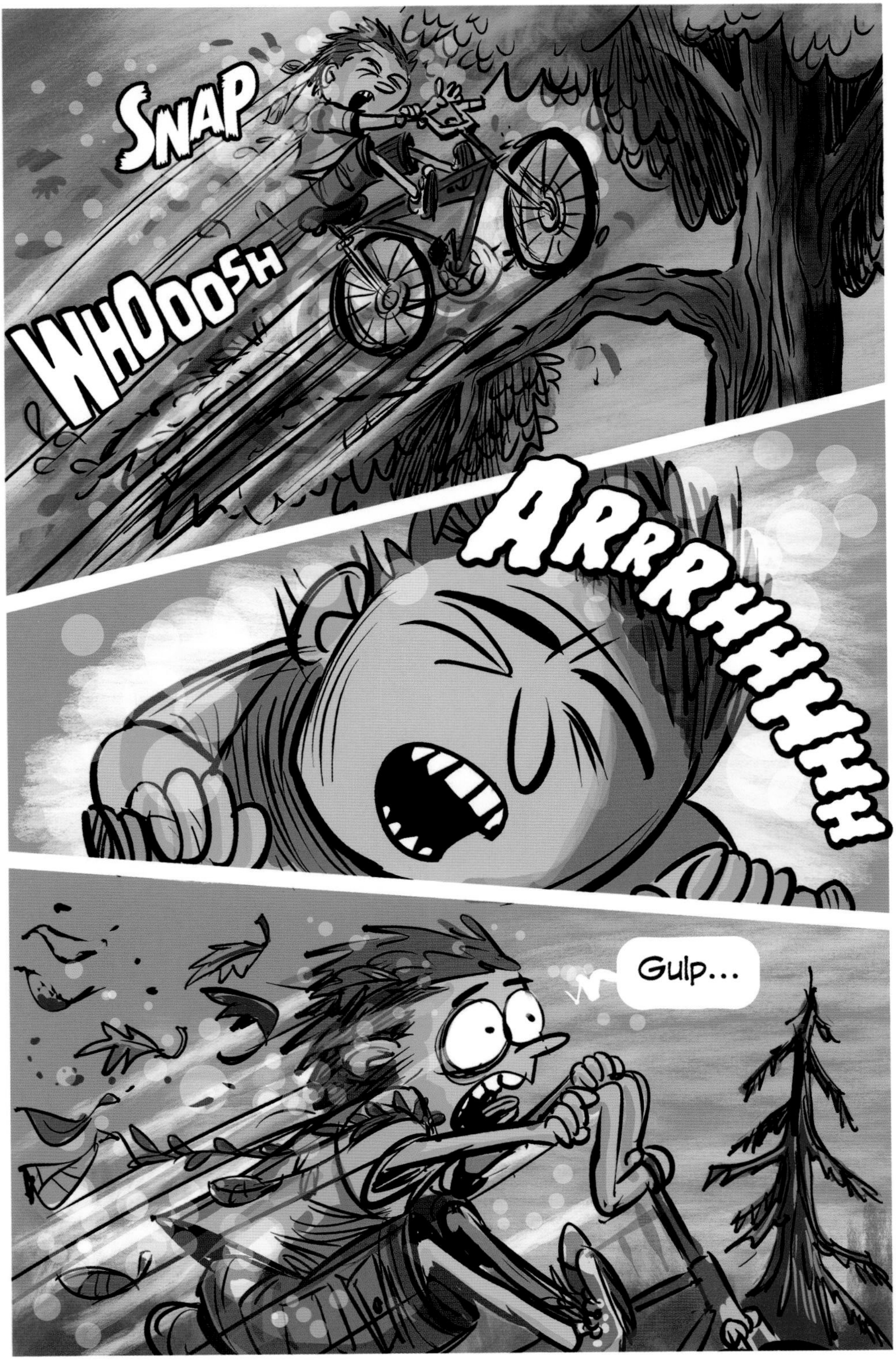
SNAP
WHOOOOSH
ARRRRHHHHH
Gulp...

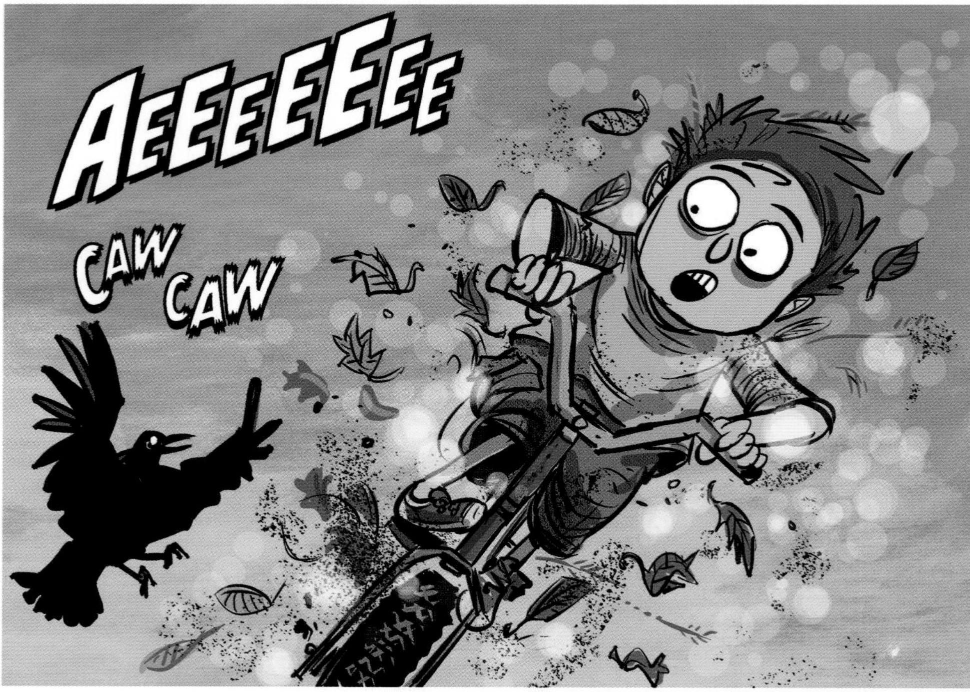
AEEEEEEE
CAW CAW

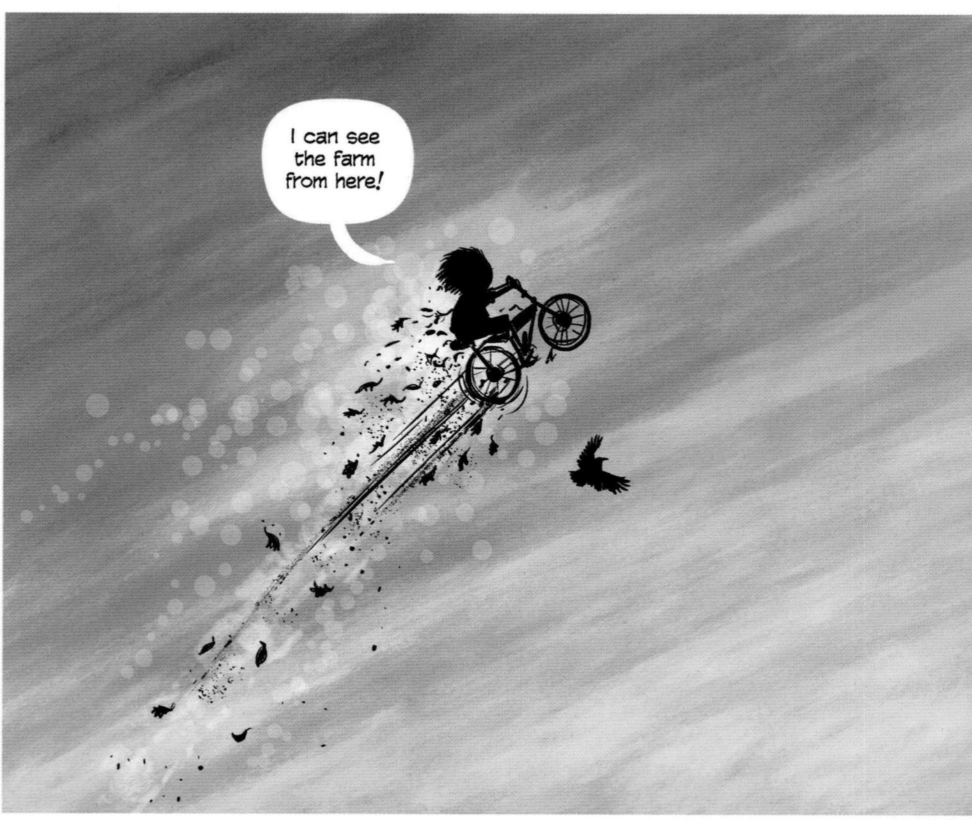
I can see the farm from here!

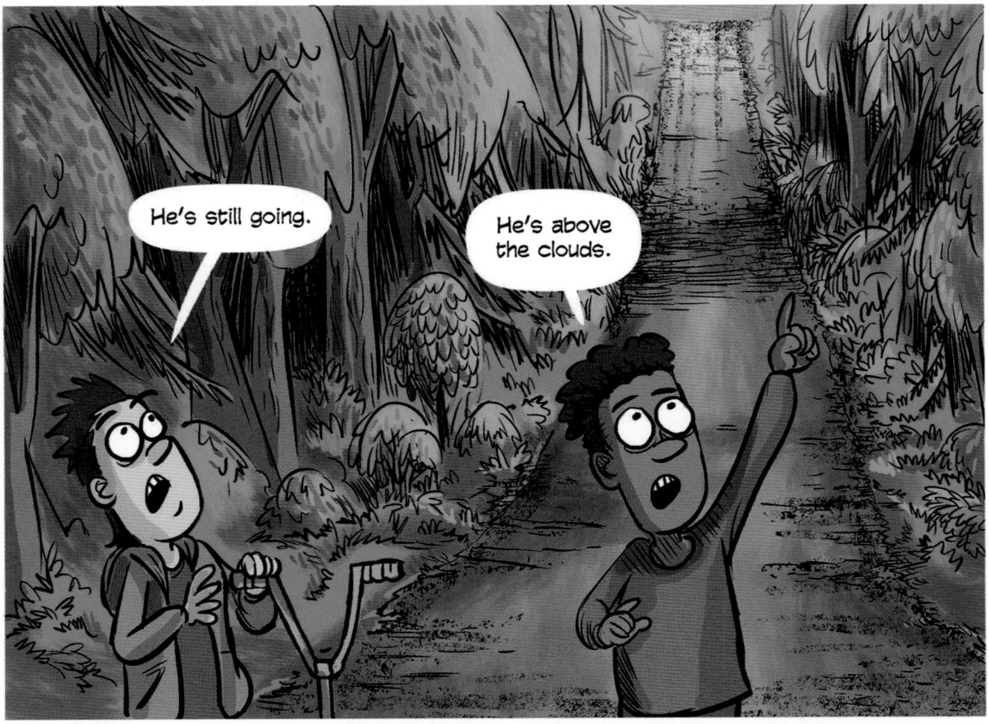
He's still going.
He's above the clouds.

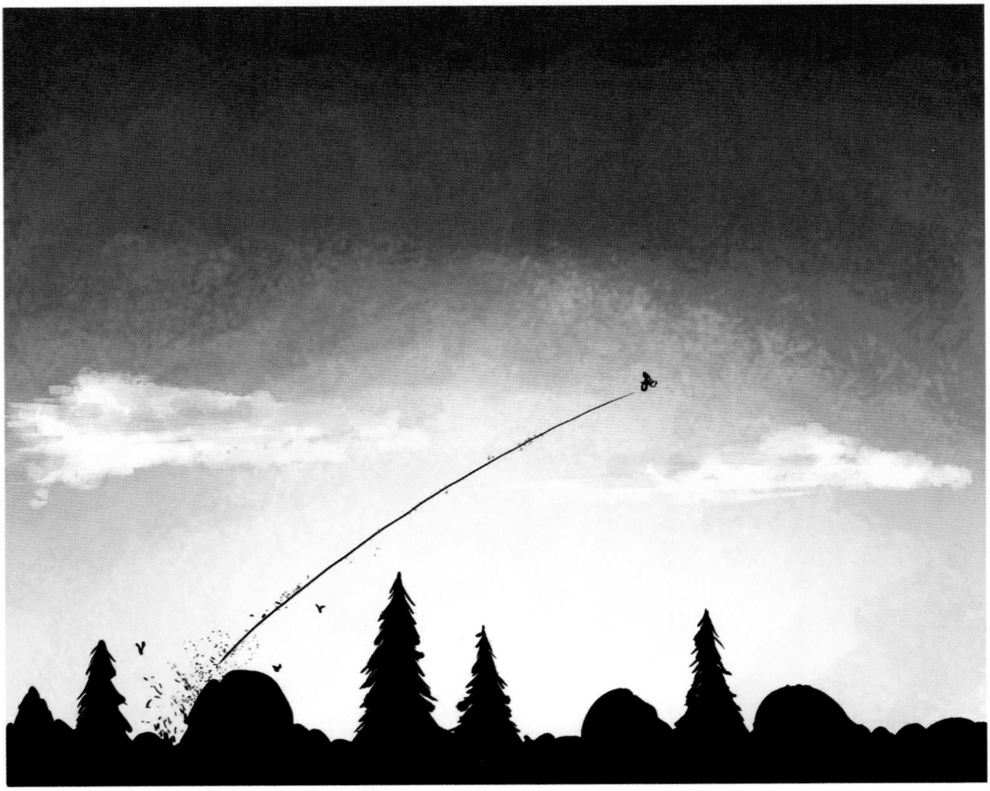

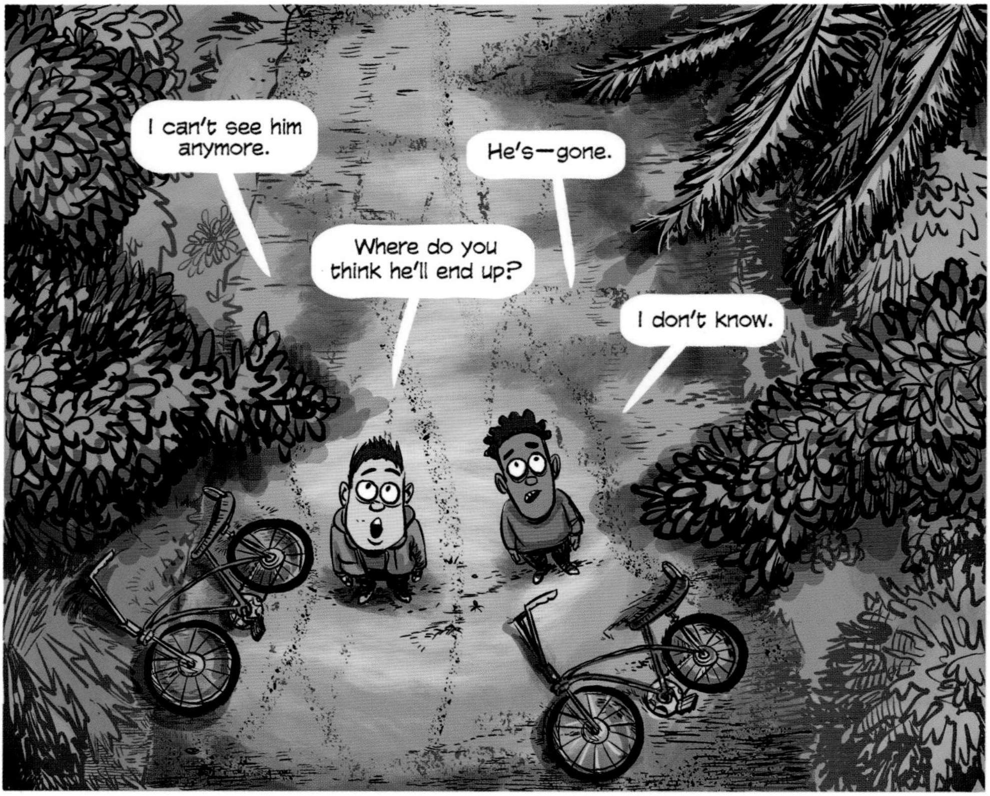
I can't see him anymore.
He's—gone.
Where do you think he'll end up?
I don't know.

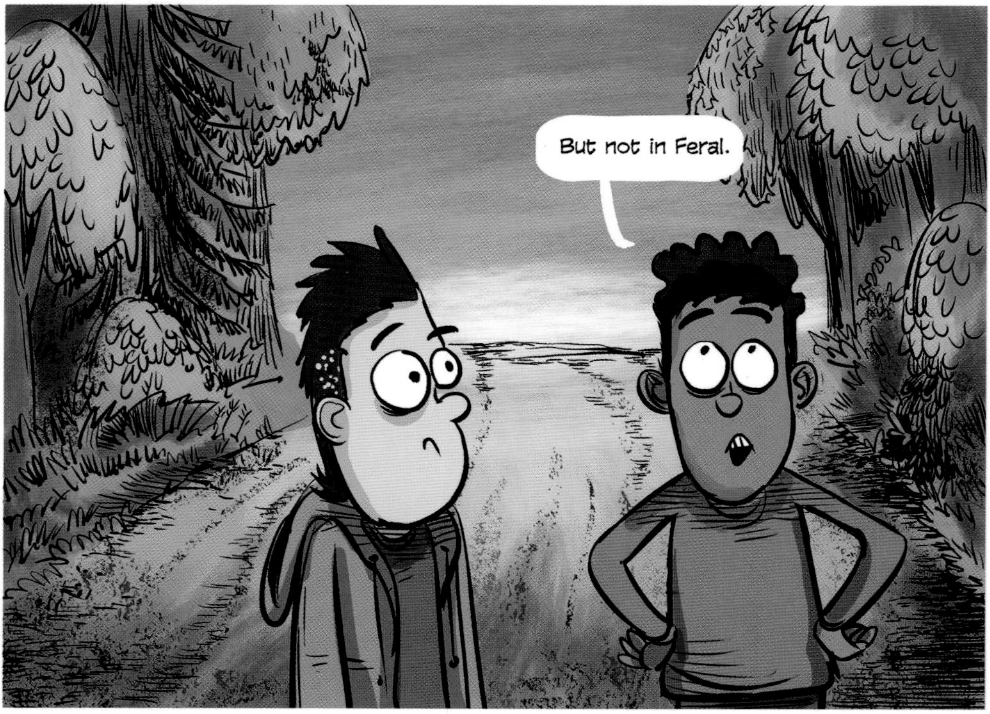
But not in Feral.

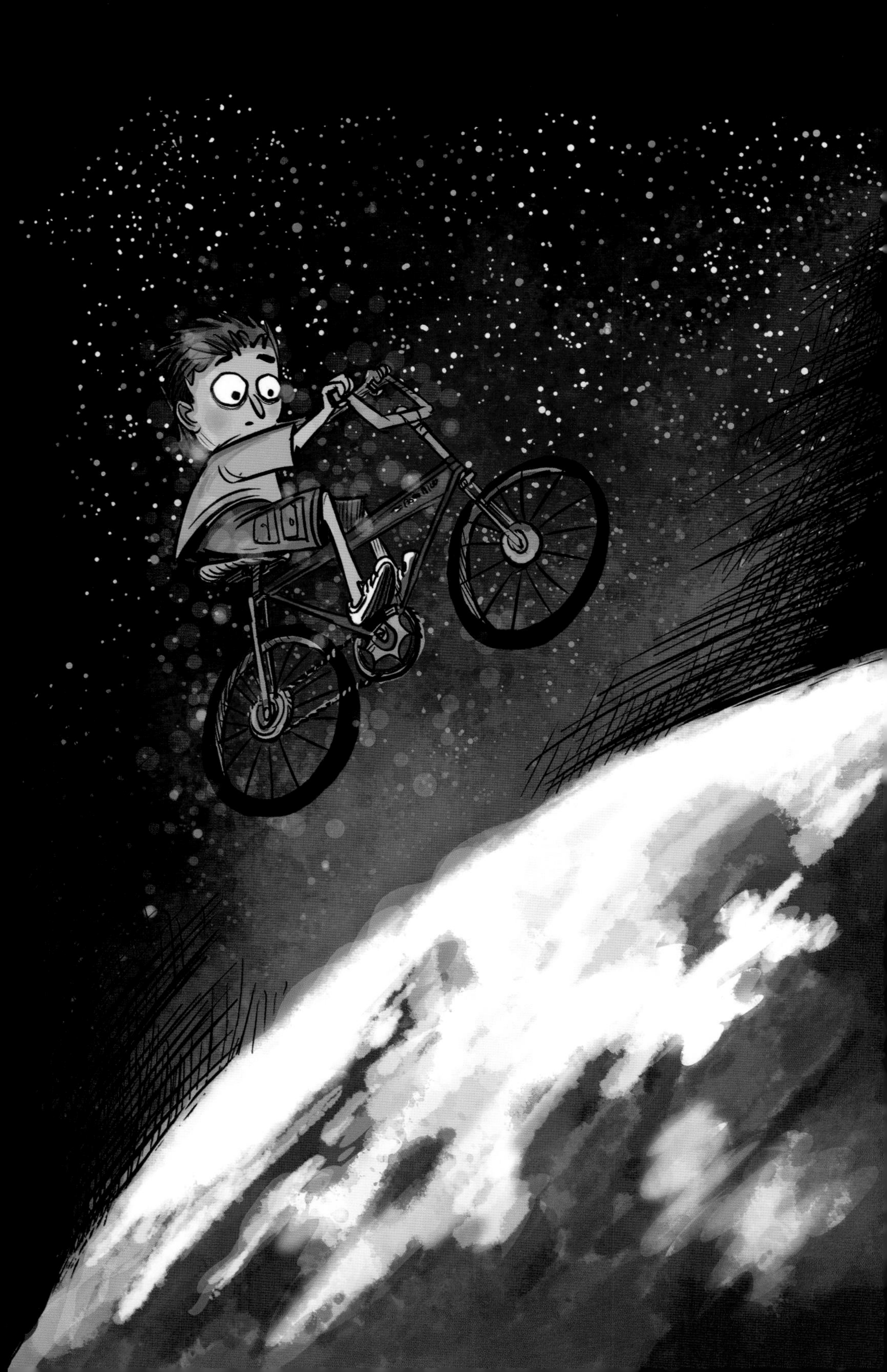

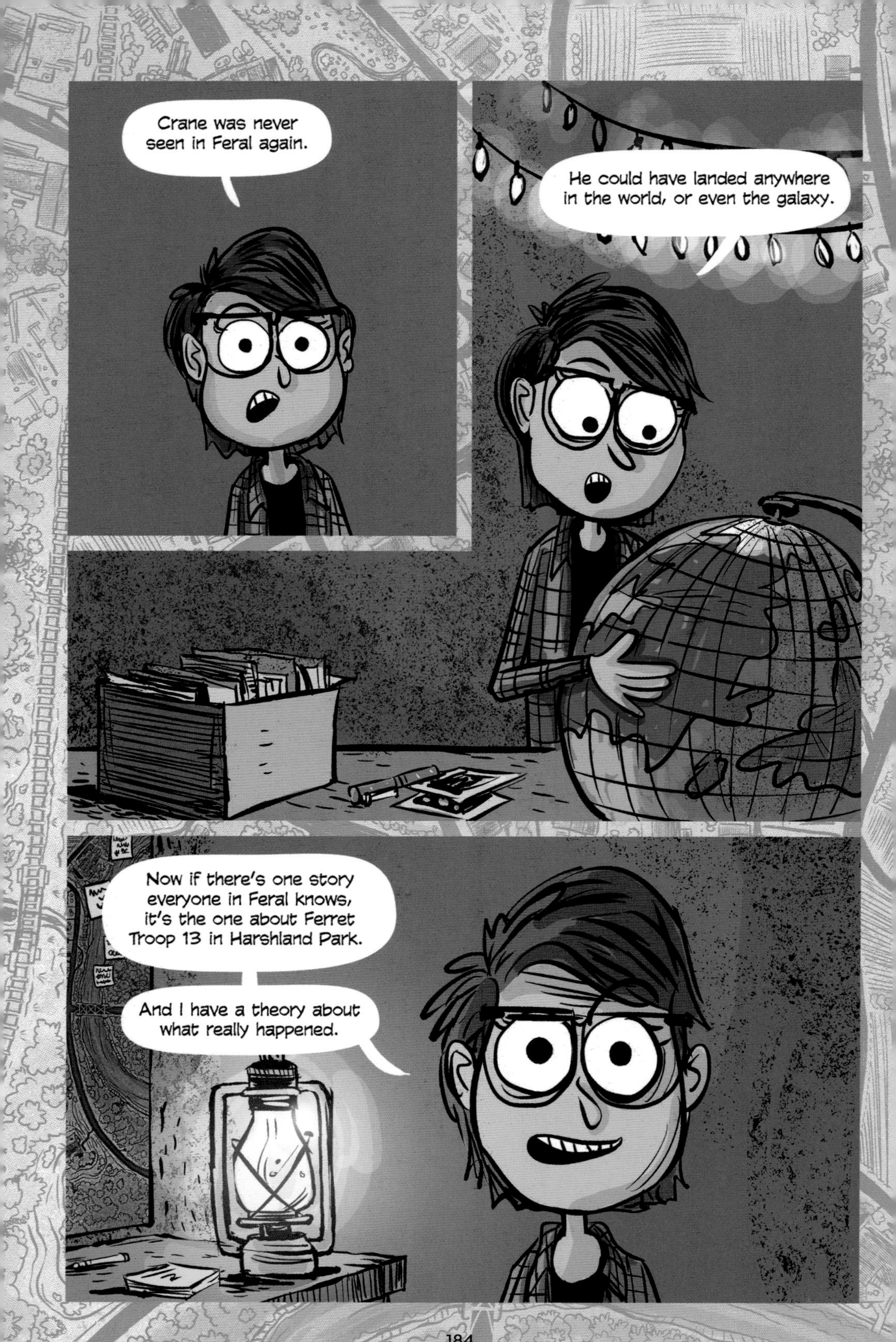

Crane was never seen in Feral again.
He could have landed anywhere in the world, or even the galaxy.
Now if there's one story everyone in Feral knows, it's the one about Ferret Troop 13 in Harshland Park.
And I have a theory about what really happened.

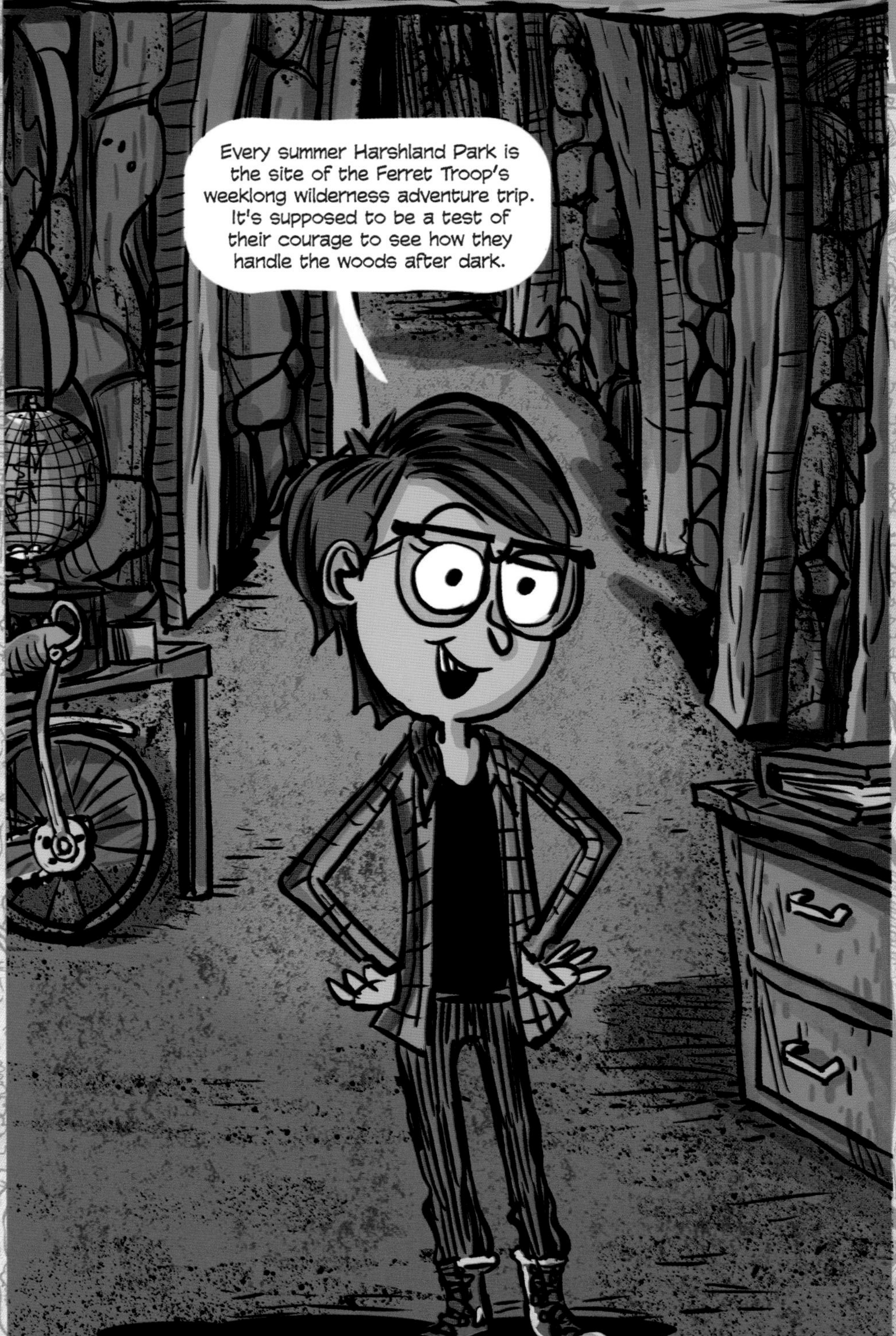
Every summer Harshland Park is the site of the Ferret Troop's weeklong wilderness adventure trip. It's supposed to be a test of their courage to see how they handle the woods after dark.

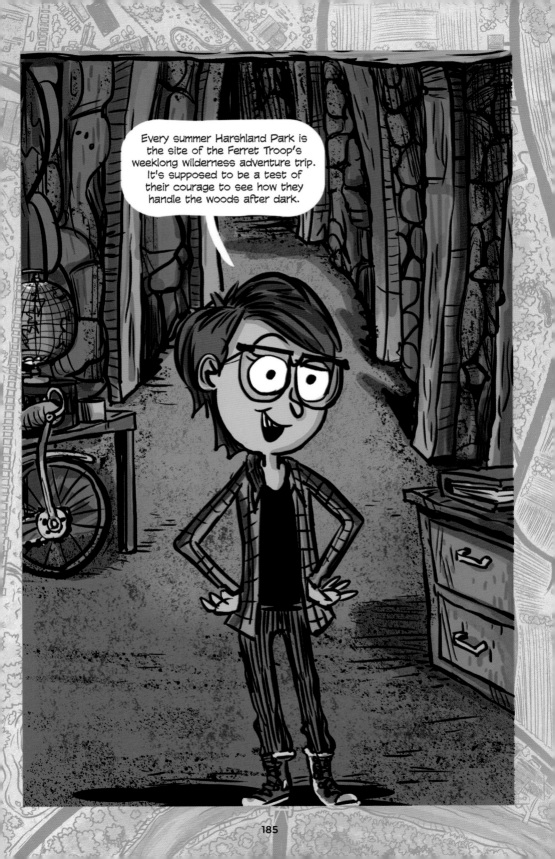

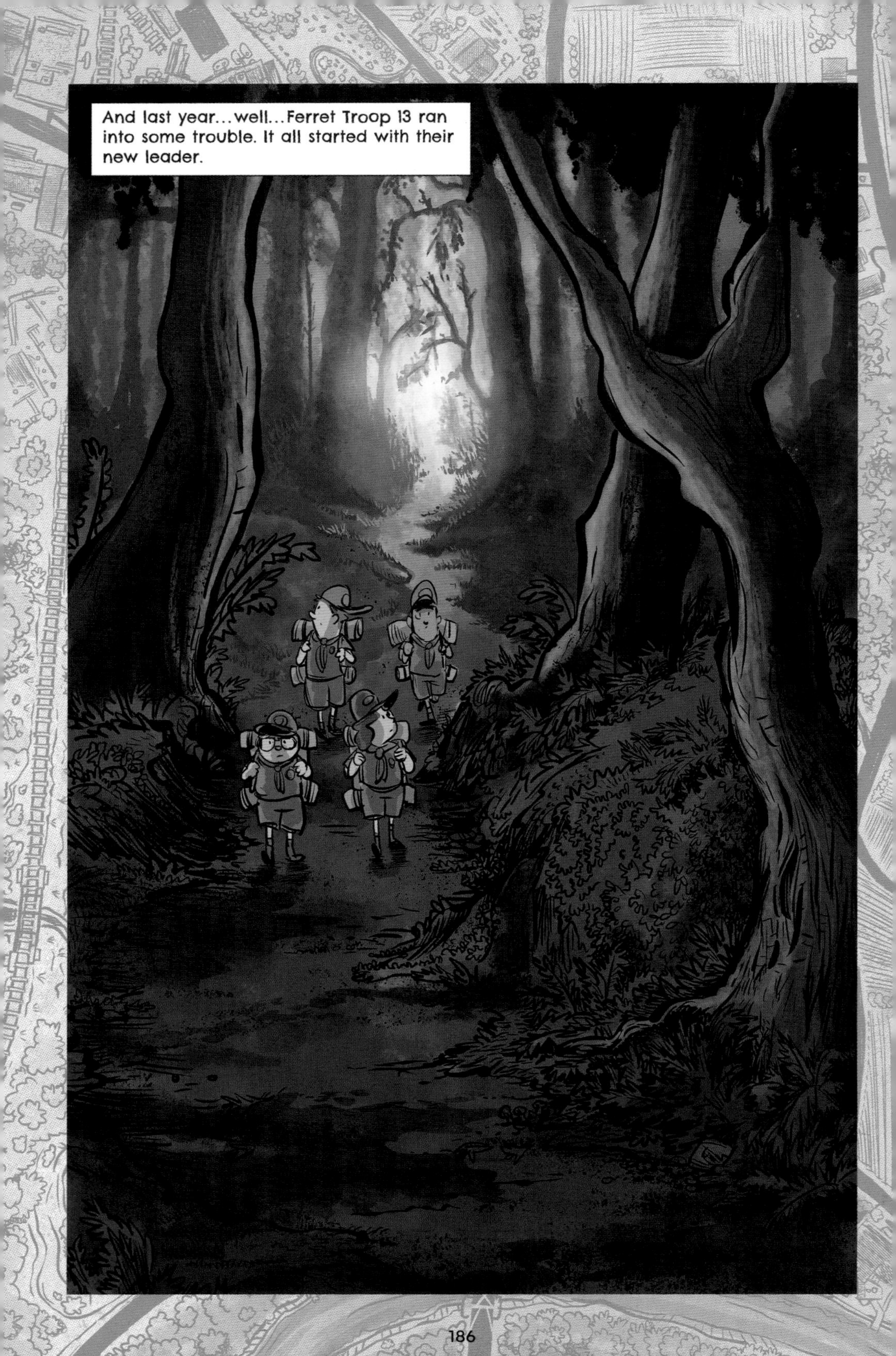
And last year...well...Ferret Troop 13 ran into some trouble. It all started with their new leader.

FERRET FROLIC

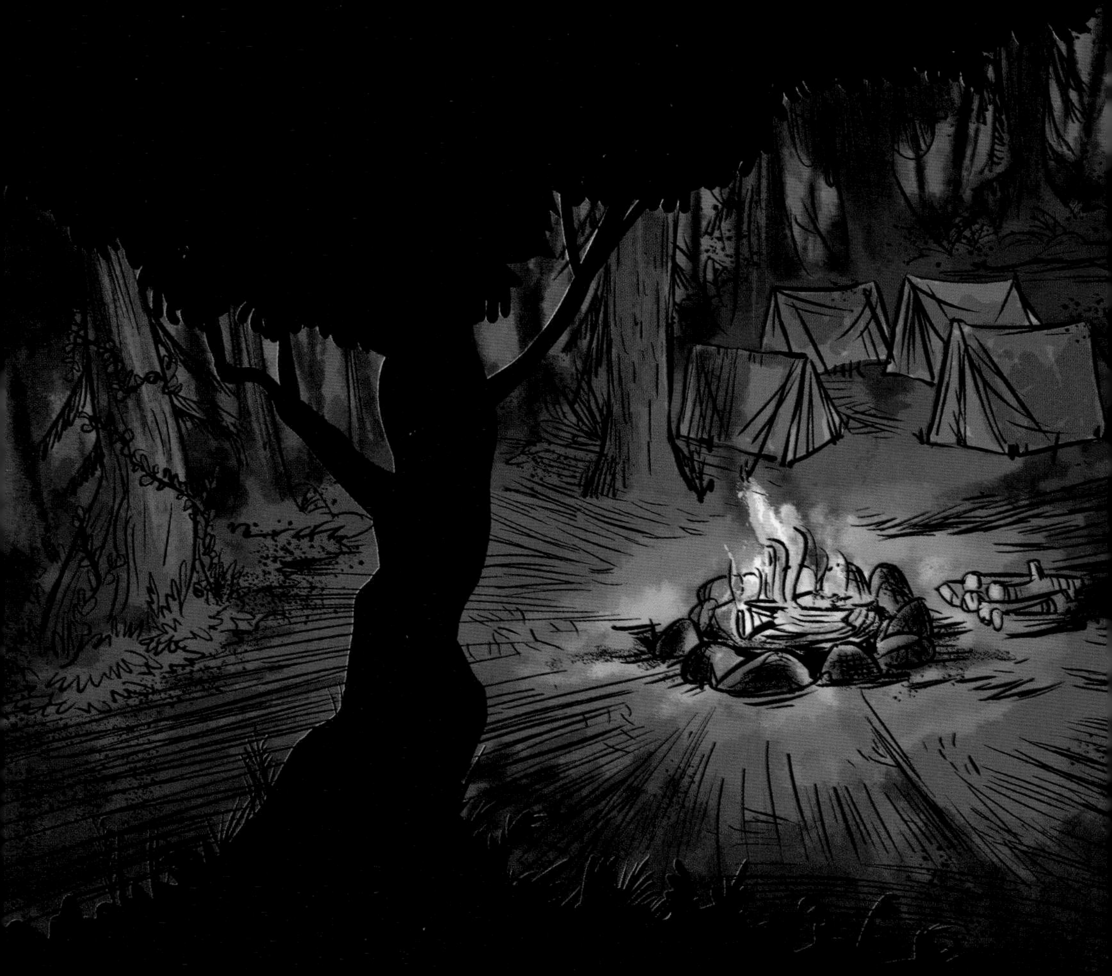

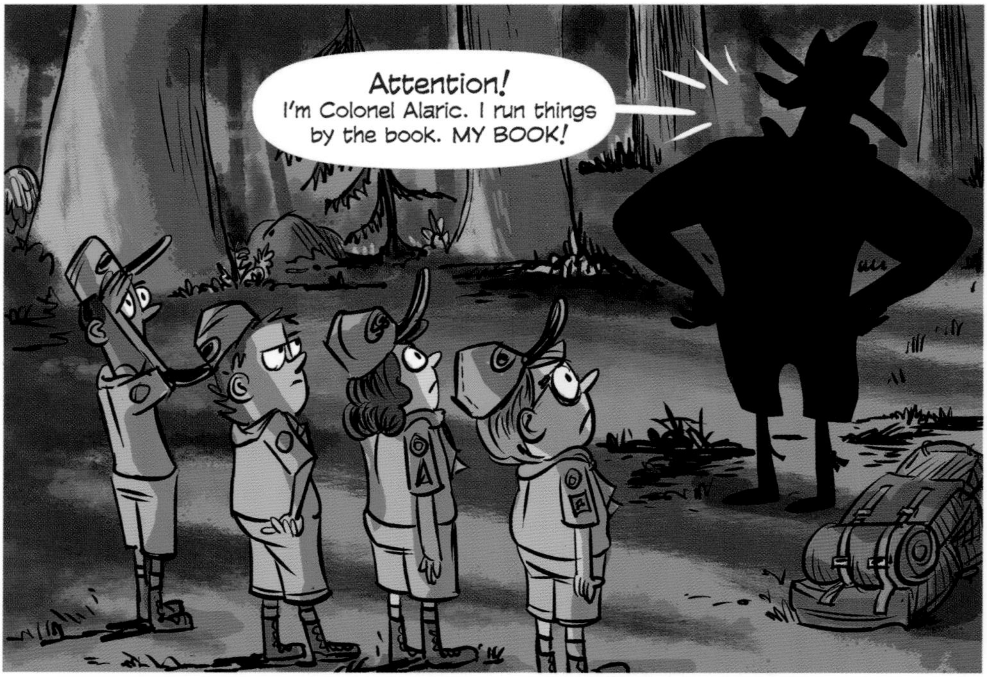
Attention!
I'm Colonel Alaric. I run things by the book. MY BOOK!

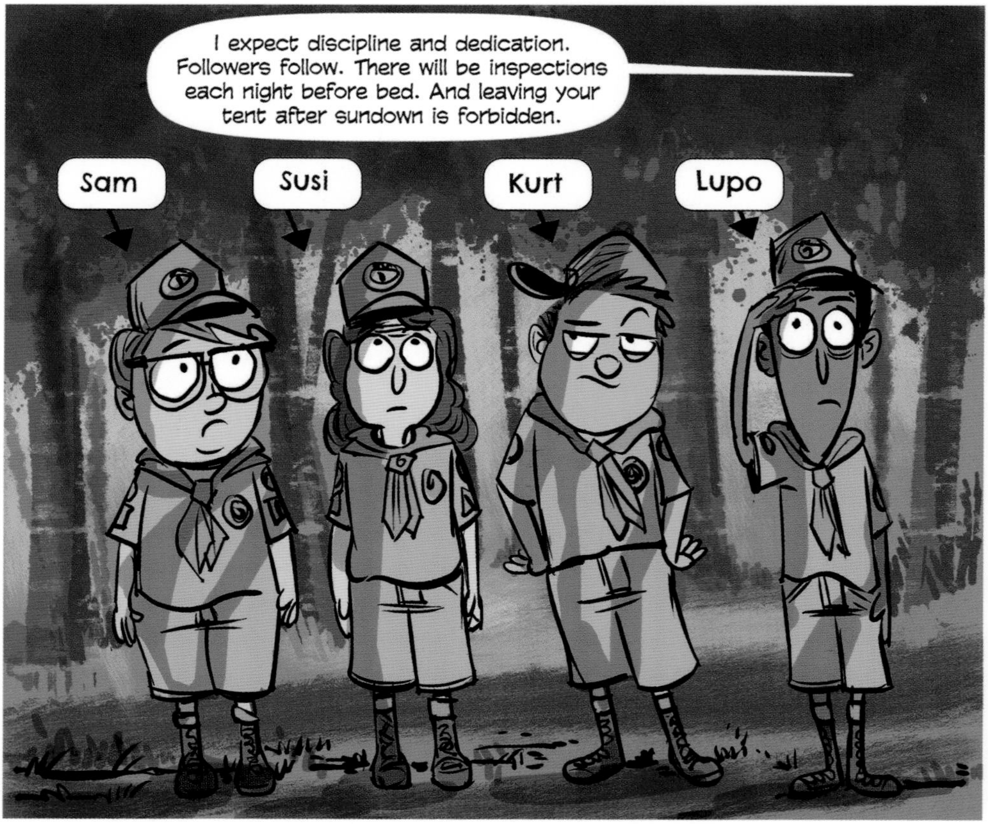
I expect discipline and dedication. Followers follow. There will be inspections each night before bed. And leaving your tent after sundown is forbidden.
Sam
Susi
Kurt
Lupo

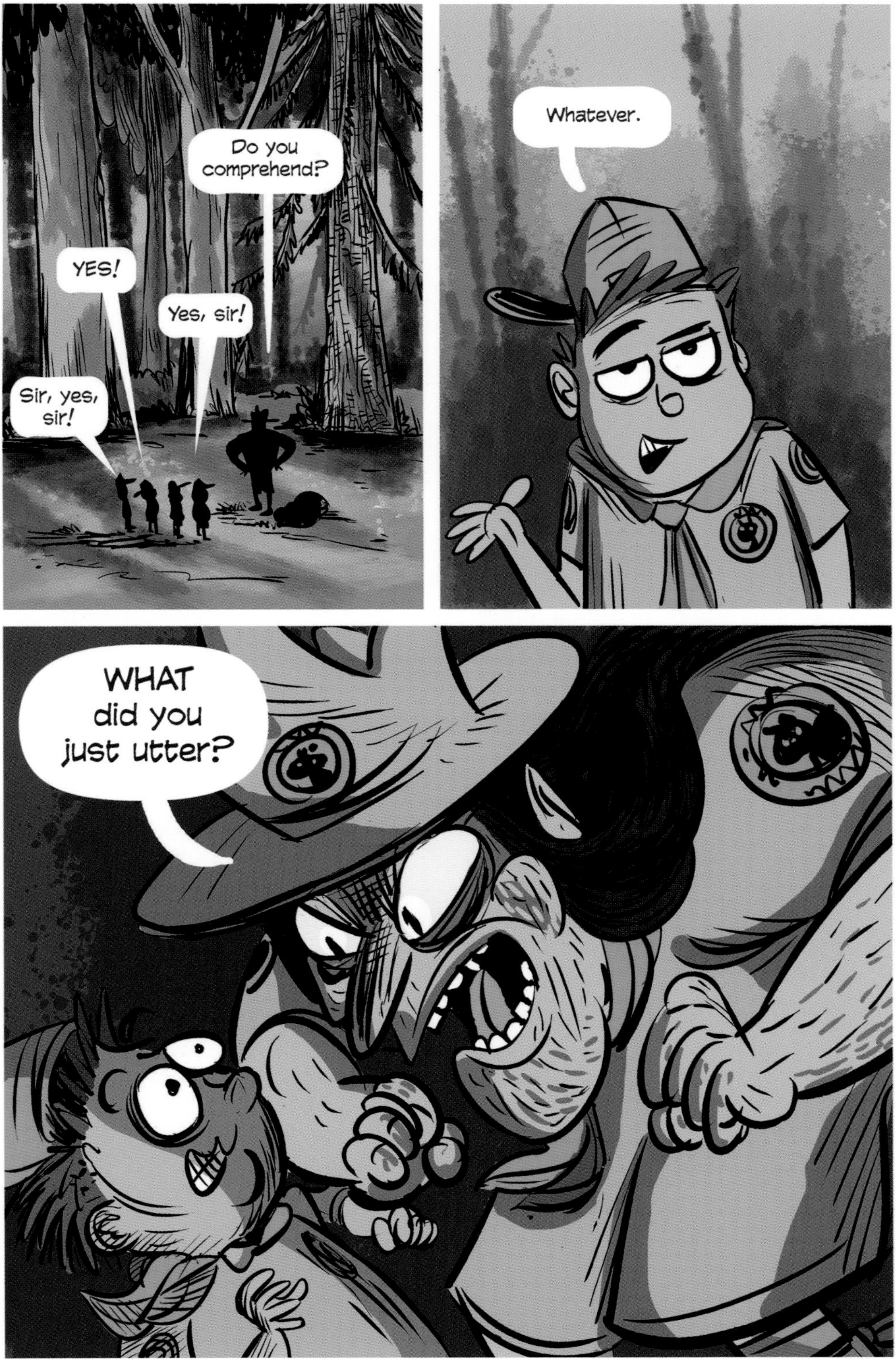
Do you comprehend?
YES!
Yes, sir!
Sir, yes, sir!
Whatever.
WHAT did you just utter?

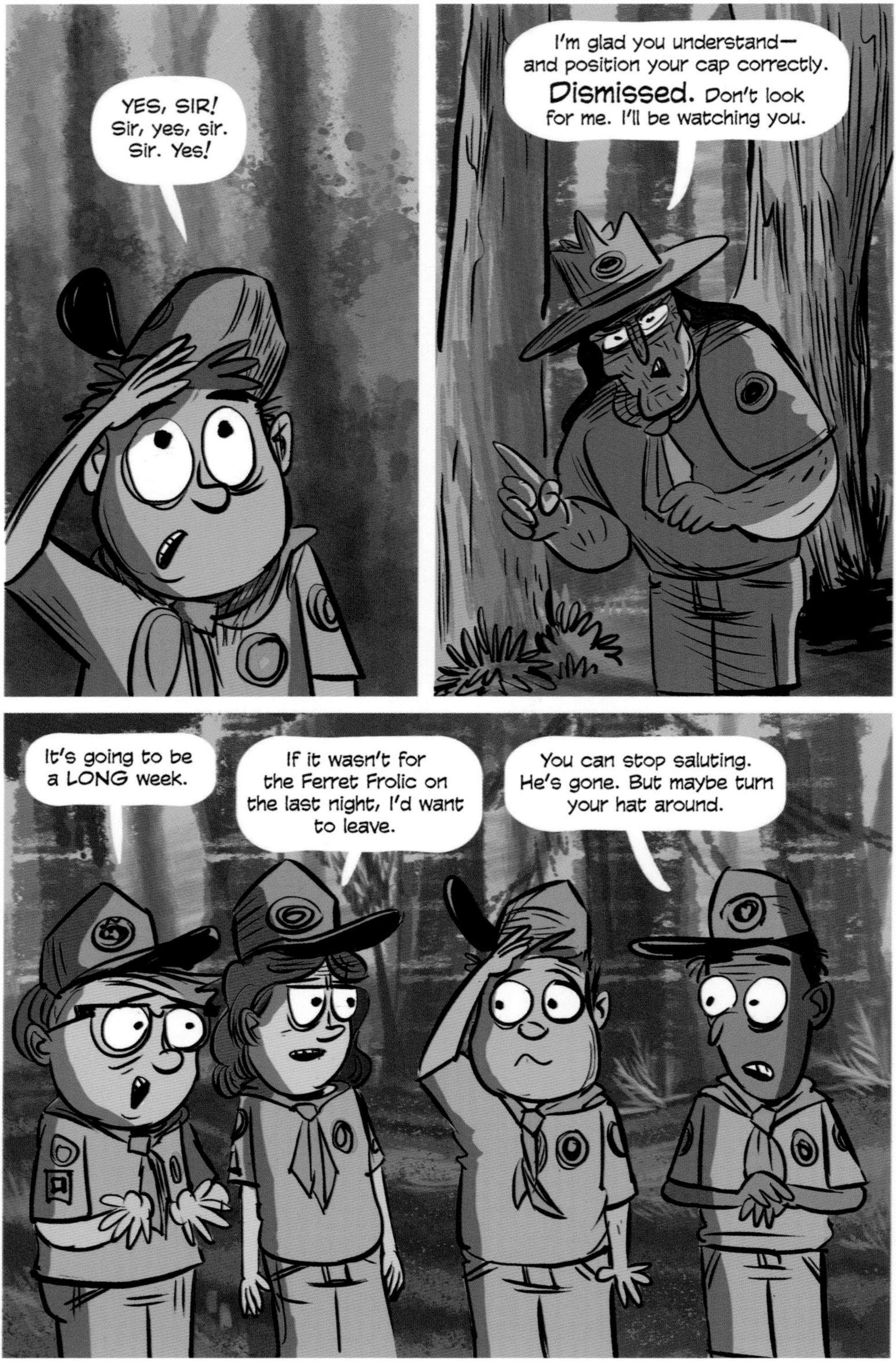
YES, SIR! Sir, yes, sir. Sir. Yes!
I'm glad you understand—and position your cap correctly. Dismissed. Don't look for me. I'll be watching you.
It's going to be a LONG week.
If it wasn't for the Ferret Frolic on the last night, I'd want to leave.
You can stop saluting. He's gone. But maybe turn your hat around.

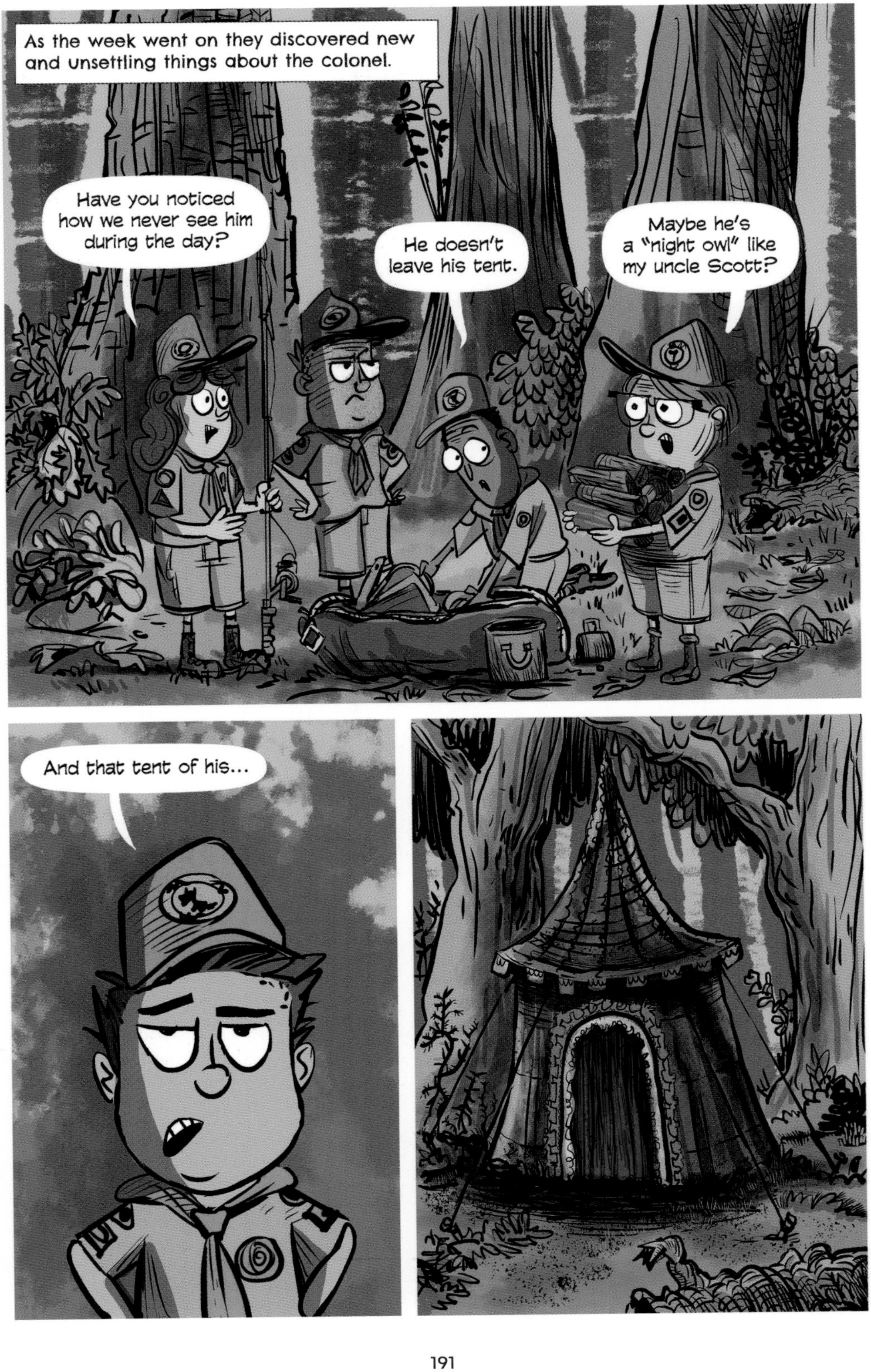
As the week went on they discovered new and unsettling things about the colonel.
Have you noticed how we never see him during the day?
He doesn't leave his tent.
Maybe he's a "night owl" like my uncle Scott?
And that tent of his...

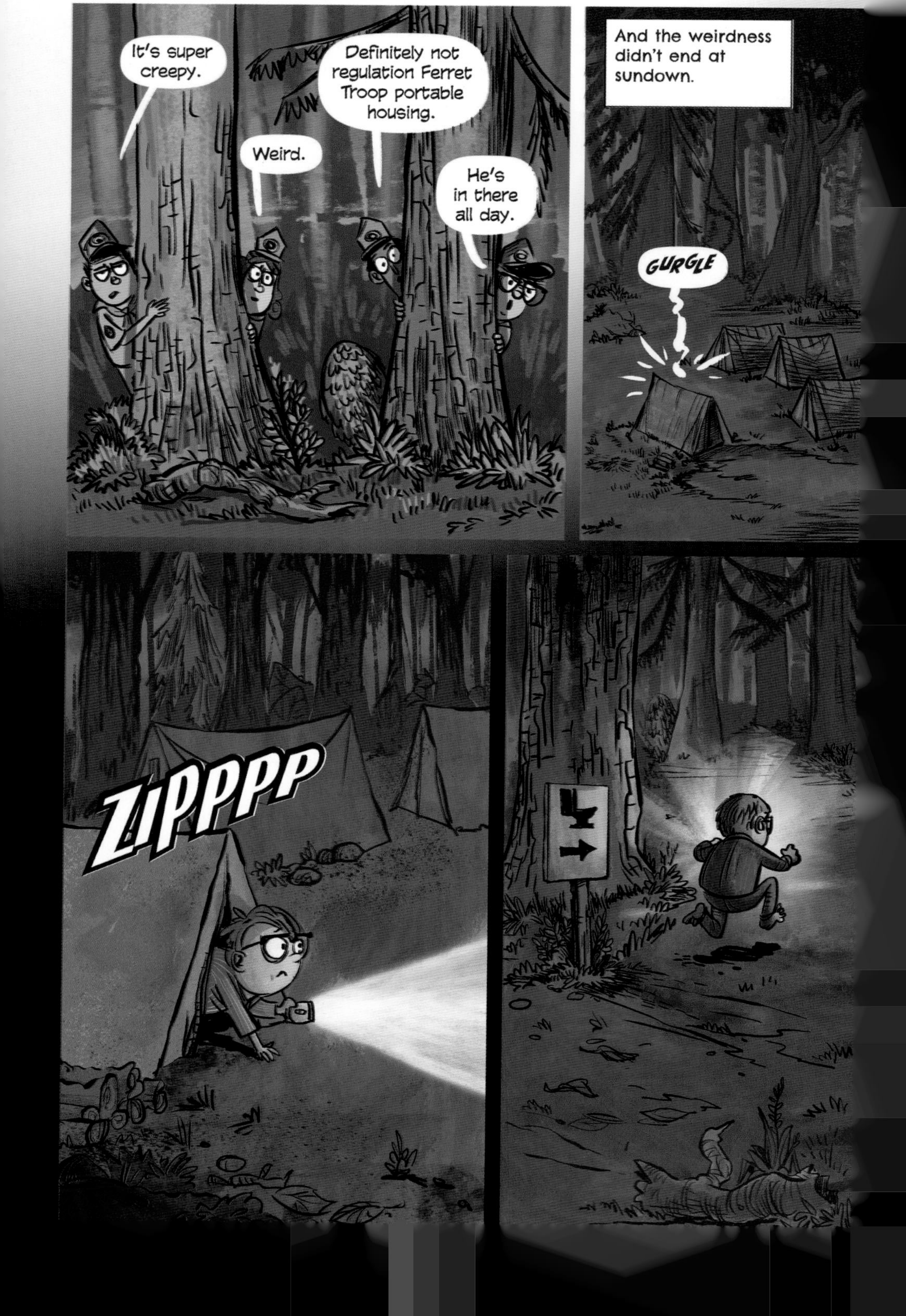
It's super creepy.
Weird.
Definitely not regulation Ferret Troop portable housing.
He's in there all day.
And the weirdness didn't end at sundown.
GURGLE
ZIPPPP

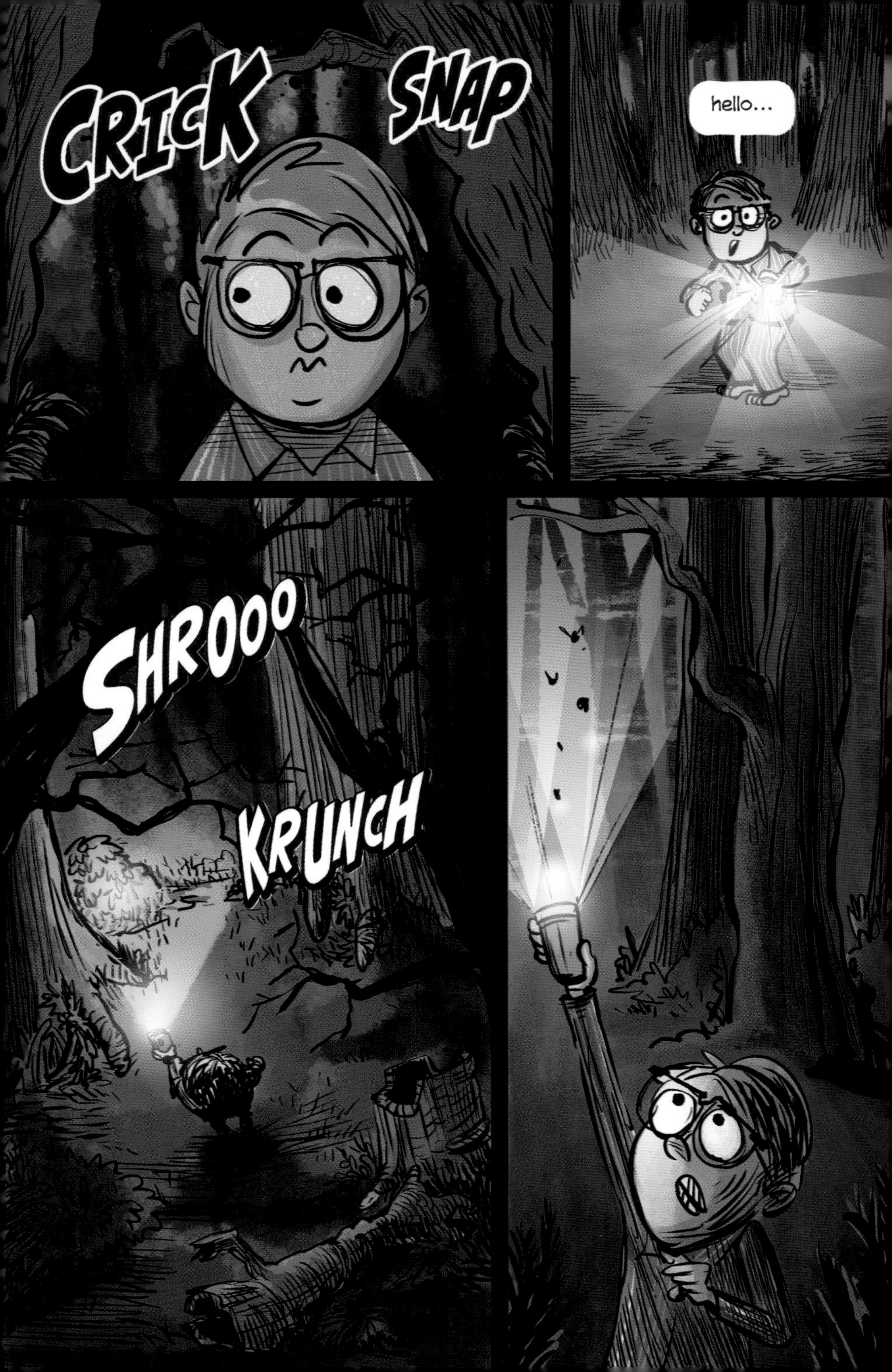
CRICK
SNAP
hello...
SHROOO
KRUNCH

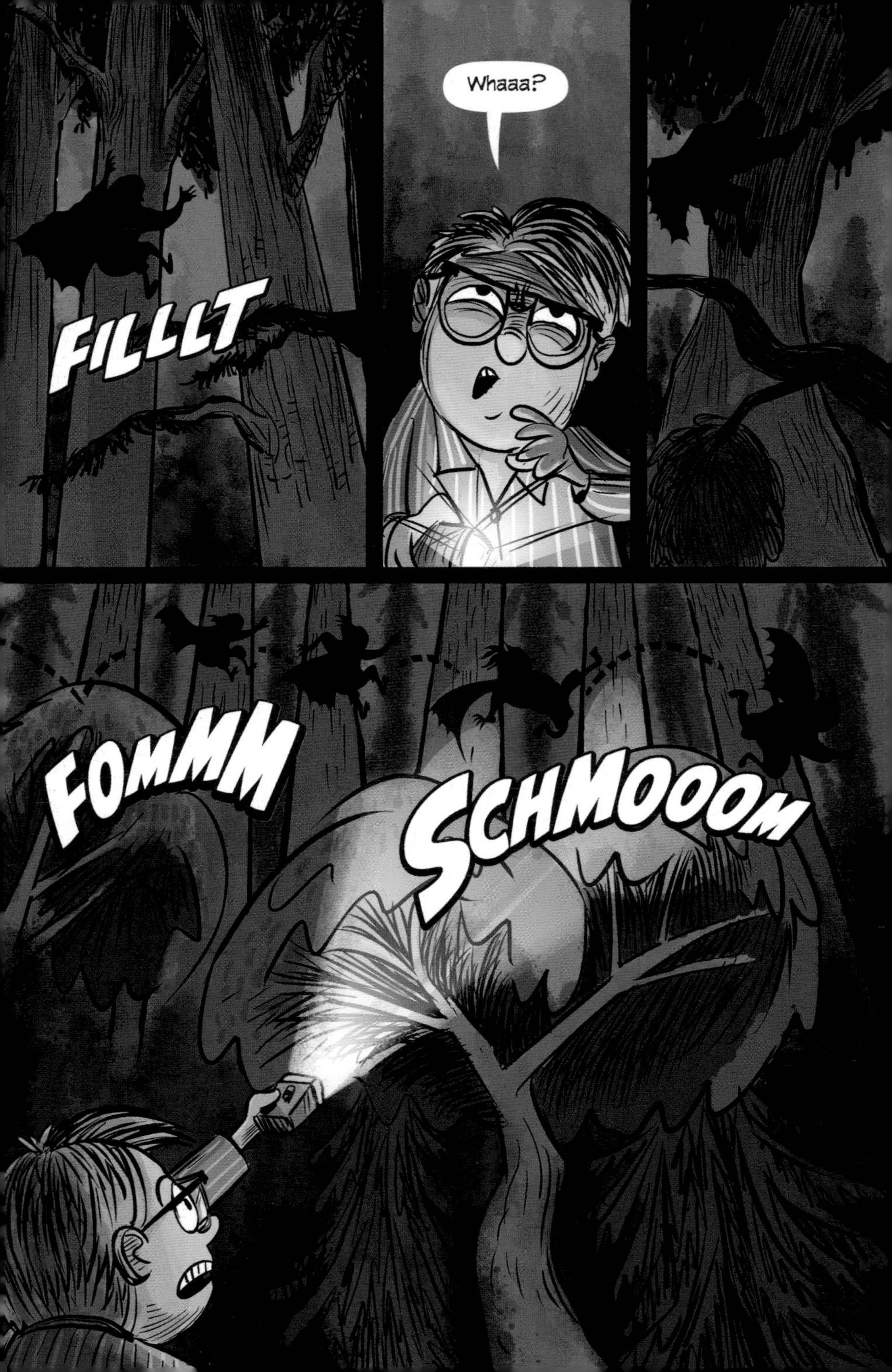
FILLLT
Whaaa?
FOMMM
SCHMOOOM

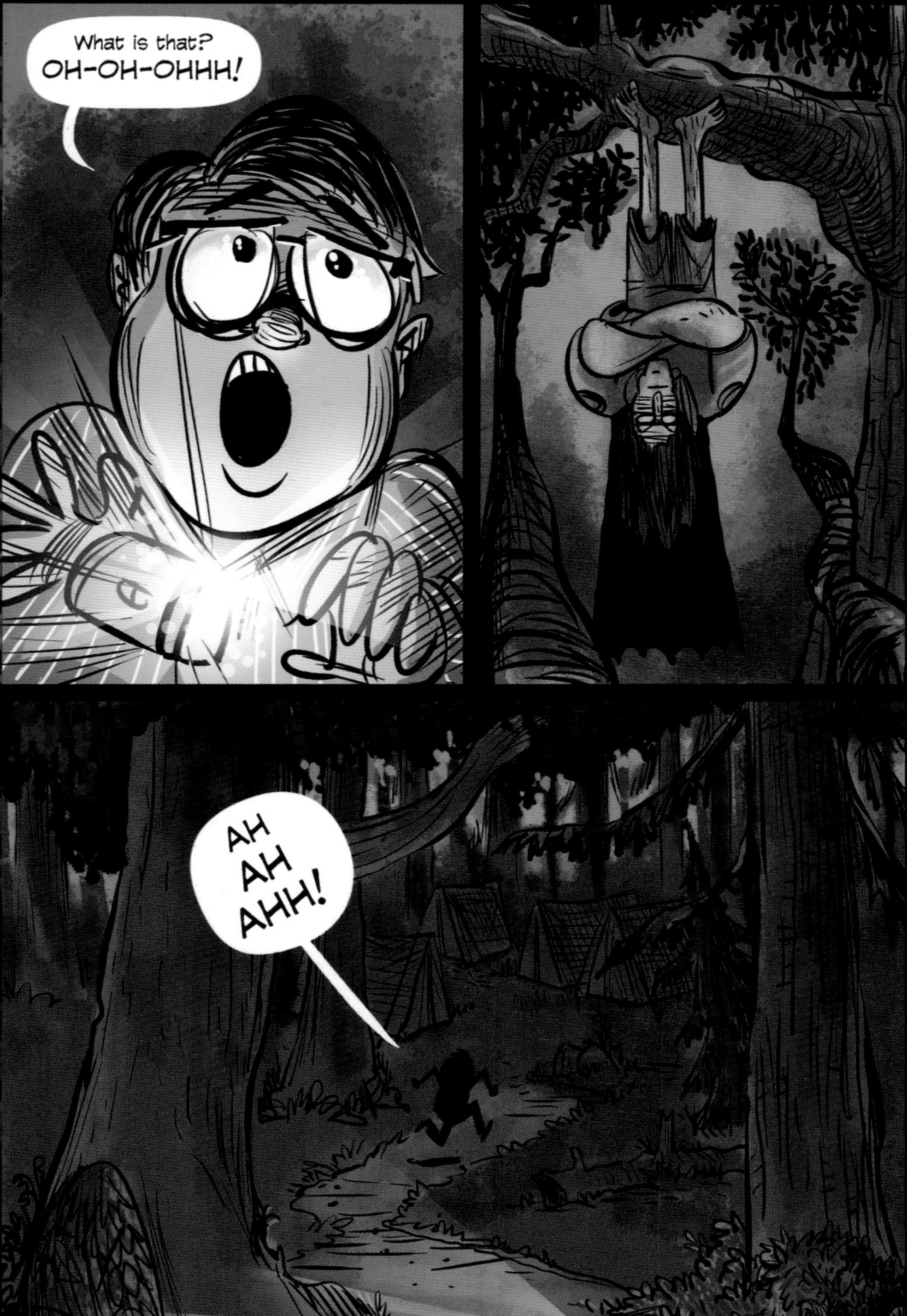
What is that? OH-OH-OHHH!
AH AH AHH!

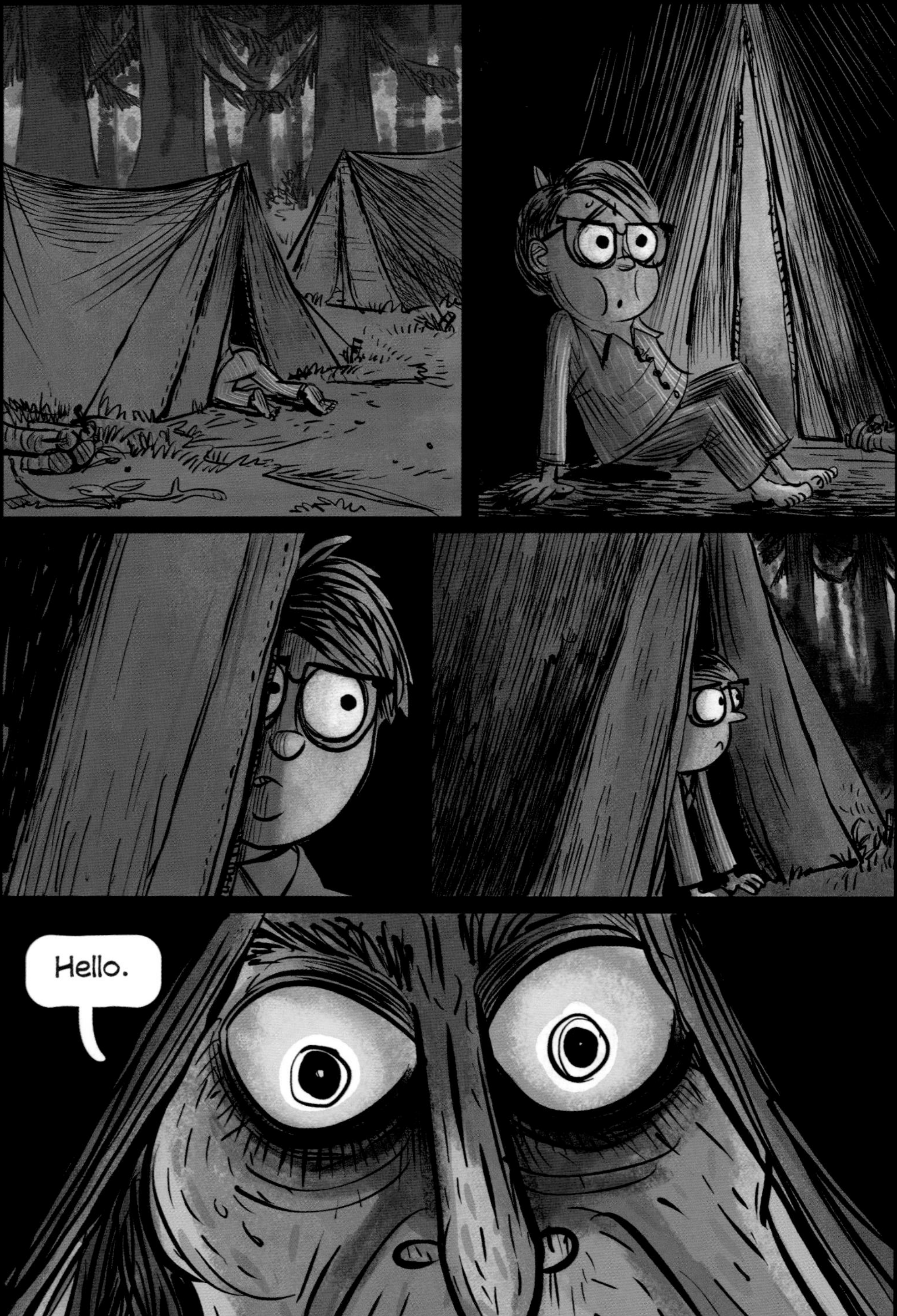
Hello.

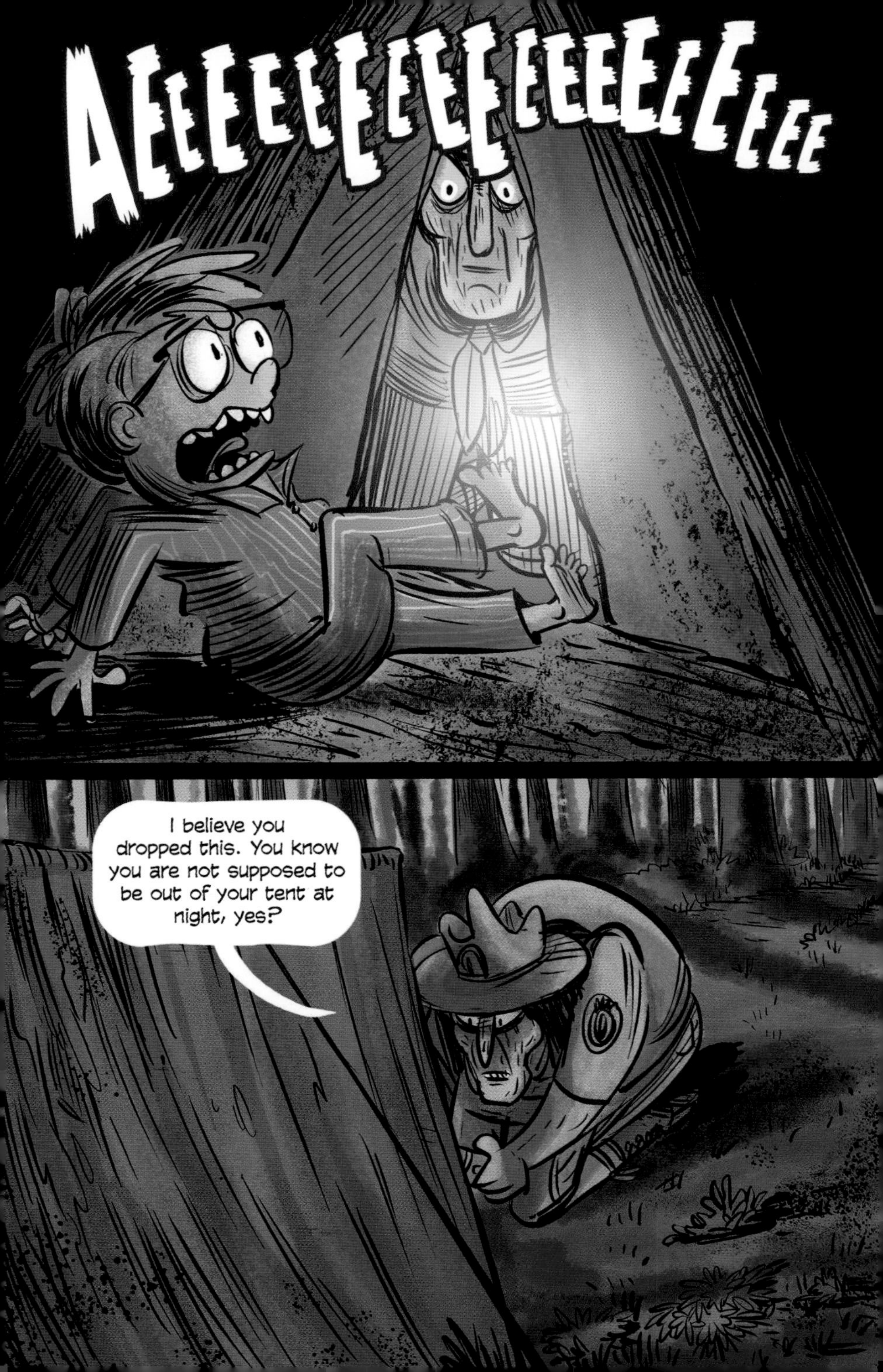
AEEEEEEEEEEEEEEEEEEE
I believe you dropped this. You know you are not supposed to be out of your tent at night, yes?

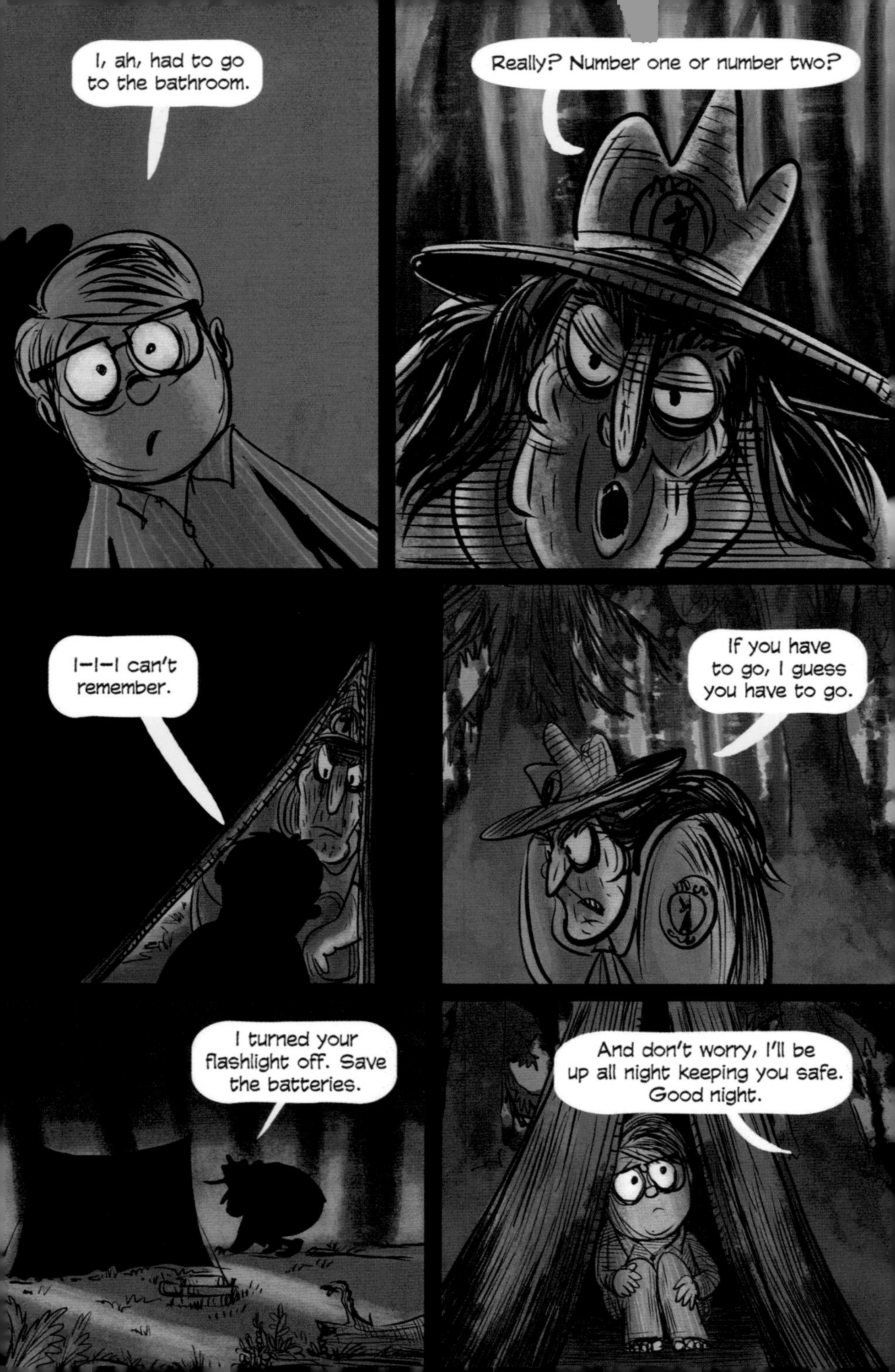
I, ah, had to go to the bathroom.
Really? Number one or number two?
I–I–I can't remember.
If you have to go, I guess you have to go.
I turned your flashlight off. Save the batteries.
And don't worry, I'll be up all night keeping you safe. Good night.

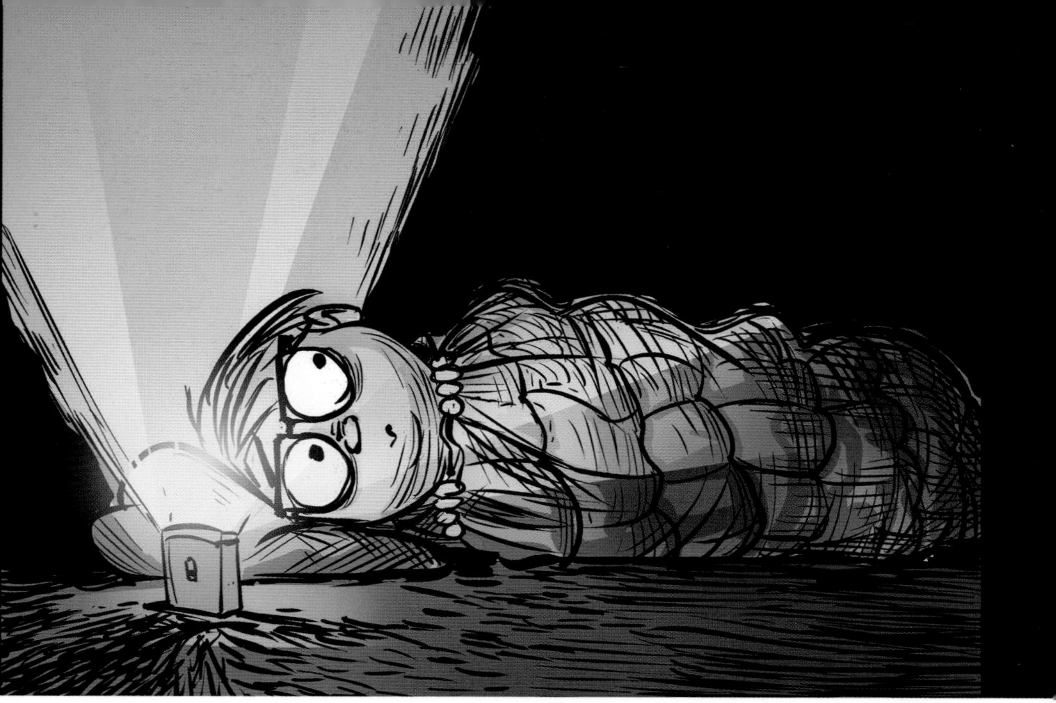

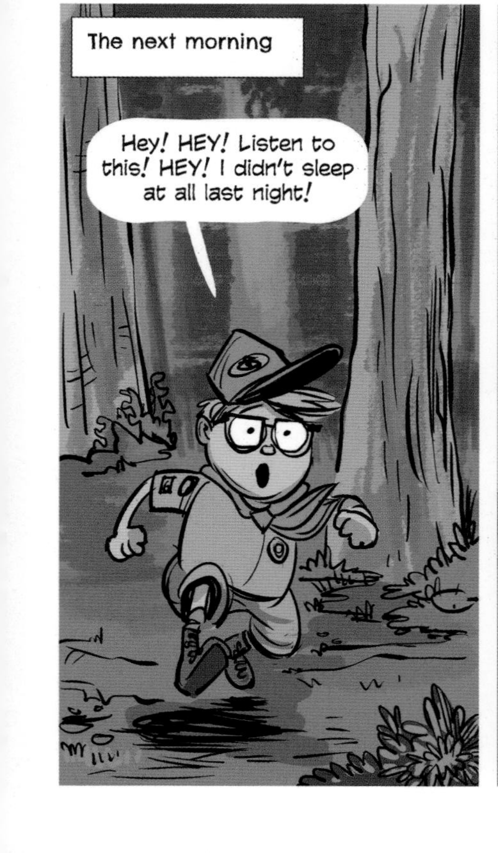
The next morning
Hey! HEY! Listen to this! HEY! I didn't sleep at all last night!

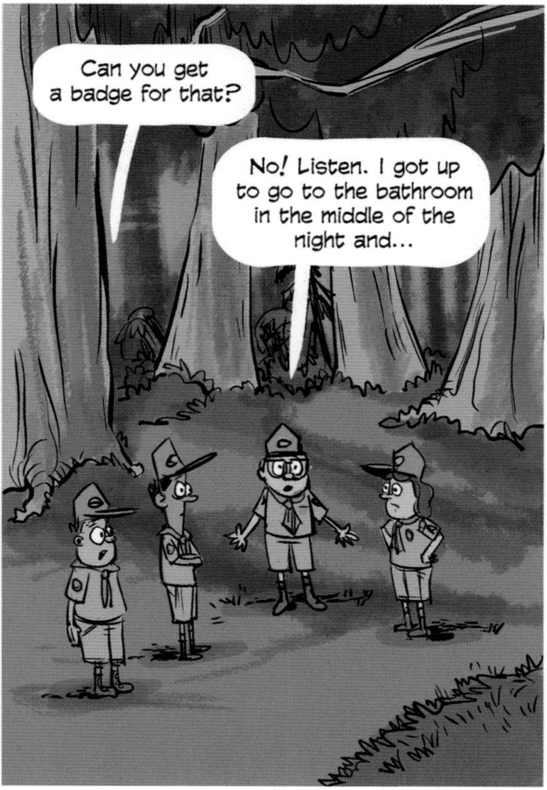
Can you get a badge for that?
No! Listen. I got up to go to the bathroom in the middle of the night and...

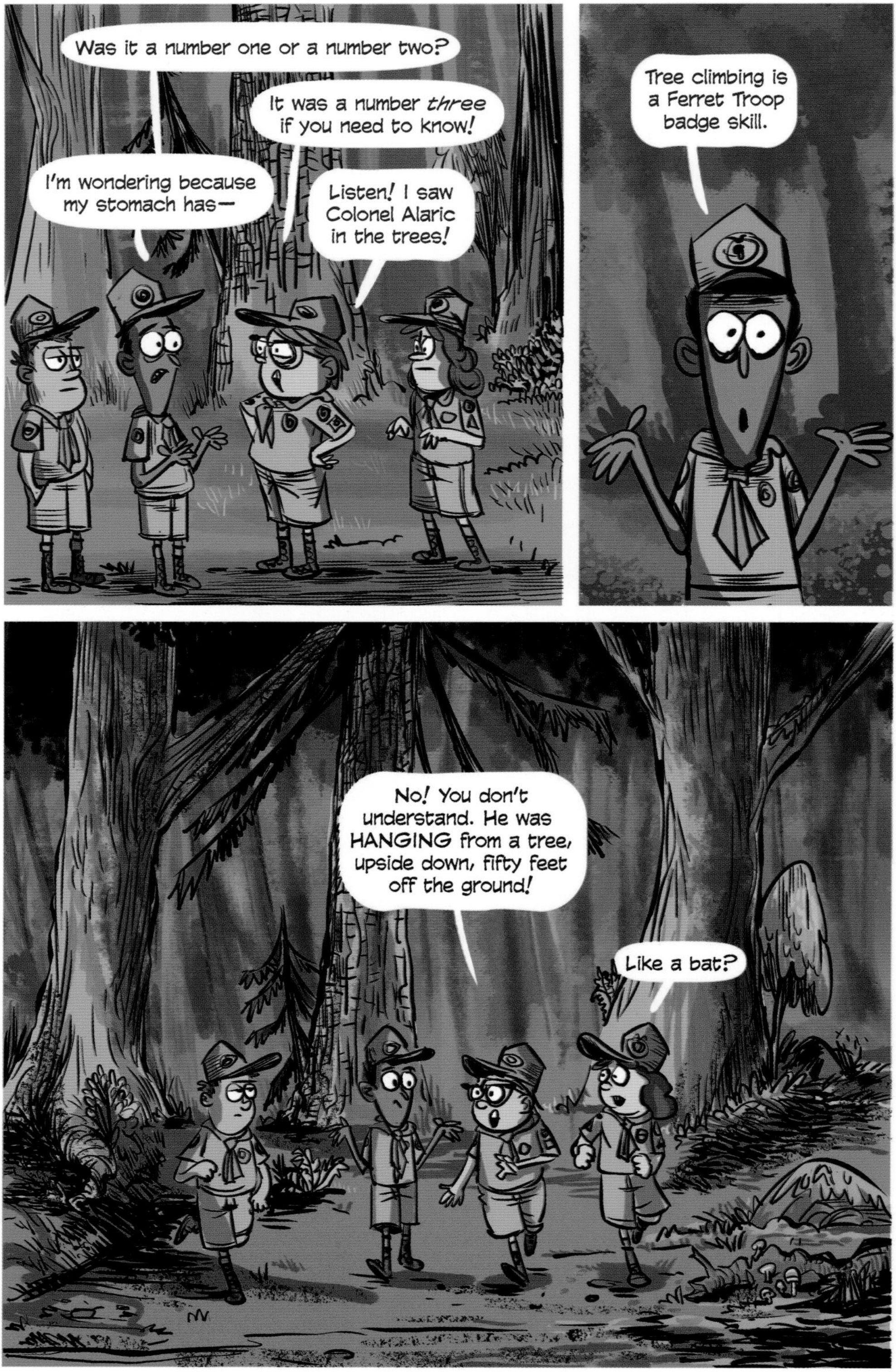
Was it a number one or a number two?
It was a number *three* if you need to know!
I'm wondering because my stomach has—
Listen! I saw Colonel Alaric in the trees!
Tree climbing is a Ferret Troop badge skill.
No! You don't understand. He was HANGING from a tree, upside down, fifty feet off the ground!
Like a bat?

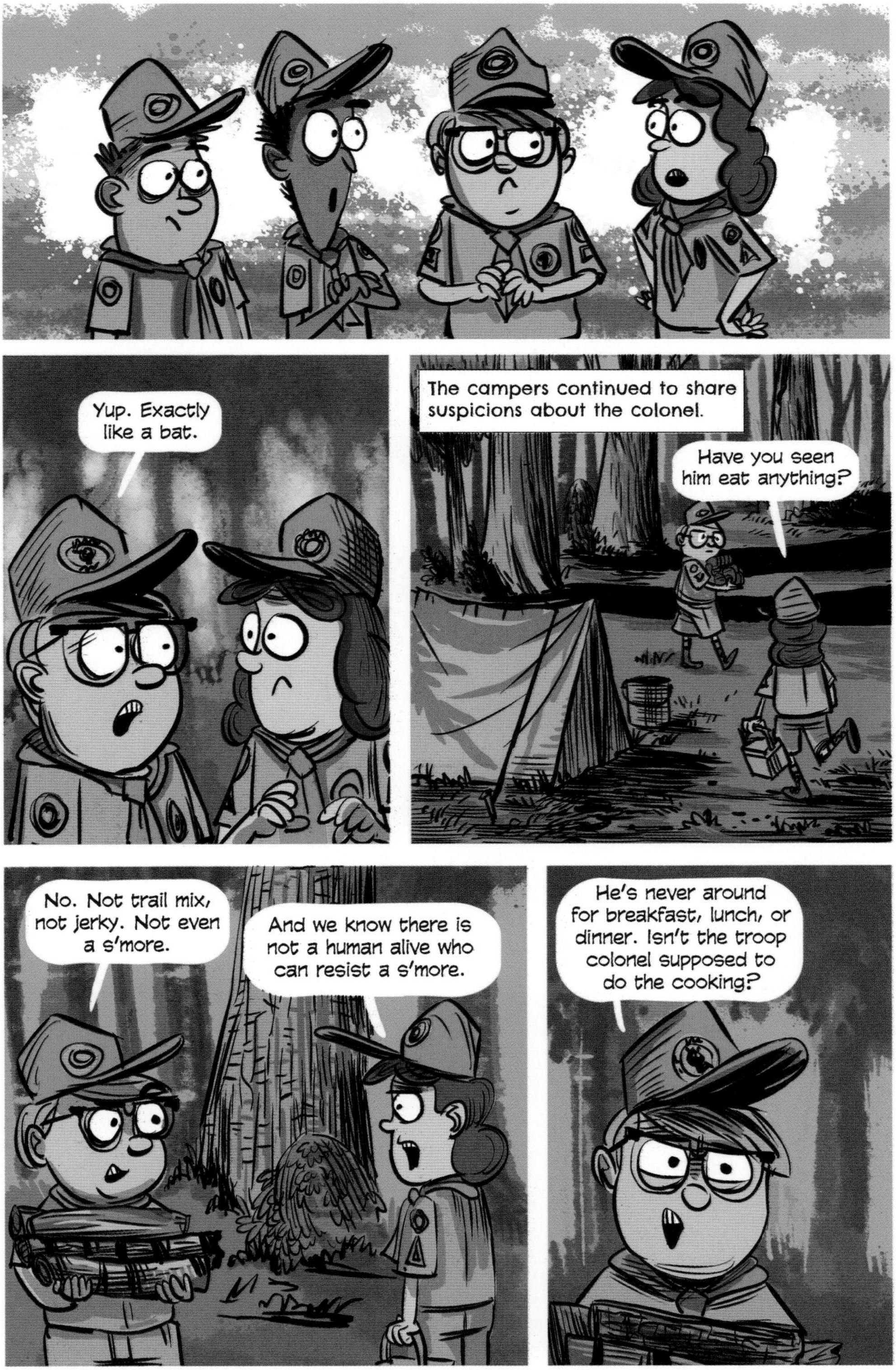
Yup. Exactly like a bat.
The campers continued to share suspicions about the colonel.
Have you seen him eat anything?
No. Not trail mix, not jerky. Not even a s'more.
And we know there is not a human alive who can resist a s'more.
He's never around for breakfast, lunch, or dinner. Isn't the troop colonel supposed to do the cooking?

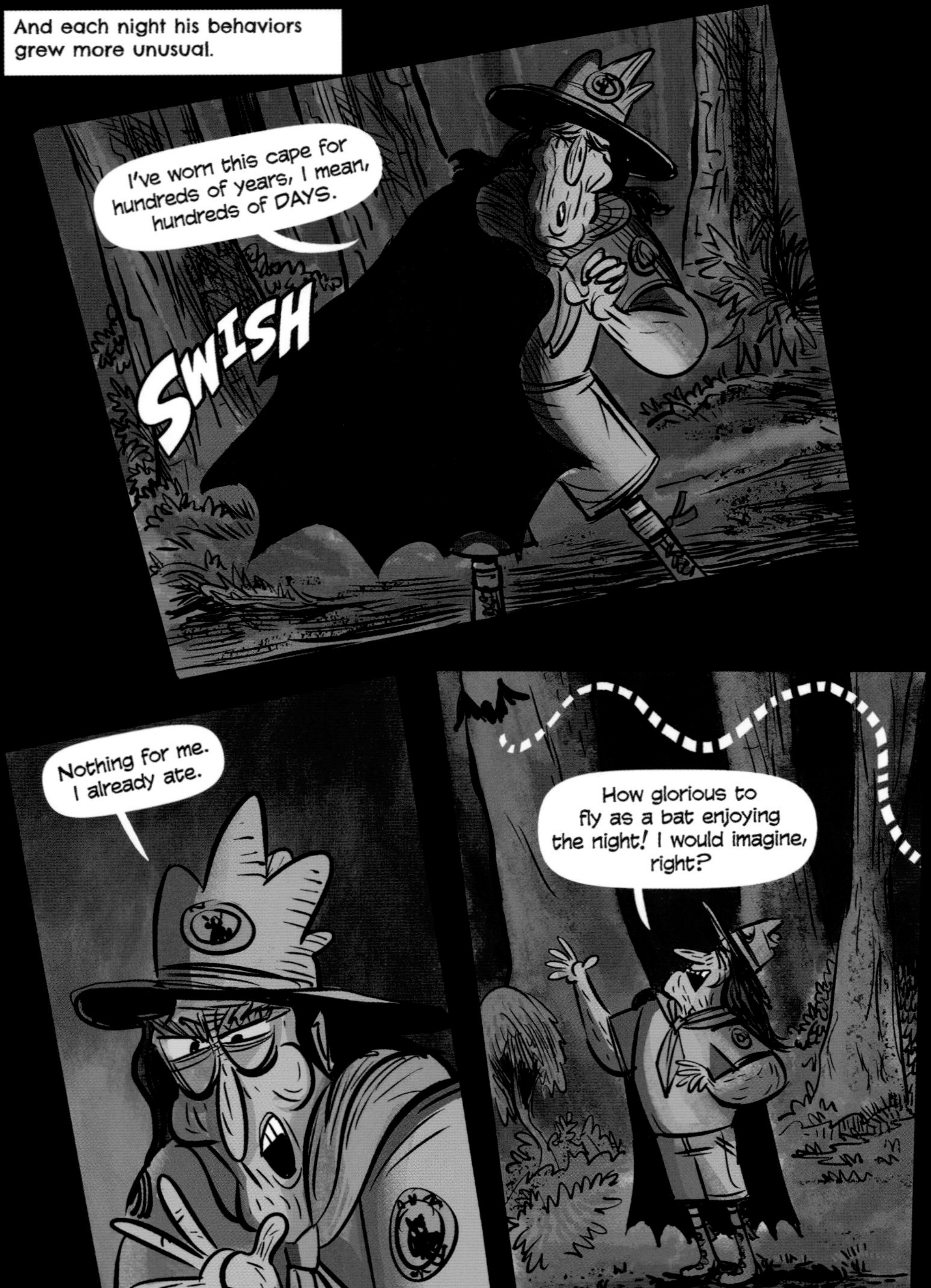
And each night his behaviors grew more unusual.
I've worn this cape for hundreds of years, I mean, hundreds of DAYS.
SWISH
Nothing for me. I already ate.
How glorious to fly as a bat enjoying the night! I would imagine, right?

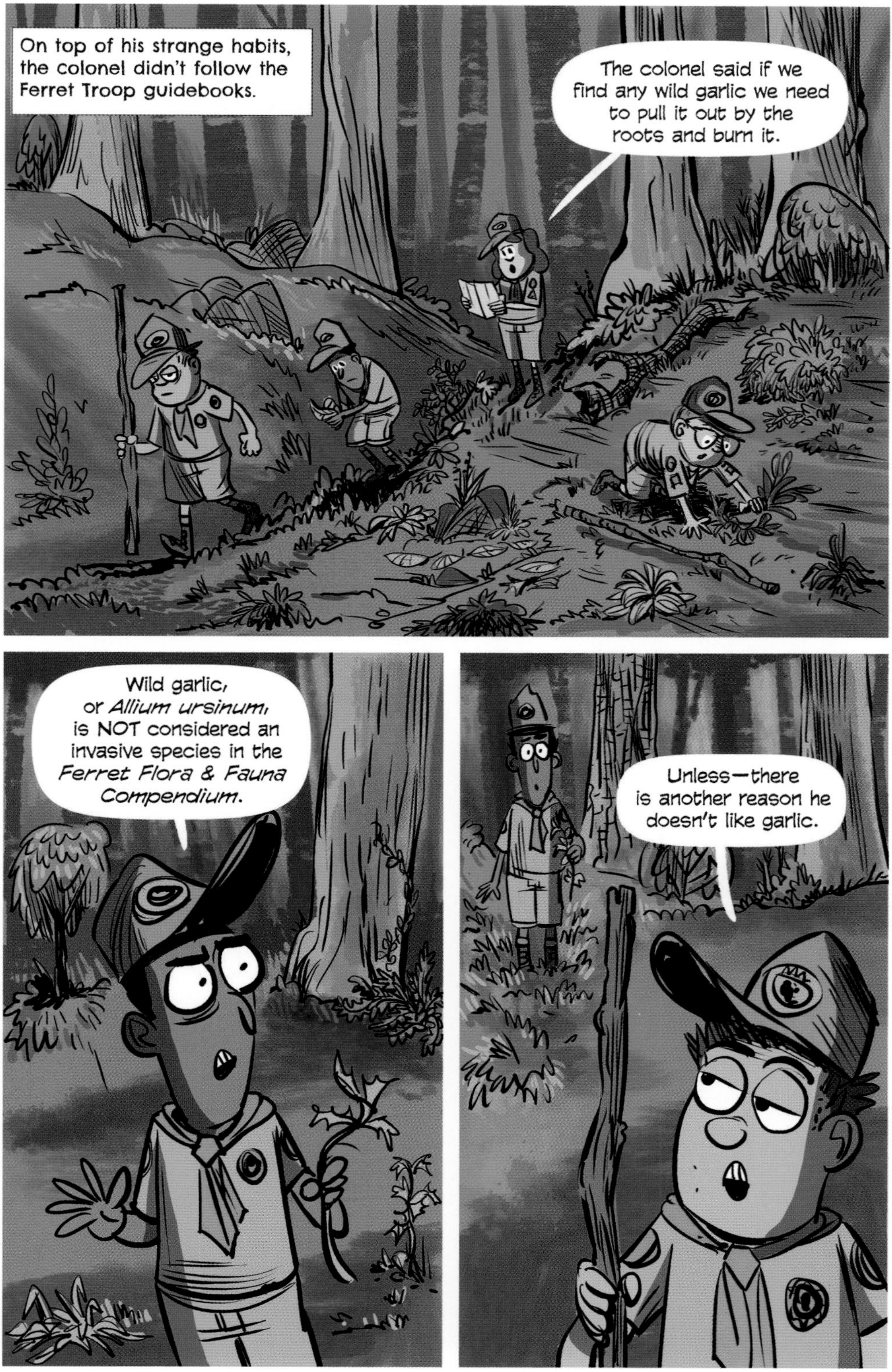
On top of his strange habits, the colonel didn't follow the Ferret Troop guidebooks.
The colonel said if we find any wild garlic we need to pull it out by the roots and burn it.
Wild garlic, or *Allium ursinum*, is NOT considered an invasive species in the *Ferret Flora & Fauna Compendium*.
Unless—there is another reason he doesn't like garlic.

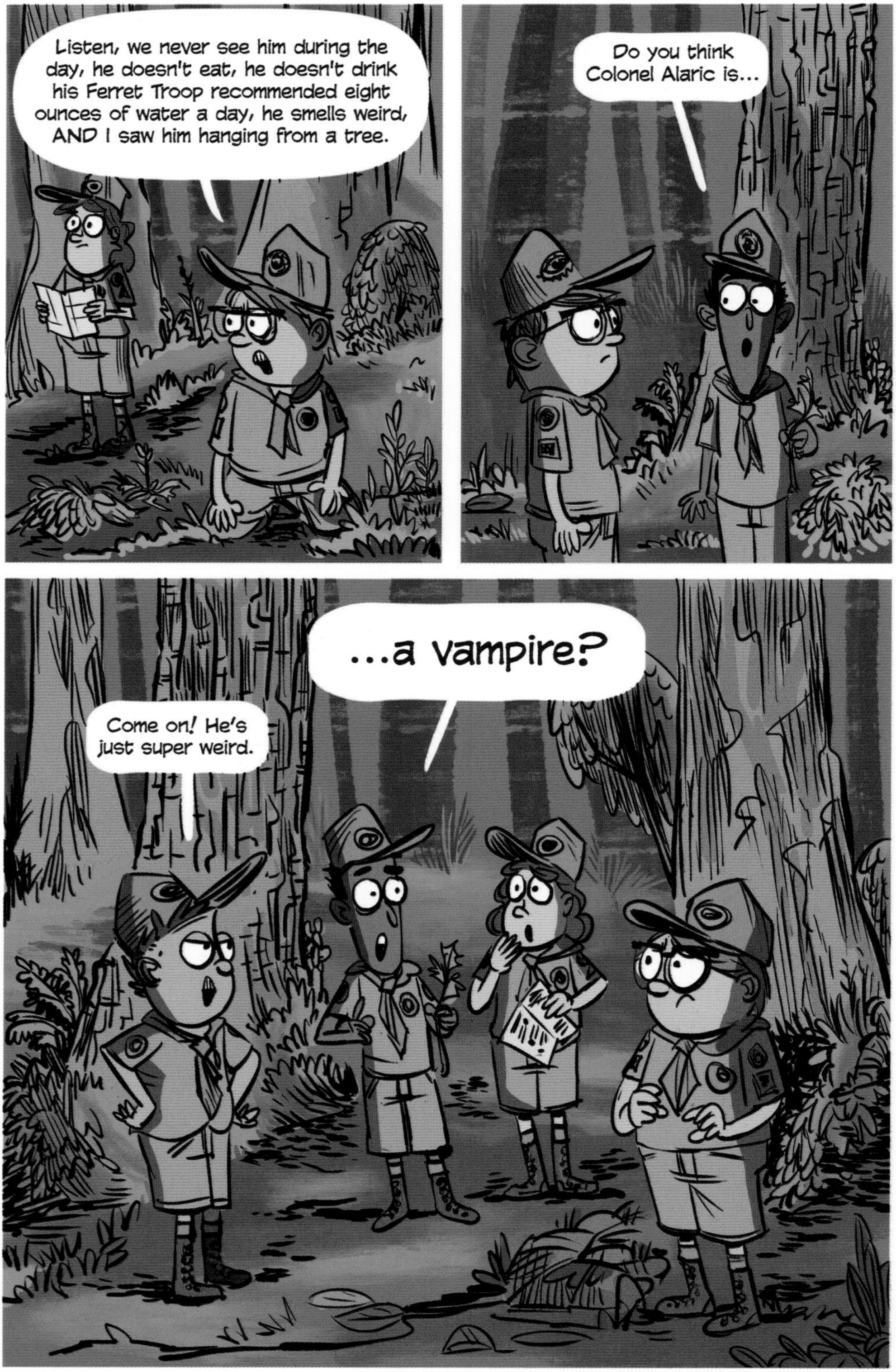
Listen, we never see him during the day, he doesn't eat, he doesn't drink his Ferret Troop recommended eight ounces of water a day, he smells weird, AND I saw him hanging from a tree.
Do you think Colonel Alaric is...
...a vampire?
Come on! He's just super weird.

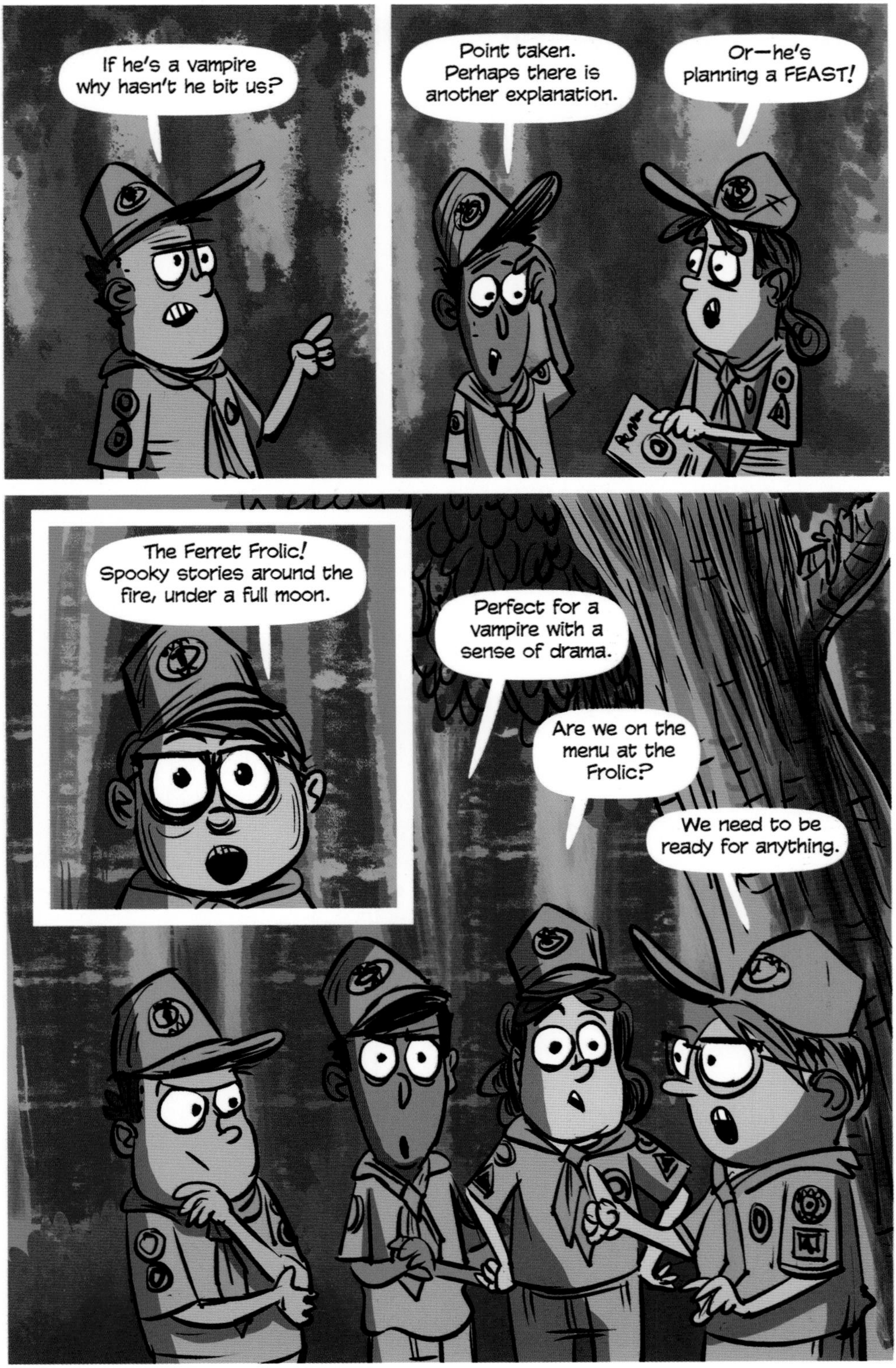
If he's a vampire why hasn't he bit us?
Point taken. Perhaps there is another explanation.
Or—he's planning a FEAST!
The Ferret Frolic! Spooky stories around the fire, under a full moon.
Perfect for a vampire with a sense of drama.
Are we on the menu at the Frolic?
We need to be ready for anything.

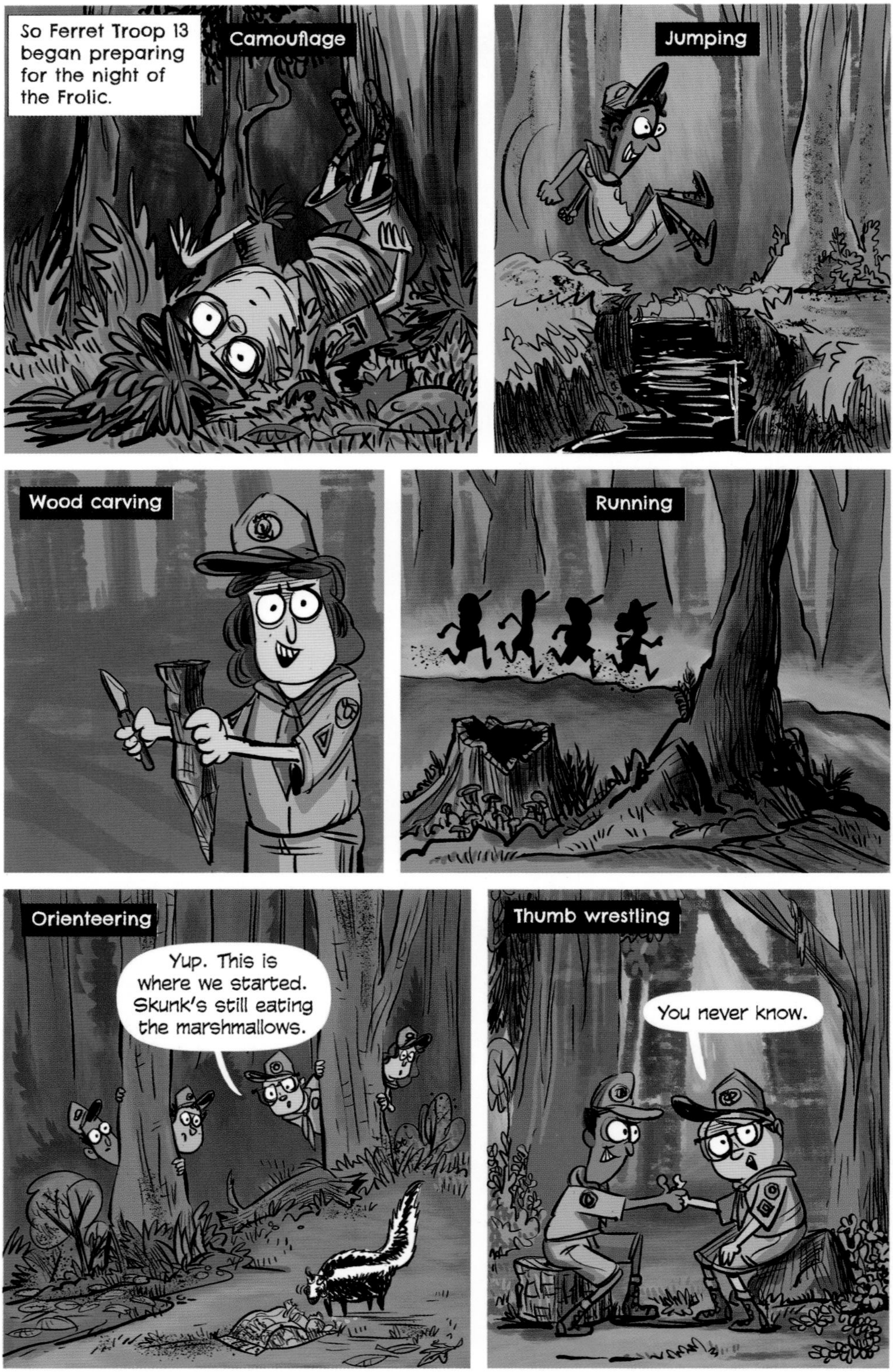
So Ferret Troop 13 began preparing for the night of the Frolic.
Camouflage
Jumping
Wood carving
Running
Orienteering
Yup. This is where we started. Skunk's still eating the marshmallows.
Thumb wrestling
You never know.

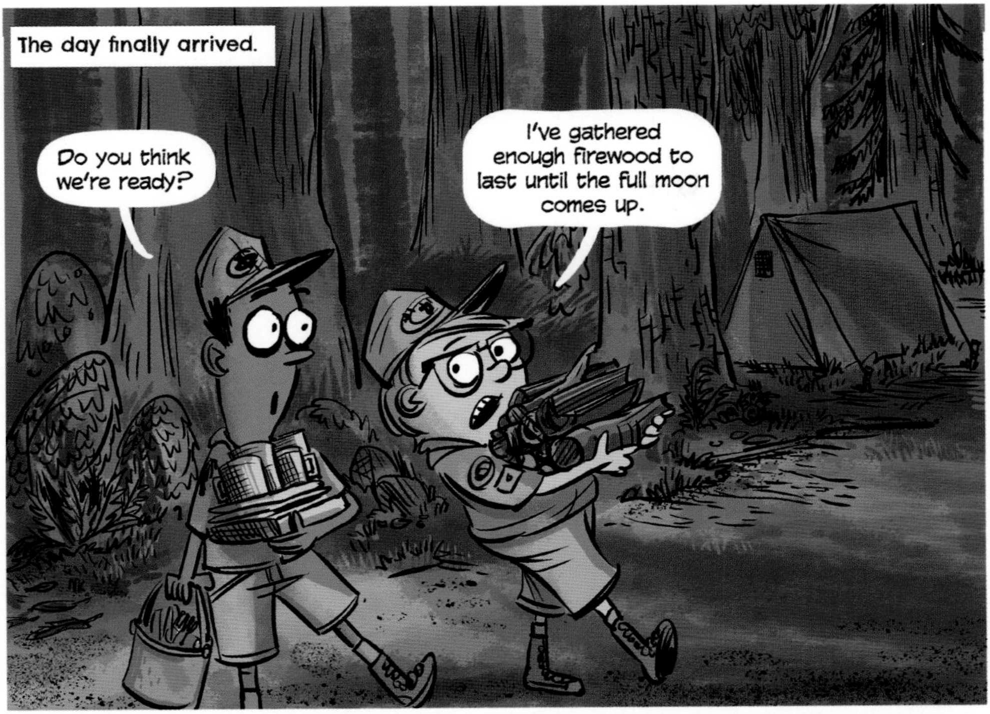
The day finally arrived.
Do you think we're ready?
I've gathered enough firewood to last until the full moon comes up.

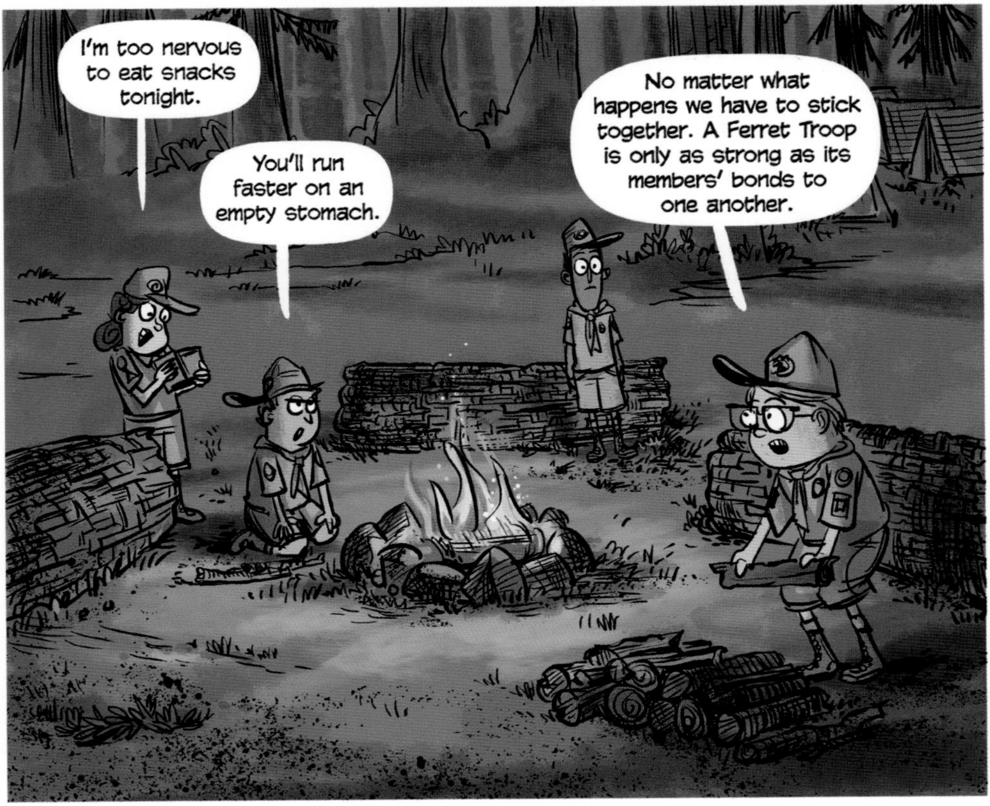
I'm too nervous to eat snacks tonight.
You'll run faster on an empty stomach.
No matter what happens we have to stick together. A Ferret Troop is only as strong as its members' bonds to one another.

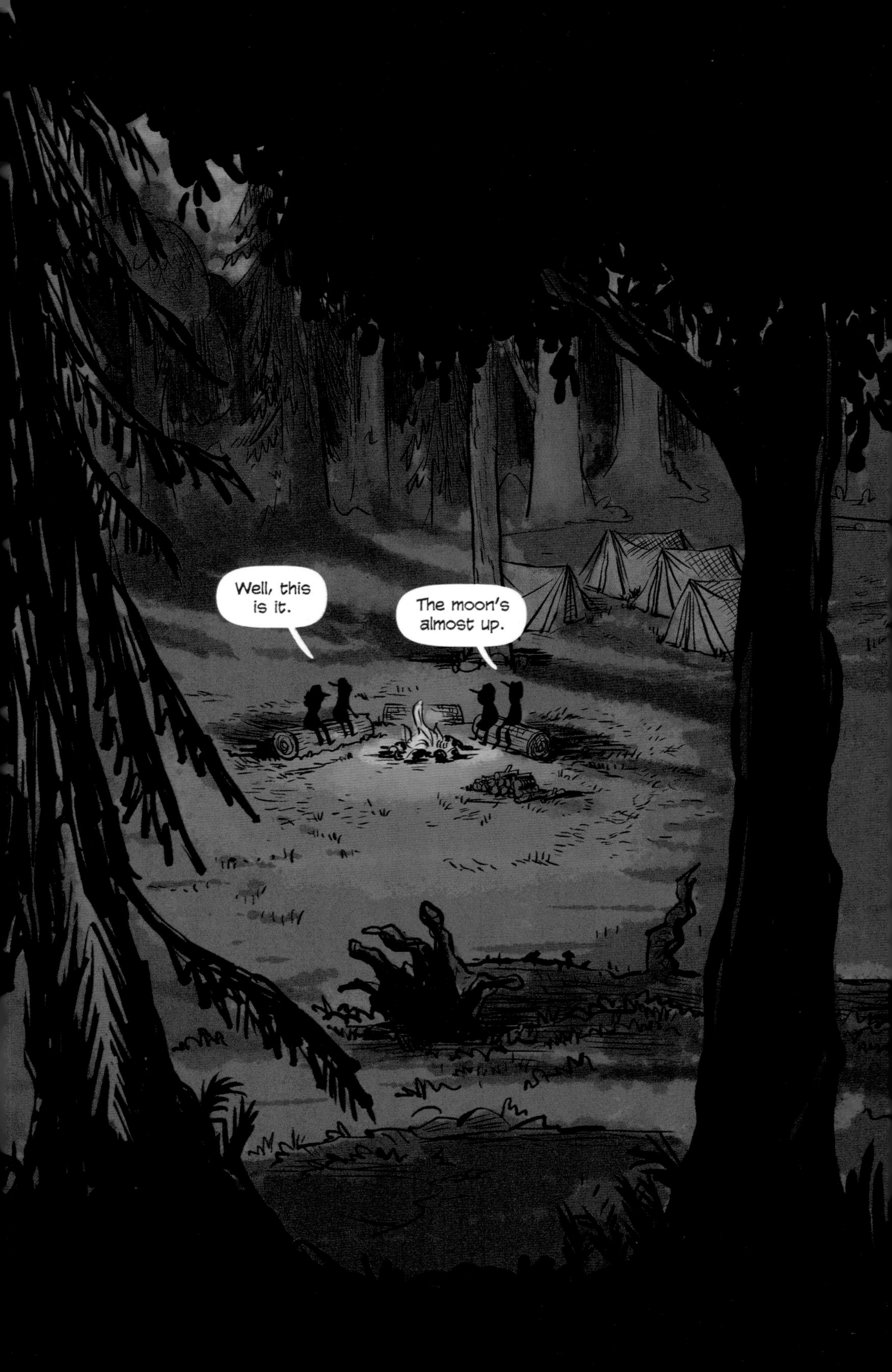
Well, this is it.
The moon's almost up.

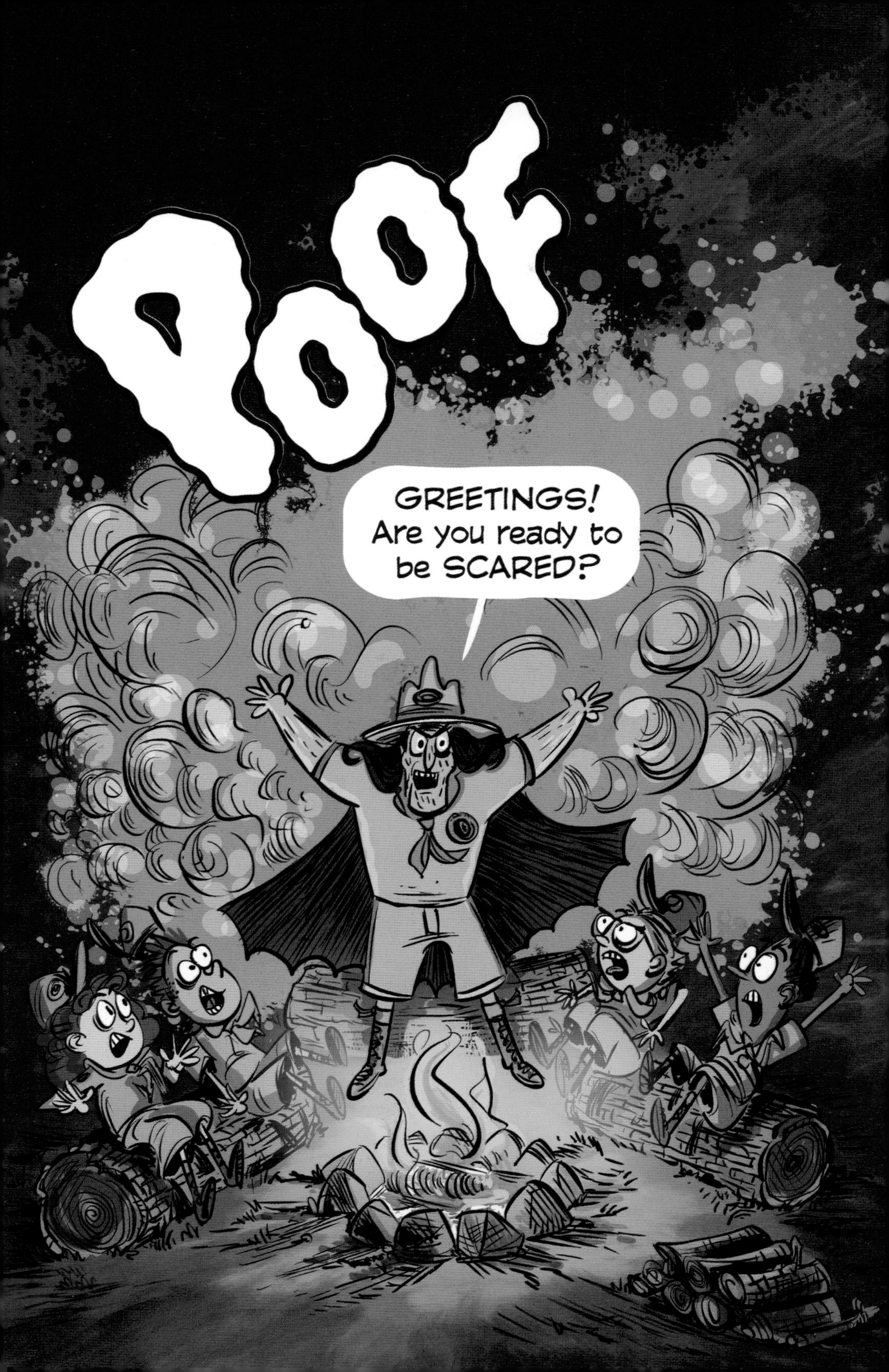
POOF
GREETINGS! Are you ready to be SCARED?

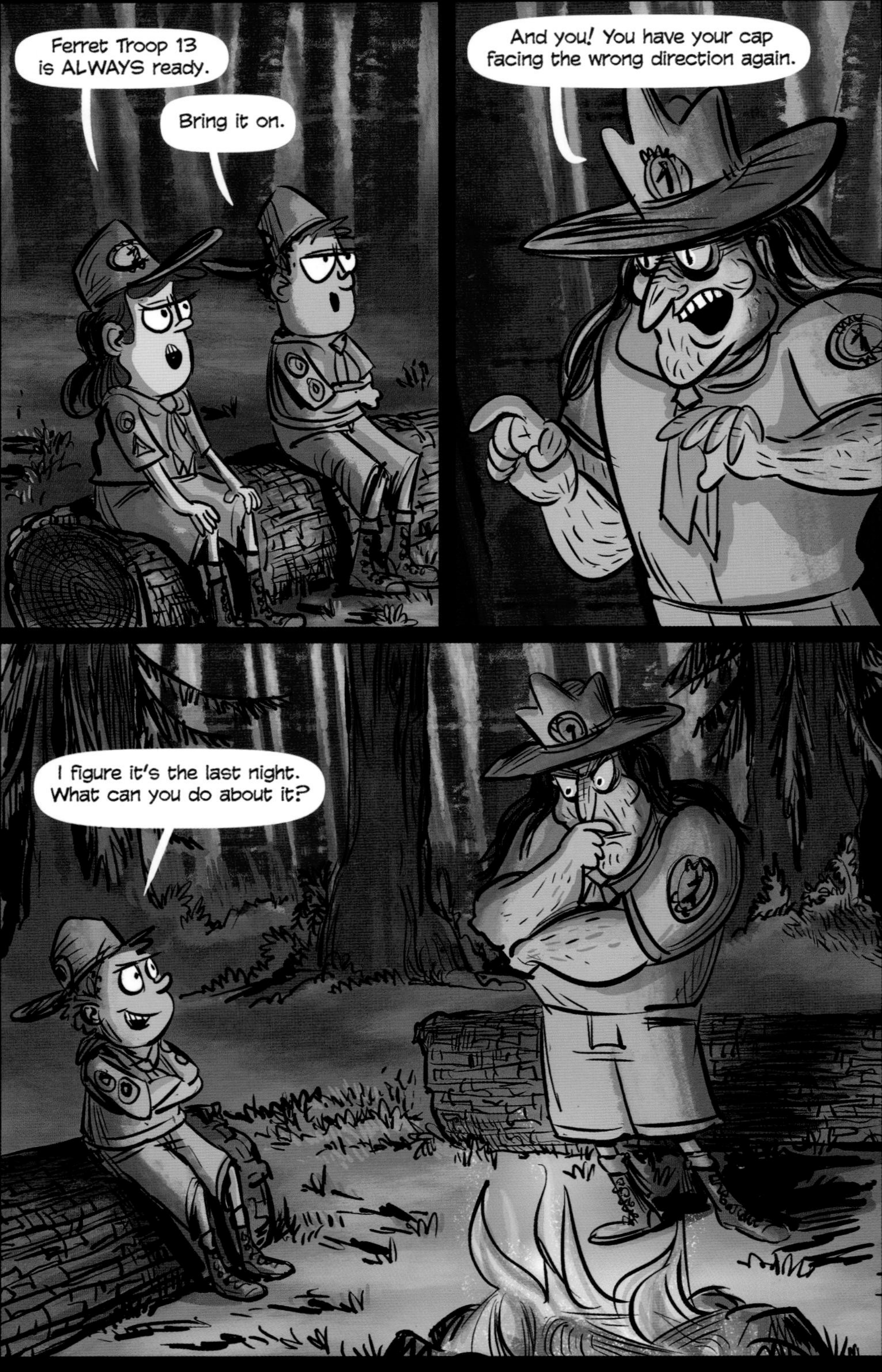
Ferret Troop 13 is ALWAYS ready.
Bring it on.
And you! You have your cap facing the wrong direction again.
I figure it's the last night. What can you do about it?

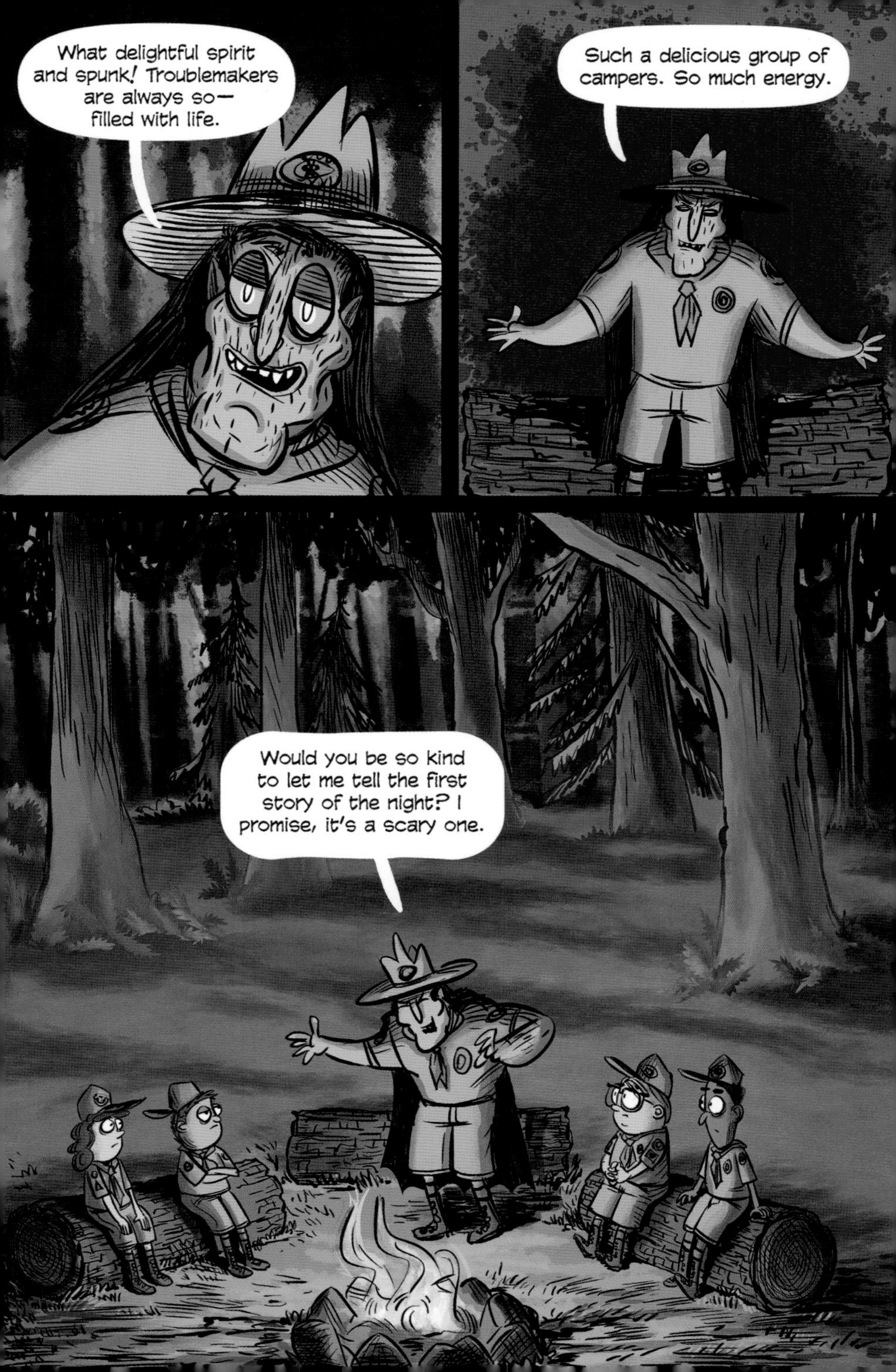
What delightful spirit and spunk! Troublemakers are always so— filled with life.
Such a delicious group of campers. So much energy.
Would you be so kind to let me tell the first story of the night? I promise, it's a scary one.

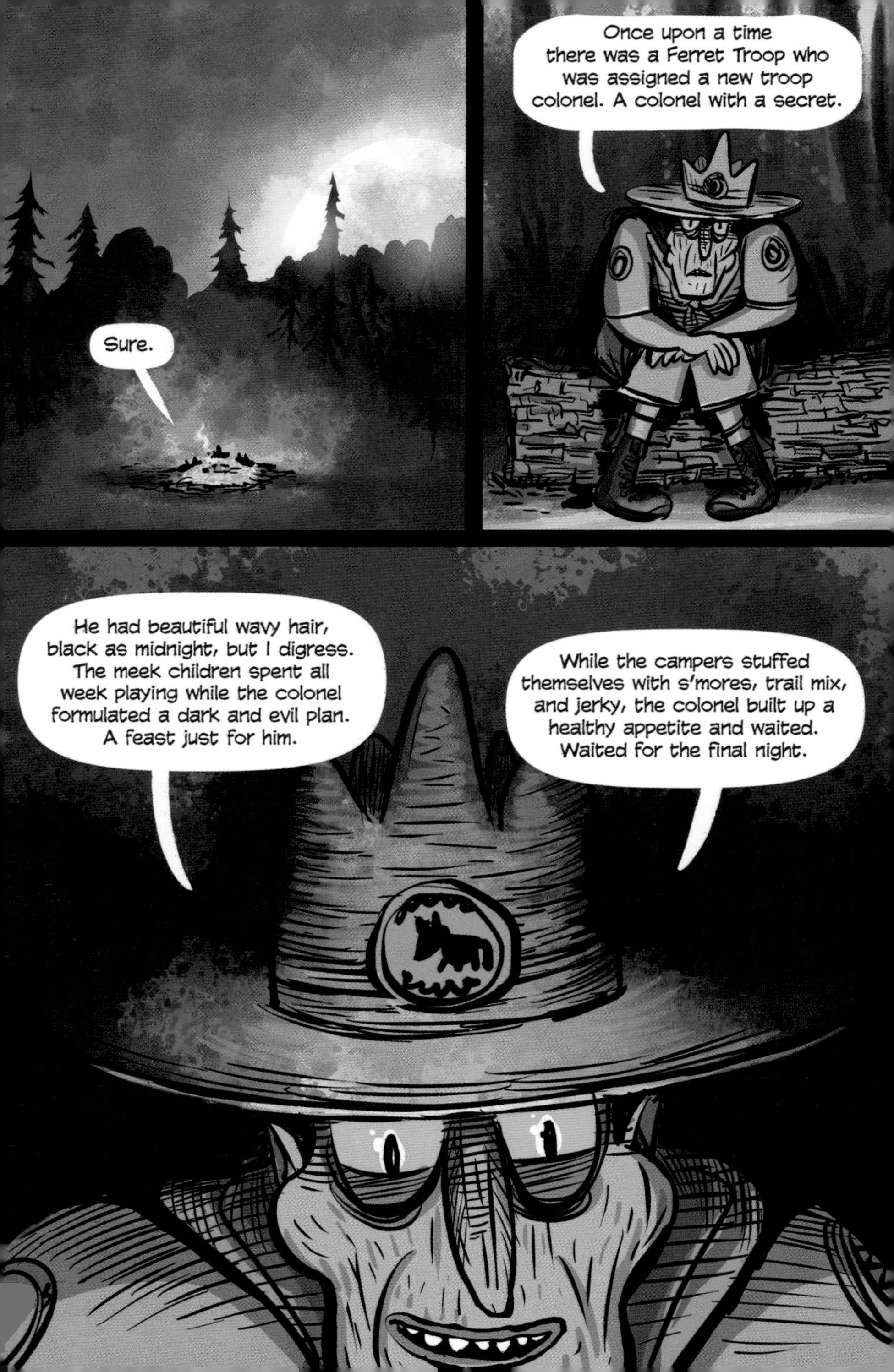
Sure.
Once upon a time there was a Ferret Troop who was assigned a new troop colonel. A colonel with a secret.
He had beautiful wavy hair, black as midnight, but I digress. The meek children spent all week playing while the colonel formulated a dark and evil plan. A feast just for him.
While the campers stuffed themselves with s'mores, trail mix, and jerky, the colonel built up a healthy appetite and waited. Waited for the final night.

And on the final night the colonel would share his plan and his secret with the campers.

Can any of you guess what his secret might be?

That he made a cake to share?

That the dude was way too into his hair?

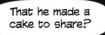

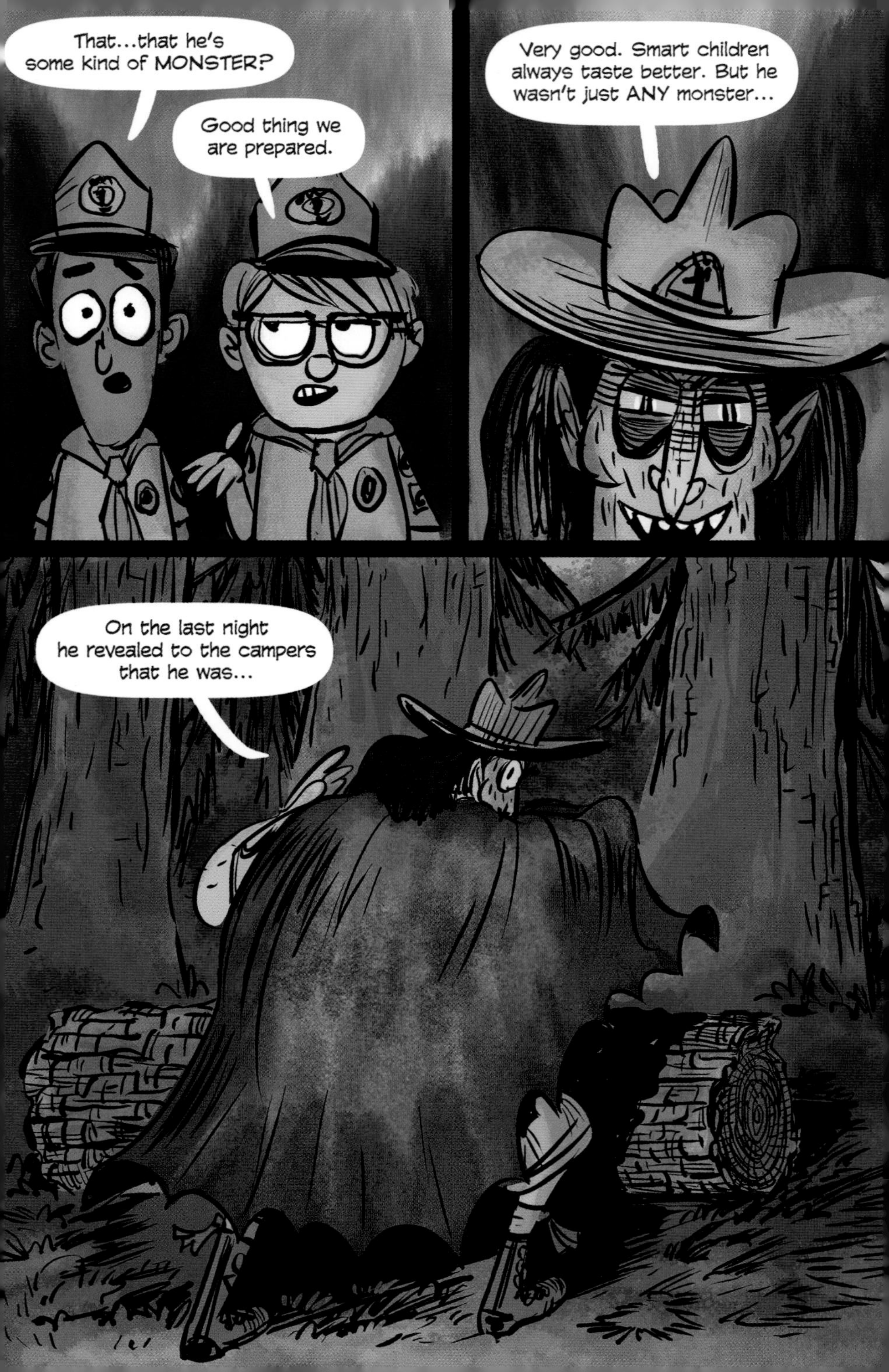
That...that he's some kind of MONSTER?
Good thing we are prepared.
Very good. Smart children always taste better. But he wasn't just ANY monster...
On the last night he revealed to the campers that he was...

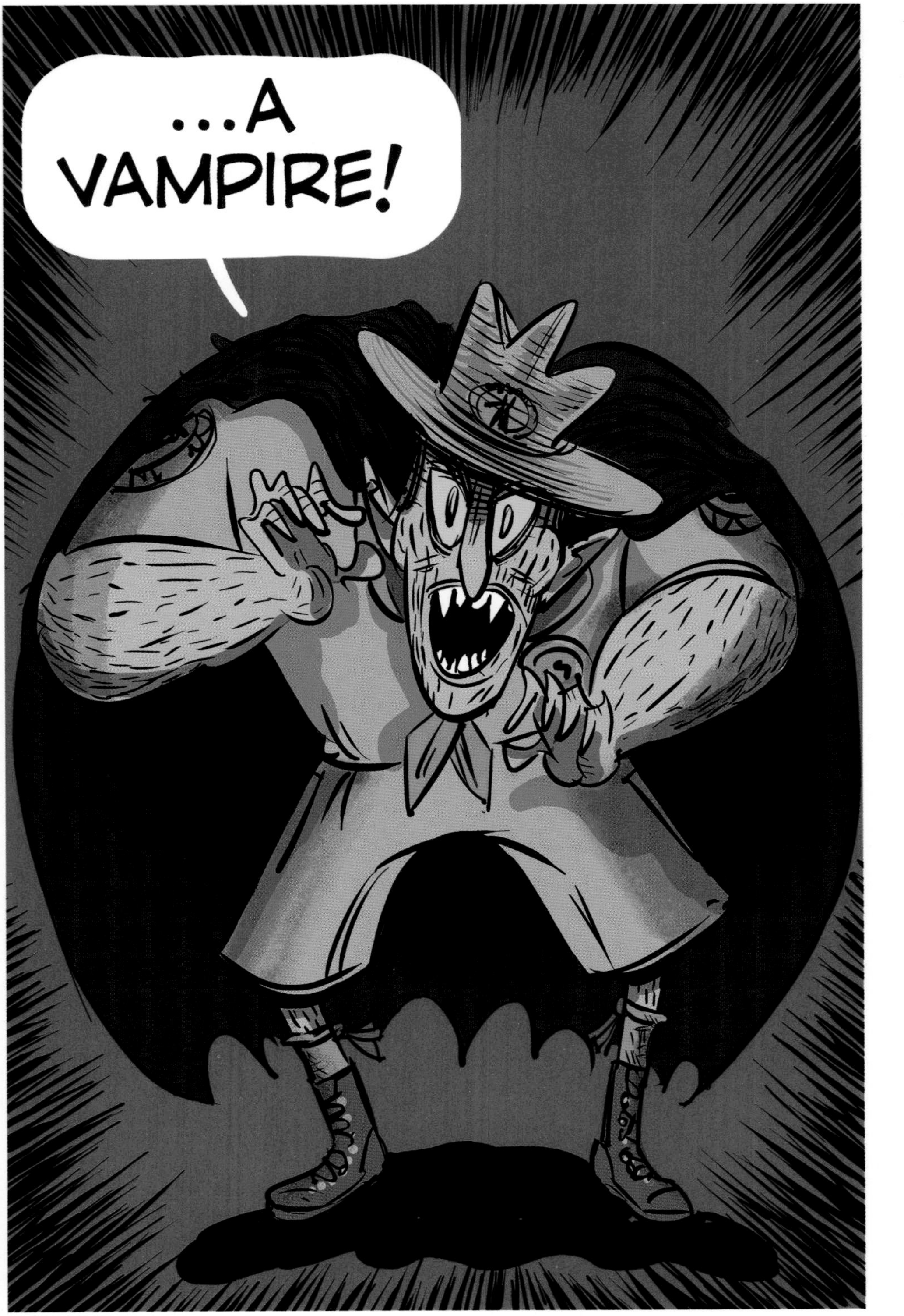
...A VAMPIRE!

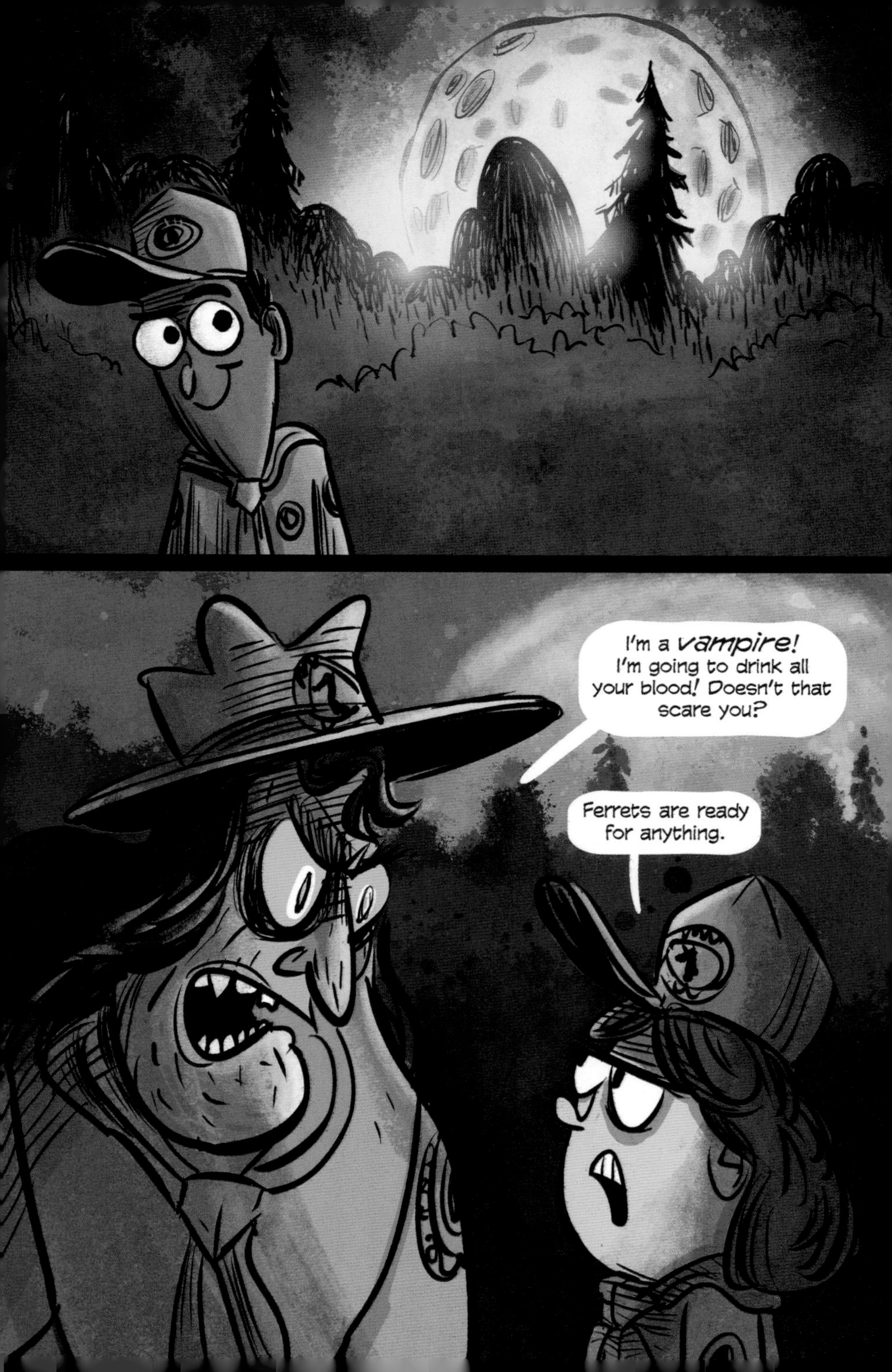
I'm a vampire! I'm going to drink all your blood! Doesn't that scare you?
Ferrets are ready for anything.

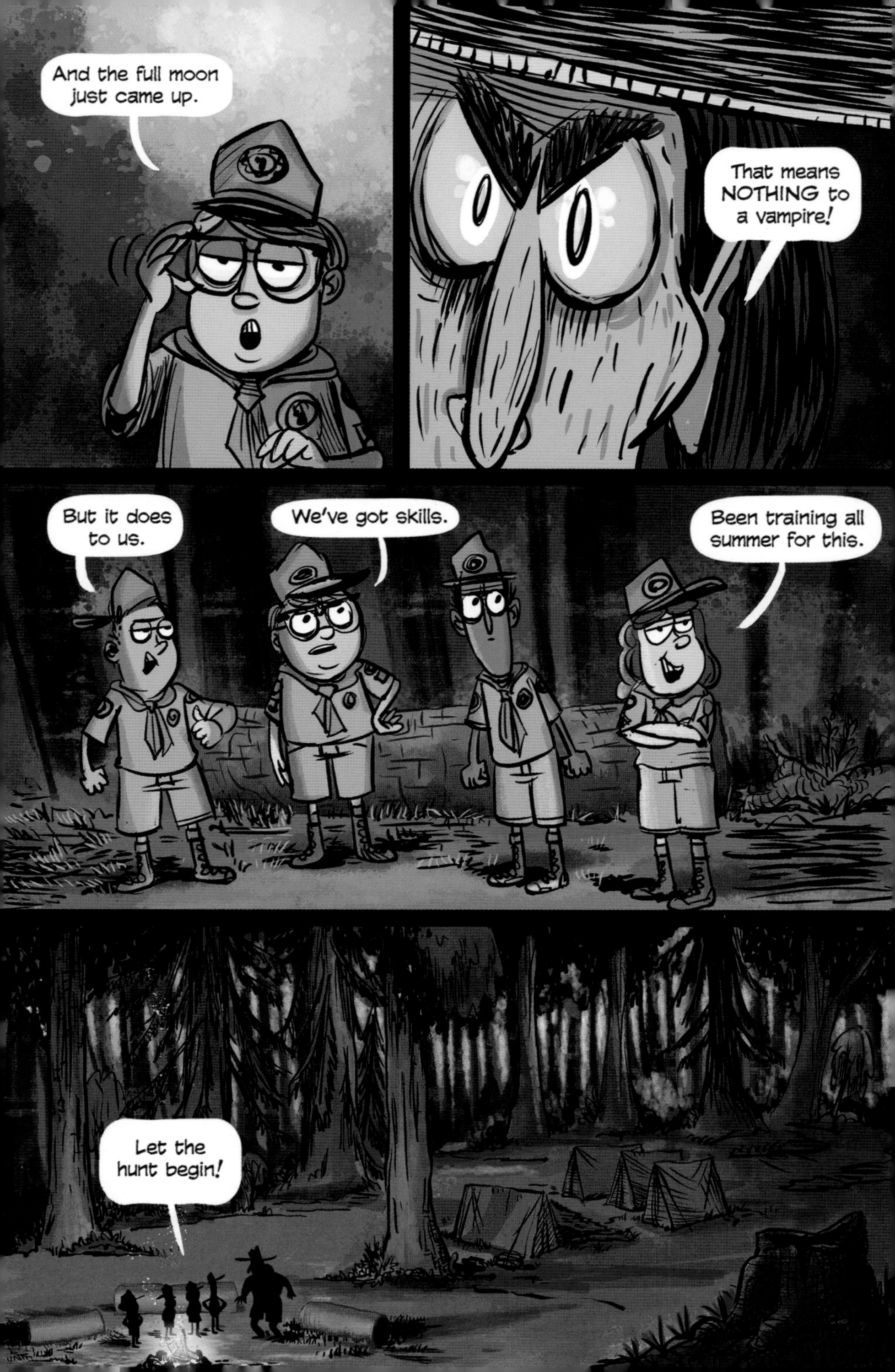
And the full moon just came up.
That means NOTHING to a vampire!
But it does to us.
We've got skills.
Been training all summer for this.
Let the hunt begin!

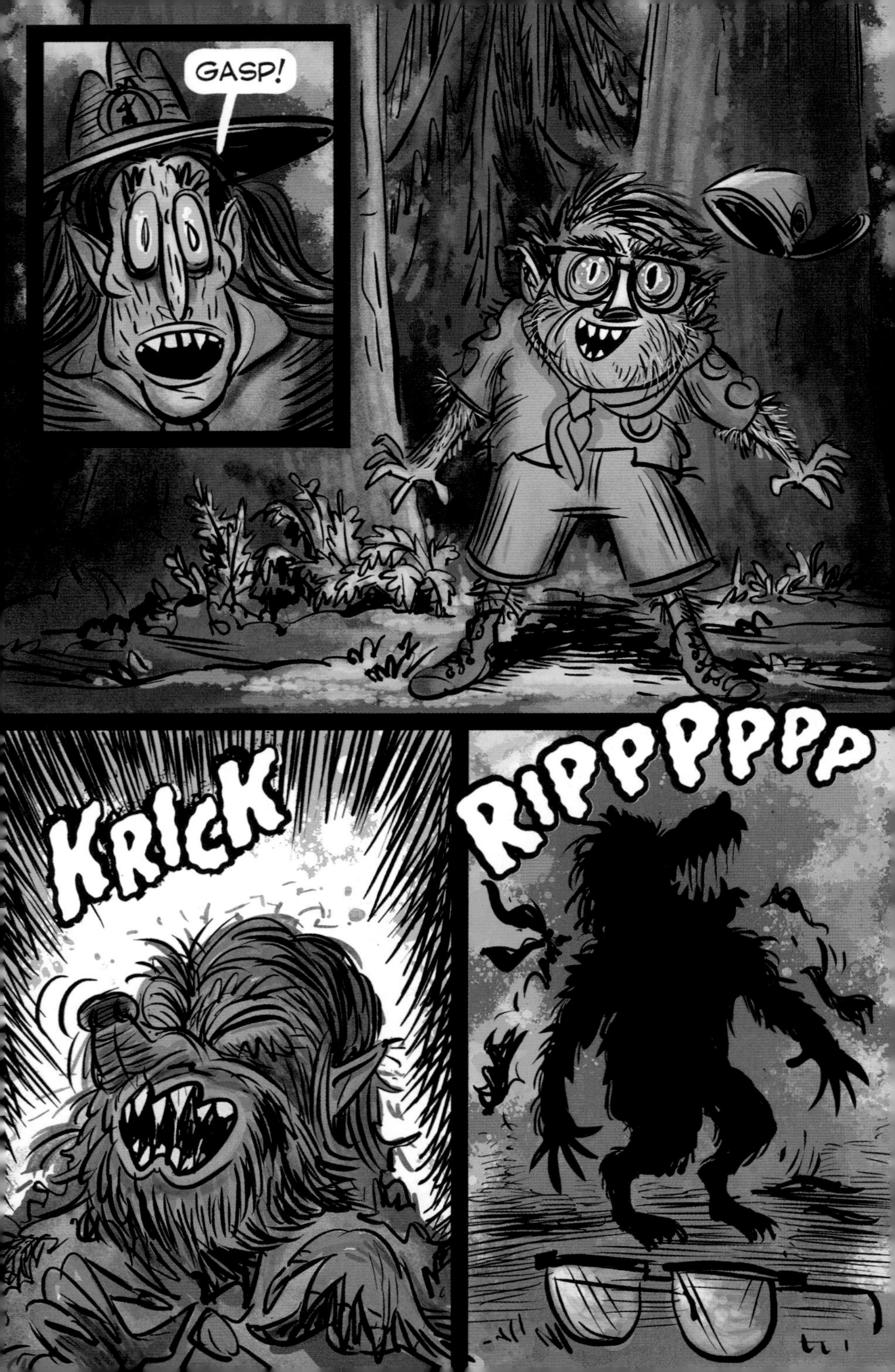
GASP!
KRICK
RIPPPPPPP

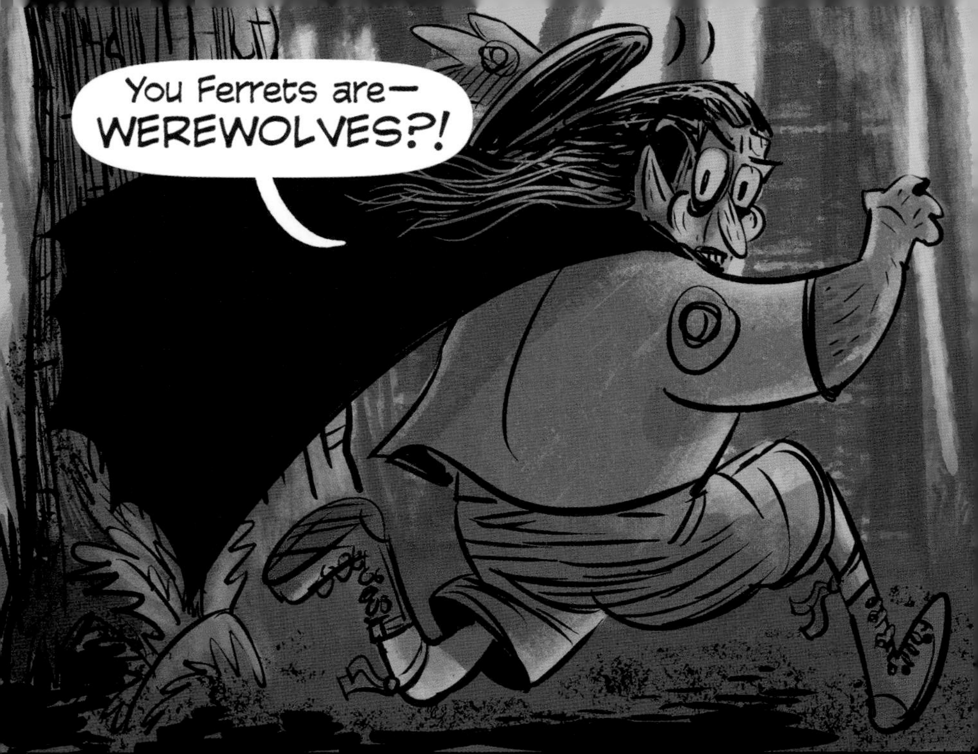
You Ferrets are—
WEREWOLVES?!

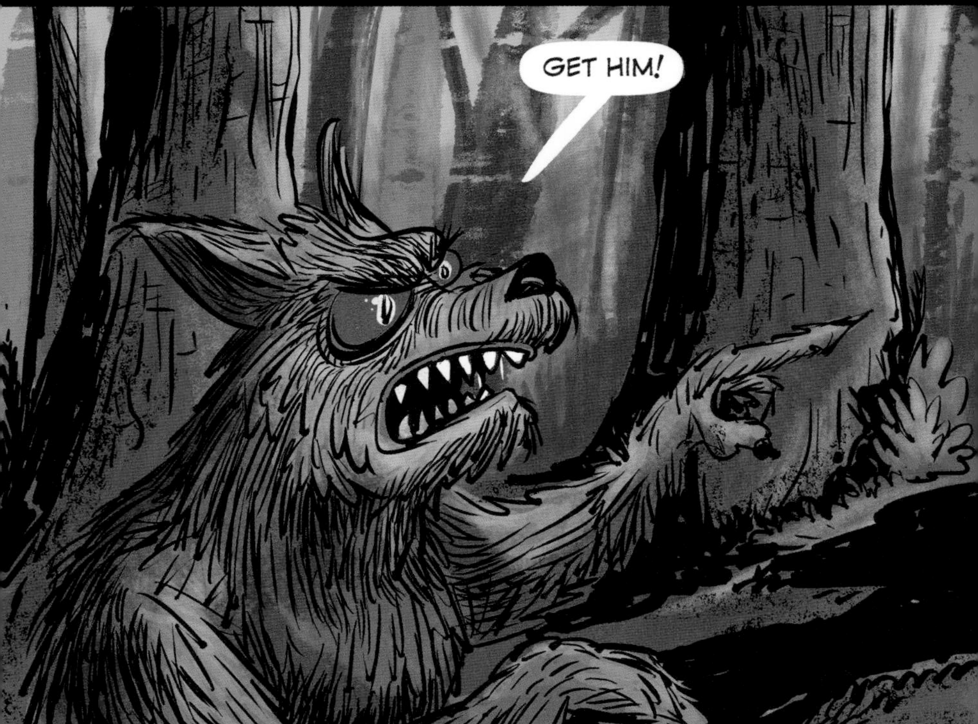
GET HIM!

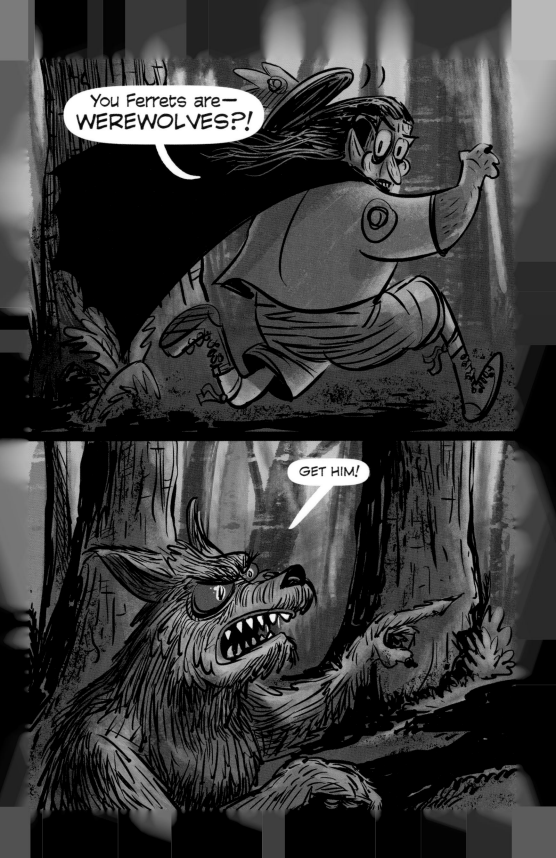

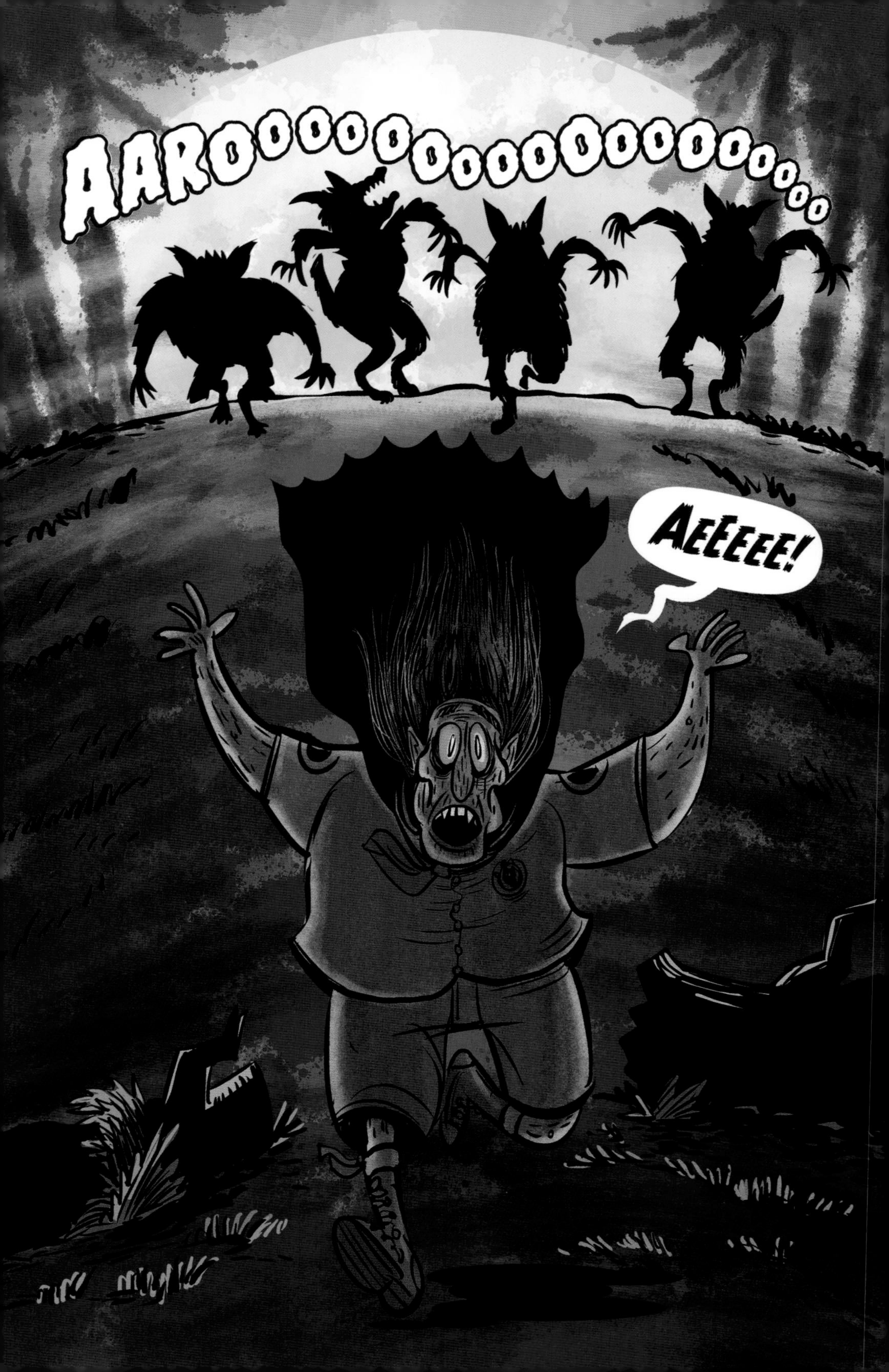
AAROOOOOOOOOOOOOOOOOO
AEEEEE!

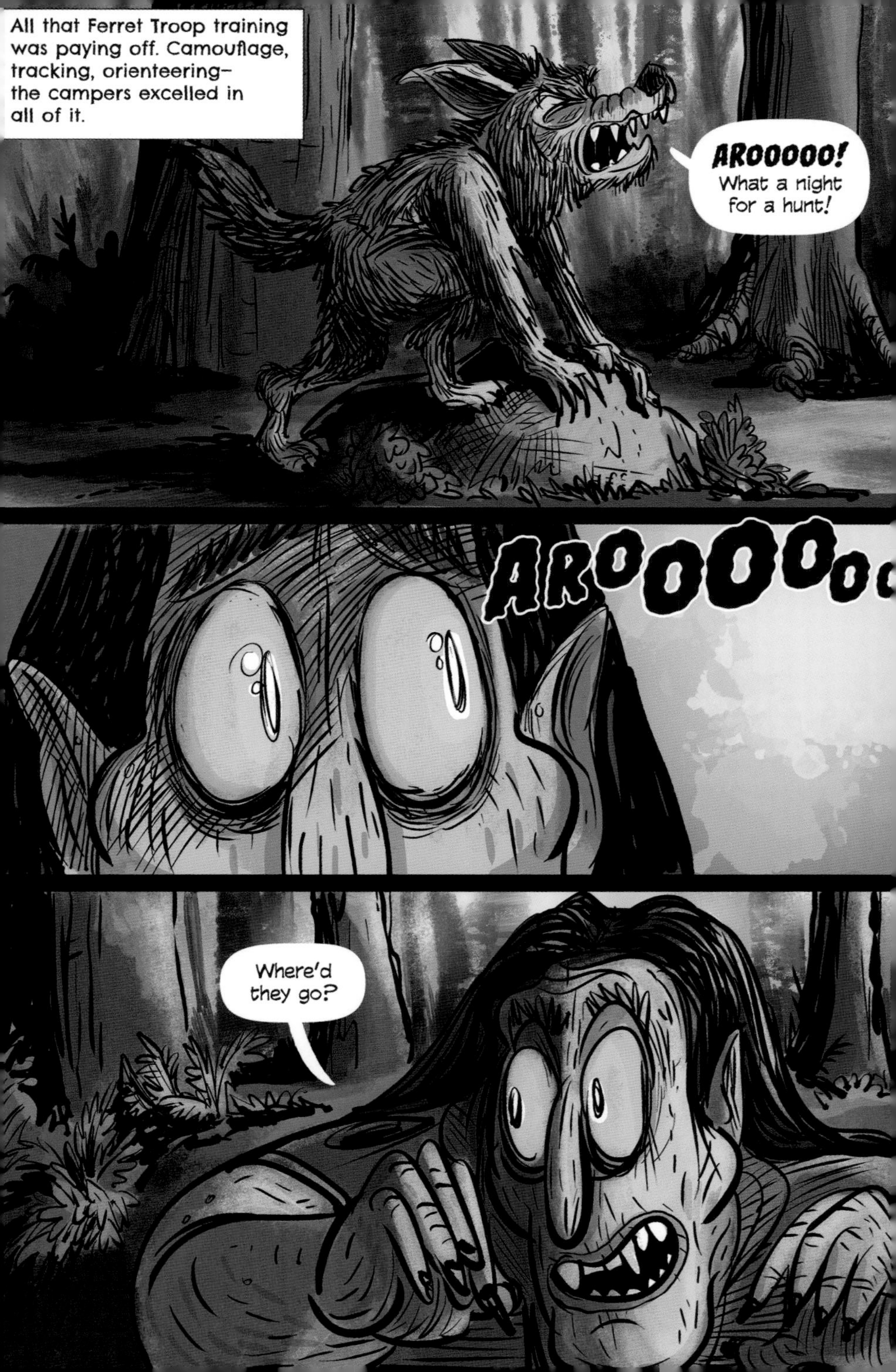
All that Ferret Troop training was paying off. Camouflage, tracking, orienteering–the campers excelled in all of it.
AROOOOO! What a night for a hunt!
AROOOOOo
Where'd they go?

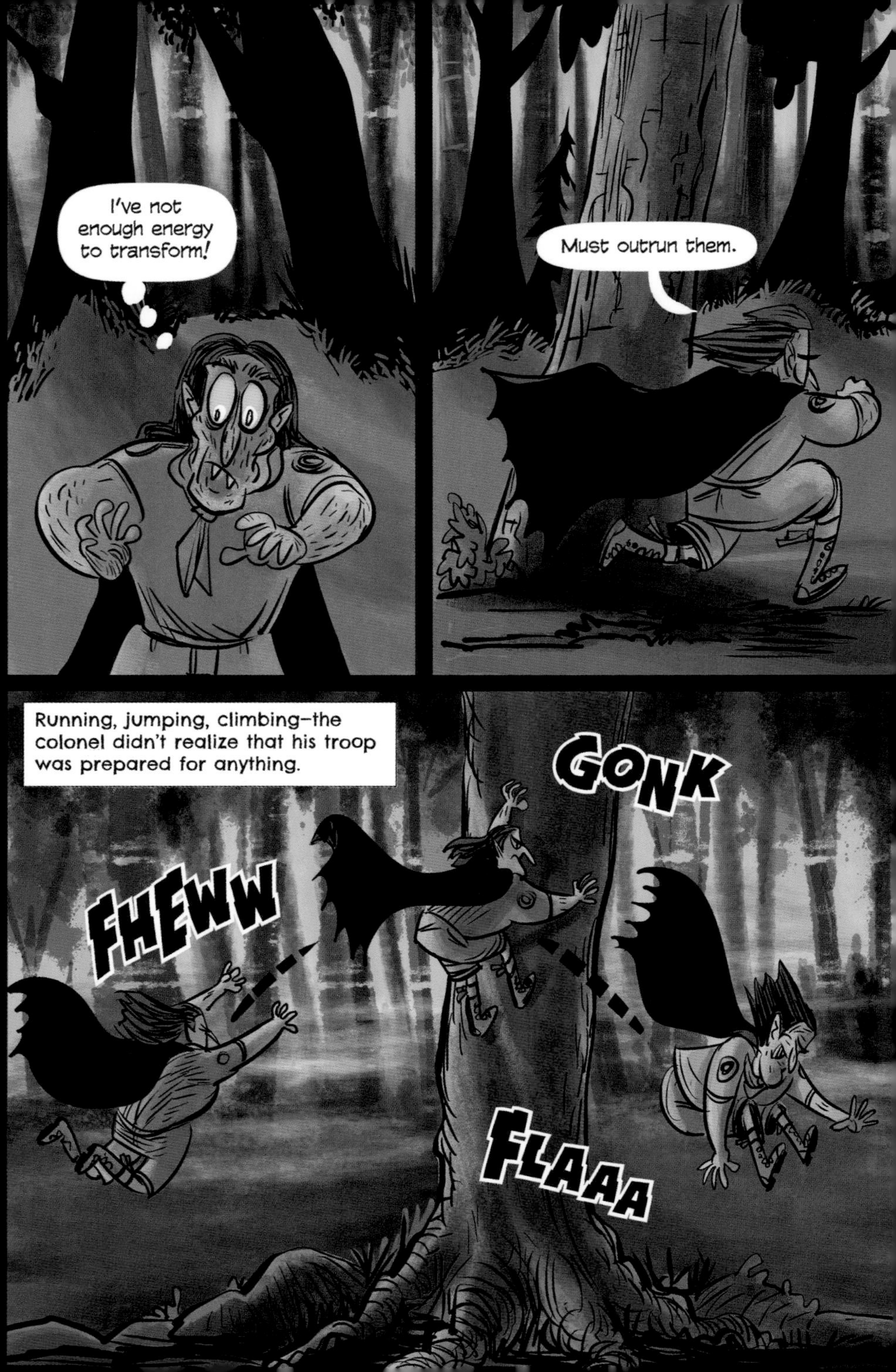
I've not enough energy to transform!
Must outrun them.
Running, jumping, climbing—the colonel didn't realize that his troop was prepared for anything.
GONK
FHEWW
FLAAA

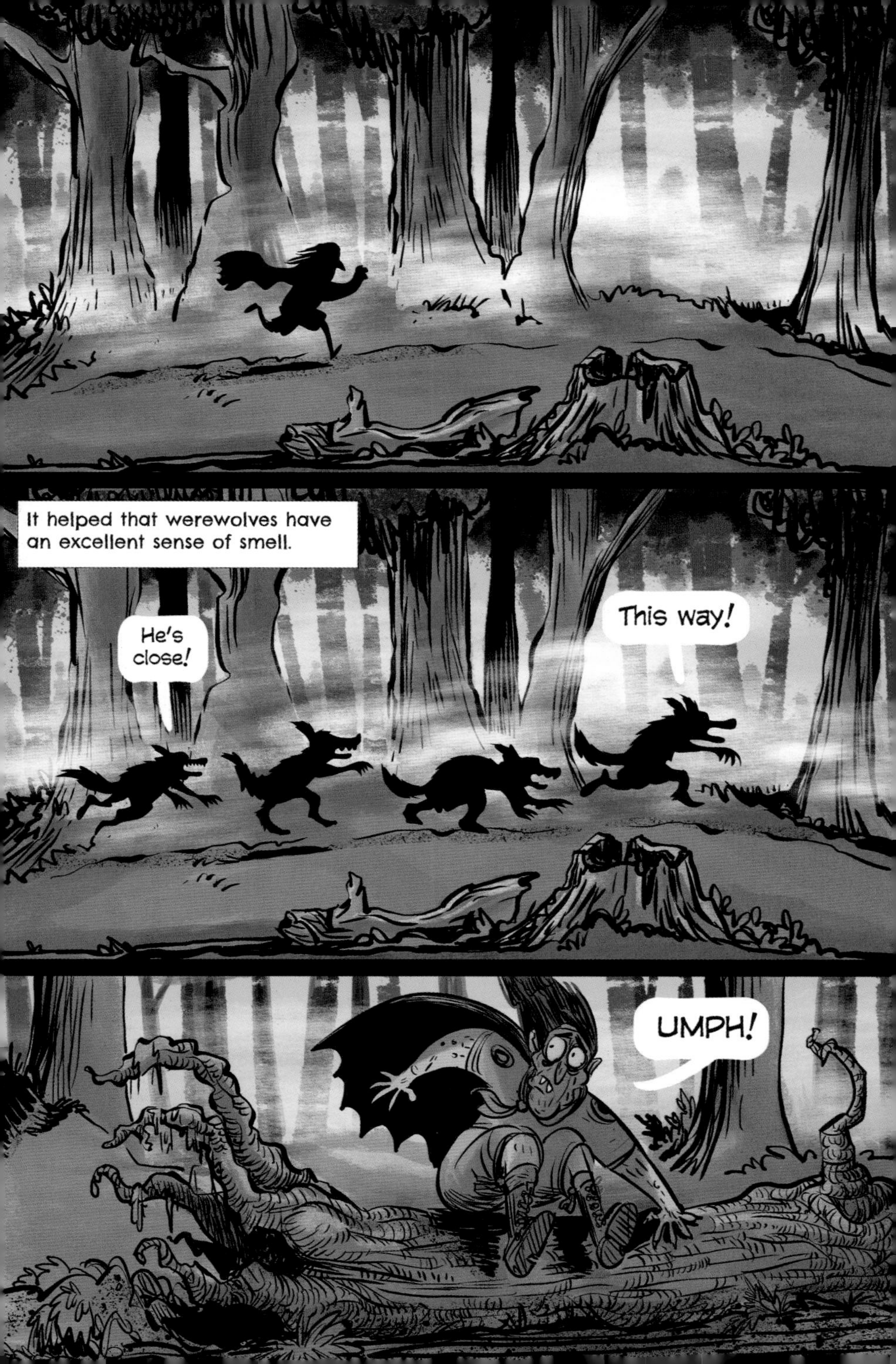
It helped that werewolves have an excellent sense of smell.
He's close!
This way!
UMPH!

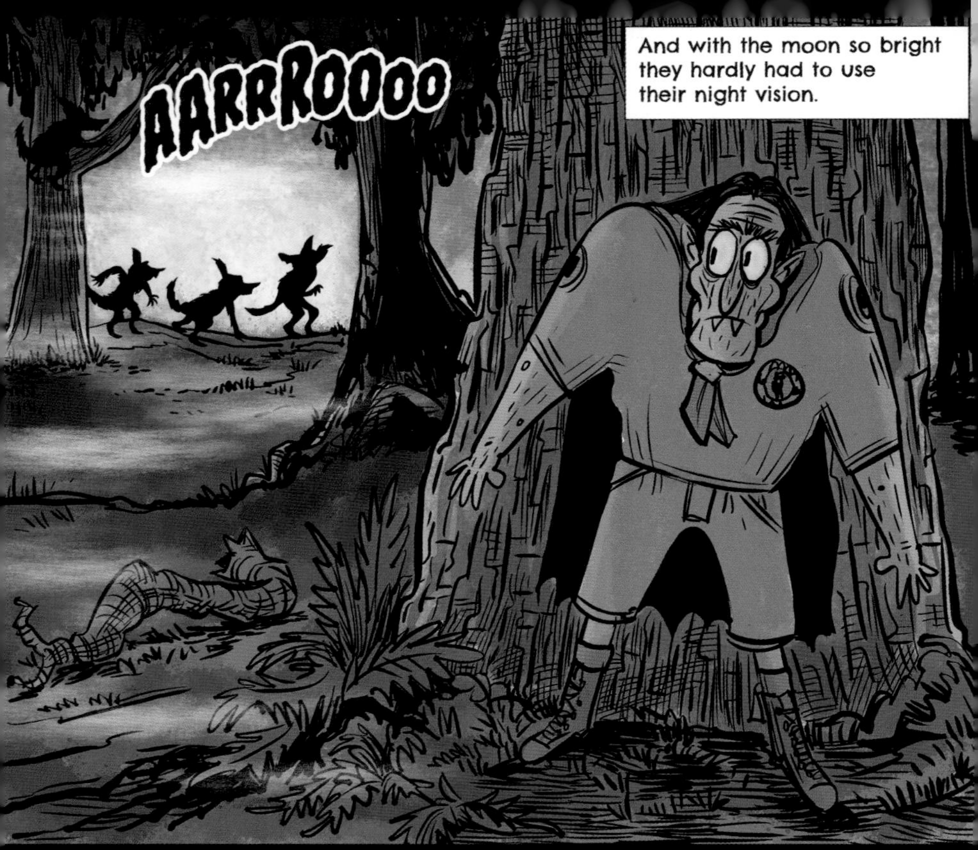
AARRROOOO
And with the moon so bright they hardly had to use their night vision.

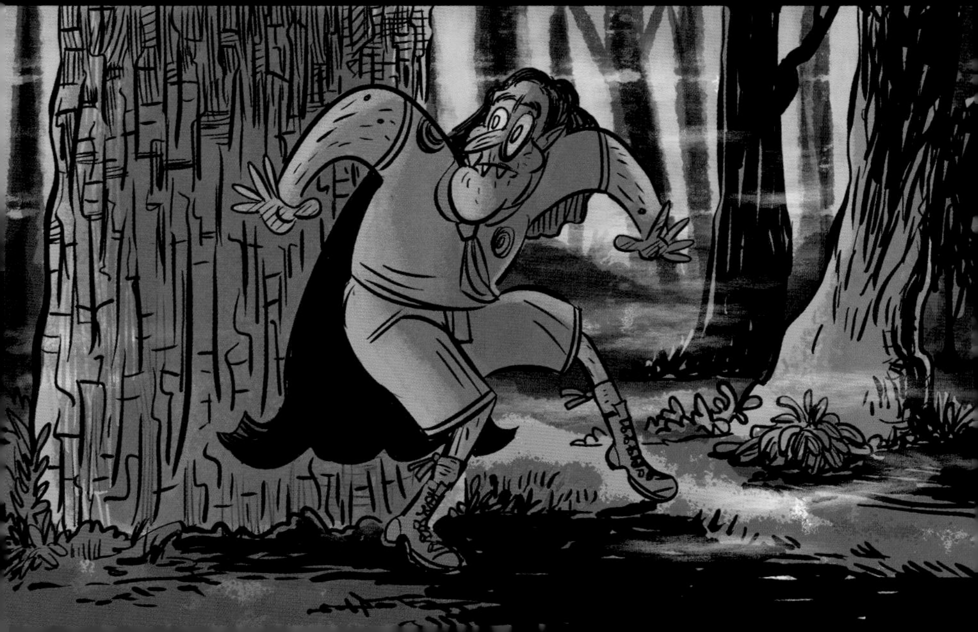

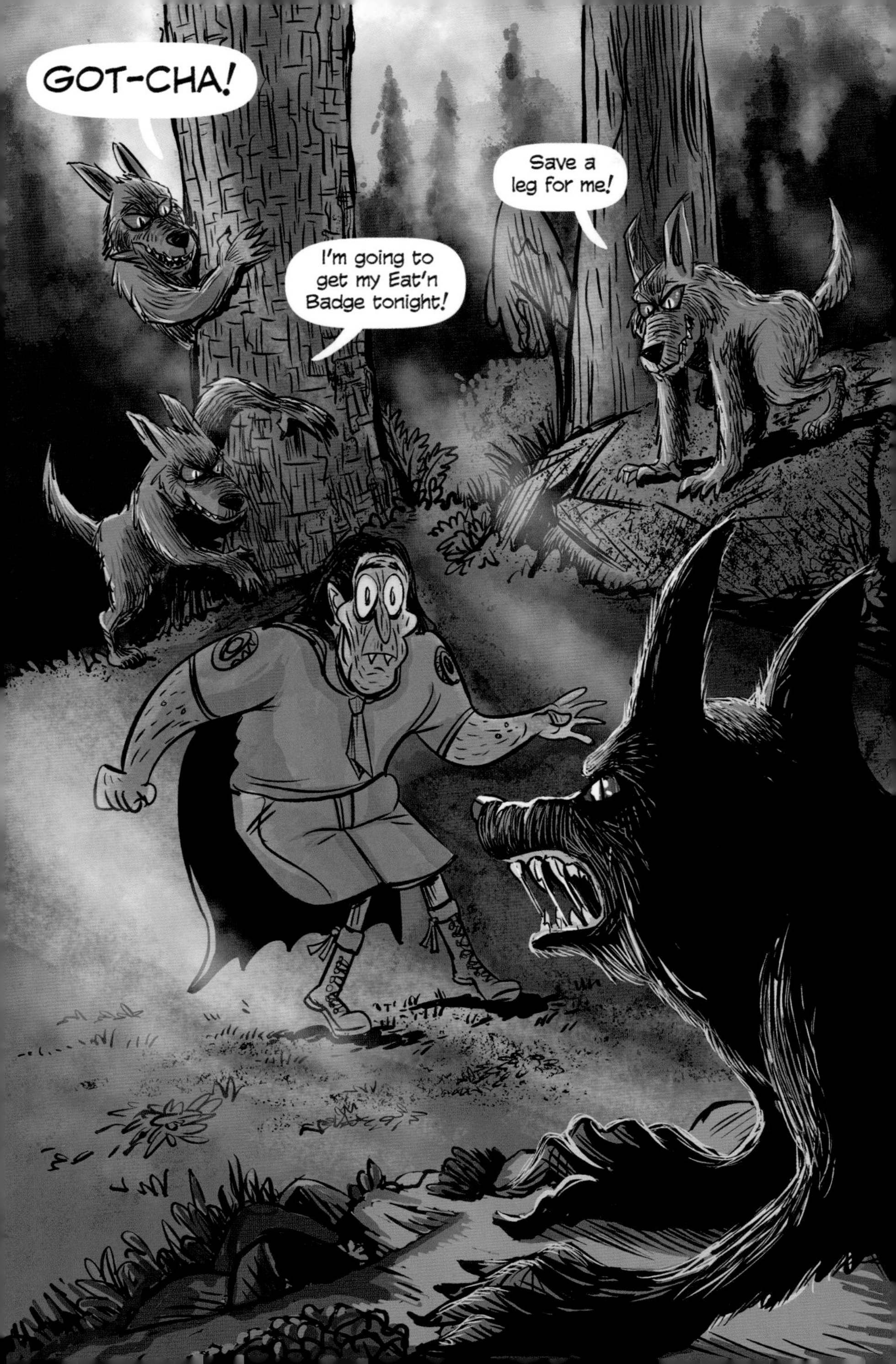
GOT-CHA!
I'm going to get my Eat'n Badge tonight!
Save a leg for me!

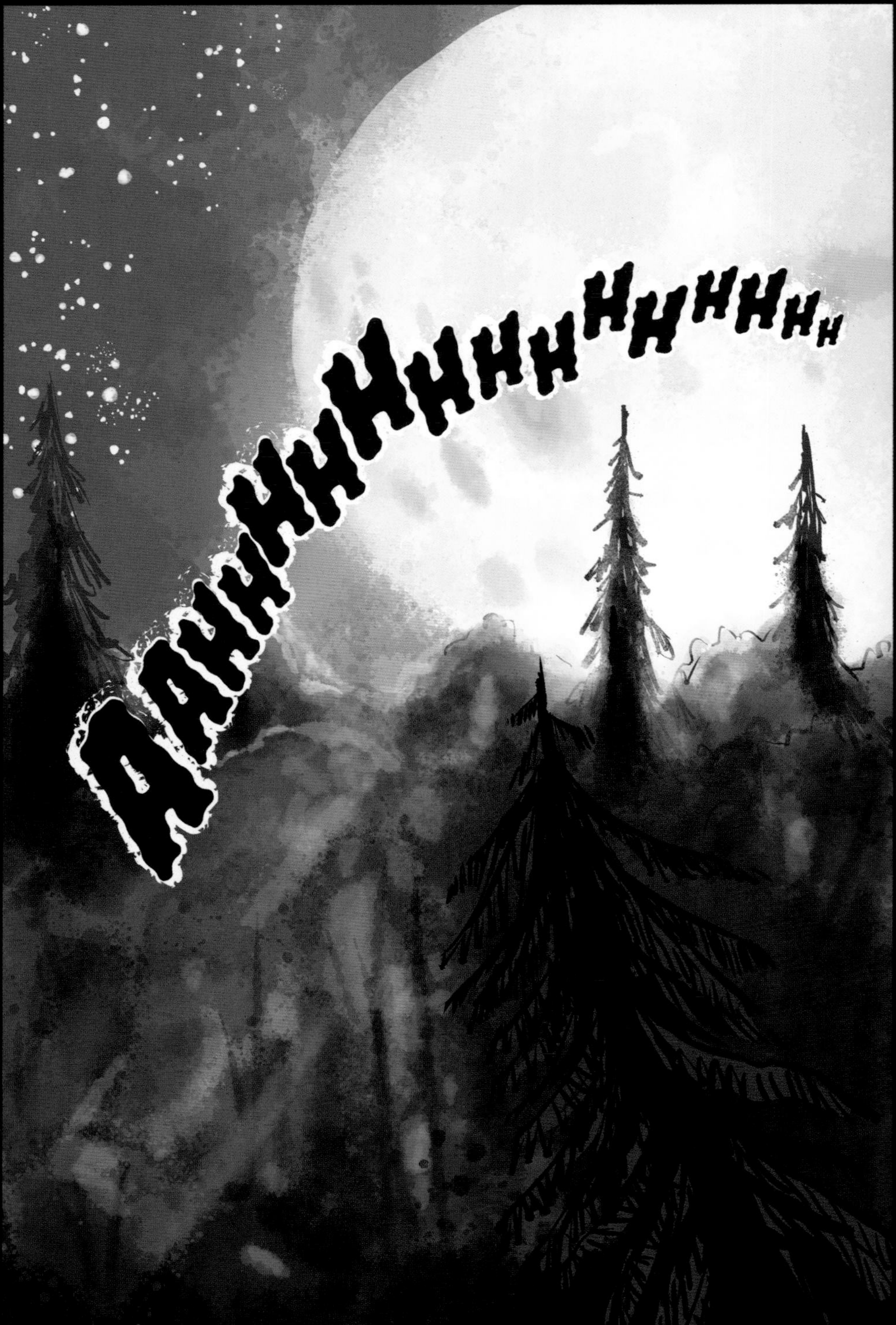
AAHHHHHHHHHHHHHHH

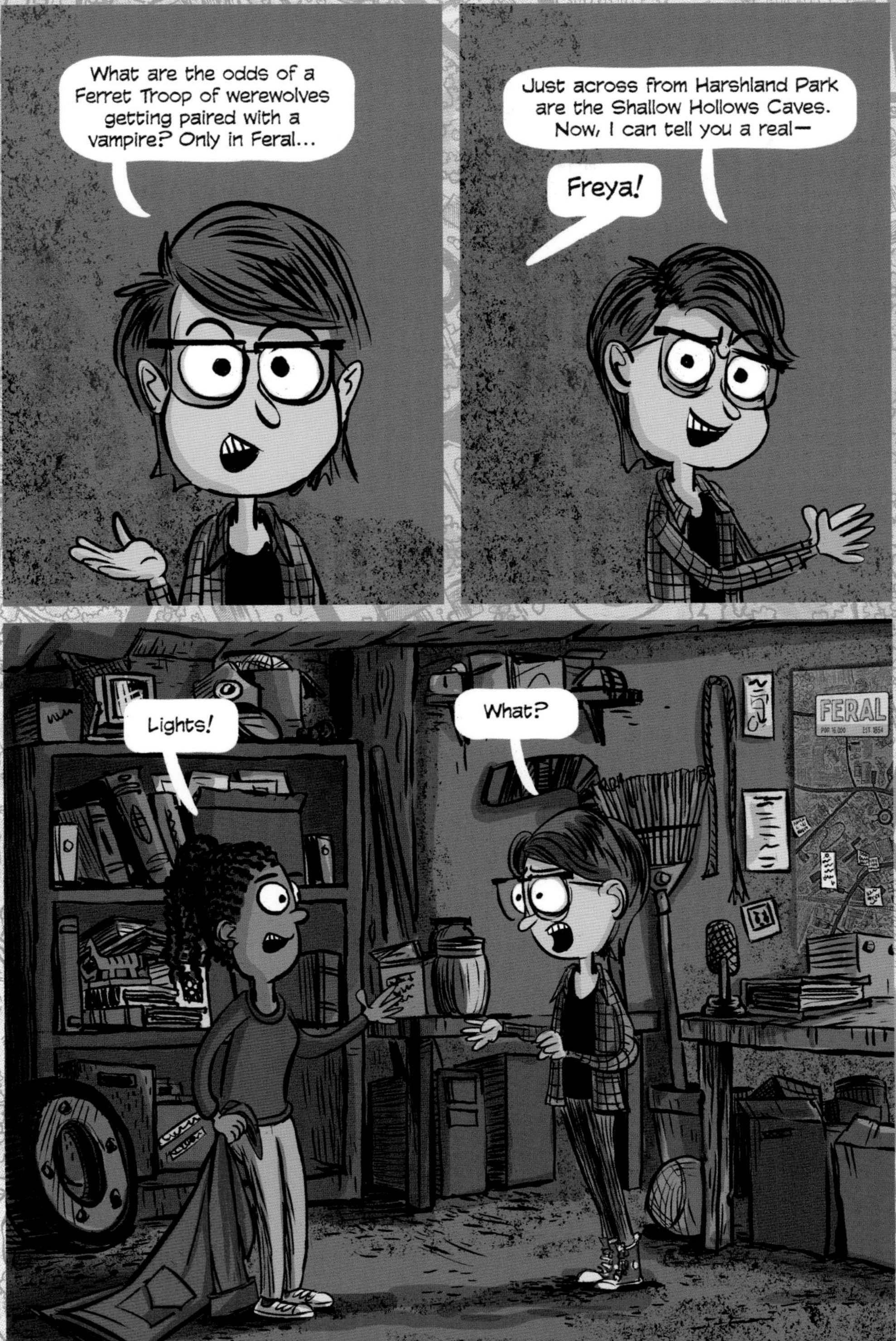
What are the odds of a Ferret Troop of werewolves getting paired with a vampire? Only in Feral...
Just across from Harshland Park are the Shallow Hollows Caves. Now, I can tell you a real—
Freya!
Lights!
What?
FERAL

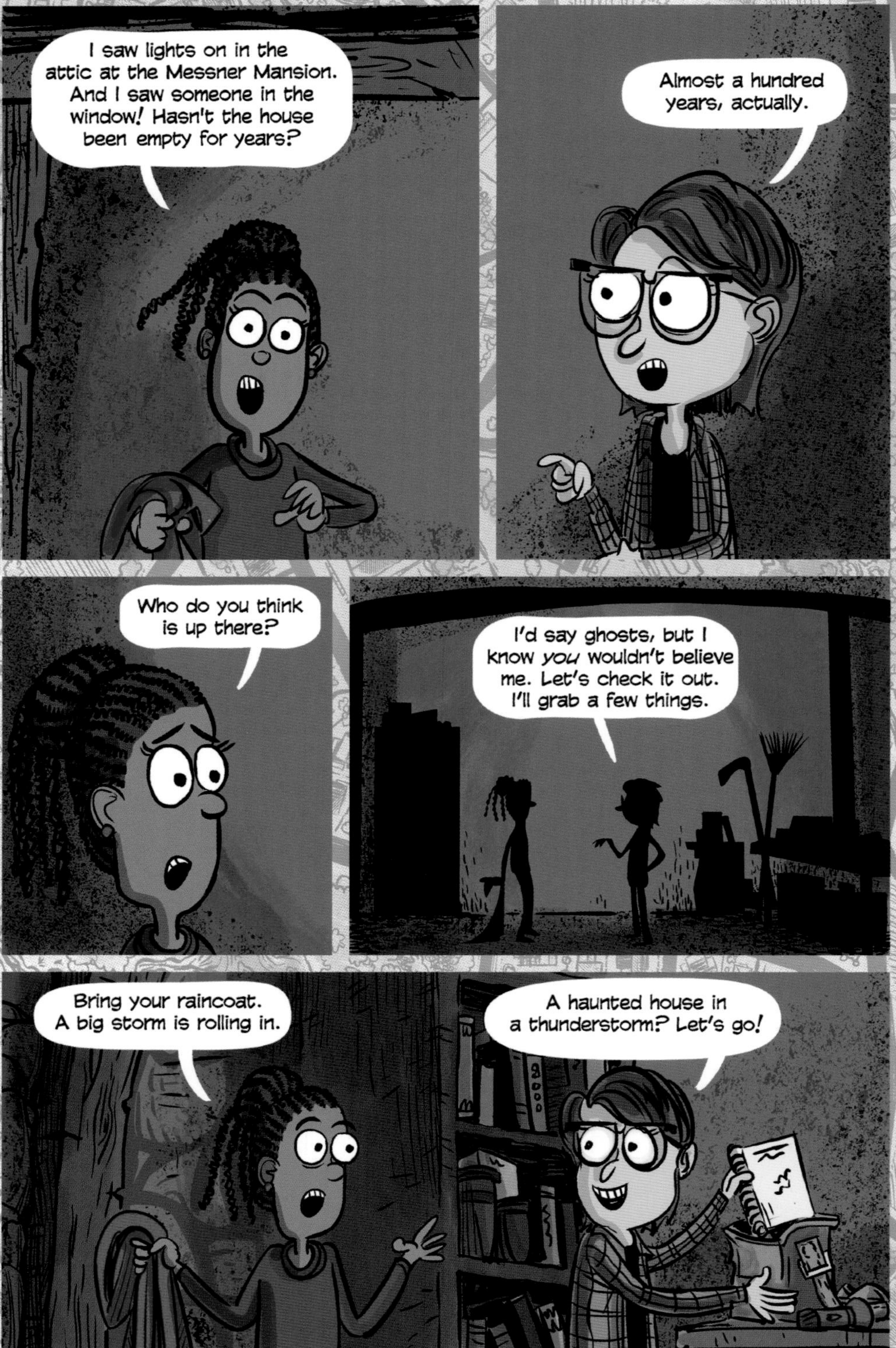
I saw lights on in the attic at the Messner Mansion. And I saw someone in the window! Hasn't the house been empty for years?
Almost a hundred years, actually.
Who do you think is up there?
I'd say ghosts, but I know *you* wouldn't believe me. Let's check it out. I'll grab a few things.
Bring your raincoat. A big storm is rolling in.
A haunted house in a thunderstorm? Let's go!

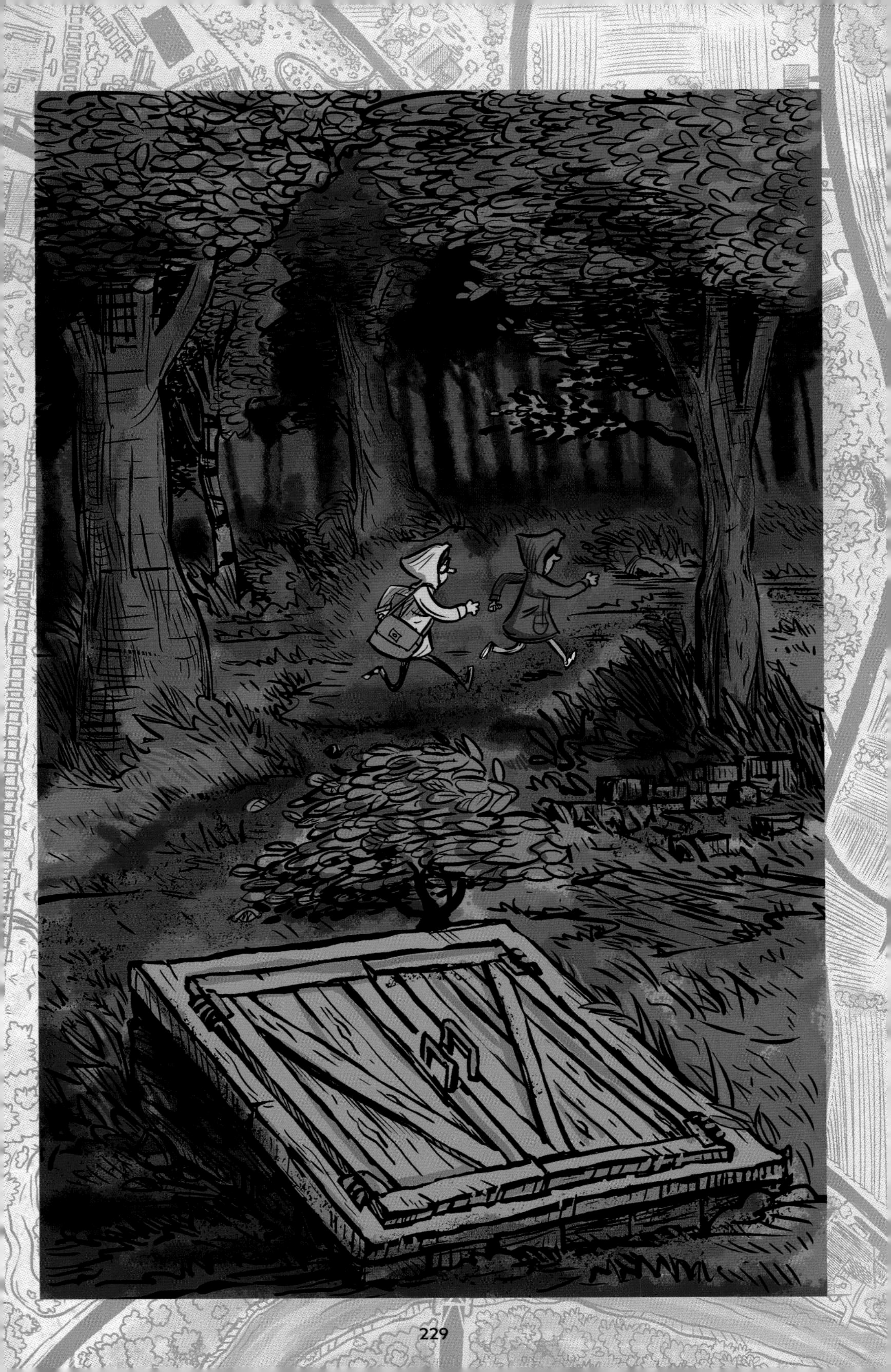

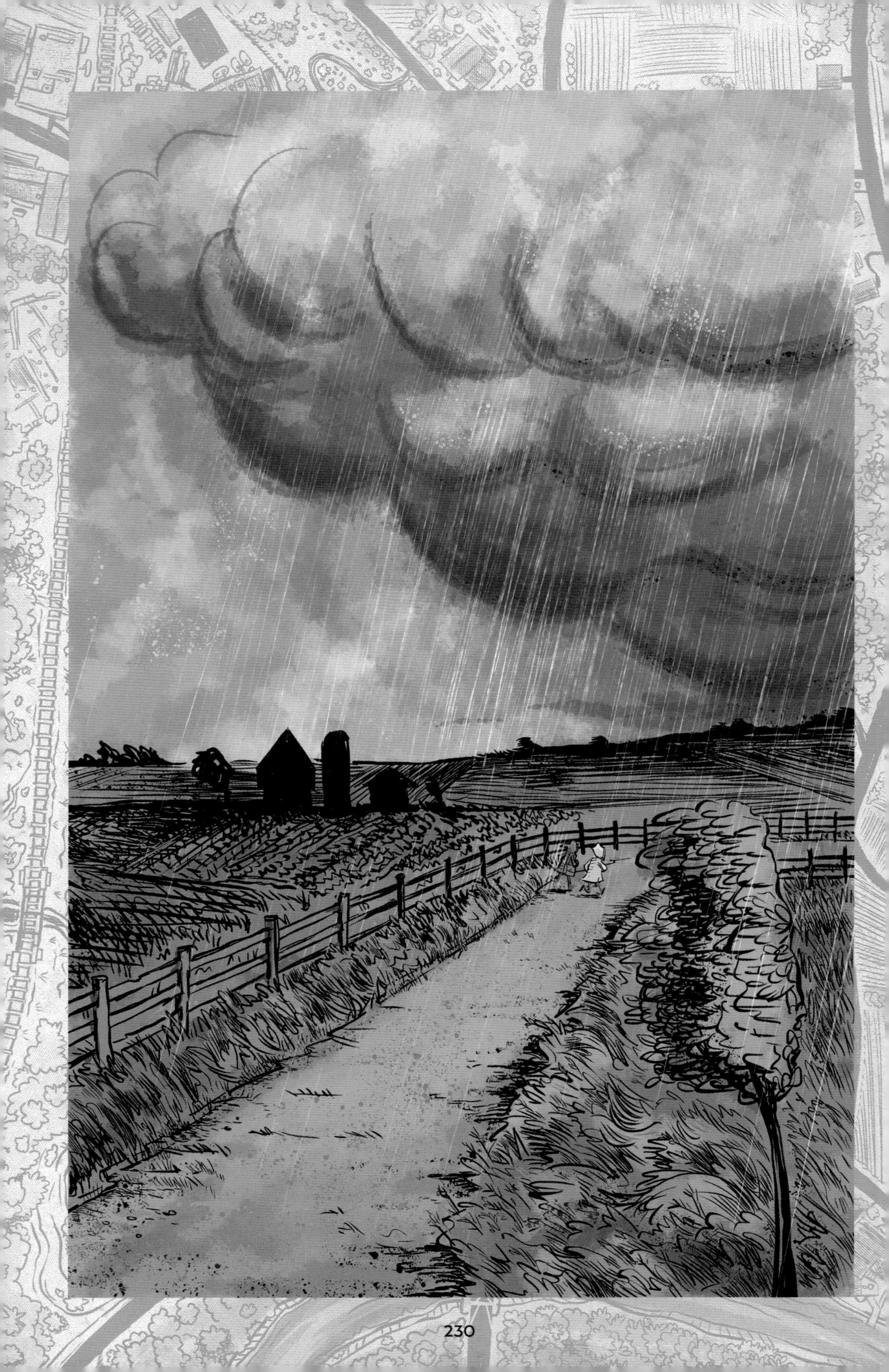

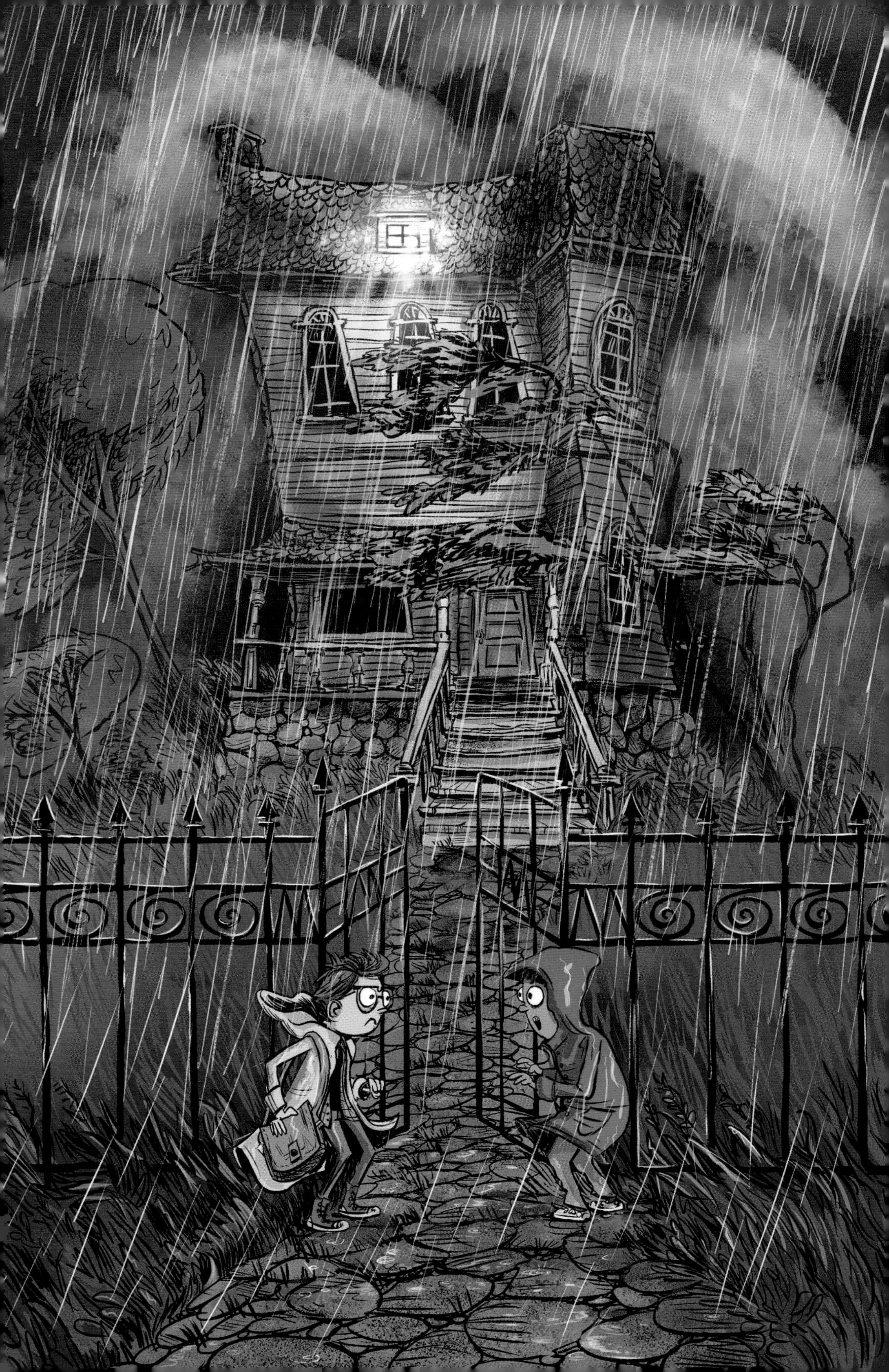

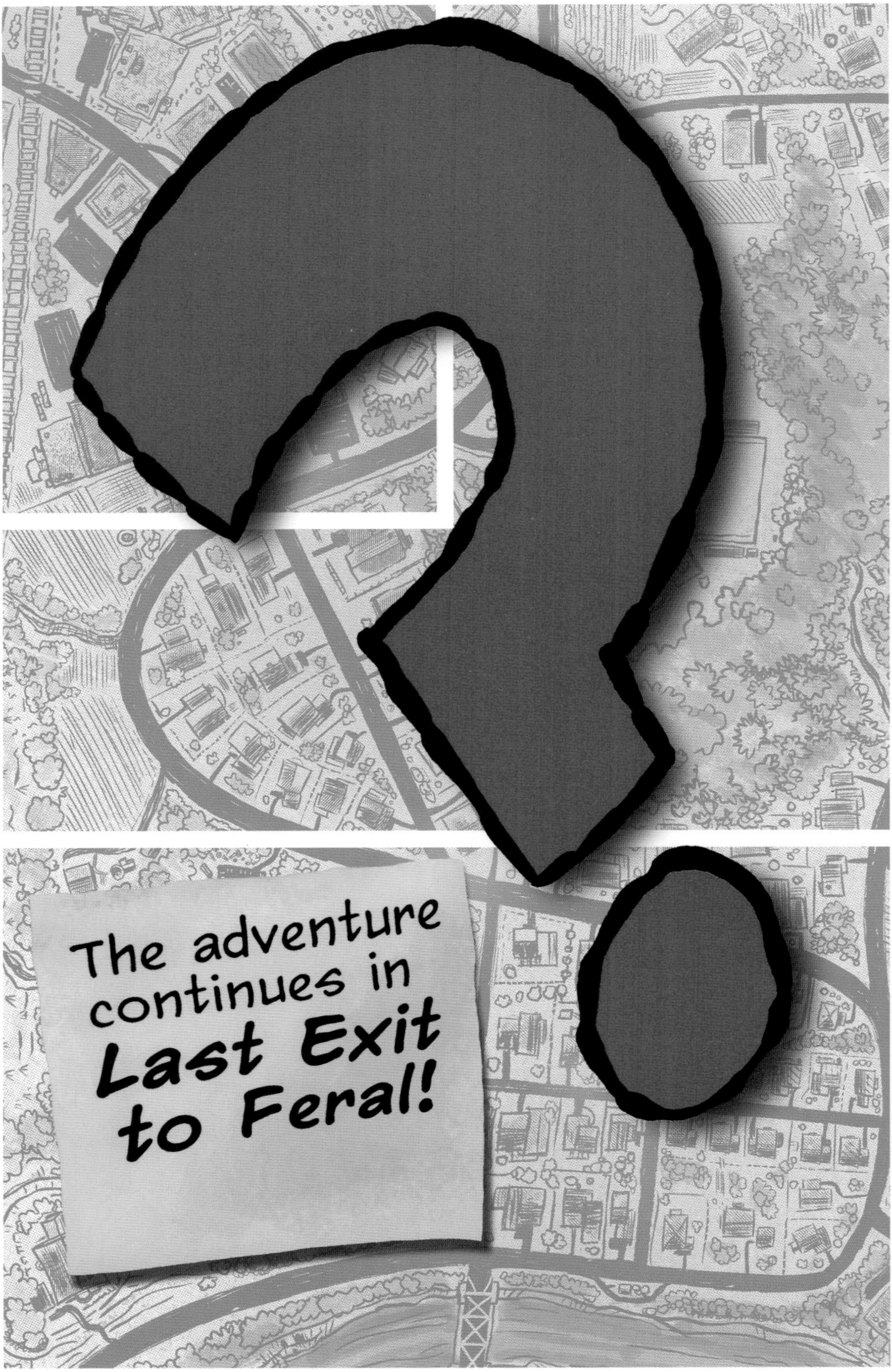
The adventure continues in Last Exit to Feral!